Victor's Blessing

Victor's Blessing

BARBARA SONTHEIMER

atmosphere press

Published by Atmosphere Press

Cover design by Matthew Fielder

Atmospherepress.com

For my children Martin, Kess and Max

And in memory of my mother Eleanor Riefler,
who gave me a *ghost* of an idea

Prologue

Ste. Genevieve, Missouri
April 1839

AnnaMargarite Gant knew she was dying and wondered if everyone felt the same odd certainty before they died. Impending death was so obvious, she wondered why her little girl Margaret or son Victor did not realize it. She wondered why her daughter uselessly sponged her fevered brow and forced water against her dried lips, begging her to drink.

This knowledge of approaching death did not alarm AnnaMargarite.

"It won't hurt anymore," she thought with exhaustion and relief. She felt death so near; she glanced toward the corner of the darkened room, expecting to see a somber specter waiting for her. Some shadowy figure reaching out with a bony white hand, coaxing her to leave the world of the living. She wondered what Father Tonnellier would think of her decidedly unchristian visions at the time of her death. *"AnnaMargarite,"* he had said countless times over the years, *"you must embrace Christianity and the Catholic church. After all, it was God that saved you, and we who cared for you when no one else would."*

Yes, they took me in. She had been sick with a strange disease the Osage did not understand, and left behind. She remembered her life after she had come to live with the family of Pierre Toulouse. Although she had been a slave for them, her life had not been harsh. She had been well fed, clothed, and shared in the family's many celebrations, almost as if she was a blood relative. She had been taught both French and English and been baptized into Catholicism. Later, her adopted family had allowed her to be purchased by Robert Gant. To further demonstrate their desire for her happiness, the Toulouse's had generously given the newly married couple forty arpents of land to start their lives. She had tried to acclimate to her new life but there were times when she felt the earlier

3

Osage teachings of the great Wah'Kon-Tah crowding out visions of the crucifix and holy virgin. She was haunted by the memories of her former life floating in and out of her consciousness like a mist. At times she could not remember where it was she belonged, or who she should be.

It wasn't an awfully long life. Thinking that at twenty-five years old she had nothing in her life but to marry at fourteen, bear six children, and bury three. Her marriage had started out well enough, but her husband's half-hearted effort to till the soil made him reach for the whiskey bottle for solace. But what shocked her was the way his demeanor changed. He began to slap her at first, then punched and kicked. For the most part, she could protect her nine-year-old daughter, Margaret, but because eleven-year-old Victor worked alongside his father in the fields, Victor often came home bruised and bloodied. On those nights after tending her son's wounds, AnnaMargarite would sob and pray to whatever God would listen to her to let it end.

And now it was ending. Although she was prepared to die, she worried about leaving her children. Her Osage grandmother had told her once that her ancestors came from a line of *long livers*. AnnaMargarite feverishly tossed her head on the sweat-stained pillow and remembered the shrewd black eyes of her grandmother, the woman with long black hair streaked with silver. The leathery face creased from a lifetime in the sun. That old, lined face was velvety-soft to the kiss. She had kissed her grandmother's cheek so many times in her life before she had come to live with the French, and she was sure her grandmother would be disappointed in her weakness.

AnnaMargarite saw Margaret standing beside her bed. Her large brown eyes were somber in her thin, serious face. Her long brown braids were messy, and AnnaMargarite tried to reach out to touch the braids that she had braided only three days ago, but found her strength seeping out like the blood onto the bed.

"Mama," Margaret choked out in a sob, putting her small arms around her mother's shoulders.

"It's all...it's all right..." AnnaMargarite tried to speak, but her feverish brain would not let her.

"Victor's back, Mama," Margaret exclaimed with hope, hearing the wagon.

AnnaMargarite heard the wagon too and closed her eyes, swallowing hard, wanting in her last hours on earth to commit to memory the faces of her beloved children and hoping their lives would be better than hers.

Yvonne Riefler hurried out of the wagon. It was already beautifully warm that spring night. The sound of a wild wind rustling the new buds would have normally filled Yvonne's soul with happiness and wonder about the spring planting and wonderful summer harvests to follow. But a wail of pain from the house mocked the calm of the twilight.

"Come on, child! *Dépêche!*" Yvonne whispered, exasperated, lapsing into her native French.

Yvonne wished she hadn't had to bring her frightened daughter Celena, along. But When Victor had run the two miles to the farm begging for her help, frantic because his father refused to call a doctor, Yvonne had no choice but to drop what she was doing.

"Robert...how ez she?" Yvonne asked nervously.

"Not well." He mumbled and hung his head as he stood on the threshold of the small, dilapidated farmhouse. His homespun shirt was not clean, not buttoned up properly, and showed more chest covered in gray hairs than a disapproving Yvonne wanted to see. His sandy-colored hair was graying and lay in unruly greasy clumps against his head. The gray whiskers on his chin and hard lines around his gray eyes made him look older than twenty-nine years.

"This way Miss Yvonne," Victor said, walking backward, leading them into the house. But when Celena realized where they were headed, Yvonne had to drag her in.

Once inside Yvonne shivered. The house was filthy. The dishes had been left on the table for days, the sticky wooden floor pulled at her shoes, an empty whiskey bottle on the floor was surrounded by mice droppings. A foul smell permeated the air and Yvonne tried not to gag as she entered the only small room off the kitchen.

Never in Yvonne's life had she seen such a hideous sight as where her neighbor lay in a mess of rank bodily fluids. And although she was not totally coherent Yvonne knew AnnaMargarite was embarrassed by her condition when seeing Yvonne, she began to cry.

"Oh, *Anna!*" Yvonne choked back the bile that rose in her throat. An uncharacteristic anger shook her, horrified that AnnaMargarite's husband would let her lay on the mattress already soaked with sweat, blood, and urine. The vile smirk Robert had given her as he sat on the porch drinking made the spark of anger in Yvonne burst into flames.

"I'm sorry, I'm so sorry!" Anna began to sob. Her long black hair in a hideous matt against the stained pillow. "The baby just won't come, I don't understand, I keep pushing..."

Yvonne knelt near her friend and noticed that her eyes were glassy and unfocused and that her normally tanned complexion looked sickly, tinged with yellow.

"Do you remember when your water broke?" she frantically glanced around for something to clean up her friend and realized because of the whiskey, Robert would be no help. "Where's the water?" she shouted in frustration, and then wished she hadn't when she spied Margaret huddled in the corner laying on yet another filthy quilt. Her face was dirty but there were clean marks on her cheeks from her tears, and her trusting eyes were almost more than Yvonne could bear.

"I—I need light."

"I'll get it," Victor said and disappeared.

"*Oh, mon Dieu!* Anna!" Yvonne exclaimed, letting her blue woolen shawl drop to the dirty floor. Again, Yvonne had to stifle the urge to gag as the rank smells of stale urine, feces and blood permeated the room.

AnnaMargarite's first child Adam had come easily enough, and barely nine months later another son, was born. She remembered nursing them at the same time. But no matter how much Adam ate, he seemed to shrivel before her eyes as her second son Victor grew strong. Adam died before his sixth birthday, and she could still see Victor solemnly at the graveside, holding onto his little sister Margaret who was too little to understand what was wrong. AnnaMargarite had twin boys that followed Adam into the earth, two years later. She remembered the morning she had found them cold and lifeless in their crib, wondering how they managed to leave the world without so much as a sound. And now here she was again trying to give birth to a baby, that refused to be born.

Victor came in with a lit lantern, which had a cracked glass flute. The light further illuminating the hideous mess, and for a moment Yvonne was so horrified by the sight, she could not remember the words in English. "I'm. I'm going to need *d'eau...water!*"

Victor darted out of the room, not bothering with the steps, jumping off the porch instead. Yvonne heard the splash of the bucket as it hit the well.

Yvonne paused; her heart afraid about the task in front of her. After all, she was no doctor nor midwife. And although she knew something of childbirth, having birthed seven children of her own, still felt woefully unprepared for what had been suddenly asked of her.

AnnaMargarite and Yvonne were more than acquaintances, but not quite friends. Because the Riefler farm was larger, and Yvonne's husband John, a better businessman and farmer than Robert, the Rieflers always had much more than the Gants. And Yvonne feeling bad for her neighbor had a habit of making sure the "extra" canning or leftover children's clothing quietly made its way to the Gant farm. The husbands were not friendly, John Riefler disapproving of the way his neighbor managed his land and family. Even though the Riefler farm butted up to the Gant's small farm at the edge of town. The Gant farm had not always been small, but Robert Gant's long illicit affair with whiskey garnered him few friends, and he lost arpents of land during his drunken binges, and idiotic renegotiations with the bank.

The alcohol was not the only thing that bothered Yvonne, it was the way Robert Gant treated his young Osage wife. He professed to love her, or at least Yvonne realized with a flush of embarrassment he managed to get her pregnant every year. Yvonne did not have proof he beat her, but it was rumored he did, and it made every cell in Yvonne's body recoil with disgust.

"Anna, how long has sis been going on?" Yvonne leaned near her gently, trying to assess what on earth to do. She watched as AnnaMargarite tried to answer but could not.

To Yvonne's relief she heard Victor running up the steps with a bucket full of water. Although he was fast, she realized he did not spill a drop as he carefully put it down. She noticed he was already tall for a boy of eleven. His eyes like Margaret's were full of hope and trust.

"When did she take to her bed?"

"Three days ago. I asked Pa if I could come get you—"

"Three days!" Yvonne shrieked "Why did you wait so long?" she wished she hadn't spoken then when she saw the guilt and pain on Victor's face. Yvonne closed her eyes briefly and shook her head. Wishing she had gone to the fields and gotten her husband John, or gone into town and gotten Dr. Casey, anyone to help her. Yvonne gasped unable to hold back, as uncharacteristic anger shook her.

She put her hands in the cool well water and traced her hands across AnnaMargarite's hot, feverish face. Yvonne's hands shook at the sensation. Never in her life had she felt someone that hot to touch and knew right then it was too late. The nauseating sensation that they had waited too long engulfed her.

"Are you cold Anna, m'm?" Yvonne asked rearranging the disheveled bedclothes and gasped when she pulled them back seeing that from the waist down, AnnaMargarite was soaked in blood. "Just let me.... clean you up a bit," Yvonne bit her lip as tears pricked her eyes. She felt sweat run down the middle of her back and under her arms, as she mopped up the blood with a discarded shift. It was horrifyingly obvious to Yvonne that in effort to have her child alone, AnnaMargarite had urinated, defecated, and nearly bled to death.

"Why doesn't it come?" AnnaMargarite asked weakly.

Trying not to gag as she smeared blood along AnnaMargarite's thighs, Yvonne gulped. "The afterbirth, Anna...it came first." She wiped a tear off her face with the back of her hand, unknowingly smearing blood on her cheek.

"I knew...I was dying, but I...thought the baby would...live." Anna-Margarite looked down at her swollen belly. "One of us should have."

At the frank words Yvonne felt the strength drain out of her. She noticed that AnnaMargarite was still in pain because her breathing was labored, and Yvonne wished she could do more to help her.

"Is there any whiskey or tafia *left* in this house?" Yvonne wailed, but in the wake of Anna's pain and the children's fear, ashamed she had done so. When no one answered, she turned toward Margaret and Celena. Looking down Yvonne realized her arms were painted in blood up to her elbows, the two little girls stared at the ghastly sight, dumb struck.

"I—I can't find a cup," Victor stammered a moment later producing a dusty bottle of whiskey. She managed a weak smile as she took it from him and had odd sensation of security when he was near. Yvonne remembered how Anna used to brag about him, how capable he was, how helpful. At the time Yvonne had merely regarded it as a doting mother's praise. But Yvonne had to admit there was something comforting about his strong demeanor. His gray eyes silently watching his mother die, his broad back resigned to take on the burden.

"Here Anna, zis may help a bit," Yvonne poured a bit of the amber liquid into Anna's mouth. Although she had difficulty swallowing, she quieted, and Yvonne hung her head forcing back her tears.

Celena stood in the doorway watching the grim happenings paralyzed with fear. She didn't understand about birthing babies or dying, but she knew her mother, who could manage *everything,* was afraid, and that terrified her. She looked over at the tall boy that was her neighbor and felt sorrier for him than she had ever felt for anyone in her young life.

Unfortunately, for another twelve hours AnnaMargarite stayed in a place that was neither life nor death, and Yvonne and the three children stayed with her. At times Yvonne sponged her fevered forehead, other times praying at her bedside. In the middle of a beautiful spring night, she painfully gave birth to a stillborn daughter. When the pale light of morning came AnnaMargarite asked for her son.

"Victor," she breathed, opening her eyes, wanting to smile at him. "You've been such a great...help to me..." she felt the tug at her mortal soul and tried to fight it long enough just to tell him that she loved him, depended on him, and that he had never not done what she asked. She wanted him to promise to look after Margaret, wanted to tell him to learn to read and write, something she had not. She felt her eyes closing and fought desperately to re-open them, as her body began to drift away from the weight of life. She could barely feel Victor place her hand against his heart, and although she heard him call her back, felt the pull intensify. For one last moment she was torn between staying with her children or going to that place where there was no more pain.

The fingers of his mother's hand arched up, and Victor leaned closer to his mother's face. Straining to hear comforting words from her lips. As he studied her still face, he liked to tell himself that she had managed to smile at him right before she died.

Celena too remembered the moment. She had been sleeping but was awakened by the muffled sobs of Margaret who stood with her face buried in the bloodstained skirts of Yvonne. Celena realized their mother had died, and she too began to cry.

She watched Victor straighten up from his mothers' bedside, still staring at his ghastly sight of his lifeless mother.

Celena walked silently next to him, and reached up and put her small arms around his waist trying to comfort him.

Victor's tortured eyes blazed down at her, and for a moment she was afraid. Then he leaned down and dissolved into tears in the arms of Celena who was only six.

Part

One

Chapter 1

1849, Ten Years Later

Victor Gant was dreaming he was young again and swimming in the Gabouri River with the Riefler brothers, Laurence, James, Will, and others like Ethan Stanfield, Caleb Charbonnier and his younger twin brothers Danny and Davey. The eight of them took turns shimmying up a favorite twisted sycamore tree, the one that snaked a limb as big as a thigh over the Gabouri river. They would balance atop it, staring down at their reflections waving in the green waters. Hollering taunts and dares as they jumped not dove into the water, because the river was not deep. Victor splashed into the water and sunk down, daring to open his eyes into its green murky depths. Touching the soft bottom, felt mud ooze up between his toes before he pushed back to the surface.

He was laughing then at Will's antics as he fell into the water when Will's older brother James gave him a shove, Victor flipped his wet black hair out of his eyes as he swam to shore.

But then he was hurled further back in time to the chilly morning he dug the graves for his mother and stillborn sister Catherine. Stepping on the cold shovel as it pierced the earth, the red Missouri clay felt so heavy he could barely lift it. He needed to sniff for the tears and mucus were running into his mouth, but he knew with his father watching, Victor dare not make a sound. Suddenly he was on top of their cold, stiff bodies in the bottom of the damp grave.

Victor's gray eyes opened, and he rubbed his face with his hand. Although it was morning it was still dark, as the sun had not breached the tall trees that circled his cabin, and early enough that no birds were singing. He rolled off the mattress and stood to stretch his long spine until he heard the pops of cartilage against bone. He moved silently to the fireplace, careful not to wake his sister Margaret. Squatting down he placed a split log on the dying embers and stoked the fire until a faint glow appeared. Staring into the orange fire he rocked back and forth on his heels, his big hands rubbing his arms for warmth.

He had a full day of work ahead of him. Although a blacksmith—or a *forgeron* as his French friends referred to him—and not a farmer, he had been lending his help to friends and neighbors at harvest time for as long as he could remember, and his friends welcomed his help and depended on him. Plus, he enjoyed the change of pace, the camaraderie, the jokes, and meals he shared at their tables. Tonight, he would be able to chow down on Yvonne Riefler's baked barue, or chicken fricassee, followed by her crusty bread, with baked apples or custard for dessert.

Located between St. Louis and New Orleans, Ste. Genevieve was a surprisingly cosmopolitan town for its small size. There were German, French, Spanish settlers, and Indians as well. And a good deal of intermarrying between the groups. In fact, in the earliest days of the village the Catholic priests had encouraged the men to marry Indian women. White women were scarce in those days and the Jesuits thought it a good solution to the illicit liaisons they were unable to prevent anyway.

Victor moved his left shoulder experimentally, knowing it was going to be a long day. He sighed quietly, hoping his bruised shoulder was up to it. Polly, Phillippe Charbonnier's mare had kicked him yesterday. He had shod her countless times before and hadn't bothered with a *twitch*. But then his striker Claude came barreling in the shop and startled her.

Victor helped Andy Stoddard cut his corn two days last week and helped Jean Gustave with bundling yesterday, but the weekend he had saved for John Riefler. He knew John was ecstatic for this corn crop. With the money from its yield, he would be able to help his son James buy land like he had done for his older son Laurence three years back.

He didn't want his sister to have to empty his chamber pot, and made a quick, chilly trip to the outhouse. A delicate white haze of frost coated the ground, and he breathed in deeply, wishing he could smell the dampness that rose from the Mississippi. He couldn't see the river from the blacksmith shop, but, across the street and behind the Woolrich's general store knew there was an early morning mist rising from it.

Back inside his little log house he dressed quickly and crammed a cold biscuit into his mouth while pouring water from the pitcher into the basin. He splashed his face with it and then dragged his wet hands through his black hair. It was getting long again. In fact, he could tuck it neatly behind his ears, and knew Margaret would be after him to cut it soon. He picked up a short piece of leather and bound it tight behind his head.

Sitting at the worn maple table, he tugged his boots on and glanced over at the book he'd been reading last night. He had borrowed from Laurence Riefler, and it was about ships. Victor was fascinated by their designs, their cargo capacity, and what propelled them from steam to wind to brawn. He glanced at another book lying next to it and frowned. It was a book of poetry by John Keats, also lent to him by Laurence. He remembered how Laurence had hardly been able to keep a straight face when he handed it to him. *"Victor, the book of ships I know you'll enjoy, and one of poetry—for your delicate heart!"* Laurence's pretty wife Lisette interrupted them. *"Don't pay any attention to Laurence! They are lovely romantic words. I'll think you'll enjoy it if you, unlike my stubborn husband, can keep an open mind!"* Laurence had wrapped his long arms around her waist. In the three years they had been married, Victor had seen Laurence with his arms around her often, and he was glad Laurence was happy. He was closer to Laurence than anyone else in Ste. Genevieve—except Ethan, but Ethan was still gone.

He sighed again when he looked at the poetry book. He tried to read it, but it seemed to him the Keats fellow used a lot of extra words to describe things and Victor spent half the time looking up the unfamiliar words in the dictionary. But somehow, he would muddle through it. Keats was Celena's favorite.

Standing up he pulled his coat on. The sleeves were too short. Although Margaret tried, she had trouble properly fitting him. As a result, he always looked like he was wearing someone else's clothes, and that someone was smaller than he was.

He stood a solid 6'5" in bare feet and weighed a lean but muscular 230 lbs. He was a whole head taller than anyone in Ste. Genevieve and always sat in the last pew in church, aware that no one would be able to see over him. Occasionally he was reminded of how much bigger he was when a newcomer would stare at him. Only last week he overheard a captain of a steamship stop his bubbly conversation with Jean Gustave, to stare nervously as he went by. Jean who had only given him a cursory glance explained: *"Oh oui! That's our local giant Victor Gant, he's a forgeron. But don't trouble yourself, he may be half savage, but he's friendly!"*

At twenty-one, his face had lost all awkwardness of youth, and the features of his mother's Osage people became more prominent. He might have looked all Osage had it not been for the alarming gray eyes. There was no doubt looking at him that he was of mixed Indian blood, or as the

French of the village affectionately referred to him as *metis*.

He was solid too. The years of walking and helping at harvest time had made him lean, and the years of blacksmithing had made him incredibly strong. In the past during the local celebrations of Bastille days, or Oktoberfest they had wrestling and weightlifting contests-but they stopped having them three years ago. Not a single man in the Village had been able to beat him in any strength test and laughingly the men of the village crowned him "*Le fort!*" with no contest at all.

It was chilly as he quietly left the house, and trotted a bit to get his blood circulating, crunching dried oak and sycamore leaves under his feet, playfully kicking the dried sweetgum balls as he went.

Ste. Genevieve nestled on the banks of the Mississippi river was a diverse town. It was born a French settlement when the Canadian trapper Louis Jolliet and Jesuit priest Jean Marquette pulled their flatboats over and declared '*le pays des Illinois*' and drove a flag into the ground in France's name.

His blacksmith shop was near the Mississippi on the corner of South Gabouri and Third Street, and he wished he had time to go look at the river. A huge expanse of moving water full of strange eddies and sudden boiling's, pulsing with a life of its own as it rolled by Ste. Genevieve. His mother told him that the Osage believed there was a demon that lived underneath the water and that its roar could be heard for miles, and that this demon could drag you down to its home in the depths. He smiled as he began the two mile walk to the Riefler farm, thinking it was indeed *Rivière a la grand* as Jean Gustave always referred to it.

There had been floods, hideous floods that all but destroyed the French settlement. There had been a terrible one in 1785, but that was years before Victor was born and he only knew what the gregarious old French farmers told him about it. How they had merely moved their beloved Ste. Genevieve back a half mile and started over.

But there had been another flood only five years ago that left Ste. Genevieve gasping for breath six feet under water. Thankfully, there had been no loss of life, but it had been for the residents, a catastrophe. Although everyone now joked about how neighbor Don Fisk had jumped off his chimney into the water, the rebuilding and clean-up had lasted for months. Victor could still remember the stench of decaying fish and livestock that had been trapped by the murky waters, and the mud that had been everywhere. Others in town like Mrs. Blay, the boarding house owner, and the Woolrich's who owned the general store had lost a lot in the flood. He and Jonah had merely cleaned up the mess in the shop, polished off their anvil and started anew. Yet it was just this petulant nature that so enriched the Mississippi valley, making her alluvial grounds so ripe for harvesting.

He'd fished for catfish in the river when he was younger and would now if he had more time. He smiled remembering the horrified look on Ethan's face when he'd first been served catfish or as the French called it *barue* fried in bear oil.

Thinking of Ethan, the smile faded. Joe Kurth from the telegraph office had been in the shop last week and told him Ethan was coming home. He'd received only one letter from Ethan, a short time after Jonah, the local blacksmith's, death. It had been a condolence letter brimming with apologies, one that Victor had found difficult to read.

He wondered how Ethan had changed. He heard as everyone else did the boasting of Ethan's mother Abigail, of how well Ethan had done in school, and how they had then sent him on a grand tour of Europe to further his studies. Annoyingly Victor felt his stomach muscles tighten with jealously. He had no illusions that his scant education could compare to Ethan's, but wanted to know enough to never again be at the mercy of someone like Ethan's father, Frederick Stanfield.

Victor shivered as he walked and, seeing his breath in the air, jammed his hands into his pockets. He knew more than likely he'd be sweating by noon with the autumn sun beating down on him. A gust of wind blew yellowed maple leaves into a funnel at his feet. Glancing up at the towering tree he smiled, remembering that August night he and Ethan had sat under the southwest corner Pecan tree that served as a marker to separate Jean Gustave's land from Widow Chomeau's, drinking hard cider.

"...No, it's true, I swear it! The cicadas, they sing faster the hotter the night!"

"What sort of old wives' tale it that!" Ethan quipped.

"It's not an old wife's tale, its true!"

"Have you a thermometer?"

"A what?"

"A thermometer, with which to measure the heat of this night."

"I don't need one. They're singing faster than last night. That means it's hotter!"

"I suppose you're still walking around wagon tongues rather than over them?" Ethan teased boldly, poking fun at Jonah's superstition that it was bad luck for a smith to step over one.

Victor shrugged, "better safe than sorry!"

Glancing up at the trees, he thought they looked black and strangely delicate as they lost their leaves. He remembered when he and Margaret were children how they used to stand in the woods on a windy autumn day trying to see who could catch the most leaves without moving. It always amazed him how surprisingly loud a single leaf could be as it rustled slowly through the empty branches on its descent to earth. Yet at other times, a leaf could be utterly silent as it fell.

A hickory nut dropped as he walked, then a pecan fell too. With a laugh he wove his way through the woods dodging the falling nuts, wondering with a mile still to walk if he would escape being hit.

Passing Jean Gustave's house, he smiled when he saw the smoke rising out of the stone chimney. It was, Jean liked to brag, the best-looking log home in Ste. Genevieve. Victor had to agree with him. It was an ingenious design these vertical log homes with their wooden shingles, enormous hewn oak trusses and sturdy pegged and mortised joints. The house then sat on a stone foundation that protected the vertical logs from rot and decay. The French filled in the cracks between the logs with '*bouzillage*' a mixture of clay and straw, to keep the frigid air out. The entire house was then covered with a whitewash that not only sealed it but gave it a homey, attractive appearance.

The *galerie* or porch that wrapped around Jean's house not only shaded the house in the summer and protected it from rain, but it gave the gregarious fun-loving Creoles another place to socialize. Victor had spent many a summer night on Jean's porch. That porch was where he'd had his first glass of tafia, and his second and his third!

The log home Victor and Margaret lived in was nothing like that of the French *poteaux-en-terre* houses. The German blacksmith Jonah Schaeffer had built it, and he had put his logs horizontal, or as he liked to joke, '*the way God intended logs to lay.*' Victor was proud though, it had wooden shingles and not a leaky vermin infected thatched roof.

His stomach was growling as he climbed the last hill. He tried not to think about how flaky Yvonne Riefler's croissants were. At one time or another, he'd eaten at almost everyone's house in the village. And although the German ladies like Annalise Stoddard and Martha Fisk's fixed scrumptious liver *knaflies* the French cooking was his favorite.

Nearing the Riefler's big, red brick house he could see the pale-yellow light spilling out onto the *galerie* that Yvonne, insisted her German husband wrap around the house. There was a tightening in Victor's chest. It happened whenever he got near the Riefler's house, or near the church on Sunday—anytime he thought he might catch a glimpse of Celena.

He heard the youngest son William laughing as he entered the hang--on and waited a moment nervously before walking in. He thought it was smart the way John Riefler had attached the kitchen to the house, and most homes didn't for fear of fire. But John had built a stone break between the kitchen and house. If a fire did start, the stone break would stop it before it caught on. In addition to that there was a hang-on at the back. A humorous term Victor always thought, referring to a hastily added porch where coats, boots, tools, and supplies were kept.

"Morning Victor, come on." John Riefler encouraged; his smile bright as he motioned for Victor to join them in the warm room. John's face was weather-beaten and more lined that it should have been for a man of fifty. His eyes were a gray-blue and his hair although blonde once, was graying as well as thinning. Although he was slender, he did not give off the impression of weakness. Even though he had the money to pay for field hands, or even slaves if he'd wanted to, he still did the farming with his three sons Laurence, James and Will. On his 640 arpents of land, nearly two miles long and a mile wide, he grew corn, wheat and sometimes tobacco and had the good luck to have some of the most productive, fertile land in the valley. He raised cows, hogs and chickens and had an orchard of pear and apple trees that were the envy of Ste. Genevieve. Although he provided nicely for his family, he was frugal. Always in his mind the worry what a late freeze or long draught would do to his beloved crops. "Did you walk?"

Victor nodded. "Couldn't see the point of using up Alpha. Thought I'd better let the horse rest up before the barn raising."

John couldn't help but like someone who thought so much like he did.

"Morning all," Victor mumbled, feeling like a giant when all eyes in the room were suddenly cast on him.

"Bonjour, *Victor*." Yvonne said, her French accent thick. She smiled sweetly up at him, her eyes as blue and clear as Celena' s. Even at forty-one it was easy to see why she had caught John Riefler's attention. "Did you eat?" she asked, and then turned to her son James and said something in French as she replaced the coffee pot on the stove. Victor grinned when James answered in English. James had complained to him before that it was sometimes difficult to understand when his mother insisted speaking to him in French while his father spoke to him in German.

Victor nodded. "Yes ma'am."

Yvonne murmured something in French he could not catch and wrapped up two hot *croissants* with a chunk of sausage in the middle of each and handed them to him. Knowing no matter what time of day it was, he was *always* hungry.

She sighed happily, wiping her hands on the apron tied around her waist, which was still trim despite having born seven children and buried one. Turning to her husband, she helped ease him into his coat. "When do you want your meal? Usual time? *Le déjeuner?*"

Despite twenty-five years of marriage, John Riefler's face softened when he looked down at his wife, who was still as feisty and nearly as pretty as the day he'd married her. "That would be fine. *Gut.*" When she kissed him full on the mouth, he blushed.

"Come on Vic—we got harvestin' to do!" William said, grabbing two croissants from the table. Juggling them, he caught them behind his back.

"You drop one of sos and no more food!" Yvonne admonished.

Will's blue eyes got huge. "Ah *Maman*! Don't you have any faith in me?"

Yvonne didn't. Will was a wild child. He would tangle with anyone who came near. Countless times the cool head of Laurence or the brawn-iness of James had rescued Will. Although he was eighteen, he still showed no signs of settling down. He tried his father's patience to no end, and although his mother loved him dearly, she wondered what would become of him.

"The court jester!" James grinned at Victor. "Laurence will be by later." He pulled his boots on, his chest puffing with pride at being in charge, at least until his older brother arrived. "Glad you're here today, Vic."

"Why's that?"

"With you workin' maybe we'll actually get something finished! Besides, you can keep this runt in line." James said, rubbing his younger brother's head.

"Who you callin' a runt?" Will ducked away from his brother and straightened his skinny shoulders.

"When you gonna *grow,* boy?" James said, standing up. He was six inches taller than Will and outweighed him by thirty pounds.

"Here James, I found them," Celena said, walking into the kitchen, brown leather work gloves in hand.

A jolt went through Victor's chest.

She was wearing a simple gray blouse tucked into a plain blue skirt, but her voluptuous figure was poorly concealed. Even though her blouse was properly buttoned up to her throat, the fabric strained across her breasts, and the waistband of the skirt nipped into a tiny waist. Her light brown hair was pulled back in a single skinny braid that fell past her waist. He noticed the end of the braid was streaked gold by the summer sun.

Nervously, she swiped at the long sun-lightened strands, pushing them behind her ear. Her sleeves were rolled up past her elbows, and her hands were red. He noticed a damp line along the bottom of her skirt and figured she had been out milking cows that morning.

"Thanks, Celena." James smiled.

"A *tout a 'l'heure*. Have a good morning, and don't worry, we'll have good food for you. Celena and I will be cooking all day." Yvonne said, standing behind Celena and, leaning forward, lovingly wrapped her arms around her daughter, easily resting her chin on the top of Celena' s head.

Embarrassed yet proud, Celena smiled, and reluctantly the palest of blue eyes shyly met Victor's.

Walking outside with William and James, Victor could now see a brilliant pink cresting the dark horizon, and that clustered next to the barn was yellow goldenrod mixed with the honeysuckle ripe with tiny red berries.

"It's gonna be a long day. *And* a long night." Will groaned, knowing that his father wouldn't think of letting up until all the work was done.

"Probably, but that's all right. I've always rather liked working under the harvest moon, it's sort of mystical."

Will laughed. "That's the Indian in ya with notions about the moon! I don't feel nothing but happy that you and everybody else are here to help!"

Victor smiled, then saw Will turn and glance back at the house.

"Glad to be out of the kitchen?" Victor asked, knowing Yvonne's insistence that each one of her teenage sons spend a winter working in the kitchen. They would prepare the slaughtered meat, cook meals, bake, milk cows, churn butter, gather eggs, can vegetables and fruits—about the only thing Yvonne *didn't* insist her sons learn was quilting! When Will's winter of 'purgatory' was over, he ran just like his brothers had back to his own work in the fields.

"Hell yes," Will laughed, adjusting his suspenders. He was so thin the straps were forever cutting into his shoulder, "but I did like getting to eat the things I messed up on."

Yvonne was ready to start the noon meal when she realized her sixteen-year-old daughter Celena was still watching the men from the window.

"Celena?" Yvonne breathed, trying to gently break the spell.

"Yes, Maman?"

"You help Eva wis za dough. We'll need to get bread started for tomorrow, but let's do zez biscuits your Papa likes first." Yvonne said piling the last of the breakfast dishes on the cupboard. She smiled at her second oldest daughter seventeen, busy adding baking soda and salt in a large porcelain bowl. "We'll do zez dishes later, I want to make sure we've got enough biscuits. Zar's going to be even more people for dinner."

"The Charbonnier boys, and Stephan and Seth Stoddard?" Eva asked, sifting the flour with a precision that drove her older sister Carlene crazy.

"*Oui,* and Victor and Henry too." Yvonne sighed. It was wonderful to have help with the harvest—but it made more work with the additional mouths she had to feed. Besides that, with her husband and sons working such exhausting hours she often found herself acting as peacemaker when egos and arguments flared. She smiled when she saw Carlene, the oldest of her girls, ambling into the kitchen from outside.

"That chicken coop needs to be cleaned out," Carlene said, wrinkling her nose. She placed the eggs from the basket into the bowl. Not only did the chicken coop smell bad but she hated the beady eyed stare of the hens when she searched for their eggs.

"It was your turn, Carlene," Eva said under her breath. When she felt her older sisters' eyes on her, she stopped mixing, wooden spoon still in hand. "What?"

"I don't see why I have to do it when Celena doesn't mind—"

"Of course she minds, we all *mind*! What makes you think you shouldn't take a turn?"

"Girls, hush! *Mes petites filles!* No fighting eh? We've much work to do!"

"It's all right—" Celena began.

"No, it's not, Celena!" Eva cried. "You and I do plenty. In fact, you do *more* than I do, and I do a lot!"

"All I'm saying is let Celena do the eggs and let me hang the wash out. She can barely reach the line."

"*Chut, paix! Mes filles!*" Yvonne barked. She sighed and looked at her oldest daughter, who tried to get out of chores every chance she got. "Carlene, do eggs when es your turn. Eva, ze dough." Yvonne nodded toward the neglected mixing bowl.

"Carlene, boil water. Celena, biscuits for Papa."

Celena went to the hang-on where they kept the extra flour. Yvonne watched her tug the flour barrel open.

Yvonne sighed and shook her head.

"What's the matter *Maman*?" Eva asked quietly, cutting the butter into chunks.

"I don't know if your Papa is ready yet," Yvonne mumbled.

"Ready for what?" Carlene asked.

"Do you *ever* pay attention to anything besides yourself! Victor and Celena are sweet on each other," Eva spat.

"Oh, that." Carlene scoffed. Eva already had a beau in Danny Charbonnier who was courting her, and if Victor was sweet on Celena, she would be left chasing after Eddie Fisk. She was the oldest, it wasn't fair. She sighed, thinking of all the work to be done, and went out to lug the water in. "I hate harvest time."

Chapter 2

At nearly midnight after eighteen hours, the Rieflers, Charbonniers, Wilburns and Victor were finally done for the day.

Laurence was leaning against one of the wagons, grinning with satisfaction over the newly cut cornfields knowing that they had more than enough to feed the cattle that winter. He turned towards the sound of the muffled voices of his brothers and friends. His wife Lisette standing next to him, absentmindedly touching her stomach as she had done constantly since realizing she was pregnant again.

"We did it, I think we're done," Laurence said as he loaded the last of the corn onto the wagon. "Go ahead, Stephan, that's the last of it for now," he called to his friend, who shouted back happily and drove off.

"You look so tired. We should go home now," Lisette said, looking at her husband. He wasn't particularly handsome with his washed-out blue eyes and dishwater blonde hair. He was too thin and was in the habit of not eating until the work was done. Consequently, there were days when Laurence Riefler didn't eat at all.

"No, I'm all right," he said, forcing a smile down at his pretty mixed race wife. Turning he saw the Charbonnier boys, Caleb and the twins Davey and Danny, waving goodnight.

"*Merci beaucoup!*" Laurence said with a grin, waving a bony hand.

"*A pas de quoi!*" the twins responded, grinning as well. It amused them when any of the Riefler brothers tried to speak to them in their horrid French.

The Charbonnier boys' parents Caleb Senior and Esther were both French, and their children took to the language easily as they did English. Unlike the Riefler brood that had one parent that spoke in German, and one in French, leaving them not only *not* bilingual, but mostly confused.

"No problem," Caleb called, smiling at Laurence, and then turned specially to smile at pretty Lisette. She was a half French and half African, and totally gorgeous. He wondered sometimes what she saw in skinny Laurence Riefler. Maybe it was his brains. Laurence could add up columns of figures in his head like no one Caleb had ever known. He was smarter even then Father Tonnellier who'd spent *years* in a missionary somewhere in France studying.

"This makes up for all the times you and your brothers have helped us! *Au revoir!*" Caleb said, sweeping a low bow that made Laurence snort.

"Night Davey, night Danny," Laurence called, smiling at the seventeen-year-old twins.

"Other way around," Danny said with a laugh *"Je est beau*! I'm the *good* looking one!"

Davey smacked his twin on the back of the head as a lighthearted argument in French ensued.

"Well damn, I *still* can't tell you apart," Laurence laughed, as James joined him, rubbing his tired neck.

"We have one more load from Victor's side and we'll have it licked," Laurence said to his brother.

"Where's Pa?" James asked, looking for the familiar gray head of his father.

"Maman made him go on in couple of hours ago."

The three of them turned their attention to Carlene and Celena riding up in the wagon.

"One more and we're pretty much done," James said excitedly to his sisters.

"Lordy...y'all got a lot done today!" Carlene said, jumping down from the wagon, putting her hands on her hips surveying the newly cut fields with shocks of corn already bundled up dotting the silver ground. She smiled at her plump-with-pregnancy sister-in-law, Lisette, and then hugged her. The happiness was contagious.

"We better get you back home, you look like you need to be off your feet," Carlene said, putting a protective arm around Lisette.

"Go on in honey, you're starting to shiver out here—" Laurence urged, taking off his brown corduroy coat and wrapping it tenderly around his wife. "How are the boys?" he asked Celena.

"I gave them a bath, read three stories, but it took me awhile to rock Gabe to sleep." She rolled her shoulders, trying to get the kinks out. Gabe at three was already heavy.

Laurence grinned thinking how lucky his sons Gabe and Nathan were to have such doting aunts and uncles.

"They're sleeping now like tiny blonde angels," she said, stepping out of the wagon with a pitcher of water and tin cups, placing them out of harm's way.

Laurence laughed knowingly. "I sincerely doubt *that!*"

"We made soup, we have *les saucissons* biscuits, and we've even got some chocolate," Carlene told Lisette as they went towards the wagon.

"Celena, coming?" Carlene asked impatiently.

"I'll come back with Will," she said, smiling at her brother, who was driving too fast and kicking up debris, forcing her to shield her eyes.

Shivering, Celena wrapped her thin shawl around her shoulders, and wished she'd put on a coat. In the moonlight, the tall stalks of bundled corn cast long, eerie shadows and she remembered as a little girl always being afraid there would be ghosts hiding within them.

"What a day," Laurence said, smiling at his little sister. "You know what this means, don't you? Means Pa will have extra feed and hopefully he'll get a few new heifers. Maybe some more pigs too."

Celena smiled. All her brothers worked hard, but Laurence was the one who worried about the dollars and cents. He read everything he could about new techniques and had finally convinced his father to buy a reaper on the installment plan. Word was it could cut six times the wheat in a day that a man could with a simple scythe. It worked so well they'd even lent it to their neighbors for their harvests too. He had also talked his father into getting the new '*singing plow*' or John Deere and they'd had good results with it.

"Hey, you got water there." Nearing her, he poured a cupful and downed it. He hugged her hard and she laughed, infected by his happiness. "Lordy this is good, Celena. I know Pa is overwhelmed; I am too."

"How much would we make with more cattle?" James asked, crossing his arms over his big chest.

"I'm not sure. Depends on the market, and I haven't put pen to paper."

"Just do it in your head." James smirked, remembering jealously when Laurence had been eleven, he'd won the arithmetic contest in school. James had spent many frustrating afternoons secretly out in the barn with his slate honing his math skills.

"Well, do you want the right answer, or want me to guess?"

The conversation was interrupted when Henry Wilburn and Victor joined them, dirty and weary, but smiling. With their appearance, the rest knew the lion's share of the harvest was done.

"We did it!" James exclaimed, slapping backs and giving bear hugs.

The hugs were going around and after hugging her brothers, Celena leaned against Victor. He wrapped his arms around her, and it was a few blissful moments before they realized what they were doing and awkwardly let go of each other.

"To the harvest moon!" Laurence said, raising his little cup.

"What are ya'll? a bunch of damn sissies?" William sneered and triumphantly produced a bottle of whiskey from under his coat. Standing in a circle they began passing the bottle around. But when the bottle reached Celena, Laurence reached to take it away from her.

"Oh come on, Laurence! She's sixteen now and *Maman* will never know, what harm could one little drink do?" Will pleaded.

"Are you drunk already? Maman would tan my hide."

Celena waited, feeling the excitement that always went along with doing something wild with her brothers.

"Oh, all right. Just a little one, and don't tell *Maman*, she'll lecture me on the evils of drink for days."

Celena tipped the bottle up and took the smallest of drinks, embarrassed by their cheers. The whiskey burned her throat and tasted terrible. In fact, she felt tears welling up in her eyes, but desperately not wanting to sputter like a child, downed it. She handed the bottle to Laurence while Will hooted with laughter.

"Give it here, to a *man!*" Laurence grinned, taking another long swig of whiskey. Re-corking the bottle he tossed it to an unsuspecting James.

"Did you see that?" William squealed in horror. "Damn fool almost dropped it!"

"Shut up, runt." James tipped the bottle, then tossed it back to William who, much to Laurence's dismay, downed much more than he should have.

"Have a drink Will, not the whole damn bottle," Laurence huffed, ready to yank the bottle from his brother. But before he could, Will tossed it to Victor.

"Here, *forgeron,* want some firewater?"

Victor shook his head. "Nah, I'm fine." Drink was, after all, what had ruined his father, and he was not terribly enamored of it.

"Oh, come on! Be a man. Be a *brave!*"

Begrudgingly Victor uncorked the bottle, took a swig, and then handed it to Henry, who also took a timid drink.

"We better get going in—besides, I'm hungry. You cooked, right Celena?" James asked as he, Henry, and William got into the wagon.

"Yes. Soup, sausages, and biscuits." The color rose in her cheeks when they began to whoop and holler about her cooking.

"I've got to get the horse, Boots," Laurence said, walking away. "Victor, have you still got one of the wagons?"

"Yes, I'll bring it in. I've got a few tools to get."

Will slapped the reins and started the other wagon with a lurch before Celena could get in. She stood, watching her rambunctious brothers and Henry thunder down the path. Sighing, she realized she would have nearly a half-mile walk home.

Laurence laughed. "They forgot you, didn't they? I'll take you back." He wondered how comfortable the two of them on the horse would be.

"I can take her back, if that's all right?" Victor offered. Out of the corner of his eye he saw her turn to look at him.

Laurence shrugged. "It's all right with me. All right with you, Celena?"

Her mouth had suddenly gone dry. Her heart pounded in her ears. Unable to do anything else, nodded.

"All right then, I'll see you back at the house in a bit. Don't be long or Maman will be after me for *that* too!" Chuckling, Laurence disappeared into the moonlit fields.

The first thing she noticed was how quiet it was. There was no wind, nothing to disturb the stillness. When she saw Victor walking towards her, she hoped he could not hear the thunderous pounding of her heart.

"The wagon is back this way," he said, stretching out his arm, seeking her hand. Standing so tall in the moonlight, he reminded her of a picture of a Roman god she had seen once in a schoolbook. She gave him her hand and felt the warmth and strength of his encircle hers even through his gloves. He smiled down at her, and such joy burst forth that they both laughed.

"Come on! Let's go." He began to run.

Because of the laughter she was short of breath, and her long skirts getting tangled up didn't help. She was afraid she was going to trip, when mercifully they reached the wagon.

They were panting from their sprint when Victor came up beside her and clumsily pulled her head against his chest, and could feel and smell the leather gloves against her face. It was an odd, affectionate thing for him to do.

"That was some harvest. Your Pa and brothers still have a lot to do, but at least most of its cut and bundled." He knew as soon as they were done with the corn, it would be time to sow the wheat. The work never ended.

She didn't want to spoil the moment with talk and merely nodded.

The farm looked endless in the half dark, and she looked up at the inky sky. The moon was gargantuan, surrounded by thin, wispy clouds. The moonlight was so bright even at midnight, still casting shadows on the ground.

"Are the stars brighter in the fall than they are in the summer?"

He looked up. "I don't know. I'm sure Laurence could tell us why... Something to do with an equinox, I suppose."

She shivered, looking over at the stalks of bundled corn. "Carlene used to scare me at harvest time—she told me that at night the bundles of corn turned into witches; the stalks were long withered hands, and the tassels were their straggly hair. It still scares me a little bit."

He chuckled. "That sounds like her."

If someone had told her a half hour ago that she'd be standing alone in the moonlight with Victor's arms around her, she never would have believed it.

"Lena, look at me." He pulled her arms up around his neck, causing the shawl to fall from her shoulders. He stooped to try and kiss her, but she looked down and his lips brushed against the small mark under her left eye.

"We better go in." She dropped her arms. She had on one of Carlene's hand-me-down blouses, and it was too tight. As it was, one of the buttons had popped open and she realized with a flush of embarrassment she could see the top of her camisole.

"Hey, put those arms back up there."

She put her hands against him to push him away. His chest was hard packed with muscle, almost like marble but warm with life under her fingertips. She was too self-conscious to meet his eyes and stared at his shirt instead. "You're going to lose that button."

Straining, he put his chin on his chest to see the round culprit. "I'll fix it later."

"I could do it for you," she offered, meeting his eyes finally.

"Maybe later. Lena, come her just for a minute." He laughed, feeling her resistance as he pulled her closer.

"We should go, Victor; my father will have a fit—"

"I know, and we will soon. I promise," he soothed, "but we'll never get a chance like this again. I've been trying for *weeks* to find you alone."

"You have? Why?"

"You know why." He grinned and, leaning down, kissed her. It was better than he dared to imagine having her in his arms, and he had

29

imagined often—and vividly—in his dreams.

His arms tightened around her like a vise, crushing her against his chest, flattening her breasts and making it hard for her to breathe. His tongue forced its way into her mouth, and although she wanted to kiss him, was unprepared for his passion that had been too long bottled up.

He realized finally her palms were against his chest trying to push him away, and it broke the spell. "Oh, sorry, are you okay? Are you hurt?"

"No, I'm all right, I only need to catch my breath." Gulping air into her lungs, she wanted nothing more than to feel his lips on hers again.

But instead of leaning down to kiss her again, he jerked his head up.

"What? What's the matter?" Reluctantly she followed his gaze.

Standing in the moonlight, watching them, was Ethan. Looking as handsome and as prosperous as ever. His dark eyes swept appreciatively over them, and he was smiling. The moustache he was sporting was perfectly trimmed over his full red lip. He was dressed in a stylish brown worsted wool suit and had on newly shined knee-high calf boots. He looked every inch the refined, well-educated Boston man. He was only twenty-three but the aura around him was of someone older and much accomplished.

"Victor!" he exclaimed, flashing a brilliant smile that showed straight white teeth. "It's great to see you again." He approached them, stretching out his hand to greet his best friend.

For an agonizing moment, no one spoke.

Ethan had written the letter, trying to apologize, and wondered if Victor was just a bad correspondent as he suspected, or if his disappearing when Victor needed him, had ruined a treasured friendship.

"Welcome home." Victor shook Ethan's hand, but Celena noticed it was not an entirely friendly gesture.

"Celena!" Ethan exclaimed as his eyes roved over her, not failing to notice she had filled out nicely in the three years he'd been away. Her heart-shaped face, he realized, was perfect. Other than the small beauty mark under her left eye, she was flawless. Her skin was pale, but rather than appearing ill, she appeared to be made of pearl. Her mouth was plump and slightly pink, and he found himself wondering if her lips were as soft as they looked.

But it was her eyes that took his breath away. Those *astonishingly* pale blue eyes! He'd forgotten how lovely they were. He suddenly wished he could paint, wanting every goddess he created to possess those aquamarine eyes.

"It is so wonderful to see you again." He took her hand between both of his. It was odd how callused and unladylike her hands were when the rest of her was spectacularly beautiful.

"Everyone's up at the house. I hear it was a fabulous harvest and that you are all to be congratulated for a job well done. I walked out here to greet the mighty *Hephaestus!*"

The old nickname didn't used to bother Victor, but now it seemed mean spirited.

"You're not on a trip, you're back?"

Ethan felt traitorous not responding, but he could scarcely keep his eyes from her. Had she *always* been that lovely? "Yes. I am back. I am back for good."

Much to her displeasure, Ethan turned his eyes on her again.

She looked down. It was the way men in town stared at her, or how the local boys did when they thought they could get away with it. She didn't have Carlene's cool confidence of staring back in such a way that made the men clear their throats and shuffle off. Instead, she always ended up dropping her eyes pretending there was something remarkably interesting on the ground that needed to be looked at.

Ethan was someone that could keep a roomful of people enthralled, someone who enjoyed having everyone's attention, something she detested. She had through the years often found herself the subject of his remarks and never realized until this moment, how much she disliked his attention.

"You must be getting cold, Celena." He took off the suit jacket and, before she could protest, wrapped it playfully around her, holding the lapels close around her face so that the fabric caressed her cheeks. He smiled down at her. "You're up awfully late."

She could feel the warmth of him still in the coat and had to fight the desire to fling it off. She noticed his glance drift down to her breasts and made her mind up that the blouse she was wearing was destined for the quilting basket! Again, she dropped her eyes and stared at disintegrating acorn shells underneath her feet, wondering if they had been there since last year's corn harvesting.

"Well...yes, but Maman said it was all right." She wished desperately he had not showed up. Not on this harvest night when she was, by some wonderful chance, alone with Victor.

Since Ethan had forgotten Victor was there, he said, "We better go." Without looking at her, Victor grabbed her around the waist and placed her effortlessly up in the wagon. Retrieving the shawl, he stuffed it clumsily around her feet.

"Victor—"

"Not now."

Ethan jumped up into the wagon. His shoulders brushed against her on one side as Victor's brushed against her on the other. As they made the half-mile trip back to the house, she heard them talking, but for the life of her, could make no sense of the words.

Chapter 3

Victor sat stiff as a board in church, trying to pay attention. But as the morning dragged on, he found himself turning to stare out the small clear panes within the stained glass to the blue sky and puffy white clouds waiting for him outside. He cleared his throat once, but when Davina Woolrich turned to stare at him, refrained from making any more noises.

Leaning to the side he touched Margaret playfully with his shoulders. He saw the corners of her mouth go up in a smile she was trying to conceal. The sleeves of her dress went to her elbows, but he could still make out the faint scars of the terrible burns she had gotten that day in the shop with Jonah, and he stared at them with sadness. He sighed then, and forced it from his mind, and wondered if Margaret was as bored with church as he was. They had an errant father who worshiped drink and an Osage mother that worshipped the sun, and Victor and Margaret were at a loss when it came to faith. Victor tried to embrace Catholicism, but it seemed to him that Father Tonnellier spent an inordinate amount of time telling his congregation what they were doing wrong, and little time what they did right.

Looking around the crowded Catholic church, he knew they were all simple, hardworking people. He just didn't understand why father Tonnellier was convinced God was so angry with all of them.

Besides, his mother had ingrained enough of her Osage teachings for him to be totally confused. The Osage believed in a supernatural life force Wah'Kon-Tah, which resided in all things on earth and in the heavens. The sun's daily journey over the earth filled the Osage with awe and reverence. During the daily dawn chant, the Osage would sit facing the sun to pray for long life and health. The sun was so central in their lives they placed their lodges so that the door faced east, so they could greet the rising sun.

Father Tonnellier had a hard time with the Osage trying to change their idea of revenge with forgiveness. Victor jokingly referred to himself as an *'Osage-Catholic.'*

Bored, Victor looked down at his rough hands absentmindedly, rubbing the thick calluses, praying ironically that Father Tonnellier would finish his homily and church would end.

"Mass has ended, go in peace," Father Tonnellier said, looking surprisingly devout in his dark suit and white soutane that Victor knew Celena had embroidered for him last Easter. Father Tonnellier did not look the part of priest. He was a muscular, handsome man whose wit was as quick as it was sharp. Like all Jesuit priests, he was something of a rebel. The majority of things Father Tonnellier and he debated down at the shop, Victor was sure the Vatican would *not* approve of!

"Thanks be to God," the French and German villagers chanted in unison.

Victor smirked and leaned near Margaret. "It always seems funny to me that we thank God that mass is over, but then it's not over because we have to sing another song."

"Victor! Hush!" Margaret scolded, although her liquid brown eyes were dancing with mirth.

Mercifully, the last hymn was sung, and they began filing out of the church. The morning was crisp and cool, and seeing Margaret's fiancé Henry nervously waiting for them, Victor grinned.

"I still don't see why Henry won't let you take Jonah's house," he said, shaking his head as he carefully moved through the groups of neighbors who stopped to chat. He was big after all, and spaces that most men could easily fit through, he could *not*.

"We've been all through this."

"I've got money, Margaret, money that I want to give to you—"

"Money that *you* worked hard for."

"Like it's *easy* being a laundress?"

He'd seen the work it was to do laundry. She had to first haul buckets of water, get the wood to heat the water, boil the water, and soak the sorted clothes for a day. Then scrub them on the washboard with the lye soap that left her hands red and rough. Then the clothes had to be rinsed in clean water and he'd spent evenings with her on one side of a large garment wringing it before putting it on the line to dry. And in the winter their little cabin became a maze of drying clothes. And the next day she had to iron.

It touched her how much he worried about her, how hard he tried to take care of her. She looked up at her brother. "Henry wants us to do it on our own. He feels bad taking anything else from you Victor, since you were good enough to hire his little brothers." She forced a smile at him as they waited for Esther Charbonnier to finish chatting. Idle suddenly she reached up to straighten his cravat.

"But that's ridiculous. Why shouldn't I give you things? Besides, if Pa hadn't lost everything, you and Henry would have the land the Toulouse's gave Mama."

Gently she brushed away a piece of lint from the black suit. "I know that, but he's proud." Again, she forced a smile. "Besides, you might be needing that house you seem so eager to give away for your *own* bride before too long." She glanced over to where Celena sat in the wagon with her sisters, her parents chatting amicably with the Stoddards.

Victor sighed. "I don't know. I'm not sure she'll ever talk to me again after the other night."

"Victor, trust me on this. I know what I'm talking about. Do it the *right* way. Ask her father if you can court her and then apologize to her and tell her how you feel. You can't just go from hardly ever a private word to...*mauling* her."

He shrugged, thinking it was an apt description. "Courting seems like a big waste of time to me. It's silly. Why do we all the sudden have to act like we don't know each other? I must show up at her house all formal, like I haven't known her all my life."

"It's not silly. It's called manners. You know how protective John is of his girls. You're going to do it."

Henry joined them as they left the church.

Even after a good night's sleep, Henry's face looked tired and drawn. He wasn't short but he was too thin and, next to the vitality Victor exuded, Henry looked pathetic.

"Morning Henry, how are you?" Victor asked, reaching out his hand. Pleased that despite his weak appearance, Henry's grip was strong.

"Right as rain. How my little brothers doing for you, Victor? They give ya any trouble?" he asked, his Adam's apple nearly poking through the skin of his throat.

"Not a lick," Victor lied. Henry's brothers Claude and Thomas were likeable enough fellows, but it was puzzling to Victor how long it took them to catch on to things.

"That was some harvest they brought in the other night," Henry said, a bit of a jealousy creeping into his voice as he watched the Riefler brothers talking with the Charbonnier boys.

"Yes, it was," Margaret agreed, smoothing her coal black hair neatly under her bonnet.

"Sure wish my Pa and me could get a bumper crop like that."

Margaret forced a smile. "Maybe they got lucky with the ground." Frank Wilburn, Henry's father, had never been able to make a farm pay. His sons Isaac and Henry were trying, but so far, they were having as gloomy of results as their father.

"Yeah, maybe." Henry sighed, unconvinced. "Victor, you don't mind if I take Margaret to my folks' house today do you? I'll walk her home before dark. We've got some things we need to talk about."

"Fine with me."

"I want to stop home first; I've got two yellow cakes cooling and I want to take them to your parents' house." She wondered if there would be any sort of supper to go along with the cakes.

As she turned to leave, she leaned up to her brother. "Good luck. It'll be fine, just do what we talked about." She said a quick prayer, not sure she could bear it if he were hurt.

Knowing he had to do it now, Victor straightened his big shoulders and started towards the Rieflers. Normally, after church neighbors lingered in the nice weather to visit, in fact in the summer it was common to bring a picnic. But the farmers still had harvesting to do and couldn't waste precious daylight. Seasonally Father Tonnellier noticed that his congregation shrunk, and swelled depending on crops and harvest.

Victor knew he had to make his move quickly. He had hoped for a more private venue, but the thought of waiting another couple of days to find out if he could even *court* Celena, was too much agony to bear.

He saw her brothers and sisters all gathered by the wagon. They were a close family, and he remembered that Laurence who was thirteen years her senior, continued to give her piggyback rides long after Celena was able to walk.

Victor took a deep breath and adjusted his black suit jacket slightly and cleared his throat. They were the best clothes he owned even if they were hand-me-downs from Widow Chomeau's dead husband. Margaret had let out the sleeves, but they were still too short. He had on a gray cravat that was not long enough because his throat was so big, but with the suit coat buttoned up, hoped it didn't show.

"Victor," Laurence greeted, moving from Lisette to shake his hand. "Have you recovered from that marathon harvest the other night? How backed up are you in the shop after putting in so much time helping us?"

"Not too bad," Victor fibbed. "I told James I like working under the moon."

"It's that wild Osage blood!" Will laughed.

"I hate to ask after you've already done so much, but you'll be able to help us all with the barn raising, won't you?" James asked, but deep down he knew the answer. Victor never said no to helping anyone.

"Oh, I'll be there, but I may have to go back to the shop during the middle of the day."

"Just as long as you're there to help us lift up those damn broadsides," Laurence said, shaking his head. "Besides, you'll want to come back for the dance."

"Me. Dancing. Now there's a horrible thought." They all laughed, including the girls who were listening from the wagon.

"Yeah well, dancing is a good excuse to get your hands on certain things," Will said under his breath, eyeing the current object of his affections, Loriel Gustave—even if he was too shy to inform her.

"You won't be getting your hands on anything," James taunted, glad that he and Alice Renaud were getting married soon and had been given a small farm to call their own by his parents.

"Morning Victor," Carlene said, butting into her brothers' conversation. She hadn't quite heard what Will said, but by the way her brothers were laughing, she didn't approve.

"Morning Carlene. I'd like to stay here and talk, but I've got to ask your father something."

Leaving them, Victor walked toward John Riefler.

John saw him approach and shook his hand. "Beautiful morning, Victor. If this fall stays mild, we might be able to get eighty arpents of wheat in this fall."

Victor nodded.

"*Bon jour* Victor!" Yvonne beamed, touching him affectionately on the shoulder. "Don you look grand ziz morning," she said, but couldn't help but notice that despite Margaret's efforts, the suit still fit him badly.

"John," Victor began, "I was wondering if I might have a word with you."

The bright smile disappeared from John's face. "Certainly," he replied, hoping nothing bad had happened. Victor and Margaret had already had their share of misfortune, and he hoped nothing else plagued them.

"I don't know exactly how to say this," Victor began, nervously clenching and unclenching his hammer hand. "Would it be all right...can I, can I ask permission to...court Celena?"

"Well...this is quite a surprise Victor. I don't know what to say—" John stammered, having absolutely no intention of letting his little girl court *anyone*. He was pleased that Victor came to him first, unlike that renegade Eddie Fisk who he found out was seeing Carlene behind his back.

"John? You don't have any objections, do you?" Yvonne asked sweetly.

John, who would have liked to strangle his pretty wife, paused, trying to figure out a way to say no while still preserving Victor's feelings. "I don't know, she...*awfully* young."

"She's sixteen."

"Yes, only sixteen, and when you're that young sometimes you don't know what you're getting yourself into. Sometimes you can get all caught up in something for the idea's sake. Do you understand? besides, I worry about her."

"I know you do. But you've known me all your life. You know what kind of a man I am."

"Yes, I have, and I do. I know I'm her father Victor, but I can imagine how a young man might feel when he looks at her. Let me make this crystal clear." His blue eyes were hard. "I expect you to be a perfect gentleman with her. I'll tolerate nothing less."

"Nor should you," Victor answered, breaking the spell.

For the first time that day, Victor turned and looked into the eyes of his beloved, feeling his heart move in his chest.

Celena had on a blue plaid dress that had decorative black ribbons stitched horizontally across the bodice. Even though it was properly to the neck, it was snug and looking at her made his temperature rise. On her head was a black bonnet with a silky ribbon tied neatly under her chin, and he wondered how she managed to tuck all her hair up underneath. She had on gold filigree earrings, and each time she moved the diamond shaped fringe on the earrings danced. Not only was she beautiful, but she was also practical and a hard worker. And he had been silently in love with her for as long as he could remember.

Possessing great beauty though did not make her confident. When she glanced up and caught even someone she was fond of like Victor looking at her, she pulled the crocheted shawl tighter around her shoulders, and dropped her magnificent eyes to the ground.

"Yvonne, it looks as though Victor here will be joining us for Sunday dinner," John said, wanting Victor to court Celena where he could keep his eyes on them.

"But before zat he's going to take Celena out for a little ride and zen you'll be back in time for Sunday supper?"

Victor was shocked by how easy Yvonne was making it for him; for a moment he was speechless. "Yes! Of course, well in time for supper." He hurried off to ask Celena.

"It's all settled zen. *Bien.*" Yvonne smiled but, turning, saw her husband glaring at her. "Relax John," she soothed, patting his rough hand, "it's our Victor."

"But he's with our *Celena!*"

"They're young. Let zem have a moment alone without everyone watching everything zey do, listening to everything zey say." Realizing he was still unconvinced, she squeezed his hand. "Do you realize zat I was never once alone wis you, never alone with you until the night we wed?"

Despite being fifty years old and married twenty-five years, John still blushed at the memory of that rapturous night. "Are you complaining, Yvonne?"

She laughed at her husband, whom she still thought was too serious. "Of course not. But Celena es not like me. She is shy; she'll need more time."

"Time for what?"

Yvonne shrugged. "To relax and fall in love. To let life happen."

John shook his head. He didn't care what Yvonne said; he didn't want *anything* to happen concerning Celena.

"Lena?" Victor said, offering her his hand to help her out of her parents' wagon. "I've talked with your parents, and I was wondering if you'd like to take a ride with me?"

Eva giggled, and Carlene had to nudge Celena.

"All right," Celena said, blushing, unable to look at him.

They walked the few steps to his wagon.

He lifted her up onto the seat but didn't drop his hands right away.

"Are you all right with all this? I realize it would be difficult to say no in front of everyone."

"It's all right."

"Good. We need to talk." Victor jumped up into the wagon.

"Forgeron!" Jean Gustave shouted. "No billiards ziz morning?" and seeing Celena in the wagon, grinned at the sight of his neighbor's pretty daughter.

"Not today, Jean."

"Bonjour, mademoiselle Riefler."

"Bonjour, monsieur Gustave. "

Even though Jean Gustave was as old as her father, the French farmer acted and looked younger. His hair was still dark, and his skin a healthy brown. Although he had a bit of a paunch, was known to suck it in when an attractive female went by. He still joked and drank with the young men of the village and danced and flirted with all the pretty girls. He had five daughters that he embarrassed regularly and a *very* understanding wife.

"That man loves to annoy me!" He grinned, ignoring Jean still calling out to them in French. "He comes into the shop every week, sometimes he doesn't even have anything with him for me to fix."

She turned and smiled. His skin was a healthy reddish brown that got darker if he spent time in the sun-unlike her own white complexion that burned. "I wondered why you brought the wagon when you usually walk." She glanced down at the old wagon. He'd bought it from Alvin Woolrich who'd given him a good deal because of all the work Victor had done on the steps to the general store.

The wagon was clean, all the screws were tight, and the springs had been oiled. The boards were sanded smooth, and it had a fresh coat of black paint. It was so like Victor to do the best with all the old things he had. Always able to either fix something or salvage the parts and transform it from the heat of the forge into something new.

"Where are we going?"

"To the shop." He pulled the reins so Alpha turned on Fourth Street and then left on South Gabouri. Jumping off the wagon he trotted around like an excited child to lift her down. His hands went up and squeezed her by the waist, pulling her off the wagon, but instead of releasing her, held her playfully aloft.

"Are you going to put me down?"

"If I must." He grinned, delighted to have her in his arms. As he slid her down, he held her so close she had to smooth the ribbons stitched on the front of her bodice.

"Come on, let me show you what I'm working on." Finding her hand, he pulled her into the shop, closing the door behind them.

She hadn't been through the huge double doors of the blacksmith shop in years. There was no need for her to go since her brothers took what needed repairing. Besides, the blacksmith shop was a place where men congregated, and it had a rough reputation. There were a lot of arguments, political debates, gossip and swearing that went on by the glow of the forge. It fascinated little boys like her nephews Gabe and Nathan. For them, the blacksmith shop was a place of mystery and excitement.

The shop was thirty feet long, and as wide as her parent's keeping room. Turning she looked at the massive brick forge. It rested on a stone foundation, and the squared brick chimney went straight through the roof. On the side of the chimney was a boxy brick thing, waist high, five feet front to back and eight feet long. On top of the brickwork next to the chimney was the hearth itself. A square tub about twelve inches deep and nearly five feet wide. At the bottom of the hearth was a slab of iron with a strange pipe attached to it. The inside of the forge was black and peering into it she half expected to see it glowing red, instead of banked for the night like it was with a stub of apple wood and bucket of ashes to trap the heat.

Near the forge was a wooden crane and above, the enormous pulley that worked it. It made sense to her now how Victor could move such enormous pieces of farming or carriage equipment in and out of the fire.

Other than the church, the blacksmith shop had the tallest ceiling she had ever seen. There were various pieces of iron hanging from the rafters, and if she wasn't mistaken she recognized a template for a buggy body. She smiled when she noticed a bird's nest atop one of the rough beams, and wondered if Victor knew he had company.

Two of the walls were lined with workbenches. One she could tell was specifically for repairs on wagons because there was a saw, plane, square, chisels and spoke shaves. Next to that was a small foot-treadle lathe, in case he needed to make a new spoke or rim.

Another bench was reserved for finish work, because even a master smith like Victor had imperfections in his work. That bench was fitted out with files, tin shears, punches etc. Looking at the finish bench, she remembered the day she helped him fix that old butter churn. He'd been so patient, so meticulous in his work. She smiled realizing they were still using it at the house.

Close to the forge, she saw a heavy iron vise mounted on a post sunk into the floor. Next to that was a foot treadle grindstone, and near that a large wooden tub full of water.

On the other walls were wooden racks where Victor neatly stacked his store of metal. They were sixteen feet long and, looking closer, she saw that there were square, rectangular, oval, and even flat ones. She realized Victor would know when and where to use each kind. Smiling, she knew Margaret was right. He never threw anything away that was made from iron.

Glancing toward the door, she saw the leather apron he always wore hung on one of the wooden pegs. She realized she'd seen him in that apron more than any other piece of clothing. Last August she remembered walking by the shop with Laurence and glancing through the open doors, catching a glimpse of Victor sweating at the forge shirtless with that apron on.

Embarrassed by the sudden tingling in her abdomen, she glanced down at the brick floor. It was swept clean, except for a neat pile of iron shavings from the horses he had shod that week. Even though there were an incredible number of tools hanging, she suspected he could instantly lay his hands on whatever he wanted.

She felt him come up behind her, and wondered with the sensation deep in her stomach again if he was going to kiss her.

He pulled an iron out from the side of forge and placed it proudly in front of her. The morning sun was streaming in the windows that faced east and quickly heated up the shop.

Ash she inspected it, she slid off her shawl. "It's an iron, Victor. Lord knows I've seen one of those before." Laughing, she began to untie the black ribbon from under her chin.

He watched her smooth the blond strands from her face and realized he might die if he couldn't touch her. He found himself fantasizing about how wonderful it would be to live with her and share his life with her.

"Is there something special about this one?" she asked, her eyes sparkling up at him.

"Look at the handle," he said, taking off his coat and rolling up the sleeves of his white cotton shirt. She'd never seen anyone with arms like his. There were knots of muscles and tendons like ropes.

"It's not connected to the bottom like my iron, is that what you mean?"

He reached out and took a hold of her hands and turned them palms up, and her heart fluttered because he bent his head as if to kiss them.

"Just as I thought," he said, looking back up triumphantly, "burn marks from ironing?"

"Well yes, some, and from the other things in the kitchen." She pulled her hands away self-consciously, rubbing the dim brown marks on her wist and hands.

"Those hot pads you put over the irons slip. I know because Margaret has burned herself more than once." He walked over to one of the carpentry tables and brought back a piece of carved wood and screwed it deftly onto the threads of the iron handle. "Here. Now you won't burn yourself anymore."

"Oh! That's *lovely!* It will make things so much easier, I mean I wish all irons were made this way!"

"I made them all for Margaret. Especially the ones for goffering, crimping and polishing."

She smiled. It was sweet how much he knew and cared about Margaret's laundry business.

"I, a...made you a set." He walked to the other side of the shop and, reaching under one of the carpenter tables, brought them to her. He waited uneasily, not sure if she would like it. He'd gone to the Woolrich's store yesterday and had a roll of silk ribbon in hand, but then couldn't decide the length or color. Then he'd picked up talcum powder, and after accidentally breathing in the stuff, had a coughing fit. The last thing he'd looked at was a pretty hair comb that had a dragonfly on it, but one of the pearl eyes was already loose and he was ashamed to give it to her, and he'd left, frustrated and empty handed.

"Victor, they're wonderful! That was so sweet of you." She looked down at the various irons and noticed that in the removable wooden handles he'd taken the time to carve an elaborate curving letter 'L.' It was a useful gift, one that Carlene would make fun of when she found out.

"An 'L'?"

"For Lena; like I told you years ago, it's too big a name for you. Three syllables you are *not!*"

She laughed, hugging one of the irons against her chest. "Have you any other treasures stowed away in here?"

Nodding, he walked eight quick steps to the end of the shop and pulled out a carriage wheel. Lifting it above his head, he swirled it by her. His exaggerated, playful gestures made her laugh. "My goodness, first an iron and now a carriage wheel!"

He crossed his big arms against his even bigger chest. "You disappoint me. Look again."

It had a rim like all the others and twelve spokes, and she felt badly because she could not see what was wrong.

"This is the hub..." He pointed to the center of the wheel, where the spokes came out. "Skein fits inside the hub. Spindle into the hub from the axle...of course there are washers and nuts to keep it in place...the spokes fit into the felloes." He motioned to the curved pieces of wood that constituted the outside of the wheel with holes in them to accommodate the spokes. "When it's all fit together, the smithy—me—fastens individual iron plates to the outside of the rim, and then they're bolted together, like a puzzle. The problem is...if all of this is not tight, as you can see," he tugged on one of the metal plates, "it all falls apart." When he pulled on the iron plate, part of the spoke slipped out of the felloe, and loosened the others near it.

She nodded to let him know she was listening.

"That got me thinking." He reached over Celena' s head and pulled a large iron circle off a hook, placing it on top of the wheel. "Everything has to be tight to work...right?"

"Yes, otherwise all of the parts will fall out."

"All *eighteen* parts to be exact," he said, thinking back to the countless hours he had spent fixing carriage wheels. After all the carriages and wagons that the farmers and everyone else drove around town in and through their fields took a terrible beating. And they all came to him for their repairs.

"But Victor...it doesn't fit," she said, trying to force it around the carriage wheel.

He nodded patiently. He reminded her suddenly of the way Sister Rita Marie used to encourage her to question when she'd attended Our Lady of Mt. Carmel School run by the Sisters of Loreto. It occurred to her suddenly that would be a good trait for a father and blushed from her thoughts.

"When I heat it, it expands," he said, grabbing one of the mallets and demonstrating toward the rim. "I slip it around the rim when it's red, then drive it hot onto the wheel. When it cools, it winches all the parts together...tight as a bow string." He put his hand over Celena's that were still on the wheel and squeezed to emphasize what would happen.

She was silent, amazed that something so ingenious could at the same time be so utterly simple. "Why doesn't everyone do it that way? I mean it seems so obvious that one piece of iron would work better than many bolted together?"

"Probably because they didn't think about it. Jonah was a master blacksmith, and was taught by a master as well, even so neither of them rimmed a wheel this way. And you do have to measure accurately."

"But you did!" she said, feeling the fluttering in her chest. "You should tell someone about this; you should get a-a patent for this and the iron cover!" She felt tears prick her eyes, wanting him to succeed and be given recognition for his hard work and ingenuity. "When on earth did you have time to do all of this? With working here and at my parents, when did you have time to invent things?"

"When I wasn't working on orders, or working on your parents' farm, I stayed out here in the shop thinking and drawing."

"At night? Alone?"

He nodded. "It kept me company after Jonah died. I felt close to him out here." He stopped then, remembering well the man that had taken him and Margaret in.

She feared it would always weigh on his heart what had happened to Jonah. She wondered if Ethan ever felt guilty about his part in that mess. If he even tried to stop his father. After all, if Victor hadn't been gone, there would have been no reason for Jonah to have gone into that blacksmith shop with those crippled arthritic hands. And no reason for Margaret to have tried to save him and gotten hideously burned while doing it.

"Besides, Margaret was spending a lot of time with Henry, and I wanted to give them some privacy. Where else would they go? They certainly couldn't go to Henry's house with all his brothers and sisters around. I came out here. It's where I wanted to be anyway."

Although she understood, it did sound lonely. Especially to someone like her who lived in a house filled with so many happy, loving people.

He suddenly smiled at her, nervously remembering he had to ask her how she felt about him, but not having the faintest idea how to broach such a subject they fell awkwardly silent.

"I dare say I've never seen so many tools, and you know what to do with all of them?"

He laughed, remembering he felt the same thing ten years ago when he first walked into the shop as Jonah's striker. "Yes. There are hammers with different points for different tasks. The first day I ever spent in this shop with Jonah he had me making nails. I honestly thought my arms were going to fall off by the end of the day."

"Was it hard to work for Jonah?"

"Not really, especially once I learned to understand him. I think I still know more swear words in German than English! Jonah was good to me.

He was a great smith. He taught me well."

She walked to a line of tools; aware he was watching her. She touched one, turning to him. "What's this?"

"A drift hammer."

She touched another.

"Sledge, mandrel, cross peen, ball peen, straight peen."

Smiling, she walked to another line of tools.

"That's a link, hollow bit, hoop tongs, swags, hot set, twisting bar, scroll fork, vice, wedge, bending fork."

She laughed sweetly. "Yes, I suppose you *do* know what to do with them all!"

"I wouldn't be much of a smith if I *didn't*."

"I've always wanted to ask you, why are there holes in it?" she asked, touching the anvil standing on an ancient oak stump next to the forge that, with no brick flooring underneath, was sunk deep into the ground. The base of the anvil forked out into four legs that were secured to the tree stump with quarter inch rods driven into the trunk and bent over. It was a strange looking thing, with its flat top five inches wide and twenty inches long; it also had a graceful looking horn on one.

He took two steps towards his anvil and touched the small hole. "Pritchel hole, for knocking the old nails out of horseshoes; the hardy hole is where I put the forging tools while I do my work. Here," he said, handing her a three-pound welding hammer. They both laughed when she nearly dropped it. "Have you ever swung one?"

"No, could I try?"

He nodded and grabbed a piece of iron and put it on the anvil.

"What's that for?"

"To protect the anvil. It may be 250 lbs. but believe it or not it can be damaged, and I am not about to order a new one from the foundry, but go ahead."

Shrugging, she lifted the hammer and it fell with a loud din on the anvil which stood like a knight at the edge of the rectangular forge. "It's heavier than it looks!" Letting go of the hammer, she shook her arm.

"It's the wrong height for you; you'd wear yourself out at it."

"What do you mean?"

"The height of the anvil is supposed to match the smith's swing. I spent almost half a day last year digging the stump out and raising the anvil."

"'Cause you'd grown again." She smiled, hoping he didn't get any taller. He was a foot and a half taller than she was, and as she found the other night, it was uncomfortable to reach up so high. "What is it Jonah used to say, the anvil is the heart of the shop?"

Something warmed inside him. Not only because she had spoken of Jonah, but she remembered the little details of his life. "The other way around—the forge is the heart of the shop, but the anvil is its soul." He walked near the anvil. "Yes ma'am, this is where I spend my life. This is a good anvil."

"I didn't know there was such a thing as a *bad* one."

He grinned self-consciously. "Well, what I mean is this one has a convex face." He reached for her hand and smoothed it over the top. "Feel that, it's slightly rounded. It makes it easier for me when I'm fullering things, flattening them."

"Oh, I see." She bent slightly, staring at the anvil. "Victor, I think it's crooked."

"It's mounted at an angle so that when the loose slivers of scale come off, they'll slide off without me having to knock them loose."

"Oh, I'm sorry," she said, still trying not to laugh. Obviously, he took blacksmithing *very* seriously. "What's the little anvil for?"

"The *little anvil* is a bickern. I use it for hollowing out things, pots, and kitchen utensils, for example."

She looked past the bickern. "I've never seen bellows so big."

He nodded with pride. "Took a whole ox hide that one did. And it's a double stroke meaning it pumps air on the up and down stroke."

"I've always wanted to ask you; how do you adjust the heat?" She wondered if the forge was as temperamental as the stove in her mother's kitchen. After all, it was common practice to stick a hand into the stove and count to ten when it could not be tolerated any longer the stove was deemed hot enough to cook with.

"Air. It goes from the bellows, through a pipe under the forge into the tuyere or nozzle." He pointed into the blackness of the forge. "I can point a blast of air from one side of the fire to the other this rod here makes it move. I have Thomas on the bellows usually while Claude and I are at the anvil. I can tell by the color of the fire if I've got it the right temperature. Too much air and you'll only eat up the coal in the middle, making it hollow. A red fire is good for working, but a white fire is the hottest. I keep telling Claude that a bigger fire doesn't get more smithing done it just costs more money—but I still don't think he believes me."

She smiled, looking around, aware that he was watching her. She was comfortable with him. She found him pleasant and easy to be with, like when they were children.

"Lena...I asked to see you today because I—I wanted to talk to you about the other night."

She dropped her eyes from his and studied the basket weave pattern on the floor. She was afraid he might be sorry he had kissed her. He might be feeling guilty about it and brought her here to apologize.

He cleared his throat. "I wanted to tell you that I'm sorry about what I did after the harvest. It was wrong. I—I don't know what came over me." Even as he said the words, he was afraid he sounded ridiculous. He knew after all *exactly* what had come over him. "I hope I didn't...hurt you. I know I was sort of...rough." He tried not to think about how wonderful it had been to crush her to him and kiss her. "I didn't, did I? Hurt you, that is?"

She shook her head.

"That's a relief." He forced a smile, still concerned. She was not responding like he thought she would. He wasn't sure what he expected, but silence was not the desired result.

He waited a moment and then too stared at the brick floor. He had the feeling in the pit of his stomach that things were suddenly not going well. He racked his brain to try and think of what else Margaret had told him to do. Ask permission, he had done that. Apologize to Celena, he had done that too! Now he remembered, the most difficult one of all, ask how she felt about him. How on earth was he supposed to do that, he wondered cursing silently for getting himself in this predicament.

"Are you thirsty? I could get us a drink?"

"No," she said quietly, her eyes leaving the floor finally. There was a puzzled, hurt look in them that he was alarmed to see.

She opened her mouth to say something, then thinking better of it, shut it, and said nothing.

He felt his opportunity slipping like sand through his fingers.

"I guess you'd better take me home. It's getting late, and I need to help with supper."

His heart fell inside his chest. "All right." But he did not move from his place. "I asked if I could see you today, to apologize for what I did the other night...and I would have apologized right then but Ethan showed up and I-I didn't have the chance."

At the mention of the kiss and his regret over it, Celena's eyes left his and again returned to the floor. It was humiliating to her that she had been transformed by the encounter and all he could do was tell her he regretted it.

"But also, to ask you—" His words dried up. He hoped she would somehow finish the sentence for him, but try as he might, he could not get his brain and his mouth to work in sync. He felt ridiculous saying the silly, flowery words he knew he was supposed to. How did anyone ever get married he wondered, if men had to turn into such ardent fools?

"Ask me what, Victor?" Suddenly her blue eyes were on him.

To his displeasure he realized he did not have the luxury of waiting for another time. "Lena—" He sighed, and leaned heavily against the forge, running both hands savagely through his hair dislodging the piece of leather that held it back. Wishing suddenly, he had Ethan's way with words, Ethan would know what to say. "Would you—could I talk you into—"

Another pause, during which they heard the clock at the church chime the eleventh hour, and listened 'til the sound of the chimes faded away.

"What is it, Victor?"

"God dammit."

"Victor!"

"I'm sorry," he rubbed his face with his hand, "this is torture."

"For heaven's sake, say it!"

He stood upright. "All right. I'll say it if you tell me beforehand you'll give me the answer I want."

Her brow wrinkled in confusion. "What answer is that?"

"Yes."

"But how can I answer yes when I don't know what it is I'm agreeing to?"

"Humor me. Just say yes."

"I can't do *that!*"

"Why?"

"You're being difficult."

Victor shook his head. "Oh no, no, no...I'm not being *difficult!* I'll tell you what *difficult* is—difficult is walking up to your father in front of Laurence, Will, James, Eva, and Carlene and asking him if I can...*court* you." He said the word 'court' like it was dipped in vinegar.

Her eyes widened. "You asked my father if you could *court* me?"

"Yes."

Unable to control herself, she laughed.

He was annoyed. "Why is that so funny?"

"Oh, it's not!" she said, trying to recover her composure. "I—I never thought you'd *do* something like that."

"Why not?"

"Well because—" She hesitated. "You're not *like* everyone else." It was, after all, one of the reasons she had always liked him so much.

"Is that good or bad?"

She laughed again.

"I do wish you'd stop laughing."

"I'm sorry Victor! I've never *seen* you like this."

"It's not pretty, is it?" He sighed, staring at the floor. "Yes or no."

"What was the question again?"

He looked up impatiently. "Will you marry me, yes or no?"

Her eyes widened in astonishment. She hadn't been expecting that, even though she had lain awake many a night hoping one day he would ask. "Sakes alive, are you *serious?*"

"As serious as a hammer hittin' the anvil." He rubbed his face. "Sorry. This isn't going like I planned."

"You *planned* this?"

"Badly, yes. I was supposed to ask your parents, then I was supposed to apologize to you about the other night because I didn't know if I'd hurt you, then I was supposed to see if you were...fond of me, then I was supposed to ask you...you know. All this seems stupid to me by the way. I can't do this...*courting* shit—"

The pounding of Celena's heart was so strong she placed her hand against her breast and felt it nearly leaping out of her chest. All she could think of was that if he was her husband he could hold her like he had the night of the harvest—always. She could see him and talk to him whenever she wished. It was the purest most wonderful idea to be his wife!

"You want...to marry me?" she asked carefully, wanting to make sure she had not imagined the wondrous words.

"Well of course." He shrugged as if there was no other alternative. "I mean especially after what happened the other night."

"But you just finished apologizing to me about the other night!"

He stared at her, annoyed. "I'm not apologizing because I *kissed* you, I was apologizing because I thought I'd sort of...*crushed* you. I'm just doin' what Margaret said."

"Margaret knows about this?"

He swallowed hard. "We're getting off the subject." He placed his big hands on his hips, staring down at her. "Don't make this hard on me. Are you going to marry me, yes or no?"

"But you already told me what I had to answer before you asked the question." She had to bite her bottom lip to keep from giggling.

He frowned. "Indulge me. Just say it."

"Oh, all right, yes! Are you going to be this crabby when we're married?"

"I doubt it."

Before she knew it, he was right in front her. Reaching down, he tilted her chin up. "Okay, we've got a deal, right?"

"Right."

"Good. Kiss me."

His mouth was warm against hers. Her knees felt weak, and her heart thumped painfully. Without giving a thought to what she was doing, put her arms around him. She was disappointed a minute later when he suddenly broke free, pulling her linked hands from behind his neck, leaning his forehead against hers.

"I know I don't have a lot to offer you right now, but I'm good at my trade and I made a decent living. And you saw, I've got things I'm working on. We'll never be rich, but I am dependable. I know I don't know anything about..." He glanced down at her in a way that made her blush. "*Womanly* things, but I promise you, I'll take good care of you. I realized the other night at your parents' farm...that...I *needed* you...and I don't need much of anything." He waited for a response.

Staring up at him, she thought about leaving her parents' home on the rolling green hills she loved, of coming to town and living in the tiny house adjacent to the shop. She imagined cooking, sewing, and washing for him. Imagined babies with their father's gray eyes.

"Am I making a...*fool* out of myself here?" he breathed quietly. "Will it be enough for you, Lena?" he asked softly, holding her so close she could feel the warmth of his breath on her lips. "Will I do?"

"Oh, it's enough, it'll do."

He grinned down and it made her blush from the part in her hair to the tips of her toes. "I'll *do*, will I!" he mocked, but there was no sting to it.

He laughed then, and it was a wonderful release of tension, and she did too. Looking down at her with shining eyes, he cupped her face with his callused hands. "God help me."

"Why should God help you?"

"Because I am lost to you."

She realized then with a fluttering in her heart that no matter he was twice her size, she had the power to make his life joyful or destroy him. Reaching up with both hands she touched his cheeks. "I like it when you smile. It rather transforms your face."

"Does it? How so?"

"You don't look...*cruel* anymore."

He laughed it off.

"No, I've seen it Victor, I've seen people that get off keelboats or steamers in town, stop and stare at you, and they're *afraid* of you. It's not only your size, but also the coldness in your eyes. But when you smile...it changes everything."

Shrugging, he took her hand and pressed it to his lips. "I don't care who's afraid of me—just as long as *you're* not. Now pick up the back of your skirt." He began gathering the fabric around the cumbersome hooped skirts and then simply picked her up and sat her down on the edge of the bricked forge. "There, now this is much better," he said, adjusting her skirts with ease like he was *always* grabbing women and rearranging their skirts. "They'd be tripping up and, in the way otherwise. I don't know why you women insist on wearing these ridiculous things, they are *always* in the way. There now, I can concentrate on properly kissing you without you going weak in the knees and slipping down." He chuckled then, like a man going happily insane. He placed his big hands neatly around her waist and, bending, nipped a little kiss on the mark under her left eye. "I've been wanting to kiss you there for a long time."

"Oh really, how long?"

"I think the day I first thought about doing it was the day you came into the shop with that butter churn to be fixed. I think that was the first uh..." He grinned nervously, remembering the first stirring of physical passion he had felt for her. "Just think," he mused, staring down. "All this will be mine! You are so tiny here." His hands slid tidily around her waist, but then looking up he added, "Not so *tiny* in other places!" His thumb gently touched the bottom curve of her breast.

She batted it away. "Victor, don't!"

"I'm sorry!" he said, but the healthy grin on his face betrayed any true remorse. "I am...*breathing* after all and I couldn't help but notice."

"You should at least be a little ashamed of yourself."

"Why? You want me to be ashamed because I want you? There's that Catholic guilt again."

"You're Catholic too."

"Osage Catholic," he corrected. He pulled her arms up around his neck again, and making good on his opportunity kissed her cheeks, her forehead his favorite place under her eye. But when he leaned closer to her, felt her knees in his groin.

"What are you doing *now*?"

"Open so," he said and had no trouble wedging apart her legs with his strength, "so, I can be against you. I want to be right next to you. I can't see anything anyway with what it is…twenty yards of fabric?"

"Twelve."

"Whatever—besides, I wouldn't *do* anything. I just wanted to have my heart against yours and your knees were well almost in my—!" He gave a short laugh.

As he kissed her, her slumbering passion for him awoke, and although she was being swept up in the pulsing new emotions, knew they shouldn't be kissing like this. She was embarrassed to admit how much she was enjoying these open-mouthed kisses and in the recesses of her mind wondered what *other* things they would be able to do once they were married. She had the distinct feeling, as Victor's hands inched upward on her breast, that being his wife, would be wonderful indeed, and yet at the same time, it terrified her. "We…we shouldn't be doing this."

"Why?"

"What if Margaret comes in?"

"Margaret's not in the house, she's with Henry." Seeing the shock register, he grinned. "You're all alone with me. There's no one here to save you."

"It's not…proper what we're doing."

He stared down at her for a moment, trying to decide how best to manage the situation. He put his hands on the sides of her face. "I only want to kiss you. Do you like it when I kiss you?"

Too ashamed to admit how much, she nodded.

"Then kiss me."

Giving in, she closed her eyes and released herself to the man who would be her husband. She wanted nothing more than to melt into his strong arms and feel his open mouth on hers. She reveled in the warmth of him next to her. She could faintly smell the soap he had bathed with and could hear the steady pounding of his heart. Her hand gripped his bicep. Even with her hand fully stretched she could not cradle the entire muscle. She pulled back. "Why are your arms so hard?"

He laughed. "Trust me, that's not the *only* thing hard at the moment."

"What?"

"Never mind. It's one of the many benefits of smithing, you become strong like an ox."

"Are there any other benefits?"

"Oh, I don't know, I guess if a door hinge breaks or anything else, you know I can fix it." He cleared his throat. "Lena, I want to explain something to you. I've got money saved, but I've been saving it for Margaret. And I figure I owe her something since I've been able to learn a trade to support myself and I have a place to live—"

"Whatever you decide to do is fine by me."

He looked down and paused. It wasn't that he minded her being agreeable, but he felt a twinge of worry. And for a moment he wondered if she was in love with the *idea* of being in love-more than in love with *him*. Unhappily, the meaning of her father's earlier words became annoyingly clear. *What's he going to say when I want to marry her?* He decided he'd better take it slow and give John Riefler time to get over what he was afraid would be a big shock for him.

"I know I've rushed you, and I didn't mean to. I wasn't planning to just...blurt it out about getting married today."

"It's all right. I'm glad you did. I want to."

He paused a moment. "Do you realize what you're getting yourself into? It's a one room house, and it may be a long time before we have anything better."

"I don't care, it's all right. And if you think I'm old enough to get married, I hope you understand I'm also old enough to make decisions. Victor, I think you should try and get a patent."

"A *patent*? I wouldn't know the first thing about applying for one. Besides, I've got more work already than I can keep up with."

"I could do it for you!" she exclaimed as two bright spots of pink suddenly colored her cheeks.

"You don't know anything about smithing—"

"I don't think I would need to be a blacksmith to apply. I could write it all down and draw it out—like you do, to scale. I bet Laurence could tell me where to find the address to the patent office. Where is it do you think, New York or someplace?"

"Washington would be my guess because it's got to be registered. Are you sure you want to go to all that trouble?"

"Why wouldn't I? that's what a wife would do for a husband, isn't it?"

He grinned wickedly, liking to think of her as his wife. "I guess you're right." He hadn't considered that when he married, he'd have someone to help *him*.

"When do you want to—to get married?" she struggled on the question, so excited she could barely speak.

"Yesterday."

"I'm serious."

"I am too. I don't know. Your father still thinks you're in pigtails."

"Maybe if we give my father 'til next spring to get used to the idea."

"*That* long?"

Celena shrugged.

"Spring is too far away...let's give your father...three months? Dead of winter when he's not too busy. He can't complain about that."

She smiled sweetly at him, but they both knew it was time they left.

"I guess I better get you home before your father yanks my courting privileges." He tapped her playfully on the nose and lifted her off the forge, holding her aloft. He chuckled in amusement. "You don't weigh *anything*!"

When he returned her to her feet he leaned down and made sure the yards of fabric were properly over the hoops. He was so practical; he was able to make her feel at ease with things that would have normally horrified her.

Putting his coat on, he smoothed back his hair and retied it with the piece of leather. It reminded her of when last week James teased him about being a 'dandy' with his long hair. She'd looked the word up in the dictionary and thought it described Victor not at all!

"I still find it hard to believe you asked my father if you could court me. I *know* how much you hate all that sort of stuff. Besides, I know what effort it took especially in front of my brothers. You'll never hear the end of this, you know that don't you?"

He shrugged. "I didn't have any choice. Besides, how else was I going to be able to do this..." Because they needed to leave, he meant it to be a sweet kiss. But she had already learned to open her mouth up to him, and it was another moment of ecstasy before he could force himself to pull away. "You're good at this Lena, I knew somehow you would be."

Her eyes flew open with embarrassment. When she tried to look away, he grabbed her chin and pulled her face back up. "Why do you keep doing that?"

"Doing what?"

"Pulling away from me, being so silly and embarrassed! Don't do that anymore, all right? It's *me*..."

She had to swallow hard. She felt one of his roaming hands gently touch a breast. "I'll stop pulling away, if you stop—" Too shy to say it, she pushed his hand away.

He laughed. "All right. I'll behave myself. For *now*."

Chapter 4

Victor knocked at the door of the Stanfield house and realized it had been over three years since he had been inside. Not since Ethan left for college had he crossed the threshold of the formidable house.

It was a grand house with tall Roman columns, and slim lace covered windows tightly nestled between the pink brick. There were Hawthorne, dogwood and redbud trees and he remembered that every tree in the front of the Stanfield house flowered in the spring. The formal gardens in the back had been designed by an architect who specialized in recreating English gardens. He knew there was a large fountain whose shallow pool reflected the different hues of roses that were painstakingly tended by the old gardener. The house should have been a gathering place for friends and relatives, it should have been a house that hosted parties and reunions. But instead, it was spoken about in hushed tones, and neighbors hurriedly rushed by as if whatever evil lurked there would infect them.

Waiting, he noticed how shiny the brass knocker was, and stooped to see if the place he nicked himself with the razor that morning had stopped bleeding.

The door opened and there was Arvellen, smiling at him. She was a mixed-heritage woman with clear green eyes. There wasn't a man in the village who didn't stop and stare when she sauntered by.

"Morning Arvellen."

"*Bon Jour* Victor," she purred with the unmistakable French accent that always seemed to be more pronounced when she was trying to curry favors. She had been raised in Ste. Genevieve and was bilingual, having lived with English speakers all her life, and Victor had heard her speak perfect English when it suited her. "Is Ethan up yet?"

"Oui, he ez jus finishing hez breakfast in ze dining room." She refused to move enough, forcing Victor to brush against her as he passed.

The plank floor of the entryway had been thoroughly waxed and Victor's booted footsteps were loud as he walked across it. Gilt frames with the likenesses of deceased relatives were all over the walls, and he smirked, realizing they were there for show, knowing how little the Stanfield's cared for their family, much less their only son.

He filled the doorway to the dining room, and Ethan looked up from his waffles.

"Victor," he exclaimed, jumping off the tufted dining room chair. "You're up with the sun as usual. Sit down, sit down. Arvellen, a cup of coffee for Mr. Gant." He settled back down as Arvellen went to the sideboard to retrieve the silver coffee pot.

Victor thanked her and couldn't help but notice that her bodice was not buttoned all the way, and that she lingered making sure he had time to see, as she set his coffee down. Looking away he settled his large body on the too small chair, glad when she disappeared. He knew all about Arvellen and the relationship Ethan had with her, and always thought it both unhealthy and unwise.

"What brings you here; is it that financial matter you wanted to talk to me about?" Ethan asked, settling in the chair, comfortable as the new lord and master. Even though his father was alive, he was ill and had begrudgingly turned over running of the beloved bank to his son

"Yes, it is," he said and squared his shoulders, knowing that Margaret's happiness and future depended on what happened next. "I want to make you an offer for a piece of property that your bank owns."

Ethan nodded, slowly chewing the last mouthful of waffle, dabbing his mouth gently with a rose-colored napkin. "What property exactly?"

"My farm that had been my mothers. The farm widow Toulouse gave her when she married—married my father." It was hard for Victor to mention someone he loved so deeply in the same sentence with someone he had grown to hate with every cell of his body.

Thoughtful, Ethan leaned back in the chair. It was not a large farm and years ago when his father had foreclosed, it rendered Robert Gant and his children homeless. He remembered how pathetic Robert Gant had been staggering into the bank demanding to see Frederick. How his father had humiliated Robert pointing out to him that his wife's owners had given her the acreage, it wasn't *his*. At eleven, Victor had been apprenticed out to the old blacksmith and worked as a field hand for the Rieflers to try and make more money to pay off the debt.

"Well, let me see what the price would be—"

"I already know the price. It's been the same price for years—and since your father can't unload it anywhere else, I won't pay any more for it." Victor reached into his pocket and pulled out a piece of paper. "As you guessed, I don't have enough money for it. So, I have a proposition for you."

Ethan tapped his fingers against the polished table, wanting to help but fearing if he offered too much, Victor's pride might rear its ugly head.

"I have enough to pay for most of it. And Henry and I can pay you back the rest in the sale of the crops until it is paid off in full. Then I want that deed, free and clear and in writing.:" Although he was speaking quietly, his words had an unmistakable undercurrent of anger in them.

It was exactly the kind of banking that Ethan's father loathed! Money. Green pieces of paper—or better, gold—were how people acquired great wealth and security. Demanding as much capital up front and foreclosing whenever possible was how his father had gotten the house, the land, the horses, and a host of other luxuries that almost no one else in the town had. It was bad business his father had always told him, to trust anyone's word, and he knew if his father got wind of this, he'd be furious.

"*Henry?* What's Henry got to do with you buying your farm back?"

"I plan to give the farm to Margaret and Henry, as a wedding present."

Ethan looked up slowly from his reflection in the polished mahogany table. There was a small, nagging feeling in the pit of his stomach, an emotion he was not used to dealing with. He had after all, his entire life, had the advantages of wealth and power, and all the material comforts that went along with it. He was unaccustomed to this raw feeling of jealousy.

"You plan to *give* them the farm?"

Victor nodded.

"Well, I must admit I'm surprised. I thought you had desires to live on that farm."

"I did. Once."

"But that was your dream—"

"Things change."

Ethan opened his mouth to speak and then shut it. "That is tremendously generous of you." Again, the annoying feeling of envy. Secretly he wondered, if the tables were turned, if he would have the strength of character to do the same thing.

Victor shrugged. "She's my sister; she's my blood."

A haunting memory flooded over Ethan of when his own little sister had died. He had not thought of her in years! He glanced quickly to the empty chairs around the table. Wondering how different or better his life would have been if she had lived. He tried to imagine her sitting there in one of the chairs, but had trouble conjuring up her face.

"It—it's..." Ethan began, wondering why on earth he was the one stammering, "it's a great proposition. I'll have the papers drawn up to-day." He smiled more confidently than he felt.

Victor smiled too and felt a tremendous weight from his shoulders. Margaret would have a home, and their mother's home at that. An embarrassing wave of happiness flooded over him when he thought about the pleasure it would give him to tell her what he had done for her. He was still not sure what Henry would do, but he would deal with Henry's protestations, if he had any, later.

"I am curious though," Ethan began, "why, such an...*extravagant* gift. By God Victor, you've been saving to buy that farm ever since I've known you! You and I had talked about what you were going to do with it when you got your hands on it. This will put you back *years* to having a farm of your own. After all, you can't expect to marry or raise children in that tiny shack you call your home."

Victor had thought about that. He was not pleased that the small house would be his and Celena' s home, but now that he had the promise of her love, he was full of hope that he could better their lives quickly. "I have thought about that," he said, placing his long arms on the spotlessly clean table, "which is why I want you to come to the shop with me. I have an idea. You told me once about that lawyer friend of yours—"

Ethan's mind was blank, then he recalled the thin, incredibly smart fellow that had so helped him through so many of his college classes. "Avery Smith; yes, what about him?"

"He can get patents, right?"

"Yes."

"I might need him."

Ethan couldn't believe what he had heard, surely, Victor had not come up with something as important as *that?* "But what about your future?"

"That's what I'm working on. I've learned to be patient." He leaned back in the chair carved with flowers that were now poking into his back, and thought that if he ever did acquire any wealth, he'd buy chairs that a man could sit in comfortably.

"But what about your immediate future?"

"Well for the immediate future, I'm still the busiest smith in town and I make a good living. You've been gone three years. I have no trouble supporting Margaret or myself, especially since I have a clear deed to the shop and the land as well." Although Victor resigned himself to forget the past, he could not help but remember when he had needed Ethan the most, he had abandoned him. "Anyway, speaking of work, I have a lot to do. We better get a move on." Victor picked the up delicate teacup, hoping he wouldn't get his finger caught in the tiny handle.

Ethan's thoughts raced wildly to Celena. He had always thought there was something between Victor and Celena. In fact, as children they had been quite close, and wondered why that bothered him. Assuredly, Victor would not be giving away every cent he had literally worked his fingers to the bone for if he planned to marry soon. Surely, he did not plan to marry Celena on these pipe dreams of his about inventions!

Pushing Victor out of his mind, he imagined how beautiful she would look in his grand house. Imagined her soft, gentle voice, filling the too-long-quiet halls.

"I still have work to get done in the shop. Let's go so I can show you what I'm talking about."

Startled from his daydream, Ethan jumped to his feet. "To the farm and Henry making it a success!"

"Don't worry; I'll see to that," Victor said, knowing that unfortunately Henry had not proved to be particularly good at anything, but Margaret loved him. And one way or another, Victor would make sure she was taken care of.

It was after midnight when Victor entered the house. Quietly he opened the door, carrying the small lantern with him set it on the table, careful not to disturb Margaret. A small fire burned in the fireplace and kneeling he added another log, holding it in place for a moment with a poker to ensure it did not tumble forward. Watching the sparks brightening to engulf the log he smiled at the andirons he had made years ago. It had been his first try at twisting iron, and Jonah had said they were hideous.

Sitting down, he pulled the boots from his feet, and massaged his aching shoulder. He dropped his face into his hands and rubbed his eyes, which were burning.

Through his fingers he saw the baskets of freshly washed and folded laundry. Touching one of the shirts on top realized that they were sprinkled with water and knew that tomorrow would be ironing day and wondered how late Margaret worked.

The bed was partially hidden from view from a quilt that hung from the ceiling, and he peered around it. It was too dim to see her, but the sound of her steady breathing was comforting.

It occurred to him that Celena had never been inside their home. It was small at fifteen-feet square. One wall was covered with a gray fireplace whose stone hearth spread out nearly three feet before butting up to the four-inch pine plank floor. The mantel above it he'd added only last year and was proud of the ticking clock and small porcelain box that sat there. He'd made all sorts of trammel hooks and utensils to help Margaret do the cooking and had even built a sink board where she could bring in water to wash and store dishes. There were two large windows covered in oilskins, that he planned on replacing. The furniture was sparse. There was a jack bed that was nestled into the wall where Margaret slept. It was tight around the bed, but Victor didn't realize it since he had never slept there. There was a table and two chairs, and an armoire and he shrugged when he looked at it. It held Margaret's things; he kept his clothes in two baskets.

Staring into the fire, his mind was flooded with thoughts of the gleaming hallway of Ethan's house. The white painted spindles that adorned the curving staircase. The formal dining room with its crystal chandelier, where he and Ethan had discussed their business on a mahogany carved table and drank coffee out of white china cups with pink painted rosebuds.

Am I a fooling myself? he thought suddenly, easily able to picture Celena sitting in one of those damned uncomfortable chairs at Ethan's house, but for the life of him, he could not picture her in his house.

Standing, he pulled the mattress that was neatly rolled and tied with a small piece of the rope away from the corner. He blew out the lantern and rolled out the mattress. Grabbing an old quilt he laid down. Tucking one arm under his head, he tried to dispel the disturbing thoughts. Closed his eyes, and sighed with exhaustion.

Before he drifted off to sleep, he thought of Celena the night of the harvest. Moonlight shimmering on her face as she looked up at him. Remembered taking her into his arms and touching his lips to hers. It had been truly an enchanted moment, one that had changed him forever.

Chapter 5

The young men assembled with their hammers, hand drills and saws for James Riefler's barn raising two weeks later. Nearly everyone in town was there to help including the four Wilburn brothers, including Henry, as well as Eddie Fisk and his brother Mason, newly back from law school. The Stoddard boys, Andy, Seth, and Stephan, Joe Kurth and lastly the twins Davey and Danny Charbonnier and their older brother Caleb.

It was a good-natured competition of sorts, to see which five-man team could get the wall or broadside of the barn ready to go up first. At barn raisings in years past the competitions had run the gamut, from serious races to lighthearted attempts. For the first time in a long time there was a lot of young men that were the same age and had known each other forever. They knew each other's weaknesses, and strengths, and everyone wanted bragging rights.

Victor, Laurence, and James had dug the foundation into the side of the hill and ordered enough lumber to build the sixty-six by thirty-four-feet barn. The stone foundation using mud not mortar, had already been laid. But for part of the construction, they needed the muscle of their friends to get the wooden sill built, and then the enormous broadsides would be neatly pegged into the mortises. They also needed help to the get the *summer* in place—a jumbo sized beam fourteen inches thick that was one of the main supports of the ceiling. Once all that was done James and his brothers could finish the rest. But the hoisting of the broadsides and fitting together of all the mortise-and-tenon joints was like fitting parts together of a huge puzzle. It was heavy, hard work, and impossible to do without help.

It was also a wonderful excuse for a party, as well as 'payback' time for the neighbors who had accepted the generous help always offered by John Riefler and his sons. Although the men involved did a tremendous amount of work, they still found time when the heaviest work was done, to enjoy themselves at the evening picnic and dance.

It was a bright sunny morning, and the intensely blue sky was cloudless. The fall sun was beginning to take the chill off the air even though summer was waning. Celena shivered in anticipation of seeing Victor. They were officially courting after all, and that meant that she could at least dance with him and talk with him openly. Maybe if they were lucky, they could sneak out if only for moment.

James smiled nervously as he surveyed the crowd. "Mornin' ya'll!" he shouted, trying to be heard over the group. It was a big gathering, and James, who was sorely lacking in public speaking skills, began to sweat. "We need four five-man teams." Counting quickly, he realized he already had a problem because they had an uneven number of men.

The men, realizing this, immediately began to argue, and a bewildered James suddenly had pandemonium on his hands. He tried to be heard over the talking, he even yelled once, but no one was paying any attention to him. He felt a panic rise in his chest, knowing how much work they needed to do and knew precious daylight was slipping away.

"But we've got to have an even number of men on each team. The team with only four won't stand a chance!" Will said, nearing his brother.

"I know, I know," James said. Too many people were all talking at the same time, and he couldn't think, much less get anyone to listen to him, and knew if they stood there and argued all day, he would never get the rest of his barn built.

"Hey, this isn't going to work. We got an uneven number of men. I ain't bein' on the team with only four men!" Eddie Fisk said loudly. "Ain't that right everybody?"

Feebly James looked to his older brother for help.

Laurence looked at Eddie. It was so like Eddie to make things more difficult than they were. "Listen up, lets divide the teams and get a move on," Laurence said, his strong voice was rising over the din.

Celena was watching from the perimeter as did the rest of the townspeople, which were busy unloading tables to line with food.

"Es a wonderful turnout," Yvonne said, turning to smile at John, but her smile faded when she saw the strained look on her husband's face, knowing he was itching to organize the gathering.

"Won't make any difference what kind of turnout it is if they don't all stop arguing."

Yvonne hoped he would not jump in to save James, knowing that it only wounded her son's already compromised confidence. James and his father argued more than she liked.

"We won't have enough daylight left if those young pups don't get started," Don Fisk joked, knowing how eager his own sons Eddie and Mason were to try and outshine the Riefler brothers. Eddie had tangled with James and Will for years. They'd fought and competed in almost everything they could think of. Now that they were in their teens the competition was naturally turned up a notch, with the desire to impress women.

Eddie was always getting in fights, but their son Mason had changed for the better, most people said. In fact, he had changed so much his family joked they didn't know where he came from. He shunned farming and gone to St. Louis to law school, and everything about him was different now. He no longer spoke with the faint country accent, his grammar put theirs to shame, as did his table manners, and stylish dress. He could name rivers in countries that his brother and parents never even knew *existed* before! And he had 'views' his father liked to say about things, and he could 'discuss' them with you at length without getting into an argument. His parents were so proud of him they hadn't started a conversation for months without first asking: *"Did you hear the good news about our boy Mason? he's a regular lawyer now!"*

John smiled at his friend, and they shook hands.

"Mornin' John, Yvonne," Don said, taking the hat off his balding head and sweeping a bow, which given his girth took considerable effort, smiling at his neighbor's pretty wife, noticing she kept her figure even after all the children she had borne. He glanced over at his own wife Sarah, whose round cheeks bulged as she chewed a cornmeal biscuit from her interrupted breakfast, and shuddered.

"Morning Don," John replied, forcing a smile. "I told James to organize this before he got us all out here."

"Nonsense John, it's a great excuse to get out of the house and watch the young people." He spied John's daughters. "Is that little *Celena*?" Don asked, trying to get a better look. "My my, she's growing up fast. Why, she gets prettier every day!"

Turning, John looked at his daughters, who smiled and waved. He nodded, thinking that they were growing up much faster than he liked.

"Okay, okay, we've got three even teams, and one lesser," Laurence said, trying to calm the agitated group. Against the protests and complaints of everyone. No one wanting to be on the lesser-manned team. "I need a team, who else is with me?" Laurence pleaded to the unruly crowd.

No one answered, not wanting to come in last place and be heckled for the rest of the day. The five Wilburns always worked together, the Stoddard boys were teamed up with the Fisks, and Will had already told Davey, Danny, Caleb Charbonnier and Joe Kurth that he was with them.

"I'm with you," Victor said, joining Laurence and James as the teams began taunting and teasing each other as if it were a sport that they could win.

"Hey there, iron giant, come join a *real* team!" Isaac Wilburn laughed.

Victor merely grinned in response.

Once during the picking of teams, Laurence rolled his eyes at Lisette, who stood at the sidelines watching. She smiled back lovingly at her mature, levelheaded husband.

"We are going to get our ever-livin' butts kicked!" James said under his breath to his brother, all the while smiling and resisting the impulse to answer the taunts.

"You think I don't know that?" Laurence said through clenched teeth. "But we'll get your barn built, that's the important thing."

Although James agreed, he still raised a hopeful hand to the group. "Who else is with us?" James pleaded, trying to get one of the older men from the crowd to come forward and even out the teams.

"I'm in," Ethan said, hoping he would not make a fool out of himself. His homecoming had not been as warm as he would have liked. His father had done even more damage to the Stanfield name and Ethan felt the subtle implications in the way he had been greeted since returning. He hoped that if he could make a decent impression at the barn raising, he could repair the damage.

There was a great deal of hooting and laughter when they saw Ethan join their team. Ethan, everyone knew, had *never* done any manual labor. He was, if anything, a handicap.

Celena was having trouble seeing over the crowd and, frustrated, stood in the wagon. Eva climbed up with her and, giggling, they hugged in excitement.

"Have you seen Danny yet?" Celena asked, eagerly scanning the groups of men for Eva's beau.

"No. Have you seen Victor?" Eva asked, squeezing her sister's hand.

"You'd think I could find him with how much taller he is than everyone else."

"That's true," Eva agreed with a laugh.

Happily, a moment later, Celena spied him. "Oh, there he is!"

He did not see her, and she had the pleasure of merely resting her eyes on him. His shirt sleeves were rolled up high, and his arms were folded in front of him. She was too far away to hear, but someone must have said something funny because she saw him laugh, and saw the coldness leave those clear gray eyes.

"Okay I guess we're ready," Laurence shouted, shaking his head as he watched the four teams assemble on each side of what would eventually be his brother's barn. It was amazing to him to hear them still taunting each other and yelling age-old insults.

"Hey Will!" Seth Stoddard grinned nastily. "Gonna whip up on ya, boy!"

"Hey Seth, hope your girl is not around, 'cause your britches are open!" Will shot back.

By the time Seth realized it was a joke, he had already checked and flushed hotly at the laughter his actions evoked from the amused crowd.

"You always were a bright one!" Will said, shaking his head. "Yes siree, the biggest toad in the puddle!"

Seth, his embarrassment now fueled with anger, grabbed a tape measure and waited impatiently to start.

Laurence shook his head, laughing to himself with the ridiculous way Seth's face flushed, wondering if any of these men could stop irritating each other long enough to build the barn. *They're all crazy.* But even he was not immune to the fun.

Will did not reserve his antics just for the Stoddards, because his brother James was across from him. They grinned devilishly at each other with a sibling rivalry that started in the cradle and would go 'til the grave.

"You're gonna lose!" Will yelled.

"We'll see about that, runt."

"Okay gentleman," Laurence said. He looked to his right; Ethan and James had their hands on the lumber, ready to start joining the hewn boards together and assembling the frame on the ground and in the final leg of the 'race' lift it up the heavy frame and then secure it perpendicularly in the wooden sill. "We all know what to do." Laurence heard anxious, nervous laughter rippling through the crowd.

"Let's go!"

At once the crowd erupted with a happy cheer as the nineteen men started to measure the eight-foot squared logs, shouting at each other.

"James, give me those two long side pieces," Victor said. "You all get the uprights and lay them inside. I'll start chalking them and mortise 'em." Fumbling in a dirty burlap sack, he tossed James a pump drill. "When I get it, all chalked you drill the tree nail holes, but you won't have to drill them all the way through because I've got an early 'wedding' present for you—" Victor reached down into the bag and produced thirty long nails he had made as well as six enormous hinges for the doors. Although James was grateful for the nails and hinges he was perplexed. They had never done it this way before.

Straining under the weight of one of the long boards, Laurence dropped one end on the ground. "What's the problem James?"

It was Ethan who answered, leaning near James, whispering, "If we can't out-man them, James...we're going to have to outthink them. I think we should listen to the mighty Hephaestus."

"Who the hell is Hephaestus?"

Laurence neared him with a smirk. "The Greek god of the forge. He had been born so ugly and lame that his own mother tossed him off Mount Olympus."

"Jesus," James chuckled, thinking it was a vile yet funny nickname.

Laurence looked over at Victor. "Got it all figured out?"

Kneeling, Victor pulled out one of his hammers from the shop and with the chalk line snapped it, marked it at the base with a roman numeral, and went on. "Yeah. I think so."

"You're shittin' me?" Laurene asked, incredulous.

Sitting back on his heels, Victor laughed. "Actually...I'm not."

It occurred to Laurence that, even outmanned and with *Ethan,* they still had a chance. Not that any of it meant anything; Laurence would like to be able to look down at all those hollering fools and laugh at them.

Standing up thirty minutes later, Victor turned to James and Laurence. "Start drilling."

Victor turned to Ethan and tossed him one of his hammers. "Come on banker boy. We've got some nailing to do." He had to point Ethan in the right direction.

The crowd, which had been mingling and nibbling, began to cheer when the four-man team finally started to nail.

"What the hell are they cheerin' at?" Eddie sneered. "We been nailing for a spell now and no one started cheering when we did."

"They're coming along!" Keith Stoddard said. He had been watching his own sons Stephan, Andy, and Seth, but now was watching the smaller team wreak havoc on the broadside.

Bending down, Ethan took a nail and pressed it into the freshly cut boards. One, two, three, four, smacks and he had the nail set. He was pleased with himself, never having done any manual labor before. The yells of encouragement from the crowd spurring him on.

When they finished mortising the last of the huge logs an hour later, Victor had James and Laurence fit them neatly into place.

Will whistled annoyingly to his brothers who were sweating. "'Bout time you boys started doin' something!" Will said, trying to flip blonde strands out of his face that were skinny with sweat.

Laurence shrugged it off with a laugh, but as always it got under James' skin. "Shut your fool mouth, runt."

Edging around the side, Victor caught sight of Celena, and he hit his hand. "Mornin' Celena, mornin, Eva," he called happily despite his throbbing finger. After all he'd not hit his hand with a tool in *years!*

Victor's teammates noticed that every long nail that took him four blows to drive into the log, Victor did it in three.

"We can't expect to—to do that. The man's a *blacksmith* for God's sake!" Laurence laughed.

Moving swiftly around the big box, Victor glanced up and saw Celena again, smiling briefly at her. He mumbled, "Watch your fingers, boy." Although he would have rather died than admit it, seeing her unleashed more adrenaline into his body.

Looking up at the team directly across from them, he had to stifle a laugh seeing that they had mortised one board too short. Worse yet, they were arguing about whose fault it was. It was costly to make a mistake with the lumber—and embarrassing.

"Measure twice and cut once!" Victor shouted, and they glared up at him, daggers in their eyes.

But Victor was not the only one who knew how to build something right. The Stoddards were still ahead. Stephen grinned maliciously at him as they neared each other at the corner.

The crowd was pleased at the frivolity and breakneck speed with which the teams worked, especially since they had the added interest of the underdog team that was doing its damnedest not to lose.

"I've never seen anysing like et," Yvonne said after almost two hours of mortising, drilling, sawing, and hammering. They smaller team started to lift the huge skeletal broadside up by hand, the logs over twenty feet long and heavy.

Laurence, Ethan, and Victor got on the outside and lifted the large frame until it was almost upright. Then they used long pikes and pushed the massive wall the rest of the way up onto the wooden sill, jockeying the tenons into their proper place within the mortises.

"Little help!" James yelled, straining under the weight of the broadside. Will and Davey darted over to help. If not pegged in right, it could topple and fall the wrong way. By its weight alone, there would be no way to stop it.

"Is it in?" Laurence yelled, his shoulders shaking under the weight as an annoying line of sweat trickled into his eyes. He watched Will, Davey and Seth scampering around making sure it was all intact.

"Lord, have a soul," Will said from underneath him. "If this doesn't cap the climax!" He was impressed that the four-man team already had a broadside assembled and upright.

"Are you sure you've got it?" Victor yelled, his arms trembling under the weight while Seth and Danny made sure the tenons were in.

"*Oui!* We got it!" Davey yelled.

Ethan and Laurence let go of the pikes and they began to shake their arms out from the strain, laughing as they walked back a few steps to turn and admire their handiwork.

A horrified gasp came from the crowd when the unstable broadside began to fall.

"Hey!" Victor shouted and felt a jarring of tendons and muscles as his arms shot up to stop the broadside from falling.

A second later they were all at his side straining to force the broadside back in place.

"I thought you said you had it in place!" Victor panted, still feeling the jolt reverberating painfully through his arms.

"I thought I did. I'm awful sorry, Victor!" Davey exclaimed. "Are you all right?"

"Yeah, I'm fine," he replied, though when he grabbed his left shoulder, he wondered if he had torn something.

A buzz started through the crowd: "*Did you see that? Victor lifted the blasted wall himself!*" The little French ones of the village even started happily chanting, "*Le forte, le forte, le forte!*"

"Good God Victor! You are one *strong* son of bitch!" Laurence exclaimed.

A shocking emotion sliced through Celena. Victor had been working with James, Laurence, and her father for two weeks in preparation for the barn raising. They'd measured the ground, dug and built the foundation. He'd given freely of his precious time, skill, and strength. It occurred to her that the people and things she held dear, because he loved her, he did too.

She knew suddenly he would never have let that broadside fall, and if it had taken the strength of five men, somehow he'd have pushed it back up. For a moment, the enormity of his devotion was daunting. She swallowed hard, wondering if she could return the intensity of his love; wondered if any single person was *ever* worthy of another's total adoration.

She realized with an embarrassing schoolgirl's flush that when she said she'd marry him only a few weeks ago, she had no idea what she was dealing with, and suddenly had the fierce desire to protect him. Knowing that anyone who could be that *giving* could also easily be hurt. She smiled, thinking of protecting him *from* the world. But she knew she would gladly stand between him and any heartache.

"We got you licked, better give it up!" Eddie said, taunting James, who was scrambling with the ladder to climb up to nail.

"Now all you boys be careful up there! Don't want anyone falling and breaking their necks," Don Fisk warned, although everyone knew his words were directed to his own son Eddie.

Victor trotted over to James. "I'll nail them."

James stared at him, knowing the other teams had several men hammering. "Fine by me, but I'll help you."

"Don't need ya." Victor stuffed the hammer through his belt and scurried up the ladder.

The neighbors were rooting for different teams as they watched as the men up on the boards hammering away.

Victor was fast but careful as he hammered since he was up sixteen feet. When he hit the last nail, he looked up and smiled at the appreciatively cheering crowd. He wiped a line of sweat off his chin, and laughed seeing James, Laurence, and Ethan hollering and dancing with delight—"We did it, we did it, we *won!*"

As Victor sat on top of the wall in the warm, bright autumn day in front of the jubilant crowd, he thought that it was one of the best days of his life.

Neither Seth nor Will realized Victor was finished, because to their credit they were pounding nails as fast as they could, determined not to lose to the smaller team.

William finished next and, thinking he had won, raised his arms in jubilation. But then he looked over at Victor, whose broad arms were folded in front of him, the hammer tucked into his belt. For one of the few times in his life, Will was at a loss for words. But it didn't take him long to see good in it—they'd come in second. The Wilburns' team still hadn't even lifted the broadside yet.

"I can't believe they did it!" Annalise Stoddard said. She congratulated her tired sons, Seth, Andy, and Stephan as they came to get a drink of water.

"Glad that's over," Stephan said, smiling, tossing his sandy damp hair out of his eyes. He smiled over at Eva, trying to catch her eye. But she did not notice him and, sighing, he looked away, disappointed that she was more interested in Danny Charbonnier than him.

Victor climbed down and was mauled by his teammates.

"You did it, we won! I can't believe it!" James gushed.

"Miraculous Victor, you never cease to amaze me!" Ethan said, his face flushed. He and James looked at each other and smacked palms in jubilation.

"Let me get a drink," Victor said, wadding through the throngs of well-wishers pummeling him as he went by, slapping him affectionately on the back.

"Okay, listen up everyone! The new rule is that whoever has the *blacksmith* on their team next time has to start an hour *later* than the rest of us!" Laurence quipped.

"Boys that was some spectacle." John smiled, shaking his sons' hands proudly. He turned to Victor. "I can't believe you all pulled it off!" He awkwardly hugged him then. John was normally not the hugging type.

"We used our vastly superior intellect!" Laurence laughed, wiping an annoying line of sweat out of his eyes. Taking the cup of water from Lisette, he put his other arm around her waist. He pointed to Victor with his cup. "And the brute strength of Victor. How in the *hell* do you *hammer* like that?"

Victor shrugged. "It's nothing special. It's what I do all day long."

"It wasn't bad enough to be outmanned, but then the damn thing almost fell to the ground," James remarked in horror.

"Oh Lord, don't say that. I don't even like to think about what would have happened if it would have fallen all the way," Victor said. "We'd have had to start over; those tenons would have broken off for sure." They all agreed.

"Yes sir, we've got ourselves a regular Samson here. Instead of pulling the walls down, though, he's puttin' 'em back up! Now we have to find what *his* weakness is," Laurence joked.

Everyone laughed, and although Victor did his damnedest to suppress the urge, he found himself looking over at Celena.

Someone touched him lightly on the arm. Turning, he saw Margaret's proud eyes looking up at him. Her black hair pulled back in a braid, her lips stretched in a smile. "You are a mess." She pulled her sweating brother to her for a hug.

"I've been working."

"You know what I mean." She looked up at him lovingly. "What am I going to do with you?"

"I don't know what we're going to do with *him,* but somebody better let me sit down before I collapse!" Henry joked, staggering toward them.

He smiled at Victor and shook his hand. "Nice work." Henry coughed nervously into his hand. "You're sure it's all right with you if I marry your sister? It wouldn't do for you to be *mad* at me! It wouldn't do at all!" As he intended, everyone laughed.

"Henry my friend, you're welcome to her, that is if you can stand being hen pecked to wash your neck, and chew with your mouth shut and clip your nails—" Margaret's small hand shot up and clamped over her brother's mouth.

"I get the general idea, and don't think I don't appreciate the warning, Victor, but I'll take her anyway," Henry said, grinning, tugging her hand away. Victor chuckled when he heard Henry mumbling to Margaret as they walked away: "...but I *do* wash behind my neck, darlin'!"

"Here Victor, you mus be sirsty," Yvonne said, handing him a cup of water and a towel and basin to wash up in. "You were wonderful. *Magnifique!*"

He was proud that he had made Yvonne happy.

"Victor...thank you so much."

Turning, he saw it was Alice's freckled face beaming up at him, and clumsily took the hand she offered him.

"I was just doing what everyone else was doing," Victor said, trying to minimize his importance.

"No, I appreciate the way you fired everybody up today. It means the world to James and me. We want to be married as soon as possible, and we needed that barn built."

"Well, you're welcome Alice."

She surprised him by leaning up to hug him.

"Not only the admiration of all the men in town, but the affection of the *women* too." Ethan chuckled when Alice left.

"Out-thought them a bit."

"We duped them," Ethan said with a grin. "Did you see the pissed off look on Eddie's face?"

Victor shrugged. "Eddie's always pissed off. The barn's mostly built, that's the important thing." Victor couldn't help but think about what Alice had said about wanting to get married soon. He had only two weeks ago asked John if he could court Celena and knew it was much too soon to ask to marry her.

"Here's a towel, Victor. Ethan I've got one for you too," Celena said.

Straightening, Ethan smiled warmly down at her. He couldn't help but notice that he could see a bit of her breast pushing up from her stays. It took all his willpower not to feast his eyes on the peak of tantalizing cleavage and wondered how John allowed her out of the house like that.

Ethan knew a lot of different girls when he had been in school in Boston, and later during his trip to Europe. Most of them were proper, well brought up girls. Daughters of his parents' friends or acquaintances of his relatives from back east. He had spent countless afternoons chatting politely with them. He'd sat with them in richly carpeted parlors, seen their reflections in beveled mirrors, been in the company of so many different girls in his years away that he couldn't remember half of their names. But he did remember some had been pretty, some had not. Most of them were proper in their demeanor, a few he had happily discovered, had not. Fumbling clumsily on the couch with the annoying looping buttons on the front of their bodices, or stealing away into the garden, safe from prying eyes, to satisfy his curiosity about women's mouths, necks, and breasts. It was that feel, of a woman's incredibly soft breast heavy in his hand that suddenly leapt forefront into his mind as he looked at Celena.

It was a shame he thought that none of the women, no matter how soft their mouths were, or how firm their calves, could hold his interest for long, and he did not know why. It wasn't because with some of them he was successful in seducing them, because his disinterest happened with all of them. The ones that fell prey to his charms, as well as the ones that didn't. He wondered why women in general seemed to have no depth. Although he did enjoy the long conversations he had with Penelope.

"Thank you, Celena. You're looking exceptionally radiant today; barn raisings must agree with you! Is that a new frock you're wearing?" He noticed the light flush in her cheeks which astonishingly made her even prettier. He noticed how slender her neck was; thought it would fit neatly within his grasp, and felt a part of his anatomy react with an embarrassing swelling.

"Oh, my dress? Yes, it's new." Instinctively she put a forearm across her chest, realizing he was looking at her. It was frustrating—she had used the same dress pattern her sisters had, and it looked fine on them. But on her it was too revealing, and to correct it she had edged it with one-inch lace, but now wished she had used a wide ribbon. "And yes, barn raisings are great fun to watch." She turned Victor. "Are you hungry?"

"Yes, I'm starved!" Ethan answered

"Hello Celena, my, isn't that a pretty dress. You worked long and hard on that I can see!" Margaret greeted her, noting the excellent tailoring. Margaret was straightforward, not like some of the girls who were nice to your face and whispered behind your back, and Celena liked her.

"Thank you, yes I did."

"I wish I could sew like you." She turned to her brother. "Victor, I know you've got to be hungry, and I brought enough for you and Henry both."

He nodded to his well-meaning sister, not wanting to disappoint her, and then turned to Celena. "I'll see you later."

Celena forced a smile back. Victor and Margaret were close. In fact, Victor had been father and brother to Margaret for so long, people in town had been afraid that when she wanted to get married, Victor would stand in her way. But he had welcomed Henry's proposal, and Margaret and Henry's wedding was set for New Year's Eve.

"So, my dear Celena, what have you been doing with yourself all this time I've been away?" Before she knew what was happening, Ethan had tucked his arm inside hers and began leading her back toward her family's picnic spot. "You've finished your convent schooling, and you've no desires to go anywhere, do anything?" He realized it was absurd question; he'd yet to meet a woman who had any plans.

"Oh no...nothing." As usual he'd caught her off guard, and she was ashamed to admit she'd not been listening to him. "We've been awful busy with all the land Pa's been buying first for Laurence when he got married, and now for James and the houses and barns to be built."

"Yes, I'd heard how well your father was doing." He couldn't help but notice how long her eyelashes were.

She was relieved when Carlene joined them.

"Hello Ethan, that was quite a show you were part of up there."

"You're looking lovely Carlene. Nothing lovelier than a blonde in emerald!" He realized it was the exact same dress pattern and had to stifle a laugh. No self-respecting Boston debutante would have been caught *dead* in the same dress as her sister. The only difference was one was blue and the other green.

"Why thank you! Thank you for noticing. How are you? You must be bored back here after having been in Boston. And I hear you're back to stay?" She tossed her head so that her earrings swayed, wondering when he asked if he could court her, if she wanted to. He was handsome enough, and he was rich. She wondered if being with him could make her forget Eddie.

"Yes, I believe so. I thoroughly enjoyed my time away, but Ste. Genevieve now just feels like home." He smiled at Celena. It was strange. Carlene and Celena looked alike. They were both blond, blue-eyed, and pretty. But Carlene's face was thinner than Celena's and had a sharpness to it, or perhaps it was her tongue. It was odd that they could look so alike and yet one was pretty and the other gorgeous.

"Have you seen Mason? You've heard, I suppose, that he's back from school. He's a lawyer now," Carlene said, wondering why he kept glancing at Celena.

"I saw him, but just during the barn raising. I didn't get a chance to talk to him about his new career, but I will tonight it will be good to see him again. In fact, it's good to see everyone again." He wished Carlene would leave.

"Half of us in town were betting you'd come back with a wife," Carlene said demurely under her lashes. Annoyed when she looked up and saw that he was again looking at Celena. She feebly hoped that if the handsome banker's son showed some interest in her it might make Eddie jealous.

"A *wife*?" Ethan choked, knowing that he might have if his father's illness hadn't called him home suddenly. He thought of Penelope. There was a certain loneliness about her that was familiar to him.

"No. I've no wife." He smiled at the eager Carlene and turned again to

Celena. "Not yet that is."

"Well, it's good to see you," Carlene said, annoyed that he wasn't paying more attention to her.

"Excuse me Ethan," Celena said, escaping. "I see my mother and Eva getting the food out and I want to help."

Celena was looking forward, now that the meal was over, to spending a languid afternoon of watching Victor. In years past the men building the barn would take a mid-afternoon break to eat, and afterwards they would start on the roof, while the rest rived the logs for the clapboards to be nailed overlapping on the sides. A day or two later, her brothers would finish by cutting in for the doors and a window, careful to insert blocks of wood on either side of the openings to keep the structure from sagging as they sawed in. Then they'd put in the doors and the window chinking the spaces between the clapboards with a mixture of mud and clay.

They would not attempt much more than nailing clapboards for the rest of the day because well before dark they would clean the area, light the lanterns, and open a keg of whiskey and *tafia* happily supplied by John. The fiddlers in town namely, Alvin Woolrich, Keith Stoddard, and Phillippe Charbonnier would then start the music.

Glancing up from her cleanup, she was relieved she had been able to shake Ethan. Happy to be free of his company, she busied herself wrapping up the leftover biscuits. She felt warm breath on her neck.

"Need any help?" Victor asked, startling her.

A torrent of pink flooded her face. Seeing her reaction, he couldn't help but laugh as he straightened back up. "You all right?"

Nervously smoothing her hair out of her face, she nodded. "Of course."

"I've missed you." He reached for her hand.

"I've missed you too." She smiled up at him. Absurdly, madly, happily. She wanted to tell him how proud she was of him, how wonderful he had been, and how terribly, *terribly* in love with him she was. But was tongue tied. How did someone start a conversation *like* that anyway?

"You were so wonderful today—"

"Oh, stop. Not you too, please. I've had enough of it to last me a lifetime. Truly, it's embarrassing."

"But you were!" she said, noticing that as he hadn't let go of her hands.

"I don't want to talk about it. I have to leave."

The smile vanished from her face. "What? Where do you have to go? Why do you have to go?"

"The shop for work of course, I've got a lot to do still today." He tapped the end of her nose. "But I'll be back by tonight for you."

"Can't you stay? Couldn't the shop just...go for the day?"

"Well...*no!*" he said in revulsion. "You forget we're getting—getting married soon—" He stammered as the visions of her that woke him from his torrid dreams came to mind. "And I'll need to work if I want to take care of you. Properly..." He stopped talking suddenly and simply held one of her hands between his own. "Have you—have you told anyone about us getting married yet?"

"No, have you?"

"Margaret, but only Margaret, thing is she knew before I told her..." Feeling exposed, he looked down.

"What's wrong? Why don't want anyone to know?"

"I'm worried what your father's going to think, and well, I just thought we could keep it to ourselves for a while. Besides, everyone will know soon enough tonight of my wonderful good fortune, when you're standing next to me—"

"And dancing."

"Dancing?" he exclaimed with horror. "I can't dance. You *know* that! Trust me, if you enjoy being able to walk and value your toes, you'll not risk injury."

"Surely you're not that bad."

"I am and you know that."

"Well, that's a pity. I was so looking forward to dancing tonight, but I suppose I shan't be able to."

"All right. I see my patience is being tested here, dance all you want. I'm a reasonable man. I not going to lie and tell you I'm going to *like* seeing anyone else with their arms around you, but it is a cross that I will bear for you." Although they had been teasing, she was reminded for the second time that day how deep his love was for her. Reaching up, she touched him gently on the shoulder.

"I'm so very—" But the magnitude of her feelings caused her throat to suddenly constrict, and she knew it was neither the time nor place for such an intimate conversation, and took a step back, trying to control the emotions in her heart and brain. She wanted to tell him things that only a week ago she would never have dreamed of saying to anyone.

"What is it?"

She smoothed his shirt front. "Nothing, go on. You go back to the shop and get your work done." She looked up at him with those eyes that completely mesmerized him and said, "I'll be waiting for you."

It was starting to get dark by the time Celena sat down. She had been rocking Laurence's son Gabe to sleep. Now that the small blond tot was safely asleep tucked in the wagon under two quilts, she sighed, her arms aching from holding him. She glanced down at the round-cheeked little boy, thumb securely stuck in his mouth, angelic in sleep.

"You about wore me out!" she cooed down at him, and unable to resist she leaned down and kissed the pudgy cheek when she felt a warm hand on her shoulder.

"Took six choruses of 'Rock-a-Bye Baby' and two of 'The Cat in the Fiddle,' but he's sleeping now Lisette." Turning, Celena was shocked to see not Lisette's hand on her should, but Ethan's.

"Sweet when they're asleep, aren't they? Little ruffians when they're awake, though. Always wanting to be chased around or thrown in the air!" But the fond look on his face made it clear he regarded children as anything *but* little ruffians. He hoisted himself up into the wagon next to her. "You best be careful with those," he said, raising his eyebrows and smiling warily at the bunch of scruffy weeds neatly bound with leather lying next to her.

"Oh, I know, they have some spines...well a lot of spines, but I love these wildflowers."

"A *wildflower*? I believe it's a weed."

"I know, but I love their star-shaped blossoms, I love the color. You know they'll grow anywhere, in any field; why, I've seen them practically growing out of a rock before."

Ethan raised a skeptical eyebrow "A fine botanical specimen indeed, one that is so *discriminating* it grows straight out of a rock!"

Celena laughed and smiled down at her scruffy bouquet. Although she did not want to hurt his feelings, she moved a bit farther from him. "They're hardy little things. My father jokes when he sees the 'purple weeds' on the table. I think they're pretty, and yet it's obvious they want to be left alone with all their thorns."

Ethan had the feeling that she too wanted to be left alone. Regardless, he reached to touch one of the blooms and nicked his finger.

"Are you all right?"

He nodded, examining the flower. "It looks like a thistle, the emblem of Scotland."

"You mean my little wildflower here is someone's emblem?"

"An old legend says that when the Norse invaders came to Scotland, it was night and they were wading barefoot through the moat to attack Staines Castle. The moat was dry though and filled not with water, but with thistles. Their cries of pain as they stepped on the prickly flowers woke the guards in the castle, thwarting their attempts at a surprise attack and they were defeated."

She beamed, proud that her little flower had such a lofty history.

"So, you see, you're not alone in liking them, they may be common, but they have spirit!" He realized he enjoyed imparting little bits of wisdom to her. No one ever found the information he had at his disposal interesting. He also found her affection for the spiny weed charming.

There was a definite chill in the air now that the sun was starting to go down and shivering a bit she pulled her blue shawl tight around her shoulders as she carefully laid down her wildflowers. She watched the setting sun paint wispy pink and orange streaks across the pale blue sky. The stars were faint blue dots, and the waning harvest moon was still doing its best to light the sky. She sighed deeply, taking in the spectacular view of the twilight sky and waning crescent moon above.

"At school I had a friend from Nova Scotia. Said the northern lights were a magnificent spectacle to see." He paused, watching the dying lavenders and corals of the sunset. "It's hard to imagine anything more beautiful than this moment...than that sky though..."

Celena searched her memory from her not-too-long-ago school days, going over the globe in her mind. "I don't remember studying Nova Scotia. That's not in America, is it?"

Ethan smiled at her in the growing darkness, thinking that she was sweet and innocent. "No, it's not. It's in Canada."

"Oh," she said with a blush, looking down. "I'm sorry, I know I must seem awfully ignorant to you."

"Why?"

She shrugged.

"You didn't know something, you admitted it and now you do. It takes courage when you don't know something to admit it. I admire that."

She couldn't think of anything else to say suddenly and murmured a weak "thank you," before looking away again.

Because she was not looking at him, he had the pleasure of gazing at her profile. He studied her smooth forehead, perfect nose, pale unblemished skin. When she turned and looked at him shyly, he realized how finely drawn her features were. In the literature a woman's mouth was sometimes compared to a rosebud. The description had always seemed silly to him, until now. She was perfectly beautiful.

"There's another name for that, Aurora...Aurora—"

"Aurora Borealis."

"Yes, that's it!"

"I believe that's the technical term for this luminous phenomenon of electrical origin, that we mere mortals call, many, *many* shooting stars."

She laughed, and Ethan moved closer to her as the twilight descended and the air cooled.

"So many, many stars." Her face was turned up to the sky. "There is so much I don't know, and I'll probably never know...do you know I've never been out of Ste. Genevieve? I've never been to St. Louis or New Orleans. You've been to college and traveled to Europe...you've able to see and learn so much."

It never occurred to him that women worried about education or about their lack of knowledge. "Yes, I have been."

"I wish I knew more...it's such a big place, the world, and so much that I don't know about and that I'll never see...so many things that I've never even thought of!" When Victor had showed her his inventions, it sent her own imagination soaring. And she liked it, she liked the whole idea of being with him and about the plans they would make together and the whole future that opened to her being his wife.

"What things would you like to know; where would you like to go?" Ethan asked, his curiosity piqued that actual thoughts went on behind the gorgeous facade.

"Oh...I don't know exactly." She didn't want to talk about these things with Ethan—these were the things she wanted to talk to Victor about. She wished it was Victor who sat with her now. Perhaps he would be holding her hand, and they would talk about his ideas and inventions, and what plans they had for their future. It was not with Ethan that she wished to open her heart and her head. Though she did not think he meant to, he always made her uncomfortable. Always his eyes seemed to hover too long on her face, always he pulled her into a conversation that she had been content to listen to. Now as he inched closer to her, in the growing darkness, she was more uncomfortable than ever.

"Where would you like to go?"

"It's nothing. I don't know what I was going on about...it's not so much that I want to *go* so many places...I'm just interested in...things." She cleared her throat nervously, quickly scanning the darkened horizon, hoping for a glimpse of Victor.

"You can go anywhere, *everywhere*," he whispered, envisioning her suddenly on one of the small arched stone bridges over the Seines River, the St. Michel Bridge. Imagined hearing the wonderful sound of her laughter as they sat snuggling in an open-air café in Paris drinking claret. "You're right, there is so much world and life out there...and it would be shame not to experience it." He wondered why his heart was beating so quickly and, reaching out, touched her hand.

She looked down at his hands. They were smooth and soft, and the nails on his slender fingers looked almost manicured.

She drew her hand away. "But I already have the world...after all I have the emblem of Scotland right in my own backyard." Wanting to change the conversation and discourage him from touching her, she said, "So things will be different at the bank I hear? With the loans and principle and interest?"

It annoyed him that she mentioned the bank, and all the uncomfortable feelings that went along with it. "Yes. Now that I'm in charge things will be better."

"I'm glad to hear that. There's nothing wrong with earning a living." She thought about the grand house that the Stanfields lived in, the multitude of slaves, the fine horses. "But there *is* something wrong with deliberately taking advantage of people, like letting people think they are paying off a debt when all they are doing is paying interest, making the loan go on longer than it should. It's wrong to let people think they are paying off something when they aren't." He knew she was referring to what had happened to Victor and his parents' farm and shifted uncomfortably next to her. But Frederick had done that, not him, although he suspected his father had forged the documents and changed the details of the note. But Ethan had been heading off to college, and did not have the courage to confront his father.

"That's all in the past. It's history."

"I've never forgotten it. Sometimes you need to remember the past, so you don't make the same mistakes again."

"Like I said...things will be better." He had no idea she knew about his father's nasty business dealings.

They heard Alvin Woolrich tuning up his fiddle. "Oh, it's time." She scampered down from the wagon, eager to get away from him, but he jumped down with her.

James and Laurence were tacking up lanterns and other lanterns appeared lit on top of tables and wagons to light along with the moon, what would be the makeshift dance floor. The first song the men played was a lively tune, and Carlene and Eva rushed over to Celena.

"Oh, let's go!" Eva said, nearly pulling Celena's arm out of her socket and away from Ethan.

"What about Gabe?" Celena asked, glancing toward her still-sleeping nephew, and Yvonne waved them off, saying, "His *grand-maman* will take care of him."

Carlene was right behind them as they made their way to the perimeter of the would-be dance floor. Alice came up beside the three and they smiled. Celena was disappointed though, looking around there was still no sign of Victor.

James came up to Alice and, smiling broadly at her, whisked her away.

Eva was pulled from the side by handsome Danny Charbonnier with his black hair slicked back, his dark eyes smiling. "Eva...dance with me?"

Happily, she obliged.

"Where's Victor?" Carlene asked.

"He's still at the blacksmith shop. He said he'd be here, though."

Both watched the dancers stepping out.

"Do you see Eddie?" Carlene whispered.

Celena wished Carlene didn't care. The only thing Eddie was good at was breaking her heart.

"There he is." Celena reluctantly pointed him out, dancing with Lorien Gustave.

Carlene stared at them, trying not to cry. "I could tear her eyes out!"

"It's *Eddie* you ought to be mad at. Lorien doesn't know he's two-timing."

"I know, you're right. God Celena, I hate him sometimes." Celena took Carlene's hand, squeezing it consolingly. "I wish I hated him all the time."

Will grabbed Carlene's other hand. "Come on Carlene, let's dance."

"Stop it, Will!" Carlene was embarrassed when she felt the hot sting of tears.

"What's wrong with you?"

"Nothing, just leave me alone." She threw his hand down and ran off.

"What's got into her this time?"

"Eddie...always Eddie."

"That asshole again?"

"Shh! Go on."

"No, come on lil sis...let's have a spin."

"I don't want to right now, Will, no!" she scolded, annoyed at the way he dragged her. But not wanting to hurt his feelings or make a spectacle, she relented.

He was laughing and smiling as he twisted and turned his little sister as fast as he could. He was a particularly good dancer, and although both Carlene and Eva were good dancers, he preferred to dance with Celena. He told Celena it was because she was the most talented, but it was because she was the shortest, and when he danced with her, he felt taller.

"Will, not so fast!" It was not a true dance floor, and she found the uneven terrain difficult to negotiate.

"All right, I'll slow you down." His palms were hot and sweaty on hers, and he continually flipped the fine blonde strands out of his eyes. "Hey, where's the mighty smith?"

"I don't know, I was just looking for him."

A few spins later Will spotted him. "There he is! Sticks out like a sore thumb doesn't he?"

There he was, standing at the edge with Margaret and Henry at his side, watching her. He'd changed into a clean shirt, and his hair was tied back tight with the leather band, his long arms folded in front of him.

His eyes spoke to her.

"I'll take you right to him," Will said and spun her over. But as it was with everything Will did, he did it with too much gusto, and sent Celena stumbling into Victor's arms.

"Are you all right?" Victor said with a laugh.

Several hairs had worked themselves free from her delicate chignon and Celena, flushed with embarrassment, murmured that she was as she brushed the errant strands from her face.

"Will!" she admonished, glaring at her brother, who merely laughed and went out in search of another unsuspecting female.

Victor had one arm about her waist, and the other on her hand. "Well, shall we have a go?" he asked, grateful that the lively dance song was over, and a calmer melody played.

Happily, she stepped out with him. "I thought you weren't going to dance with me?"

"Maybe a few." He held closer than anyone else was doing, and although she liked it, she did worry what her father would think. Victor had not lied—he was not a good dancer. She even heard him counting, but so far they had not bumped into anyone.

"Did you get caught up on your work?"

He laughed. "That'll be the day. And how did you spend your afternoon, with your sisters?"

Suddenly she felt Ethan's soft pampered hands on her. "Yes, mostly." She traced one of the calluses on his palm.

The second song ended, and they lingered together on the dance floor, using the pretense of having been dancing as the reason they still had their arms about each other. Gently she felt him touch the nape of her neck with his hand. When she met his gaze, he leaned down and openly kissed her.

Astonished, she pulled back. "Victor, no," she whispered, and nervously he cleared his throat and led her into the crowd.

"That was such fun to watch," Lisette said, smiling. Laurence and Lisette's two boys, Nathan and Gabe—roused now from his late afternoon nap—were darting in and out from between their parents, chasing each other. Both boys favored their mother and had smooth olive complexions and pecan-colored eyes.

"Fun? We almost killed ourselves out there!" Laurence said and laughed when Victor caught Nathan and effortlessly lifted him up into his arms and onto his shoulders.

"Can I touch the moon, Victor?" Nathan squealed.

"I'm not *that* tall Nathan!"

"Go on your tiptoes," Nathan suggested, and again they all laughed.

Victor elaborately flipped Nathan down.

"Victor, again!" Nathan pleaded wanting to be back up on his shoulders and repeat the trick.

"Me too, Victor!" Gabe begged and Victor leaned down and picked him up as well.

Celena was enjoying the antics when someone grabbed her hand.

"You are far too exquisite to be on the sidelines."

"No!" She pulled back but he tugged her onto the floor.

Ethan was an excellent dancer. He had years of practice, and they whirled together as if they were in a grand marbled ballroom instead of the yard by James' unfinished barn.

"Shall we turn up the tempo a bit?" Without waiting for an answer, he sped up their twirling until they were being exclaimed about and pointed to by the neighbors that watched.

"Oh my, don't they look marvelous!" someone exclaimed.

"They make a striking couple!" remarked another.

Ethan was holding Celena so that their bodies were pressed up against each other, and she disliked the feel of his warmth against her. The pale blue of her skirt swished back and forth around almost like a wave. Ethan's posture was perfect, and he made it look effortless and graceful.

Victor felt a faint, uncomfortable spark of jealousy.

Thankfully, the song ended, and Victor waited in the crowd for Celena to come back to him. He lost sight of her with so many people walking by. He scanned the area hoping she was able to extricate herself from Ethan, but when she did not return, he walked to the Riefler's wagon.

But before he could find her another song started, and he spotted her again in Ethan's arms. Victor sighed silently. One dance was fine, but it was time for Ethan to bring her back where she belonged, with him. Victor also found himself wondering why with all the other girls that would have died to dance with the handsome banker's son, Ethan picked Celena.

He knew the reason though as he watched them effortlessly glide around as if they were on glass. She was exquisite, and if any man were given the chance, knew they would gladly take her. It was obvious by the murmurs he heard from the other young men around him as they commented to each other about how pretty she was, and other things none of them would have ever *dared* mention in front of her.

He tried to get to her before the next song started, but he wasn't quick enough and to his annoyance saw that now she was dancing with Mason! He realized then that there seemed to be a line of men that were hanging around one corner, and that they were all waiting to dance with her. He stepped gingerly toward the 'line.'

"Lena!" he called, trying to shout and whisper at the same time. "Lena!"

"*Pardonner!* The line! It starts back there!" Davey yelled.

"Sorry, Davey, no problem," Victor apologized. He turned and went to the back of the line, but then feeling ridiculous waiting in line to dance with the girl he was going to marry, merely stood to the side. Although he wished he was alone with her, he did have to admit he enjoyed simply watching her. Knowing that no matter what these young men had in mind, she belonged to him.

Her eyes looked even paler lit by the light of the lanterns, and even though her hair was coming messily out of its pins, it gave her the appearance of just having gotten out of bed, which made him think of *other* pleasant things. He noticed how all the different shades of light brown and blond there were in her hair when it was all wound up. *She could have any one of them on their knees begging,* he realized soberly as he watched her line of eager dance partners lengthening.

Restless, he stepped away, pacing for an entire song. He talked to Jean for a while, couldn't help but glance up now again, looking for the blue dress. He saw that Ethan had somehow circumvented the line and was again dancing with her.

"Oh, enough already!" he scoffed, and then turning felt like a fool realizing people had heard him.

"She's only dancing Victor," Eva soothed, feeling badly for him.

"I know...you're right."

"You realize, she waited all afternoon for you to come back. She spent most the day looking down the road for you," Carlene added.

Hearing this, Eddie snickered. "Relax ol' Vic, you'll get ya *some* soon enough!"

"*Eddie!*" Carlene cried in shock.

"Don't be crass, Eddie!" Eva scolded.

Spying Margaret on the dancefloor Eddie tilted his head toward her. "Unless, of course, you're *already* getting some."

Victor grabbed Eddie by the shirt collar, choking him. "You shut your filthy mouth!"

Will and Laurence, hearing the commotion, jumped in to pull Victor away.

"I was just funnin'" Eddie sputtered.

"You shut your filthy mouth! If you don't, I swear to God I'll shut it for you!"

"Victor, Victor come on, let go!" Will pleaded, trying to pry Victor's hands off.

"Not without kicking his ass first!"

"If Pa sees this shit I guarantee you won't be courtin' Celena anymore!" Laurence warned.

Eva stood next to her sister, who was close to tears. Eva hated it when Eddie was around—there was always trouble. She hated that Carlene had set her cap for him.

"Eddie, you disgust me!" Humiliated, Carlene darted away in tears.

"What is *wrong* with you Eddie?" Eva hissed and took off after Carlene to console her.

Furious, Victor turned away and flung their well-meaning arms off. He walked until he could barely hear the noise of the party, until the lanterns became little pinpoints of yellow light. Sighing, he turned his attention up to the heavens to calm himself and wondered who Celena was dancing with now.

He spent nearly an hour looking at the night sky. Searching for all the constellations he knew like Orion, Pegasus, and Leo, but no matter how hard he tried he could never make out the others, like Aquarius and Andromeda like Ethan could. He smiled, remembering how he used to enjoy annoying Ethan by referring to them the 'big and little dipper' instead of Ursa Major and Minor. It also seemed to him the ancients had taken liberties with their 'fleshing' out of the stars. Leo never looked like a lion to him.

A gentle wind touched his face, and he thought of his mother. He wondered how she would have felt on a night such as this.

Looking up at the night sky, he listened to the rush of the wind and wondered where his mother was, wondered where her heart and soul had gone. Was she still on the Earth? Had her spirit ascended or had she been condemned to earth where in Osage lore the spirits of those who failed went often into the body of a screech owl. She had told him that if you listened closely you could hear the spirits of those left on earth, weeping, and wailing at night while their host flitted about the woodlands.

He wondered if she felt like she had failed. She'd been a good mother, but her marriage had been full of pain and suffering. It still bothered Victor that he had not been able to do more to defend and understand her.

The wind crossed over him again and he breathed in deeply the smell of fall, the dried leaves, the crisp and chill in the air. And felt a sudden odd pull and dropped the hands that had been resting on his hips. It was not a physical thing, but it was there. A gentle prodding, a tug at his soul. He glanced up at a faraway line of trees looking black against the horizon, and felt a strange, sudden weightlessness. He had the sensation that, if he so much as took the smallest of mental steps, he could simply go. But realized, as he stood on this threshold, that Celena could not go with him.

Then the feeling was gone, and he shook his head to rid it of the eerie sensation. Glancing back up at the lights of the party, realized he was able to hear the music again.

"What the hell am I doing out here?" He walked back.

Up at the party, Victor searched for the whirling blue dress. He saw Will and Lorien, James and Alice, and other neighbors laughing and enjoying themselves. When he had scrutinized the dancers twice, and had yet to find her, he looked to the sides where people stood after dancing. Maybe Celena and Ethan were done finally, and *he* could be the one to have his arms around her! He searched the entire perimeter twice, but there was no sign of them. They were gone.

For a minute he did not move, listening for her voice. But it was too noisy, and he began to walk slowly at the edge of the party. He saw Margaret and forced a brief smile at her. He saw Laurence, and Stephan and Davey, they greeted him warmly, not suspecting the tension that was growing in his body with each step.

When he got to the Riefler's wagon he thought he'd see if Yvonne had seen her, and asked as politely and as aloofly as he could muster, not wanting to alarm them or signal anything was amiss.

"No Victor, ze last time I saw her she was dancing wis Ethan."

Victor nodded and moved on. He stopped and talked with Seth Stoddard and Jean Gustave, all the while quietly searching for any sign of them. He saw Eva talking with Danny Charbonnier and asked them if they'd seen Celena. Everyone had the same response; she was with Ethan.

After fifteen minutes, he circled around until he was back where he started, and found that his jaw was tense, and he kept clenching and unclenching his hammer hand.

Where is she?

A cold, rather large lump formed in the pit of his stomach when he realized that if he couldn't find her, with his head always rising above the crowd she could have easily found him! *If she wanted to!* He shook his head, trying to make sense out of what was happening. He wondered if Ethan had spirited her away somewhere, knowing from experience how persuasive he could be, but what was more perplexing was, why would Celena go with him?

His heart was speeding at the awful possibilities when he heard a rustling, like someone in great flight. He saw movement on the farthest side of James's half-finished barn. Realizing then that it was Ethan trying to slip unnoticed behind the barn, he took off after him like a shot.

He nearly knocked down thirteen-year-old Becca Stoddard, who was crossing to her family's wagon for a much-needed drink of water, and he quickly righted her, apologized, and was gone before she had a chance to tell him it was all right.

Bolting around the corner, he was horrified to see Ethan with his hand under Celena' s chin, bending as if to kiss her. Since he hadn't been trying to sneak up, his big feet alerted them, and they jumped apart at the intrusion.

It was an embarrassing moment for all of them, and for three agonizing seconds no one spoke. Although Victor would have choice words for Ethan later, it was Celena who had his attention. Her cheeks were flushed, and her chest was heaving but it was her eyes so guiltily downcast that nearly broke him.

"What's going on here? Where have you two been all night?"

"What do you mean where have we been all night? We were dancing. I was not aware that we were under obligation to check in with you?" Ethan scoffed, trying to act confident, but he was embarrassed at the interruption.

"*What?*"

"What in the world is the matter with you Victor? Can't you see Celena and I would like a moment alone?" He nodded to Victor, dismissing him as an unwanted intruder.

"Wait a minute! Lena—you *want* to be out here with him? You want *me* to leave?" He took a step toward her, but Ethan blocked his way.

"You needn't raise your voice to her Victor, she's done nothing wrong."

"I didn't say she had, but she *can* speak for herself can't she, and I want to talk to her!" When he moved again Ethan put a hand out to stop him.

"Ethan don't—" Celena implored.

"What do you think you're doing?" Victor's gray eyes narrowed to slits.

"*Victor!*" Celena sobbed and placed herself between the two of them, fearing that if she didn't they'd be throwing fists. "Victor, please—"

"Obviously, no one's told you." Victor scowled, ignoring Celena pleading to him.

"Told me what?"

"About Celena and me. I was sure you knew already; I've always been..." Humiliated suddenly, he could not finish. "Besides, I thought you saw us together the other night after the harvest—"

"What does any of that have to do with any of this?" Ethan interrupted.

"Because if you'd seen us you would have known!"

"It's my fault Victor—I should have told him—" Celena interjected.

"Known what?" Ethan asked.

"That Celena and I are...that—that we are—" But Victor's eyes shifted down suddenly and there was an edge of doubt in his voice.

Celena felt a physical pain in her heart to see the hurt and confusion on his dark face. "I'm so sorry—" she gasped, still trying to get Victor's attention.

As Ethan reached a hand out to her, Victor viciously knocked it away. "What do I have to do to get you to understand, Ethan? Get your damn hands off her!"

She wriggled free of Ethan's hold.

"Celena, I think maybe you should come along with me."

"What the hell for?"

"I'm not sure she's safe out here alone with you."

"Are you out of your *mind?* Don't be ridiculous!"

"Celena, come along with me—"

"I'm fine," Celena said sternly to Ethan.

"Are you *trying* to get me to hurt you, Ethan? 'Cause I'm just about mad enough to do it!"

"Victor don't! It's all my fault." Celena began to cry, feeling so wretched she could not look at either of them. She cursed herself for not getting away from Ethan sooner. But now, with hot tears pricking her eyes, she realized she had managed to do the thing she promised herself she would never in life do. "I'm sorry Ethan, I should have told you, I should have told you when we were dancing."

"How the hell could you with him talking his damn head off!"

"Then why didn't you tell me?" Ethan yelled.

"I wish now I had!"

Ethan again reached out to touch Celena, and Victor shoved him back so hard he stumbled. "You touch her one more time and I'll drive you head through that barn wall! *God damn it* Ethan! What do I need to do to get *through* to you?" He sighed then and hung his head. It was foreign to him to be mad at Ethan, who, after all, was the closest thing he'd ever had to a brother.

"I suppose then, I should leave you two alone." Ethan made one last glance in her direction. "Celena, are you sure you're all right?"

She nodded silently, wanting more than anything for him to simply leave.

Turning swiftly on his heel, he was gone.

Victor stepped four paces away and hung his head.

"Victor, I'm sorry, it's all my fault!" Although she tried, she couldn't keep the tears from spilling down her cheeks. She gasped, trying to fill her lungs with enough air to speak. Overcome again with the realization of how much Victor loved her, and because of it, how she had the power to hurt him. She never realized before how vulnerable love could make one, that if used vengefully, love could be the most lethal of weapons. "I'm sorry, he talks *so much*! I tried but I couldn't get away from him, and I didn't want to be rude or hurt his feelings, but I wanted him to leave me alone. When I finally got away from him you were gone, and I looked for you, but couldn't find you *anywhere*. I only came out here to get away from him so I could keep looking for you and he followed me."

But at the end of her tearful apology, he did not gather her into his arms and tell her that everything was all right as she hoped he would. He merely stood, hands on his hips staring at the ground.

"It doesn't matter. It's all right. I shouldn't have lost my temper."

"I'm so sorry, I never meant to hurt you! Before I knew it there was some sort of *line,* and somehow Ethan kept being right there."

He nodded grimly. "Yes, I saw."

Sniffing back her tears, she realized that even though he was saying the right things, something was wrong.

"We better get back; your folks will be looking for you." When he moved to leave, she grabbed his hand, stopping him.

"What's the matter?" she pleaded, looking up to him, her eyes frantically searching his dark face.

"Nothing."

"You—you don't think I *wanted* to be out here with Ethan?" Although he said nothing, his down-turned face confirmed her worst fears. "You're wrong! You're all *wrong*, it's *you* I want!"

"It's been a long day and I'm tired, I want to go home."

Panicked, she reached up and grabbed his shoulders. "But why are you acting like this?" She quickly went over what she had done. She'd done nothing but dance, there was nothing else in her behavior that was suspect. "What have I done to upset you so?" There was a panic in her voice even though her words were faint. "Victor please—" She stretched up to kiss him, but it was impossible if he would not accommodate.

"I can't...do this Celena," he said with a finality that nearly undid her. He was shaking his head, getting ready, she feared, to tell her that things had changed for him.

Oh my God it is a weapon!

"Let's just call it a night."

When she tried to embrace him for the second time, he grabbed her hands from him, and hurt her when he jerked her face up to look at him. "You obviously have no idea what I want from you, or how I feel about you."

"Oh yes I do!"

He let go. "Celena please, I can't...do this. I'm not good at it. I wanted to marry you; I was serious when I asked you."

"And I was serious when I said yes."

He shook his head. "You're young, you're too young. And I guess I didn't realize it 'til tonight, although I suppose I should have," he mused bitterly, thinking how she looked having so much fun dancing with all the different young men.

"But I'm not too young, and I want to marry you." She tried to embrace him again, and he batted her hands so roughly from his shoulders she wobbled.

"*Stop doing that!* This is *not* a game for me. I don't want to be one of your many dance partners. And since you obviously don't feel for me what I feel for you, let's call it quits!"

"But—but I do feel it for you! I love you so much—why don't you believe me now?"

"Because you were having an awfully damn fine time tonight *without* me!"

"But you were the one who told me to dance, you said you'd watch me."

"I—I know that, but I didn't think you'd be gone from me for the *entire* night!

"It's *you* that I want!"

For what seemed like an eternity she stood staring up at him, shaking with frustration, then smacked him as hard as she could with both fists on his chest.

"Don't *hit* me!" he hissed, grabbing her wrists.

"Then don't tell me what I feel! You don't *know* what I feel! How dare you act like you know what's in *my* heart!" she wailed, struggling to free her wrists from his hands. "I've been waiting all day...*all day* to tell you, and if you hadn't had to go back to that stupid blacksmith shop, I'd have told you already and we wouldn't be having this ridiculous argument!"

Having absolutely no idea what to do, Victor was silent for a moment. "All right, I won't tell you what you do or don't feel." Although it was the right thing to say, things were still skewed between them. "What have you been waiting all day to tell me?"

"I realized today that you love me, and that you've loved me for a very long time..." She paused to see what effect her words were having on him, and he gave a nonchalant shrug of his broad shoulders. Despite his downcast face, she felt a little burst of relief when he did not deny it. "And that you want me so much your heart actually aches, and that you hope you're—"

"Must we go on with this? I mean, it's *embarrassing*! I think we both already know how *I* feel!"

"I only wanted you to know that I know all of this because I feel the same way."

He stood looking out over the fields of James' farm and future. *He has a barn already*, Victor thought, and realized he wanted it too. He straightened and she moved into his arms. "I feel like I'm rushing you again."

"No, you're not. Victor, I've known these boys all my life and I never wanted anything to do with any of them. I'm ashamed of myself now because I know the only reason I danced with all of them tonight is because I knew you would be watching me." She looked down guiltily, but felt his fingers under her chin, lifting her face back up to him.

"I'm sorry, and I wouldn't mind you, dancing with other people, as long as I knew that it was me you—"

"Oh Victor, I *do* care for you! I love you." She waited a moment for him to say the same.

"Will you let me try and make you happy?"

Reaching up, she softly stoked his cheek with the tips of her fingers. "You already have."

"But...I mean, after we're married, for always—"

"Je t'aime..." she whispered sweetly, "I will love you 'til the day I die," she breathed, her words choked with emotion, tears suddenly pricking her eyes again. She hoped he wouldn't think her silly to make such a poetic declaration and blessed him silently when he bent and kissed her tenderly on the forehead.

"Only until you *die?*" he teased, grinning down at her.

"That's not enough?"

He kissed the top of her head, shrugging. "Why put a time limit on it? What I feel for you will last much longer than that—"

"Put your arms around me."

He did.

"For being as big as you are you are bad at hugging."

"Is this...better?" He laughed, trying clumsily rearrange his arms around her. "I don't want to hurt you."

"You're not going to hurt me." Reaching up, she pulled his mouth down to hers. "Now kiss me."

He was trying to control the wild range of emotions he was feeling and struggled to keep a clear head. But with her so willingly in his arms, and opening her mouth to him, it was getting harder to ignore the raw need building in his body.

"I want so much to be your wife."

"You know what that means don't you?" he teased, pausing to kiss her quickly on the mouth. "It means you'll have to cook for me...sew for me...sleep with me."

A hitch caught in her heart.

His mouth was bruising her lips. At first, she felt a hand on her face, then it was on her neck, and before she knew it he was squeezing her breast. She was shocked and embarrassed but tried to force the thoughts from her mind. *I love him—he can have whatever he wants from me!*

But when he pushed her down on the ground by James' unfinished barn, she felt a stab of fright.

"I want you," he whispered hoarsely, his body pinning her uncomfortably to the ground. Frightened, she felt him moving against her. "*God I want you.*" He fumbled angrily with the hoops and petticoats.

She was terrified when she felt one his hands moving up her leg under her skirt. He was laying on top of her, crushing her with his weight. She squeezed her eyes tight to keep the tears from slipping past and let out a tortured sob when she felt his other hand reaching up around the neckline of the pretty blue dress. His hand was hot and rough against her breast. Her hot tears were leaking into her ears when he began to knead her breast savagely, while the other hand was tugging frighteningly with her pantalets.

His tongue was in her mouth, and when he'd kissed her like this the night of the harvest it had sent the most magnificent chills up and down her body, but it was not having the same effect now, and she wrenched her mouth from his.

Shockingly, she felt his mouth travel down to her breasts, leaving a warm wet trail. Forcing a breast out of her corset, he bent and sucked hard enough for her to wince in pain.

But he was an animal and didn't notice that she no longer reached her arms out lovingly to him, that she ceased to kiss him back. Because his hands were reaching underneath her bottom, pulling her up painfully against the hard place at his groin.

She was mortified about what was going to happen. Knew it was terribly, terribly wrong, and knew she would feel unbelievable regret and shame when it was over. This was not how she had pictured it, grabbing and panting in the dark on the dirty ground, and, she thought with an intense flush of shame, not yet wed.

He was thrusting himself against her and not only did it hurt but it was degrading. Opening her eyes, she saw him fumbling madly with the buttons on the front of his pants, and a desperate sob escaped her lips when she saw him reach inside.

"Victor *don't!* Please don't do this to me." She turned her face from him, bracing herself for what was horrifyingly going to happen.

She could breathe again. Felt relief from the unbearable pressure of his weight when he rolled heavily off. Cold suddenly without his big warm body pressed against her, she began to shiver.

He was sitting with his back to her in the darkness, his head in his hands almost panting. She glanced over at him. He was still sitting, elbows on his knees, face covered by his hands, bearing little resemblance to the lusting fiend he had been moments ago.

"Thank you..." she began as a new rush of tears choked her words, "thank you for stopping."

"Don't thank me. I don't deserve to be thanked." Unable to look at her, he dropped his throbbing head into his hands again, fighting the wretched knowledge of what he had almost done. Mortified that he had come so close to doing such a vile thing and doing it to someone he professed to love so much. Bile built up nauseatingly in the back of his throat. "Did I hurt you?"

"No. I'm all right."

"Do you realize..." he began, hating himself, "that's the *second* time in mere month I've needed to ask you that?" Standing, he re-buttoned his fly and tucked in his shirt. His eyes met hers briefly before dropping back down. His face had gone peculiarly pale, and his eyes had a look of such deep shame that she felt sorry for him. She watched him nervously run both his hands through his hair.

"Lena." Unable to bear seeing the tears in her eyes, knowing he was the cause, he looked down again. "I am deeply sorry. Please...please forgive me."

Her heart aching for him, she reached up and surprised him by softly tracing his cheek with the tips of her fingers. "I forgive you."

Cautiously he reached for her, unsure she would trust him now, and blinked back tears of gratitude when she laid herself against him.

They held each other for a few moments without speaking. She expected to be overcome with feelings of shame and guilt and surprised herself when she wasn't. Puzzled by her own feelings she simply rubbed her cheek against his chest, nestling against him. Understanding better than she ever had before how a woman could be a wife to her husband. She was glad they had stopped, knowing it was not right for them now, but it would be soon. She would do it because she knew how much he wanted it from her, and because she loved him, she would figure out a way to reconcile herself to it, and the eagerness to please him caused a wonderful little shudder deep in her heart.

He gently pulled away from her. "I am thinking that I had better...not see you again for a while."

A cold panic assaulted her. "But why?"

"Because..." He paused, tortured.

"Because why?"

"Because I don't know how long I can control myself. I'm sorry I'm just...God help me!"

"Then let's get married right now, and then you won't have to worry about—" But she was embarrassed to put a name to it, and they looked nervously at each other and then both looked away.

He was relieved however, that his display of wanton lust hadn't completely terrified her. "Like I said we, or at least *I* need to cool off a bit."

"But I don't want you to stay away from me. Let's get married then, let's just get married, right away."

Staring down at her he wondered suddenly if he was dreaming since the intense object of his affection was begging *him* to marry her!

"Please Victor, ask my father right away. Ask him tonight."

"No, no it's far too soon. Your father will have my head on a platter."

She ignored the joke. "Please ask him."

"No."

"Please!"

"*No!*"

Refusing to be put off so easily, she reached her arms out to him, and seeing a nervousness cross his face couldn't help but smile. "Please ask him, do it for me. I don't want to wait and not see you. Don't you...want to marry me?"

"You're going to drive me mad," he said, pulling her arms from him.

"Ask him now." She threw her arms back up.

"I can't. It's too soon." He was trying to resist, but she pulled him down towards her. He knew he should not kiss her like this, but he had dreamed about it for so long, and she was after all so very, *very* willing.

"Don't you...want me to be your wife?" she whispered, wondering if she looked as silly as she felt, but guessed she didn't, seeing as how he was helplessly falling into her little snare

"You're being cruel."

"Please ask him tonight. Promise me you will. I don't want to wait. Don't you want to be with me?" she asked, gently stroking his cheek.

"You know I do."

She could see him wavering, went up on her tiptoes to run her fingers gently over his lips. "Please ask my father. Do it for me, promise me you will?"

"All right. I promise."

She kissed him sweetly once more and forced a smile up at him. "It's getting late, we better go."

"You're right," he agreed, swallowing hard, regaining his composure.

They finished dusting off their clothing, neither of them wanting any signs of their frolic on the ground to be visible. As they made their way back around the barn, were shocked to see the party was broken up-and nearly everyone was gone.

Victor had a bad feeling in the pit of his stomach but forced a smile down at Celena as they made their way back from behind the barn hand in hand. It would be obvious to anyone that was left that they had been alone together if they weren't careful.

"You go out first," he said, stopping at the edge of the barn, dropping her hand. She turned back once to smile at him and was gone.

"...Have you seen Celena?" Yvonne asked Margaret as she and Henry loaded their picnic baskets to get ready to go home.

"No, not in a while," Margaret answered, but sensed something was wrong. "The last I saw of her she was dancing with Ethan," she added, trying to be helpful.

Yvonne thanked Margaret and turned back to John.

"Celena?" he asked, meaning *where was she*, and Yvonne shrugged.

"I don know, John. I've asked everyone—no one has seen her." Although she was a bit worried, she turned to Carlene and Eva and helped them pack what was left of the picnic dinner.

"Ethan! Have you by chance seen Celena?" John called.

Leaning against his horse, Ethan turned to him, the four whiskeys he'd downed since the earlier humiliating scene coursing boldly through his veins. "The last I saw of Celena she was being rather forcibly spirited away by our fine blacksmith friend. Perhaps when you see Victor you should ask *him* where your daughter has been tonight." He grinned nastily as John stared at him in confusion.

John then overheard Henry asking Margaret where Victor was, and it sent a ripple of annoyance through him when she answered that she had no idea.

"Time to go?"

Turning, John was overcome with relief to see Celena.

"Where on earth have you been? We've been looking for you!" He was so happy to see her, he leaned down and kissed her on the forehead.

"Oh, zar you are!" Yvonne said. "Zat was quite a day, let's go home."

John let Yvonne take her to the wagon and then realized with a sinking feeling in his heart that Celena had not answered him.

"Celena!" Carlene said in an excited whisper. "I did it! I gave Eddie the mitten."

"I'm glad if you actually did." Celena had heard all of this before.

"Of course I did! I'm through with him."

"She danced three times with Mason," Eva interrupted, keeping her voice low, not wanting their father to hear.

"With Mason?" Celena asked in surprise. "Tell me you're not using him to get back at Eddie?"

Carlene made a face. "No. He's sort of...interesting," she said, although he'd bored her with his conversation. She cared nothing for politics and he'd talked at length about President Polk and his acquisition of something called California and the New Mexico country, and how it had heated up the quarrel over the expansion of slavery.

"What's the matter, don't you like him?"

"Oh no!" Celena exclaimed. "In fact, I like him, I like him a lot. But he's a lot different than Eddie." She hoped her sister wouldn't find the calm, even-tempered Mason dull after all the turbulence with Eddie.

"Guess who's coming over on Sunday?" Eva whispered, her eyes sparkling, wanting to share her good news.

"Who?"

"Danny Charbonnier!"

Smiling, Celena leaned over to hug her.

"We're going to have a houseful, what with Mason coming for me and

Danny for Eva—and Victor for you!"

"Oh heavens. Poor Pa," Celena said, biting her lip. "I hope of all this at one time isn't too much for him."

Carlene laughed. "He'll be fine." She'd show Eddie, she'd make him sorry. She couldn't wait until he found out she was now seeing his older brother. "Besides, it's not like any of us are getting *married* yet!"

Wincing, Celena looked up at the stars, hoping everything would be all right.

Carlene and Eva were already upstairs, and Yvonne was on her way tiredly up as well when she heard a knock at the door. She and her husband exchanged puzzled looks. Curious, John crossed the room and opened the door.

There in the dark stood Victor, a tight, serious expression on his face. He made no move to enter, waiting for them to ask him to come in. Celena, who had been waiting in the kitchen, heard the knock and froze.

"Victor, what brings you here? It's awfully late."

"Nothing's es wrong? Victor, Margaret all right?" Yvonne asked, coming from her perch on the step to stand next to her husband.

Victor shook his head. "No, no it's nothing like that. Nothing's wrong. May I come in?" He noticed John did not look happy to see him.

"Oui, of course." Yvonne apologized for their rude behavior. She was uneasy, though, because she could tell her husband was tense and did not know why. It was Victor, after all.

"John, Yvonne..." Victor began, nodding to each of them politely. His palms were sweaty, and he wiped them nervously against his pants leg. "I'm sorry for bothering you all so late, but you know how fond I have always been of Celena..." He wasn't sure but thought John recoiled at the mention of his beloved daughter. "And I know this is sudden, considering I just asked you if I could court her...but...I wanted to ask you if I could marry her. I want to marry Celena, right away."

Celena could not see her father's face, and although she knew he would be surprised, she figured he would slap Victor on the shoulder, give them his blessing, and tell them congratulations.

There wasn't a sound in the room save for the ticking of the clock and the thunderous pounding of Celena's heart. Dying with suspense, she moved from her hiding place in the kitchen to peer anxiously into the living room at her father and Victor standing across from each other.

"John?" Yvonne asked, confused as to why he wasn't answering. She noticed he was shaking, his rage barely under control. She could not remember ever seeing her husband so angry.

"Absolutely not."

"*What?*" Celena gasped from the kitchen, unable to believe what she was seeing and hearing.

"John, what on earth es za matter?" Yvonne begged, realizing her husband was dangerously close to losing his temper.

"You want to get married *right away,* Victor?"

"John! What are you *saying?*"

"Is there something you *need* to tell me, Victor?"

Looking down guiltily, Victor shook his head.

"Well, is there?" John shouted, and it was humiliating to Victor knowing full well what he was being accused of.

Summoning all available courage, he met John's eyes. "No. There's nothing I need to tell you."

"I was nice enough to allow you to court her, gave you my blessing. I asked you that day after church, Victor—you knew *damn* well what I was talking about! I told you I'd accept nothing less from you! How *dare* you touch her!"

"But—but I haven't!"

"How dare you do all this behind my back, after all the work we've done together over the years! Why, you've been almost like another *son* to me! And *this* is how you pay me back?"

"I want to marry her..."

"Where was she tonight when she was missing? Where was she when her mother and I were worried about her and looking for her? Was she with you?"

Although his eyes never left John's, it took Victor a few seconds to collect himself enough to answer. "Yes. She was with me."

"And that's how you repay me? That's how you repay my trust? You've *betrayed* me!"

Yvonne saw Victor flinch. She knew he could have endured any tongue lashing or punishment, but losing John's trust wounded him.

"If you've done anything to hurt her, so help me God Victor—"

"But I haven't—I haven't done anything!"

"That's a God damn *relief!*"

"*Mon amor,* please, get ahold of yourself," Yvonne begged, putting her hands on her husband's chest. He dropped his eyes and apologized under his breath to his wife. "Now everybody juz needs to calm down and talk ziz through." Her hands remained on her husband, not sure she could control him.

"I don't want to talk it through, Yvonne."

"But we must *mon amor,* et is our daughter's happiness we are talking about." Yvonne looked at Victor with his guilty downcast face and felt her heart move in her chest. She saw him suddenly as the frantic eleven-year-old boy who had run the two miles to their farm, trusting her to save his mother.

Victor felt terrible knowing he was the cause of their arguing and, cursing himself, silently dropped his head in shame.

"*Mon amor...*" she began, looking up at her husband, "I sink we both know how Celena feels about him."

Victor thanked her silently; she was pleading his case and doing a better job than he had. "You'll only end up breaking her heart if you stand between zem."

Thank you Maman! Celena thought, still poised in the kitchen.

Turning from them, John began to pace, his footsteps the only noise in the room. He sighed loudly and shoved his hands into his pockets.

"You had no right; you know that, don't you Victor? No *right* to ask me for her, it's too soon and you *know* it."

Victor nodded.

"I need time to think about it."

Victor nodded again, hoping now that John's tirade had subsided, he would calm down and tell him that he had their blessing.

"I'm sorry Victor," he began, "sometime...a few years from now, if you can prove to me that you can conduct yourself in a proper fashion and that you have some way to *provide* for my daughter...well then—then you'll have our blessing."

Victor's heart felt too big in his chest. He realized John wanted to make him pay and pay dearly for what he'd done. "I have a house, I have a trade, I can provide for her now."

"I don't say this to be cruel Victor, but everyone knows that you're barely surviving."

"I don't know where you hear that, but it's not *true!* I'm doing fine! I paid back all the money on Jonah's land and kept it from being foreclosed on, I earned enough to buy my sister back my mother's farm, and I've got an idea for a patent—"

"And the thought of my daughter living in that tiny house with oil-skins still for windows—"

Furiously Victor wondered why everyone felt entitled to attack the little house he lived in. "We won't always live there; I know she deserves better."

"Well, when you can prove it, you can marry her!" John screamed. His normally tan complexion took on a furious purple tinge, his eyes nearly bulging out of their sockets.

Victor stood straighter and knew talking right then would do more harm than good. He swore silently for getting so worked up and letting his emotions rule his head. "All right...then," he said finally, sounding more confident than he felt. "I understand," he added, though he didn't. Sighing, he walked heavily to the door. "I've bothered both of you long enough." He dropped his head then, knowing he better leave but hating to with John so furious with him. It hurt him on all levels.

"I'm sorry that—" Victor sighed again, thinking he had done so many things wrong that night that he hardly knew what to start apologizing for. "I'm sorry for arguing with you. I do..." Victor began and then paused, trying to keep the frustration and disappointment from taking over his voice. Trying for once in his life to say the right thing. "I do not want to quarrel with you," he pleaded, and then his eyes fell to the floor, feeling his control slip. "When I have your blessing, John, I want to marry Celena. And I swear to you, she'll never want for anything. I'll take good care of her." He opened the door and walked out, shutting it firmly behind him.

Celena didn't care what Victor said! Blessing or no blessing, she was not going to wait *years!* She ran into the hang-on and, pushing the door open, ran out of the house and around to the front yard where she knew Victor was getting on his horse to leave.

Yvonne heard the back door bang and wondered if Celena had been listening—she was sure of it a second later when she heard her frantic voice outside pleading with to Victor to stop.

Victor was already on Alpha when he saw her running around the side of the house.

"Don't go! *Don't go!*" As she ran to him her shawl fell off her shoulders.

"What are you *doing* out here?" he barked, staring down at her.

She came up to him, tears on her cheeks, chest heaving, arms outstretched.

"*Damnit!*" He swung a leg over the saddle and slid off the horse, grabbing her by the shoulders.

"Please don't go! I don't care what he says, I can't wait!"

"Stop," he hissed. Wary about touching her, he held her literally at arm's length, knowing that John was watching from inside the house and might even be on his way out to confront them.

"Victor...I can't...I *can't* wait years," she began, her words choked with emotion. "Let's run away! They can't stop us; I don't want to wait to get married!"

"Settle down." Sighing with frustration, he stared up at the sky, wondering how he had gotten himself into such a ridiculous situation. How had this evening turned into such a nightmare? He was ashamed when he thought how he'd nearly gotten into a fight with Eddie, ashamed that he'd nearly hit his best Ethan, horrified that he'd nearly raped the woman he loved. "We're just going to have to wait. We don't have any other choice."

"But—but—" she stammered, and he squeezed her shoulders so tightly she winced in pain.

"Listen to me." His eyes were cold. "You think I *want* to wait? I don't like this any better than you do."

"But we could run away—"

"Don't talk like a child."

"But we could! We could just leave."

He let go and stared down at her. "And have your father disown you and hate me? I know what your family means to you. Do you honestly think I'm that selfish?"

"No! I don't think you're selfish! I want to get married!" she wailed, the tears drenching her cheeks. Embarrassed, she had to wipe her nose with the back of her hand. "But...it's *so long* to have to wait! If he'd said a few months...but he didn't, he said *years*! He's not being fair. I'll make him see that it's not fair!"

"I know it's not fair, but we should have expected this, they had no idea we were so serious. We should have kept quiet about it like we were planning to." Silently he chastised himself for the mess he'd made.

"I don't want to wait. *I can't do it!*" she burst out and suddenly felt more frustrated than she had ever felt before in her life. "You're so good at your work. You could be a smith anywhere, any town would be glad to have you, we could pack up the tools and the anvil and—go."

"No. We're not going to run away. I'm not going to take you from your parents and home that you love. Believe me...I don't like this any better than you do. We'll have to prove to them that we're old enough." But she had the annoying sensation that he meant that *she* was old enough. He took a deep breath. "We can do it; it'll just be for a little while." He forced a weak smile, but deep down he had the feeling that John hoped their desire to marry would not survive the waiting.

"I looked forward for two weeks to this night," she said, and looking up at him wondered how it had all turned out so terribly wrong.

"I did too." They fell silent again, united in their disappointment.

"Victor," she whispered, sniffing back her tears and wanting nothing more than to lay her head against his chest, to feel his strong arms around her.

He pushed her away. "You better go on in now. Lena *please*...don't tempt me. We have to stay apart from each other."

She bit her bottom lip to keep from crying when she saw him guiltily lower his head. "You...heard everything in there?"

She nodded.

"Then you know how mad he is. And besides, he's not all wrong. I almost didn't control myself tonight—" He hung his head even farther, thinking what John had been accusing him of was not that far from the truth. Ethan's accusation that she was not *safe* alone with him darted unpleasantly through his mind. "I don't...ever want to do that to you again."

She felt a fresh wave of guilt, knowing that after he'd been decent enough to stop, she had used his desire for her to coerce him into asking her father. They stood silently, heavy between them was frustration and defeat. Yet at the same time Celena was not without hope. She knew her father, knew how much he loved her, and she would force him to make good his promise. After all, he'd only said they had to *wait*, he hadn't said *no*.

"It's late. I've got to go." Without looking at her, Victor got back up on his horse. He was used to being physically tired, but the emotional exhaustion he was feeling was worse than anything he'd ever felt. "Good night." Spurring Alpha, he left.

She stood in the darkness watching him until she couldn't see him anymore. Then she lifted her face to gaze at the still-bright moon. Although she couldn't put her finger on it, she felt changed. Turning, she went toward her house and bent to retrieve the shawl, picking up her heavy skirts to ascend the steps, squaring her shoulders as she went.

They would wait until they had her father's blessing, and then nothing would ever keep them apart again. She had the feeling that Victor was doubting her maturity, doubting her commitment, but she shrugged as she got to the porch. It didn't matter; she'd make him understand what she knew to be true. After all, it was simple. They belonged together.

Part Two

Chapter 6

"Morning Victor," John said without looking at him, ushering Celena protectively into the wagon after church the next morning. Yvonne too murmured good morning without looking at him. Even Will and James, who always stopped to talk, steered clear of him.

Victor stared down at the ruts the wagon wheels made in the street. He'd slept badly, his shoulder was aching from stopping the broadside yesterday, and the Rieflers' avoidance of him only added to his misery.

When he caught sight of Celena earlier that morning in church he had to swallow the hard lump that formed in his throat. In the morning light her face looked so innocent and beautiful that his heart ached in his chest for wanting her. She had barely smiled at him before she looked away, fearful to ignite her father's anger.

"That was some barn raising last night, John. Did we go through both those kegs of whiskey?" Don Fisk asked.

John nodded but the last thing in the world he wanted to talk about was the cursed barn raising.

"Yes, sir, that was something all right. I still can't believe you stopped that wall from falling, Victor!" Keith Stoddard said, coming up near Victor grinning, oblivious to the tension.

Normally Victor would have been proud of his feat. But with the way John was treating him, he felt proud of nothing.

"Hey strongman!" Andy Stoddard yelled. Coming over, he gripped Victor's hand hard and shook it. "This man is a *brute* if there ever is one!"

Wincing, Victor forced a smile, wishing he had used a different word. He listened to the other men banter a bit before getting ready to go home. When he realized the Rieflers hadn't stayed around to socialize like normal, his spirits sank even further.

Jean but a hand on his shoulder. "Somezing wrong?"

They walked companionably, out of the hearing of the other men.

"You could say that."

Jean's bushy eyebrows went up in question.

"I asked if I could marry Celena." He half expected Jean to laugh at him and was relieved when he did not.

"He said no?" Jean was incredulous, half wishing Victor wanted to marry one of *his* daughters.

"He said...maybe." Victor shrugged non-committally. "In a few years."

"Give him some time, eh?" Jean consoled. "He's a stubborn German, that one. But he'll come around. She'll convince him."

"Yvonne?"

"No. *Ce-le-na*," Jean enunciated; his French accent made the name even prettier. "Trust me. I have five daughters myself. Little girls have a way wis zare fathers. You'll see, *forgeron*." Jean gave his friend a reassuring smile and left.

An hour later Victor was working in the shop when Ethan breezed in.

"Victor, good afternoon," he trilled, but stopped when he saw the way Victor was staring at him. "I-I don't know what happened last night."

"You were there, weren't you?"

It was ten seconds before Ethan could bring himself to speak. "I had no idea that my dancing with Celena would upset you so much." He knew he should say that he had no idea that they had feelings for each other, but it was hard to say words that he knew were false.

Victor shook his head, wanting to give Ethan the benefit of the doubt. "It's too late now, it's done. Besides, it wasn't the dancing that bothered me, it was what you did...later." He was torn. He had always thought good things of Ethan. Even though Ethan had done terrible things at the bank, Victor rationalized that it was because Frederick forced him. But now a nagging doubt gnawed away at the valiant perception he had always had of his dearest friend. "It doesn't matter now...you couldn't possibly have known," Victor said, wanting to believe Ethan innocent.

Relieved, Ethan smiled. "You certainly don't look like a man who has the respect of the entire town, as well as the affections of the fair Celena. Last night you were the hero—"

"Last night I made a fool out of myself."

There was an awkward pause, and Ethan lightly changed the subject. "I see not much has changed since I've been gone."

"Some things change, some don't. Jonah's dead, that's a change, Margaret's getting married, that's another change. I work all the God damn time—that's *not* a change." There was such bitterness and disappointment in his voice Ethan felt a burst of affection for him. But he was not sure he could ever talk to Victor about what his father had done to him and Margaret; there was too much guilt for him to deal with.

"So, since I've been gone you've...seen Celena, from time to time?" he asked nonchalantly. He had after all spent the night convincing himself that since he had been away at school, she had to make do in his absence. Now that he was showing interest in her, surely she would favor him for a sweetheart, the handsome, well-educated banker's son, over the perpetually sweating blacksmith. He had a wonderful time with Celena last night, and found himself for the first time in his life interested in a woman not merely for her beauty. Celena had touched his heart, and he liked the way he felt when he was with her. Even when she had scolded him about his father's dealings with the bank, he knew she was right. He felt that if she were in his life, he'd be not only a better banker, but a better man.

"Yes, as a matter of fact we have been...courting," Victor said. Hating the word, hating the formality, hating the waiting period.

Ethan's heart rate doubled. "You've been courting Celena?"

"Yes."

"You didn't say that last night. You didn't say *courting* last night!"

Victor stared down at him. "What do you want me to say? Do I have to spell it out for you? I'm—" He stopped short of saying '*in love with her!*' but it burst through the air as clearly as if he had shouted it. He sighed and slumped back against the forge. "Besides...I—I can't *say* things like that. They just won't come out of my mouth."

"*You're*...courting Celena?"

Victor shrugged. "Well, I don't know now if I'm still *allowed* to court her, but one thing is for sure, I'm going to marry her."

"*What?*" Ethan cried, more alarmed than he had ever been in his life.

"I asked John last night."

"You asked Celena's father *last night* if you—if you could...*marry* her? What answer did he give you?"

"He told me..." It was painful and embarrassing for him to think about, much less talk about, especially with Ethan. "He told me that I'd have to wait a...few years...that I'd have to prove that I could take care of her. I don't think he's fond of my little house."

Ethan let out the breath he didn't realize he had been holding. And as much as he cared for Victor, he was certain John Riefler had no intentions of his cherished daughter ever marrying the son of an Osage slave and the town's most notorious wife-beating drunk.

"Have you discussed this with Celena?"

"Of course."

"You asked Celena to marry you, and she said *yes*?" He could not keep the shock out of his voice.

Victor, keying in on it, eyed him curiously. "She didn't say yes, she said that I'd do. Does that surprise you so much?"

Under the weight of the steel gray eyes, Ethan felt a dampness under his arms. Yet at the same time he was encouraged. "Well Victor you must admit, it does not sound like much of a love match if the prospective bride can't think of anything more endearing to utter than *that!*"

Victor shrugged, self-conscious.

"I had no idea things were settled with Celena."

"Well, they *aren't* settled, in fact they aren't settled at all. At least not for a...long while..." Victor sighed, giving in a bit to the despair he felt. Fighting the knowledge that it may be years before Riefler gave them their blessing to marry.

"How long have you been seeing her?" Ethan asked, needing details.

"About a month," he hedged.

"You've courted her a *month* and you already asked her father! Why that's preposterous!" Ethan had to suppress a laugh. "What did you expect? How serious could you two be in a month?"

"I know that! But I had to ask last night—she begged me after what happened. Things sort of...got out of control."

Ethan watched the gray eyes shift to the floor guiltily. "What do you *mean* out of control?" A cold panic swept through his heart. "Last night did you—"

"*No!* No, I didn't! But I..." Victor stammered guiltily. "Let's just say I got close to it." Ashamed again, his eyes left Ethan's, and he dragged both hands viciously through his hair. "The worst thing is I was in such a... rage and wanted her so badly, I think I hurt her—" he said, needing desperately to admit his regret and shame to someone. Wanting someone to loosen his burden. Knowing this was *not* the sort of thing he could ever bring himself to admit to Margaret.

As Victor stood there in front of him with his head hanging, a part of Ethan wanted to console him. Tell him of his adventures and his *own* difficulties in control. But he said nothing, offered no comfort. He did not, because a part of his personality, the part he was least fond of, was glad. Glad Victor had made such a mess of things

"Anyway..." Victor sighed. "I've got to go. I'm going to go work on the roof at Margaret and Henry's house." Picking up the tools in the box, he glanced around to make sure he had everything.

"So, you'll be at your farm all day?" Ethan asked, opening the door, as afraid to look at Victor—afraid his eyes would reveal too much.

"Yes. I guess it's not much of a wedding present with a leaking roof." It was Victor's first genuine smile of the day.

"No, I guess not. Could we play chess later this week?" Ethan asked hopefully, eager for the rift between them to be gone, wanting the "Victor" who was always calm and trusting back.

"That would be fine."

By midday Celena was restless and in a bad mood. She was determined to prove to her father that she was ready to be married, and prove to Victor she was old enough to love him. She had barely even looked up at him that morning at church when she felt her father's arm around her elbow protectively leading her away from Victor.

The house was quiet and still. Her mother and sisters had gone to Josephine Chomeau's and even though they pleaded with her to go with them, she had declined. Her father and brothers were out in the fields and she knew they wouldn't be in for hours. Even though it was Sunday, there was a host of things that needed to be done, and John Riefler was never one to be idle. Besides, he couldn't bring himself to meet her eyes. She knew it was weighing heavily on his heart, that he had hurt her, and she was simultaneously angry with her father and felt badly empathy for him.

Celena was working on a needlepoint she had started last spring. It was a seat cover of a grapevine wreath with a pink rose vine entwined and bluebirds perched along the top. She had stitched all the wreath, but now as she concentrated on the bluebirds, the stitches were not neat, and had to go back and yank them out. Normally, she was content when the housework was under control to lose herself in her needlework.

Agitated, she put the needlepoint down and stepping out the door faintly hearing Laurence and Will hammering. Even though they were far away, she could hear snatches of their conversations as their voices traveled in the cool afternoon air.

Carlene and Eva asked her what happened last night, having heard the argument from downstairs. It was sweet Celena thought how both her sisters were on her side, and how they too thought it wrong of her father to make such demands. "But Papa *likes* Victor!" Eva exclaimed. She was worried suddenly about Danny, knowing he didn't have any idea the hornets' nest he was stepping in. "Papa's too strict!" Carlene wailed, thinking he was going to throw a fit when he found out she was now seeing Eddie's brother Mason. "I mean, I'm already nineteen, does he *want* me to be an old maid? One of these days I'll show him!"

Celena looked at the maple tree and saw they were rapidly losing their brown and red leaves and that without them the branches looked black against the dazzling azure sky. The smell of earth and dried leaves filled the air, and breathing in, closed her eyes. Trying to let the serenity of such a perfect fall afternoon seep into her soul.

She was certain she could convince her father but knew regrettably it would take time. Trying to be patient, she went back inside to resume her needlework. Calmer, she was making headway on the bluebirds when she heard someone coming up the drive. Her sisters and mother had barely been gone an hour and could not possibly be home yet.

Victor!

Jumping up, she threw the needlework into the basket and raced to the door, flinging it open.

"Well good afternoon to you too Celena! That certainly was a heartfelt welcome!" Ethan said with an amused laugh.

The door bounced against the side of the house and bumped Celena, who was standing in shock, mouth gaping. She had to drop her eyes to mask her disappointment, wishing to God she had not even come out of the house! There wasn't another person in the world she wanted to see less at this moment than Ethan.

"It is a spectacular afternoon, I thought I would come by and see if you'd like to take a stroll with me." He walked up the last step of the front porch. She noticed that his eyes traveled up and down her, and that they lingered too long in certain places.

She took a step back.

He looked eager, dressed simply for once no cravat or suit coat, in brown pants, and a white shirt. His hair neatly combed back. Smiling sweetly, he reached out and took hold of one of her hands and began gently to pull her towards the steps. "It's a shame to let a beautiful afternoon like this go to waste," he urged, tugging playfully at her hand.

Panicked, she wished suddenly she had gone to Josephine's, wished her father was sitting inside the house, wished James or Laurence were within earshot. But she was alone. She would have to take care of him herself.

She pulled her hand away. "Thank you, but I don't feel like it."

He made a face of mock hurt, but she did not laugh as he expected. "Well...we'll sit then."

As she stood staring down at him, she couldn't help but wonder why he didn't have the sense to leave. She didn't want to sit with him on the front porch no matter how beautiful the afternoon.

"Will you sit?" he asked. He knew what effect his charms and looks had on women and figured her to be no different.

"No, I won't."

He was puzzled, totally unaccustomed to dealing with rejection from the female sex. "Why ever not?"

"It just...wouldn't be right," she managed, wanting him to leave. It certainly wasn't *all* his fault, but still she couldn't help but think that if it not for him, last night wouldn't have turned out the way it did.

"Why wouldn't it be right?" he asked, ignoring the flutter in his gut.

She wavered, not wanting to hurt his feelings. "It just wouldn't be."

He stood. "Why? Where's the harm in sitting with me?"

"Because—because I don't want to." She felt an embarrassing flush of color coming into her cheeks and looked down.

"You are wounding me terribly Celena!" he said, taking another step toward her. With her eyes downcast and her lashes lowered she looked so gorgeous that he could understood why Victor had nearly lost control. Gently he touched her chin, wanting her to look at him.

"Don't touch me!" She batted his hand away with a shudder.

Anger and humiliation sprang into his eyes. "You don't want *me* to touch you, but you relish the feel of *his* dirty blacksmith hands!"

"What is the *matter* with you?" she screeched, suppressed her first furious reaction to slap him. But it was *Ethan*, Victor's best friend. Besides, she was going to prove to everyone that she was old enough to get married; slapping him seemed childish and she vowed to rise above it.

"Celena, surely you can't be serious about him. You can't be serious about marrying him!"

"Yes! I am serious. I want, and since you've obviously talked to Victor, you already *know* this." She was certain now his motives for coming to see her were not innocent. But it was hard to think bad things of Ethan; he was a person Victor had trusted, and because Victor trusted him, instinctively she had too.

"But you'll have *nothing* as his wife!" he lamented, fearing the future he so desperately wanted was slipping through his fingers like water.

"I'll have everything I need and want."

"But you *can't!*"

"Why can't I?"

"He's...he's...too big for you for one thing, you look *ridiculous* together!" It humiliated him when she stared at him as if he'd lost his mind. "You can't marry a simple *blacksmith!*"

"He's not *simple!* And *you* of all people should know that."

Ethan shut his mouth, fearing if he attacked Victor's sterling character it would make more the loathsome beast he feared he already personified. "But he's...not right for you."

Annoyed, she crossed her arms in front of her chest. "Tell me, Ethan, why isn't he right for me?"

"Well...he's—he's poor for one thing."

"He may be, but as long as I have a roof over my head and enough to eat, I don't care." Looking at him, she wondered if he wasn't coming down with something. He had turned a peculiar shade of green.

"But I'm back now—" He stopped again, realizing he was at a crucial point. He had been so sure the affection between them was one-sided, but now he was afraid all hope for him was lost. "My coming back..." He paused to find the right way to phrase it. "...makes no difference to you?"

She blinked her sparkling eyes. "Of course it makes a difference. I am glad you're back. You are Victor's dearest friend, and he has missed you terribly these last few years."

Even though she had mistaken his words, he understood hers and their horrible implications. He turned his back to her in desperation, not wanting Celena to see his eyes, fearing they would reveal his torment. If he was not careful, he would lose not only Celena, but the man that was his best friend. "I'm—I'm sorry Celena," he mumbled, unable to look at her. "Please forgive me for what I did earlier. I-I was worried about you, and I wanted to make sure you knew his situation. I only meant that I'm glad you and Victor waited to get married until—until I came back." Weak suddenly, he had to sit down. The brutal knowledge that he and Celena were never to be was making it difficult for him to breathe.

She smiled at him, having no idea that her well-intended warmth was breaking his heart. "Well, we'll be waiting a while longer still," she confessed, and no longer worried he was going to try and touch her, sat down on the steps.

He could feel her concerned eyes on him. Humiliated, he could not return her gaze. "Yes...Victor said something about waiting, why is that?"

"My father said that Victor has to prove that he can take care of me." She brushed away the thin strands that worked themselves free from her braid. "It's complete nonsense and I told my father so...but something made him angry last night." She leaned near him and he realized she was going to divulge something private. "It was almost like he *knew* Victor and I were alone somewhere together, like someone had told him, and now he's furious with Victor. And we did nothing wrong, Ethan. Anyway, we're going to have to wait to get married. I'm going to have to be patient. I don't want to be, but Victor told me I have to, and I guess he's right, he's usually right about most things."

He felt his heart turning to stone inside his chest.

They sat quietly. He listened to her quiet breathing and realized she had no idea how desperately he wanted to lead her to the meadow and lay down with her under the dappled shade of some tree. How desperately he wanted to kiss her and make her see that he, not Victor, was the one for her.

"You've changed. Do you realize that?" he asked quietly, fighting the impulse to brush away the sun-streaked strands from her face. She had always been pretty, but when he had seen her in the moonlight the night he had returned, something happened to him. Again, when he danced with her the night of the barn raising, he realized he was falling in love with her. She already seemed different to him than the quiet beauty he remembered.

"I know I have." Turning, she looked at him squarely. "I feel different too, but I didn't know it showed so much."

"Yes, you're more radiant and confident. I suppose it's because you've found your soulmate. It was destiny I suppose." Although he said the words easily, he felt that the course of his entire future had just been altered. In the depths of his soul, he knew that it was an unfortunate turn his life had taken, yet he was powerless to change it. "He is a fortunate man to have your love."

Feeling the color flooding her cheeks, she looked down. "I'm the lucky one. You've known him a long time, Ethan, you must know he's not like anyone else. He's not like anyone I've ever known. I feel safe with him."

"Safe from what?"

She shrugged, looking down, uncomfortable to be talking so intimately with Ethan. "All my life I've been...stared at and whispered about. I guess all things come with a price, even—"

"Beauty?"

She nodded. "Yes. I know that sounds silly. I know I should be grateful I wasn't born blind or deaf, and I am. But looking like the way I do and being noticed *all the time.*" She shook her head at some hard memories. "I can't tell you how many times I've been cornered. Everyone expecting me to be witty and carry the conversation. I always ended up feeling that I'd disappointed them, that they were thinking that '*Yes, she's pretty but...*'" She paused for a moment, thinking. "And even when I did try and talk, none of them wanted to talk to me, they just wanted to *look.* Carlene told me once being pretty was wasted on me because I didn't know how to *use* it. But Victor listened to me, even when I was a little girl. He's always paid attention to me, and not only because of how I looked. There was more to it. There always was. And he's been in the background of my life quietly waiting. I feel like he was waiting for me to grow up so I could marry him." She smiled at the wonderful thoughts. "Do you know he's even made me a wooden cover for an iron?"

"An iron cover, in the tenuous balance of life, is what tips you toward him?"

She smiled. "Actually yes. He made it because he cares about Margaret and wants to help her, and when I'm his wife he'll help me too." She sighed again, looking up the brilliantly blue sky. "He always told me I could do things. He made me feel that the little things I did, like the mending and cooking were as important as what my brothers did in the fields. I know that must sound silly."

"Actually...it doesn't sound a bit silly. After all, isn't that what we all strive for in this vast universe—to find the one person that makes us feel important, unique...significant."

"I suppose so."

"I'm jealous of you actually, you've found what you want in life... you're so sure of yourself," he said on the brittle hope that she would be harboring any doubt.

"I've never been surer of anything before in my life!" she said with a smile and then looked away. "Victor lives in my heart, and he *always* has. I want nothing but good things to happen to him, and I want to protect him from anything that would ever hurt him. He's the first thing I think of in the morning, and the last thing I think about when I go to sleep at night. I find myself wanting to tell him everything...I can't wait to be his wife!" She reached out suddenly and put her hands on his. "Oh Ethan, I want you to be as happy as I am. I truly hope you find this love, this connection with someone someday, it's too magnificent to believe!"

I did find it, he thought sadly, savoring her warm hands on his hands, knowing it would probably be the last time she would ever do so.

And I lost it.

Chapter 7

The snow started at midday on New Year's Eve and was still falling, even as darkness fell. Victor helped Margaret out of the wagon in front of church as she wrestled with the wide hoops of her wedding dress. He noticed that her face was flushed and her hands were hot and damp inside his.

She looks pretty, he thought. Celena had helped her make a dress out of pale blue muslin. It was a simple design with a high virginal neck, a slim long waist, and long sleeves. Although it was plain and did not have rows of seed pearls or bundles of lace like most wedding dresses of the day, she still looked every inch the happy bride she was.

Her dark hair was pulled up away from her face and Carlene and Eva had spent nearly three hours curling the heavy tresses. She had on a long lace veil that she had borrowed from Lisette, and it hung loosely over her face. Through it her brown skin looked pale and Victor took a second glance, never having seen her look pale before in his life!

Carefully they started up the steps that, although Victor had shoveled, were still icy. She slipped once and, holding onto her, he noticed with a pang of sympathy that she was trembling under his hand. As he pulled open the heavy oak door Margaret felt a rush of warmth. Eva was at the piano, smiled at the two of them, and began playing.

Margaret blushed when she heard the hushed exclamations from the crowd of how pretty she looked. Seeing Henry dressed in a brown suit, standing stiff as a board at the altar, she smiled.

She wanted more than anything to marry Henry and start a life with him but knew that meant leaving Victor and it caused tears to form in her eyes. Besides the fact that she was going to miss Victor, she was worried about him living alone in the house. He would of course have Mrs. Blay at the boarding house cook him two meals a day, but he would still be alone. It bothered her that no one would be doing the little things for him that she had always done.

They were at the altar suddenly and Victor let go of her.

Victor took a full step back and happily watched his sister marry Henry Wilburn. He looked around the ornately decorated Catholic Church with its marble communion rail and whitewashed walls and thought of his mother. Wondered again where she was, wondered if her soul wandered the land as he feared it did. He imagined her soul soaring along the wide expanse of the Mississippi's edge, sometimes felt he could almost hear her voice as the wind roared through the leaves of the tallest oak trees. Was she in their heaven with angels dressed in white robes and halos of gold? Or was she with the Great Spirit, Wah-Kon-Tah? Try as he might he could not picture her in either place and wondered if her soul still wandered the earth looking for a place to belong, like she had done in life. He had the strongest, almost frightening feeling suddenly that he could find her. Quickly as the feeling came, it was gone.

Only someone watching him closely like Celena would have noticed his intense preoccupation, and that something had in a split second happened to him. She wondered where he had gone when he should have been listening to the service, where his soul had gone when it had left his body.

The small reception was toasting the happy couple after the vows were said and mass completed. Celena baked an enormous wedding cake, three layers tall, and the fluffy white icing was flawless. She had painstakingly embellished it with dried red and green fruits in the shape of a Christmas wreath.

Near Victor, Ethan whispered, "Are you going to spring giving the farm on her now, and have her faint and ruin poor Henry's wedding night?"

Victor grinned. "I think I'll wait a bit." The two of them stood companionably at the edge of the merry making.

Victor had purposely kept his eyes from Celena but could not help himself from looking at her. She was wearing a silk dress that hugged her body, not leaving much for his overactive imagination to work out. Her hair was center parted and pinned up, and she had on small silver filigree earrings. He looked at the little mark under her left eye and remembered what it felt like to kiss her there. Looking away he sighed, silently wishing it was he and Celena that had wed.

He could still remember when he had shown up that next Sunday after the barn raising, still trying to court her. He could tell John was shocked and annoyed to see him at the door but could not turn him away. The courting consisted of Victor coming by for an hour on Sunday afternoons, where Celena, her parents, sisters, and sometimes Danny and Mason all sat uncomfortably in the parlor. She and her sisters did needlepoint while Victor and her father sat across the room from each other and had stilted conversations with long pauses. The only time they were remotely close was when they sat opposite each other at the table working on the patent request. Other than that, they had not had a private word since the night of the barn raising, or even so much as touched hands.

"It's so beautiful Celena, it seems such a shame to eat it." Margaret beamed, silver cake knife in hand.

"Well, you'd better eat it—Celena whipped the batter 'til I thought her arms would fall off!" Carlene quipped.

"Well, I need a piece!" James said, smiling at Margaret as she began to cut the cake into wedges for her guests. He was bursting with happiness—he'd married Alice a month earlier and was still reeling with joy. Will came over to both Ethan and Victor and refilled their punch cups.

"Don't want you two going thirsty."

Victor watched Laurence and Lisette and their two boys and brand-new baby girl Estella, and everyone else like the Stoddards, Fisks, and Gustaves enjoying themselves. It made him proud how they were all shaking his hand and congratulating him as the head of the bride's family. It was wonderful to have so many friends.

When the cake had been thoroughly destroyed and lay in discarded crumbs on the crystal platter, Victor knew he could not wait any longer, and clearing his throat reached out to touch Margaret's arm. Most of the guests that were not family were gone, which was fine with him. He wanted to do this for Margaret but did not think it needed it to be a public spectacle.

Turning, Margaret looked at him, her face radiating happiness.

"Henry," Victor said, reaching out to shake his hand. "Margaret, I have a wedding gift for you." He reached into his coat pocket and pulled out a folded piece of paper.

"What is it?"

"Well, I suppose we should read it darlin' and find out," Henry said, taking it from her and unfolding it. As they read, Margaret's eyes flew open with astonishment.

"You couldn't have—please tell me you didn't do that!" she exclaimed, her eyes filling with happy tears. She searched the faces around her. "Ethan—is this true?"

"It's true, you've a place to live."

"I don't know what to say, Victor...thank you. I'm truly beholden to you—not only for Margaret, but for the farm." Henry swallowed hard.

"It needs a lot of work, Henry, don't be thanking me too soon. Besides, it's not all paid for yet, but Ethan has generously agreed to let you pay off what's owed with the sale of crops, and I plan to help you."

"Victor," Margaret said again, pulling him down so could hear her whisper, "that had to have cost you everything you've *ever* saved. You'll have nothing left!"

"It did cost me everything, but I have a house and land and a trade, what more do I need?"

"I can't take this...it's too much, I can't let you do this."

"Of course you can," he scoffed, straightening so she could have no more private words of refusal with him.

Sniffing, Margaret took the handkerchief Ethan handed to her, and stood staring up at her brother. He was protecting her. A little shiver went through her suddenly, remembering the time she spilled a bucket of water on the floor, and how Victor shoved her behind him. How she'd crawled in terror under the table, curled up into a ball, and jammed her hands against her ears to blot out the sounds of Victor taking the beating meant for her.

"Thank you," Margaret whispered to him. She hugged him again, pressing her face against his chest. Drying her eyes, she let go and turned to the family and friends who wanted to congratulate her and talk about plans for the farm.

Henry's mother leaned toward Celena. "Did you know about this?"

"Yes, he told me what he planned to do."

"This is so generous of him. He must have been saving for years!" Mrs. Wilburn exclaimed, pleased to death her son suddenly had a farm and wondering if he would consider taking in one or two of his siblings. "It's such a kind act. You must be proud to death of him."

"Yes, I am." Celena's eyes ran riot over the man she loved.

Ethan looked at Victor, who only moments earlier had been simply a blacksmith, but now with the gift was transformed into a martyred saint. It was an uncomfortable paradox for him to feel love and jealousy for Victor at the same time. After all, Victor had told him last month that his outlandish attempts to coerce the wealthy widow Josephine Chomeau into a partnership had worked. Because Josephine had let Victor install and create the new parts for her sawmill, she had given him half-ownership instead of paying him. Ethan was incredulous that Josephine would do such a thing. But he had the formal papers tucked away in the bank, spelling out Victor and Josephine's business arrangement. Ethan begrudgingly realized, despite his lack of schooling, Victor was a savvy businessman.

Margaret and Henry were saying goodbye to their guests and Victor, seeing an opportunity, neared Celena. She was brushing the crumbs from the table into a cup, collecting stray forks, and carefully wrapping up the crystal platter to be taken home.

"I hope Margaret's happy," he said softly, his eyes on the floor, careful to stay a respectful distance from Celena, knowing John was still there.

Celena glanced at Margaret who was, by her flushed face and laughing eyes, overwhelmed with happiness. "Oh, yes," she said, proud that the person she loved had made them so joyous. "Victor, you've made them happy."

He nodded and shuffled his feet. "I wasn't sure at first. She cried," he said, thinking it was odd that women always cried when they were *happy*.

"I don't think she's had a good night's sleep for days worrying about this wedding, and I know she's worried about you being alone now. Then you shock her with the deed to the farm, I think after all that, I might burst into tears too!"

"Well, if you say so."

Daringly, Celena looked up into his eyes. "You know nothing of female natures, do you?"

He grinned, embarrassed. "I guess not." He knew it was time to go, heard everyone getting on their coats and shawls to brave the frigid air, and he was anxious to show Margaret and Henry all the work he had done, and how good the house looked. But he was not ready to go yet, not quite ready to leave Celena.

"A few hours from now," he began, his eyes on the floor, "if by chance you're still awake...when you hear the clock from downstairs strike midnight, it will be a new year, 1850. If we're lucky, it will be the year you and I marry."

A painfully large lump formed in her throat, and she nodded.

"I'll be awake to hear it, Victor. I'll be very much awake."

Chapter 8

Margaret stepped silently into the shop, motioning to her brother-in-laws Thomas and Claude to be quiet. Stealing up behind Victor, she grabbed him around the waist.

Turning, he dropped the saw he had been sharpening to hug her.

"It is so good to see you!" she exclaimed, smiling up at him. "You're losing weight, are you eating? Is Mrs. Blay still cooking for you? I don't know why you won't come over to our house and eat more often like you promised you would!" she admonished. The almost three months she had been married she'd seen so little of him.

He laughed and shook his head. "I'm fine, I've been working a lot. And how are you? You look grand!"

"Victor!" she whispered excitedly, her hands drawn up in little fists under her chin. As always, the scars on her arm looked angry against the smooth skin of her face. "You're going to be an uncle!"

Victor's healthy laughter filled the shop. "Already? I didn't think ol' Henry had it in him."

"Oh, you men are all the same!" she shot back. "I was so busy and had so many things I wanted to do; Henry would hardly leave me alone that first month! It's a wonder I got any work done at all with him after me all the time! It's going to be a boy, I just know it, and I plan to name him Henry Victor—for the two most wonderful men in my life." Leaning up, she noisily kissed her brother on the cheek.

Chapter 9

Walking into the Rieflers keeping room on Sunday afternoon, Victor noticed that Celena was more dressed up than normal. She had on a starched white blouse pinned with a small cameo at the throat, and a brown skirt. He noticed she'd pinned her hair up again and wished she wouldn't. He wondered if she thought she looked older with her hair knotted to the back of her head and couldn't wait as her husband to pull the pins out of that hair. He sighed silently, knowing John and everyone else was in the room, and chased those thoughts from his mind.

Victor grinned at Danny and Mason, both sitting uncomfortably in chairs, looking like possums caught in a cage.

Celena greeted him. "Hello Victor."

He offered her a multicolored bunch of wildflowers he'd been hiding behind his back. There were creamy white daffodils, a twig of lavender from a redbud tree, and a bright yellow forsythia branch. Most of them were still budded and barely opened. She hugged it gently against her chest, careful not to crush the delicate buds.

"Hey Vic, you're makin' all the other boys look bad!" Will laughed, looking at Danny Charbonnier, who looked almost green, and Mason, who looked like he might lose his lunch.

"They're beautiful," she whispered. "I thought you'd never get here." She gently rubbed her cheek against the soft petals.

"I know I'm late. I would have been here sooner, but I busted a handle on one of the hot sets." He shook his head with frustration at how long it had taken him to fix it. "Besides, I wanted to bring you something."

"Bring me something, why?"

"It's been six months. Six months we've been...courting, or as I like to think of it, *waiting*. And we've made it this far. I wanted to mark it somehow, but by the time I finished up in the shop the store was closed, and I didn't want to show up empty handed. I think I got everything budding between my shop and your Pa's farm."

She bit back happy tears. It hit a sentimental chord in her knowing he had been thinking about her each time he stopped to pick a different flower. "It was so sweet of you to think of me."

He shrugged. "I'm always thinking about you."

Chapter 10

When Alexander Pickering from the patent office in Washington, D.C. wrote back requesting a meeting with Victor, Celena could not have been happier! She was excited Victor was going to Washington and tried not to think about how much she would miss him while he'd be gone.

But when the day came for Victor to leave, she was irritable, distracted, and annoyed with Ethan who, when she had asked him to accompany Victor, had been non-committal. She knew Ethan would have no trouble talking to the important men in the patent office, whereas Victor might, and was disappointed that Ethan was unwilling to help.

"Thank you for bringing me to town, Laurence." She slipped out of the wagon, grabbing the lunch she had made Victor for the steamboat ride.

"Do you want me to wait for you?" he asked, feeling a pang of sympathy and wondering why his father couldn't see how silly it was forcing them apart and how miserable he was making her.

"No, I'm all right. I'll meet you over at the store in a little while." She walked to the blacksmith shop and pulled one of the heavy doors open.

A shaft of sunlight slid into the shop and Victor looked up. "Just a second Claude." Getting off the stool he came to her.

"You're *working* today?" she asked, seeing the tools and bits of iron spread out on one of the carpenter's tables along with paper and pen.

"I was giving Claude some last-minute instructions."

She handed him the bundle to divert the gaze of his gray eyes. "I knew you'd be hungry on the trip. I made you three egg sandwiches, and there's two apples and biscuits, almost a half of a pecan pie." He took the bundle from her. "Careful, there's a jar of apple butter for your biscuits. Try and bring it back if you can." A welling-up of dread caused her to drop her eyes, afraid suddenly she might burst into tears.

"Well...thank you. No one cooks like my Lena."

"My heavens Victor! You should have told me you didn't have a decent suit; I could have made you something that fit!"

He looked down at his clothes in surprise. The black tweed coat would not stretch over his chest, the shirt collar was too tight to be buttoned, and he had merely cinched the cravat up to disguise it. The sleeves of the coat and the shirt were too short, his hands hanging out of them looking unusually large, and the pants legs were only long enough because the hem had been completely taken out.

"Well...it's all I have," he said with a disinterested shrug. "Margaret ironed the shirt. It's stiff. I did shine the boots though."

Taking a small step towards him, she noticed he'd gotten a close shave that morning because there was a small cut on his chin. "Well...your hair looks nice," she said, not wanting to send him off to Washington with only criticisms filling his head. It was such beautiful hair, so shiny, so black. "Have you got everything?"

He reached into his pocket and began laying things on the carpentry table. "Money, steamship passage up to St. Louis, then another steamer up the Illinois river to Chicago. I'll buy the train ticket to Washington when I get there...patent request...letter from the patent office...the sketches, the rim—" He motioned toward the burlap sack on the floor.

"You've got the address of the patent office-and Mr., Mr.—" She couldn't believe she had forgotten the name of the man in the patent office, after all *she* had written all the letters.

"Alexander Pickering. Yes, I've got the address."

"I guess that's everything then," she said, afraid to look up at him.

"I guess so."

But they both knew that it was not everything. He laid his hands on her shoulders and tried to pull her towards him.

"What about...Claude?" she asked nervously.

Victor glanced over at his striker who was furiously bent over the notes. "He's trying to read the notes I left him—it will take him awhile, trust me. He reads about as well as I dance."

"Victor, have you got everything?" Margaret called, bounding into the shop, startling them apart.

"I'm sorry, Celena, I didn't know you were here," Margaret said, flustered. "Victor, I brought you a lunch." She heaved the large picnic basket on top of the table.

She looked, Celena thought, quite healthy and happily pregnant in the loose dress she wore. Her cheeks were flushed, and her breasts had doubled in size.

"Oh, heavens," Margaret cried, spying the bundle on the table. "You've already got a lunch. I'm sorry, of course you'd make him lunch. I'm so used to looking after him. Victor, take Celena's lunch—"

Before they could settle the lunch dilemma, Ethan breezed into the shop. His charcoal gray suit was lightly padded across the shoulders and made him look broader than he was. It tapered to his waist, giving him a trim, athletic look. The perfectly tied silk cravat was black and gray with an elegant stripe of burgundy. He even had on kid gloves that perfectly matched the color of his hat. In one gloved hand he held a walking stick with a shiny bronze wolf head, in the other a gorgeous leather suitcase.

"Hello all! We've got two lunches here I see, and two travelers as well, that will be perfect. I'm famished already. Victor, we had better be off," he said, sweeping out of the shop and past a surprised Victor.

Victor turned to Claude. "Mind the shop."

"I-I will! Have a safe trip."

Victor stuffed the papers into his coat pocket as he hurried out of the shop with Margaret and Celena on his heels. "What are you doing here?" he asked, catching up to Ethan, who was making his way across the street towards the telegraph office where they would wait for the steamship.

"I am going to accompany you, my dear Victor, to Washington."

Victor stared down at him and dropped his carpet bag and burlap sack on the dusty sidewalk. "Why would you want to do that?"

"Because we are going to be partners. I must admit what you did with the repair for the steamship was ingenious—you impressed *even* me, which is a feat in and of itself. And if this carriage rim idea is half that good, well let's say there may be a small fortune to be made." He polished the wolf's head with his glove.

"Since when do you need another fortune?"

"Let's just say...I'd like to make a fortune for you or help you make one. You know nothing of business Victor, and I know nothing of metal work. Together we should be quite the team."

"Thank you, Ethan," Celena whispered.

He bowed to her. "At your service, my dear, always." He turned back to Victor, inspecting him. "Besides, if you showed up alone, you're likely to scare the civilized inhabitants of Washington out of their wits. They might think the savages are rising again!" He shook his head at the fact that Victor refused to cut his hair and look like everyone else. "But never fear, I plan to use it to our advantage. After all, who could not be persuaded, given my negotiating skills? But if for some reason they are not persuaded by my oration alone, I'll have a wild Indian by my side!"

Before he boarded the ship, Victor gently touched Celena's chin and whispered, "I'll be back before you know it."

"All's we can do now is hope and pray," Margaret mused, wrapping an affectionate arm around Celena as they watched the giant paddle wheel of the steamer cruising upstream make white, frothy waves out of the muddy Mississippi.

Chapter 11

In the day's ride to St. Louis, Victor and Ethan worked out their plan for talking to Pickering. Victor agreed that Ethan would introduce them both and show the sketches. When it came time for the demonstration, Victor would take over. Victor was relieved to have Ethan with him. To someone like Victor, who had never been outside of Ste. Genevieve, St. Louis was an adventure, and the capital was downright daunting.

Looking out the window of the steamship, Victor watched the wild green of spring plunge upon the countryside and was excited about talking to someone about the carriage rim. There was no one in town he could talk to about all the jumbled ideas in his head. He hoped the other smith Jedidiah would be interested, and although he conceded it was a better way to rim a wheel, was set in his ways. It had been wonderful the way Celena had listened, how encouraging she had been.

When Victor stepped off the steamship in St. Louis, he felt as if he'd been transported into another world. The streets were not dusty or muddy like they were in Ste. Genevieve because they were *paved* in cobblestone and sometimes brick. Tall brick buildings soared from every corner and looking both ways was shocked he couldn't see from one end of town to the other. There were so many people, carts, and carriages in the streets that he almost knocked into a gentleman headed the opposite direction and was nearly trampled by a fast-approaching bakery wagon. There were brick and stone churches, and shop after shop, and he marveled that one town could support so many businesses.

"This is one big town!" Victor exclaimed, looking from the busy streets to the river, noting the number of barges and steamboats tethered up and down the muddy, steep banks of the Mississippi. Ste. Genevieve herself had a fair amount of river traffic but nothing like this!

"It's almost hard to believe it's the same river that flows past Ste. Gen," he mused, watching all the roustabouts loading and unloading cargo brought by train that had to be transported by boat over the mighty Mississippi. Looking across the water into Illinois, Victor realized that the railroads would need to build a colossal bridge over the Mississippi to link them and that it would be an engineering feat to do so.

"Yes, the infamous gateway to the west. Of course, that doesn't do us much good since we'll be travelling east," Ethan said drily. "It'll be good to stretch the legs." He tossed Victor his carpet bag and hoisted his own heavy trunk over his shoulder. "We leave a little past five to catch the next steamer." Ethan rubbed the back of his neck. The long ride on the crowded steamship had tired him. "I'm parched...do you want anything?" He eyed a local tavern and wanted desperately to sit somewhere that was not moving, enjoy a beverage, and try to work the kink out of his neck.

"No. I'm all right, you go ahead, and I'm going to look at the train," Victor said spying the station in the distance. He could hear the whistle and see the smoke coming from one of the stacks. He had heard about trains, seen pictures of them, and worked on a steam engine for a ship, but since there was no train in Ste. Genevieve, he had never come face to face with one and was compelled to learn about them.

"There you are!" Victor said, finding Ethan dozing in the rear of the steamboat. His hat was tipped down to his nose, the fine leather boots crossed at the ankles and the gray frock coat off and folded smoothly on the seat next to him. "Been looking for you."

"I knew you'd find me," Ethan said, removing the hat and sitting upright. "What have you been doing?" He fumbled with something under the seat.

"I've been talking with a young fireman at the trains. His name is Brian, and he was telling me all about what he does. He's the one responsible for gathering the pots of mutton tallow. Listen to this, he must crawl out the cab window onto the locomotive running boards and edge along the boiler to the cylinders, now mind you, they are red hot. Then he's got to pour the tallow into the steam chest to lubricate the valves."

"Sounds like a dangerous job."

"It is."

"Why does he do it then?"

"He said if a 'tallow pot' does his job well he will be promoted to engineer."

"Sounds positively fascinating."

Grinning, Victor sat down across from Ethan, knowing he was anything but fascinated. "I had no idea the running of a train was so complicated, or that it took so many men to operate it. You need engineers, switchman, signalman, brakeman, and conductor's baggage masters—"

"Victor, spare me please," Ethan pleaded, his hands up. "I venture that there will be many more things on this trip that you had no *idea* of! You'll be a great deal enlightened by the end of our adventure than you ever dreamed possible. But I would appreciate it if you would not apprise me of every nuance that those of us who have seen a bit of the world, take for granted. Truly, I find it annoying!" He pulled the chessboard from under the seat and went about positioning the pieces.

"All right then." Victor grinned good-naturedly. Waiting until Ethan had made the first move, he leaned near and made his. "I'll keep my enlightenment...to myself."

"Thank you!" Ethan sighed and looked down at the chessboard, irritated that Victor had already taken one of his pawns.

Two days later they boarded the train, and when it stopped in Ohio, Ethan and Victor got out to catch a quick bite when Victor noticed a man standing between several of the cars.

"What are you *looking* at? We've scarcely got an hour before we'll be pulling out again. If we don't hurry we won't have time to eat!"

"Go ahead—I'll be along," Victor murmured, walking toward the brakeman.

"The man's *obsessed* with metal!"

Later when they were settled back in the train, Victor sat staring out the window. Although he was enjoying the changing countryside, realizing trees he had never seen, he kept reworking the strengths and weaknesses of the link and pin system of attaching the railway cars. If the pin would stay up, it could hook itself without the man having to stand between them. He kept envisioning different mechanisms that did the same, but then discard them, realizing a flaw in his design.

He sighed, leaning his head against the glass, reworking it for what seemed like the thousandth time when something occurred to him. He jumped up straight in his seat, startling a sleeping Ethan.

"Have you got anything to write on and with?"

Ethan rubbed his eyes. "What do you need it for?"

"Never mind." Victor went up the aisle and asked every passenger if they had a pen and ink.

Three minutes later Victor returned to his seat. "Look at this." He had an old train schedule—apparently torn off the wall, the corners of the paper ripped off where they had been tacked up—and a small bottle of ink and a pen.

"Where did you get that?"

"From an old man near the front of the train. Now watch."

Ethan watched as Victor furiously sketched what appeared to be two opposite facing hooks. "They look like hands."

Victor grinned at the observation "Hands or knuckles if you will. So, they can 'shake hands' and put the cars together." He continued to draw with a determination that impressed even Ethan. "This way the brake man will be way off the tracks," he explained, adding more detail to the sketch. Then, dissatisfied with the width of one of the pins, he crossed it out and redrew it.

"What is it...exactly?" Ethan asked after another few minutes.

"It's a simple but better way to attach the railway cars to each other. It would be more efficient, because it will work the first time, and faster too—to say nothing of it being safer for the poor brakeman out of the way."

"Is this a big problem for the railroads, this attaching of cars?"

Victor shrugged. "I don't have any idea. But each car must be hooked to another—it must take a while to do that with the sheer number of them, especially if they don't get fit in right the first time."

Ethan sat up, his interest piqued. "Your little idea here, they will attach the first time?"

"I think so."

"But how would you...do this? Wouldn't you have to vastly overhaul everything to do it this new way?"

Victor shook his head. "Look at it again. I planned to use the existing parts, only adding what I would make. Have you seen the link and pin on the train?" He realized Ethan had never studied how the cars were attached. "Anyway, look at it when we get off and you'll see what I mean, and besides that, it pretty much solves the brakeman's problem."

"Sorry?"

"Being crushed or maimed, or if the cars were moving swiftly...even killed."

Ethan shuddered, grateful he did no such manual labor. He imagined striding into the powerful offices of the Central, Baltimore, and Ohio railroads and showing them this improvement over the old system. After all, here was a better, faster way to attach the cars, a problem that had (he hoped) plagued the railroads for years. Here was a simple solution, and not only would it efficiently fasten the cars, but could also spare the brakeman accidents.

"Will it work? Are you absolutely sure it will work?"

"Let me get to a forge first, and I can be sure."

Ethan looked out the window, failing to notice the pink sweet Williams blanketing the hillside. "Do me a favor," he said, checking his gold watch, realizing happily that the train was running only a bit behind schedule. "*Make* it work."

By the time the train pulled into Washington, Victor was again amazed at how much bigger Washington was than even Chicago. There was a whole universe out there he that he never even *dreamed* existed.

Snapping his watch closed, Ethan straightened his aching back. "I can't believe I let you talk me out of sleeping berths!"

"We saved money this way. Besides, even you wouldn't fit in one of those and I knew I wouldn't."

Ethan rolled his stiff neck, irritated even though he knew from experience that the sleeping berths were so small they were not much better than sitting up all night. "Our bags," he said, and motioned for Victor to follow him. But instead of following, Victor gaped at the new city that suddenly opened before him.

"This is it, my friend," Ethan began, putting a friendly hand on Victor's shoulder. "The beginning of it all."

"But the beginning of *what*, I wonder."

Ethan laughed. "We've got a few hours before our meeting with Pickering, let's get ourselves a hotel room, and get presentable for the occasion." He hoisted the trunk over his shoulder as he scanned the busy street for an idle carriage to hire. He found an old man who was willing to take them and quickly loaded their trunks on the back.

"Where to?" the old man asked. He'd been in Washington all his life, and was used to all kinds of passengers. Not much surprised him, but even he thought the two made an unusual pair.

"A hotel."

"A *good* hotel!" Ethan settled back as the old man took them down Delaware Avenue and closer to the nation's capital, turning the carriage onto Pennsylvania Avenue. It was a broad, busy street already shaded by the Lombardy poplars that lined it, and the cherry trees were starting to show their delicate pink blossoms amongst the dark green waxy leaves.

Victor was struck by the sight of the capital.

It was three stories tall, and had a domed copper rotunda, with two wings on each side. Victor could not be sure what it was made from, but the tall white columns that flanked the front were fluted. It was already an enormous building, and yet it was still under construction because there was scaffolding against it.

He could not help turning to look at it as they drove on. He felt a rush of warmth and patriotism towards a country he had never thought of much before. It was true what Ethan said, he knew so little of the rest of the world. He had done as much reading as he could, but still realized how insulated he had been in Ste. Genevieve at the forge.

He glanced into the shops as they drove by. Bakeries, butchers, goldsmiths, clock makers, jeweler's shops—not at all like the Woolrich's general store, which housed nearly everything a household needed. A huge park seemed to go on forever as they drove by. In it he saw marble statues of famous people whose identities baffled him.

He swallowed hard. A feeling of impending doomed weighed heavily on his chest, and he couldn't help but wonder what difference his little idea would make to a city so grand. Staring out at the modern city, his little creation seemed trivial.

Sighing, he sat back against the leather seat, knowing it was too late. He was here and he had to try, no matter how futile it seemed.

He had made a promise to Celena.

"The Willard," the old man announced happily as he pulled the carriage in front of the hotel.

"Thank you, this will be fine."

"Good God! It runs the *entire* block!" Victor exclaimed as he got out of the carriage. He had to turn his head to see the entire length of the building.

Ethan paid the man, who smiled warmly at his generous tip and scrambled on agile legs to get their bags down quickly.

The inside of the hotel was no less spectacular with its enormous two-story lobby, complete with polished wood, gleaming brass, and luxurious yellow velvet curtain that graced the huge windows. Looking up, Victor was astounded to see that the ornately decorated ceiling was painted to look like heaven with a lovely blue sky, white clouds, and fat cherubs.

Ethan ordered their rooms, baths and even asked for a late breakfast to be sent up. He had to nudge Victor away from his study of the elaborate brass metalwork on the desk.

Having bathed and put on a clean shirt, Victor entered Ethan's room later that morning. "This place is something else."

"Yes, it is," Ethan agreed, calmly sipping his coffee at a small round table and nibbling a piece of toast slathered with strawberry preserves.

"Aren't you going to eat?" Ethan asked, seeing how long Victor' hair was laying wet against his shoulders.

Victor shook his head as he looked out the window, his stomach in knots. "Not hungry."

"Well, that's certainly a first." Ethan laughed, swallowing the rest of the tepid coffee.

"Are you ready now, should we go?" Victor asked, eager to get to the patent office, see Pickering, and get the day over with.

"All right now Victor, we've got some serious negotiating to do here, and please let me do the talking," Ethan instructed as they made their way down the stairs. "For God's sake you're looking around Washington like you're a man from a foreign land rather a few days ride—no more backwoods ignorance if you don't mind."

"I like the backwoods."

But when Ethan turned to argue, he was struck mute.

"What is it?" Victor asked. Following his gaze, he saw a young woman standing in the lobby below them.

She was dark-haired and wore a dress of pale rose. Although she looked to be at least twenty, her figure was childish, and did not seem match her chronological age. The straw bonnet on her head was pretty, but her ears were trying to poke out from her chignon. Her coffee-colored eyes were in stark contrast to the paleness of her complexion. All together the effect was pleasant, but she just missed being pretty.

"Penelope," Ethan breathed, walking down the remaining steps.

Turning, the woman's eyes flew open wide with shock.

"*Ethan!* What—what are you doing here? It's so wonderful to see you!" Two violent red spots stained her cheeks as he bent to kiss her hand. "Papa!" she exclaimed, tugging at the sleeve of the man standing next to her trying to reconcile the bill, "look who's in Washington."

The white-bearded man with a balding head turned. His eyes flicked distastefully over Ethan, but he recovered his composure quickly. It amused Victor that the man was obviously not fond of Ethan.

"Why, if it isn't Ethan Stanfield," he said, reaching to shake Ethan's outstretched hand. "What brings you to Washington? The last anyone heard was that you'd gone back to run your father's bank in Missouri." His shrewd eyes did not fail to notice how well dressed Ethan was, and wondered how much it had cost him.

"I'm here today on business. Professor Harrison, I'd like you to meet my new business partner, Victor Gant."

"Good morning Professor Harrison," Victor said, leaning down and surprising Ethan by the confident way he shook the older man's hand.

"The professor was my history teacher at Boston College. Those were some spellbinding lectures about the Mesopotamians I must say."

Professor Harrison smiled at the compliment, but then not sure it was genuine, his back stiffened.

"This lovely creature is his daughter Penelope."

"Good morning ma'am." Victor smiled and bowed his head, seeing that her cheeks were still bright with color.

It was only because she was able to call upon her years of polite training that she was able to smile up at him at all. She had never seen anyone so tall and broad shouldered. His hair was the blackest she'd ever seen, and he looked dangerous with it tied back from his face like a pirate. His hand was rough and callused as it grasped hers, and she was both repelled and attracted to him at the same time.

"Business? What sort of business would that be? Don't tell me you're buying another bank," Professor Harrison exclaimed.

"No, it's nothing like that. My friend has an entrepreneurial spirit, I'm afraid. He's an inventor of sorts and I'm here to negotiate with him.

We've a meeting at the patent office this morning, which we hope will be a success. What brings you and Penelope all the way from Boston?"

"I've accepted a position here at George Washington University."

"Why, I never imagined you'd ever leave Boston with you being so close to becoming dean of the history school, and Penelope and her dreams of teaching the violin. I would have thought you were indeed well rooted."

Victor noticed that Professor Harrison's jaw jutted out at the words, and it was obvious that the Professor was not nearly as happy to see Ethan as his daughter was.

"We had best be off. It was a pleasure to meet you Professor Harrison," Victor said, stretching his hand out again. "Perhaps we'll see you again this evening...are you staying in the hotel tonight?" he asked, eager for them to make their way to the patent office get the business over with.

"Yes, as a matter of fact we will be."

Penelope stared at her father. Hadn't they been trying to barter with the bill, which he had said was astronomical? Now he was committing himself to staying another night? She wished he would be more concerned with their limited finances.

"Well then please be our guests for dinner tonight...say around seven?" Ethan asked warmly.

"We'd be delighted," the professor said, forcing another smile.

The patent office was a three-storied building surrounded by an ornate wrought iron fence that Victor would have stopped to inspect if he thought Ethan would let him. The eight marble columns that held up the roof were as large and mighty as sycamore trees against the banks of the Mississippi. They walked up ten polished granite steps to the building, and when Victor pushed open the heavy paneled doors, the white marble floor was so shiny he could see a reflection.

There was a humorless fellow with spectacles low on his nose at the desk in the foyer. He took their names, barely concealing his irritation at their presence, and told them with morose pleasure to simply '*wait*.'

Sighing, Victor settled on the hard bench with Ethan and glanced around. It seemed like an orderly place, with a central hallway and dozens of doors on each side. Occasionally, muffled voices from one of the offices echoed in the corridor, but other than that it was terribly quiet.

"You've got the letters?" Ethan asked in a low voice, careful not to disturb the ill-humored man at the desk while trying to get comfortable on the straight bench.

"Yes."

"And the application and the fee, and the rim and all the drawings?"

Victor nodded. "All I need now is my forge."

Two hours later, a door opened at the end of the corridor and Victor's head shot up from his study of the veins in the marble floor. The man walking briskly toward them was barely five feet tall, and obviously enjoyed the fine cuisine the capital offered because his suit coat was so tight the buttons looked ready to launch. His hair was gray and sparse, and his ruddy head was shiny. Small glasses perched precariously on the end of his nose, and his face was round and full, and unlined even though he was advanced in his years.

"Well, you must be Victor Gant?" Alexander Pickering asked, offering his soft white hand to Victor, who eagerly stood up.

"Yes. Good morning Mr. Pickering."

"My!" Pickering said, looking up and chuckling. "You *are* quite a large fellow aren't you! What sort of work did you say you did?"

"I'm a blacksmith."

"Oh, my word! Well that rather explains it though, blacksmiths usually are big fellows—must have something to do with all that pounding and hammering all day. I've a cousin here in town who's a blacksmith, I dare say he's not as built up as you are though."

"Mr. Pickering, this is my partner, Ethan Stanfield."

"Good morning sir!" Pickering said as he bowed from the waist flamboyantly, clicking the heels of his boots. "Both of you follow me and we'll have a look at things, shall we?" He led them down the corridor. "Here we are," he said a moment later, ushering them into a small office. "Jed, coffee, please," Pickering called out before turning to Victor and Ethan. "Cream and sugar?" When they shook their heads, he said to Jed, "Two black coffees and one fancy." He scurried around the large messy desk that was piled high with papers and catalogs. The floor-to-ceiling bookshelves that lined the walls were crammed with books and catalogs precariously, an avalanche that could happen any minute. The fine Persian rug under their feet looked as though it had the misfortune to have had coffee spilled on it more than once.

"Felix, out!" Pickering scolded as he picked up a snoozing black and white tabby from his chair. After kissing the soft head lovingly, he replaced the sleepy cat in the window seat.

Victor couldn't help but grin, already taking a liking to the little man who made no apologies for loving his cat.

Jed, an unsmiling, thinly built man, appeared in the doorway, delivering the coffee on a silver tray. He expertly laid the spoons, cups, and pot of coffee down, complete with a tray of cookies, and promptly disappeared without a word.

Ethan looked around the office in mild horror, wondering how Pickering kept anything straight in this mess! Ethan could not imagine running a business this way and couldn't imagine what his father would say if he dared to bring a *cat* into the bank! He realized Victor had been lucky that Pickering had even been able to *find* their patent request and returned any response at all, given the condition of the office.

"Well now," Pickering began after he had made sure everyone had their coffee and quickly eaten two of the shortbread cookies on the tray, scooting closer to them on his swivel chair on wheels.

"That is quite a chair." Victor grinned.

Pickering smiled delightedly. "An invention of our own Thomas Jefferson—handy, don't you think?" He spun on the rotating chair "Although his enemies said it was merely so he could 'see all ways at once!'"

Victor smiled.

"I believe you've got a carriage rim to show me?" Pickering asked pleasantly, wanting to get down to business.

"Yes." Victor produced the carriage rim from the bag he had been carrying all the way from Ste. Genevieve. Not knowing what else to do, he simply launched into an explanation. "Carriage rims are normally made with individual pieces of iron..." He pulled out two such pieces from the bag to compare. "They are fit on hot to the outside of the rim. The problem is when they get loosened it causes everything else to fall apart."

Pickering listening to him silently, crossed his plump legs at the ankles, and crossed his arms across his round belly. He nodded to encourage Victor to continue.

"If I take one continuous piece of iron and heat it to expand to fit snug around the wheel, when it cools—"

"It tightens up and keeps everything in place." Pickering wiggled to get more comfortable in his chair.

Since Pickering grasped it so quickly, Victor was quiet.

"It is a far superior way; I'll give you that. Simple and yet ingenious at the same time." Even though his words were complimentary, Victor sensed the next words would be ones of rejection.

Pickering took off his glasses and, pulling out a lace-edged handkerchief, began buffing the lenses. "Let me see the specifications." Finished with his glasses, he took another cookie from the tray and absentmindedly brushed the crumbs off his chest as he read the papers Celena had spent hours preparing.

Felix jumped down from his perch in the windowsill and walked on the desk in front of Pickering as he studied the papers. The morning sunlight streaming through the windows showed the cats hair coming off all over the desk. Ethan thought he'd die before he'd have a shedding cat all over his papers at the bank and wondered why Pickering was allowed such a pet! But the shedding bothered Pickering not at all as he merely stroked the purring cat as it walked back in forth in front of the papers, forcing Pickering to adjust the papers as Felix rubbed against them.

It was two minutes before he spoke. "It's...remarkable. It's classic, and simple and the only way in which they should be rimmed...however, I most certainly cannot grant you a patent for it."

"Why not? It's remarkable, you said so yourself!" Ethan exploded.

Pickering was used to dealing with spoiled, conceited would-be inventors who sulked, cried, and ranted when their creations were rejected. "Because it is un-patentable," he said carefully.

"How can that be?" Ethan demanded, trying to control the angry pounding in his own chest. *He had made a promise to Celena.*

"Because I cannot guarantee non-duplication. It is remarkable yes. There is no doubt in my mind that once you show this to a carriage manufacturer, they will all be producing them this way." He nodded in approval for his ingenuity. "But the reason for patents is to garner the individual sole ownership so to speak—rights and royalties, if there are any, to a patentable design. Meaning one that is unique enough to be cataloged and patented. This idea, this rim, is so perfect, so ingenious in its design it is its inherent *simplicity* unfortunately, renders it un-patentable."

Although Victor was disappointed, he understood.

"I was so impressed by your diligence in sending in the requests so thoroughly filled out that I was hopeful there would be something unique in the process...you are quite the author and artist!"

Victor nodded, knowing it had been Celena's hand.

"Is there *nothing* else we can do? What about the carriage manufacturers? How will there be any money to be made with them? We can't sell them the rights to an idea that has no patent?" Ethan asked.

"No, you can't," Pickering said, carefully folding the pieces of paper and handing them back to Victor. "Forgive me for sounding so negative, it's simply that there are rules and regulations here that I must abide by. I have extraordinarily little latitude so to speak. I am sorry." He brushed more cookie crumbs from his chest. "I am in the position to see many wonderful ideas, and I must say yours is the type I like the best. I see some ridiculous patent requests for the most absurd things! Yours is not only universally useful, which is by the way, one of the prerequisites, but also classic in its simplicity."

Victor shrugged. He knew his life would go on with or without the patent. He would go back to Ste. Genevieve, work in the shop, marry Celena and never think of it again.

"Then we've got to produce the wheels ourselves...and sell them to the carriage shops," Ethan said, his eyes bright.

"Yes. I suppose that would work," Pickering mused, leaning back leisurely in his chair, enjoying their company. This was one of the reasons he had taken the position with the patent office; to see bright young minds at work, be on the edge of greatness, see the technological future unfold before him. He had been disappointed by the deluge of ridiculous patent requests and irate would-be inventors. It was the reason he had asked for the formal meeting with the two from the charming-sounding little town in Missouri.

"Where would we get the money to start building carriage rims?" Victor queried.

"I've got money...my money. If we can't sell it to the carriage makers, I'll *buy* a carriage maker. That rim is going to be on wheels, I promise you that!" Ethan said, flushed. "Mr. Pickering, I believe it is public record what patents the manufacturers have, along with what they produce, and their addresses—I wonder if you would be kind enough to direct me to the individual who could give me that information?"

"Ethan, you don't have to do this—"

"Show our friend here the other request," Ethan interrupted, silencing Victor's protests, nodding toward the bag. "The hands...the knuckle. Whatever you're going to call it!" Ethan stammered, trying to mimic the drawing Victor had done on the train. "Mr. Pickering, your guidelines for granting patent requests require that it be useful, unique. What would you say to the idea for the railroads, of a coupler that linked the cars together, that worked more efficiently, and for all intense purposes did it the first time? And I might add, as a human element, avoided smashing the brakeman on the tracks altogether?"

For a moment Pickering was quiet, not sure if Ethan was taunting him, or if they had such a creation. "I'd say it would be beneficial to the railroads to have such a thing, *if* one existed. I am familiar with the link and pin couplers, and it certainly is an area where a design improvement could be especially useful. And a brakeman's job is certainly one I wouldn't like to have," he said with a feminine little shudder.

"It exists," Ethan said, and then turned to Victor, who wished he had something to show him rather than the frantic scribbling on the old train schedule.

"It's like this...two opposite links that hook together...as they draw together...the weight of one flips the other open." Victor wished he had an actual model, and knowing he needed a spring suddenly remembered he had seen a clock maker's shop as they had ridden into town. He tried again to draw it but could tell Pickering was having trouble visualizing it.

Victor discarded the drawing. "Mr. Pickering, is your cousin working today?"

Within the hour Victor was coatless, shirt sleeves rolled up, working at Cyril Pickering's forge. Cyril had been shocked to see his plump, over-dressed cousin at his shop, and even more shocked when the man behind him asked him if he could borrow iron—which of course he offered to pay him for—and his forge. Cyril was happy to lend his forge to another smith, especially he could tell was a master at his craft. And both of Cyril's strikers were more than willing to abandon their work and watch the stranger.

During it all, Alexander Pickering was as excited about the possibility of an invention of real merit as a child would be with a new toy. He rubbed his dimpled hands together as he watched Victor work. "Do you?" Pickering asked Ethan, motioning toward the anvil.

"Oh no. I own a bank in Ste. Genevieve."

"I must say I thought when I first saw the two of you that you were an unlikely pair. Have you been partners long?"

"No, just since I returned from college and took over my father's bank."

"Oh. I see, and he came to you for backing...difficult to make a decent living as a smith in a small town I suppose."

"Actually, you'd be amazed. He does well. And he didn't come to me for money, in fact he's never asked me for my backing or for money. That was my doing and the offer still stands."

"Yes, and an interesting offer it is. I'd like to talk to you more about that later if you don't mind, but right now I'm intrigued why you'd take it upon yourself to have such an interest in his work?"

"We grew up together, like brothers. And I want him to succeed. I thought I could help him," Ethan said, watching Victor plunge the red-hot iron into the slack tub and pick up a file to smooth down the piece he had made. "But to tell you the truth, I don't think he needs my help. He's doing fine on his own."

By the end of the day Ethan and Victor submitted another patent for a coupler for the attachment of railroad cars. Pickering himself had helped them write it, and even helped with the sketches. Victor paid the patent fee, signed his name to the request, and handed it to Pickering who assured him when he met with the other patent officers and the directors of the Board of Arts, that the request would be granted.

"Gentlemen, I think this calls for a bit of a celebration," Pickering said, checking the time on his silver pocket watch to see that it was nearly three o'clock. Since they had all missed their noon meal, he decided he was done with work for the day. "I know a lovely little place to get a beverage and a morsel before dinner." He petted Felix's silky head, pouring the remainder of the cream from their morning coffee into the tabby's bowl. He grabbed his hat and walking stick and made his way out of the patent office, his short stubby legs propelling him faster than either Ethan or Victor thought capable, and they had to hurry to keep up with him.

"Right this way gentlemen," Pickering said as he nodded to the humorless man at the front desk, who didn't appreciate the flexible hours Alexander Pickering kept.

As they walked down the street in the late afternoon, F Street was bathed in shadows from the trees that lined the boulevard and the tall structures haphazardly built along the street.

"Ah...spring, there's nothing like spring in Washington," Pickering said, puffing his chest full of air. He acknowledged nearly every other person they passed, and would comment on them after they were out of earshot, often not kindly. "Ah good afternoon, Mr. Dunbar, so nice to see you."

Then, when he was sure Mr. Dunbar was out of hearing: "Penniless dolt—lost all his money in one of the gaming houses. You know what they say—never gamble what you cannot afford to lose. Are you much of a gambler Mr. Stanfield?"

"Not really, a bit of horse racing and billiards occasionally, but true gambling…" Ethan shook his head as the three of them walked companionably down the street.

"And you Mr. Gant?"

"No," Victor replied with a grin, not wanting to admit that he'd never even heard of such a 'house' until that moment. Ste. Genevieve had its vices—horse racing, card games, as well as billiards—but he never had the inclination to bet his sweat-earned money on a game of chance.

Pickering stopped suddenly in front of a restaurant. There was a wrought iron arched gate leading from the street, and neat red bricked walkway to a white painted building. "I wonder, Mr. Gant, if you would consider gambling just this once."

"Depends on what I suppose."

"Would you consider taking a gamble on me?"

There was a short pause.

"I don't understand," Victor said, and did not follow Ethan and Pickering as they made their way to the steps.

"It's simple really. Let us have a beverage with which to discuss my proposition for you both." When Victor still did not move from his spot, Pickering smoothed back the wayward strands of hair on his balding head before replacing his hat. "You see, I am sure that the request will be granted for the coupler for the railroads."

"Are you personally acquainted with any of the gentleman with interests in the railroads? I sincerely wish to speak with them," Ethan interrupted.

"Unfortunately, no, but I may be able to introduce you to a man that could help you. I was thinking rather about the now long forgotten idea for the carriage rim. I rather fancied that idea, and I rather think you might be able to make a go of it."

"Are you trying to…go into *business* with us, Mr. Pickering?" Victor asked, surprised he would be willing to invest money with two strangers, on an idea he would not even grant a patent for.

"Well, that depends…but it is from my viewpoint, a definite possibility." He smiled kindly. "Come along then and we'll discuss it inside."

Reluctantly Victor followed them.

"Afternoon, Mr. Pickering," a middle-aged man said, forcing a polite smile as they entered.

"Good afternoon, Rolly."

"The usual table, sir?" the man asked, taking Pickering's hat and walking stick to be checked by the pretty maid at the door.

"Yes, thank you." Pickering led Ethan and Victor through the maroon and gold velvet dining room to a table by the tall windows with mini panes that faced the west side of the street.

Even though it was luxuriously furnished, Victor immediately felt comfortable. It was decorated with senators and representatives in mind, and was, despite it its finery, a masculine dining room. The mahogany furniture was large and comfortable for a man even of Pickering's weight or Victor's height to accommodate. *Not at all the like dining room chairs in Ethan's house!* Victor thought. Even the framed pictures that graced the walls were pictures of famous battles with valiant armies charging up green hills, or large schooners braving turbulent seas. Although the table was crowded with china and crystal, they were not delicate. The china had a bold gold rim, and the crystal goblets had stems thick enough for a man to get his hands around.

"Let me see," Pickering mused, the waiter at his elbow. His glasses low on his nose as he perused the wine list, he said, "I think we'll have a chardonnay—or a chablis, or meatier burgundy."

"Not for me, thank you," Victor uttered, wanting nothing less than to start drinking what he feared would be expensive bottles of wine. .

Pickering turned to the waiter. "Bring them all, and a plate of cold salmon and some breads and cheeses—I've had the most interesting day, but I must say that all this tinkering and inventing has left me famished." When he saw the look on Victor's face, he leaned in. "My dear Victor, you must learn to enjoy some of the finer things in life! For Pete's sake man, drink good wine when it's offered, savor fine food when it's placed in front of you. Life is exceedingly short, my large friend, experience the pleasures the world has to offer."

"Alexander, I've been telling him that for years!" Ethan corroborated. The two of them laughed in agreement. Before Victor could protest, Pickering spotted another acquaintance, offered a polite excuse, and promptly left the table to greet his friend.

"He is something else," Victor said, "not at all what I expected."

"Nor I!" Ethan laughed, leaning back comfortably in the padded hair when the waiter appeared with the wine, asking which bottle they wanted opened first. "Chablis," Ethan replied, and a moment later raised his crystal glass to Victor. "To a successful partnership."

Nodding, Victor took a mouthful of the wine and decided that although it was too sweet for him, it was an improvement over the gut-wrenching whiskey Will secretly made at home. When he finished his glass, Ethan quickly poured him another.

"To the railroads and the coupler," Victor said, trying to be a good sport, and downed the wine. It burned in his empty stomach.

"To the railroads and their *buying* of the coupler," Ethan corrected, finishing his wine. He straightened when he saw Pickering returning to the table. "Humor me, will you, and let me do the talking. With any luck we're about to acquire ourselves a well-connected new partner *and* a carriage factory!"

They had demolished the plate of cold salmon, baked breads and cheese that had been artfully arranged on the silver platter, but Pickering, undeterred, scraped up and ate what bits were left as he finished his wine.

It had been an interesting afternoon with Pickering jumping up every few minutes to introduce friends to his guests at the table. Victor had never met so many new people in his life and did not realize how long they had been there until he glanced out the window and saw that the sun had long sunk behind the horizon.

Although it had been a wonderful afternoon, drinking and talking to so many different people wore on Victor, and he was grateful when Alexander Pickering finally made to leave. When he and Ethan made to pay for the wine and the hors d'oeuvres, Pickering adamantly refused. "Nonsense! I invited you both, and I enjoyed the afternoon tremendously. Remember to be back in the office in the late morning. I'll have spoken with some of the other officers by then, and they might want to have a look at the coupler." He smiled at both of them as he took his hat and walking stick from Rolly and, shouting goodbyes to his friends, left the restaurant. The three of them stepped outside onto the dimming street.

"Where are you staying?" Alexander asked Ethan.

"The Willard."

"Let me take you back there then," Pickering said, summoning a waiting carriage. Not waiting for their answer, he stepped inside.

Victor, relieved to be out of the restaurant, gazed at the sights of the nation's capital rolling past him in the waning twilight. "What *is* that?

Why it looks like a *castle!*"

Ethan looked out the window. There was a tall, red stone structure with towers which he had to admit looked like they could have been turrets for a castle. It saddened him suddenly, the memory of how he had once wanted to create such masterpieces. He had been in the midst of obtaining a secondary degree in architecture when his father's illness summoned him home.

"Oh that," Pickering said, looking briefly before turning his attention to adjusting his suit coat over his large stomach, "that, my dear boys, is the Smithsonian."

"I'd heard something about that, it's a museum of sorts, isn't it?" Ethan asked.

"Yes, we Washingtonians think of it as the chief cultural agency in the nation. A fabulous building-and new too, been finished shy of two years now. It was done by a James Renwick, a remarkably interesting man. Calls it his Norman castle." Pickering was now admiring how trim and neat his nails were.

"What's inside?" Victor asked.

"A number of things actually...a museum, an art gallery, a chemical laboratory, and a well-stocked library."

"Must have cost a fortune for all those things," Victor said, amazed.

"Actually, it was a gift from an Englishman by the name of James Smithson who never even stepped foot in our proud nation! Seems he willed some ungodly amount of money with the stipulation that we found an establishment for the diffusion of knowledge among mankind. Must have been an awfully remarkable fellow."

"He gave away his entire fortune to a country that he'd never even seen?" Ethan asked.

Pickering nodded.

"Generous indeed!" Victor said, turning away from the window, disappointed that he could no longer see the red castle that housed James Smithson's dream.

As the carriage rambled along the uneven street, near the Willard, Pickering fumbled with something in his pocket and, finding it, handed Ethan a small, engraved card.

"What's this?"

"It's one of my calling cards. There's a lovely little place that I know you'd both enjoy. Besides a certain gentleman by the name of Sean Walker who has considerable influence with the railroads is known to frequent the establishment. He shan't be there 'til much later this evening though. I've written the address on the back. It's exclusive, but my name should get you through the door. Whatever else happens is strictly up to you though."

Victor and Ethan thanked him for all his help, as well as for the wine and carriage. Ethan placed the calling card safely in his pocket, and waved goodbye as the carriage rambled down the street with Alexander Pickering.

"Remarkable gentleman," Ethan said as they walked into the hotel, putting a brotherly arm around Victor.

"Oh! Mr. Stanfield," the concierge called, trotting up to them in the lobby. "There was a young lady who had inquired as to your and Mr. Gant's whereabouts."

Ethan's mind was clouded by the bottles of wine they had all drunk, and for a minute could not fathom what lady could possibly be looking for them.

"Your friend Penelope! Is it that late?" Victor burst out. Glancing at the large clock in the lobby, he realized they were a half-hour late for the dinner engagement they had made with her only that morning.

"What room is she in?" Ethan asked, knowing that the Professor would not be pleased that they were tardy for their dinner.

"On the second floor in room 211. Shall I send a maid to tell her you're here?" the concierge asked, never dreaming that the two young men were about to burst upon the young lady in her hotel suite.

"No, thank you," Ethan said, and motioned with his head to Victor as they dashed up the stairs. "I had no idea it was that late! How many bottles did we have?" He didn't like feeling rushed, and wondered if Penelope had already eaten or if she had taken their invitation seriously at all.

"Four or five, I think," Victor said, touching his forehead, feeling that if he did not eat something soon, he would either be sick or asleep!

They knocked at the door of the suite. When Penelope opened the door, it was obvious she had not forgotten the dinner invitation, for she was dressed in a gown of dark green muslin. The neckline was low, fashionable for evening and showing no hint of cleavage since she was small breasted. Her hair had been carefully arranged to cover her ears.

"Hello! I am terribly sorry we're late, is your father in?" Glancing behind her, Ethan was surprised he did not see the Professor.

"No, I'm afraid not. He said to send you sincerest apologies, he's forced to dine with faculty members tonight. It simply could not be avoided."

Something about the way her eyes drifted nervously to the floor made Victor think she was lying, but then his stomach rumbled and he didn't care. "Have you eaten?"

"No."

"Then let's be off." Victor shocked her by not only taking hold of her hand but tucking her arm neatly under his. "I am much in need of a large meal." He laughed and she did too.

"Penelope my dear," Ethan said, offering to wrap her other arm around his. He walked down the hallway between the two of them.

Ethan summoned a carriage and as they got in Penelope realized her palms were damp with excitement. She had never been out alone like this before in her life with one man, let alone *two!* Not only was it a terrible breach of propriety but thrilling too! She was glad they had believed her story about her father, not having the heart or the courage to tell them that he had not even returned. She knew more than likely he was still out gambling and knew that it might be any number of days before she laid eyes on him again. Although she was scared about the future, for the moment she pushed the thoughts of her mind. She was with Ethan.

She sat as far as she could on the side of the carriage, tucking the bulky skirts down around her as Victor stepped in, and she was relieved he sat across from her and not next to her. And as Ethan stepped in he sat next to Penelope. Although he sat as far from her as he could, she could feel the warmth of his body against her. Trying to calm the pounding of her heart, she looked at Victor and asked cheerfully, "How was your meeting today at the patent office?"

"It went well."

She noticed that when he smiled the hard edge to his eyes softened. He was such an unusual looking person, she found herself wondering what his parents must have looked like. She recognized *Gant* as an English surname and was at a loss as to figuring out his parentage.

"Splendid, actually," Ethan said, looking out the window to the street.

"You were granted the patents?"

"No not yet. But we are hopeful," Victor said, and again his face seemed to transform when he smiled at her.

The restaurant was elegant, but it wouldn't have made any difference if they were at a seedy tavern. Penelope felt as if she were dreaming as the maître d' led them to a small table near the arched window facing the street. It was set with an ecru tablecloth with three-inch lace piled with more silverware and crystal than Victor had ever seen in his life.

"You'll...help me here, won't you?" Victor whispered, surprising her by leaning close. When she turned a questioning face up to him, he motioned toward the table settings. "I don't have any idea what to do with half of this stuff."

She laughed sweetly.

"We'd like a bottle of your best champagne to start, and oysters," Ethan said, handing the wine list back to the waiter without even bothering to look at him.

"Champagne? Ethan, I need *water*." Victor smiled but wished the dull throbbing at his temples would go away.

"My dear friend, you may have both!"

Settling in, Victor knocked one of the tall, fluted champagne glasses, but caught it before it fell.

"You're not used to all this extravagance I see? I would have thought that being Ethan's partner you would be more accustomed to all this!" Penelope had the feeling tonight would be like no night, and the excitement left her heart pounding and made her unusually bold.

"Hardly!" Victor began, grateful when another waiter brought a silver pitcher of water to the table, and after downing a glass of it said, "Penelope, I'm not a banker. I'm a blacksmith in Ste. Genevieve, and we're partners simply because we've been friends forever, and he's been good enough to help me."

Immediately, a little pain went across her heart, realizing that if Ethan had ever let her get close to him, she would have known that. Masking her discomfort, she forced a smile. "Ste. Genevieve—such an enchanting sounding town, it's French is it not?" In truth though she had thought so often about Ste. Genevieve, she felt like she knew the place.

"Yes, it is, and I suppose it is a rather enchanting little place." Ethan smiled as he refilled the champagne glasses.

"I don't know if its enchanting or not, but it's home to me," Victor replied, careful as he reached for his water goblet, not wanting to knock over any more crystal with his clumsy paws.

Although she was still smiling, a dull ache started in Penelope's heart. She had not wanted to leave her home in Boston and wished desperately she belonged to a quaint little town somewhere instead of plunked in the middle of the nation's capital, knowing no one and having to start over.

"But what's in a name?" Ethan mused, sitting back in the chair as always, liking when he was the center of attention.

Victor shrugged. "I imagine that rather depends on the name."

Swallowing the champagne, Ethan nodded. "So right you are. Take your name for instance. Victor, Latin for victorious! To the victor go the spoils!" Ethan turned to her then. Although she may have imagined it, his eyes seemed to caress her face.

"But *your* name, my dear Penelope, the unspeakably beautiful, long-suffering wife of the mighty king Odysseus, or in Latin if you prefer, Ulysses. Who patiently waited for her beloved husband to return after the long battle of Troy. But he was not to return to her yet, and spent another decade lost at sea while the gods trifled with his destiny. But so, captivating were Penelope's charms and beauty that not even the enchantress Circe nor the lovely nymph Calypso, not even the bewitching song of the sirens were able to deter him from his desire to return to his homeland of Ithaca and her loving arms. For years she spurned the affections of the would-be suitors who sought her hand in marriage, waiting, waiting for her king to return.

"At long last the great king Odysseus returns home. When Penelope lays eyes upon her adored husband who had set sail so many years ago the tears she wept were so full of joy that the goddess Athena took pity on her, and restored Penelope's beauty to that of her youth. The newly reunited couple spend the first night together after their long separation telling each other their adventures and making love, and to give them more time alone, the goddess Athena delays the very sunrise—" He silently upended his champagne glass.

Penelope had, of course, heard the ancient tale before, but never had the meaning been as personal. Never had she ever remotely thought anything so wonderfully romantic about *herself*. She realized she should be offended; he had mentioned 'lovemaking.' Instead, she found herself trying to imagine what it would be like to be so entwined with someone that a night would not be enough time to satisfy the passion.

"Ten *years* lost at sea," Victor cried, "this Odysseus fellow must have had seriously *bad* directions!"

Ethan laughed, but when he returned his attention to Penelope, wondered why her eyes did not reflect the candlelight. He cleared his throat. "You must help me Penelope, teach my friend here to enjoy life a bit more. He's been chained to a blacksmith shop since he was a boy though, it shan't be an easy task!"

"If all goes well, I'll soon be tied to a carriage business," Victor said.

"And a railroad coupling deal as well. I'll have you so busy making fortunes for us both that I'll be hard pressed to keep track of all the money you make us!"

"Things went as well as that?" Penelope asked, their happiness and excitement infectious.

"Yes. We were shot down for the carriage rim patent, but now have the idea to produce them ourselves by purchasing a carriage factory on the brink of bankruptcy. The coupler is for hooking the railroad cars together. My ever skilled and thinking companion here, got the idea for it on the train from St. Louis. In fact, the three of us made a detour to a blacksmith shop today so that we could have the actual parts to show the railroads. We wrote the official request for the patent today and we are encouraged that it will be approved." Ethan refilled their glasses, casting his eyes on her, and lifted his champagne for a toast.

"To success with old friends." Ethan turned to Victor.

"How do you suppose they do that?" Victor asked, watching the tiny amber bubbles floating to the top of the champagne glass.

"It has to do with the fermentation process. The yeast in the grapes converts into sugar, which gives us the coveted alcoholic properties," Ethan began with a smile. "When the winemakers desire to make champagne, they take new wine and mix it with already sweetened wine, and this adding of them together, along with the additional aging causes a secondary fermentation process to take place in the bottle and the result, is the famous effervescence, or if you prefer—bubbles!"

Victor took a tentative sip of the champagne, surprised that he liked the taste. "And the different colors?" he asked, thinking back to the afternoon's burgundy.

"Depending on the color of the grape and the time the winemaker leaves the grape skins in the tank—a white wine is fermented with only the must—the inside of the grape. For a rose they leave the skins in a short time, and for a Claret longer, and so on."

"And do they all do the same thing—give headaches, that is?""

Ethan laughed. "Actually no. Some are more potent."

"The longer the fermentation the stronger the wine?"

"The longer the fermentation the *drier* the wine! The ones you need to stay away from are the dessert and appetizer wines. The winemaker has added brandy to them which increases the potency."

"I'll remember that!" Victor grinned, then took a small sip of his champagne. "Must have been an interesting fellow to figure out a way to make wine sparkle."

"Indeed, he must have been. He was a Benedictine monk by the name of Dom Perignon."

Victor snorted. "Oh, that it explains it then. He was a *monk,* right? A lifetime vow of celibacy would drive *any* man to drink!" He realized what he'd said. "Oh! I'm-I'm terribly sorry Penelope! I guess I'm showing you a bit more of my colorful upbringing than you'd like to see."

He was so genuinely remorseful that Penelope giggled, red blotches warming her cheeks.

"Good night, Penelope, it was a pleasure to meet you," Victor said, smiling at her. He took her small hand inside his, squeezing it. She could not help but notice again how rough his were, yet it was not unpleasant. She had no siblings, but wondered if this was what having an older brother would be like.

"It was a fabulous evening. Do tell your father that we missed his company. I hope all goes well for you both here in Washington." Ethan reached for her hand, and after planting a respectful kiss on it, murmured good night.

"Good night then," Penelope said, touching her hand where Ethan had kissed it. Ethan and Victor watched her ascend the stairs, her dark green dress lightly brushing each step. When she was safely out of sight Victor covered up an enormous yawn.

"Come on," Ethan said, turning swiftly on his heel.

"What? Where are you going?"

"Where all gentlemen go after the proper women they've had dinner with head off for bed...*out!*" He grabbed Victor by the shoulder, ushering him out of the lobby.

As they walked up to the '*establishment*' as Pickering had called it, Victor felt uneasy. The brick building was down a long side street, and had tall windows that faced the front, heavily curtained.

"This is it, come on." Ethan stepped spritely out of the carriage. Victor noticed a gold sign next to the front door that read '*members only.*'

A large man opened the door. He stared unblinkingly, not recognizing them, but when Ethan offered Alexander Pickering's card, he moved and suddenly the front porch was flooded with the soft candlelight. There was the sound of piano music, and the muffled sounds of talking and laughter.

"Wait here," he said and walked quickly over to a table where five people sat talking and laughing.

A middle-aged woman walked up to them and stretched out her hands warmly in greeting. "You're new in town, and friends of Alexander's. Welcome, I'm Beverly but everyone calls me Bev. How naughty of him not to have come with you himself." She peered behind Ethan and, not seeing Pickering's short round form, cast her gaze back on Ethan, who she decided was handsome.

"What can I do for you gentlemen this evening?" She glanced up at Victor and grinned. "You're a big one aren't ya?" He was even bigger than her dear Jake, and until this moment Jake, her doorman and protector if needed, had been the most long-lasting lover she had ever had. She swept her eyes up and down Victor, wondering if sleeping with him would be as enjoyable as it had been in years past with Jake.

"Good evening. I'm Ethan Stanfield and this is my partner Victor Gant—we were wondering if you knew if a Mr. Sean Walker was here this evening?" Ethan tried not to notice that even though she was a good twenty years older than he was, she must have been gorgeous in her day.

Her silk blue dress was shockingly low, and it was with tremendous effort that Ethan did not stare at the snowy white breasts spilling out of it. Her face was pretty, even though the small lines around her bright blue eyes hinted that she was not as young as she was trying to appear. Her mouth he noticed was painted a most provocative red, and she was jeweled all over. Glittering diamond barrettes held back her dark blond curls. At her throat, a black velvet choker from which dangled a cameo, on her bare arms, gold bracelets rattled, and on her soft hands with finely manicured nails were rings on every finger, even one on her right thumb

"Let me see where he is at the minute, we wouldn't want to interrupt him." Winking at them, she tiptoed off to inquire as to the whereabouts of Sean Walker.

"Where the *hell* are we?" Victor said under his breath.

"An exclusive, and surely expensive whore house. Let's hope we can get our money's worth," Ethan said, watching Bev return to them, her breasts jiggling as she walked.

"Mr. Walker is still here; I believe he's upstairs on the second floor enjoying a game of chance. Do you both partake in games of chance? Could I interest you in that or some *other* form of entertainment this evening?" Ever so lightly she traced her tongue over her lips to moisten them. She grabbed both of Ethan's hands.

Because Ethan was suddenly mute, Victor answered. "No. Thanks anyway. We only need to see Mr. Walker."

"All right then," she said, but the look in her eyes caused Ethan's heart to speed up. "Can we get either of you gentleman a drink?"

"None for me," Victor said, wishing that Ethan had not filled his glass so many times with champagne. Besides, he still thought it was a bit too early to be celebrating.

"A glass of cognac I think."

Beverly motioned to one of the young girls that stood dutifully with the tables of talking gentleman.

"Good God," Ethan said under his breath as he and Victor stared openly at the young girl like hormone-crazed adolescents.

She looked to be in her late twenties, and when she came back with Ethan's cognac and a large tumbler of water, neither of them could resist looking at her figure. She was in a red and black striped silk dress that was so tight she looked as if he had been poured into it. Her breasts, pushed up by a whalebone corset, nearly popped out of the skintight bodice. Victor had never seen a woman's breasts displayed like this before, and to his embarrassment felt a stiffening in his groin. Her jet-black hair hung past her waist and was pulled back from her face by a red satin bow. When he finally looked at her face, he realized she was not particularly pretty, but with a figure like that it didn't much matter.

"There is a lot of...um...cleavage in here," Victor said, swallowing hard.

"Yes, there is," Ethan said with a small nod and an appreciative smile at a plump pretty redhead batting her eyes at him. But her efforts would be for naught. Bev had already sniffed him out.

"I'll...hmm...be back shortly," Ethan said.

"Where are you going?" Victor protested but stopped when he saw Bev with her head flirtatiously tilted, smiling up at Ethan. He watched with annoyance as Ethan headed up the narrow stairs after her.

"*Now what am I supposed to do?*" he mumbled and, throwing his arms behind his back, paced over to the window. His head was throbbing now, too much wine, too much champagne, if he could sleep for a little while. He sat down at one of the empty tables, wondering what in the world he was supposed to do, and hanging his head for a minute dragged his hand through his hair. He toyed with the idea of walking but wasn't sure of the way back to the hotel. Besides if Ethan did find Walker, they might need him to explain something about the coupler. Sighing, he resigned to wait.

As he glanced around the room and saw the small groups of men talking, noticed that all the women in the room were dressed for a man's pleasure. For there was no neckline that was not shockingly low, no gowns of demure grays, no hint of feminine blush that had not come from the bottles and round boxes from the dressing table. No coquettish flirtation that would end with an un-satisfying kiss on the hand at the end of an evening.

He noticed a deck of cards in a leather case and took them out and shuffled them. Thinking that if he had to wait for Ethan, at least he could entertain himself by playing solitaire. Laying the cards out, he realized it was no ordinary deck of cards! There were black and white drawings of women, and not just any women. Woman in various stages of undress, and then finally naked women in painstakingly vivid detail. Astonished he began leafing quickly through the cards, seeing more desirable womanly form than he had ever seen in his life. The Ace's he soon found out showed men in the cards as well. And they were performing sexual acts on the women, and he stared in disbelief at the cards, never imagining anything of the kind. He shuddered involuntarily with sexually charged energy and could not bring himself to put them down. Staring at the explicit drawings before him he decided women were indeed beautiful creatures, and it made him want Celena suddenly more desperately than he had ever wanted her before.

Damn John and the waiting period!

Giggling wrenched his attention from the cards. Looking up he saw two girls pointing at him and snickering. Feeling like a naughty schoolboy caught behind the barn, he stuffed the cards in their case and stood up.

Eager to be somewhere dark and quiet, he strode across the room, opening the first door he saw, walked in. There were two girls and one man inside, and he must have interrupted something interesting because he saw one of the girls throw her skirts back down, and the other jump guiltily from the man's lap.

"Oh! Um...sorry," Victor stammered, wanting more than anything to escape. Seeing another door, opened it and to his relief found it empty and dark. It was chilly inside since no one was there, and the great marble fireplace was dark, but he was relieved to have found somewhere quiet and dark, that he simply slumped down on the couch. A line of light came from under the door and he leaned his head back and closed his eyes for a moment, forcing the images of the lewd playing cards out of his head.

Tomorrow they would go again to the patent office and see Pickering, hopefully they would be granted the patent, and he and Ethan could make their way back the next day to Ste. Genevieve, home. Thoughts of home had a calming effect on him and him, laid his weary body down, careful to hang his booted feet off the end of the brocade couch.

He closed his eyes, wanting nothing more than to sleep, and have the fuzzy uncomfortable feeling of too much drink and sexual arousal to ebb away. He wondered how Claude and Thomas were getting on at the shop and did not even want to think about how much work he was going to have to do when he got back. He thought of Margaret and Henry and tried to remind himself that he needed to go over what they still owed Ethan on the farm with Henry.

His mind wandered as it always did to thoughts of Celena. Wondered if she thought of him as often as he did her. He imagined her in the kitchen at her parents' house. Her hair in the long braid that had so many different colors in it. The sleeves of her blouse rolled up to her elbows, white apron around her waist, working furiously at the stove, whipping up the most incredibly tasty meals.

Just a hint of smile could send his big heart racing. He desperately wanted to make her proud of him and please her, like he'd never wanted to do with another person. He thought again about the night of the barn raising when he'd kissed her and how right it felt to have her in his arms. He could clearly see the gorgeous face looking up at him in the moonlight.

'I love you Victor,' she had breathlessly whispered, gazing up at him with those incredible blue eyes of hers, glistening with tears.

He remembered the feel of her underneath him. The feel of her neck and breasts and touching her like a husband would. He imagined her slowly unbuttoning the front of her dress, saw her hand waver shyly before she pulled it off. He watched her as she untied the little satin ribbon on the camisole, loosening it for him, watched her smooth down the quilt on the bed. Saw her lean up and reach for his hand to pull him down on the bed and lean towards him, felt the light touch of her long hair brushing against his arm. Noticed the faint smell of flowers or perfume, and it reminded him of the fragrance of the wildflowers that he always brought her. Then he felt the light touch of her sweet moist mouth against his, and the glorious weight of her breasts laying against his chest. Felt her unbutton his shirt and slide her hand against his chest.

"Lena," he whispered as she trailed her hand down his bare chest, and he reached out to pull her closer and skimmed a nervous hand over her breasts. He paused a moment, quivering at the wonder of being able to touch her. Then overcome with desire, slipped his hand all the way inside the camisole. His breathing quickening as he kissed her.

He felt a hand cross over his belt and hips and then, to his astonishment, lower to gently fondle his groin. It was an erotic sensation he'd never experienced before and he felt himself becoming powerfully aroused.

The strange smell was stronger now, and he realized that it wasn't the wildflowers but perfume, and it confused him because he could not remember Celena ever smelling of anything, save the wonderful scent of soap. He struggled to open his eyes. He dropped his hands from her and tried to focus on the darkness. He thought he saw a woman sitting on the couch next to him, her long hair touching his chest.

"Celena...Lena?" he whispered in the darkness, knowing that at any moment he was going to be powerless to stop himself, blessing or no, married or not.

"No...Leticia," a soft voice said, crashing into his dream.

For three agonizing seconds, he could not fathom where he was. Then he remembered. He was still in Washington D. C. In an expensive whorehouse. Not with his beloved Celena.

Bolting up from the couch, he knocked Leticia to the floor. She landed with an undignified thud, hurting her tailbone.

"What's the matter?" she asked, struggling to her feet and rubbing her injured backside.

He recognized her as the shapely girl who had brought them their drinks. "Nothing...nothing," he stammered, "I-I was sleeping. And you startled me...I was dreaming!" Shakily he began to re-button his shirt.

It amused her to watch a man with an obvious desire to bed a woman try desperately to conceal it. She was sure any moment he would ask her to go upstairs.

At first, she dreaded servicing him when Bev told her to. But when she found him sleeping in the dark, found his dark face without the hard eyes, handsome. Leaning down to kiss him, she found his tender reaction to her wonderfully surprising. She had the notion that he was not experienced with women. At times she hated servicing the 'experienced' kind. They were often awkward, sloppy, selfish, and even brutal in their pairings. But she had the impression that pairing with this virginal man would be nothing at all like that.

When he started to leave, she ran after him. "Where are you going?"

"I'm awake now, I'm not dreaming anymore." He shut the door firmly behind him. He noticed the adjoining salon was empty now and that the three-some had left. *Probably tired of being interrupted!* he thought, glancing around the room.

He was going to leave with or without Ethan. Whether he'd made his deal with Walker or not! Besides, it did not seem to him that since keeping a clear head was important for making a business deal, that *this* would certainly not be a good place to try it.

He entered the main room and saw that it was nearly empty now. He had no idea how long he had slept, and what time it was. From the looks of the quiet salon, it must be late. He wavered a minute, wondering if he should go up and look for Ethan, but realizing he was not *about* to go barging through doors, decided he'd find his way back to the Willard.

He was at the front door when he heard them coming down the stairs.

Bev had changed into a pink silk dressing down. It was obvious that she had nothing else on, because her breasts, without the stays pushing them up and out, wobbled and sagged under the thin silk. Her barrettes and most the jewelry was gone, and her perfect curls were a bit worse for the wear.

Ethan was behind her and although he was all buttoned up, it was obvious what he had been doing.

"Did you ever even find Walker?" Victor asked with irritation, tiring of the whole sorry business.

"No actually I didn't—I had more pressing things to address."

Victor sighed loudly. "Come on. Let's go." He headed for the door. When Ethan did not follow, he turned to see him tugging playfully at the thin belt tied around Bev's waist. He considered picking Ethan up by the scruff of the neck and dragging him out. "Ethan, come on. Let's go!"

Sitting in front of him, Bev purposefully crossed her bare, shapely legs.

"*Come on!* I'm quickly losing my patience!"

Bev let out an ugly snort and poked Ethan in the stomach. "That's not the only thing *quick* around here, eh?"

The next thing Ethan knew Victor was pulling him out onto the street, but not before they heard her erupt into peals of laughter.

As they walked back in the dark to the Willard, Ethan turned suddenly to Victor. "You won't...you won't mention—"

"*Never!*"

They looked at each other and started to laugh, shaking their heads over the bizarre night.

Chapter 12

Out behind the house, Celena pulled a sheet from the washboard. She had to fold it several times and then wrung it as tightly as she could, her hand aching from the pressure. It was hard to wring or hang something that large alone, and as she walked to the maze of clothesline that zig zagged behind the house had to go up on tip toe the throw the damp sheet over the line. A gust of wind blew it back on her, plastering the sheet against her, and straining up on tiptoe threw it again over the line. Shaking her hair out of her face, she pulled the wooden clothespins out of her apron and, carefully skimming along the clothesline pushed a clothespin in every few feet.

It was late in the day to be hanging out the wash, but it had been a bad day, with her father frustrated because he could not get the reaper to work, that her chores had gotten rather interrupted. Besides that, she had been unsettled with Victor in Washington. Even though during a normal week she only saw him once a week on Sunday, the knowledge that he was not merely two miles down the road, bothered her more than she thought it would.

Sighing, she pulled one of her father's shirts from the wash bucket and wringing it out, again reached up to get it on the line. Another gust of wind blew the strands of hair that always worked themselves out of her braid across her face, and she shook her head impatiently to get them out of her eyes. She was concerned about her father. He was sick with worry about the reaper, and he was not thrilled with how Carlene was seeing *both* Eddie and Mason. It was causing a rift within not only the Fisk family with one girl for two brothers—but their own family as well.

"Poor Pa," she whispered, leaning down to get the last garment, a petticoat, out of the wash bucket. After wringing it out, she stretched up to throw it over the line.

Two hands grabbed her around the waist.

"*Victor!*" She threw her arms around him, laughing when she realized he had the wet petticoat against his back. She quickly peeled it off him. "When did you get back?"

"Now. I hitched up the wagon and came right over." He took the wet petticoat from her and stretched it carefully over the line.

"I'm *so* glad you're home."

"You have no idea how good it is to hear that. How good it is to see you." He brushed the stray hairs from her face, smiling uncontrollably.

"I missed you so much."

"Did you now?" He grinned, his eyes darting all over her upturned face. "I missed you too." He gently held her face in his hands. He knew he must look foolish gazing down at her madly but couldn't help himself. It was both liberating and exhilarating to have found one's soul mate on earth.

"How did everything go? Were you granted the patent?"

"No."

Her pretty face crumpled. "Oh, I'm so sorry." But he was smiling so happily down at her that she was puzzled. "You don't seem...upset about it?"

Shrugging, he bent and kissed her on the top of the head. "I'm not."

"What happened?"

"Oh, it was too simple a design to be patented, but it's all right, we filled out a form for another patent."

She pulled back in surprise. "*Another* patent? what do you mean?"

"For a coupler. Something that links the cars of a train together. I came up with an idea, another way to do it."

"Just like that?" she asked, impressed by the way his mind worked.

"Yes, but anyway...enough of that now." He pulled her toward him. "You're a sight for sore eyes."

"My heavens, I guess I am." She looked down self-consciously, knowing her hair was a mess. She had on one of Carlene's old aprons, the one with the rip in the pocket. And the dark green dress was a hand-me-down from Eva, faded to a dull gray where the apron did not shield it from the sun.

"Don't look down," he said, putting a finger under her chin to lift it. "You look fine to me."

"But Victor, what happened, what is this about another patent?"

"It's a long story, I'll tell you later. Come here. Please."

Knowing what he wanted, she looked nervously around, wondering if they were hidden amid the flapping laundry. She didn't want her father to erupt again; he was already in a bad mood. "Do you think we dare?"

He bent to kiss her.

"Victor! Welcome back. I figured that was your wagon in front. I'm sorry to bother you, but we've got a problem," James chirped, but he felt bad for interrupting. He liked Victor and hated to immediately bring him their problems.

"What's wrong?" Victor asked, holding Celena against his chest, hoping he could somehow solve whatever was wrong and still have the much-anticipated kiss.

"It's that damn reaper. It's got Pa foaming at the mouth. Laurence was here all afternoon and none of us can figure out how to fix it. We don't even know what's wrong with it. I hate like the devil to bother you, I know you just got home and all, but can you look at it?"

"I don't have any tools with me." When he saw the dejected look on James' face, he added, "I'll take a look at it, but if there's something seriously wrong I'll have to take it to the shop." He followed James through the maze of hanging laundry, shaking his head.

"No problem, we appreciate you lookin' at it—I think we can all lift it up there. It's a heavy son of a gun though."

Weaving through the clotheslines toward the barn, Victor did not let go of Celena's hand even when he came face to face with John.

"Hey Vic! How was Washington?" Will said, trying to lighten the sour mood.

Victor, knowing that the last thing John wanted was levity, merely nodded. "It was fine." He turned to John. "What's it doing?" Finally he let go of Celena's hand as he squatted near the machine to get a closer look.

"What's it *doing*? It's more like what's it NOT doing! I don't know— the blasted thing won't stay straight or cut or do half the things the brochure said it would. I'm so frustrated with it I feel like throwing the damn thing in the river!"

"If you want me to, I'll take it to the shop and take a look at it."

Looking at Victor, Celena realized he hadn't stopped to change because he still had on the black suit. His suit coat and shirt were badly wrinkled, and his pants legs had street dust on them, but she had never seen anything more wonderful than his road-weary clothes, because they meant he had traveled *home*.

"Would you mind, Victor?" John asked reluctantly.

"I'll get the wagon."

When they finished lifting the reaper into the wagon, Yvonne came out on the back porch to tell them supper was ready. She smiled when she saw Victor. "Well, you're a pleasant surprise, welcome home." She planted a kiss on his cheek. John walked up and, standing next to his wife, forced a weak smile.

"Stay for supper, won't you, Victor?" he asked, mustering enough courage to look Victor in the eye. It was an odd situation to be telling a man to keep his distance one moment and in another asking for his help.

Victor smiled. "I'd like nothing better."

Three days later before supper Victor sent an excited Thomas to the Rieflers to tell John that he needed to see him. John was cranky as he hurried his wagon down the familiar lane to town. The reaper so far had been a financial nightmare, and his stomach was in knots as he stepped off the wagon at the Victor's shop.

"John." Victor smiled as he trotted over to him.

"Go ahead give it to me straight—it's shot, right?"

"No. Not at all."

The response took John so off guard that for a minute he couldn't think of anything to say. "You fixed it?"

Victor nodded, folding his big forearms in front of him.

"What in damnation was wrong with it?" John asked, coming closer and listening for better than five minutes as Victor explained what had been wrong and how he had fixed it.

"But those are new pieces of iron—" he interrupted, peering into his reaper and noting the pieces that weren't painted blue.

"I know. I had to add things, and I changed some things, but don't worry, it'll work. I couldn't figure what it was not doing so I had to take it almost all the way apart—but you see here, frankly I was concerned that you might have the same problem, so to prevent that from happening I added this part here," Victor said, his words muffled because he had his head nearly all the way in the reaper. "What you have now is a new improved version. A McCormick-*Gant* reaper. Go on, look."

John listened for another few minutes as Victor went on about the workings of the reaper and how, though a great invention, it had a minor fault which Victor assured him he had remedied.

"Are you sure, are you sure it works now?"

"Of course. I tried it out last night, works like a charm. In fact we'll load it up for you to take back home now."

John nodded. Part of him was overwhelmed with relief that Victor had been able to fix it, but again felt the uncomfortable feeling of being beholden to a man he was trying to keep at arm's length. "Well...thank you. You've done a good job as usual," he stammered and tried to smile. "I appreciate it. What do I owe you?"

"Don't worry about it, John."

A tiny spark of anger flitted through him. "Come on Victor, what do I *owe* you?"

"You don't owe me anything."

For a moment they fell tensely silent. John looked past Victor to the sign that still said "Schaeffer's Blacksmith," even though Victor had owned it for years. John had liked Jonah, and he admired when the old German blacksmith had taken Robert Gant's children in.

"I know how long this must have taken you, and besides that I know you've got your own work to do without spending two days on my equipment alone. Now let me pay you."

"It's all right."

"It's *not* all right!" John bit back, even though he knew everyone in town thought he was being an idiot. In fact, even Laurence asked him why he was dragging his heels when it came to Victor and Celena. "I don't want to be in debt to you and you know I've got means to pay you. At least let me pay you for your iron."

"Like I said, it's all right. Don't worry about it," Victor replied calmly.

"Dammit Victor, how much money do you want?"

"It's not *money* I want from you!" he snapped back, shocking John. For all his calm exterior, his blood was boiling underneath his skin as John's was.

John forced himself to wait before speaking, wanting to cool off before he said something he knew Yvonne would make him apologize for. "Well...then...what do you want?"

"John, you know *exactly* what I want." Victor hung his head, trying to quell the anger growing in him. "I have a trade, I have a house, I make a good living. I want Celena. I want your blessing." He opened his mouth to add more, and then thinking that he'd maybe said too much, shut it.

John thrust his hands deep into his pockets and paced silently around the reaper, kicking small stones as a storm brewed in his mind. He had seen the way Celena looked at Victor, and it broke his heart a little more each day to hurt her. She was such a sweet child, such a dutiful daughter and he knew she was patiently waiting for him to give her his blessing.

"You know how...how much we love her—"

"Yes, I know that. And I feel the same way, haven't I *proved* that by now?"

There was another uncomfortable pause.

"Yes, I suppose you have, haven't you?" His eyes met Victor's. "She's young."

"She's not *that* young." Sighing with frustration, he put his big hands on his hips. "She'll be seventeen on her next birthday. She's not a child."

John recognized the posture of a man who had heard it all before and was growing weary of a father's reluctance to let go of his little girl. John realized he had run out of reasons. "Her mother will want a...big fuss made over this."

"When?" Victor's heart beat faster.

John scratched the top of his graying head, pondering the timetable. "I've got acres of wheat to cut and thrash and too much work to do now to even think about it...and in the fall, I'll be busy sowing—"

"You're never *not* going to be busy, John. I mean, there's *always* going to be something you've got to do. Can't we just...get it over with?"

John nodded weakly in agreement. "I suppose you're right. I guess next winter would work."

Victor's heart suddenly felt too big for his chest. "But that's *months* from now!" He thought he would go *mad* if he had to wait another eight months. "How about Sunday?"

"*This Sunday?*"

"Why not?"

Putting his hands up, John backed away. "No, no, I couldn't agree to that! Yvonne would be furious with me."

"You'll be cutting wheat in June and thrashing in July?"

"Well...yes," John stammered, confused by the sudden subject change.

"Then let me marry her in August. That gives you time to finish up the summer work before you get busy again in the fall and lets Yvonne plan...*whatever*."

John tried to think of a reason to tell him no, tried to delay what he knew was inevitable. He sighed. "All right."

August. Four months away. John was finally giving them his blessing.

Victor stretched out his hand in a gesture of respect, an offer of friendship and, he hoped, the end of the quiet feud between them.

"You'll take...good care of her, Victor?"

"Of course."

"It was nothing personal, Victor. It wasn't because I didn't like you."

Embarrassed, Victor had to look down. "I know."

"It's just...well...I'm fond of that little girl."

"I am too."

John nodded. "Yes, I believe you are."

The next Sunday Victor listened patiently to Yvonne's plans for the wedding for over two hours. When he finally stood up to leave, he shook John's hand and said goodnight to Yvonne, but stalled at the door, wanting to be alone with Celena, if only for a few moments. If nothing else to be able to look at her without being watched, and bolstered by the happy talk of their impending marriage, cleared his throat and reached out a took a hold of one of Celena's hands.

She turned to her parents. "I'll just walk Victor out."

Outside, Victor immediately pulled her close and stood smiling down at her, not sure what to do with the sudden treasured time alone.

"Do you really have to go right away?"

"No, I—"

"I know, all that wedding talk was getting to you."

He smiled with embarrassment.

"Sit?" she suggested, and they moved to the porch swing.

It was a lovely cool night. The summer sounds of crickets and cicadas had not yet started yet, but the meadows and woods seemed poised for their songs. The air was fresh and clean from the spring rains and damp grass and budding flowers. Even the nascent leaves looked freshly washed. The porch still retained the heat from the afternoon sun, and the darkening sky was dotted with brilliant stars that peeked through wispy clouds. They rocked back and forth quietly, simply content to be together with no one watching what they did or listening to what they said.

She shivered.

"I'll warm you." He put his arm around her, pulling her against him.

Nodding, she rested her cheek against his chest and daringly put her arm around his waist.

"Better?" he asked, looking down at her in the growing darkness. He stroked her hair, liking the feel of the silky tresses under his fingertips.

"Yes, much better," she said, and then glanced at the purple, blue, and pink morning glories that had closed their horn-shaped flowers for the night. She realized how fragile and beautiful they were. Only to venture and unfold their trumpeted selves to the soft morning light. She wondered where at Victor's house she could plant her own growing latticework of shy flowers.

"This is so nice," she said breathlessly. Choking up with embarrassing emotional tears pricking her eyes, she was grateful for the darkness so he would not see.

"That it is. You all have sure made a lot of plans for the wedding."

"Yes, we have. Maman is so excited, it's all she has talked about since Papa gave us his blessing. She's already started making a dress for me, and next week we are working on altering Maman's dress for Eva. I didn't want such a fuss, but my mother does, especially after Carlene. And my father said if I am going to get married, he is going to make sure I get married properly. Anyway, it makes my parents happy."

"How is everyone?" Victor asked, nodding toward the house. The town was still buzzing about Carlene and Mason eloping last week. Victor could not help but feel sorry for John, who had tried so hard to protect his daughters and failed so miserably.

"Carlene seemed better today. We washed every piece of laundry yesterday, and ironed them today. Then we washed all the windows inside and out, and Eva and I went right out into the garden with her and pulled weeds until be all about dropped dead. Carlene did nothing but cry for the first two days, but she did not say a word about it today. She seemed annoyed when Mason finally came to get her. Maman seems to be over the initial shock, but Papa is not taking it too well. I know he's devasted that Carlene has done this. I don't think she had any idea she would hurt them this much." She watched him quietly trace the outline of her hand with his fingers. "And frankly Eva and I are confused. First Carlene was mad for Eddie, but then to make him jealous starts seeing his brother, and when Eddie comes back around she goes too far and goes off and marries his brother! Did you hear the day Mason and Carlene came back from Cape Girardeau, Eddie showed up and Mason and Eddie got into a shoving match on the front porch and it took both Laurence and James to break it up?"

"Yeah, I heard."

"Eddie's a bully, and I'm glad Carlene didn't marry him, I don't think he'd ever make her happy. I doubt he'll ever make *anyone* happy."

He took one of her hands a kissed each finger.

"You and I thought about running away once, remember?"

"*You* thought about it, I did *not*."

"How did you know it would hurt my parents this much?"

He shrugged. "I just knew. I didn't want to hurt you like that or your parents for that matter. Besides, I know how much they love you, and because I feel the same way, I've always been able to understand how they feel about you."

"That's a rather roundabout way to tell me that you love me."

He grinned self-consciously. "You've never *doubted* it have you?"

"No, but it might to nice to actually...hear it."

Victor's brows furrowed. "It would? But why? Why does it need to be said if you already know?"

"Oh Victor!" She laughed at the look of worry on his face. "I guess I'll have to settle for knowing you love me. Besides, its' getting late."

"You're right. I best be on my way. I've got to see Josephine Chomeau in the morning, and I'm already backed up at the shop." Yet even with these solid reasons for leaving, neither of them moved. He hated the thought that such a wonderful evening would end with a chilly ride back to a dark house and empty bed.

She turned her face up to him, resting her chin against his chest. "To see if she'll sell you the land for the coupler factory? She will, I think. She's fond of you."

"Let's hope so. I still think it's too soon to be doing all of this, but Ethan says that's how business is done. He says we have to be ready."

"What still bothers me is that Mr. Pickering would not give you the patent for the carriage rim. I still think that was a wonderful idea."

"It was worth a try. Ethan still thinks Pickering will contact us about a carriage factory. Who knows." He smiled at her. "That was so sweet of you to do all that work, although I don't know why you would bother with it."

Surprised, she raised her face to look at him in the starlight. "I did it because I love you, and it's a wonderful idea and you deserve to have wonderful things happen to you. I want nothing more in this life than to make you happy."

He wrapped his arms around her as she nestled her head under his chin. "You have," he said, his heart was jerking painfully in his chest. "I am happy." He realized it sounded a little flat given the feelings he had for her that shocked and frightened him. He also felt the stirrings of unrequited sexual passion begin to build in his body and pulled back from her.

She shivered in the cool spring night without his big body warming her. It was suddenly awkward between them, because she seemed to be waiting for him to add something. "I better go in." After hugging him goodbye, she went back into the house.

He walked down the steps in the darkness, but as he headed home an uneasiness stayed with him.

Chapter 13

On a warm afternoon two weeks before Victor and Celena's wedding, Margaret gave birth a month early to a son. It had been a long day and a half and Henry Wilburn had never been more relieved in his life to see his mother and sister Grace walk in and take over. When Henry expressed his doubt about the value of walking his weak, trembling wife about the room, his mother shot her sixth child of eight a look and said, *"I know a bit about babies and birthing them."*

Victor was there that night to see his sister.

"He'll probably take after his Mama, at least I hope he does," Henry said proudly.

"He's got a lot of dark hair that's for sure!" Victor laughed, looking down at his nephew.

Margaret gently stroked her tiny newborn's cheek and then smiled up at her brother. "Did Henry tell you? We've named him Henry Victor Wilburn—Henry Jr."

Victor grinned. "He may be Henry Jr. to you...but he looks like a *Hank* to me." He leaned down and kissed his sister's cheek, glad she was happy with Henry and relieved she had lived through childbirth.

"Hank," Margaret cooed to her son, "later when you can open your eyes, I'll introduce you to everyone. Your grandmama, Aunt Grace, and your Uncle Victor. Uncle Victor's big and noisy but he's a good big brother, he's always taken care of me, and he'll always take care of you too."

"You did well Margaret. He's a fine son," Victor said, touching the baby's red cheek.

"Of course he is." Margaret smiled, her brown eyes caressing the face of the brother she loved. "He's related to you after all."

Chapter 14

Celena didn't know what time it was, but knew it had to be early because it was still dark outside. She laid an impatient arm across her eyes and tried to tell her anxious brain to *sleep.* Rolling over on her side she could hear the comforting sound of Eva's quiet breathing. Celena smiled a small, sad smile, knowing it would be that last morning she would ever wake in her parents' house, in the bedroom with the maple four poster beds she had shared with her sisters since she had been old enough to sleep out of a cradle. She glanced at Carlene's unslept-in bed with the star of Bethlehem quilt, and hoped that across town where she lived with her new husband, she was enjoying a restful, undisturbed sleep.

Sighing, Celena turned over again and lay on her back. She stared up at the ceiling, liking the way the old, whitewashed boards looked in the darkness. As a child she used to imagine all sorts of animals, trees, and flowers in the wood grain peeking from behind the whitewash. She wondered idly what patterns there were in wood grain above Victor's bed.

Her heart sped up. Only last weekend her father and brothers had finished their summer harvest, and the waiting period she thought would never end suddenly had.

It was her wedding day.

"It'll be all right," she whispered and rolled to the other side, wondering why the thought of being alone with Victor scared her. It was all she had wanted for so long. But now when it was within her grasp, a quiet fear gripped her heart. "I'm being ridiculous," she said quietly, tucking her hand under her head. Finding no comfort laying in bed, she sat up in the darkness, and drawing her knees up, stretched the cotton nightgown over them.

Looking out the window, she could still see faint blue stars in the slit between the curtains and wondered how late her mother had worked. Celena felt guilty when she saw the fatigue all over her mother in the mornings. She glanced over at the dress her mother had been married in, carefully laid over the arched leather trunk. It was a beautiful shade of pale blue satin and had tiny pleats of white ribbon stitched on the front of the bodice. Celena adored it. But ten years ago, when Queen Victoria married Albert, she had bucked the tradition of wearing brocade and velvet and been married in an all-white lace gown trimmed with delicate orange blossoms. Yvonne, wanting the best for her daughter, insisted that Eva wear the blue dress and that they make a stylish white wedding gown for Celena.

Quietly Celena got up and went to the window where her new wedding dress had been carefully laid on a chair. She touched the soft satin that, when spread out over the hoops, fell in the most magnificent folds. The waistband was three inches wide and nipped in at the waist. There was a modest scoop neck embellished with tiny seed pearls, which had taken she and Eva two months to sew in. There were short cap sleeves, and tiny satin corset lacing that closed the back. Even though she had adjusted the pattern to a less full train, she still worried it would trip her on her way up the aisle.

It was a beautiful dress, but being fair skinned, it made Celena look paler than usual. Her mother's blue dress looked better with her skin tone and especially complimented her eyes, and Celena would have much preferred to wear it. But the dress, like so many things about the wedding, had gotten away from her.

Sighing, she looked away from the dress and glanced out the window. Craning her neck, she could see the hint of coral light rising from behind the hill. Looking down at the yard, she saw that James and Laurence had finished bringing in the tables for the wedding reception. She thanked God it hadn't rained last night. After all, so many neighbors had lent tables and chairs; she would have felt terrible if it had rained.

One tent was already set up, and underneath it was the long table that she and Victor and her family would sit at to eat dinner. Next to that was the place they had reserved for the string quartet that Josephine Chomeau had so generously offered and would not take no for an answer. Celena would have to remind James to pick them up from Mrs. Blay's in town today. They had come all the way from St. Louis, and Celena could not even imagine what it had cost her. Josephine had offered a whole host of things. Some her parents had taken her up on, like the music, and use of some of her furniture, and others like shipping in flowers and a fancy St. Louis cake, they had not.

Eva and Margaret had been cooking for days. The menu had grown to ridiculous proportions, Celena thought, but she knew Margaret wanted to be a part of her brother's wedding and the wedding *'fever'* that had seemed to grip everyone. And gifts poured in! The most wonderful gifts—from an entire set of new china from Widow Chomeau to the sweetest and most innocent homemade gifts like new quilted hot pads from Esther Charbonnier.

She shook her head at the embarrassing memory two weeks ago of going to the general store and having the silly Alvin Woolrich fawn all over her. Telling her that her pending marriage had been great for business, and that so many women were coming in to buy bolts of cloth to make new dresses, and foodstuffs to make their heartfelt contributions to the wedding feast. And that even the men were buying things like new razors and God forbid—new socks!

"It's not every day," he told Celena, straightening the black bow tie that pinched his skinny neck, "that Ste. Genevieve's own famous inventor marries the prettiest girl in town—why, it's a bigger celebration than the Fourth of July event."

"It is indeed turning into an event," Celena murmured softly.

The sound of a cardinal's singing pierced the quiet and sent a shiver through her soul. Looking up at the sky, she knew the only thing that could spoil the day was rain, and so far, the lightening sky looked clear. She smiled again as the awakening robins, and blue jays chimed in.

"It's finally time," she whispered. "Time to get married."

By the time Celena and Eva gathered the eggs and milked cows, the normally orderly house was in upheaval! Laurence, Lisette, their boys, and baby Estella had come to help with the preparations, as well as Alice and James. As much as Celena loved her nephews, they were rambunctious little boys and so excited by the wedding that more than once Lisette had to scold them. Finally, Lisette appealed to Will to take them outside where they were put to work lining up chairs. There was also a steady flow of neighbors coming and going, bringing the food they had prepared and the gifts they had made, stopping to chat and talk about what a wonderful day it was going to be, and how everyone hoped it wouldn't be too hot.

There was so much commotion that Celena was relieved when her mother said it was time for her to go upstairs and dress. At least in the sanctuary of her bedroom she could try to keep calm.

By ten o'clock that morning, Victor sent Claude and Thomas home. They had been laughing and joking all morning, and were more than happy when their benevolent employer cut them loose. After all, they had to get home to bathe and change for the wedding, just like the rest of the town.

When Victor finished bathing and shaving he dressed in the new gray broadcloth suit Celena had made for him. He was solemn as he buttoned up the shirt sewn by Celena, and stiffly ironed by Margaret. It was difficult to see much of himself in the small mirror he had propped up behind the washbasin, but made sure he had tucked everything in right, and buttoned properly, wanting to justice to both Celena and Margaret's handiwork.

He was surprised when he heard a knock on the door.

"Good morning. Almost ready, are you?" Ethan queried, walking in before being asked. He noticed right away that the small house was immaculate, and wondered again how on earth three people had ever lived there together. At least Victor had finally replaced the hideous oilskins over the windows with glass! The bed had been carefully made, and few dishes he had were at least washed and stacked neatly. It made a lump form in his throat seeing that Victor had worked hard getting his little house ready for his bride.

"Yes," Victor said, taking a drink of lukewarm coffee. He sat down in one of the un-matching chairs to pull on his shined boots. "At least it's not raining. I'd hate to think of what will happen if it does." Standing up, he shook his pants leg over the boots. "What time is it?"

"You've got plenty of time. I've taken the liberty of hitching my carriage up. Thought it was my duty as best man to give you a grand escort to the wedding and then to the farm for the reception."

Victor pulled on his suit coat.

Ethan realized suddenly that his boyhood friend looked different.

Maybe it was because for the first time in his life, the pants Victor was wearing were long enough, or that for once he could button up the white shirt to his throat without looking like he was about to pass out from lack of oxygen. His shoulders looked positively massive in the light gray suit, and when he gently tugged at the shirt sleeves to have them peek out from underneath the suit sleeves, Ethan realized that it was the first time he had ever seen Victor in clothes that fit him properly, and realized jealously that Victor had an exceptionally good build and was a striking figure of a man.

If Victor's appearance was not enough to rattle him, he noticed a new aura about him as well. A quiet maturity, a self-assuredness that surrounded him without any trace whatsoever of vanity or conceit.

"Here." Ethan grinned, offering him a drink of whiskey out of the flask he had cleverly hidden inside his suit coat. "I've never known a bridegroom in my life that didn't need a little fire in his veins to go through with it."

Victor smiled and took a swig. "Trust me, I'll go through with it."

As Celena climbed into her family's wagon in her heavy satin wedding dress, she had to wipe a line of perspiration off her top lip. The stiff curls she could already tell were wilting in the humidity and she felt guilty at how much time and effort her mother and sisters had put into curling her hair. Sitting down in the wagon she forced a smile at her sisters.

More than once Celena had to close her eyes and grip the rails of the wagon as nausea overcame her on the bumpy two-mile trip to town. She tried to enjoy the hints of yellow in the foliage of the cottonwoods, elms and sycamores, elms signaling the waning of summer. Tried to look up and enjoy how intensely blue the sky was, marvel at the fat puffy clouds, but it was difficult with the nausea coming in waves.

Nervously taking her father's arm, she followed her sisters up the limestone steps up to the church. The rest of her family went in, and she and her father were to wait outside until Eva started at the piano.

For what seemed like an eternity, she stood with her father poised outside the church, the sun on her back. She felt a faint nausea ripple through her as a trickle of perspiration ran down between her breasts.

Her face was gray, dampness at her hairline already darkening her hair, and fine beads of perspiration on her forehead and above her top lip. She swayed slightly, and it occurred to him that she might faint.

"You all right?" her father asked, leaning down.

James and Laurence opened the tall oak doors of the church, and she heard Eva at the piano. She felt the gentle tug of her father toward the dark coolness of the church. She had to use the back of her bouquet holding hand to wipe the sweat off her lip.

Laurence smiled encouragingly, feeling sorry for her when he saw the bouquet jiggling madly in her hand. "Celena, stop worrying. He's here."

"Yeah and wait 'til you see him!" James said with a grin. "All slicked up with war paint and feathers!"

"*What?*" John cried, his eyes widening in horror.

"I'm kiddin' Pa. Relax." James chuckled. But the trick had worked—his joke had made his sister smile. Besides, it served his father right after what he put Victor and his sister through this last year. His father was too rigid, thinking bitterly back to all the arguments he had with his father about buying slaves. After all, James had talked with rich planters who stopped in Ste. Genevieve on their way north, he still couldn't understand why his father was so against it.

The church was full and a sudden panic swept through her. She glanced up at her father for support, clutching his hand so tightly that his fingers were turning white. She was afraid she was going to make a spectacle of herself and vomit. "Papa...I can't do this. I think I'm going to be sick."

He stopped walking. "You don't have to do this Celena. If you don't want to, if you've changed your mind, we'll turn around and march right out of here."

She knew he meant it. That he would endure the ridicule and humiliation of walking out on everyone if that was what she wanted. Her heart swelled with love for him. "Oh no Papa, that's not what I mean." She gulped. "I-I'm all right. I'm just a little shaky."

"Are you sure?" he asked, unconvinced.

She nodded, trying to force down the bile in the back of her throat.

"All right then," he said, lovingly patting her hand wrapped around his arm. "You hold onto me."

Looking down the impossibly long aisle, she saw Victor waiting for her.

She was grateful some wonderful soul had thought to open four of the slim stained-glass windows, and a warm breeze briefly revived her. All she could see was a blur of happy smiling faces, and miraculously she was at Victor's side. Letting go of her father, she clung to Victor's arm instead.

She stared steadfastly at Father Tonnellier for much-needed support, and he did not fail her. She tried to listen the sermon, tried to accept the wonderful sacrament of marriage being bestowed on her. She could see Father Tonnellier's lips moving, but could make no sense of the words because her heart was pounding so loudly in her ears. She was afraid to even turn and look at Victor, as if he was an apparition, and if examined, would vanish.

The church began to spin. She tilted forward, forcing the hideous taste of impending vomit back down her throat. Before she hit the hard marble of the communion rail Victor caught her and hauled her into his arms.

She heard a distressed intake of breath from the worried congregation

"I'm all right. You can put me down now," she forced out, trying not to vomit all over him. She hoped her pantalets were not on display to the worshipers.

"You are not," Victor whispered, rearranging his arms underneath her and turning to the concerned crowd. "She's all right everyone, I've got her." He knelt on one knee with Celena propped up on top of it like a seat.

"Yeah, having you as a groom would make any girl faint!" Will quipped, but the congregation heard him and it was a welcome relief of tension and everyone laughed nervously.

Swallowing the taste of vomit, Celena repeated her marriage vows, staring at the knot of Victors cravat.

"I Victor," his voice was strong and loud, "take thee Celena, to be my lawfully wedded wife."

When Father Tonnellier asked for the ring, he slipped an iron ring on her finger. Whispering to her then, much to the amusement of Father Tonnellier, "I forgot about the ring part, I promise I'll get you a gold one later."

"You may kiss your bride," Father Tonnellier announced.

With the vows finally said and the ring on her finger, Victor tried to kiss her. "*Lena*," he whispered, his hand forcing her chin towards him. "*Kiss me*. Everyone expects you to."

Summoning all her courage, she looked for the first time that day into the eyes of her beloved. It had been almost a year since he had kissed her, and the feel of his lips against hers was so wonderful that she poetically thought she could die happy, having felt completely loved and fulfilled by her moment on earth.

The rest of the mass, all Celena could do to steady the pounding of her heart was to stare down at colors the sunlight sifting through the stained-glass windows made on the polished floor. The host got stuck in her throat and she nearly choked trying to get it down. It seemed like an eternity as she knelt beside Victor on the hard marble floor, shaking, perspiring and sick to her stomach.

"Mass has ended, go in peace."

The cheering started, and Eva began to play the piano again

"Shall we?" Victor said, offering his arm.

She nodded, smiling up at him. Grateful to have him next to her as they began their walk through the throng of people, who stopped them frequently to kiss the bride sweetly on the cheek and shake the hand of the lucky groom.

At the Riefler farm, Victor had suddenly become Ste. Genevieve's most popular man. Everyone was congratulating him, asking him about the patent, laughingly telling him how well he had been heard. They came up to Celena too, telling her how pretty she looked, to inspect and chuckle at the iron ring, and she smiled and said: *"It's one of a kind, sort of like my groom!"* It was polished with intricate lines. She would have to ask Victor which one of his infinite tools he used to do the minute work.

Celena was grateful a half-hour later when Yvonne announced it was time for everyone to sit and eat and began ushering people to the tables.

"This is some feast," Victor said happily as he dug into the side of a roast suckling pig. There was a whole side of slowly barbecued beef the Stoddards had brought, as well as bowls of vegetable soup heavily seasoned with peas, cabbage, and onions. There was catfish fried in refined bear oil, boudin as well as German sausage and mashed and boiled potatoes, carrots, and turnips in at least four different variations. There were biscuits and fresh bread that, judging from warmth of the basket, hadn't been taken out of the oven too long ago. Celena had expected apple and cherry tarts, but the blackberry ones impressed even her especially since she knew how difficult it was to keep the pastry shells crisp.

"He's a lucky man, zis *Forgeron!*" Jean Gustave said loudly, wanting Victor to hear him, and seeing his friend looking so confined dressed up couldn't resist the temptation to tease him. *"Bon Jour* Madam Gant!" Jean said, sweeping such a low bow that Victor laughed.

"Bon Jour Monsieur Gustave," Celena said with a smile.

"As the bride, you will dance with me, mm?" Jean asked, taking Celena's hand. He bent to kiss it, but when he saw the ring, he stopped, horrified. *"Forgeron!* Such an ugly *iron* ring you give to such *une jolie femme?"* Jean said loudly, making everyone laugh.

Celena tried to pull her hand away, not wanting to hurt Victor's feelings.

Grinning with embarrassment, Victor looked down and endured the taunts of the men in the crowd.

"That man lives to annoy me," Victor laughed.

Ethan came up to one of the tables and proudly placed a bottle of champagne in the middle.

"What's this?" Don Fisk asked with surprise, pleased. He knew that if Stanfield had picked it, it was expensive.

"There's a whole crate of it over there if you need another." Straightening his shoulders, Ethan marched to the wedding table. He smiled at Victor and, with a dramatic flourish, put the bottle down. "With my compliments to the happy couple."

Celena was touched seeing yet another gift to wish them well. Innocently, her hand went to heart, trying to calm the happy pounding of it as a gentle summer wind blew the thin floating about her shoulders.

Ethan stared at her, thinking, like he had so often, that she was untouched and pure. She reminded him suddenly of Botticelli's *The Birth of Venus*. He had studied the painting in Paris, and good-naturedly argued with the art history professor. Ethan held fast to the controversial belief that Botticelli had depicted her as a symbol of both Christian and pagan love, and spent a delightful afternoon debating with the old professor. As he looked at Celena now, knew without a doubt that he was right. Because looking at her filled him with not only a sense of awe and worship, as in Christian love but also with pagan desires to have her submit to him with her body as well.

He imagined suddenly running away with her.

"Celena—" he choked out, daring to gaze deeply into her ice blue eyes. "You look...*beautiful*..." He had to shake himself once. Hoping to see a bittersweet longing for him, perhaps a tinge of regret.

He lifted his glass. "I want to propose a toast." Taking a spoon, he tapped it noisily against one of the crystal glasses borrowed from Josephine. "Everyone!" he thundered, the large amount of whiskey he'd consumed making him reckless. "To Victor, Ste. Genevieve's own inventor, my business partner, and most importantly—my friend! All the happiness in the world!" Respectfully he nodded to Victor as the happy crowd shouted their approval. "And to the ever, *ever* fair beauty Celena..." His voice cracked under the strain. Even with as much as he'd had to drink he wondered if he should stop now, before he embarrassed himself, before he made a horrible declaration. The guests were silent, all eagerly waiting for the best man, who had suddenly stopped talking, to say something. "Best of luck!" he finally said, and the crowd—having been anticipating a grander toast and a bit disappointed—went back to eating.

Ethan filled up another wine glass, smiled at something Seth Stoddard said, and then trying to go unnoticed up ended the glass, finishing it in one noisy gulp. He filled another glass and downed it, and then walked away and sat down and hung his head, but he was careful to appear normal, not wanting to attract attention to his torment.

Looking up, Ethan noticed Victor staring at him. Wanting desperately to escape, he turned to person closest to him. "You're looking beautiful today Carlene! Weddings must agree with you."

"All but my own," she said, but smiled her prettiest smile. "Thank you Ethan." She thought back to the night of the barn raising when she had tried flirting with Ethan, hoping that if the handsome bankers' son showed some interest in her it might make Eddie jealous. It seemed like a lifetime ago.

"I've yet to congratulate you on your marriage."

She sighed. "Thank you."

"I hear his law practice is growing."

"Yes. It's terribly interesting. He reads all the time," Carlene said flatly.

Ethan shook his head, feeling a little sorry for Mason. He'd never heard a bride sound so bored.

"She looks pretty doesn't she?" Carlene critiqued, watching Celena who was smiling at something Esther Charbonnier was telling her. "She looks better in blue though, I told her the white made her look sick. But Maman wouldn't listen." She leaned toward him, took the glass of wine out of his hands, and took a long drink.

"Would you like your own glass, Carlene?" he asked, surprised by her familiarity.

"No. Yours will do fine." She handed him back the empty glass.

"Hope your Papa doesn't see you."

"He can't do anything anymore, after all I'm someone's wife now." Carlene stared at her sister. "She's in for a rude awakening tonight."

Ethan laughed, a bit caught off guard by her bluntness. "Is that how all brides feel?"

"That's how I felt." She shrugged. "We're a pair, aren't we?"

Ethan flushed. "I don't know what you mean." He refilled the wine.

"Yes you do. But it's all right. I've got enough of my own troubles to keep me busy without worrying about yours." She again took the glass of wine out of his hands, took another long drink, and returned the glass to him. "Enjoy your wine." Spotting Eddie talking with Joe Kurth, hoping Mason wouldn't see, she slipped off to talk to her old beau.

When the meal was finished, Will marched over to Victor and pulled him to his feet, hauling him over to the group of drinking men.

"Victor," Laurence greeted, moving to shake his hand. "That string quartet is tuning up; better get your dancing shoes on, son! Groom's gotta dance with the bride."

"Jesus, do I have to?"

They laughed as the Charbonnier and Stoddard boys joined the group.

"*Bon jour!*" Laurence said in his horrid French, shaking the Charbonnier boys' hands.

"Nice wedding," Caleb said, slapping Victor hard on the back, "long as the tafia holds out."

"Thanks," Victor said, wincing in pain.

"Iron man." Will poured him a shot of whiskey. "One for the bridegroom and one for me." The crowd of men chuckled approvingly.

Victor protested when Will poured him a second shot, but he was met with so much heckling that to silence the rowdy bunch, he simply upended it, which unfortunately only made the rambunctious group of men howl with appreciative laughter and shouts for him to do it again.

"No," Victor said when one of the twins quickly refilled the shot glass and forced it under his nose. "You take one, Danny."

"I'm Davey! Why can no one keep us straight, hmm?" Davey said with a grin. "Like I keep saying, *Je suis le beau*; I'm the *good*-looking one!" A roar of laughter went through the rowdy group of young men as well as heated objections in French from his twin brother.

Across the yard the women began clearing away the dishes. They watched the obnoxious antics of the men, rolled their eyes, and shook their heads in loving disapproval

"My Henry better not be joining in on that foolishness," Margaret scoffed, ready to thrash her timid husband.

"Don't look now Margaret, but Henry's over there too, and he's dared Victor to take another drink," Lisette whispered. The group of women turned to see Henry with Hank cradled in one hand, taunting Victor to take another shot. Again, the obnoxious cheers from the young men. Not knowing how else to get rid of it when he found it thrust into his hand, Victor simply downed the shot to silence them.

"I'm sorry Celena, you wait 'til I get Henry home!" Margaret huffed, embarrassed Henry was part of such boorish behavior. Besides that, she wished Victor wouldn't drink so much.

"It's all right," Celena said, "they always get wild like this after weddings—funerals too. Maman says it's because they have too much pent-up energy." She watched then with disappointment as her bridegroom downed another shot from a steadily-pouring Caleb Charbonnier.

"Yes, pent up energy indeed," Josephine Chomeau said, overhearing. She smiled warmly down at Celena and took her hands. "You are possibly the most...*beautiful* bride that I've ever seen, my dear. And you did a lovely job on his suit, he looked so tall and handsome. What a lovely ceremony!" Then she heard the antics of the men behind her and was struck by the possibility that all of them would be dead drunk if they did not find a cure for their idleness soon. Yvonne and John happened on the same conclusion and wandered over to hug Celena and comment on how well everything was going.

"John, I was just about to ask our minstrels to play a little something lively, rather to get the young people dancing and on their feet."

Yvonne smiled at her in agreement. "Es a grand idea. Ze perfect time. John, would you mind?"

John walked over to the musicians, who were annoyed to be called on to play, having been greatly enjoying their blackberry tarts. When they began to play, Victor sat down in a chair, surrounded by the swearing, laughing men, prepared to watch the dancing when he saw Margaret marching towards him.

"Look out Henry! Your wife's coming," Seth warned in a low voice, which made the rest hoot with laughter.

When Henry saw that she was truly coming, he jumped up to his feet, a sleeping Hank still in his arms, frightened to death that the other men would never forgive him for letting a female cross the sacred threshold of male bonding.

"What's the matter darlin'?"

She glared. "I don't want *you* Henry," she said, but seeing the hurt look on his face quickly kissed him on the mouth, which she knew would send him into fits of embarrassment. She tugged her brother to his feet.

"It's time for the groom to dance with the bride," Margaret said, and laughingly Victor obeyed. Halfway across the yard, she let go of his hand, and he affectionately put his arm about her waist. "You look grand! You don't clean up half bad when you've got something that fits. We've come a long way, you and I," she said, embarrassed when she felt tears prick her eyes. It was painfully wonderful to have him as her blood.

"Yes, we have," he answered and the smile on his face was wistful. But it lost all trace of sadness when his eyes fell on his Celena. "Margaret says the bride and groom need to—to dance together," he stammered nervously, realizing how many neighbors were watching. Awkwardly he offered Celena his arm.

Amidst the melodic chords of the string quartet, Celena and Victor danced their first dance.

"Why are you shaking?" Victor asked her in a whisper.

"I know they mean well but...they're all...*staring* at us. Isn't there something else they could do?"

"They're all staring because they're amazed you actually *married* me. Half of them here probably had odds that you wouldn't even show!" He meant to console her with his joke but realized he failed when she buried her face flat against his chest.

"I-I don't feel good."

"Where don't you feel good, your head, your stomach?"

"My stomach. I couldn't sleep last night. I can't eat, I'm afraid I'm going to be sick." She tried to calm herself. She'd gotten through the wedding and the meal. It would all be over soon.

"Well, marrying me would be enough to upset *any* girl's stomach!" But she didn't laugh as he had intended her to do and he was at a loss. He was used to solving problems, and this one was perplexing him.

"I want to go home, Victor."

He wondered if she went in and took a nap if she might feel better and glanced in the direction of her parents' house.

"No, not here—home. *Our* home."

His heart nearly burst out his chest but before he had a chance to say anything Claude tapped him on the shoulder. "Dance with the bride?"

Celena watched Victor step back and Claude take his place. Celena did her best to smile at the well-meaning Claude. Out of the corner of her eye she noticed with relief that other couples were beginning to dance.

"You sure look pretty Miss Celena," Claude said, thinking he had never seen anyone more beautiful in his life, and she was *nice* too!

"Thank you, Claude."

"Been good to us," he said, his eyes brimming with admiration for the man he labored long hours for in the hot blacksmith shop.

"I'm glad," Celena said, annoying tears beginning to well up in her eyes, and before she knew it James had taken Claude's place.

"My turn!" James said with a big smile. "Didn't rain...good turnout... good food. Nice day." James ticked off what he considered to be the important points, and she nodded in agreement. "Old Vic is really in some trouble now. I must admit I wasn't sure he was going to make it. Lord! I thought he was going to crack under the pressure of coming to the house and still trying to court you after all that. I gotta hand it to him, he put up with some *stuff*. Pa can be an ass."

"James," Celena pleaded.

"Sorry. It makes me so mad. It's my money, Celena. He can't tell me what I can and can't buy."

"You know how he feels about slaves."

"I'm gonna do it when Alice and I are set up. In the spring."

"He still won't like it, James. Don't do it." Before she could extract a promise from her brother, Danny Charbonnier took his place. Would this dancing with the bride never end? Even though Victor danced with a few girls, somehow he had been able to stop. She saw him talking with Laurence and Lisette, watched with amusement at the way he tossed Gabe and then Nathan up in the air. The little boys squealed, delighted. Celena watched her mother come over and hug him, watched him shake hands nobly with her father.

Ethan and William called for him and she watched the most popular man in town go back to his flock! She was disappointed seeing the men were up to their antics again as they poured Victor another drink. She watched him put both hands up refusal, but it did little good because he was met with thunderous protests by the men that wanted nothing better than to see the bridegroom drunk and staggering.

"Come on! You're the bridegroom; take another," Andy Stoddard taunted, forcing the shot glass into Victor's face.

Celena was now surrounded by bustling, happy females, but her attention kept being jerked back to the loud group of drinking men.

Victor couldn't help wondering as he looked at the sun edging toward the hillside, how much longer until the reception would end, and he could finally take his young bride home. "I can't be drunk; I've got to keep my wits about me for later." A roar of laughter went up from the men, and from across the yard his eyes met hers.

Hearing Victor's words, anger rose so suddenly in Ethan's heart and he had to walk away. He knew this day was coming, had known for months. But suddenly the knowledge that sometime tonight his precious, untarnished Celena would be in Victor's callused hands crushed him.

A half-hour later the neighbors and friends reluctantly began to leave the wedding reception, and Celena couldn't have been happier! She said her obligatory thanks, breathed a quiet sigh of relief, and, feeling idle, suddenly picked up a dish to help with the cleaning.

Lisette shooed her away. "Celena, we can manage, you go on home now. You look so tired." She stopped and embraced her. Overhearing the conversation, Yvonne agreed. As she hugged her daughter she couldn't help but think she'd made a mistake by having such a large affair. It was obvious by the faint gray circles under her eyes and the strained whiteness of her face that the attention had been almost too much for Celena.

"But you all have done so much, and I haven't done *anything*," Celena said. knowing how hard everyone had worked.

"And we'd do it all over again," Margaret said to cheer her up, and then took her hand. She caught Celena looking at Victor loading the wagon with the gifts and things for them to set up housekeeping. "He's madly in love with you, you know that don't you?" Margaret asked, and it had the desired effect of making Celena smile. "And he'll be good to you. After all I know first-hand how kind he is. He was always good to me." Sensing Celena was still anxious, Margaret—a new bride herself, privy to the worries flitting through Celena's brain—whispered, "It will be all right tonight. I was scared, too. Just remember that he loves you, and it's the best way for men to show their love."

"You about loaded up?" John asked, hands in his pockets as he ambled up to Victor at the wagon. "Turned out to be a real nice day...a good day." Gently he reached for his daughter, and Celena hugged him. He kissed her on the top of the head, and then for the first time in his entire life, pulled away first. "You two best be off."

As if it had all been scripted, Victor filled the void and put his arm about her.

"Goodbye, Celena," Carlene said, leaning down to hug her, Mason standing quietly behind her.

"Come along Carlene, we should let them be on their way," he said, smiling adoringly at his wife.

With her back to him, Carlene rolled her eyes.

"We've packed up some eggs in this bundle—be careful not to crush zem," Yvonne said after placing the bundle in Ethan's wagon. She hugged both her daughter and Victor goodbye.

"See you tomorrow at church," Eva said to her little sister.

"You've all been so wonderful!" Celena exclaimed, wiping the irritating tears from her cheeks.

"Are you sure you've got everything?" Victor asked, having already loaded what wedding gifts they could fit into Ethan's wagon along with her trunk of clothes and carpetbag, gifts of food from her parents, and Luann, a good milk-cow tied to the back.

"I think so."

"Then, I guess we're off."

Victor sat on her right side, Ethan on her left. And the whole odd situation seemed vaguely familiar, but she could not put her finger on it.

Ethan took off with a jolt and she suddenly was sure she was going to retch. *Not now!* She tried to get her mind off her stomach. She looked down at her iron wedding band and closed her eyes for a moment, taking it in. But the jostling of the wagon made her eyes again fly open. She hated the way the wine she had been expected to drink was now sloshing in her queasy stomach.

And although it had not been hot, still she had been too warm all day in the heavy satin wedding dress. Even though it was cooling now as the sun began to go down, when a breeze touched her sweating skin, she shivered. Her face ached from smiling, and she was sick to death of making polite conversation, something that took a toll on her in the best of circumstances. She had a dull headache and wanted nothing more than to simply lay down in a cool, dark place and sleep.

She was squished between the two men and again felt the annoying trickles of sweat under her arms, down her back, even between her breasts. *I'll stain the dress—Eva won't be able to wear it!*

"Ethan, can't you drive any faster? I simply have to get this dress off!"

"Good Lord, what an *eager* bride you have here, Victor!" Ethan exclaimed with a thunderous laugh.

Mortified, she bit her bottom lip to keep the tears welling in her eyes from spilling down her cheeks. She was never so relieved to finally see the blacksmith shop. She bolted up and climbed clumsily out of the wagon. She was trying to be careful with the dress, not wanting to rip it as well as stain it, but had to get away from them. She grabbed her carpet bag and made for the house.

"Lena! I can get that for you," Victor called uselessly.

Darting inside she leaned against the door to regain her composure. She looked around. "It's not a bad little house at all." It was always how she had pictured it, simple like water. She noticed the pine plank floor was swept clean; the entire little house looked immaculate. Two straight-backed chairs were tidily tucked against a worn maple table, and an old rocker was shoved unused in the corner. She smiled seeing a porcelain vase that although had a chip around the mouth was filled with yellow daisies. It made tears prick her eyes knowing Victor had worked hard getting his house ready for her.

Hearing them outside and needing a refuge, she darted behind the hanging quilt that separated the sleeping quarters from the other room, and opened the carpet bag on the bed, pretending to be doing something.

"You all right?" Victor asked, a moment later startling her so badly she gasped.

"No...yes! I'm-I'm fine," she lied and then to divert the gaze of those concerned gray eyes, asked, "Have you brought it all in? I...I need my trunk, and make sure Luann gets a drink." Putting her hand against her throat, she felt her pulse hammering in her neck.

"Not yet, but we'll do it right now." He did not leave right away. "Are you sure you're all right?"

She nodded.

Sighing with relief when he left, she eyed the pitcher and washbasin in the corner and pouring a bit of water into the bowl, hungrily reached her hands into the water to wet her face, careful not to splash it on the dress.

"Here's your trunk and the rest of your things," Victor said quietly, placing her trunk near the quilt, not wanting to startle her again.

She heard Victor tell Ethan that was the last of it a few minutes later and stepped cautiously out from behind the quilt and looked out the window to see him talking with Ethan in the front yard. Since they looked to be deep in conversation, Celena decided it was safe to quickly get out of her dress. Stepping behind the quilt, she unpinned the veil and then began the arduous process of undoing the laces in the back of the dress. It was devilishly hard to do alone, and she nearly burst into frustrated tears. Finally, though she pulled it off and finding a small stool in the corner carefully laid it there. Stopping to inspect under the arms and along the waist for signs of staining and not seeing any, breathed a sigh of relief.

Pouring more water into the bowl, she rinsed her face liberally. The water was not especially cold, but felt wonderful on her dusty, sweaty face. In fact, it felt so refreshing she let the cool water drip down the front of her. Getting a washcloth from her bag, dipped it in the little bowl and quickly wiped her chest, under and along her arms.

Miraculously, the camisole was not too wet from perspiration as she stepped out of the cumbersome hoops, unhooked her boots, and took off the stiff petticoats. She had to pull the corset down and turn it to unlace the cursed thing. She took a deep breath released from the lacing and tried to decide if she should change into a fresh camisole.

It was stuffy and warm in the little house, and although a large tree shaded it, she still wished she had thought to open a window to let in fresh air.

Once again, she dipped her hands into the basin and greedily splashed water across her face and stood for a moment with her eyes closed, letting the water run down her front. She stood with the wet cloth against her chest, realizing it would get her camisole wet unable to bring herself to stop. She was letting the water cleanse away the tenseness and nervousness she had been feeling all day. She took another deep breath, relieved that the nausea was subsiding.

Opening her eyes, she saw Victor standing at the edge of the quilt, watching her. She was aware she had on only her camisole and pantalets, and the water she had so liberally splashed on her face and neck was making the thin cotton of the camisole nearly transparent.

She could feel the weight of his eyes all over her. There was an unmistakable look in them that she'd only seen once before. Now that they were married, there would be no stopping him.

"Compliments of Ethan," he said, producing a bottle of wine and two mismatched cups. He filled the cups with the dark red wine. Putting the bottle down on the convex of the trunk, Celena watched the bottle wobble.

Looking masterly down, Victor handed her the cup. "To us." Tilting his head, he downed it.

She wondered if his head throbbed with a dull ache as hers did, after all he had been drinking all afternoon. He barely waited for her to finish taking an unwanted sip and grabbing the cup from her leaned down and roughly pressed his mouth to hers. She could taste and feel the cool red wine still on his lips. He tried blindly to find the trunk but missed it in his frenzy the cup shattered when it hit the floor.

Her strangled breath caught in her throat at the sound.

But it didn't seem to matter to him, seemed almost to add to his urgency as his hands dug into the delicate chignon and pinned up curls at the back of her head. He tugged at it until it loosened, and she gave a little cry of pain as the offending pins took a few hairs with them.

She was paralyzed as she watched him unbutton his shirt and toss it carelessly to the floor. She noticed a tattoo on his chest but what caught her eye was the nasty five-inch scar near his right bicep. He'd had it, she knew, a long time; she'd caught glimpses before of the ugly twisted mark. Through the years if he'd caught her looking at it, he would cover it up with his left hand, but made no move now to shield her from the ugliness.

She looked down nervously, but his hands went up forcefully on the sides of her face, pulling her mouth up to his. The feel of her body in his arms indescribably intense to a man as starved for her as he was.

His kiss was rough, and it surprised her that something as wonderful as a kiss could hurt. She wanted to pull away but was afraid to hurt his feelings. While she worried about hurting her bridegroom's feelings, he was trying clumsily to untie the pink satin bow that closed her camisole.

"Take it off. I want to see you." His voice was hoarse and muffled in her neck.

The thought of suddenly disrobing in daylight was mortifying to her! Instead, she tried to divert him by kissing him back. But even that did not work because he was so erratic, kissing her lips then her cheeks than her forehead that she could not keep up. Frighteningly he was pushing her back on the bed, and instinctively she put her hands across her chest for protection. The weight of his body on top of her was so horrible she thought she was going to suffocate.

"Move your hands." He stopped his pawing long enough to grab both her wrists in one hand and pull them up over her head, pinning her underneath him. It was humiliating and even frightening when she realized no matter how much she struggled, she could not free her hands.

He stared wildly down at her for a moment, and then his mouth came down to hers. He shoved his tongue into her mouth and began to tug awkwardly at the satin ribbon. He ignored her muffled cry of refusal as he bent to kiss her bared breast. Taking the mound into his mouth, he sucked hard enough to make her cry out. A moment later he felt her hands frantically pulling his head up from his greedy work at her breast.

"Victor," she pleaded in a sob, wrenching his face from her breast. *"Victor stop!"*

For three heartbeats he merely stared down at her breathing heavily. He pulled up and, sitting on the edge of the bed, turned his back to her. His booted feet made a loud thud as he swung them down to the floor. He stood then and simply disappeared around the quilt.

It was horrifyingly silent in the little house. Celena sat up in bed, rearranging the camisole back where it belonged, her heart hammering in her chest.

When she heard the door open, she scrambled off the bed in search of him. A roar of rambunctious laughter arose from outside, and she jerked her hand back from the doorknob as if it were hot. Careful not to be seen, she peeked outside. Seeing the crowd of drunk neighbor men that had been lying in wait right outside the door, she burst into tears. They were hooting now, screaming with laughter at the spectacle a stunned, shirtless Victor made bounding out the door.

"Done *already* boy?" Don taunted, laughing as he sat on his horse.

Victor flushed hotly with humiliation and embarrassment.

"Got your britches done up right?" Seth asked, grinning.

Confused, Victor mistakenly looked down, which only caused the drunk bunch to laugh uproariously again.

"Was it good?" Davey asked. He wanted to be with all the other men and raze and cajole, but he was quite shy himself, and in truth wasn't particularly good at it.

"Yeah, it was damn good!" Victor lied. Summoning all his courage he forced himself to grin.

"Did you know where to put it?" teased Jean Gustave, but his good-hearted laughter after the taunt made it much less effective.

Completely mortified and not knowing what else to say, Victor merely nodded, wondering if Celena was able to hear all the off-color jokes from inside. He hoped more desperately than he hoped for anything other than being able to marry her that she could *not*.

"Well, there is more than *one* place to put it!" Eddie added obnoxiously, causing another round of laughter.

Victor watched them toss around a flask and looked down, placing his trembling hands on his hips to steady them. He listened as they insulted and joked with each other as they drank. In a way he had expected this—it was common after all to torment newly married couples. And although he desperately wanted them all to leave, knew that if he didn't appear happy and contrite, they'd stay for God knew how long and torture them.

"Hey, where's the best man?" Stephan asked, wiping whiskey from his lips.

Victor surveyed the group. Seeing no sign of Ethan or Celena's brothers, he felt relieved. He had heard before the painful way the Riefler brothers had hounded the newly married couples. In fact, Henry had told him that they'd stayed outside their house for nearly an hour until the cold finally chased them away. But it was August, and he wondered how long the obnoxious group would wait drinking and hollering outside his door. He was glad Ethan was not there, nor Celena's brothers who apparently found the teasing and ridiculing of a nervous groom not nearly as appealing when it was one's own little sister he had married.

"He's too drunk! Didn't ya see him at the party, I never saw him not with a drink in his hand! He couldn't get back up on a horse, hey you're not having that problem getting it up are ya Victor?" Eddie asked nastily.

Although another drink was the last thing in the world Victor wanted, he tilted his head back and pretended to swallow a mouthful of whiskey. "No," he said, shaking his head, "no problem there." The unpleasant memory of Celena fighting him and pulling him from her breast spun sickeningly through his mind. Again, his words were met with laughter. He forced another smile, wondering how long he would have to put up with this anguish!

They stayed talking and joking for almost an hour, and Victor did his best to appear calm and happy, when in truth he was in excruciating agony that they go. Jean, the unofficial leader and the least drunk of the group, suggested after they'd stayed what he thought was a respectable amount of time that they leave. He liked Victor and sensed his friend's quiet torment.

"Come on, *mes amis*. Let us play some billiards," he suggested and gave Victor a knowing wink.

"But your old lady, won't she be hoppin' mad?" Seth said, a bit unsteady as he sat in his saddle—he'd drank way too much, but it would not do good to let anyone know. "She won't mind. Come on. A*llons-y*." Without complaining the group began to amble along.

Victor shivered once, tucked his hands under his armpits, turned, and walked into his house. He saw Celena kneeling with her back to him at the fireplace. "What are you doing?" he asked, startling her.

"I-I was going to light it," she said, motioning to the lantern on the table. "It's getting dark," she explained unnecessarily.

"Where's the flint?"

"I-I dropped it."

He bent to retrieve it and took the tinder box from her shaking hands. He struck it once and lit the lantern. When his eyes met hers, she looked away. "All right then." Not sure what to do, sat down hard in the straight-backed chair.

She surprised him by stepping over to the door and bolting it. He noticed that from behind the quilt she had smoothed the bedcovers, and that they were invitingly turned down. And that instead of her underclothes, she had changed into a nightgown. "We've had quite a day." She forced a smile, hoping he would pick up the threads of the conversation.

He did not.

"Do you want anything to eat or to drink?"

"No. I don't want anything."

Her courage faltering, she forced another weak smile, noticed that her heart was skipping uncomfortably in her chest. "You must be tired, I-I know I am."

More dreaded silence.

"You were sure...sure out there a long time. I put some of my things away."

"Good."

Quickly running out of idle chatter, she began to wring her hands. She could tell there were hundreds of thoughts swirling around in his head, but it was clear he was not going to share them with her, and it made the little pains in her heart get stronger. "I'm—I'm sorry about earlier. It just that...it was all happening so fast and I was afraid."

He stood up, and it startled her into silence. It hurt him that everything he seemed to do—even something as simple as getting up—frightened her. He sat back down, shaking his head in disgust.

"I don't know why I was so frightened..." she stammered, still wringing her hands. "I mean, I'm your wife now and—"

"It was my fault. I didn't mean to frighten you." His eyes still on the floor, he couldn't help but think that was *all* he'd ever done. "It's just, it's just that..." Thinking better of it, he did not finish. She looked more beautiful to him now than she had when he first caught sight of her walking toward him in the church today. He was glad she had taken the rest of the pins out of her hair, and couldn't help but notice the nightgown was so thin he could see the outline of her body. He felt a stiffening in his groin. But when she caught him looking at her, she wrapped her arms in front of her self-consciously.

"It's...what?" After all, she was *trying* to make amends. She had put on the nightgown, cleaned up the smashed cup, turned down the bed-covers, and apologized.

His eyes met hers. "You're my wife. I want you, Celena."

She racked her brain to think of something appropriate to say. Words that would explain the complexity and depths of her feelings. She loved him, and despite her naiveté they were married and now and she expected to be a wife to him. But she expected being in his arms to feel like it had the night of the harvest.

He must have somehow understood her fears because he got up from the chair and came gently to her placing his hands lightly on her shoulders. "Let's start over." Leaning down, he kissed her softly, sweetly.

She closed her eyes, enjoying the feel of his arms around her. She put her arms around his neck and daringly opened her mouth to him. She could feel the heat from his body building, felt his chest moving against her, felt the shocking, immediate hardness at his groin. And although she had just finished telling him that she wanted to be a wife to him, at the same time was afraid of the things she imagined, and realized they were already at the terrifying threshold again. How did it *happen* to men so fast?

"I'm...I'm afraid!" she cried, breaking free from his kiss.

This time he refused to let go of her. "No, no, no, no, no. No, you're not. You're not afraid of me. What am I, a foot and half taller and outweigh you by what...130 pounds, how could you possibly be afraid of *me*?" Seeing she was still not convinced, he whispered, "Celena, you love me." He leaned down to kiss her. "*You love me.*"

"I'm...I'm not ready!" she cried, pulling back from him yet again, her hands flat against his chest.

He couldn't help but laugh knowing how much stronger he was. "Yes, you are."

"Can't we wait?"

"Nope." He slipped his arms underneath her and carried her to the bed. "We're married. I'm your husband, it's time now."

"But I'm afraid!"

"Then let's get over with so you can stop *fearing* it!"

Despite everything she laughed because it made sense. He smiled at her underneath him on the bed. The black hair falling forward into his eyes. The dark chest was smooth, but she could see the pack of dense muscles underneath and wondered with a catch in her throat if someone as big and strong as he was, was even capable of physical tenderness.

She turned away, embarrassed when she realized he was tugging off his boots and slipping off his trousers. He slipped into bed next to her.

"I-I don't know what to do," she whispered, feeling totally unprepared for what was now expected of her.

"I don't either. But I'm certainly willing to figure it out." His mouth came down on hers, and he gently slipped his hand inside the loosened drawstring. A minute later his lips traveled down to her neck and her throat. And then, shocking her, he kissed her on her breast. Tugging impatiently at the drawstring until the bow unraveled and he pulled the gathering apart, the cool air on her breasts made her shiver.

"You have no idea how much I *want* you," he whispered, and then pulled up to look at her, feasting his eyes on what he had wanted for so long. Tracing his rough hands up and down the tender underside of her arms, gently over the curve of her shoulders, lightly touching over and around each breast and down to her ribs. "Take it off...please," he whispered, pushing the nightgown out of the way.

"I'd rather not, if you don't mind."

"Why? And I *do* mind."

"Because." She bit her bottom lip.

"Because why? Because you're embarrassed of that gorgeous body in front of me?" He laughed when her eyes widened with embarrassment. "Shall I rip it off you then?"

"Don't you dare! I spent a week embroidering it with cross stitches."

"Yes, it's pretty, but I'd rather see what's underneath."

Swallowing hard, she forced a nervous smile. "It was a lovely wedding, wasn't it?"

"Nice try. You're stalling. It's not going to work." He let his wandering hand travel down to her leg and massage her calf.

"It's not?" she asked weakly, feeling the warmth of his lips against her neck.

He smelled lavender in her hair, but realized the wilted curls were stiff. "What's in your hair?"

"Olive oil and wax."

"What, why?" he asked, amused, touching the firm curls.

"My mother and sisters decided to curl my hair for the wedding."

His brows furrowed in concentration. "How on earth do they do that?"

"First you melt the wax, add some olive oil, and lavender water so it smells nice. Then they take small sections of hair and wipe the mixture down it, then wind each section of hair around a hot rod from the coals."

"Really?" Victor tried not to laugh. He had no idea women had to go through such trouble for fashion. "Well, it smells nice," he said, resting his face in the fragrant hair. He had a hand on her plump, bare calf.

"What should I do now?" she whispered suddenly.

"Stop talking for one thing."

"I'll be quiet."

He beamed down at her in amusement. "You don't have to be *quiet*; I just don't want to hear talking anymore."

Her brows creased in confusion. "Then what do you expect to hear?"

"Sighing, moaning, panting. Begging would be nice."

Her eyes widened again in shock.

He chuckled. "Yes, I know I'm a vile, wretched, sex-obsessed beast! But I'm also your husband and you're stuck with me." He kissed her.

Trying to relax, she let him do what he wanted while bracing herself for what was going to happen next. She had no idea what to expect but hadn't expected the hand that had been on her calf to be rapidly moving up her thigh.

He was pushing the nightgown up out of the way and she feared that at any moment she would be exposed *there* as well! When she struggled to protest, he shoved her back on the bed.

"Don't *fight* me!" He still had one hand between her thighs that she had at first touch clamped firmly shut around him, but he didn't care, and rather liked the thought of his hand snuggly encased by her firm white thighs. He inched the hand upward and her whole body jolted.

"*Don't do that!*" she gasped in embarrassed horror.

"Why not?"

"I-I don't think you're supposed to."

"According to who?"

When she could come up with no reply, he continued.

"*Let me!*" he barked, exasperated a moment later when he felt her trying to pull his hand from her body. He stared down at her, breathing heavily, trying to decide what to do. "Let's think of this logically. There's no way you can stop me, I am way stronger than you. Chances are it'll all go better if you *don't* fight me." He hung his head in frustration. "Please Lena...*please* let me touch you. Let me do what I want. I will try my best not to hurt you, but struggling will only make it worse."

He was worried—he had heard the stories about virgins and pain, and wanted to spare her as much discomfort as he could, but never having been with a woman, was not sure how to do that. Ethan had told him about many of his escapades with women and how if they were properly '*primed*' by a man's hand, they were more '*receptive*' to being bedded.

Nearly mad with desire, he hoped he had done a good enough job of readying her, and tried clumsily to guide himself in. She felt something brush against her bare stomach, was too mortified to look, and suddenly wanted to just get it over with. She felt him bump her low on her stomach, then on her thigh. It was dreadful waiting for him to get it right while he stabbed about her. She grabbed him and he nearly leapt off the bed.

"What are you *doing?*" he exclaimed, horror mingled with pleasure.

"Here...I think," she whispered, her eyes frighteningly slammed shut.

He had no trouble then following her lead, and did his best to ease into her, and for a moment did not move. His eyes nearly crossed with frenzied lust at being at long last inside her.

It felt so huge she was afraid she was going to split apart and thought there must be something terribly wrong. When he began to thrust himself against her, she felt such a horrible stab of pain and instinctively tried to push him off.

"Lena I'm sorry!" he burst out, but knew he couldn't stop now, and reaching down tried to pull her legs apart a bit. "Open for me!" he begged, hoping that would ease her pain.

The weight of his body was pinning her to the bed, and his chest against hers painfully flattened her breasts. The agonizing feeling of being pried apart and having her internal organs shoved up into her body was almost too much to take.

"I don't think this is right!" She felt warm tears somehow slip past her tightly shut eyelids. "It hurts! Victor, it hurts!"

He felt her small body shuddering with pain. "I won't move. Let yourself get used to me." He desperately hoped he could stop himself long enough for her to be able to accept him. A moment later her tear-filled eyes opened, and he leaned to kiss the salty tears off her cheeks. "You all right?"

When she nodded, he began to move slowly, realizing as he did so that it was the most intense pleasure he had ever, ever felt in his life. He stared down lovingly at the angel underneath him who was pleasing him physically and emotionally more than he ever dreamed possible. Ducking his head down he kissed her madly. A breathless burning intensity building in him so powerfully that he wondered if there was anything better in the world than being with this woman.

He gasped, realizing he couldn't stop any longer, and hated himself when he felt her crying underneath him. He put his hands on the side of her face and turned her up to him.

"Lena, you *love* me!" he pleaded, confused as to why he could still feel pleasure when he knew he was hurting her. "You...*love* me!" he repeated in a tortured voice into her parted mouth, wondering why he was stating the obvious when *he* was the one that needed and wanted to make such a declaration.

"Yes, I love you." Even as naive as she was, she knew she was pleasing him, and even in the wake of her pain it made her proud. She was glad to please him as no one else ever had before and as no one else ever would again. Relaxing a bit, she wrapped her arms as far as they would go around his broad back. He did look wonderful looming over her! His sleek muscled body above hers, the taut smooth skin of his dark chest, the gray eyes with a look in them that she alone had put there.

The sweet warmth of her young body underneath him was too much for him. He knew suddenly no matter how many times he made love to her over the years, he would always remember how she had accepted him and given him the greatest gift she could.

It was with these powerful feelings of absolute love that he had always felt for her that he realized with a pounding in his heart that something was happening to him. It shocked him with its blinding intensity, almost with its rage, and jolted his body. It was as if the strength of his entire body had simply flowed out of him.

Relieved it was over, she tried to move him enough so she could breathe. Her movements roused him, and he slid slightly to the side of her, resting part of his large body against the bed, knowing his weight was too much for her. She could still feel the pounding of his heart against her own chest, and it was curious to her how his body was shaking, and leaning in she gently kissed him.

He opened his eyes slowly and smiled at her in exhaustion. Trying to settle the wild pounding of his heart, tried to remember simply how to get air in his lungs and to breathe.

"You're trembling," she whispered, hoping nothing was the matter with him.

"I'll be all right." Summoning what energy he had left, he pulled himself off her.

Although it was a relief of pressure when he moved, she was cold now without him covering her.

"*Jesus!*" he exclaimed with a weak laugh. "If I'd known it was going to be *this* good, I *would* have run off with you!"

"Don't swear, Victor."

Leaning on an elbow, he grinned so devilishly at her that she blushed. He kissed her noisily on the cheek and then went about the business of adjusting the covers over them, sighing with contentment.

She was suddenly more tired that she had ever been in her life, and closed her eyes.

With the pounding of his heart lessening, he turned and gazed at the perfect face next to him on the pillow. Noticing that her lashes tilted up at the ends. Noticing how delicate her cheekbones looked under her flawless skin. "My God you're beautiful," he whispered, then smirked at his bad timing. One of the few times he had worked up the courage to *say* such a thing and she was asleep. "And what by the grace of God did I ever do to deserve this?" He watched her quiet breathing. "I'm a plain, ordinary man. I'm not worthy of your love. But I promise you. I promise you on my life and on my death, that I'll honor you, take care of you...and love you." He marveled at the straight perfect nose, the smooth unlined forehead. "And I've always loved you." His thoughts wandered back to the morning he watched his mother slip from his life. Remembered that as a little girl Celena had comforted him. He leaned in and lightly kissed his bride, his very own sleeping beauty, and contently drifted off to sleep.

Celena was not sure how long she dozed but knew it couldn't have been awfully long because it was not completely dark yet, and the birds were still calling goodnight to one another with their songs. He was laying so close to her that even turning her head on the pillow woke him.

"Well, hello there," he said, grinning anew.

Nervously she smiled back. She was shy since she only had on her thin nightgown, and he was naked with his warm thighs pressed right next to her. It hadn't seemed so embarrassing earlier when they had both been so caught up in the moment, but now she felt modesty overcoming her.

"Feeling okay?" he asked, rolling onto her as lightly as a man who weighed well over 230 pounds was able to do. He smiled at her underneath him, ridiculously happy to have her in his life, in his house, in his bed.

She nodded.

At first his mouth was gentle on hers, but it did not take long for him to become aroused again. She felt not only the hardness down by her hips, but his movement against her. A stab of anguish went through her, realizing he wanted her again.

"I'm glad," he said, propping himself up on an elbow to gently trace the curve of her cheek with his fingertip. She would have enjoyed the closeness, the gentle touching, if she did not know that he was aroused and what to painfully expect. The kissing felt like it had the night of the harvest and she tried to let herself float off on the cloud that lifted her up whenever he kissed her. But she knew what was coming and it was a shame she thought that she would be so brutally hurtled from her celestial perch down to the earth.

"You're so soft," he whispered, trailing his callused hand across her smooth shoulders, marveling at all the gentle curves and slopes on her body. "There's nothing sharp on you, everything is rounded," he mused, his hand traveling up to her slender throat that he had no trouble gripping neatly in one hand. "And curved," he continued, his hand sliding up from her throat briefly brushed her chin, and he bent then and kissed the little spot under her eye as his hand traveled back slowly down to her neck. He touched her shoulder and then ever so lightly down to her breasts. But when she shivered suddenly under his touch he stopped. "Do you not like them on you, are they too rough?"

"No," she breathed, her skin tingling wonderfully under the caress of those rough calloused hands. It also amazed her how remarkably light his touch could be. "I mean, I don't mind."

"I used to wonder—" he began, his hand tracing gently down her inner arm. "If any woman would want my hands on them."

"That's something you needn't worry about anymore, at least not with *this* woman!"

"You know I mean you."

"Do I?" She smiled up at him

"It's always been you." He kissed her, and his hand softly trailed down her breasts, nearer her ribs, and as if to illustrate how much she loved him, she arched her back in response, wanting to be touched. Gently his hands slid down and caressed the indentation of each rib.

"Put your hands on me," he whispered, looking down at her, his hair falling into his eyes. Taking both of her hands, he kissed the palms and then laid them against his chest.

They looked unusually white, she thought, *against his dark chest*. Shyly she trailed her hand across his chest, and for the first time allowed herself to look at his body. Everybody in town joked about size of his arms. Her brothers always referred to them as 'hams.' She slid her hand across the uneven terrain of his chest, felt how smooth the dark skin was, felt the mass of densely packed muscle nestled next to bone. She smiled impishly realizing he was as hard as she was soft.

"You don't have any hair on your chest."

His eyes widened, and he glanced down regretfully. "I've got hair," he began, searching his body for something pleasingly hairy. "*Other* places."

The mortification and shock in her eyes made him laugh out loud. "Come here you!" He nipped three kisses on her mouth. "Any other comments you'd like to make?" he teased, his eyes radiating happiness.

"You are—"

"Yes?"

"Sort of...heavy."

"That's it!" Before she knew it, he had taken her by the shoulders and rolled her to the opposite side of the bed, and suddenly she found herself on top of him. And if all of this was not enough to shock and bewilder her, his hands were happily planted on her bottom, pulling her full against him. "Not too heavy now, eh?" he asked, grinning madly at her.

"Victor...please!" she wailed, flushing with embarrassment as she tried to shake the long hair from her face, mortified at the thought of her breasts exposed and heavy against his bare chest.

He shrugged and instantly she was on her back. "Makes no difference to me," he said with a laugh of man going quite happily insane. "I'll take it any way I can get it!" and his mouth dropped to her breast.

"Do you have to do that?" she asked weakly, trying to reconcile herself to the improper suckling of a grown man at her breast, and realized with a flush of something like shame that what he was doing had a most curious effect on her heart rate and breathing. Involuntarily she felt herself lifting towards his mouth not wanting him to stop, but thinking she should command him to do so.

"Yes. It excites me."

A few blissful moments later he was fumbling below, and she felt again the unmistakable shock as he entered her. She slammed her eyes shut, waiting for the hideous stab of pain, and although he still felt uncomfortably large for her body and foreign to it, to her relief, the intense discomfort did not come.

"You all right?" he asked, noticing that she was rigid as a board underneath him.

As she looked up at him in the growing darkness, she realized with a catch in her throat that from the way he trembled and moaned, he enjoyed this lovemaking. *I'll just learn to live with it.* She reached up and touched his smooth chest, liking the way the muscles flexed and moved under the tight skin. She glanced over at the arms heavy with muscles, propped up on either side of her as he thrusted with his hips. They were powerful arms, and yet she knew he was trying to be gentle with her.

He collapsed a few minutes later in a sweating heap, and with nearly superhuman effort pulled himself out of her warmth and landed with a thump next to her. He concentrated on breathing, and looked over at her.

"It rather...takes a lot out of you!" he explained to his bride. He sighed then with contentment and closed his eyes in sated fatigue. "I don't know why you women aren't ruling the world with that a...well...you know what I mean."

She giggled. "Do you mean that I have you in my powers?"

"Yes." He felt her move away from him and sit on the edge of the bed. Cracking an eye open, he was amused to see her modestly retying her nightgown.

"Makes you sleepy...makes me hungry!" She leaned over him to rearrange the covers.

"Makes me hungry too!" He reached for one of her breasts dangling enticingly above him.

She slapped his hand away. "For food!" She hopped lightly off the bed.

He heard her footsteps, saw the room grow light through his closed eyelids as she turned up the lantern. Hearing her moving pans and dishes, he forced himself to get up.

"What are we having?" he asked, coming around the quilt. He had put his trousers back on but hadn't bothered with the shirt. His long hair was tousled and made him look like he had been tumbling around in bed, which of course he had.

She smiled. "Breakfast." She felt suddenly like a child at play and not a married woman in her own home. It was now their little house after all, and she rather liked the idea of being the wife and in charge. She placed a pan on the gridiron in the fireplace and knelt to get the flint.

"I'll get it." Jumping up to help, he filled the small hearth with dry wood. He added another log and held it place a minute with a poker and watched as the small sparks flew and the flames jumped up to engulf it.

She smiled, noticing the lopsided andirons in the fireplace. "Did you make those?"

"Yes. It was the first time I twisted iron. Jonah said they were hideous and not fit even for horseshoes."

"Is it hard to do?" She loved the feeling of being able to ask him about anything.

"Not anymore. But it was then."

He sat down at the table and watched her place brioche in tongs to warm in the fire. Watched her deftly crack the eggs with one hand. She then whipped them quickly with the cream from Luann. He let the wonderful smell of bacon grease and simmering omelet fill his senses. She asked him occasionally where something was, but in truth the little cupboard hid so little, she didn't have trouble finding things. She poured him a tall glass of water as the omelet puffed in the pan.

The excruciatingly wonderful thought occurred to him that at any moment he could pull her into his arms, kiss her and make love to her. No more courting, no more watchful eyes, no more God-awful waiting.

"Aren't these pretty?" she asked, carefully setting the table with the new dishes from Josephine.

He had been so mesmerized watching her, he hadn't even noticed them. "Yes, yes they are," he murmured, forcing himself to at least glance down at the plates.

"And these are from Margaret," she said, carefully placing a napkin under the fork and knife precisely laid at the table.

Looking down, he saw embroidered napkins, a blue and green cross stitch pattern with yellow flowers. "Very nice." He grinned, not looking at the napkins, but rather at his wife's lithe form through the thin nightgown.

She slid the perfectly crisped omelet out of the heavy iron skillet and onto the plates. She snatched the brioche before it burned and placed the large chunk of butter along with a pitcher of water on the table. She sat then and smiled across the table at the man that was now her husband.

He knew he was grinning like a madman, but frankly did not care. But when he began to devour his omelet, the gaze from her blue eyes stopped him. He then folded his hands in prayer like she had done.

"Thank you, Lord, for this food, and this our wonderful wedding day. Amen!"

"Amen." He dug hungrily into his food. "Good," he mumbled, thinking that he was the luckiest man that had *ever* walked the earth.

She smiled her thanks to him, glancing casually around the house.

"Did you find a place to-to put all your things?" he stammered, still not believing that she would stay there with him that night and every night for the rest of his life.

"Did there used to be an armoire?"

His spirits sank a fraction. "Yes, but I gave it to Margaret and Henry." He decided he'd build her or buy her a new one immediately.

"Oh no bother, I can put my clothes in a chest of drawers," she offered agreeably, but looking around realized there wasn't one of those either. "Victor, where do you put your clothes?"

"I've two baskets...one for clean and one for dirty." He nervously wished he had asked Margaret more than he had about the peculiarities of women.

"And Margaret came and picked them up once a week—yes, I know!"

She smiled broadly at him. "Well, she won't need to do that anymore now that I'm here." Standing up then, she pushed part of her omelet and half a piece of brioche onto his plate, and he glanced at her with surprise. "I'm full, besides, I've seen you eat. I know how hungry you always are." She planted a kiss on his cheek.

He ate his food and the rest of hers and watched as she collected the plates and pan for washing. She reached under the sink board for the rinse bucket and then stood up placing her hands on her hips. "No bucket?" she asked, brushing away the sticky cobwebs

He shrugged lamely.

"It's obvious that this house has not had a *woman* in it for a long time."

He brought his glass to her at the sink board and placed his hands neatly around her waist. "No, it hasn't." His thumbs inched up to brush the bottom of her breasts.

"How am I supposed to earn my keep?" she asked, having to tilt her head back to keep her eyes on him as he neared her.

"Oh, believe me, you *earn* your keep, with or without doing chores!" He laughed then seeing the violent red staining her cheeks. "Come on, let me show you a few things." He took her hand and cautiously pulled her outside, anxiously looking around hoping no more "friends" were lying in wait to ambush him!

It was dark and she giggled, realizing she still had on her nightgown. Looking around, she saw that all was quiet and shrugged, deciding to add it to the day's list of things she had never done before!

He showed her where he kept the wood for the house, and that it was *not* to be confused with the wood for the shop. Seasoned oak was his favorite to use in the forge-but she was informed that other hardwoods *would* do. He made it perfectly clear that nothing was to be tidied up inside or outside the shop. He assured her that all the haphazard pieces of metal stacked outside would be used.

He showed her how the pump at the well was temperamental at times, but if coaxed, would work. He showed her the barn, and the only horse he had, Alpha, and where he kept the oats, wagon, tackle. They gently patted Luann and made sure she had enough water, and talked about that it was a good thing they already had a fence around the part of the land they had for her to graze.

They walked away from the barn, and he showed her where Jonah's wife Hilde was always going to put in a vegetable garden. He let go of her hand finally in the darkness and knelt. Sensing his sadness suddenly she knelt next to him as he touched the untilled earth.

"I never even knew her, but Jonah talked about her all the time. In the beginning I half expected her to walk into the shop one day and give me one of those damn spritz cookies he always talked about. Anyway, Jonah never started the garden, and Margaret had a small one closer to the house, but it was too shady, and didn't do well." They stood up then and she reached for his hand. He couldn't help but miss Jonah, miss his mother, miss the people that had cared about him. He hoped if they were looking down, they would be proud of the man he'd turned into.

"Will you till it for me? I'd like to put in a garden."

"You'd want that?"

"I'm a farm girl after all. I'm used to tending a big garden full of all sorts of things, besides, when the babies start being born, we'll need all sorts of things to feed them once they've cut a few teeth. And we can't let good ground go to waste."

At the wonderful mention of babies and their future, he pulled her to him and kissed the top of her head. "How big do you want it?"

"Big."

"My mother had a garden, I used to weed it with her. I wonder sometimes where she is," he mused, looking up at the crescent moon and star-studded sky.

Celena reached up to gently touch the face of the man she was desperately in love with. "She's in heaven, don't you suppose?"

He took her hand and, turning it palm up, kissed it. "Is she?"

"Of course."

"I wish I could be so sure. Life, death, the afterlife, I've always felt the lines between them were rather blurred." A warm wind crossed over him, and he breathed in deeply the smell of late summer. "I swear sometimes, I can almost *feel* her."

"What do you mean?"

"I don't know. I can't explain it. She's not here, but she's not gone. And I've tried for years. You know I've tried. You see me there every Sunday on my knees in that church, but I don't *feel* anything in there. I feel it...out *here*." He glanced at the dark sky, hoping he was not shocking his Catholic wife.

"At least you feel it."

He looked at her, puzzled. "Don't you with all those rosaries you do?"

"I feel better after I've done them. Better like I feel after I've taken down all the wash and folded it. It's like a chore, that I feel guilty if I don't do. I asked Father Tonnellier about it once."

"Did he have an answer for you?"

"No, but he was kind."

Victor chuckled. "He and I have had many discussions through the years about what the Osage believe."

"What do the Osage believe?"

He shrugged. "In a lot of the same things you do. They believe in an overall creator, a sustainer of the Universe. Wah-Kon-Tah created the world to function in peace and harmony. Things that you and I take for granted, like the sunrise, was an event to the Osage. My mother used to sit on the ground and chant waiting for the rising of the sun." But he had to look away then remembering one of the last times he heard her dawn chant, she got her face bloodied having done it.

"Doesn't sound so bad."

"It isn't. The Osage live close to the earth, and everything they do has a symbolic place in the world around them. They plant and hunt, killing only what they need. They are monogamous and for the most part stay married for life. Children are coddled and nurtured, I know Margaret and I were. And although they are warlike and have a terrible reputation for stealing horses, a lot of the times instead of killing each other they were proving their bravery by touching their enemy, counting coup." He wrapped his arms around her. "I mean, there are things I disagree with Catholicism-like what you talked about and the whole welling up of guilt! But at the same time the Osage have a few traditions I'm at odds with."

"Like what?"

"Well...for instance when an Osage chief dies an enemy scalp is necessary for their mourning ceremony."

He laughed when her eyes widened in horror. "Do you realize that if we were Osage we would have been able to be married in four days?"

"I would have liked that."

"Me too."

"Did I tell you Father Tonnellier came over to the house to talk to me before the wedding?"

"Was he trying to prepare you for life with a savage?"

"No, of course not. You know how fond he is of you, even if he does refer to you as a reluctant Catholic"

That made him laugh. "I've told him more than once I'm an Osage Catholic. He doesn't like it much."

"I think he was worried about our children..." She couldn't finish.

"That our children would be raised to worship Wah-Kon-Tah rather than Jesus Christ?"

She nodded shyly.

"Typical priest! Worrying about the devotedness of his congregation before they're even *born!*" It was amusement in his voice, not anger. "Of course we'll raise them Catholic, although I hope you don't mind if I tell them some of the things the Osage believe."

"Not at all. What could possibly be wrong with teaching children to love and respect the earth?"

"I-I hope I can make you happy," he stammered.

"You already have."

"It's easy to be happy in the beginning when things are...new. But...I mean, through the years, when I'm old and gray and the house is bulging at the seams with children. You know...later...for always."

She kissed him and when she let him go, he was panting.

"We...um, better go back in the house." Reaching down, he adjusted his groin.

"Would you carry me over the threshold?"

He frowned. "But you've already been in."

"Would you do it anyway? It is my wedding night."

Grinning, he picked her up, amazed at how little there was of her.

"It's true what my brothers said about you."

"What did they say about me?" he asked warily as he walked to the house, knowing that the multitude of nicknames he'd been called at the shop were not fit for female ears.

"That you are strong."

He scowled, fumbling to open the door. "This is no test of strength." Once inside he kicked the door shut. "You don't weigh anything. What's this supposed to mean anyway, this carrying over the threshold?"

"What if I was pregnant?"

"You can't be pregnant already," he scoffed, laying her on the bed.

She looked up at him, her eyes wide. "Can't I?"

"Well...I mean...you're *probably* not, anyway," he said, shivering with anticipation with the wonderful thing he got to do to get her pregnant.

Seeing that he was undressing, she turned away shyly. "They used to carry the brides over the threshold because stumbling was thought to be a bad omen. Still others think the practice comes from the custom of marriage by capture."

"*Capture?*"

She nodded. "I imagine a good deal of them weren't happy with their abductors."

"Kicking and screaming were they?"

She laughed.

"Well, I didn't stumble, and you weren't kicking or screaming."

"No, I came willingly." She smiled.

He realized it would be a perfect time to tell her how much he loved her, imagined himself saying something memorable and poetic. But before he screwed up his courage she kissed him, chasing all thoughts of talking out of his head.

Chapter 15

Victor was not even fully awake and felt a stiffening in his groin. He had woken like that many times before but had never been able to do much about it. He wanted Celena underneath him again, wanted her soft breath in his ear.

Reaching, he found an empty bed.

He heard a kettle being placed in the fireplace and, bolting upright, swiped the quilt from out of his view and saw her kneeling to put more wood in the hearth.

Grabbing the sheet, he hastily wrapped it around himself and coming up behind her grabbed her by the waist and kissed her neck.

"I thought you—I thought maybe I'd been—" Feeling like a fool, he blurted out, "When I go to sleep with you, I expect to wake up with you!" Sighing, he pulled out a chair and sat. He patted his sheeted lap. "Come here. Have a seat."

"*Victor!* It's daylight, and Sunday after all, what would people say?"

"What's Sunday got to do with it? Besides ,you're in your own house, with your own husband who wants you to come sit on his lap, now come here."

She was embarrassed to tell him how sore she was and gingerly stepped near him. Though she knew he was quick, he surprised her with his agility, pulling her onto his lap. He had his lips on her before she had a chance to speak.

"I got the pump to work...I milked Luann..." she said between kisses, "and I've almost got your breakfast ready."

He nipped a kiss on her nose. "Oh good, breakfast *again!*"

She knocked him teasingly in the ribs.

"Oh! I like it when you touch me there, do it again!" He held her hand against his bare middle and laughed when she could not move her hand.

"Good heavens Victor, you're a beast!"

Letting go of her, he shrugged, seeing nothing wrong with his behavior. "Let me put some clothes on so I can eat with you like I am civilized." He planted three quick kisses on her lips. Setting her on her feet, he chuckled, looking down at her. "You are a *little* thing."

She placed her hands on her waist, staring up at him defiantly. "I am not *little*. I'm a grown, married woman, thank you."

Chuckling, he went behind the quilt to dress. He glanced down at the bed where he had so happily had his way with her, and noticed a dark stain on the sheets. Upon closer examination, he realized it was dried blood. He had heard about virgins and bleeding, but never expected to see the crimson symbol of lost innocence so cruelly displayed on his bed. He realized he had physically hurt her; that in his frenzied, selfish lust, he had ripped through her. He walked silently around the quilt, his neck bent.

"If you sit and eat now I might have time to get the dishes washed before church." She stopped when she saw the look on his face.

"Are you all right?"

She stared at him in confusion, a pitcher of water in her hand. "Yes, of course I'm all right. Why wouldn't I be?"

"There's blood on the bed." He hung his head. "It's certainly not mine."

"Oh," she said quietly, and dropped her eyes with embarrassment to the floor. Noiselessly she put the pitcher on the table and smoothed back her hair. "I think I can get it out of the sheets."

He jerked his head up. "I don't care about the *God damn* sheets!"

"Don't swear."

"Then don't act ridiculous! Like I give a shit about—"

"Why are you swearing at me?"

"I'm not!"

"You are!" she said, her eyes filling with tears.

"I'm not worried about the *damn sheets!*" he yelled. "Lena—I'm sorry, I don't mean to swear at you—"

"Then don't! Don't you think I'm embarrassed enough by all of this without you..." Mortified, she looked down.

He had to bend to look her in the eyes. "I only brought it up because I saw it on the bed, and I was worried about you. I feel like some sort of...*monster*. I-I didn't mean to *hurt* you like that. Oh, Jesus, come here!" He pulled her into his arms.

"I need a handkerchief."

"Use my shirt."

Despite everything she laughed. "Are you sure?"

"It's the least I can do for you," he said with a smile, feeling her tears dampening his chest. "Especially after what you've done for me."

She sniffed and wiped her face again. "It's nothing special Victor, I mean I'm not unique, this happens to every woman. It's nature after all. I'll bleed once a month you know, and I'll bleed way more than last night when I give birth to our children." She could hardly believe she admitted all that to him.

He shook his head, rattled by the mechanics of her body. "I think I'm glad I'm not a woman."

She smiled. "I'm glad you're not too."

"Are you sure you're all right?"

"Yes. It hurt less each time."

"And there were a lot of times," he murmured, having lost count sometime during the night.

Nestling against him, she couldn't help but wonder if *all* new husbands woke in the morning worried about their brides. Feeling the thumping of his heart next to her, she didn't think so.

Later that morning as they made their way into church, Celena couldn't stop smiling. Everyone was coming up to her, hugging her, congratulating them on their marriage, and talking about the wedding. It was easy to smile at them and answer all the women's squeals of *"How are you this morning Celena? We had a wonderful time at the wedding!"* Because she was simply happy. As she stood to begin the opening hymnal, she felt an all-encompassing wave of love. Love for her family, love for her friends, love for Victor.

She happily took her place next to Victor even though in the back she couldn't see a thing! She felt sweet tears in her eyes as he fumbled trying to find her hand, and when he did, held it for the remainder of the mass. He only let go when they had to kneel or make the sign of the cross—and each time his hand would quietly seek hers again.

Although she couldn't see Father Tonnellier, she listened intently to his sermon. On her knees in the pew after Communion she closed her eyes and, wanting to thank God for blessing her, said four Hail Mary's by the time Father Tonnellier resumed the mass.

"Celena," Yvonne said as they left the church.

"Good morning Maman."

Lovingly Yvonne gathered Celena in her arms, closing her eyes for a moment as she held her daughter. "How are you?" she whispered.

When Celena pulled away Yvonne saw that Celena's eyes were sparkling with happiness. "I'm fine Maman. I'm just fine."

"Morning Celena," Eva said and hugged her sister, missing her already. The three of them walked arm and arm down the steps until she saw her father.

"Papa." Celena folded herself against him.

John was glad to see his daughter. He knew deep in his heart everything was all right, but just the same he was glad to see the same sweet face smile back at him when he had caught her eye in church. Relieved to see that they were the same light eyes that had mesmerized him as they had done when he'd held her as a baby in his arms moments after her birth and were still mesmerizing him to this day.

"Good morning Victor!" Laurence said with a grin so broad that Victor could not help but grin back. Nathan and Gabe, hanging on to his hands, also smiled up at their 'new' uncle.

Will and James joined them along with the Stoddards and a severely hung-over Davey and Danny Charbonnier. As Victor listened to them talk about what a wonderful time they all had at the wedding, he scanned the thinning groups of people for Ethan. Even though Ethan was not Catholic, he always made a habit of milling around when mass was over to visit.

He felt hands on his sleeve and was delighted to see Celena had wandered back over to him

"Victor, would you mind if I went to my parents' for the day? There's still cleaning up to do, and no one would let me lift a finger yesterday, and they've all be so kind and worked so hard, and I want to help. Besides I've the rest of the gifts to get. Will said he could bring me home later in time to cook supper if it's all right. That is, I'd be grateful?"

He wondered madly what excuse he could come up with, wondered what he could fabricate to prevent her going. It was not that he minded she go to her parents, he just wished he could find a reason to get her back to the house, wanting only to kiss her goodbye properly.

"That'd be fine. Do you want me to go too, and help with all the cleanup?" he asked hopefully but noticed that her parents and Eva were already waiting patiently in the wagon.

She shook her head, knowing that her parents would never have said no to Victor accompanying her, but that they wanted her to themselves.

"No, but thank you for the offer." She flashed him a thankful smile and leaned up to hug his solid chest. Making good on the opportunity he whispered, "You'll show me later how *grateful* you are?"

Her cheeks flushed hotly.

Letting go of her, he smiled at Yvonne as Celena walked toward their wagon, and waved goodbye as they drove off.

Margaret came up alongside him, and instinctively Victor reached out to hold his nephew.

"Is that Celena?" Margaret asked in surprise.

"Yes, it is. She's going to her parents' for the day. Seems they already miss her."

Margaret nodded in agreement when they overheard Dr. Casey talking to Father Tonnellier and an enthralled Davina Woolrich.

"It's a shame, Mr. Stanfield's a relatively young man still..." Dr. Casey was saying, knowing that he was only a few years older than Frederick and did not like to think about his own demise.

"Don't you think he could come out of it?" Davina asked, her large eyes full of admiration for the good doctor.

Dr. Casey paused and shook his head, reveling as he always did when he had the attention of what he called *simple folk.* "Highly unlikely."

Victor reached over and touched the doctor on the arm, annoying him. "Sorry, but I couldn't help but overhear; did you say something was wrong with Mr. Stanfield—Ethan?"

Dr. Casey wasn't fond of Victor. He always had the feeling Victor thought he did not do enough for Jonah when he had been burned, and that in some way held him responsible for the pain he had been in those last two weeks of his life. Dr. Casey knew medically it was preposterous, that he had done all he could do. That there was no need to keep administering costly laudanum to a patient that he knew had no chance for survival. What difference did it make if the poor man was more comfortable—he was going to die anyway.

"No, not Ethan, rather, his father, Frederick. He's had a rather debilitating apoplexy or stroke, I'm afraid...paralyzed now, and mute. I was called there early this morning. Nothing I could do by then, nothing can be done now for him, seems he and his son got into rather a nasty row." Dr. Casey took out his engraved silver timepiece, looked at it, then snapped it shut. "Well, I've got to check on my patient."

As he walked away, Victor wondered how a man who seemed to care so little for people's suffering ever became a healer.

"Poor Ethan," Margaret sighed. "What will you do with yourself today? Would you like to come out to the house for lunch?" She smiled at the way one of his big forearms was able to comfortably cradle Hank.

"No, I'll be all right. She said she'd be home to cook supper, and I've got work to do." They began walking slowly across the lawn, and she turned to smile at Henry as he talked happily with his brothers.

"It's *Sunday*, Victor."

"Never stopped me before. I think I'll go by later and see Ethan too, he may need an ear."

"Good afternoon Arvellen."

"*Bon après-midi*, Victor," Arvellen purred, smiling slyly, "tell me, ow iz our little Celena ziz morning, eh? Tired, sore?"

"Is Ethan up?" Victor pushed the door the rest of the way open, forcing Arvellen out of the way.

"Oui, he iz up."

"I heard ya'll had a bad night last night."

With the mention of the screaming match between Ethan and his father, her interest in Victor's wedding night faded.

Hearing Ethan's voice, Victor headed to the parlor.

"Mother like I told you, I'll take care of things..." Ethan and Abigail both looked up when Victor filled up the doorway.

"Oh!" Abigail cried, and melodramatically put the lace-edged handkerchief to her mouth as if some hideous apparition had appeared.

"Afternoon Mrs. Stanfield. Dr. Casey mentioned that Mr. Stanfield had taken...taken a turn for the worse."

Abigail looked away, not wanting to believe what the damn doctor or the idiotic blacksmith said about her beloved Frederick.

"I'm sorry to hear he's not doing so well."

Ethan interrupted the uncomfortable silence by getting up and pouring himself a mid-afternoon brandy. Looking at him, Victor realized that he still had the same suit on from wedding and that his shirt was badly wrinkled. His hair was tousled, and stubble covered his chin. It was a shock to Victor, for in all the years he had known him, he had never seen Ethan anything but impeccably dressed.

"Yes...my father has decidedly taken a turn for the worse." He threw his head back and finished the small snifter of brandy, even though it burned in his empty stomach. He felt *awful*, terribly hung-over. Worse than even the outrageous binges of drinking and gaming when he had been in college. And he knew why. When he had been drinking in college, he had been happy, but yesterday's binge did not come from wild young antics, but rather from grim and deep-felt torment. He could hardly believe when he'd staggered inside last night that his father wanted to see him.

"Ethan, I'm going to check on your father." Abigail stood.

"If you wish, mother," Ethan said, putting his arms out dejectedly and lowering his head.

In a flurry of skirts, she left the room.

"Want one?" Ethan asked, pouring another drink. He handed Victor a brandy in a cut glass cup.

"It's a little early, isn't it?" Victor asked, taking the glass, not knowing what to do with it since he had no intention of drinking it.

"Early—or late—depends on one's perspective I suppose. Since I've not had the benefit of sleep, I think it's safe to say that it is indeed *late!*" He poured the drink down his throat. "God...what a frightful night." He stared into the blackness of the fireplace, placing his hands on the cool, marble mantel. "And the worst thing is, I of course, caused it. I have caused all my father's sufferings and disappointments." He paused a moment, still trying to rid himself of the frightening parallels between his father and himself. "But surely you know all of this Victor, because I in turn have caused all *your suffering and disappointments!*"

Victor was silent.

Annoyed he was not getting a reaction, Ethan trudged on. "Did you *hear* what I said? I'm the cause of all your misery and heartache!"

"What in the world are you talking about?"

"Didn't you ever think it *odd*, that in all those years your mother's farm was never sold? Do you know what he was doing when he couldn't sell it at first? He purposely held on to it—even years later when he could have finally sold it and been rid of it, he didn't. He was holding on to it, knowing that it would eat at you every day as you watched it lay in ruin. He didn't derive any income from it, which was the only thing that's ever mattered to him. He was holding onto it merely to be cruel, merely for spite—" The guilt was weighing heavily on his soul, and it irritated him when Victor merely shrugged as if his confession was of little importance.

"It's in the past. That means it's over, there's nothing I can do to change it. Besides, it doesn't matter now, I've got it back."

"It *does* matter! He was furious with me when I stole those bank papers for you and figured out the asinine terms of the debt you'd never pay off—"

"But I did pay it off," Victor interrupted calmly, hoping somehow it would rub off.

"Do you realize that Margaret was burned, and Jonah died because you had the misfortune to know me?"

It took Victor several heartbeats to answer. "I don't want to talk about that."

"My father only tried foreclosing on Jonah's land...because he hated *you*! Because you had the extreme misfortune to befriend me. Though *why* he hates you so much, I've yet to completely figure out. It's a domino effect to the absurd degree—he does absolutely as he pleases...he decides who to hate, and the rest of us suffer the enormous repercussions!"

"He didn't take Jonah's land," Victor said flatly, as if he needed to remind him unemotionally of the facts.

"Only because you were lucky enough to have Josephine Chomeau's steamship break down at precisely the right time!" He reached for the decanter to pour another drink, but Victor pulled it out of his reach.

"You don't need any more."

"But I do! I *do*! He should have *died* last night. It was gruesome. The coughing, the flailing on the bed, the hideous gasping for breath—the idiot doctor needlessly telling us things were serious. Like I'd need to be a damn *doctor* to see the cold hand of death in the room last night! And yet remarkably, Frederick is still here. White as a ghost, crippled and silent, but nevertheless he's still here." Successfully wresting the decanter from Victor, Ethan poured and took another large drink. "And regrettably, I *am* still here."

There was a painfully long silence during which Victor realized how ominous the ticking of the grandfather clock was in the large house.

"Before his fit last night, he disowned me," Ethan said softly, his brown eyes meeting Victor's gray ones. "Told me I was nothing and that I'd *have* nothing. Told me I had not the fortitude or talent to accomplish anything in this world...told me that I did not have a chance in hell of making it on my own. It's quite touching don't you think to hear my father speak so highly of me?"

Victor shook his head grimly, knowing what a cruel father Frederick had been. He promised himself right then that when he and Celena had a child, he would be careful. After all it was a *life* he would be shaping.

"Right before he went into his fit, I told him that the reason he didn't die was because there was no point. I told him he didn't die because he had no soul! I then told him how much I hated him. And I-I didn't *want* to hate him! It goes against all the laws of a *decent* world to hate your father, your own blood. And now that his health has incapacitated him, I suddenly have all the control. I have everything. I may do exactly as I please." He shook his head despondently. "What an odd twist of fate." He turned then to look at Victor, who was sitting in one of the leather armchairs, quietly listening.

The silence between them was uncomfortably tense. Especially for two men that had known each other for so long and were such good friends.

"What? No congratulations on my newly acquired position as bank president? No comment on my immense wealth and fortune? Look around the halls of the great house, the gardens, the land, the stables...it's all *mine* now!"

"What about your mother?"

Ethan laughed and it was not a pleasant sound. "My *mother*? She'll not get in my way. She wants her life to go on exactly as it has, and full well expects me to run everything. She is harmless as well as useless." He was trying to project sarcasm, but it was pain that came through. "Aren't you going to commend me on my resting my fortune from the clutches of my father? Commend me on ridding the town for the last time of its evil banker, the scourge of Ste. Genevieve! Well...aren't you!"

"No."

"But it's my *father,* the misfortunes are Frederick's! I thought *you* of all people would be glad to hear of his near demise."

"I find it hard to find pleasure in anyone's misfortune, even his."

Ethan shook his head and smirked. "The inherent goodness in your soul overwhelms me."

Victor's eyes were cool. "No one is naturally good. We all have to try."

Newly humiliated Ethan downed another shot of brandy. "Oh yes! *Always* the noble blacksmith. The man whose sense of honor is so great, it is a measure that we should all strive to attain."

Staring at him, Victor wondered why he was being attacked.

Ethan swallowed a bit more brandy to bolster his courage. "Well then, revel in my windfall in my good fortune...my ability to do exactly as I wish. And now that I have all the control, I must be careful though, careful not to repeat like a chilling prophecy, the sins of the father—"

Abruptly Victor got to his feet. "You've had too much to drink."

"Oh, you're brilliant Victor! How did you come to that conclusion?" Having said it, Ethan regretted it. He knew better than to think Victor would hit him, but it was unnerving suddenly to be the target of his cool eyes; frightening to think that the man he had just insulted he'd seen easily lift an anvil.

"Simple, you're talking nonsense. There's no ridiculous *prophecy*, there are no sins for you to repeat. You are nothing like him, you're nothing like Frederick."

Hearing Victor defend him only sent Ethan further into the abyss of regret and shame. He shook his head as he looked at Victor, wondered what he had done to deserve his friendship. Realized anew how easy it was to be like Frederick, doing exactly as you pleased, not worrying about the consequences or who was hurt. He remembered wanting to hurt Victor and Celena the night of the barn raising, how he had caused the argument between John and Victor and the waiting period. And although it had turned out all right, feared what else he was capable of.

"Perhaps you're right, I'm not to fulfill an ancient Greek tragedy, perhaps I'm just an ordinary soul, agonizingly caught in a life I've no control over. Perhaps I'm just another bitter martyr...tormented by what is lost to me...another tormented Heathcliff."

"*Heathcliff*, what the hell are you talking about? You need to sleep it off!" Victor walked to the door of the parlor.

"Heathcliff of course! The demon-ridden hero, the passionate, brooding man so frustrated by what cannot be—that he destroys two generations and drives himself mad with unfulfilled love and hate. It's a fascinating book, I'm surprised you've never read it."

"You *know* I've never read it!" Victor spat, annoyed at Ethan's sudden lunacy. "Here! I've got a prophecy for you. You don't want to be like your father and manipulate, lie, and cheat, then simply don't. You want to pine away and waste your life with this martyr hogwash—then you're a bigger fool than he is!"

Ethan heard Victor's boots pound through the hallway. The front door slammed and in the ensuing silence Ethan slumped weakly in the chair. He dropped his aching head into his hands and waited for grief to overcome him. But in a few minutes, he felt strangely better. It was odd the good Victor's tongue lashing had done him. Besides, Victor made it seem possible. For the first time in a long time, Ethan felt in control.

"I did wrong to them, but I never will again," he reflected quietly, closing his eyes as feelings of regret but also relief because they would never know. Sighing, he stood up and walked to the window and looked out to the beautiful gardens. He noticed there were waning pink and scarlet roses near the window as well as bright yellow asters. The garden was well tended as the neat beds and tightly pruned plants showed, and yet looking at it saddened him because no one ever went out to enjoy it. It seemed sacrilegious to have something so beautiful be so unappreciated.

A brown sparrow flitted down and landed on one of the statues that dotted the garden. It was of a young girl holding a water jug, and its simple innocent beauty made him think of Celena. He remembered the conversation he'd had with her the night of the barn raising and how she asked him if he would change things at the bank, and knew she was hoping he would do the honorable thing. Despite everything, it was a good memory, cleansing almost. He knew with a painful sigh from his heart that it was too late. It occurred to him with that he had not even asked Victor about her, and that Victor had left his bride to offer condolences about Frederick's health.

"He's better for her anyway," he whispered, knowing that Victor had always been the better man. Clasping his hands behind his back he walked out of the parlor and laboriously made his way up the stairs. *I cannot have her love, but I can have her friendship and admiration, and it will be enough.* As he walked into his bedroom, amazingly a part of him, believed it.

Chapter 16

It was still dark outside when Celena felt Victor get out of bed. He dressed hurriedly and she knew he was leaving to milk Luann. When the door closed, she got up quickly to use the chamber pot. It was wonderful being married and she loved Victor to death, but it was a tiny house and impossible to have any privacy. Patting herself dry with the linen cloths that she would use when it was her time of the month, she was reminded of how sore she was. So sore in fact that, after putting the lid back on the pot, she hobbled back to the bed. Her lips were chapped from kissing, her breasts sore from his mouth, her hair a snarled, ratty mess in back.

Regardless, she had a ton of things she wanted to do and tried to sit up but dropped back down. After all she hadn't gotten much uninterrupted sleep with her active groom waking and making love to her every few hours. Closing her eyes, she promised herself she'd get up in a minute, and dozed off.

"Good morning," he said softly, the mattress sagging under his weight as he climbed back into bed. He kissed her sweetly, smiling. "I lit the fire for you, brought in water, and milked our cow." Another mad grin and he kissed each cheek and her forehead. "I've got to get to the shop pretty quick this morning, but..." His hands took over where his words left off.

But she had been loved often enough by her virile new husband to know full well where this was leading. "Victor, I'm sore."

"Oh," he said, hoping this bit of news did not mean what he was afraid it did. "Sorry about that. It'll go away, mine has," he confessed and bent to kiss her forehead.

"You were sore too?" she asked in surprise, feeling another bond with him, not thinking she could admit what was bothering her to another living soul.

"Yes. Is it...bothering you now?" To his disappointment she nodded. "We'll have to get you fixed up then." He planted a chaste kiss on her forehead. "I suggest then, dear wife, after breakfast you take a long, hot soak, do you a world of good. Kiss me, we've both got things to do."

She obeyed, grateful for his understanding.

Victor washed his face and hands, reached for the clean clothes in the basket, and pulled on a shirt, trousers, and socks. He combed his coarse hair out of his face with his fingers and, grabbing the piece of leather, bound it behind his head. By the time he came to the table to pull his boots on, Celena had coffee waiting for him on the table and pancakes on the griddle.

"What time do you want your lunch, straight up noon?" she asked, placing the perfectly browned pancake on the pretty new plates.

"That's fine, give or take." He hurriedly ate, his mind wandering to all the work he needed to do. The week of the wedding there had been so many interruptions, with people coming in to offer their congratulations and tease him that he had fallen behind. He did not like to be behind, and since he had two able strikers now, rarely was.

Walking to the door, he saw the delicate pink light of early morning creeping up the hillside and breathed in deeply the cool air. The sky was brilliantly blue without a trace of clouds, and he hoped it would be a mild day, one where he could keep the shop doors open while he worked.

Turning, he picked up his cup and drained it of coffee. "Lena, there's a box on the mantle, there's money in it. Take some and get whatever you want at the store today."

Curious, she wiped her hands on her apron and on tiptoe carefully reached for the rectangular porcelain box and lifted the lid. She was surprised to see several neatly folded bills unpretentiously stashed inside.

"Now don't get too carried away, I'll go to the bank this month and put some of that in." He reached for his boots, pulling them on, wanting to get the fire going in the shop before Claude and Thomas got there.

"Why, there's almost eighty dollars in here, Victor! How long have you been saving that?" She wondered how many long, hot hours he had labored in the shop for that money.

"A month. That's this month's earnings."

"You mean to tell me you make that much *each* month?"

"No, it's usually more. I had a lot on my mind this month, I've been a bit...distracted lately." The lazy way he grinned made her blush.

"But...but you're not *poor*!" she cried as if cheated.

"No, we're not *poor*! But most of that is seed money as Ethan calls it and we're to make deposits every month—invest, and not spend it all. You get whatever you want today though." Finished with his boots, he motioned for her to come closer. Pulling her against him as he sat in the chair, he looked up at her with a frown. "Who told you I was poor?"

"I'm sorry. I-I always thought you were."

"Well," he began, his words muffled because his mouth was against her breasts, kissing them. "At one time I was, but not anymore. I make a profit in the shop. I pay Claude and Thomas decently and turn over my share of the sawmill for Ethan to invest." He nipped a kiss on her mouth.

She laughed suddenly at the absurdness of it all. After all she'd never had a conversation with someone who had his head buried in her breasts, much less a serious conversation about money!

"I've got money put away for the coupler," he paused to kiss each breast, "and money put away for our new house."

She caught his face in her hands, forcing him to look up. "You never said anything to me about a house?"

"Well, your father and I *sure* talked about it! It won't be right away, but once those babies start coming..." he nipped playfully again at a breast, "...we'll bust right out of the seams in this place!"

She pressed his face tight into the valley between her breasts and kissed the top of his head. Wanted more than anything suddenly to show him how much she loved him, how happy she was, and—despite being sore—considered leading him right back behind the quilt!

She heard something. Looking up she was horrified to see Claude standing at the open door, his mouth hanging open in shock, his eyes nearly bulging out of their sockets. She jumped away.

"Good morning Claude!" Victor called to his striker who was nailed to the spot. "Go on to the shop, I'll be right there."

"Oh. Sorry! Morning Victor, morning Miss Celena. Be going—going to the shop now—Thomas will be right along," Claude stammered, his face as red as Celena's. He darted away.

"It's all right," Victor said laughingly to Celena, whose pale cheeks were blotchy with embarrassment

"For heaven's sake Victor! You—you shouldn't kiss me there!"

"Don't worry about Claude. He's more embarrassed than you are!" he said with a laugh. "Come on, give me a kiss. I've got to go to work, or we *will* be poor!"

Celena straightened the little house in no time, and discovering to her amusement that there was no mop, added that to her list of things to buy. She stripped the bed and remade it with clean sheets she had been given as a wedding present. She treated the stained sheets with a paste of baking soda and began soaking them in cold water in an old pot that had been long forgotten in the back of the cupboard. She would have to remember to get blue indigo to add in the final rinse to see if she could get them white again.

She cleaned out the ashes in the fireplace, saving them to fertilize the garden she would plant, and re-laid the fire. She finished unpacking the gifts from the wedding, like the fine white tablecloth from Annalise Stoddard that she proudly spread over the worn maple table and the new blue and white pads from Esther Charbonnier and pretty coverlet Martha Fisk had made with the two-inch tatting that she placed over the old rocking chair. She placed new candles in iron candelabras that stood on the mantle and arranged the pretty china on the cupboard, careful as she stood the new plates up in the groove so they would not fall.

She toted in three buckets of water and soaked in a hot tub as Victor suggested and having done so, felt surprisingly better. Then proud as a new wife, changed into her best everyday dress, a dark green cotton twill with tiny white buttons up the front. It was hard to see how she looked when all was done though, because the small mirror that Victor had propped up behind the water pitcher barely showed anything. She started to quickly braid her hair but stopped then, wanting to look mature, and wound it up on the back of her head, securing the bun with three hair pins and two combs.

"There now," she said, smoothing the dress flat against her stomach. Giddy with excitement as a newly-married woman shopping for her own home, she grabbed her drawstring purse with her husband's money safely tucked inside and walked out into the blinding sunshine.

It was different living in town than on the farm. It was noisier for one thing. She could hear the street behind the shop, *La Grande Rue* which was the central thoroughfare through town. Then the noise from the shop was at times loud, even though there were walls and ground separating the shop from house, other times depending on what Victor was doing, she could not hear him at all.

She walked past the shop, and a little flutter happened in her stomach when she heard the wonderful sound of Victor's deep voice telling Claude to add more air to the fire. She wavered a moment wondering if she should stop in and see him, but then decided against it. She was looking forward to bringing all of them their noon meal. Just imagining the look of welcome on Victor's face made her shiver with happiness. Besides the embarrassing encounter with Claude was still fresh in her mind, she would have to face him soon enough—no need to hurry it.

She made her way across the dusty street then towards the Woolrich's store. It looked busy; from all the heads she could see through the large windows. As she walked up the steps Victor had rebuilt for the Woolriches two years ago, noticed that the red paint was chipping off. They took a terrible beating from the western sun, and she feared all Victor's work would be for naught if Alvin didn't at least try and maintain them by keeping them painted. She smiled then, realizing that nearly everywhere she looked in Ste. Genevieve she could find something Victor had worked on, a wonderful little reminder of him.

Seeing her enter, Alvin immediately came around the counter. "Good morning Miss Celena, or should I say, Mrs. Gant! Got shopping to do for your new home? Isn't she looking lovely this morning!" he gushed to no one in particular, and to her embarrassed surprise, a man she didn't know agreed with him.

"Morning Mr. Woolrich." She looked down at her list and proceeded to put the skinny shopkeeper to work getting cans off shelves, measuring out bags of sugar, coffee, flour, baking soda, salt, and spices. She bought a new rinse bucket and marveled at the style of mop he had before happily telling him to add it to the list. She bought potatoes, shocked by the cost of them, deciding that if she had time that afternoon she would start to till the garden, and splurged on a whole pound of bacon and cocoa.

"Will that be all?" Alvin asked, grinning at her.

"And borax and blue indigo."

"That was a wonderful wedding you had! Those fiddlers, those fellows from St. Louis were the best I've ever heard, and the food, well it was enough to stuff me for more than a day!"

"Well thank you Mr. Woolrich, we're glad you enjoyed yourself." When the groceries were paid for, she began to carefully bundle up her parcels, and realized she had bought way more than she could carry.

"Looks like you could use my assistance."

Ethan grabbed two of the parcels that were slipping out of her hand, and then hoisted one sack over his shoulder. He was well dressed as ever in a black suit, gray vest, and starched white shirt, but there was a tiredness or maybe a sadness around his eyes that she did not fail to recognize.

"Yes, that would be wonderful. Thank you." Waving goodbye to Alvin, she walked out the door with Ethan but made it no more than two steps before Mrs. Blay stopped them.

"Celena, child, how are you!" Because of everything Celena was carrying, Mrs. Blay gave her an awkward hug. "You made *the* most beautiful bride, and my Victor, well he looked so tall and *almost* handsome! It was truly a lovely ceremony Celena. I see you've got cooking supplies, I must admit, I'm going to miss cooking for him—he never was chatty, but always such a pleasure to cook for and so prompt with his payments. Anyway, it's so nice to see you—and I'm so glad that now that you're in town I'll get to see more of you!"

As they made their way across the street Ethan commented, "You're quite the new celebrity in town."

"It's not me, it's Victor they all adore." Celena smiled, falling perfectly in line with the rest of the town in her admiration of her husband. "Thank you so much for helping me, would you like to come in and have some coffee or tea?" she asked nervously at the door. She had never entertained anyone socially on her own before and wanted to make a good impression.

"Well, I need to be getting to the bank," he said, mulling over what he should do. In a way he wanted to go and sit with her. Sit in Victor's house and prove to himself that he could see her, be in love with her and still be her friend. "All right."

She rewarded him with a smile, and he followed her into the house.

"Tea or coffee?" she asked, tying what looked to be a brand-new blue apron around her waist as she got down the new teacups and saucers.

"Tea would be nice I think." He eased himself into the straight-backed chair. "So, you've settled in?" Glancing around the house, he noticed the new womanly touches and that she seemed at ease in her little house, quickly reviving the banked fire and putting the kettle on to make tea.

"Yes, and quite nicely too."

He couldn't help but glance toward the quilt. Knowing that behind it, Victor had laid down on the bed with her, that he'd held her in his arms and made love to her. He remembered with a shudder what his father had snarled at him during the argument. "*I bet that young girl has been fouled by that dirty Indian by now!"*

"Do you take anything in your tea?" She set the steaming pot before him, hoping he didn't want sugar because she hadn't had time to put it in the matching sugar bowl.

"No this is fine." He forced a smile. "It was a wonderful wedding Celena."

"Do you think so? I was afraid maybe it was silly; it was rather larger than I expected."

"No, it was nice." He did his best to sound aloof. "I don't think I've ever seen a more striking couple. And by the way it was refreshing to see Victor for once in some clothes that actually fit him!"

She beamed. "Thank you. I worked long and hard on that suit, and he is such a big man. I don't think I ever knew how big until I measured him, and my heavens what he must weigh—" Suddenly realizing the intensely personal direction her thoughts were headed, she clammed up, flushed hotly, and forced a nervous smile. "Anyway, I'm glad the wedding's over."

He could not look at her. Finishing his tea, he placed it carefully back on the saucer and got to his feet. "I best be on my way, thank you for the tea. Your home is most becoming with all the things that you've done."

Even though she knew her house was nothing compared to his, she said. "You're sweet." Walking to the door, she opened it for him. "Victor told me your father's not doing well, I just wanted to tell you I'm sorry."

He shrugged to make light of it. "It's only Frederick." But her concerned gaze was so full of compassion he had to look away.

"I know you've never gotten on with him, but still, he's your father. If you need anything, you know Victor is always here for you, and now I am too. You've got both of us now, two friends." He noticed she was absentmindedly twisting the iron ring around her finger.

He nodded as he stepped out of their house into the humid August morning. "Thank you, I appreciate it. Tell Victor I'll see him later." He knew sadly she meant what she said with all her heart.

Celena wiped a line of perspiration off her forehead. She had already opened the front door and loaded the tray with the three plates heaping with food. But when she lifted it, it was heavier than she anticipated, and quickly put it back on the table

She had been working on their lunch since Ethan left. She had made a terrine, lining the sides and bottom of a pan with bacon fat, then spread ground deer spiced with nutmeg and allspice. It cooked slowly in a pan of water just until boiling and then she added potatoes and carrots. The slow cooking ensured the deer would be tender and the perimeter would not burn. She then mixed, rolled, cut, and cooked biscuits 'til they were golden brown, and lastly made a white gravy flavored with bacon grease.

"Maybe not the water pitcher." She moved the heavy pewter pitcher off the tray. Lifting it, she realized it was manageable and walked through the door and the twelve steps to the blacksmith shop.

Thomas saw her first, and smiling broadly motioned to Victor that someone was at the door.

"Is it that late already?" Victor asked, reaching behind to untie the leather apron, tossing it carelessly to one of the carpenter tables.

"Afternoon Miss Celena!" Claude and Thomas said, grinning at her. When their eyes fell on the tray of food their mouths dropped open.

"I didn't know she was going to *cook* for us too!" Thomas gushed happily to his brother. "Gosh Miss Celena, I know you are darn fine cook!" He turned to his brother. "I can't believe we get to *eat* it!"

Victor rolled his eyes at his less-than-brilliant helpers. "Shut up and eat." Taking his plate, he moved over to one of the carpenter tables and grabbed the only other decent stool in the shop for Celena to sit on and pulled a crate over for himself, wanting even if they were in the shop to have a bit of privacy with his wife.

"You're not eating?" he asked, seeing only three plates.

"I sampled enough along the way."

"Did you go to the store?" he asked between sloppy bites.

"Yes. I got a mop and bucket. I ran into Ethan on the way out, and he helped me home and I made him a cup of tea."

"How is he?" he asked a second later, having inhaled his food and stuffed an entire biscuit into his mouth. She shook her head, wondering how she was going to teach their children decent table manners when they watched their father cram whole biscuits into his mouth!

"He seemed fine. Said to tell you he'd talk to you later."

She watched him take the last biscuit and sop up every drop of gravy.

"Did you...do as I suggested? Are you feeling any better now?" He picked up his water and drank. The mere thought of her naked, soaking in a tub, was enough to immediately harden him.

"Yes," she felt the pink creep into her cheeks, "I feel much better." Their eyes met.

Clearing his throat noisily, he stood up. Not sure exactly what to do, he took her awkwardly by the shoulders and placed a light kiss on the top of her head, as if dismissing her.

"That's all the thanks I get for the lovely meal I spent all morning cooking for you?"

"That's all you get for *now*. Don't you think we've shocked Claude enough for one day?" Unable to control himself when she looked up, he landed a swift kiss on her mouth. But her body responded more than she intended it to, and he felt it. "Unless of course...you'd like me to thank you...*another* way?"

Before she could answer he was loading the plates on the tray and barking instructions to Claude and Thomas as to what to do while he was gone.

"What are you doing?" she asked, trotting to keep up with him as he went toward the house.

"Open the door and get inside."

Rattled, she did as commanded and watched him carry the tray in, set it on the table, and close and bolt the door.

"What—what are you doing?" she asked, her eyes widening in surprise as he untucked his shirt.

"Get on the bed," he said, stripping the shirt off and struggling to tug off the boots while standing up. She had yet to move. He stared down at her, resting his big hands on his hips. "I suggest you do as I ask. I don't think you'll be comfortable there on the floor, splinters and things. Or would you prefer I haul up your skirts and bend you over this table?"

"*Victor!*" she moved toward the bed as little shivers of excitement started up and down her spine. "Aren't Claude and Thomas going to—to miss you in the shop?"

He climbed in after her. "They can get along without me for a bit." He knew he would not be able to take as much time with her as he'd like, but smiled, thinking there was always tonight. He bent and kissed his favorite little spot under her eye, and then his hands went softly to her hair. "I don't...like it like this." He pulled out the pins. "Can you go back to wearing it in the braid like you used to?"

She nodded breathlessly.

"By the way—" He began to clumsily undo the tiny buttons on the front of the dress. "You can still bring a tray of food for Claude and Thomas in the shop. But from now on, I'd rather eat in the house alone with you, if you don't mind, that is."

Pushing his fumbling hands away she undid the buttons herself. "I don't mind," she whispered, closing her eyes. "That would be wonderful."

Chapter 17

"Carlene!" Celena exclaimed with delight. "Come in, come in!"

"I've been to the store, since we're so close I thought I would come by," Carlene explained, but as she walked into her sister's little house, immediately felt sorry for her. Celena was sweating; the house was terribly hot, and she looked like she wasn't getting enough sleep because there were gray circles under her eyes. Her hair was a mess, straggling out of the braid, and her apron was soiled. The wooden table was dusted with flour and loaded with bowls, spoons, measuring cups and a wheel of butter that looked like it had been hacked on with a dull knife.

"I'd have been furious if you didn't!" Celena said, hugging her. "Have a seat and make yourself at home." Her smile was innocent and welcoming.

"Well, it is small isn't it?" Carlene said, looking critically around the tiny house, thinking that at least she and Mason had three rooms rented above the Post Office.

"Oh, well yes I guess it is," Celena murmured absentmindedly. "Truthfully I've been so busy since the wedding, I scarcely noticed. Would you like some tea? I've got the most darling new tea set, and I was getting the last of the bread out of the oven. I should have enough for the week." She smiled and wiped her forehead. "We could have a slice while it's warm and visit for a while, I could use a breather."

"All right." While her little sister got down the new teacups and saucers, Carlene inspected the house. She noticed the pine plank floor was in good shape, in better shape than the floor above the post office, and they had a real stone hearth to warm the house and cook on. Not like the temperamental pot-bellied stove she had. She looked at the iron candelabras on the mantle, the sconces on the wall, hooks in the fireplace and realized everywhere she looked there was Victor's handiwork. She glanced towards the bed, noticing there was precious little space to get around Celena's trunk and the water basin and stool. Although it was cramped, it was a place Carlene could happily imagine laying her head.

"You know we've got Luann here. Victor's been milking her, and I've cream I need to churn and extra milk. Victor and I can't possibly use it all, so I was thinking we could share her," Celena said, knowing Carlene was still angry at her parents for being unhappy about her eloping, and thus no wedding gifts.

"That would be nice," Carlene said, watching Celena with envy as she happily set the table with the pretty new china and napkins. It was a little house, but it was *hers* and not rented rooms.

"I'm so glad you came by, and I want to come see your house too, I've been so busy getting settled. Who'd have thought taking care of one man would keep me so occupied."

"I see," Carlene said, dreading the free time that she had. The solitude of living with such a quiet man after living in her parents' busy household was almost too much for her.

"I went to the store a few days ago to get some things. Victor had almost everything, but you know what they say about bachelors. Then I met Ethan at the store, and he had to help me home I bought so much. He stayed until I started to make the noon meal for Victor, Claude, and Thomas, so I didn't get around to making bread until today—"

"You have to cook for *them* too?"

"Oh, I don't mind."

"*I'd* mind! What does Victor think you are, hired help or something?"

"He thinks I'm his wife."

They fell awkwardly silent.

"Like I said, I've been making bread all day, least I'll have that done for the week." Sitting, Celena wiped her face with her corner of her apron and cleared her throat, trying to think of something to say. "What day are you going to do your wash?"

"What *wash?* I can do my own and so can Mason."

Celena nodded, trying to understand. "Well...I was thinking Monday, then Tuesday could be ironing day. Remember that time in the summer we forgot we left a basket of damp laundry, and it spoiled with that awful orange and black mildew before we got to ironing it!"

"Yes," Carlene sighed, her boredom obvious. "I remember, they had little black spots of mold we never got out again." She glanced down at her hands, and seeing her wedding ring flash, quickly dropped her hands into her lap impatiently.

Celena stood and went to a basket on the floor. "Look, Victor made me a wonderful set of new irons. I'd be happy to share them with you."

Confronted with the iron, Carlene looked at them and realized the wooden handle screwed off. "I do hate getting burned." She noticed the crude cursive "L" carved in the handle. "He does know your name starts with a 'C' doesn't he?"

Celena tilted her head, annoyed. "Yes, he knows Carlene. But I'd love the company if you'd like to come over every washday. It might be less of a chore if we did it together."

Carlene sighed almost imperceptibly. "I...guess I...could."

Sitting back down, Celena smoothed down the pretty napkins, still trying to coax a conversation out of Carlene. "Oh, and did I tell you Victor's going to put a garden in for me—"

"A *garden!*" Carlene exclaimed jealously. Celena had been the seamstress and cook of their house; Carlene had always seen to the garden.

"I thought I'd better. Besides, I can't see letting good ground go to waste." Celena smiled as she poured the hot water into the teapot and then sat quietly waiting for the tea to steep.

"How are you settling in?"

"Fine."

"How's Mason's practice coming?" Celena asked, trying to find a subject that would interest her. After all, Victor was never far from her thoughts and she loved to have a reason to speak of him.

"Fine," Carlene said, glaring at the pot as if staring would make tea sooner.

Celena poured their tea, and then watched Carlene take one sip and set the teacup down impatiently, rattling the cup in the saucer. "What's the matter?"

Carlene's blue eyes flashed. "Everything. I hate it when Mason kisses me goodbye...or hello or...*during*—"

"Oh Carlene—"

"I'm sure Victor's the same, men are *pigs!*" Carlene said bitterly, thinking how disgusted she felt every time Mason, fumbling with his nightshirt, climbed on top of her. "Thinking of nothing else, the *disgusting fiends!*"

Celena couldn't help thinking that Mason had a tough road ahead of him.

"I hate it Celena. I've gotten so I dread sundown!" Carlene angrily swiped at her teary eyes. "He touches me everywhere and the way he looks at me like I'm something to eat! It's sinful!"

"It isn't sinful. You're married. He's your husband," Celena said, on her knees now in front of Carlene, trying to comfort her. "He's trying to show you how much he loves you. He married you, Carlene, despite his family and Eddie, I think he genuinely cares for you."

"Oh yes I forgot! The minute we're married they have all rights to our flesh. Nothing happens during the courting. My God if you *kiss* some-one before you're married they treat you like some sort of tart, but the minute they put a cheap gold ring on your finger you're expected to sur-render your body. I wish to God someone would have prepared me for this!" Although when she'd been intimate the one time with Eddie, she'd so wanted to please him she'd put up with it. "Don't tell me *you're* im-mune to these monthly pawing sessions?"

Celena's cheeks flushed hotly. "No, of course not."

"Isn't it awful?" Carlene moaned, wiping her face with the back of her hand. "And I'm always such a God-awful mess afterwards! Stuff leaches out for *hours,* even after I've taken a bath!"

Celena blushed at the accuracy of the description. "Well..." she tenu-ously began. "I must admit at first I was afraid, and it certainly was painful, but it's gotten better." She was rendered mute by the horrified way Carlene stared at her. Nervously she got up to slice one of the loaves of bread.

"But what? Don't tell me you're swallowing that it's our *'woman's duty'* hogwash are you?"

"But it *is* our duty. Just like it's theirs to take care of us and the children that no doubt we're going to have! Honestly, Carlene, it's not *that* bad."

"I can't believe you're *saying* this! It's something unfortunately that must be endured! Only street walkers and tramps like it! Why you almost act like you—you *enjoy* it!" She squealed in a tone bordering on accusation.

"Well I don't...hate it!" Celena exclaimed, feeling her heart speed up uncomfortably in her chest. Not wanting to have to defend to anyone how she felt at night with her husband. It was intensely personal to begin with, and she was having a hard enough time dealing with all the new things being a wife entailed without Carlene making her feel guiltier than she already did.

"Why not?"

"Oh, I don't know! It's not *all* bad. I-I love falling asleep with his arms wrapped around me, and I love waking up in the morning the same way. The *hugging* is wonderful, certainly you don't object to *that?*" Celena wailed.

"Maybe if I wasn't hugging Mason I might like it." The dam broke then and Carlene started to sob. "I made a mistake, I've made such a horrible mistake! I should have married Eddie. It would feel different if it was Eddie. Everything would be different if it was Eddie."

"Yes. Everything would be different. Your heart would be broken."

Carlene glared at her. "How can you say such a thing?"

"Eddie's nothing but a *bully* Carlene. He's always been mean. How many times did he and James get into it? How many times did you wake Eva and me crying over Eddie at night?"

"At least life with Eddie would have been exciting."

Celena nodded. "It would have been that."

"You don't *know!* You don't know how horrible it is living with Mason. He's so...boring, all he does is read!"

"He might not seem so boring if you gave him a chance."

"I doubt it."

"Give it some time—"

"I don't want to!" Carlene wailed and then burst into tears again.

"Maybe you're just tired Carlene," Celena soothed. She wanted to reach out and hug Carlene, but Carlene was not the hugging type

"I'm not tired. I'm pregnant." When she saw the look of happy surprise on Celena's face, Carlene snapped. "Don't say anything nice!"

"Oh, certainly. I shouldn't say anything... *nice.*"

Despite everything, Carlene smirked, knowing how silly it sounded. She shook her head pathetically. "Look what marrying Mason Fisk has done to me. Turned me into a blubbering idiot."

Knowing it might anger Carlene, Celena reached for her hand anyway and held it affectionately. "You're not an idiot. You need to settle down and think things through before you do them. Let me help you. We are both newly married, we can help each other."

"I guess it's a little late for thinking things through now," Carlene said, bitterly glancing down at her flat stomach, knowing a baby was already growing inside her. "I'm scared to death to have this baby. I never liked diapering Gabe and Nathan that much, and I hate the spit up. I bet you can't *wait* to get pregnant, and you'll be a great mother. I know I won't."

Celena ignored the jib. "Have you told Mason?"

Carlene nodded, dabbing her eyes with a clean dishtowel. "He told me he hopes the baby has my eyes. I wish I liked him Celena..."

"You might in time if you let yourself. He's crazy about you, you know that don't you?"

"Yes, I know. But that only makes me want to hurt him. Especially, when he looks at with me with those eyes of his. I don't know whether to scratch him behind the ears or toss him a bone."

"Carlene don't."

Sighing then she wiped her face dry. "I'm sorry. I'm a bit out of sorts these days. I shouldn't take it out on you." She watched Celena deftly wrap up some of the sliced bread in one of the napkins Margaret had embroidered. "It still doesn't seem fair that marriage can suddenly change everything." Carlene shook her head, discouraged. "So, you're happy... being married?"

Celena turned and met her eyes. "Yes."

"It's not fair...you're the prettiest, you're the youngest, now you're the *happiest*."

Celena laughed, "I've got plenty of bread, why don't you take some? And we can start the garden together if you like. I could certainly use your help."

Reluctantly Carlene got up and went to the door, the bundle of still-warm bread under her arm. "All right. I guess I'd better get back home. Mason will be wondering where his lunch is."

Celena smiled but knew that most nights Mason took Carlene out to Blay's to eat because she wouldn't cook.

"I'll come back next week?" Carlene asked, a tremor in her voice—the fear of not being wanted.

"Of course. Please give Mason a chance. He's a good man, Carlene. You might find out you actually like him."

Upon entering the bank, Victor made his way to Ethan's office in the back and rapped lightly on the door that sported an insert of frosted glass.

"Ah, I see it's my able business partner. I'm glad you're here I was about to come over to the shop when I finish my coffee. I need a bit more to begin the day."

"Some of us have already started our day." Victor smirked, knowing he had been at the forge at least an hour before Ethan had even gotten out of bed. "I've come to make a deposit." He wanted to get a semblance of his old life back but knew at the same time it was absurd; as jumbled as his new life was proving to be, he would never want to go back.

"I got a letter this morning, from our friend Mr. Pickering from the patent office in Washington," Ethan said, leaning back comfortably in his chair, pausing in that way that always rather annoyed Victor. "Seems the old coot has bought a carriage factory in town, a failing carriage factory but a carriage factory regardless."

Victor waited for him to continue and, when he did not, said, "Good for him."

"He wants your rim. He wants you to change over how they do it at the factory, and he's offered to pay us quite well but—"

"But *what*, I can't lord anything over him with the rim, I've got no patent for it."

"That's true, but he still needs you. He wants your expertise." He eyed Victor speculatively and made a steeple with his fingers under his chin as he leaned on the desk. "And I'll go with you to negotiate the deal, I am however thinking of something with more teeth than *merely* money." He smiled, thinking lustily of how he was going to coerce Pickering into giving him what he wanted.

"Go *with* me? I'm not going *anywhere!* I'm backed up with work as it is already, I've got the coupler factory to tool, organize and men to find and hire and train, if I don't work on the actual patent we *do* have I'll never get it going." His mind was racing how he would fulfill all the new obligations, and although he would never have admitted it, leaving Celena to go to Washington was simply out of the question.

"But I need you to teach them the rim."

"It's simple. Pickering said so himself. Any smith worth his salt could do it."

"It's easy for *you!* But that's because you have a gift. You have a unique talent for iron working—you're more skilled than the average smith."

"It's not a gift. It's called hard work. I'm not going."

"But the money we could make—"

"I'm making plenty of money! I've got *way* more work than I can manage right now." Knowing how late he got home last night after helping Henry, and how late he was going to be from now on with all the things he needed to do to get the factory going, to say nothing of keeping up with the regular smithing—taking on something new would only take more time away from Celena.

Ethan watched him quietly, perturbed that Victor would not jump at the chance to earn more and annoyed that he expected Celena to live like she was living. "All right, I'll tell you what I'll do, you sketch it out for me in detail, and—and teach me and once I negotiate with Pickering, I'll teach them at the factory."

Victor grinned slowly. "You realize you'll have to work at the forge, don't you? That means sweating, and...getting dirty?"

"I am not pleased about my venture into the realm of manual labor, but I suppose I must bear it, if I am to make us a fortune."

"Are you too tired?" Victor whispered, leaning down to kiss her before she could answer. He was always noisy when he came home late and although he tried not to, invariably he woke her.

Even in the semi-darkness she could see him smiling down at her, and reached for him. It was nearly impossible for her to tell him no, knowing as she did how desperately he wanted and even *needed* to make love to her. Besides, it made her happy to be able to please him so.

As he kissed her, she felt the familiar wanderings of his greedy hands. Although she would have never admitted, his hands sent the most magnificent shudders through her body.

"I want you. I want you so much," he whispered.

"I want you too."

The next few minutes though were rather a blur for Celena. She only knew that as he reached underneath her and pulled her to him, a different and violently strong emotion gripped her. She had done her best to reconcile herself to all the shocking new things being married had opened for her. She had to admit she did agree with Carlene on a few points—they did seem to surrender their bodies! But she thought that, in less than a week she had done a remarkably good job at accepting all the new, and she was happy. But the alarming feelings that were now building low in her body were not only confusing but overwhelming her.

She found herself pressed up against him like she hadn't been before and couldn't help herself from moving urgently against him, which unbelievably only seemed to excite him more. She didn't realize she let out a little gasp, feeling the odd, desperate need building. It was strange, once close to that little '*place*,' found she couldn't help herself for want to go toward it. She reached around and grabbed his hips, pulling him harder against her and ignoring her own shyness opened her legs. Knowing only that she wanted him suddenly even more deeply—more closely to her.

The second little gasp she let out he noticed however and opened his eyes and looked at her. She let out another cry as these new feelings of want and desire kept escalating until at once they all came together, shocking and bewildering her as the pleasure coursed through her in bursts and waves.

A few moments later it happened for him too and he collapsed next to her in a panting, sweating heap. Although she was still coming down from the excruciating joy of what had just happened to her, part of her felt guilty. Felt guilty and ashamed for having so enjoyed it.

It was nearly midnight when Victor returned to the house. He'd spent the last two evenings working with Ethan on the rudiments of the carriage rim, as well as the drawings and text to go along with it. And as against it as he had been about it in the beginning, he was excited about the carriage rim in use somewhere.

Awakened, she heard him pull out the chair and sit and eat the fried catfish and two-day-old bread she had left for him under a towel. Done eating he brought the lantern to the other side of the quilt, and she heard him set it quietly on the table. Felt the mattress sag under his weight as he sat and pulled off his boots. He undressed silently, and pulling the covers up, slid in next to her.

She opened her eyes and smiled at him, and he smiled back, thrilled that she was awake.

"Sorry. I didn't mean to wake you. I always do, don't I?"

"It's all right. I don't sleep well when you're gone anyway. How are the plans coming?" she asked, trying unsuccessfully to stifle a yawn.

"Quite well actually. I'll never make him a smith that's for sure, but he'll do fine. Hope Pickering can pull it off. Guess we'll see what happens when Ethan gets back." He wondered if she was awake enough to make love. It had been three days since he'd made love to her and felt an actual pulsing ache in his groin. He wasn't sure why she had refused him, not sure if it was because he'd come home so late or that she'd merely been tired but would cease to worry about any of it if she'd have him now.

"What time is it?"

"Midnight," he said, reaching out to touch her cheek. The flawless skin of her face looked so soft; her warm, young body so inviting.

Before she knew what he was doing he was rolling on top of her.

He thought he felt her stiffen underneath him but hoping he had imagined it gently turned her face to his and kissed her like he had missed doing, and she responded at first opening her mouth to him. But when his hand reached down to stroke her breasts it was obvious that she did not want him to touch her.

"What's the matter?" he asked, wondering why she was avoiding him. She was sweet and affectionate enough when he was standing up, but when he laid down with her, something changed.

"I'm still a bit...sore."

"Again? Even with the soaking, is that what's been bothering you?"

"Yes, but..." She bit her bottom lip and looked away.

"But what?" he urged, pulling her closer, hoping that when the talking stopped, the loving could start.

"It's so...often." She lowered her lashes, unable to look at him. "It's just that it seems a bit...much," she said, not wanting to hurt his feelings.

He sighed, knowing he had better address this concern carefully if he wanted their coupling to stay as outrageously satisfying as it was now. "Well, let's talk about this for a minute," he began, thinking himself remarkably in control for a man whose wife was complaining to him that their lovemaking was not only too *rough* but too *frequent!* "I am pretty sure that when I'm with you the next time—the soreness will be gone for good," he said, desperately hoping he could try out his theory that night.

She nodded, hanging trustingly on every word.

"And as for how often...well, I think every morning and sometimes noon and every night is perfectly normal." But it didn't sound normal-even to a lusting fiend like *him*, it didn't sound normal, and he knew it! Knew he was luckier and more shamelessly satisfied than any other man he knew!

"It's not that exactly." She swallowed, timid to talk about it, especially with the things Carlene said.

"What then exactly?"

"I never thought, people *did* this that often. Do you think we're odd because we do?"

He would have laughed if she hadn't looked so genuinely worried. "No, we're not odd, just young and healthy that's all." His voice shook a bit, wanting to get on with it.

"It's just, it seems...almost sinful to like it so much. The church talks about it as a duty for women, it almost makes it seem like it's...*wrong*," she said, trying to blot out the contrast between the Blessed Virgin's immaculate conception and the way *less* blessed women had to conceive. "It's hard for me to think about marriage being a sacrament when we're—"

"When we're what?"

She shrugged, embarrassed "I can't imagine the church would condone such—"

"Such what? Excitement? Passion?" He noticed she flinched with embarrassment at the words. "What could possibly be wrong with two married people enjoying their lovemaking?" But when he saw her cheeks turn pink, he was exasperated, thinking she was past the ridiculous shyness by now. "Look at it this way. You know I'm not terribly religious, it's no secret that I'm not a great fan of some the things they try to make us all think, but I believe in living my life honorably. I believe in trying to do right and avoiding doing wrong. I believe in some kind of God and maybe even angels." He paused a moment and stroked his own angel's cheek. "It's a special gift from God. The sacrament of marriage, of intimacy, of the children that their union creates." His hand trailed across her flat stomach as if expecting to feel the bulge of impending motherhood on her already. "I don't see how it makes any difference to God or the church or anyone else, whether it's once a day that I love you or ten times, as long as we both want each other and enjoy it."

"But I feel guilty when I enjoy it, I'm not supposed to—"

"Why ever not?" he interrupted, and for the first time in the conversation felt a real measure of worry. "Why does the Catholic religion *insist* on making women feel so guilty about sex? They could stand to learn a thing or two from the Osage!"

"I don't know, I can't help it! I always thought that part of it was only for...men. Marriage for women is security, to be taken care of and have children. For women it's—it's more a duty, something to be endured, you are the only ones that are supposed to like it." Although she was not looking at him, she could feel him staring at her.

"Why would the world be set up that way? Why would such a kind and benevolent God *only* give the pleasure to men? Why would God be so cruel to *women?*"

"I-I don't know!"

"Are you telling me you that you don't like it...ever?" Horror and disbelief edging into his voice. "*Are you?*" Suddenly the gentle hand that had been on her chin was no longer gentle. "Are you merely *enduring* me?" Although she was still shy in the darkness unless he was a conceited idiot—she seemed to be doing much more than *enduring* him!

"When you kiss me, is it only for *duty?*"

"*No!* that's not how it is, you're my husband and I-I love you! It's what I've been taughtI'm so confused! Only girls that aren't *nice* enjoy it, and I can't help it, I felt so guilty that one time—"

"*One time!*" he shrieked. Mortified when he thought of the times he'd already made love to her, ashamed he had not realized she hadn't even enjoyed it, embarrassed and humiliated at his own incompetence as a lover. "You've only enjoyed it *once* in all these times? Is that why you've been pulling away from me—afraid you might enjoy it again?"

Although she did not admit it, her eyes gave her away.

"*Don't!*" he shrieked, pulling her flat on the bed underneath him. Looming over her, she could see the rise and fall of his muscled chest, could feel his breath against her as he hovered over her like a giant. "We were married in a church in front of our families, friends, and God! Chose each other freely, wanted each other as partners for life," he said, the anger in his voice giving way to anguish.

She hated seeing the pain on his face. "It's all right, I don't mind—"

"I *mind!*" he shrieked again. "It wouldn't matter if I didn't care about you—if I only wanted to satisfy my own selfish wants, but I want you to enjoy it! I *want* you to enjoy being with me! I don't want you to endure it and have it be a damn duty! Half of my pleasure is seeing that dazed look on your face after I've loved you!"

Knowing guiltily that her face had held that dreaminess, she looked shamefully away from him, but he grabbed her face back to look at him.

"I want you to want me, and not because of the vows, not because I'm taking care of you, not because of obligation, but because I—because I—" He broke off but she knew what he wanted to say.

She wanted to apologize to him but before she could he took both of her wrists inside his hand and pulled her hands up over her head, pinning her to the bed.

"I want you to enjoy it, and by God, I want you to enjoy it...*now!*" His mouth came down on hers with such a fury that it hurt. "Feeling guilty are you? I'll show you *guilt!*" He pushed the nightgown out of the way and took a breast in his mouth and sucked hard.

Sliding off her, he undid the bow on her nightgown, tugging it off her shoulders and pulling it down to her waist. She squirmed with embarrassment at being exposed but he ignored her. Kneeling on the bed, he began to tug the nightgown off her hips. She had never had the nightgown off since they'd wed, and it had been a minor irritation to him. Tonight, though, it was coming off.

"Victor, please!" she pleaded as he pulled the nightgown over her hips and ultimately off her feet.

"I want you," he said, his voice muffled as he left her mouth to kiss her ribs and then up slowly to her breasts. "To want me. And besides," he said, his hands skimming from her thighs up slowly to her ribs, "if what you're telling me is true, I *owe* you quite a few pleasurable experiences. And I always pay my debts." He reached down and touched her between her legs and her whole body jolted violently in protest, and she struggled to get up. "Lay down, it's *over*, do you hear me? It's over!"

"But what—what are you going to do?" she gasped; fright mingled with excitement.

"You're my *wife,* and I'm going to show you an *obligation* you'll never forget!" He knew what he wanted to do but wondered if the shock would be too much for his naive wife, but then decided he didn't care. He moved his big body down the length of the bed and shocked her nearly to death by prying her knees apart. He might have laughed at the look of terror in her eyes if he hadn't been so excited about what he was about to do.

Because of the nightgown, he'd never been able to take a genuinely good look at her, but he could now, and it was a sight that aroused him feverishly. He lifted himself up and started by kissing her navel, and then lower and lower until she was rearing up on the bed again frantically trying to pull his head from her.

"If you get up one more time, I swear to *God* I'll get straps to tie you down!" He shoved her hard back on the bed and thought about the times he dreamed of doing this, but the reality was even more intoxicating that he ever imagined it would be.

It was a sinfully wonderful feeling! Although she was mortified, at the same time new waves of deep hot, pleasure radiated where he worked, and she found herself being lifted off on waves of joy. They were a bit like the sweet clouds that used to lift her when he kissed her, and yet it was not sweet, it was basic, and primal in its gratification. And she could not help but succumb to its wicked pleasure. Although her mind was having trouble reconciling the lewd act, her body knew what it wanted. She was marveling that such magnificent, blinding enjoyment existed, and that Victor was giving it to her.

He heard the thud of her iron wedding band as her hands clawed the bed above her. He heard her suck in her breath, trying not to cry out, although she did so, twice. He felt her lifting herself up, pushing against him in an ever-increasing rhythm.

She felt his hot breath on her tender flesh, and it was all at once too much for her. Whatever it was, was building, and she thought she'd burst into frustrated tears, when it come crashing down inside her. Her body shuddered and she felt an aftershock of pleasure course through her body. Rearing up, she pulled him on top up her, her heart beating madly.

"No more—no more, I can't take anymore!" she panted, her eyes wild. Several violent, shameless thrusts later, he too was spent and lay panting against her his heart thumping in his chest.

Now that it was over, he was afraid to look her at her. Afraid she'd be angry or worse repulsed by what he'd done. But knew he'd nonetheless proven his point, knowing she had enjoyed it.

"Victor," she breathed.

"What?" he said, blowing out the lantern, leaving the house bathed in the soft glow of the fire.

"The world, it's set up fine. God's not cruel to women."

He laughed softly, kissing her sweetly on the forehead.

"Is...is that how it is for men, all the time?"

"Yes."

"Then no wonder you want it all the time!"

He laughed, amused, and took her hand and kissed each fingertip.

"You won't...ever tell anyone how wonderful it is between us? You'd never tell anyone what we...do together?"

"No," he said smiling in the darkness with relief, knowing that everything was all right "It's between you and me, always." Arranging his arms around her, sighed contentedly.

"How did you ever...*think* of such a thing to do?"

"I didn't. When I was in Washington, remember, I told you we ended up in a brothel and I saw etchings of it on a deck of playing cards. Besides, men are *born* wanting to do things like that."

"Oh," she breathed, snuggling closer to him, curious about the brothel, but decided she'd ask another time. "I guess then...we're not the first to do...something like that?"

"I assure you, we're not."

"Were there any...*other* things on the cards?"

"Am I *hearing* things? Or is my *shy bride* asking me questions about sex?"

"Who *else* am I going to ask?"

He laughed. "That's true."

"Does it...go the *other* way too?" she asked timidly, glad the lantern was out and hoped he couldn't see that she was blushing.

"Oh *my God*! Am I *dreaming*? I must have died, that's it! I've died and gone to *heaven!*" He pulled her against him in the darkness, kissing her forehead, her cheeks, and the little spot under her eye. "I am without a doubt, the *luckiest* man to ever walk the face of the earth!"

"You're teasing me."

"I'm not!"

"Then why did you say that?"

"Well, first of all, you're easy on the eyes, you're an excellent cook." He caught her face gently between his hands. "And you want me. You *love* me—"

"I do love you. I love you so much," she whispered, kissing him back. Hoping he would know she wanted him to make love to her again.

She was not disappointed.

Chapter 18

Mason was reading the contract furnished by Alexander Pickering about the new partnership with the carriage factory in Washington, as Victor and Ethan sat anxiously waiting for him to finish. Mason knew Ethan was a shrewd businessman and wanted to earn a good reputation in town. He read the entire three-page document from beginning to end, then for good measure, re-read it.

Ethan put a finger against his stiff white collar to loosen it slightly. He noticed how polished and empty Mason's walnut desk was and wondered if the poor man had any other clients.

"It does seem to be in order," Mason said finally.

A huge smile crossed Ethan's face. "You'll sign it for us then?"

"Certainly." Mason dipped the pen delicately into the inkwell. "You'll both have to sign the copies, and then of course you keep one in your possession, and we'll send one back to Mr. Pickering."

"Not a problem," Ethan said, confident that since Pickering had already written him one check, that others would be coming since they now had a three-way partnership of the carriage shop.

"Do you mind?" Victor asked, wanting to read the contract, since thus far neither of the other two men had let him. He didn't understand why they had to involve Mason, but since he figured Ethan knew more about business than he did, reluctantly agreed.

Mason leaned back in the chair agreeably. "Be my guest." He watched Victor lift one of the thick sheets of parchment. Glancing at his brother-in-law realized he must have been pulled out of shop unexpectedly, because his shirt sleeves were still rolled up, and the blacksmiths apron was still across his chest.

Mason knew Carlene was spending a lot of time at Victor's home. She helped with the garden she and Celena had dug up to be ready for next year, and she also went there all day on Monday's which was laundry day, and half a day on Friday when they made bread for the week. He wondered, if anything, what Carlene said about him. A small part of him was jealous, wishing his wife wanted to spend time with him.

"Ethan...on the second page it says here that, and I quote, I am to *'manage and train'* in the factory. How in the world am I going to manage a business in Washington when I'm here in Ste. Genevieve? Mason, I don't remember you pointing out this fact to us."

Mason picked up the other copy of the second page and felt a hotness color his cheeks.

"Don't worry about it, we'll manage it somehow," Ethan said, trying to smooth it over.

"There's no *'we'*—it says my name, Victor Gant, manager—this won't work. I can't possibly do this. I am not going to agree to this contract."

Ethan was irritated that somehow he let Pickering slip that in. He knew Pickering had not been happy to see him step off the train without Victor, and he had to admit that the demonstration he had staged at the factory had less than awed the laborers.

"Let me see that—damn it!" Ethan snatched the paper from Mason. Reading over the one error in what he thought had been such a shrewd negotiation. "Well," he said, rubbing his eyes for a minute, trying to find a way out of the mess, "how often would you have to do anything?"

"I honestly don't know," Victor said, as though his workload had been tripled.

"Victor I'm sorry, I should have seen it," Mason apologized.

Victor waved him off. "Not your fault Mason. It's Pickering, he put this in purposely, and he was hoping it would go unnoticed."

"Let's see how it goes...maybe things will run fine, and they won't even need you. It could be months before you're called on. Let's let the dust settle."

Victor was silent, considering. "You gave them the drawings and the model and all?" he asked, hoping to God Ethan had done a good job of teaching them. "We haven't got much choice—"

"Why is that?" Mason interjected, wanting to know more about the carriage rim, and the coupler patent they had just told him about as well as the factory to build it. It was all exciting, and he hoped they would come to him for his legal advice on subsequent contracts, and his business would grow.

"Because of Pickering. Even though he is a decent enough fellow, I fear he would be irritated if we change any of the points in his contract.

And we can't chance irritating the man who has, although he says he doesn't—the ear of the railroad when we are trying get them to change over the link and pin system," Victor explained, resigning himself to the fact that he might have to go to Washington soon. "Anyway, let's sign it all and be done with it." He straightened to his full height, looming over Mason sitting at his desk.

"There's mine," Ethan said, handing Victor the quill.

"What do we owe you Mason?" Victor asked, his large hands on his hips.

"I don't know. I haven't had a chance to compute it yet...I'll charge you." Mason felt foolish suddenly when Victor looked at him, knowing that Victor was in the habit of quoting a man an accurate fee for his work on the spot.

"All right, you know where to find us," Victor said.

Chapter 19

Victor looked up when Celena walked into the shop with a tray of food, and glancing quickly out the door, was shocked to see the last rays of the orange light had sunk behind the hills of the October night.

"I had no idea it was that late," he said, forcing a tired smile as she set the heavy tray on one of the carpenter tables and went about arranging the napkins, and silverware. He smiled again when he watched her drag over the stool and the crate for them to sit on.

"I know you've got to be hungry especially since you didn't stop for your lunch."

He looked worn out, worse than she'd ever seen him. The gray eyes were bloodshot, and rimmed in red, and his black hair was tousled and plastered with sweat against his forehead. The tan shirt was dirty and damp, and there were black lines of dirt under his nails.

It was proving far harder than even she thought for him to work building the factory all day and keeping up in the blacksmith shop.

"There," he said, placing the scythe he finished mending into the slack tub with a little hiss. Sighing tiredly, he stretched his aching back, working out the painful knots and kinks of overworked muscles.

She brought him a bowl of water and cloth to wash up in. He did so quietly and sat down on the crate. After they said grace, he quietly began to eat his food, she felt a pain in her heart seeing the fatigue all over him.

"It's good." He nodded later finished with the *potage parmentier*, and having devoured entire baguette, started on a second.

"Oh, I'm glad. I had such little stock; I didn't know if it would give enough flavor."

He tried to smile.

She finished her soup too, and glancing over at the anvil was surprised to see an odd contraption. It was iron and on it welded together were different parts of what looked to be vices of some sort.

"What is that?" she asked, standing up and gently placed a hand on his shoulder, surprised to feel how tight the muscles were.

Turning to see what she was referring to he winced in pain. "Oh, well I've also been working on ideas for the factory." Affectionately he placed a hand atop her hand still on his shoulder.

"Does it work, your...contraption?"

"Yes, quite well in fact." He smiled ruefully at his creation. "In fact, I think it will help with the coupler. We'll make them all perfectly sized, uniform. One piece of the coupler made in one part of the factory will easily fit into another part of the coupler made in different part of the shop. Everything uniform...identical."

"Can you do that—can you make them all so that they can be switched?" she asked, leaving him to inspect it further.

"Yes. I'm reasonably sure that I can."

"Has this been...done before?" she asked, trying to imagine things not made like Victor made them, individually and by hand.

"Yes. Your sewing machine for instance. Made in a factory with at least some interchangeable parts. And a fellow by the name of Whitney tried it years back with a munition's factory, and got people thinking about it."

"Where did you learn this?" she asked, realizing that, although she knew him well, there were still so many things about him still to discover.

"Read about it." He dropped his face into his hands and rubbed his eyes which were beginning to burn. "Believe it or not, years ago Jonah and I talked about all of this. The first I ever saw of it was a drill press. We talked about interchangeably, design uniformity like this." He smiled faintly, thinking Jonah would be pleased that he was going forward with their ideas. "You know what though, when this becomes the way that things are made, in factories quickly and perfectly...someone who labors as I do, won't be needed anymore. It's strange when I think about it that way. I'm all for it, and I think it's the way things will be and are meant to be, but I am in fact, putting myself out of work."

"I hadn't thought of it that way," she said softly, turning to look at him.

"Don't worry about it, I've got to build everything first before I put *myself* out of work!" He chuckled. Reaching for her he fit his hands around her waist and pulled her to him. Knowing what he wanted, she leaned down and kissed him.

"You look so tired," she said, kneading her fingers along his shoulders. He tilted his head back as she dug her fingers into the tight muscles along his back.

"The right shoulder, always the right shoulder," he murmured, his eyes closing with pleasure.

His hands left her waist and slowly moved up her ribs and just barely touched the curve of her breast, and a shiver ran through her. He stood up then, pulling her flush against him and bending, kissed her. It was three blissful seconds before he released her.

She was embarrassed when she saw him reach down and adjust his groin. "How does that...happen to you so fast?"

"What?"

She motioned downward.

"You kissed me."

"You poor thing!"

He dismissed it and tilted his head until his forehead touched hers. "I've only got a couple more hours in here, all right?"

She was breathless when he released her. "All right." As always when he took his hands and lips off her, she was cold, even with the warmth from the forge.

She was on her knees cleaning the ashes from the fireplace when she heard his heavy steps coming up to the door and glancing up at the little clock on the mantle realized he'd only worked another hour since his dinner.

He painfully lowered his big body into the chair. "I'm beat."

She moved two steps over to him on her knees, and without a word began to tug his boots off.

"Oh," he uttered when he realized what she was doing, "thank you."

Standing up she laid the boots by the door, and then came back around and laid her healing hands on his shoulders, massaging them.

"God that's wonderful," he said, eyes closed, head drooping back.

She kissed him then on the forehead, but as he reached up to touch her, flinched in pain.

"What you need is a good soak." She moved to add wood to the fire.

"I do?"

"Yes. I'm going to heat you a whole tub full of it, and you're going to lay in it and work some of the soreness out of those muscles."

"All right, if you think it will work."

"It'll work. You recommended it to me once, remember?" she said, putting the large kettle on the hook in the fireplace, knowing she would need more wood and water. "I'll be back in a minute with more water. Take off your clothes and leave them by the table, I'll soak them too when you're finished with the water."

"Go ahead and get in." She poured in another steaming kettle. She was perspiring now having brought in and heated not only kettles of water, but every pot with a handle she could hang in the fire.

"Ooo…"

"Too hot?"

"A bit."

"Here's a cool one. Be back in a minute."

"It's good," he said later, hip deep in steaming water, two washcloths that had been dipped in the hot water laid across his aching shoulders.

She wiped the perspiration off her forehead. "I'm glad." She took a drink of water, kneeling by the tub. She handed him a glass of water, and after noisily draining it, returned it to her.

"Thank you." He leaned back in the tub. It was a large metal tub, one that she could sit up in, completely stretch her legs out. But it did not seem big now as he sat in it with his knees protruding out of the water like tree trunks.

"You might as well wash as long as you're there." She went behind the quilt to retrieve soap, and getting a towel, carefully laid his nightshirt out across the bed.

"Couldn't reach my back."

Kneeling behind him, she began the arduous process of washing his back. He moaned delightedly as she rubbed the washcloth along him, and she watched the tiny white bubbles glisten against his smooth dark skin. She dipped the washcloth in the water again and rinsed him, watching the water run down his sleek brown skin. He was so big, and muscled, and yet at the same time he was so affectionate and sweet, and she loved him so much.

She peered at his chest. "What is that supposed to be?"

He glanced at the triangular shaped tattoo almost over his heart. "I can't remember," he shook his head, "I'm sure my mother told me."

"Did she give it to you?"

"Yes."

Celena leaned closer and traced her hand along the faint blackish marks under his skin. "How did she do it?"

"With a needle made from bone and some charcoal from a redbud tree."

"Did it hurt?"

"No. My father didn't like it though, that's why she never finished."

When her washcloth suddenly got to the place on his bicep with the twisted silvery scar she dropped it, and instead spread her fingers. She could barely touch the scar end to end. Self-consciously he moved his hand to cover it

"H-how did you get that?"

"A piece of firewood."

"*Firewood?* How would you get that...from firewood?"

He shrugged, not wanting to explain. Not wanting his sordid past to touch her. "My father got mad." He watched then how her eyes flew back in silent horror. It had healed ages ago, but since the wound had been deep and never stitched, it had scarred badly.

"He...hit you with it?"

A shudder of cold revulsion when through her when he nodded.

"How old were you?"

"Ten or so. I was already bigger than him, so I guess he thought he needed to even up the odds."

"Did it...hurt much?"

"I suppose."

"Does it hurt anymore?"

He forced a smile, not wanting to talk about it. "No."

It was horrifying to her that the man she loved had been the target of such cruelty. She had heard the rumors, but it was chilling to see such gruesome proof of those beatings. "How often...did he hit you?"

He shrugged. "It was a long time ago." His eyes dropped guiltily from her, as rank memories crept into his mind. The afternoon with the firewood was bad, but other days when he heard his mother being slapped from behind the bedroom door were worse.

"I don't remember," he mumbled, deciding he'd make something up to explain the other two scars on his body.

"I don't understand. I don't understand why he'd hurt you."

"Who knows. I probably deserved it."

Leaning near him, she held his face in her hands. "You were just...a little boy. I don't understand how he could hurt you like that?"

"He drank too much. Guess it makes it easier to do whatever you want when you don't have to worry about remembering it in the morning.

Besides when he was drunk, he didn't have to think about what he'd done."

"What had he done?"

He shrugged, but she could see humiliation creeping up on him and didn't understand why. "He ended up with...an Indian woman. He was from Philadelphia. He was educated, a schoolteacher. His family cut all ties when they found out, they never forgave him."

"But he married her—"

"Well yes, *after* he got her pregnant. She was pregnant even before he bought her from the Toulouse's, and I was three years old by the time he actually got around to marrying her. I think the only reason he even did was because Father Tonnellier insisted, saying it was a sin to simply live with her."

"He didn't...love her then?"

"Actually, I think he did love her, or at least as much as he allowed himself to. He told me once... that he'd fallen far from his place in the world. It's funny though, I always thought it was the other way around. That *she* had been the one degraded by the marriage."

"Did she...love him?"

"I don't know. I don't know how she could have. They never got along. My mother was already eleven years old when the Toulouse's found her. She'd been Osage all her life, then suddenly she's living in a brick house, speaking French and English and going to a catholic church. I don't think anything ever made sense to her again."

"She left you too soon."

They fell silent.

"My father had me dig the hole and I buried them...buried them as your mother left them wrapped up together in the quilt my mother had given birth on. Took me a day to dig that hole." He shook his head unpleasantly. "When I was finally done, I couldn't lift them, so I had to pull them into it. I couldn't believe how heavy they were. They thudded into the grave, and the baby rolled out of the quilt. I-I was desperate to put her back in my mother's arms—" He stopped then, not wanting to finish and tell her that his father furious and drunk had kicked him into the grave on top of them. To this day he could still see his mother's face smudged with the dirt from his boots. He tried spitting on his hands to get the dirt off her face.

"Catherine. Wasn't her name Catherine?"

His eyes met hers. "I can't believe you remember that—I mean you were so small yourself."

The air was heavy with sadness around them when she reached for the towel. "We better get you out of the tub before you're wrinkled all over."

Forcing a smile, he stepped out of the tub and dried himself.

Later that night when they crawled into bed together, he pulled her against him in the darkness. Gently tracing his fingertips across her cheeks. Aghast at the thought of how any man could take a hand to a woman, much less a woman he was in love with. He was horrified at the thought of striking the beautiful face underneath his fingertips.

"Maybe I shouldn't have told you all of this," he began quietly, worry threaded through his voice. "I am his son; he was my father after all. It's his blood that flows through my veins."

She gently stroked his face in the darkness, and then kissed him, keeping her lips against his heartbeat longer than necessary. "But you forget, your mother's blood is there too...coursing warmly, all through your heart."

Chapter 20

"It's remarkable. Extraordinary. Do you think we can pull it off?" Ethan asked after having listened to Victor for a half hour explain how they were going to set up the coupler factory.

"Yes, after all it's hardly a new idea," Victor admitted, glancing from Ethan back to Celena as they each sat with cups of coffee around the square table in the shop.

"And if it works as well as it should, I think we should also re-tool the carriage factory."

Ethan took a drink of lukewarm coffee. "As soon as that coupler factory is running, I'll get every one of the railroads to commit and switch over. Think of the superiority our factory will have over all the others, the power we'll have, the fortunes to be made."

"And the amount of work to be done." Victor sighed, wondering how many man-hours he had already put into the infinite details of the factory.

"I still don't like the idea of the factory here, and not in Washington. We'll have to ship everything. Everything will have to go by steamer, and that will eat into our gross profits."

"We have been through this *ad nauseam—*"

"Really, *Latin*, Victor; you are *annoyed*, aren't you?"

"Yes, I am annoyed. I am already supposed to run the carriage factory in Washington, which I never agreed to by the way. And I must oversee the sawmill here otherwise it'll be losing money again, *and* I still have a blacksmith shop to run. If the coupler factory is not built here, who's going to run it? Are you going to, Ethan?"

"I was only saying that if we had built the factory in Washington on the land that we already owned by the carriage factory, it would have been more cost effective than us having to buy that land from Widow Chomeau, who overcharged us by the way."

"And like I've told you half a dozen times before, how does having another business in Washington help St. Genevieve?"

"Why do you insist on worrying about the *town?*"

"Why start a business when it doesn't help anyone we know? We're already doing that in Washington."

"Why do we care who else it helps, as long as it helps us!" Ethan scoffed with irritation. It annoyed him that Victor was already offering people in town jobs and paying more than Ethan liked.

"I'm not going to argue about this. We made the decision."

"No, you did. Unilaterally. Against my good business sense. It'll be that much longer before we return a profit."

"But we will still return a profit, *Jesus* how much profit do *we need!*" Victor said and wished he hadn't sworn when he saw Celena flinch at the table. "I don't know if you understand this Ethan, but to get people to work, you have to pay them. And did it ever occur to you that the better you pay them, the better workers you'll attract?"

"And do you understand that's there's been money, a lot of *my* money invested in all these ventures? And if they fail, the worker you insist on paying well loses nothing, while I on the other hand, lose everything."

"My money is invested too," Victor said. "I'm done talking about this. I let you take care of all the other financial matters you wanted you, make unilateral decisions as well...like the shoe factory."

"Shoe factory?" Celena asked, looking at them both.

"Last time Ethan was in Washington he bought a failing shoe factory! I don't even want to talk about it anymore." Victor laughed and looked up at the ceiling, ignoring Ethan's vehement defense that it was a good deal. "Ethan, have you got the other plans?"

"Plans for what?" Celena asked, thinking they were indeed good friends, since they could be arguing one minute and grinning the next.

"Your life is about to change my dear Celena. After all your broad-backed husband here has surprised all of us, me included—with his ability not only to envision the coupler but also to put it in motion. I am sure that when I get the railroads to agree, the coupler will no doubt make us all rich beyond our wildest dreams."

"But—but I don't want my life to change! What are we talking about?"

Victor reached across the table and sweetly took a hold of her hand.

"Money. Victor has now a rather large surplus of it," Ethan said with a laugh. "You see, the carriage factory in Washington is paying off nicely."

"Not *that* large a surplus." Victor frowned.

"Like I was *saying* before I was so rudely interrupted—he has decided at this most inopportune of moments I might add, to plan for you a new gracious home." He reached down amidst all the bank papers that went with him everywhere and pulled out a blueprint. Victor helped him unroll it and they moved the coffee cups to keep the edges from curling back up.

Sketched was a plan for a large brick house. It was three stories tall, and had roman columns supporting the front porch with a curving balcony above, that looked simply perfect she thought for Juliet to be looking down at Romeo. Underneath it was the floor plan; two large parlors, dining room, detached kitchen with stone break. Winding staircase to the second floor, where four large bedrooms were mapped out. Above it a small stairway leading to an attic with a quaint pitched ceiling, which seemed to her suddenly perfect for a nursery.

"Where did you get plans like this?"

"I sent away to St. Louis for architect's plans, but none of them matched what I wanted for you, so I asked Ethan. He took one of their plans and re-drew it. I told him what to add and what to take out. I've got other ideas too. Do remember that fabulous coal stove we saw at the Willard?" he asked, looking at Ethan. "I am going to order a larger version." Victor began rummaging on the table through the house plans that he had drawn as well. He scrutinized the drawings, squinting a bit like he did when he was deep in thought. "I think it will work but I'll have to do some more figuring."

"Where—where will we build it?"

"On our land...the place that I showed you on our wedding night, where Jonah was to build the house for Hilde." He glanced from his plans to look into her eyes. "I'm also going to try and pump water into the house—"

"Into the *house?*" Celena exclaimed.

Victor nodded. "Yeah, I think I can pump it up to a big tank or reservoir in the attic with a Windmill. I'll have pipes to disperse it through the house by gravity. And right here, we'll put in a necessary or water closet."

Celena was so shocked she merely sat mouth gaping. "A necessary *inside* the house?"

"Look," Victor said, pointing to a series of what she thought must be pipes that looked like a sideways *S*. "I found plans for it. It's not a new design the idea was first sketched out in 1775 or so by a Scottish man by the name of Cummings, and he improved on the work of a man named Harrington by keeping water in the pipes to keep the smell away and a flush mechanism."

Impressed, she leaned forward to stare at the papers. Although they were tidily written and painstakingly sketched, she had trouble making sense out of the solid lines, dotted lines, numbers, and fractions all over it.

She stared up at him. "How did you *think* of all of this?"

"I didn't, I mean not all of it. Most of it someone else thought of, I read about them, studied them, modified them. Like I always do." He leaned back in the chair. "You like it, don't you?"

"Oh, oh yes! It's wonderful, I'm shocked. It couldn't be more wonderful." She got up and came around to where Victor sat at the table and hugged him a bit shyly because Ethan was there.

"Ethan, I don't know how to thank you." She left Victor briefly to hug him. "Thank you," she whispered, looking gratefully into his warm brown eyes, thinking that even though he was smiling, he looked sad.

"You're welcome." Ethan looked back down at his papers, not wanting to see her return to Victor's arms. "Although I do not understand my dear Victor with all we have going on right, you choose to build a house."

"I've got my reasons," Victor said, snaking his arm around a timid Celena, pulling her towards him. "I have a bit of a time frame."

"What time frame is that?" Ethan asked.

"We'll be having a child sometime in the spring. And I want at least to start planning for the house."

Dumbfounded, Ethan tried to think of something to say, of how to congratulate them. But it was hard to do any of these things when his heart constricted so painfully in his chest he could barely breathe. He looked down suddenly to mask his shock. With shaking hands, he rolled up the plans for the magnificent house he had designed. The house that his adored Celena would lay her head at night, and bear Victor's children.

"Well...congratulations to you both." A devastating realization hit Ethan. He realized he would never have children. There would never be a child to bear his name, demeanor, and values. That there would never be a woman, thrilled like Celena was, carrying his child. He didn't understand how or why the feeling came over him but knew deep in his heart it was true. Immediately, he felt the sealing off another corridor to his heart. Sealing off the corridors of communication, caring, giving, and receiving love. After more he sealed off, the less he would hurt.

"We should toast," Ethan forced out, lifting a cup of cold coffee.

"To my business partner, best friend, and to tomorrow and all the joy it brings."

Ethan nodded in agreement. And despite himself, hoped with what was left of his heart, that all their tomorrow's held joy.

Chapter 21

"I'll give it to him when I see him," Celena said, smiling at Widow Chomeau's overseer Joseph Kendrick when he came to drop off the earning check from Victor's interest in the mill.

"I hear he's also got a carriage factory in Washington and that it's doing well," Joseph said, but for a moment, their attention was diverted by the sound of a vicious wind howling outside the door.

It was the end of March and an unseasonably cold day. The gray skies were already darkening as angry storm clouds rolled in from the river. It was so chilly and gloomy outside that Joseph longed to stay in the snug, warm little house. Have another cup of hot coffee and continue chatting with the blacksmith's pretty wife.

"Yes, it is doing well."

"And I hear all goes well with the coupler for the railroad and that the factory is due to open anytime now, he must be a busy man!" Joseph said, touched by the way her pale face pinked when he spoke appreciatively of her husband.

"Well, he's not home much these days!" She saw Joseph Kendrick's eyes drift downward at her pregnant form and felt a shiver of embarrassment. "Would you like another cup of coffee Mr. Kendrick?" she offered, summoning all her courage to look him square in the eye.

"I'd best be on my way." Getting to his feet, he respectfully pushed the chair back in.

For a moment, the eerie sound of the howling wind jerked both of their attentions. Through the window they could see the oak and silver maple trees bending and twisting fitfully to the fury of the wind. Rapidly losing their emerging leaves to the sudden gale.

"Looks like we are in for a dandy of a storm. I sure do wish it'd wait 'til I get home though. Take care of yourself Mrs. Gant."

A half hour later the steady rain that had been falling turned into a torrential downpour, and Celena opened the door a bit to inspect the weather but quickly closed it when a piercing flash of lightning snaked across the sky and the clap of thunder hurt her ears. The sky had taken on an almost green tinge, and it worried her. She didn't mind rain, in fact she had for her family's well-being, at times prayed fervently for rain, knowing that it nourished the fields her brothers and fathers put so many backbreaking hours into. But this was not merely rain, it was the type of storm farmers dreaded. The kind that uprooted trees and broke tender stalks of crops painstakingly tended. For some reason, the eerie cast of white lightening that lit up the sky caused her to catch her breath and wait for the deafening roll of thunder which rattled the panes of glass in the windows. What made the storm even worse was the fact that Victor was not merely twelve steps away. She was after all, spoiled having him so near, and she missed him. He had gone to the factory early that morning and she did not know when he would return.

Walking to the sink board she carefully washed and put away the cup Mr. Kendrick had used, jumping once when a particularly bright flash of lightening illuminated the dark sky, and still jumping from the noise of the thunder even though she knew it was coming. She lit a lantern to try and cheer the suddenly dark house.

She hadn't felt right all day. There was an odd uneasiness in her mind and her body. Her back hurt, her legs hurt and there was a dull ache deep in her abdomen. She wished Victor was next door and that she could walk into the shop and lay her troubled head against his chest. She knew merely having him listen to her complaints she would feel better.

She took the check Mr. Kendrick had brought and leaned up to place it on the mantle when she felt a sharp stab of pain. It was so strong she cried out, and then feeling silly, was glad there was no one there to hear it. Unsteady, she sat down in the rocking chair with a thud. She'd had these pains during the night, but they hadn't troubled her too much. She heard from other women about the 'false pains' that often came long before the baby was due.

"It'll go away in a minute," she said out loud as if trying to convince herself and the baby and wrapped her hand around her stomach when another gut-wrenching pain racked her abdomen. "That...was a bad one," she exclaimed, patting her stomach. But before she could relax, another contraction came. Without warning vomit rose in her throat and she scrambled down to the ground as quickly as her ungraceful form would enable her. She retched violently into the chamber pot, emptying her stomach. Hanging her head, she felt a sudden clammy dampness under her arms, above her lips, and between her breasts. She felt better on all fours and merely stayed there for a few moments.

She hauled herself back up into the chair but noticed with confusion that she was sweating, as she reached for a dishtowel. Wetting it tried to wipe the foul taste of vomit out of her mouth. Another pain racked her, and she gripped tight to the edge of the table. It was the first time in her entire pregnancy that she had felt sick.

"I am going to lay down, and I am going to feel better," she said and dragged herself over to the bed. She was struggling to pull herself onto the bed when she felt something warmly trickle down her legs. Horrified that she'd lost control of her bladder, hauled her skirts up and saw a line of pink tinged liquid running down her thighs. She was certain the this was not a good sign, and no sooner had she dropped her skirts back down, than she felt a whoosh of something warm and wet splash against her legs. Shocked she stared down as the amniotic fluid seeped out around her in a quiet circle on the floor.

Thomas and Claude noticed the door open to the shop because a gust of piercingly cold rain rushed in, and when they saw Celena they both dropped what they were doing and ran to her.

"Miss Celena—are you all right?" Thomas asked, alarmed, his skinny arms grabbing her, wishing to God Victor was there!

Celena gulped twice trying to force the bile back in the throat long enough so she could speak. "Thomas, I need Victor, get him—" She grimaced then as another wave of nausea and pain gripped her. "And my sister Carlene, she lives above the post office, get her please!"

Her face crashed into the brick floor of the shop when a confused Thomas let a fainting Celena slip from his hold.

Victor was drenched from the storm and could barely see through the downpour, and stinging hail was pelting as he hurried home. He saw lights on in his house as he neared it and was relieved when he recognized his father-in-law's wagon.

He swung his leg off Alpha and led him into the stall. "I'll be back later, sorry old boy." He ran then from the barn, slipping twice in the mud.

Opening the door, it was overly bright because there were extra lanterns lit. He saw Eva placing a pot of water on the fire. When she turned to him, her blue eyes were rimmed in sadness and Victor's brittle hopes faded.

"How is she?"

"Maman's with her."

Sloughing off his wet coat, Victor ducked in behind the quilt to see Celena laying fitfully on the bed. He noticed her face was already wet with sweat, and the cotton shimmy she had on was already damply clinging to her form. Underneath her body was an old quilt that had been stuffed with straw to protect the mattress.

"It's too soon, Maman, I know it's too soon—" She gasped and braced herself for another wave of pain.

He was shocked then when she began to vomit during the contraction. He felt sorry for her seeing that the girth of pregnancy made it almost impossible for her body to bend as she needed to vomit, and the only thing she produced was a yellow-green frothy bile.

"I'm...sorry Maman, I'm so sorry!"

"Ez all right, ez all right," Yvonne soothed. Although, to Victor she looked scared as she wiped off the sweat from Celena's forehead with an already damp cloth. Carlene sat at the foot of the bed, motionless, wide-eyed, and for one of the few times in her life, utterly silent.

"Lena."

Celena looked over at him-realizing finally that he was there. Even though she forced a weak smile at him he saw fear in her eyes.

"What's happening?" Victor asked, his throat constricting with emotion when he looked down at her, wondering how long she had been in pain.

"Her water's broken, ze babies got to come now," Yvonne explained.

"It's a little soon though, isn't it?" A cold shiver went through him when Yvonne nodded silently. "What's happened to your face?" he asked, moving closer to Celena, seeing the beginnings of an ugly purple bruise on her temple.

"She fainted and slipped out of Thomas's hold." Carlene explained.

Silently Victor cursed.

"Here comes another one," Yvonne said and Victor could see the worry in her eyes. "I'm so glad you're here, shez done nothing but ask for you."

He didn't know what to do, and for a moment merely stood there feeling like a helpless fool while Yvonne sponged her. He glanced from Carlene to Yvonne, and wanting to do something, moved up towards Celena and knelt by her.

He thought he'd die when Celena began to cry. "Lena it's all right. It will be all right." They were ridiculous words to say to a woman giving birth painfully and prematurely to her first child, but he was at a loss of what to do.

"Oh. It—it hurts...and I'm going to be sick."

Victor reached under her arms and lifted her up as she tried to vomit, but there was nothing left but the foamy yellow bile and the horrible sound of her dry heaves.

"You all right now?" he asked, laying her gently back down and she nodded for a moment, and he watched her eyes close.

"I feel like such a bother." She gasped and gritted her teeth through a small contraction. "Making all of you sit here and watch this—it's not...ladylike, is it?" she said weakly of Carlene and Eva.

Carlene forced a smile, but she was terrified knowing she could also go into labor at any time. "It's all right Celena. Yell all you want. We're not going anywhere."

"How long will this go on?" Victor quietly asked Yvonne, his alarm rising a few notches.

"Could be only hours Victor, ez come on strong, but sometimes it still takes days..."

"Should we get Dr. Casey?" he asked, even though he was not sure he liked the idea of the Doctor there and wished Dr. Casey hadn't scared off the only midwife Ste. Genevieve had by spreading vicious rumors that she was a 'butcher.'

"We already talked to him, he said to call him in a few hours when zes farser along..."

Twenty-four hours later, Victor thought seriously that he might lose his mind. Every time Celena cried out in pain his heart constricted. It was hard enough to *watch* her in pain, he couldn't begin to imagine what it felt like to be *in* pain for so many hours, especially when nothing appreciable seemed to be happening. Nothing except that she was getting more tired, but seemingly no closer to giving birth to their child. Yvonne, distraught, had sent a terrified Carlene for Dr. Casey.

"Lena—"

Weakly, she looked up at him.

"You're strong, you can do this."

"But I'm so tired...why doesn't it end?" She realized she would have fallen asleep were it not the pain that kept her awake, "I can't do this anymore!" She began to sob hoarsely. He felt useless and guilty seeing her in so much pain, knowing he was after all, the reason she was in this predicament.

"Try and relax," he said, noticing that her whole body, her face her hands everything seemed to tense up with the pain and never seem to let go. He couldn't help but think that maybe her rigidness was getting in the way of what should be happening. "Come here." He started to drag her out of the bed under her arms. "Let's get you up for a minute."

"What the devil do you think you are doing?" Dr. Casey scoffed, coming around the quilt, annoyed as Victor forced Celena out of the bed on her feet, weak and trembling, holding on to his shoulders for support.

"She can't just keep laying there, nothing's happening! Besides maybe if she moves around a bit." He stopped talking when she let out a small gasp and then buried her face against his chest. "You all right?" he murmured into her hair and could tell by the way her hands gripped his shoulders how long the pain lasted and felt himself breathe a sigh of relief when her hands relaxed.

"Let it go Lena..." he murmured when he felt her tense up again, and she nodded weakly. "I know you're scared, I'm scared too, but I'm here and I'll do whatever I can. You...let it happen." He could tell she was trying to do what he said, and he felt another burst of love for her thinking that with the pain and danger involved it was a wonder *any* woman ever agreed to bear a man's child.

"We're getting closer now...won't be much longer," Dr. Casey said, having timed the contractions with his pocket watch.

"What do we do?" Victor asked, drenched now with sweat, his own mingled with Celena's.

"There's nothing *you* can do; she's got to do it!" Dr. Casey snarled. "It's time now, come on girl!" He merely stood at the end of the bed peering insanely at Celena's limp body to miraculously produce a child. She was beyond exhaustion now and Dr. Casey's standing back to watch his nearly dead wife suddenly push out child seemed ludicrous.

"Can't we sit her up or something?" Victor asked, knowing that she was simply spent after so many hours and didn't know if she had in her the reserve for this most difficult bit at the end.

"It's going to be a difficult delivery no matter whether she sits or lays. She's a small woman Mr. Gant, surely you've noticed that! And small women have difficulty bearing children!"

Paying no heed to the doctor's words, Victor moved him out of the way and grabbed a limp Celena under her arms. "If I was trying to push something out, I'd at least want *God damn gravity* on my side!" He climbed up on the bed and lifted Celena up so that she was squatting, her knees up.

Within a few moments Celena was awakened by the horrendous pressure, afraid again that she was losing control of her bowels. Yet at the same time could not suppress the primitive urge and began forcefully in her new upright position, to push. She groaned loudly and gripped onto Victor's forearms tightly. Seized with the knowledge that it was finally ending, lifted her head up weakly.

Victor knelt behind her, his arms wrapped around the front of her although he was careful not to hold her too tightly as he felt her chest heaving. He put his cheek against hers through clenched teeth prompted her: "Again...Lena...*again!*"

She was sure she was going to die and never birth this child. But she gritted her teeth and felt a burning sensation between her legs and bearing down felt a gush of wet and then the unbelievable relief of pressure. Shaking uncontrollably, she dropped her head weakly back against Victor.

But the room was oddly silent, and she struggled to lift her head back up to see Dr. Casey frantically trying to remove the sticky red mucous from the baby's face, even while the umbilical cord still tethered it to her. A second later Celena was flooded with relief when she heard the joyful sound on her baby's cry. Victor gently laid her back down and stroked her forehead. "It's a girl Lena, we have a baby girl."

She tried to smile back, but exhaustion took over and she dissolved into a weightless black void. She awoke a short time later and felt a searing hot pain between her legs. She was so thirsty she could barely move her tongue from her mouth. She could hear murmuring of voices, and tried to call out to them, but her tongue was immovable. When she tried to move, was met with a stab of excruciating pain. She trailed her hand across her stomach, it was loose and flaccid now. Not at all taut and firm like she had been when she had been pregnant. The fluid sloshing underneath her slack skin sickened her.

I had a girl!

Victor was suddenly leaning over her and pulling her head up to give her a drink. She gulped, choked, and fell back against the pillows.

"It's unfortunate," she heard a voice say, "but she was two months premature, tiny actually...nothing we could have done."

Even in her exhausted, mind-numbed state, she grasped the meaning of the awful words and fell into a ghoulish, nightmare-laden sleep.

Chapter 22

"Shouldn't she be better by now? I mean, she's not even been awake— and the fever...it keeps getting higher, shouldn't it have broken by now?" Victor asked, pacing back and forth beside the bed where Celena's feverish body had lain for four days.

Yvonne was wringing her hands, new lines of worry creasing her forehead and around her mouth. She was haggard and worn out from nursing Celena and scared that her daughter was going to die.

"Oui, I'm afraid somezings, wrong," she admitted, having watched in silent horror as Celena's fever continued day after day. How her restless body would shake with chills and no amount of quilts or blankets draped over her could stop her shivering. How she had for the last three days not been able to drink much less eat, and even the sips of water, they forced in her mouth, moments later her body would reject and vomit.

"There must be *something* we can do!" Victor shouted, the pain and frustration in his voice causing Yvonne, Eva, and Carlene to jump.

"I don't know. Dr. Casey said keep her in bed and not to agitate her," Eva repeated, looking from her mother to Carlene, who sat in absolute shock at the frightening events of the last few days. Carlene had already been afraid of motherhood and of child birth , but after watching Celena's terrifying ordeal, she was horror-struck.

"Dr. Casey!" Victor spat, shaking his head. "Idiot believes in bad humors and bleeding people as a cure." He knew the doctor thought him a fool for asking him what they could do to revive her and when he offered his own thoughts on the subject, Dr. Casey waved him off saying he was being *'outlandish and ridiculous.'*

He walked over to the bed and stared down at Celena. Her face was an unnatural gray and faint purple circles rimmed her closed eyes. Her lips were pale, and her breathing was frighteningly shallow, almost as if she was panting. She would move fitfully at times, and it was shocking because she looked already to be dead, and yet she was hot to the touch. Reaching down he touched her throat and felt her pulse hammering under his fingertips and leaning down laid his head against her chest. Heard her heart beating he knew much too rapidly. And although he knew little of medicine and the mechanics of the human body, had the feeling the accelerated heart rate was a horrible new symptom.

"If we don't do something, we're going to lose her. She gets weaker by the hour." He stared at her thin body, restless with fever on the bed. Saw the beautiful face he loved so much white as death, felt the dangerous heat of her body. "I've got to try something. I can't stand here and let her die..."

"Eva, are you sure that water is warm enough?" Victor asked, holding an unconscious Celena in his arms.

"Yes, it is." Quickly she moved out of the way while Victor carried Celena to the tub. It was frightening to see the vulgar contrast of her sister lying lifelessly against Victor's muscular, healthy arms.

"Should we take her shimmy off?" Carlene asked, her eyes rimmed in red, looking up to Victor for guidance.

"Ez filthy; get it off her," Yvonne said, leaning by the bathtub as she and Eva tugged the sticky, dirty garment off. It was strange Eva thought how they stripped the clothes off her sister while Victor watched. If someone would have said she would be in a room with her brother-in-law while her sister was stripped naked in front of her, she would have been mortified. But what did mortify Eva was the fear that one of these mornings, she would find Celena dead. And Eva would have done anything Victor asked her to do to prevent that.

Victor gently laid Celena's ghostly body in the tub of warm water.

"What should we do now?" Carlene whispered, watching trustingly as Victor began to sponge her sister's face and shoulders with a cloth.

"Something is wrong," he said quietly, having thought of nothing else for days.

"It juz...happens...sometimes," Yvonne explained, wringing her hands in worry.

"I know childbed fever. But...*why*? Why does it happen? What's wrong?" He scrutinized Celena's body, trying to discover the source of the killing fever. "If I just knew what it was." He had the insane desire to tear her open! That if he could open her flesh and look underneath he could see the cause of the sickness.

"Shez given birth Victor," Yvonne murmured weakly.

Nodding he glanced down again at Celena in the water. Immediately after giving birth, they had placed folded towels between her legs to soak up the blood and birth fluids that had gushed out of her. Carlene had for the first two days needed to change the towels every few hours—and then it had ceased.

"Shouldn't she still be bleeding? Is it normal that it stopped so quickly?" he asked, wishing again that he understood more about women's bodies, remembering that morning Celena had told him about how much she would bleed when she birthed their children. He reached down into the water, trying to touch her womb, but knew by the sound of her skin as it had ripped that she would be sore, and he would no doubt hurt her if he put his hand up. Besides, he realized hopelessly that he hadn't the faintest idea what he would be feeling for.

"Well...yez," Yvonne stammered, trying to remember how long she usually bled after birthing her own children. "It usually lasts...for a few weeks."

Victor went over again in his mind the visions of the birth. Remembering as he had held her upright in the bed, as she pushed the baby out how water and blood and other things that he had no name for come out of her. "It's not all...*out!*"

The three women turned to him for explanation.

"All the...blood and whatever else her insides have made to grow the baby—it's still inside her now, rotting." He stared at Celena laying under the water, looking gruesomely like she had drowned. "I'm going to push on her stomach."

"What will that do?" Carlene asked, afraid.

"Maybe nothing, but I'm afraid to put my hand up there—"

Carlene jerked her head up at him in shock.

"If that baby's *head* can get out, surely my *hand* would fit, but still, I don't know what should be there and what shouldn't. I'll have to get it out another way." Turning back to the tub he reached both hands down into the lukewarm water and began pushing on Celena's abdomen. "Tell me if I force anything out. Carlene, hold her under the arms—and don't let her go under!" He pushed gently at first feeling with his hands what his eyes couldn't see.

"There's a lot of, *something* in there," he said as he pressed different places along her stomach and rib cage and felt fluid sloshing inside her body. "Problem is, I don't know what belongs and what doesn't!"

"Lower, Victor," Yvonne urged and, leaning down into the water, guided Victor's hands.

"I feel something move, and then it gets away!" he barked, splashing water all over the three of them as he worked.

"Oh God Victor you're going to hurt her!" Carlene gasped seeing the force he was exerting on Celena, which looked to be enough break her ribs.

"See anything?" He stopped to inspect the water for any change.

No one spoke.

Again, he leaned into the tub of water, his large arms splashing the water noisily on the floor.

"*Come on!*" Gritting his teeth, he kept pushing. "Where the hell *is it!*" He hissed, pushing so hard on Celena that all three women were sure at any moment they were going to hear bones crack. "Wait a minute! I *feel*... something—" He pushed down violently. And then it gets away, *damnit!*" he shrieked, leaning his head against the side of the tub. Fighting the hopelessness that was threatening to engulf him. But a moment later, he lifted his head in determination and began pushing again. Felt whatever it was underneath his palms and pushed as hard as he could.

Both Eva and Carlene screamed when a mass of blood and afterbirth thickly oozed out of Celena's body.

"*Oh! Victor...!*" Yvonne cried when she saw the amount of un-expelled placenta that he was forcing of her body. It was foul smelling and he looked up from his efforts to see the tub of water now red-brown stained. There were dark red blood clots and pink tinged tissue now floating in the putrid water.

Yvonne's red rimmed eyes met Victor's for a moment and overcome with gratitude and relief she lunged over and hugged him, sobbing. His wet arms went immediately around her in a death grip. He swore silently thinking that all the damn doctor could think of to do was to keep her laying horizontal with quilts on her!

"Make zure you get it all out."

Too choked up to speak, he nodded. "Eva, would you please heat more water. We'd better clean her out again, we don't want to take any chances. Carlene would you hand me that sheet." Reaching down, he dragged a limp Celena from the tub.

As he wrapped Celena up, he gently cradled her body in his arms and couldn't stop himself from kissing the colorless lips. "You'll be all right; it'll be all right now," he chanted as he rocked her back and forth. For the first time since he walked through the door five days ago, gave into his fear. Felt the wall of strength he had built, begin to crumble, brick by brick as tears filled his eyes.

He remembered how his father laughed at him when he'd cried when he buried his mother, and infant sister Catherine. *Tears are for the weak.* Victor held Celena closer to him, trying to shake off the bad feelings that came over him whenever he thought of his father. Realizing his father was wrong again, like he had been about so many things.

Celena felt something warm next to her and turning her head on the pillow saw that it was Victor. He had been sitting on the floor, but had both hands resting on her arm, and his head was face down on the mattress, and by his steady breathing she could tell he was asleep. The pain was gone except for a dull throbbing ache. She saw her mother come around the side of the quilt, and the look of surprised joy that crossed her mother's face shocked her.

Yvonne only had to shake him once. "Victor...shez awake." She leaned down and put her hand on Celena's forehead as Victor leaned to kiss her.

"She's much cooler," Yvonne reported. "I've got to get word to John." She disappeared.

Victor lightly stroked Celena's cheek, smiling at her as if he never expected to see her again.

"H-how do you feel?" he asked, pulling the quilts protectively around her shoulders.

"Much better."

"Good. You rest now." He hovered over her for another moment, and then sighed as she drifted off into a restful, healing sleep.

A week later Victor led a thin, shaky Celena carefully into church for Sunday Mass. She smiled at everyone and tried not to react to their shocked, incredulous expressions when they beheld her.

She had taken extra care dressing for church trying to appear and act better than she felt. She wanted after all to be strong for Victor, for her mother and father and for the rest. But the dress she put on hung on her and made her look even thinner than she was. And when she brushed her hair a goodly amount of the long tresses ended up in her brush, and she had simply stared at them, not wanting to let Victor know she was in any way distressed. He had been a mountain of strength, and they were both clawing back to a sense of normalcy.

She sat through mass and respectfully prayed, thanking God for her life and the solid warmth of Victor next to her, blinking back tears when she thought of the sad events of the last few days. Gripped again with the frightening thought of how close she had come to dying.

She had little memory of the last week, only knew that bit by bit she could drink water and had the hazy memory of people by her side. She could remember bits and pieces of Anna's birth. She still had faint bruises on her wrists where Victor had gripped them and could vaguely remember being more than once in his arms, but it was almost as if they were all disjointed parts of a horrid nightmare.

"Celena," Margaret said, and put her arms around her frail sister-in-law, blinking back tears thinking she looked even worse than the rumors had reported. "I'm so glad you're better."

"Thank you...I'm getting much better," Celena forced herself to say and straightened her frail shoulders. She felt the warmth of Victor's hands resting lightly on her back. Henry came up beside them holding a fussy Hank. Margaret saw Celena's eyes wistfully caress her little boy.

"Can I hold him Margaret?" Celena asked, thinking with another pain in her heart that she'd never gotten to see or hold her child.

"Of course," Margaret said and felt a stab of guilt to have such a growing healthy boy.

Celena held him and smiled. "He's adorable." And she managed to laugh then when Hank took that cue to screw up his face and cry, wanting to be back in his mother's arms.

"We'll have none of that!" Celena teased and touched her pale lips to his forehead "I'm your aunt and you'll have to get used to me. This is what mothers and aunts do! We love babies and we kiss babies," she said, and then, not wanting to get him into a fit, handed him back to Margaret.

"I'm so glad you're better. We were all...so worried about you," Margaret confessed, then hugged her again, a squirming Hank between them. "Please let me know if I can do anything."

Celena nodded. "I will."

A moment later, Celena found her head pressed against Father Tonnellier's chest. His big, warm hand rested gently against the side of her head, as his soutane flapped around them. He told her that she would be all right, how everyone had prayed for her, and how the child that they had to bury while she was ill was now in heaven and would be all right too. As she left Father Tonnellier's warm embrace, she forced herself to talk a bit with the worried and relieved neighbors. Forcing smiles to the countless *"I'm so sorry about the baby,"* and, *"I'm so glad you're feeling better."* She had been hugged, kissed, and patted till she could hardly stand it anymore. She then turned to Victor and asked to see baby Anna's grave.

It was against his better judgment, and it made his already tattered heart clench when he heard her tortured sob as she looked at the tiny mound of earth covering their daughter and knew it had been wrong to bring her. She was still too weak mentally and physically. And in a brief lapse of strength, he lowered his head and fought back his own tears. He'd been desperate for the last week to keep Celena alive that he'd hardly allowed himself to think about his daughter. But now he let his soul ache for the tiny bundle that had stopped breathing moments after her birth and would not be revived even when he wrenched her from Dr. Casey's useless arms and coaxed her to live. He felt helpless about her death and wondered guiltily if he had acted faster if he could have done anything to save her.

"She was so...little," Celena whispered, looking at the amount of ground that had been turned to bury their daughter. It was heart wrenching to see the little one-by-two-foot space when all the nearby graves where that of adults and nearly six feet long.

A chilly wind blew across them and Celena shivered as it went right through her wool shawl. The thought of her tiny child underneath the earth caused a gush of tears to spill down her cheeks. Victor came up to her then and consolingly wrapped his arms around her, but she moved out of his embrace.

"She shouldn't be here Victor. She shouldn't be buried under this cold dark earth. I never even got to see her."

Sighing, Victor dropped his head. "I had to bury her Lena; we couldn't wait."

"But I never saw her, I never held her," Celena whispered. "I could have sworn I heard her crying last night. I'm afraid she's alone and crying for me. I should be looking after her. She should be with us, warm and loved. She doesn't belong there buried under that damp earth—"

"She's not crying, Lena, and she's not under that dark earth."

"But how do you know, how do you know for sure?"

He glanced across the windblown cemetery at all the gray weathered stones, heard the squeaking of the wrought iron gate. "I just do," he said with a shrug. "She's all right Lena. I wish she was here too, but she is all right."

Blinking back her tears Celena tried to envision her baby in heaven, that place in her mind of blue skies and blinding sunshine. She tried to think of her there, otherwise she was not sure she could survive the loss.

Unable to stand it anymore she walked off, leaving Victor standing alone in the cemetery.

Chapter 23

"Carlene had her baby, a girl named Olivia, although Mason and my mother are already calling her Livi," Celena said to Victor as she stood with him, the shop in the twilight of the May night. Claude and Thomas had left for the day, and Victor was, as usual tending to all the things that he fell behind in, working so much with the factory.

"How is she, is she all right?" he asked as he finished closing the shop.

"She made a lot of noise, screaming, cross with all of us. I'm surprised you didn't hear her over here! She's all right though. Got through it in less than seven hours." She wondered as she had so many times if she could carry a child to term and bring it safely into the world. When she held Carlene's daughter moments after her birth, she found herself sobbing not only with relief that Carlene's daughter had lived, but with renewed grief that hers had died. That was the way of things after all, more than half the babies born, died within their first year, and half the women died bearing them. Despite knowing all of this, her heart still ached for Anna.

"Well, I'm happy for them."

"You must be hungry; do you mind I planned to have a small supper." A few long strands had worked themselves free from her braid, and he reached forward to brush them out of her eyes, but she pulled away. It hurt him the way she was all the time shrinking away from him.

She was ridiculously self-conscious about her hair, or rather the lack of it! It was so thin she had to be careful when she pulled it back that she did not make rectangular bald spots. Her mother assured her that it would grow back, but her hair was not the only thing making her feel unattractive. The skin on her stomach was still not tight and hung on her body; she had lost nearly fifteen pounds. She was thankful that Victor had made no move toward her save a hug in the last two months, grateful that he was giving her body and emotions time to heal. And yet at the same time there was an unspoken tenseness between them, since neither reached for the other.

"That's fine," he said but noticed that she had moved far enough from him to prevent him from touching her again and wondered lamely what he should do.

"Victor, you've got to go with me this time. This is the second shutdown we've had in the last six months! If you would please go and fix whatever it is that they're doing wrong maybe we can finally get it straightened out," Ethan complained.

"If you'd taught them right the *first* time we wouldn't be having this problem!" Victor snapped pacing back and forth on the bricked patio, as Ethan sat comfortably in an Adirondack chair in his garden.

"Damn it! I'm no blacksmith! If you'd gone with me when you should have they would have been taught properly and we wouldn't be in this predicament now!" He remembered why Victor had not wanted to go with him and had the feeling it was the same reason holding him back again. Ethan noticed after all with concern the uneasiness between Victor and Celena in the last three months since their child died. As he watched Victor angry and pacing, knew things were far from mended.

He had been shocked when he had first seen Celena months ago with her thinned hair and gaunt face, but she was much improved now, and even jested about her appearance as she returned to normal. *"At least now I've got some hair to pin a hat to!"* But there was cautiousness with Victor that did not use to be there, and Ethan for the life of him could not understand why. She seemed almost afraid to reach out to him. And Victor too had changed. He was polite and concerned about her, and worried about her health like an old woman! Constantly badgering her to sit, rest, eat, and not tire herself. But he never seemed to spend any time with her and almost seemed to avoid her. True that he had his hands full at the factory and the shop, but it was as if he made it a point to get up and leave the house before she awoke, and usually came home long after she was asleep. Ethan would have had no way of knowing these things had Celena, in trying to make light of it, mentioned how often Victor was absent. Ethan had not known what advice to give to her when the pale blue eyes had looked at him vainly searching for answers. For whatever reason Ethan could tell that they were for the moment, lost to each other, and it bothered him that the two people he cared so much about were at odds. After all most men who were in love with their best friends' wives would be *glad* they were at odds! But he derived no perverse joy in the desperate longing that was in Celena's eyes every time she looked at Victor, no pleasure in the way Victor was sullen and more quiet than usual.

"You know, I hear Washington is beautiful in the summer," Ethan began, knowing that he was being hideously obvious, but decided unfortunately that the situation warranted it.

"What do I care about beauty," Victor sneered, not even noticing the pink and yellow roses blooming in front of him.

"Well, at the risk of sounding trite, I know you care a tremendous amount for a *certain* beauty who might enjoy a trip to an exciting city like Washington. Why don't the three of us go, you could make it your belated honeymoon if you like. Think of it, a fine suite in the Willard, dining in lavish restaurants, dancing, a trip through the Smithsonian, art galleries, the theater, the opera, visiting the vast array of shops and with the money we've made in the last six months, the means to buy Celena anything and everything her heart desires. I believe it's precisely what may be needed. To get away for a while, put things back in perspective."

Victor was staring at the delicate purple flowers on the lilac bush but wasn't seeing anything. "I don't have any idea what Celena needs anymore," he said softly, pressing his hands firmly behind his back.

"I imagine what Celena needs is to have the man she married *back*."

Victor stared at him. It was humiliating to Victor how Ethan keyed in on the tension between he and Celena. Besides Ethan was not the only one who noticed. Others who had innocently inquired had also been met with his wrath. "She has me."

"No, she doesn't! She's alone most of the time, the poor creature. You leave before she awakes, and you come home long after she's asleep! And when you are with her you're a dour-faced bullying husband who nags her to eat and rest and gets himself into a rage if she lets a few raindrops touch her brow for fear she'll catch a cold!"

Victor turned to him slowly. The gray eyes angry slits, and although he spoke quietly it was obvious he was close to losing his temper. "You weren't there. You weren't there as I watched for days as she grew weaker. You didn't watch her writhe on the bed as her fever climbed higher and still higher, until she was delirious, and then lifeless. And there was nothing I could do! I've never felt helpless like that before in my life, but I was helpless then—and I hated it. All I could do was watch her slip farther away from me and know that it was all *my fault* that she was dying!"

Ethan was silent for a moment, letting Victor's anger dissipate. "No, you're right. I wasn't there. But I have watched the exasperation in Celena with the stifling, frantic way you treat her now. She loves you and wants you to smile and laugh and stop reminding her every minute how sick she was, stop reminding her how close she came to death; stop reminding her that your daughter was lost!"

At those last words Victor glared at him and Ethan wished he had not mentioned the child, which was a subject he knew Victor flatly would not discuss with him. It was a source of constant quiet pain for Victor. An ache that Ethan feared would never go away.

"I am sorry. I don't mean to offend you." Ethan sighed, fearful that his little heart to heart with Victor would make matters worse. "Victor, truly, it's just that you seem to be caught in a most unhealthy web, you cling desperately to the fear that something horrendous will happen and because of that you take all the joy out of life for Celena and everyone! don't you see what will happen if you continue at this morbid pace? you'll have broken her spirit; you'll poison her soul."

He watched Victor pace the entire length of the garden three times. Finally, he faced Ethan. "So...I'm dour-faced...and bullying?"

Ethan couldn't help but laugh. "Well, to be honest...you can be at times."

"She's...told you...all of this? Told you all her frustrations, her unhappiness?" he asked, not looking at Ethan but rather at the finely laid brick patio, noting the superior work of the craftsman. He wondered if in her torment she had bared her soul to Ethan, wondered with a horrible grip in his chest if she told him that she refused to kiss him let alone make love. And it hurt him beyond anything to have her reject his touch. When all he wanted was to lay his head against her breast, and weep for the child they had lost, and joy that they still had each other.

"No, but for God's sake Victor, it's obvious! You have both been through a terrible ordeal."

Victor was relieved at his words. He smiled, thinking he should not have doubted her commitment to their privacy, and sighed heavily. It was true he knew, what Ethan said, he was overprotective of her, even with her reassurances that she was fine. He'd already lost his mother, Jonah, and his child, and the thought of losing Celena would simply destroy him. And yet if what Ethan said was true, he knew he would lose her anyway. He understood of course her commitment to the sacrament of marriage, and that she would never actually leave him, but she would have her spirit broken, her soul robbed of joy.

"I suppose she might enjoy a trip."

Chapter 24

By the time the three of them stepped out of Union Station in Washington, Celena was astonished at the magnificent city spread out before her.

"Oh, its's *so* pretty!" she exclaimed, looking out onto the clean cobblestone streets, watching the masses of people strolling along, the buildings and shops on every corner. Smiling, she eagerly linked her arm through Victor's as Ethan flagged down a cab.

"Shall we?" Ethan asked, grinning at Celena, wanting to show her the city, finding her happiness infectious.

Turning, she dazzled him with a smile of her own. "We shall. Why, it's enormous!" she exclaimed, looking at the capitol building.

"And it's still not finished." Victor pointed to the scaffolding. "Wait 'til you see the Smithsonian." He was so happy that before he realized what he was doing he took her hand to his lips and kissed it. To his delight, she did not pull away.

"Oh Victor, it's splendid!" she gasped, seeing the gorgeous suite they had been shown to at the Willard. There was a bedroom, a sitting room, and much to her astonishment, their own private bath of sorts. There was a tub, washbasin, a barrel on the wall which held a reservoir of water and even a small water closet.

Celena had only ever seen wallpaper before in Josephine Chomeau's home and had thought it nothing short of fascinating! The hand-blocked green and white wallpaper up the fourteen-foot walls had been imported from France, and it reflected the light from the French doors that opened out to a curved stone balcony. The carved four poster bed was so large that a step stool was needed for those not of Victor's height to climb in. And spread across it was a luxurious blue and gold brocade coverlet.

She was untying her bonnet when Ethan knocked once on the opened door and stepped in.

"How do you like the suite?" he asked.

"I've never seen anything like it! It's wonderful!" She beamed, smoothing her hair back and placing her bonnet on the long bench at the foot of the bed. "The room is beautiful, and look!" She pointed to the brocade coverlet. "Have you ever seen four-inch silk fringe? Carlene and Eva will never believe me!"

"Shall we have some lunch and then head to the factory? You'd like to see it, wouldn't you Celena?" Ethan asked eagerly.

"Oh yes, yes I would. You don't mind do you, Victor?"

Victor's mind was weighed by the problems at the factory and it took him a moment to answer. "Oh, of course not, but you may have to take her home. I've no idea what I'm up against or how long it will take."

"Not a problem. I am sure Celena and I can find something to occupy ourselves within this great city!" Ethan found himself wishing he could be her guide to all the great cities in the world.

"I think that's rosemary and maybe even a bit of thyme," she said, tasting the unusual but delicious white cream sauce. It was a fabulous lunch, full of all sorts of delicacies than Celena had ever seen before. Ethan was surprised how eager she was to try them all, and how interested she was in trying to detect the spices that were used in the veritable smorgasbord he had ordered for them.

"Don't they have boiled potatoes and meat without some yellow sauce all over it?" Victor was unimpressed by the menu; he didn't have the faintest idea what half the things were, like oysters which he had been horrified discovering what they were and that they were eaten raw, as well as terrapin which he planned to order until Ethan informed him was turtle soup.

"It's a *béarnaise* sauce, Victor." Ethan had to suppress a laugh.

"It's the middle of the day," Celena giggled when Ethan ordered a bottle of wine.

He waved his hand happily at her. "It's evening somewhere!" Smiling handsomely, he poured magenta wine into a crystal wineglass for her.

"I-I shouldn't." She turned to Victor as if for permission.

"None for me. I'll need a clear head to deal with them at the factory. Go ahead, I don't care." Realizing it sounded a little flat, he added: "Enjoy yourself, this is to be our honeymoon." He couldn't help but think '*honeymoon*' the silliest of all words, but was glad he'd said it, because she smiled at him. It suddenly reminded him how he felt looking out the shop nearing the end of winter realizing that drops were sliding off the icicles.

"I'm the foreman. God given name is Ezekiel Spunner, but I don't answer to it. Edgy is what they call me. You're the blacksmith fellow ain't ya?" Sizing Victor up, Edgy realized that this was the man they had been hoping for. Not like the dolt they'd sent before.

"Victor Gant, and I think you know my partner Ethan Stanfield."

"Oh yeah, I remember you," Edgy said, giving a large smile that showed missing teeth.

"And this is my wife, Celena. Can you show me where you're making the rims?" he asked, eager to get to work.

"Pleased to meet you ma'am." Although Edgy tried to hide it, he was shocked by how pretty she was. Washington was a large city, and he'd seen his share of beautiful women in his day, but she was head-turning pretty. "This way." He motioned to them to follow.

They passed the wheel rights, carpenters, laborers, Edgy calling to each all of them as they passed. Turning the corner, Victor saw the forge and the two smiths at work and plastering a smile on his face approached them and shook their hands. They seemed surprised to see man in suit and waistcoat coming towards them. It was summer after all, and the temperature near the forge was at a staggering degree.

"Afternoon gentlemen," Victor said, untying his cravat. He took off his coat and unbuttoned his cuffs to roll up his sleeves. Edgy handed him a spare apron and he tied it around his waist.

"Mr. Gant, this here is Roy and Marcus, they've been having a time of it with that one-piece rim I'm afraid." Edgy shook his head doubtfully, folding his arms across his barreled chest. "This is the fellow who invented the one-piece rim, and since you can't make it work, he's come all the way from somewheres called Missouri to fix it—so listen to him!"

Victor grinned at the worried looks the smiths exchanged. "Let me show you what I mean..."

An hour later Victor was certain he could re-tool what needed to be done and fix the problem, but it would take time, and he persuaded Ethan to take Celena back to the hotel. Neither Roy nor Marcus were experienced smiths as he had hoped, as a result he'd spent precious time explaining the basic rudiments of iron working. But they were eager to learn and it amused Victor that they regarded him as some sort of hero because he could get the iron to do what they could not!

"Are you sure? I-I don't mind staying?" Celena asked, looking up at him, putting both her hands on his biceps. It had been so long since she had willingly reached for him that for a moment, he fought the mad desire to sweep her up into his arms. If Edgy and the rest had not been watching, he might have done it.

"No, you go on ahead. I'll meet you back at the Willard." He was sweating after all and did not want to drip down on her.

Reluctantly she dropped her hands from his arms.

It was getting dark by the time Victor got back to the Willard. He grinned at the desk clerk who smiled back having no trouble remembering his name simply because of his height. "Good evening, Mr. Gant." The short round clerk smiled, wondering if all men from Missouri were so tall.

"Evening," Victor said, nodding politely, and then took the steps two at a time up to the third floor.

"Lena?" he called, cautiously opening the door.

She rushed to him from where she had been sitting by the window. She kissed him. "You're late! And I'm hungry...Ethan and I have been waiting for you, how did everything go?"

It was shock to him to have her so instantly and wonderfully in his arms once again. He tried to answer, but couldn't think straight. Couldn't stop the immediate reaction in his heart and body when she leaned up against him like that and opened her mouth under his. Yet still he tried to clear his head, and not hope for things that may not happen.

"They went well. I'm hungry too, but let me clean up a bit—I must smell!" He laughed, knowing he had been sweating all afternoon at the forge, and was self-conscious as she leaned her clean sweet-smelling body against his.

"All right, I'll run you a bath." She went into the little bathroom and still marveled when water came out of the barrel attached to the wall. He was behind her a moment later, stripped to the waist. "Should I call for hot water?"

"No, I'll be quick."

"Get in the tub then and I'll get your clothes ready." She left the room and pulled out the only other decent clothes he owned. "Did you teach them to use the rim correctly?" she called, smoothing out the shirt that she had hung in the armoire and wondering if she could tomorrow purchase clothes for Victor, but shook her head wondering if anything ready-made would be large enough!

"Yes, I think so. They couldn't figure it out, but they've got the idea now. I also showed them how I do the work on the wheel to keep the spokes from falling out. They are nice enough fellows, but I've never seen such shoddy workmanship. They seem eager to learn." At least that was different from Claude and Thomas whom he could not help but be disappointed in their lack of ambition.

"So, is it all under control-did you finish up there?" she asked hopefully, wanting to spend tomorrow in her new blue and white dress, her arm linked through her adored husband's, taking in the sights of the city.

"Oh no, I've got a lot more to do there. They're still not working all together. I've only spent time with the two smiths and a bit of time with the wheel right. I've still got to see what improvements I can think of with the carpenters too," he answered, having no idea how much he was disappointing her. "Have you got my razor?" he asked, standing at the threshold fresh out of the bath. Towel wrapped tight around his trim waist. The black hair smoothed back from his forehead, glistening with water, and laying like black snakes against his shoulders. His arms looked frighteningly powerful even laying calmly at his sides.

"It's still on the wash basin stand isn't it?"

Turning, he laughed at himself. "Ah, so it is!"

She stood in the doorway and watched him lather up the bar of soap and apply it liberally on his face, liking the sound the straight edge made across his cheeks.

"What did you and Ethan do?"

"He took me shopping and we bought clothes, the most *beautiful* clothes!" She was excited when she thought about the dress she would wear to the opera. "There's a blue and white day dress, and a yellow dress for church that I can wear at home. Then a fancy opera dress that Ethan picked out. They were all frightfully expensive though and I didn't even ask you! I hope that's all right?"

Patting his face dry with the towel he turned to her. "I don't care what you spent. If you want the clothes, I want you to have them." He walked past her then and, nonchalantly stripping off the towel, began to dress.

She shook her head lovingly as he stepped into his underclothes, and trousers realizing he was unashamed of his body. She watched him pull the white shirt over his massive arms and had to swallow hard and look away thinking with a flush that he was justified being so comfortable, his body was beautiful after all. She chastised herself suddenly realizing how many times in the last few months she had pushed that beautiful body away, pushed away those great impatient hands.

There was a knock at the door. When Victor opened it, Ethan flashed a smile. "How are things at our factory?" he asked cheerfully, dressed for dinner in a dark suit, gorgeous brocade shirtwaist and stark white shirt. He had shaved recently too because the ghost of a beard was gone, and the thin mustache looked to have been finely trimmed.

Celena looked from one to the other, both so different, and yet so attractive, and smiled greedily thinking that while they were in Washington, she had them both at her disposal. She laughed suddenly, and they turned to her curiously. "I'm simply...happy!"

"It's food deprivation, it's gone to her head. Victor, we must feed this wan creature immediately." Ethan took Celena by the arm.

She giggled again with embarrassment and grabbing his coat Victor followed them out the door.

"Lena, what are you *looking* at?" Victor said with a laugh. Thinking that she had already had too much to drink, he eyed her champagne glass, empty again. He realized she had already drunk two glasses by the time the appetizers came.

"Oh...um—nothing!" she stammered, feeling her cheeks hot with alcohol, and straightened in her chair. Trying to appear unaffected by the champagne and thoughts of laying once again in Victor's arms.

"As I was saying earlier, I think we should see if we can get more productivity out of them at the factory, which would increase our profit."

Victor swallowed his laughter and nodded to Ethan. "All right but let me get them up and running first. They are still not convinced that if they all work together—they can get it all done faster, to say nothing that if each man learns his part of the carriage making like a craftsman, we'll have a better product in the end."

"How long do you think that will take?" Ethan asked but could not help but notice an attractive woman in an emerald dress enter the restaurant with a man at least twenty years older and shook his head at the lascivious nature of men.

"I'm hoping that if all goes well I can finish it—maybe tomorrow—maybe the next." He glanced quickly to Celena and then back to Ethan. "Then maybe we can do the museum, sightseeing things."

Celena rewarded him by smiling.

"In the meantime, I plan to have a formal meeting with Sean Walker again," Ethan said.

"I remember, the railroad magnet."

Immediately the two men's eyes met. Vivid in their memories what happened the last time they tried to have a meeting with Sean Walker. They smiled at each other. The brotherhood of silence intact.

"About the quota," Victor said, changing the subject, "I was talking to Edgy about their wages—"

"Oh, here it comes! Let me guess, you want to increase their pittance of an earning to a slightly higher pittance of an earning!" Impatiently Ethan drained his champagne glass.

"Well, yes a bit, but I have another idea as well," Victor began, already annoyed with Ethan wondering if he ever gave a moment's thought to how much it would take to house and feed a family on what the men were paid down at the factory. "What I had in mind was some sort of incentive plan for their work."

"Isn't a day's wage for a day's work incentive enough for them?" Ethan scoffed, wondering why it suddenly sounded as though it was his father, Frederick, talking.

"What I have in mind is, if they increase the number of carriages they put out, a quota so to speak that they would get paid, say a bonus a few times a year, every quarter if they make their quota."

"I don't see the difference! If you're so worried about their blasted creature comforts—if you want to pay them more say it! You'll know I'll be opposed, but you also know that Pickering, because he is so *enamored* of you, will side with you and you'll both override my good business sense and squander the profits on the workers!" He angrily threw his napkin up on the table. "Why the long, drawn-out tale?"

Although it wouldn't be obvious to anyone else but Celena, she watched Victor clench and unclench his right hand and knew he was getting angry. "Yes, I want to pay them a bit more, but money is not the *only* thing that matters. If *I was in such a manual labor* job," he continued having no trouble meeting Ethan's annoyed stare, knowing Ethan was silently cursing him, "...and I was told that if I turned out a finely made product that I could make a higher wage, I would do my damnedest to try harder, if I could in fact *share* in the profits of the company. Don't you see, it gives purpose and worth to their tasks." He paused as if to let the meaning sink in. "But on the other hand, if I had no way to...better myself, if *my* working harder only increased the holdings of the rich men that owned the factory, I'm not sure I would do it. And if they thought so little of my efforts and raised my wages by a trifle only to quell the momentary grumbling—let's say it does not seem to be a particularly good way to run a business."

"It's essentially the same thing. Either way your precious laborers make more money."

Celena suddenly wondered why Ethan did not have the sense not to argue with a man who was bigger and stronger, and who had the *knowledge* to make or break the business deal in question.

"No, it's actually not. And that's what you don't seem to understand." His quiet words sent Ethan through the roof.

"I understand perfectly! You came from a working environment, and you sympathize with the low class, wife beating fools who don't have enough self-respect to pull themselves up out of the gutter! I understand now that you have two nickels to rub together you want be noble and self-righteous and help them." Again, Ethan was assaulted by the sense of Frederick. He shuddered suddenly realizing that was *Frederick* that would say such horrible things.

"No, you've misunderstood again, I don't want to *give* them money they will have standards to keep up and a quota, besides believe it or not money is not always the answer."

"Oh...it isn't?"

"Well. of course not. It's not the only thing people want."

"What else do your laborers want along with the soft job you'll hand them? Stuffed chicken, a twenty-minute brake every hour and bottles warm milk for lunch?"

"Ethan, please," Celena breathed, maddened with his insults.

"No. Just a chance to make a decent living, some basic self-respect. The belief that you have control over your destiny. The ability if the desire is there to better your situation. A bit of...hope if you will."

Ethan was silent, knowing he would sound like the devil himself if he tried to contradict Victor's poetic words. "Well then I'm confused now Victor—do you want to pay them more or not?"

"Not if they don't earn it. I don't see how simply *giving* a man a living, makes him much of a man."

Into Ethan's mind Fredericks's words came crashing down on him. Even though he knew Victor's words were not directed at him, still they tore at the delicate lining of his soul.

"Like I keep saying, I want there to be an incentive for them, and when they do that, they make more money, and in turn ensure a better product out of our factory-and better profits for us." Victor leaned back in the chair then, his big hands looking huge and out of place amidst the crystal and china on the table. "Don't you see? We gain as much as we give them."

"I know when I'm backed into a corner."

"I'm *not* trying to back you into a corner! If you'd let yourself think about it you'll see that it makes sense—and not only because it's simply a *decent* thing to do, but it makes good *business* sense."

Ethan waved away his words. "Regardless, I want to be there when you present this to Pickering...and we'll see if we can agree on anything." Although outwardly he was calm, his eyes showed an internal war. "You don't mind picking up the tab do you? I think I'll get some air and walk back to the hotel." He stood up and abruptly pushed his chair back to the table. "Good night Celena."

"All right...see you in the morning," Victor murmured, folding his hands on the table.

Celena reached across the table and touched his hand. "I think it's a wonderful idea," she consoled, wishing they were in their little house in Ste. Genevieve, and she could get up from her chair and go over and put her loving arms around him.

"I don't understand what he finds so offensive," he said, going over in his mind the words he had spoken, and still could not find no fault. "I'm *not* trying to simply give away the profits—if anything because of the incentive there might be *more.*"

She felt a welling up of sympathy for him.

"Besides, I've heard all about the horrors of these factories. Lena, they've got men there that have families to feed, and the owners pay them as little as possible knowing the poor workers have no choice—that they're families will starve otherwise, and the conditions they are expected to work in..." He shuddered and then shook his head. "Making a profit is fine, I'm not against profits and business, but I'm not so greedy or callused to want to make it on the hardship of others."

Celena nodded, looking at him across the table, thinking that he was all that was good and wonderful in the world. Not many people would risk arguing over the concerns of men he would probably never see again.

"In my mind, it's almost like another form a slavery—in fact, it's one of the few things your brother James and I have ever agreed on! Do you realize that the horrible conditions that workers are subjected to is one of the selling points the slave states use to condone the extension of slavery-saying that the factories are so horrendous that a well-cared for slave is actually better off? Trade one owner for the other, pick your misery. I don't understand why he finds all of this so offensive."

"It's not just that Victor, he's different that's all. He's never been hungry; he's never worked like you have. He's never had things taken away as you have. I honestly don't think he can sympathize never having been in the situation." Her fingers were tight around his hand, her heart hammering in her chest with love for him.

"Well, maybe he'll feel differently in the morning," Victor said skeptically. He summoned the waiter to pay the bill, which he was aghast to find monstrously high—Ethan had ordered the most expensive champagne.

Victor was up and dressed by the time Celena's eyes opened. She was used to getting up early to do the chores, and it embarrassed her that he was up already ready to go.

"You're going already?" she asked, trying to sit up in the bed, a dull ache in her temple. Remembering painfully how much champagne she had drank and wished she had been more prudent.

"Yes—early to work and early to rise and all that rot!" he said with a short laugh and then taking a risk leaned down and kissed her on the head. He wavered for a moment as he looked down at her in the bed. Her hair messily pulled back with a bow from her face, the thin nightgown showing the valley between her breasts.

It would be so nice, he thought suddenly, to push her back on the bed and take off the clothes he had put on. There was after all no Luann waiting to be milked, no Claude and Thomas hovering around the door or impatient customers waiting for him at the shop-what difference would a half hour make to the men at the carriage factory anyway? And she had been so receptive to him since they'd come to Washington.

He put a hand up to her face, and touched her cheek, then to the base of her throat. He watched her head drop back, saw her shoulders arc, and daringly reached down and gently laid a hand on her breast.

A hundred thoughts came crashing into his brain. He knew that if he did not stop soon, he'd have her flat on her back underneath him. Although that, in and of itself, a wonderful thought, he knew he'd get her pregnant again and wondered if that was why she would not make love to him.

"Do you...want me to stop?" he asked as he leaned down to kiss her, fearing that it was already too late, and wondered why he was so shamelessly weak when it came to this.

She didn't want to waste time talking, and merely opened her mouth to him.

There was a loud knock at the door.

"Damn it!" He jerked back, stalking angrily to the door, flung it open. "Yes?"

"Here's your—your newspaper sir!" The maid gulped, forced a smile.

"Newspaper? I didn't ask for a newspaper!"

"It comes compliments of a Mr. Pickering for you sir, as well as a breakfast for you and the missus," she explained and moved to the side to let another maid wheel a squeaky wooden breakfast cart in.

Sighing, Victor stared up at the ceiling shaking his head. He took the offered newspaper and finding two coins in his pocket, gave it to them. They both smiled at the generous tip and left.

He heard Celena giggling. "Funny is it?" he said, looking down at the Washington Post and then tossed it carelessly to the floor and came towards the bed and pushed his wife, whom he had not seen laugh in months, back against the pillows.

"It was just—your expression! I'm sorry!"

"I'm glad my expressions amuse you." Confident then that he would not be pushed away, he leaned down and kissed her, but realized the spell had been broken when he felt her laughing under his mouth.

She wriggled free from his hold and jumped up to see what was making the delicious smell on the tray. Lifting the silver dome saw poached eggs poised in silver egg cups, crispy bacon strips and toast on Delft blue plates. There was a matching pot of coffee and cups along with an oval plate of butter, two small silver pots of preserves complete with tiny spoons. She shook out the white starched napkins with a *W* embroidered in gold thread and smiled seeing a crystal bud vase bearing a single yellow rose. "We might as well eat."

Victor laughed like a man on the brink of losing his mind. He took two pieces of bacon and ate them while she poured coffee. He tasted the eggs and although they were good, liked the way she made his eggs better, and wanted simply to be back home with her.

He stood and slurped the last of his coffee. "I'd better go. You'll be all right alone? Ethan is meeting Sean Walker, do you want to go shopping again today?" he asked, tugging on his coat, and noticed her eyes sparkled. He was glad he had listened to Ethan and brought her to Washington, because it did seem that they were making a most wonderful new start.

"Do you mind? I'd like to get a few things for my sisters and everyone."

He rummaged around in his wallet and pulled out three large bills. "Here," he kissed her on the forehead, "I'll see you later."

"Is she *ever* coming down? I mean, we've got reservations!" Ethan complained, checking his timepiece for the third time.

Victor shrugged, as bewildered as Ethan. "I don't know. She gave me a new shirt to wear that *almost* fits," he said, stretching his long arms and showing a cuff that nearly came down long enough. "Then she practically pushed me out the door and asked me to wait in the lobby."

"Well...we've still got time enough, if she's down soon." He couldn't help but notice a pretty blond walking slowly up the curving staircase, admiring her beauty.

"I ran into Pickering at the factory, and he seemed pleased with the progress we're making. And as you requested, I did not mention anything to him about the incentive, we can talk to him about that another time," Victor said.

They fell silent again, watching the comings and goings of the other guests in the hotel, a goodly number of them made ready for the opera as the gorgeously trimmed evening gowns of lace and feathers suggested.

"We can talk to Pickering about it tonight. After I 'missed' Mr. Walker," Ethan said with sarcasm, "I paid Pickering a visit at the patent office. Seems he's not fond of opera, but he's fond of the society that attend and he's in the habit of having everyone over to his home. I assured him and I assume you'll have no objections that we'll be there tonight afterwards." He turned to look at Victor for confirmation and chuckled seeing he was trying to pull the too-short shirt sleeve even with his jacket.

"All right," Victor said, "tell me, how did you manage to *miss* the elusive Mr. Walker yet again?" When there was no answer, he looked up and followed Ethan's gaze to the stairway.

Standing at the top of stairs stood Celena, wearing a silk dress in a gorgeous shade of amethyst. The fabric fell to the floor in such fluid lines it looked to be made of liquid. The skirt spread out in magnificent folds over the crinoline, and the gradients of the raw silk caught the light at different angles, making the dress seem to change hue. It had a tight boned bodice, and a scandalously low boat neckline. She had worked on hard on her hair, and it did not look thin anymore, like a woman who had lost so much of it to fever, it looked beautiful and full. At her throat was a black velvet choker from which dangled a cameo.

She started cautiously down the stairs; and when she felt the weight of so many eyes on her, had the modest desire to cover herself up! But more worried about tripping, kept a steady hand on the banister.

"Took her *shopping* did you!" Victor hissed, glaring at Ethan. Glancing around he noticed jealously that every man in the lobby was staring up at Celena as she came down the stairs.

"Hello," she murmured, relieved to feel Victor's big hand pulling her protectively to him. But when she neared him, he realized to his horror that three inches of ripe cleavage was displayed for every man's eyes.

"Celena...you look *exquisite*. Like a beguiling mermaid rising from the depths of the sea—an enchantress sent to bewitch any man who casts his eyes upon you." Unable to stop himself, Ethan reached out and took her hand to kiss it tenderly. "*Beautiful...*"

Victor frowned at the antics with her hand and waited impatiently until Ethan finished. He protectively tucked her arm around his as he led her out the door but had half a mind to take his coat off and cover her up!

Victor sat bored through the opera in the National Theater. Wondering why people would pay so much money to see such a ridiculous show, which to his horror wasn't even in *English*! He didn't care what Ethan said about opera being an art form that combined music and drama, that the elements of music and the libretto could bring one to tears or leave them laughing. Besides that, it seemed to Victor that all anyone did was look at everyone else and gossip, rather than watch the show.

"Oh, that was wonderful!" Celena exclaimed, sitting down in the carriage, and taking Victor's hands squeezed it tight as he forced his big body in and sat next to her.

He was glad again that he'd agreed to go to the ridiculous opera when he saw how her eyes were sparkling, saw the flush across her round cheeks. Absurdly happy that a smile was once again across those soft lips.

"Yes, it was delightful," Ethan agreed as they made their way to Alexander Pickering's house, still not able to keep his eyes from running all over her whenever he knew Victor was not looking.

"I've never seen so many beautiful gowns, and jewels! Why I never thought I'd see anyone *wearing* a tiara! and the theatre with marble statues was beautiful. And the music was wonderful, Eva would have loved the pianist!"

Victor tried to control the range of wild emotions he felt seeing her so happy and acting like her former self. He pulled her hand up to his lips and awkwardly kissed it, wishing Ethan was not with them and he could pull her onto his lap and bury his head in those wickedly displayed breasts.

Ethan chuckled. "Victor! I think we have a new opera enthusiast here. You had better learn to appreciate the finer things in life my good man!"

Victor merely looked out the window smiling through clenched teeth, not willing to take the bait.

Celena's mouth dropped open as the carriage pulled up to Alexander Pickering's massive three-story stone house. If the gorgeous house was not enough to amaze her she saw peacocks strutting about the circular drive. Although their long tails were closed, they still displayed gorgeous iridescent blue and green colors.

"Oh, my heavens!" she said, staring at the magnificent birds as they roamed about the manicured front lawn. "No one will ever believe me."

The soft warm light of candles flooded the stone steps in the front of the house. As she carefully stepped up, she heard the faint strains of a waltz. She was speechless when the double wooden doors swung open to show a large, marbled entryway with an enormous curving staircase to the second floor.

"Good evening, sir, madam," the butler greeted and, taking Ethan's card, motioned politely for them to take the stairway to the second floor where the ballroom was.

The polished wood of the stairway felt almost slick underneath her slippers , as her hand trailed along the waxed mahogany of the banister. The lovely sound of music filled her ears as she ascended the steps with Victor at her side.

Entering the ballroom, she was astonished by its size. It had to have been at least twenty-five feet in diameter, and was stunningly round with alcoves around the perimeter. There were roman columns at the edges and she could imagine a girl coquettishly playing a flirtatious game of hide and seek with her beau. The ceiling was lit by three huge crystal chandeliers, and the floor was tiled in black and white marble on a diagonal. On the walls were large paintings in gilded frames of battleships on the high seas and landscapes of beautifully dressed women collecting summer flowers. The long casement windows had white frothy curtains that revealed large cement planters that held a profusion of red and yellow flowers.

"There's Pickering," Victor said, spotting their portly host talking amongst a group of bearded, older men.

Suddenly a panic hit her. "I'm—I'm a little thirsty—" She hesitated nervously, her heart pounding at the thought of meeting people. And seeing a waiter carrying a silver tray filled with cups of punch, wanted one. "You go ahead I'll be along in a moment."

"Are you sure?"

She nodded.

"I'll be right back then. Ethan, I am leaving Celena with *you*," he cautioned, wanting him to take Celena's hand. Reluctantly, Victor let go, and she peered questioningly at him. "I am not *about* to let go of you in here," he scoffed, having already noticed a man paying too much attention to her. "I'm afraid there'd be nothing left of you but *scraps* when I got back!" Then meeting eyes with the offending man, took her hand and kissed it. Intimidated, Celena's admirer disappeared amongst the sea of people.

"Mr. Pickering! Alexander," Victor called, boots clipping on the shiny floor.

Alexander whipped his short body around, and beholding Victor, his round face erupted with pleasure. "Victor! Good evening. Gentlemen, this is Victor Gant, the young man I was telling you about." Proudly he puffed out his rotund chest and leaned up to put his arm affectionately around Victor's shoulder.

"Ah, yes the carriage factory you bought Alexander, I hear there's been trouble!" one of Alexander's colleagues joked.

Pickering shook his head so vigorously the jowls of his face shook. "Trouble? Why that's ballyhoo! We're in the process of re-working the factory that's all. And gentlemen we have a rim for carriages that is all one piece, not pieces that used to have to be welded together mind you! This new revolutionary design virtually eliminates the bothersome trips to the blacksmith for repairs." He slapped Victor hard on his shoulder.

"Have you now sir! And who did you get to do this work for you?" another of Alexander's associates said, eyeing Victor up and down, thinking he had to be the one of the tallest men he'd ever seen.

"I did sir." Victor respectfully nodded to the pert older gentlemen.

"You? How could you?" another man asked.

"I..." Victor hesitated, not wanting to embarrass Pickering but decided he could never fool anyone for long anyway. "Am a blacksmith by trade sir. I came to Mr. Pickering for a patent for my seamless rim...which to my sincere regret, was dully rejected." The crowd of gentleman around him laughed good-naturedly. "But Mr. Pickering here was good enough to purchase a carriage factory for my business partner and myself and allowed the use of my rim in the factory."

One of the men touched him on the shoulder. "Are you formally trained in engineering or design?"

"No. I...dabble a bit, that's all. I have no formal education."

Alexander laughed loudly. "Nonsense gentleman! what we have here is a man who can fix virtually anything. Mr. Stanfield our other partner told me that he's invented a new part for their local sawmill and that it turns out more lumber than ever before! in addition to that he'd fixed a steam engine and prevented it from breaking down again, which as you all know keeps the ships on time and the profits rolling in."

"Increased profits always did interest you Alexander!" one of his friends joked and they all laughed companionably.

"And if that is not enough to awe you gentlemen he altered the design of a broken McCormick reaper, and it hasn't broken down since." Again, the good-natured laughter, and then Pickering with mock seriousness scowled up at Victor. "Although you might be wise because of his *patent* not to mention that to anyone!"

"You have a broad range of interest, is there anything you *don't* fix?" One of the men laughed as the others murmured their agreement.

"I work on what I see around me," Victor explained, shrugging "I look at things and try and think of how they can be changed or improved." When he saw Alexander was still looking at him, he knew he could never fully explain. "That's simply how my mind works."

"And since it will make me a tidy profit, I am awfully glad that it does!"

Another low rumble of appreciative laughter from his friends.

Victor turned to Alexander. "I am proud to say that things are working well now at the factory."

"Yes, things are much better now, and I dare say if you had come the first time we'd not have had this trouble," he joked.

Victor grinned self-consciously. "I was unavoidably detained."

Alexander smirked. "He could not come when we first acquired the factory gentleman, because he had recently wed, and could not bear to tear himself from his new bride!"

"Give him some time! He's young!"

"After a few years he'll be wanting to quit her company every chance he gets!" The men laughed.

Victor smiled tightly. "I sincerely doubt it, sir."

Again, the laughter of the wealthy men around him.

It was then that one of the white haired men looked up. "What an *exquisite* creature," he exclaimed, and they all turned to see what he was looking at.

"*Extraordinarily* lovely!" another remarked.

Victor felt his heart nearly burst out of his chest with pride.

"I don't recognize her or the gentlemen with her. Who is she?" another man asked, vying to get a better look.

"That woman, gentlemen..." Victor said, knowing that it was but a once in a lifetime chance to have such an honor. "Is none other than my wife."

There was a choked silence as the men watched in astonishment as Celena came over to them and shyly took the arm of husband.

"Alexander, I would like to introduce you to my wife, Celena."

She smiled at Alexander Pickering as he took her hand and kissed it.

"Mrs. Gant, it is an absolute *pleasure* to finally meet you my dear! welcome to Washington and welcome to my home." He did not release her right away, wanting simply to touch something so beautiful. But remembering himself, he began to introduce Victor as well as Celena formally to the crowd of gentleman around them.

Celena, for all her modesty and shyness, endeared herself to them. She politely asked those she met one or two key questions, and then was content to listen and knew to smile in the appropriate places. Even though she was flushed and nervous as she met couple after couple, Victor never let go of her.

An hour later Victor was leaning against one of the white painted columns as his eyes roamed the busy dance floor for a glimpse of the deep purple gown. Celena had been dancing since the introductions had ceased when a frail senator had asked. Given the man's, age, Victor did not object, but when he spied her now saw she was dancing with a *much* younger man. He felt the muscles in his stomach tighten and wondered with a smirk how this same ridiculous scenario kept happening. He watched her for a while but then she disappeared, and he pressed his hands against his back, surveying the sights, trying to take it all in.

It was almost inconceivable where he was standing. That the son of the town drunk, and Indian slave woman had been to an opera and now was standing in a polished marble ballroom in the country's capital. That he was at a party filled with senators, dignitaries, and wealthy plantation owners. That a man he was comfortable with calling friend, had invited him to an exclusive party at his estate. That Alexander Pickering had bragged about his inventions, like a proud father would about a dutiful son. That he had been discussing use of one of his patents with Washington's wealthiest people. He would have to tell Margaret that hadn't done anything clumsy to shame her and belay his humble beginnings.

And if all of this was not enough to make him shake his head in bewilderment, he knew he had the distinction of being married to the most beautiful woman in the room.

"Pickering is indeed happy," Ethan said, walking up beside him, surveying the dancers, his hands pressed firmly behind his back.

Victor nodded. Contently they watched the colorful skirts that swirled on the dance floor. "Is Walker here?"

Disgusted, Ethan shrugged. "I've had meetings scheduled with him *twice*, I'd venture a guess he's not very receptive, but I can't say that because I've still not *met* the man! Pickering says he's here somewhere. Don't know how we'll find him though."

"Any ideas?"

Sighing, Ethan shook his head. "Not at the moment. I suppose I could try again tomorrow."

They fell silent again still watching the couples dancing.

"By the way," Victor began, not looking at him, "if by some..outrageous coincidence, you are *ever* shopping with my wife again, if you pick out something that revealing—I'll beat you senseless."

Ethan chuckled. "But Victor, look around at the style of fashion. All the women tonight are in attired in dresses like Celena's."

"That may be true, but with *her* in it, that *attire* becomes positively obscene!"

Ethan laughed. "I see an opening, I'll be back later."

Victor watched him sidle up next to a dark-haired girl, gallantly offer his arm, and lead her to the dance floor. Victor grinned when he saw the way the girl's eyes widened with excitement as she looked up her handsome dance partner.

Ten minutes later Victor's patience was faltering as he spied Celena dancing with the same man for three dances now. Felt the uncomfortable tightening of his chest as he looked at the man's hand on the small of Celena's back. The man looked to be about forty with jet black hair and smiling blue eyes, and because he was on the tall side, Victor realized he would have the most wonderful view of her breasts as he whirled her laughing around the dance floor. *Didn't the man have the sense to see the ring on her finger and know that she was married? Did he think she was for his company alone? Who was he anyway?* The longer Victor watched them the more irritated he became. He stepped curtly onto the dance floor, nearly bumping into an elderly couple making wide sweeps across the marble tiles. Whoever she was dancing with was talking non-stop, and if he did not know that her heart was all his, he would have been jealous with the attentive way she was looking up at him.

"I'll cut in," he mumbled, and reaching out he grabbed the man by the shoulder, a bit harder than necessary. "Excuse me."

Recognizing the tight expression on Victor's face, Celena placed herself between them. "Victor!" she gasped, a bit out of breath, "I'm glad you're here—"

"Really, are you?"

Celena had to suppress a laugh at the touch of sarcasm she detected in his voice. "Yes. There's someone I want you to meet—" Spying Ethan close by, she reached out and touched him as well, much to the annoyance of his dance partner who objected mightily to the intrusion.

Still flushing, Celena turned back to her dance partner. "This is my husband, Victor Gant."

Victor took the offered hand and squeezed it hard enough to hurt.

"Good evening sir," the man replied, bending formally.

"And this is his partner and, our dear friend, Ethan Stanfield." The man shook Ethan's hand as well.

"Gentlemen! Allow me to introduce myself, I am Sean Walker. Mr. Gant, your lovely wife has spent the last three dances telling me all about your invention, I understand you have an idea for the railroads that I absolutely *must* see..."

Two hours later Victor and Celena were thanking Alexander Pickering for his hospitality.

"I simply couldn't believe it! She brought Walker right to us!" Victor said, beaming proudly. "Ethan and I couldn't get the man to commit to any meeting, and here Celena convinces him to see us with a few dances!" The appreciation of what she had done etched happily all over his face.

"She is an able negotiator, and a strong ally," Pickering said, and his eyes crossed over her face. He noticed both her arms were wrapped tightly around Victor's and that she looked at him with commitment that it made his own cynical view of love soften. Reminding him bitter sweetly of how he'd felt once, an very long time ago.

"Good night my dear," he breathed, peering into her pale eyes sparkling up at him reflecting the light of chandeliers.

"Good evening Mr. Pickering and it was so wonderful to finally meet you, thank you for everything!"

Her sincerity warmed Alexander's heart.

Victor leaned down to Alexander and said under his breath, "I've got one more day at the factory, and then they're dragging me to the art museums."

"I understand now," Alexander said with a fatherly smile, "why you were so reluctant to come before. Good night my dear man."

As Victor closed the door behind them, he felt relieved as he lit the lanterns on the table. "Thank God that's over!" he said. and immediately loosened the constricting cravat and tugged it off his neck. He had the confining suit coat off even before Celena had walked to the bed.

He came up silently behind her and caught her about the waist, turning her around in his arms. "You will never wear this dress again." He kissed her roughly on the mouth for emphasis.

She laughed. "I didn't think you'd even notice."

"I noticed."

"But you like this, don't you?" she asked with a smile, motioning at herself.

"Yes, I *like* it! But it's supposed to only *mine* to look at!"

"You men are so two-faced. You want us to be all sweetness and innocence in public, but then when we're alone, you want us to turn into little vixens."

He had to clear his throat. "That's...actually accurate."

Smiling, she turned her back to him. "Would you unlace me?"

"Gladly." He laid his thick fingers on the ribbon webbing and began to untie the bows one by one. "How in the world did you get into this?" he said, frowning as he struggled with the tiny strings.

"I had a maid help me. The same one you scared with our newspaper this morning." Turning, she felt the dress loosened against her.

He stood looking down at her, and the promise of what had been interrupted that morning, paramount in both of their minds.

"I'll be right out," she said breaking the spell. Taking one of the lanterns with her, she went into the bathroom.

He leaned his head back and stretched his long back. Turning he walked to the window and glanced for a time out onto the quiet gas lit street. He saw a bat flutter against the light. Glancing down the street as far as he could see there were buildings, shops, and houses. He shook his head with wonder at how big Washington was. How much there was to know in life, how much he still did not know, and probably never would.

"Victor." She watched his mouth drop open, and his Adam's apple bob as he swallowed.

"Is it pretty?" she asked, moving to expose the thin nightgown underneath the peignoir. It was pale pink rosebud silk, and had a gathered row of three inch cream colored lace dripping off the sleeves. The thin silk nightgown underneath had tiny braided pink ribbons for the straps, and another insert of lace at the neckline. The fine silk was fine and draped beautifully, and he had no trouble making out her form underneath it.

He shook his head, rubbed his chin, and laughed nervously. "Another purchase with Ethan?" Certain *now* he was going to tie Ethan to one of the anvils tomorrow at the factory and beat him senseless.

Her eyes flew open wide. "Well yes! But he didn't—I didn't tell him I was purchasing...*this*. I picked this out on my *own*."

"Thank God for small favors!" he said, staring up at the ceiling. By the time he looked down she was right in front of him, winding her hands up his chest. "You realize with you...uh, dressed, or *undressed* like this, there is a chance that I won't be able to stop myself?" he said desperately not wanting to be on the threshold of making love to her, only to have her beg him to stop.

"I wouldn't have bought this if I didn't."

It was strangely awkward between them, and the silence was overwhelming, and Victor was afraid that another second or two and he would be ripping the silk gown off her with his teeth.

"Are you trying to...seduce me?"

"Yes."

"It's working."

She laughed and thrillingly felt him pull her closer. He picked her up and carried her over to the bed, and gently placed her on the brocade cover. "You tend to pick me up and carry me a lot, did you realize that?" she asked, amused, her eyes sparkling, arms still linked around his neck.

"You're little, I don't mind." He lowered his head and nuzzled it against her neck.

She felt an aching yearning for him, and realized whatever barrier she had put between them was gone. "I love you Victor, and it's been so long. I've missed being with you."

"You're not afraid?"

"Of what?"

"We both know what will happen. Where we'll be nine months from now," he said as his hand gently traced up and down her flat stomach. Even with those sobering thoughts, he still shook as he touched her, aching with the desire that had been denied these last months.

"No, I'm not afraid and don't you be either." She took his hand and placed it firmly against her heart. "I'll never leave you, and I don't want to lay another night next to you without you holding me."

"But the risk you take, the risk I'll be *forcing* you to take. You have no idea what torment it is for me to want you, but to also know that my want of you could end your life." He lowered his head with guilt.

Touching his chin, she forced him to look back up at her. "I don't fear it. I'll have you with me."

"Did it ever occur to you that you have too much faith in me?"

"Never. You dragged be back once before from the shadows and breathed new life into me. I fear nothing if you are with me." She gently touched the long strands of his hair. She laid her lips against his, but he pulled away.

"There are things we can do, things to prevent you from getting pregnant. I read about them—"

"But I *want* to have children, I want to give you children, besides it's against everything the church teaches, and I don't even want to know *where* you read such a scandalous thing."

"In a woman's publication of all things, it out and out encourages young brides about how not to get...pregnant. There's female syringes, a sponge complete with string attached and something called a pessary which is supposed to correct whatever a prolapsed uterus is—but it's obvious what its real intent is."

"Do you have one of those—those pessaries with you right now?"

His face turned ashen. "A...er...no. I had no idea I'd be in such urgent need of one."

"I was hoping you would do your husbandly duty by me now, and since you don't have one of those things, that I wouldn't *let* you use anyway. You still want me, don't you?" she asked and traced a fingertip over his mouth.

"Yes...of course!" He realized he was at any moment about to possess the object of his fantasy riddled dreams. "Had it all planned did you?" He grinned, rubbing the silky fabric between his fingers. "You needn't have gone to all this trouble, not that I don't appreciate it!" He kissed her shoulder where he had pulled off the finely braided silk strap, marveling anew at their softness. "A simple glance in my direction would have done it."

She caught his face between her hands, "I'm so sorry. I'm sorry I pushed you away all these months. I honestly don't know why I did. I was so upset about losing Anna and being sick. I know now that it was the wrong thing to do. I realize that I should have turned to you rather than away from you."

"You needn't explain."

"But I want to! I hurt you, I know I did. I could see it in your eyes every time I pulled away. After all you lost her *too,* and I never even tried to console you in your grief as you did in mine. And I've missed you. I think this was part of my unhappiness these last few months. I was missing you, but I'd pushed you away for so long I was afraid to ask for you."

"Please don't ever be afraid of me."

"I've missed...being with you," she whispered, lowering her eyes and felt her heart start to jerk in her chest, "and I want more than anything to have another baby." Her determined eyes met his. "I know I can do it this time Victor; I *know* I can. I want to be with child again soon."

"Oh, you do, how soon?" he asked, tracing her jaw with his fingertips.

"Well...I was hoping to be carrying before I left Washington."

His eyes widened in surprise. "Are you sure?"

"Quite sure."

"Well," he said linking his hands and cracking his knuckles, "I guess I could be persuaded to give it a try!"

Leaning down, he kissed her and let his hands—which had been too long deprived—explore the soft skin of the woman he adored.

Closing her eyes, she gave her body, heart, and soul to the man who she knew would guard them with his life.

Chapter 25

"I don't know when I'll be back," Victor said, tucking the shirt into his trousers, and when he saw the shadow of disappointment cross her face, knelt on the bed, and placed his hands on either side of her face. "Don't *do* that to me!" he laughed, leaning to kiss the parted mouth. "It's hard *enough* for me to leave you like this." His eyes swept up and down her, noticing with amusement that she had modestly put the nightgown back on after he had taken it off her so many times during the night. "But leave you I must."

She forced a smile. "All right, I'll think of something to do while your away." Her mind wandered to the lovely parks they had seen as they had come into the city and wondered if she could walk there. Ethan was meeting with Sean Walker, so she would be on her own.

"Do you want to shop again?" he asked, thinking madly that if she bought another thing like that pink one she'd worn last night he'd *never* get any work done in the shop with her only twelve feet away!

When she shook her head, he was at a loss. "Do you want to come with me, then later I could take you out somewhere for lunch?"

She threw herself into his arms. "Yes! Oh yes please!"

He picked her up. "You won't be bored? I don't know what you'll do."

"No. I want to be with you," she said, kissing him quickly.

"Get dressed then," he said, letting go. "And put on something high necked—Washington has already seen *enough* of you!"

By two o'clock that afternoon Victor had the factory good enough under control to leave. As they stepped out onto the street in the hot afternoon, the air felt cool after having spent better than five hours at the forge. He took a handkerchief out of his pocket and mopped his face with it.

"Hungry?" he asked and she nodded happily. "Where would you like to go?"

She glanced around the street. "Let's walk for a bit and see what we find." She linked her arm though his as they walked along the avenue back to a more central part of the city.

"I'm sorry it took so long, I thought I'd get done sooner," he said, thinking that if Marcus and Roy listened more and talked less they would catch on more quickly. "Were you terribly bored?"

"Not at all," she said, smiling up at him. "I was with you."

Two blocks down the road she spied a small cafe. It looked friendly and homey with its white awning and roughly-hewn tables and benches. There was a large oak tree shading the outside sitting area, and wild bunches of yellow and white daisies growing in messy clumps around it.

"Let's go there."

"Didn't you want something...fancier?"

"No, this is fine."

They both ordered the daily special which was to Victor's delight was food that he recognized. Regular food like meat, boiled red potatoes, green beans with a small loaf of bread, and plate of butter. And it was delicious as they sat to eat in the shade of the great oak tree.

"I've been thinking," Victor began and took a napkin to wipe a bit of butter from the corner of his lips, remembering his manners and putting the napkin back on his lap. "When we get home, I'm going to go ahead and build the new house."

"But I thought you wanted to wait until you were sure about the factory and things?"

He reached across the table and took hold of her hand, his big fingers playing with her small ones. "I know, I did say that. But I've changed my mind. I think we should build it right away. Sometimes it's better not to be so careful, it's not always wise to wait." He looked at her and in his eyes there was a trace of pain, "Anna dying and you being so sick makes me realize that none of us knows how much time we have. And if you wait too long you might not ever get a second chance. Today is the only thing certain, whereas tomorrow." He shrugged. "Besides it would please me mightily to build a nice home for you."

"Are you sure?"

"Yes, I'm sure."

"I guess then...I shouldn't disappoint you."

He wanted more than anything right then to kiss her, but even though the cafe was mostly empty, he dared not. There was an elderly gentleman at a table, as well as the owner of the establishment, reveling in the late afternoon slump, seated with his wife, who had also been their server.

"What would you like to do now?"

"I think I'd like to walk through some of those lovely parks I saw the day we drove in," she said, smiling at him, and when he nodded she had the feeling that if she'd said she wanted him to walk back to the Willard on his *hands* he would have done it!

"Let's get back to Pennsylvania Ave."

"Aren't we on it?"

"No we're on H street—now if we just walk and go south on 5th street that should lead us back to Pennsylvania, and I'm pretty sure 5th street will run us into the mall." His fingers dug into her elbow, carefully guiding her across the busy street. "If I stay on the numbered streets or the spoke streets—"

"The *spoke* streets?"

"Well, the streets start from the capital in numeric order from north to south—the small, numbered streets being nearer the capital. The streets that come from the capital building branch out, sort of like spokes from a wheel, the capital being more or less the hub. There's Massachusetts, and Pennsylvania, and Maryland and more I can't recall now. Anyway I can find my way back to the Willard if I stay on one of those streets and I know that park or grand mall was along one of them."

She was reminded how well he took care of her. After all she had merely been ambling along, languishing in the beauty of the afternoon whereas he had made sure as they walked how to get them home. It was such of feeling comfort and security.

They spent the rest of the afternoon strolling through the mall, stopping to look at the beautiful gardens that graced it with the multicolored flowers that grew in the orderly plots of land. Both enjoying the ornate fountains and soothing sound of the water splashing into the shallow pools. They laughed as they stood watching the gentle cascade of water, when the wind shifted, and they were sprayed with a mist of water.

"It amazes me how they carve this, I mean, it's a rock," Victor said, inspecting one of the gorgeous marble statues of a Greek goddess in a flowing dress. Squatting he touched the delicate folds of her dress that looked as though the wind was back blowing them.

"It amazes me too," Celena said in awe. "She looks so real."

"I read once that before a sculptor even begins to carve he has to study the stone for days."

She turned and smiled at him in surprise, amazed as she often was not only by how much he read, but how well he remembered! "Do they?"

He nodded, standing back up.

"Studying it to decide on the design?" she asked.

"Well, yes that and if you look close there's a grain to the stone, he has to work with it. If he chips in the wrong place," he said, touching the statues face, "could take the nose off this lady by mistake."

She traced her hand against the smooth pink and gray stone. "That would be a tragedy, she has such a perfect face."

He stepped near her. "No," he said, gazing down at her in adoration. "*This* is a perfect face."

They kissed.

"We'd better head back, it's getting late," he said, taking her hand. They walked without speaking back to the Willard with the warmth of the sun on their shoulders. As they went up the stairs to their room, they saw Ethan in the hallway.

"Where the *devil* have you been?" he burst out, striding up to them.

Celena's heart sank, an argument between Victor and Ethan *not* having been how she wanted such a glorious day to end.

"We went to eat and took a walk. What's the matter?"

"Sean Walker! He's been wanting to meet with you and talk—and I had the extreme embarrassment of not knowing where in the world you were! I took him to the factory, but you'd already left, then we came back looking for you at the hotel, anyway you'd better hurry up and change we are taking him out to dinner this evening."

"When?" Victor asked, turning his back to Ethan as he opened the door to their suite.

Irritation was etched all over Ethan's face as he dug out his pocket watch. "In scarcely more than an hour."

"Fine. We'll meet you downstairs in forty-five minutes."

"I don't think you grasp the importance of the situation!"

"I understand," Victor said, trying to close the door, but Ethan blocked the way.

"No, you don't! This is vital and pertinent to our business that we make a good impression—"

"I said I *understand!* And I'll be there! Now if you don't mind I'd like to attend to my *own* vital and pertinent business!" Victor pushed Ethan out of the way and closed the door. Victor began to undo the hooks and eyes on the front of her dress.

"What are you doing?" She tried to ignore the little shivers going through her as his hands fumbled against her.

"You want to be with child before we leave Washington, and we've got barely a day and half left, so as I see it is my duty as your husband to fulfill your request."

With the bodice opened he laid his lips against the breasts pushed up invitingly by her stays.

"But—but we haven't got time for this, truly," she protested weakly.

"Truly, we do," he whispered.

When the carriage door was shut Ethan burst out, "My God what an evening! I had the intense desire to throttle you more than once my dear Victor! You nearly cost us the entire deal with your bullheadedness!" He huffed, seated across from Victor and Celena in the carriage.

"Walker had it coming. He trounced on nearly every word I said."

"But did you have to be so colorful? I mean, my God, Victor, *severed* brakeman? It's a wonder he didn't get up and walk out!"

Victor shrugged. "That's what happens to them, the cars will cut them in half."

"I'm impressed that Victor kept his temper at all Ethan. All Mr. Walker did was interrupt him every time he tried to speak, and he made light of decent and humane treatment to anyone," Celena said, shaking her head.

"I suppose that's true," Ethan said with a laugh, delighted that they would have huge orders for the Baltimore and Ohio, "but still it was a risky thing to do."

"You forget that we have the patent and without it he has no coupler. We would have merely gone to another railroad. Anyway, I'm glad the meetings over I'm done with the work here," Victor said and, finding Celena's hand, squeezed it.

She glanced up at him, puzzled. "You're not needed at the factory?"

He smiled thinking about what he planned to do with her when he got her behind the door of their suite that night. "No, I'm finished. I'm not going to the factory tomorrow. I'm taking you to the art museum, and the next day—home."

Victor was good as his word and dutifully went to the art museum. He bought a guidebook, which he quickly bored of and handed to Celena, who looked up and studied each painting. Victor was elated three hours later when they left.

"Ethan, I shouldn't have let you lead, I think we are lost," Victor said after they had eaten lunch on an unfamiliar road.

"We are near the riverfront, is that where we wanted to be?" Celena asked.

As they rounded the corner they saw a small crowd of people watching a man on a crude wooden stage.

"He's hawking some wares no doubt," Victor said.

"Not just any wares. Slaves," Ethan remarked, staring at a young woman that had been brought on to the auction block, and both Celena and Victor turned in shock.

The auctioneer with a short pole in his hand pulled the girl who was shackled and wearing a filthy dress, foreword. "Our second to last offering today is eighteen yrs. old. She's got a strong back for working," the auctioneer said pushing her to turn and display her back which was hunched over in fear and shame. "She's got most of her teeth," he said, forcing the young girl to open her mouth. "She's fresh from the farm, and she'll be a good worker for years to come. And good for breeding too eh?" the auctioneer said, pointing lewdly with his stick to her hips that were covered by the folds of her skirt.

Embarrassingly a flood of indignation washed over Celena, wondering how it must feel suddenly to have your entire sense of self-worth be diminished to one small aspect. She swallowed hard at the sexual comments she heard around her about the young girls breeding ability, and the thought of laying with any of the leering buyers that stood around sickened her. Watching the girl, Celena noticed that her eyes never left the ground no matter what the auctioneer was saying and seemed not to care which buyer would get her. Because her life would be no different no matter where she ended up.

All at once Celena was assaulted with a sense of pity, sadness, bitterness, and voracious hate she hadn't known she possessed. She'd seen slaves before working at Josephine's plantation, heard them singing their songs in the evening, seen their backbreaking labor. She'd even got friendly with Judith the maid at Josephine's, but had never seen the actual bidding and buying of another human being.

Ashamed she had fallen prey to the popular propaganda that the slaves did not 'mind' their lot of life, and that they were content. If that was true she wondered suddenly, why would they need to be shackled to be kept from running away, branded to show who they belonged to?

Turning she saw that the already purchased slaves stood still shackled together. Some of the women were weeping silently, the men had their eyes downcast, bitterly resolved to their fate.

"All right who'll start the bidding?" the auctioneer asked, wiping a line of perspiration off his forehead, and then replaced the sweat stained hat back on his head.

"Eight hundred dollars!" a man in the crowd yelled.

Immediately counteroffers went up.

"I'll give you 825," another said.

The auctioneer smiled, liking that the bidding was fast.

A sudden panic gripped Celena. She pulled Victor down to her. "Could we buy her and...let her go?"

"My God Lena, that's a lot of money."

"I know it is, but—but she's so young. She's *my* age! Victor, I'll wait for the house—I'll trade that girl for my house. Please Victor, don't let those men buy her!"

He wavered a minute, not because he had not been affected by the horrors of the slave market as she had been, but because he had no idea how to bid, or what he was doing.

"850, I'll give you 850," Victor yelled, his hand tight on Celena's as he dragged her behind him through the crowd.

The auctioneer smiled down at him from his platform when more bidding erupted.

Victor was a little confused, having thought he'd read somewhere that slavery had been abolished in Washington, and he wondered suddenly if not only he at an immoral slave was auction—but an *illegal* one as well.

"Now that's more like it! Do I hear 900?"

To Victor's horror, they did. When he looked back at Celena with a shrug her pleading eyes prompted him to continue.

"1,000!" Victor yelled again.

"What in God's name are you doing?" Ethan hissed, having finally gotten through the sweating crowd to reach Victor's side

"Do I hear 1,100?" the auctioneer bellowed, and Victor feeling the adrenaline fueling his body desperately hoped no one else would speak.

"1,150," came a voice from the crowd.

"Victor do you know you can get in a lot of trouble bidding without this kind of money?"

"Shut up Ethan!" Victor hissed, not wanting the auctioneer to realize his folly.

Ethan grabbed his arm. "Besides, there's something wrong here! There's something wrong with all of it," he said, glancing around nervously, knowing they had stumbled into something dangerous. "Why are you bidding? What in the world are you going to do with a slave—this is insane!" Ethan tried to force Victor's arm down.

"Let go of me!"

The sound of the gavel hitting the rough podium yanked both of their attention back to the auction.

"Sold to the man in the back for 1,1500 dollars."

Victor turned to look at Celena, and seeing the grief and horror on her face, angrily turned on Ethan. "I lost her! Dammit!"

"What were you going to do when you got her anyway?" Ethan exclaimed, wanting more than anything to get the wild-eyed Victor away from the grim slave auction.

"I told him to, I wanted him to!" Celena answered tearfully.

Ethan turned his horrified eyes on her. "And what the hell were you going to do with her when you got her?"

Victor was afraid to tell Ethan that he hadn't thought any farther than wanting to please Celena and see the poor creature off the block.

"My final offer today is a well-seasoned fifty-seven-year-old male—"

"He's old and used up!" someone yelled from the crowd.

The old slave looked up, panning the crowd to see who had insulted him. He had to be over six feet tall, and powerfully built. The large shoulders looked strained under the faded homespun shirt. His black hair had streaks of white in it, and the ghost of a white beard clung to his chin. His eyes met Victor's for a moment, and never had Victor felt such anguish as he did when he returned the gaze of that old slave.

"Let's start the bidding," the auctioneer said, wiping a line of sweat off his forehead.

"Give ya 300 bucks for him," a tall, thin man said, wiping his damp forehead with a dirty handkerchief and stuffing back into his faded coat.

Victor stood stunned for a second, but then felt Celena squeeze his hand. "400." He felt his heart again beat rapidly.

"Like I said what do you think you're going to do with a slave? Do you have philanthropic *delusions* that you will free him, and he'll be forever grateful to you and lead a charmed life? What good does freeing *one* of a thousand do anyway?" The shocked looks on Victor and Celena's faces told Ethan he had been right. "How *ignorant* are you, Victor? You can't just free him! First, our lovely host here would probably pick him up again perhaps even collect some runaway slave bonus-and turn around and re-sell him *illegally* again!"

"I don't know, I don't know what I'm going to do. But I can't *watch this*!"

"Well then let's get out of here and think rationally."

But as Victor listened to Ethan's commonsense words, the auctioneer banged the gavel. And Victor suddenly found himself the proud owner of a fifty-seven-year-old male slave for four hundred dollars.

The auctioneer motioned for the old slave to join the others as he began to settle the accounts.

"How the hell do you think you're going to pay for this?" Ethan shrieked, furious.

"I-I don't know! I'm not sure, I've got the money back home," Victor said, eyeing the soft cloth of Ethan's suit coat. "Give me the checkbook."

"The business' checkbook? I will not!" He put a protective hand over his coat.

"Oh, Ethan he only did it because I asked him!" Celena said and felt the tears pricking her eyes knowing it was her fault they were arguing.

"Give it to me—we're partners—I've as much right to that money as you do."

"This is insane! I won't allow you to do it!"

"What do you mean you won't *allow* me!" Victor shouted.

Neither one of them noticed the auctioneer approach them. "Something wrong gentleman?" he asked, tipping his hat off his damp brow with the tip of the cane he had prodded the slaves with.

Celena rushed over to him. "No nothing at all, my husband was discussing with his partner when we might pick up our—"

"Property, ma'am?" The auctioneer grinned at her, liking what he saw.

She smiled prettily despite being revolted by him. "Well yes. When may we have him?"

"Tomorrow morning, we cut the shackles off 'em—and there'll be someone there to brand 'em if you want."

Celena covered up her little shriek of horror by waving her hands in front of her face. "Sorry, mosquitoes—we don't have so many at home."

"And where would that be ma'am?" the auctioneer said, taking off his hat and smiling at Celena in a way that made Victor want to choke him.

"Ste. Genevieve. We're from Missouri, my husband owns a factory there," Celena said and forced another beguiling smile. "You see we hadn't planned on purchasing any...any help..." she lied and felt herself visibly shaking and swatted at another nonexistent mosquito to mask it. "And my husband and his partner were deciding how to pay-would you accept a check from our business?" she asked and when she saw a shadow of disapproval flood over the man's place she swatted at another phantom mosquito. "I can see that you'd rather not—well not to bother—do you know Mr. Alexander Pickering, or perhaps Sean Walker of the Baltimore and Ohio?"

"Yes ma'am I do!" the auctioneer said, grinning nervously, wishing in part that he had more slaves to sell to such a wealthy and beautiful woman, and yet afraid at the same time because it was illegal to sell in Washington.

"Victor don't you think Alexander would loan us the money until we can get back home to our private bank?"

"Celena this is going far enough," Ethan began.

"Oh no need ma'am, I can see as your well good connected. I'll be happy to take a check from ya'll—no need bothering Mr. Pickering for it," he said thinking that Pickering and all his well-connected friends might throw him in jail again. After all they'd already yanked his permit when it was legal, as the letter had put it for his 'mistreatment of cargo.'"

"Oh, thank you sir, you are most kind. We'll be along for him with a check in the morning," she said, turning quickly and taking both arms of the men with her who stood listening to her with their mouths gaping.

When he was sure they were out of earshot, Ethan broke away and turned an angry face to her. "What the devil do you think you're doing? You have no idea what you've done! You've bought a goddamn slave? And paid an astronomical price for him, and for what?"

"I'm sorry Ethan, I couldn't watch and do nothing—I had to do something!"

"What difference will one slave make Celena?"

She turned away, knowing that his words rang with an unpleasant truth. "At least he's one less. At least I tried in my own selfish, foolish way," she defended quietly.

"I know Ethan, it was a foolish thing to do..." Victor said running both his hands through his dark hair, as he paced back in forth in front of them, the folly of his actions coming back swiftly and painfully to haunt him. "But it's done now, and I can't undo it."

"It's not *done!* You have no idea what you're up against. You can't simply free him!"

"I understand what you're saying, maybe not here—"

"No, you don't! You don't understand—not here, not in St. Louis and not in Ste. Genevieve! *Nowhere!* He's a slave—no rights, no past, no future, nothing. He's *your* responsibility. I'm done with this," Ethan said and dramatically dusted his hands off and left them amid the auction crowd.

"I'm sorry Victor—I'm so sorry," Celena began and was relieved when he merely moved his arm up and she slid under it and against his chest. "This is all my fault! I wish I'd never seen that girl. Wish I'd never seen that horrible auction!" and he began walking with her tucked tightly under his arm. Not able to think of anything to say to sooth her, the truth and sense of Ethan's words ringing in his ears.

"I'll think of something," he whispered softly as he led her out of the throng of auction goers. He happened to glance up as they walked through the crowd and caught the older slave looking at him. Victor forced a tight smile at him, a smile the old slave could not return.

The next week was for Victor, nothing short of a nightmare! From picking up his new slave whose name he was informed was Bartholomew, to having to buy an extra train ticket for Bartholomew, which had to be in the baggage compartment-to having the steamboat captain from St. Louis refuse at first to even transport him.

As they made their way home, Victor felt a tightness in his chest as they saw the shore of Ste. Genevieve. Even though he was desperately glad to be home, hated to admit how Ethan's words about his foolishness bothered him.

"That's that," Ethan said, stepping a bit gingerly from the boat. His stomach unsettled after having been on the water so long, and he turned to help Celena walk down the plank, careful to make sure her wide skirts did not catch on anything. And as she murmured her thanks she looked up into the quiet stare of Bartholomew who stood meekly before her and smiled nervously at him.

"It must have been awfully hot down there, were you all right?" she asked with a trace of embarrassment knowing that the back of her dress was dampened with perspiration, and that riding in the bowels of the airless ship, had to have been excruciatingly hot in the August afternoon.

"Yessum ma'am," he mumbled and his eyes reverted to looking at the dust in the street below them. Celena was relieved a moment later when Victor having tipped the sailor who brought their trunks out. He lugged one of the huge trunks onto his shoulder, and leaned down to get the other one, not knowing with all the new things Celena had bought, how he was going to be able to get everything home in one trip! As he leaned down to try and hoist the other large trunk onto his shoulder, a weathered black hand touched the trunk before his did.

"Ah gits it," Bartholomew grunted and hoisted the trunk onto his massive shoulder, and then taking another carpetbag that was lying near, placed it on his other shoulder. He waited then, for Victor to direct him.

"This is fine," Victor said, dropping the trunk right outside the house, noticing that Bartholomew was silently surveying the house and land. "This is my home. The house here, the barn," Victor said. "I own about fifteen acres around it." Victor wondered why in the world he was telling the man this, and then took out a handkerchief to wipe the sweat from his neck nervously. "Like I told you earlier...I...a didn't plan on—on buying a...a slave," he explained, feeling himself grow queasy at the thought, "and I want to let you go—but you'll need some money and since I spent every dime I had getting you, I frankly don't have any now...I can give you some money when I go to the bank in the morning...and then maybe I can try and find you some work." He rambled pitifully, wondering what in the world to do.

"Ya gots no farm?" Bartholomew asked, his displeasure obvious.

Victor suddenly wished he had listened to Ethan and simply turned from the horrid auction. He shook his head. "No. No farm."

"What's I gonna do for you then?" Bartholomew asked, his dark brown eyes nearly boring a hole into Victor's face.

"I-I don't know. Like I said, I didn't intend to..." he stammered, unable to again speak of his purchase. "Have you...got any kin?" Victor asked and then felt foolish having said it. Realizing that even if Bartholomew did have kin, the trip to Ste. Genevieve would have undoubtedly separated them by hundreds of miles.

"No, suh, ah had me a wife a chillins, but my wife she gets a fever and died, five yeas now...an my chillins of the three that lived—de be sold long time 'go."

"Of the three that lived, how many children did you have?" Celena asked and felt her heart leap into her throat with thoughts of baby Anna.

"Ah had me nine chillins...six boys and three girls...three boys died from da measles...two odders died in their cribs, da odder died under da whip..." He shook his head at the memory as it passed before his eyes as if it had only been yesterday. "Dey didna listen to da foreman," he explained with a shrug of his big shoulders. "Da girls were sold a few yeahs lada...'bouts dat time my wife taked to her bed with a fever..." He was silent for a few minutes and then, sighing, said: "Yessum ma'am, dey were sold...long time ago." Although he had a great deal of practice masking his pain, still a shadow of it passed over his lined face.

"How long were you...on that farm?" Victor asked.

"Aw my life."

"What happened if you don't mind me asking...why aren't you there anymore on that farm?"

"De ole man...he told me ah gets my freedom when he up an die...but his missus she doan see it that way, an when I talks to her, she gets mighty 'fraid—be saying ah uppity and bad." He shrugged his huge shoulders again, "she sold me first chance she got..." he said, old eyes staring at the ground, and it was obvious he was humiliated at this late date in life, being sold again.

Both Celena and Victor were quiet, Bartholomew's tale depressing.

"When I...when you're free—do you have a way to make a living? Any skills? what did you do on the farm?" Victor asked, wondering how he was going to let a man with no relatives, no kin, loose in the town. Even with money he wondered how long it would be till some slick talking fellow either cheated him out of it or murdered him for it in a strange city.

The barrel chest puffed out a bit more as he spied the iron curlicues way over Victor's head holding the sign, that even after all these years still read: "Schaeffer's Blacksmith."

"Ah kin works there!" Bartholomew said, smiling broadly for the first time since Victor had picked him up. "Does ya know da man who'd be ownin' et?" he asked, still smiling, rubbing his meaty hands together "I used ta shoe all the horses, an I gots speshal good at fixun broked tools, yessuh...I ken works smiffen."

"You worked...for a blacksmith? You're a striker?" Victor blurted out incredulously.

Bartholomew violently shook his head, insulted again. "No suh! I did all the work on the farm wis da fire, ole man prentised me out when I was a youngin' on learnin me smiffen... Ah be da smiff on da big farm fo' nigh on forty yeahs," he ended indignantly.

"You must be joking?"

"No suh! Ah ain't a lyin'!"

It was an unbelievable, incredible stroke of luck. Victor felt his heat swelling out of chest with unexpected happiness. "Well then, Bartholomew, if you want it—you've got yourself a job! You can for work me, and Lord knows I need reliable help. That's my shop, I'm the smith here."

Silently Bartholomew looked Victor up and down, as if seeing him for the first time. He broke out then into a toothy grin when he realized he was in the company of man who shared his trade.

"Yours?" Bartholomew asked, pointing to the shop.

Grinning, Victor nodded and surprised the old slave by putting a friendly hand on his shoulder.

"Lena, could you start supper please? Bartholomew and I are going to have a look around the shop. I've been gone over two weeks no telling what shape it's in."

Part Three

Chapter 26

"What is it, Mother?" Ethan asked impatiently as he walked into the house. He felt a sudden chill in the air, which was ridiculous given that it was still a warm and humid afternoon. It was unnerving to him that his own home always affected him this way. Almost as if the warmth and beauty of sunlight somehow never seeped into the house. Taking off his hat and smoothing back his hair he noticed that his mother did not so much as look at him.

She sat, back erect in the parlor chair, hands folded in front of her, an even more unhappy look on her gaunt face than usual, and she was dressed monstrously from head to toe in black.

"Didn't you get the telegram?" Blankly her eyes met his.

"No. Was it important?"

"Yes. As a matter of fact, it was. Your father's dead." She turned abruptly from her son. Her head set in a posture of defiance, the proud chin trembling, unshed tears shimmering in her eyes.

A stab of pain assaulted him, and for a moment Ethan could not speak. Swift on its heels though was guilt. He had after all more than once, wished his father would die-wondered at times why he hadn't already, and thought bitterly that his own life would be much better if the cruel old man were dead. But now that he was, there was no jubilation in Ethan's heart, no wonderful feeling of at long, last freedom. Rather he felt the loss of something he'd never even had.

He knew suddenly when his father's bitter soul had left the earth-because he remembered when it passed over his own. Felt it hovering him that night in Washington like a vampire when he argued with Victor. Ethan shivered at the memory.

He heard his mother sniff and watched then as she fumbled with an embroidered handkerchief. He realized that he had never seen her cry before. And she was almost crying now, but the tears could not quite fall.

Her thin shoulders were shaking, and her slender manicured fingers covered her mouth.

He knew any other son would go and put his arms around their mother. Let her lay her head against his chest, while murmuring *things would be all right*. But it had been literally *years* since he had touched his mother, and he could still painfully remember the last time. He was seven and taken a nasty spill down the steps and went crying to his mother with a large lump on his head, wrapping his arms around her skirts. He could still remember how she had immediately disengaged herself from him, and unceremoniously deposited him in the arms of the startled kitchen maid to deal with. Although he would have risked being rejected, had the feeling that his arms about her, was the last thing she wanted.

"I'm...I'm sorry Mother," he said at last. "Have you taken care of the arrangements, do you want me to do that?"

"Yes, do make the arrangements. You are still his *son* after all."

Even in the wake of her sarcasm he hoped it could be a new start for two of them. Without his father there, he hoped they could have a traditional relationship. Maybe if his father was not always there to point and say, *"See what he's done now!"* She would smile at him, smile at him how he had seen Yvonne do when her eyes rested lovingly on her own sons, and even Victor. In time his mother would grow to like him, even *love* him.

He knew he was far from perfect, and that his parents did not like that he gambled on horses and sometimes came home after having too much to drink, and he knew his mother disapproved of his relationship with Arvellen, although it had always been Arvellen that had been the pursuer, *not* him. But he also knew that he'd done everything they'd ever asked and yet, he knew embarrassingly, that they were never pleased with him. Not pleased he had come home from his studies, not pleased that the bank was running well, not pleased that he had no life for himself, other than his friendship with Victor. No matter what he did, it never seemed like it was enough.

"All right Mother, I'll make the arrangements," he said and a bit shyly forced a smile, wondering again if he should put his arms around her.

"It's the *least* you can do, where were you when he needed you? Off in Washington!"

"I'm sorry Mother—"

"You disappointed him so *many* times Ethan, do you realize that? It breaks my heart to think of it! your father and I we had such high hopes for you, you were such a disappointment to him. Your poor father was distraught over the mess you've made of things at the bank—"

Ethan bristled. "Mother that's not true, the bank is fine," he said, knowing that it was in much better shape *since* he had taken over.

"You made your father sick night and day with worry over the terrible things you've done."

Annoyance gnawed at him. "What terrible things have I done?"

She went on as if he hadn't spoken. "And the stupid factory you insist in being involved in-dreaming fools dreams!" She stood, signaling that the conversation was over. "I suppose it's too late for you to make amends to him... apologies and such. Do make the arrangements, Ethan." She smoothed her wide skirts and left him alone in the room.

"Fool's dreams indeed," he murmured, knowing there would be no new starts in the Stanfield house.

In the four months since they came back from Washington, Victor was so busy Celena rarely saw him! He spent nearly three days in the shop with Bartholomew, showing him where things were, introducing him to the surprised customers, trying to explain to a shocked Bartholomew that he would be able to make a living in the shop, and that indeed even *'white people'* would come to him for their work. Bartholomew had been amazed at the gregarious, cosmopolitan nature of such a small town, and watched in amazement the amount of mixed-race people, the occasional Indian roaming in the town, and the various colors and nationalities of children all playing and fighting together in the streets.

"This be a strange place!" he had remarked to Victor after seeing two women, one white and one mulatto vying for freshest bread that had been taken out of the bakery window, and the mulatto women had won the coveted bread! And he had been even more amazed to learn that Victor was *metis* himself and had an Indian as a mother. He wanted to know which of the pretty women that came in the shop was Margaret the sister he had heard so much about.

But even as good as his welcome was in Ste. Genevieve there were those that flatly told Victor like Davina Woolrich that if that "black man was doing the work," she would take her business elsewhere. Victor told her while she ranted at him, that it was her right to go somewhere else- just as it was his right to hire Bartholomew. After she left Bartholomew had bleakly turned to Victor and asked, "Wat if dey all be lik dat?"

There had also been discussions about where Bartholomew should sleep. Victor felt bad putting him in the barn, and yet the shop was not much of an improvement, so that was where Bartholomew stayed.

Bartholomew refused—much to Celena's dismay—to eat with them, and instead came dutifully and took his tray every morning and evening and ate alone in the shop, and no amount of coaxing from Victor or a well-meaning words from Celena would change his mind.

"Leave him be Lena. He's had a lot happen to him," Victor said, trying to understand how Bartholomew might feel. He remembered embarrassingly trying to explain to Bartholomew that he did not want to own him, that he was giving him his freedom, and Bartholomew, annoyed had asked again why he had purchased him if he didn't need him. Victor explaining that he did need him-but as an employee and not a slave. After the first month, when Victor had dropped the bills into his meaty hand, Bartholomew had been shocked, especially when Victor had told him that he was at any time, not beholding to him and free to go.

"What's ah want te be doin that fur? An where is ah sposd ta go? Ah gots nowhere to be. Where else do ah gets a job like dis an ole? Ya told me ya goin ta gimme da house when ya gets anudder one bilt...ain't ya?"

Although in general they got along well, at times Victor and Bartholomew had different ideas about how things were to be done. But the former slave was not dumb, and he kept his thoughts to himself, and although he had all his life tried to keep his emotions buried, he found he liked the big *half-Injun*. He liked the way Victor "*could never leave well enuf alone.*" But since no one ever knew what the future had in store; Bartholomew kept his affection for his employer hidden.

All in all, Victor thought what he had been afraid would be a horrendous situation was working itself out nicely.

Three days after they had come back from Washington, while fending off the remarks about his buying a slave from surprised and concerned friends and an especially shocked James Riefler! Victor employed a five sailors who had missed their leaving, who suddenly found themselves in a strange town with no money, and Rolph Adders—the cabinetmaker who everyone knew could build anything—to help him build their house.

Shivering a bit, Victor shuffled to his door after having gone over the day's business with Bartholomew. He was happy with Bartholomew's work and felt better about being away so much from the shop. He had seen Bartholomew's tray and wondered if Celena had already eaten; he was late coming home again.

She looked up at him from her sewing when he walked in the door, and hastily putting it aside came to him. "You're so late, you must be tired." Leaning in, she kissed his cheek and, taking his coat, hung it on the peg. "How are things at the factory?" she asked, scooping a generous helping of soup from the kettle on a trammel hook in the fire.

"Good, surprisingly good," he said, sitting down tiredly. It was beyond wonderful he realized to be able to come home to her. Knowing that she would not be angry he had been gone so long, but instead simply happy to see him.

"Rolph came by looking for you—said to tell you they'd need the windows in a few days."

"If they ever get here! I ordered them a week after we got back from Washington and that's been nearly four months ago. I find it hard to believe it takes that long to ship them from St. Louis."

"They'll get here," she said softly and paused a moment. "You have to be patient sometimes." She placed the hot bowl of soup in front of him.

"Well anyway they are doing a pretty good job—and they should be done with the house by spring for sure." He picked up his spoon and attacked the chunky soup. It still amazed him how is wife could take bits of vegetables, spices, and fish and make it so delicious.

"I hope they are done in the spring, because I'm pregnant and God willing, we'll be having a baby in April."

He did a quick count in his head. "But that means you're already four months along, why did you wait so long to tell me?" He stood up and pulled her towards him.

"I knew you'd worry, and you've got enough to worry about without me. Besides in case something happened early—I didn't want to hear all those...sympathetic words from everyone."

"You haven't told anyone, not even your mother or sisters?"

She shook her head.

He was suddenly at a loss for words. "Well...I'm glad. I'm happy." He dropped a kiss on the top of her head. He felt her arms tight around his waist, and her cheek against his chest.

"I want so much to give you children. I hope I can."

"Everything will be all right; it will be different this time. But to be safe, at about month eight, I'm not letting you out of my sight!"

Spring 1852

By the time the tiny spring beauties and purple and yellow crocuses were peeking through the thawing ground Victor, Rolph, and the Stoddard brothers (the sailors having long since taken off!) finished the house, or as the Stoddard brothers referred to it *the iron giant's mansion.*

Victor stood back and looked the beautiful columned brick house that stood before him, hoping he had built the dream house Celena wanted. And when her eyes at the sight of the finished house filled with tears, he knew he had done just that,

"The house is built my lady!" He smiled happily down at her, holding her as close to him as he could given how pregnant she was. It reminded him when they had been 'spooning' as she liked to call it the other morning, he could feel force of his unborn child's kick through her body, and wondered how it felt to have something alive and obviously wanting out-kicking inside you! It amazed him how women could share their *bodies* for nine months. And he smiled every time he felt the thrust of tiny feet on his back. "You can come now baby, we are ready for you!"

"Ethan...*Ethan!*" Eva called as he left the bank at the end of the day.

Turning, Ethan saw her running to meet him, carefully darting around the many mud holes the April rains made on the streets. She was flushed and bright-eyed and her hands were hot and moist gripping his.

"Celena had her baby this afternoon, a boy! And she's fine and the baby's beautiful! Victor sent me to spread the word. He's so happy Ethan, he's given everyone at the factory and the shop an extra day's wages— and my father's opening bottles of tafia toasting his newest grandson!" Gulping, she suddenly fell limply against him. "I was so afraid. So afraid it would be like last time." She sniffed away happy tears and beamed up at him. "Ethan, you should have seen Victor! organizing everything and telling us all what to do, and he did such a good job of keeping her mind off the pain she didn't get *nearly* so tired this time. He walked her around the room for so long at the end, telling the *worst* jokes—she even laughed a few times, and then it happened."

"Are you telling me Victor *delivered* this baby?"

Eva laughed. "He's amazing! I know he was worried, but you know how he analyzes and studies everything. When he told us she was ready, by God she was! Yes, he and my mother safely brought a screaming Randell Victor Gant into the world."

"Well, that's something," Ethan said after a moment. "Tell them I said congratulations and that I'll be by the house later to see them."

She shocked him then by embracing him, her happiness at Celena and Victor's good fortune infectious, as it was with all people that knew them, Ethan realized jealously.

Chapter 27

"Should he be sleeping this long, Celena?" Ethan asked, staring down at the slumbering Randell Gant in his little wooden cradle with the carvings of the stars and the moon.

Victor shot him a look. "Why do you even bother to ask? What do you know about babies?"

"He was asleep when I got here, he slept through dinner even with your loud talking. And he's still asleep now."

Victor leaned back in his chair with a loud slump. "Tell him, Lena. Tell him how much of the night this little fiend is awake!"

"*Victor*! When you're only two months old you can do whatever you like!" she teased, knowing no matter what he said how much he adored the little *fiend*.

"Anyway, I've got the second set of couplers ready to be shipped."

Finishing his coffee, Ethan set it back down gently on the table. "All right I'll wire Walker with the details." He stopped and sighed quietly as he looked around.

It was such a nice house, large enough with its four big, whitewashed rooms downstairs, and the four large bedrooms upstairs. And quite thriftily Celena had furnished it. The living room although not fancy, was an inviting room with sturdy furniture Victor had insisted on, wanting at least in his own house, be able to sit in any chair without fear of breaking it! The bright multicolored quilts draped over the straight back benches added a wonderful homey quality. The enormous stone fireplace Victor had ingeniously built into the center of the house was three sided and could heat the other three rooms on the first floor. Celena had made white drapes for all the windows on the first floor, and the few touches of china and crystal seemed to whisper that a woman with quiet elegance lived there.

Victor had attached the kitchen much like his father-in-law had done to the back of the house, complete with a stone 'break' in case the kitchen caught fire the stone would prevent the rest of the house from also catching fire. But Celena's kitchen was a marvel of convenience because the man who built it improved *every* design he had ever seen. Victor had put in not one cooking fireplace but two, and a stove, there was also an oven built right into the wall of the kitchen with a hinged iron door. And when the fireplace next to it got the stone walls good and hot, embers would be placed on the oven floor at night, and she could slide loaves of bread in on a long wooden peel and close the door, and in the morning, she could take out her bread, brown, crusty, and perfectly cooked. And because Celena was short, he made it possible for her to adjust the height of everything, from the trammel hooks in the fire, the adjustable broiler, stew pots, even the clothesline in the yard.

Victor had piped the water from the well into the house so that Celena would not have to brave the elements. It was an ingenious design; he had fashioned the pipe to bring the water in on the first floor, and rigged a way to flush the used water back out. In fact, it was such a remarkable convenience that Ethan had urged he seek a patent, but Victor, weary of the marbled halls in Washington, had merely waved him off.

The enormous curving staircase that Ethan had himself designed was beautiful, and the large window on the landing in the middle of the stairs flooded it in the afternoon with a soft light.

He had not been upstairs since the house had been finished but knew there was a stone fireplace in their bedroom, and that Victor had asked Rolph to make an enormous four poster bed, and the first night Victor had slept in it had been thrilled for once to be able to stretch out without his ankles falling off the end of the bed! The knowledge that a happily married couple with an adorable baby already lived in the house weighed on Ethan's heart as he got up to leave.

"Good night, Ethan. Same time next week?" Celena asked, holding the baby against her, her skirt with the other hand.

"That would be lovely Celena, if it's not too much trouble."

She smiled in such a way that made his heart lurch. "No. It's no trouble at all. We love having you."

Ethan smiled at her then, unable to do anything else.

"Do you want me to carry him up? Is he too heavy for you?" Victor called. She had recovered quickly from Randell's birth, but still, he couldn't help but worry. She had to hold on to her ridiculous skirts. Women's clothing would never make practical sense to him.

"No, I'm fine. Goodnight."

They watched her disappear up the stairs.

Ethan knew it was time for him to go, yet lingered as he walked outside, looking up at the darkening sky as bright stars began to show. "It's a good house."

Although the June days were warm, the evenings cooled off when the sun went down. But Victor could still feel a warmth of the sun's rays soaked up by the bricks. He stepped onto the large veranda, his boots thudding across the wide wooden porch, and turned back around to inspect his house. "It turned out all right. There are a few things that didn't go as planned," he mused, thinking that the pocket door in the dining room must have warped because it didn't slide easily. "But all in all, it's all right."

"Well after all, what in life goes as planned?" Ethan asked, noticing Celena had lit a lantern upstairs.

Victor shrugged. "Nothing, I guess."

"Who'd have thought we'd be where we are."

Victor gave a little laugh folding his arms in front of him. "You are right where you should be in that mansion of a house you live in."

"Yes, I suppose I belong there." Ethan chuckled without mirth. "But truly, did you ever think you'd live somewhere like this?" He wished it was where he laid his weary head at night.

"No of course not, but that was before...Celena."

They fell silent.

"By the way, I got another dividend from the carriage factory," Ethan said, watching Victor kicking small stones on the drive.

"As big as you thought it would be?"

"Bigger. Do you realize we are making so much money, that I'm starting to run out of places to put it?"

That made Victor laugh. "I find it hard to believe that *you* can't find a place for it."

"I'll think of something, but honestly Pickering is thrilled with the product they are turning out." He paused a moment. "You did a good job teaching them."

"It was not a difficult concept," he laughed, remembering that when Ethan had taught them, it had not taken.

"Easy for you."

Again, Victor laughed.

"And I got another letter from Walker. They plan to switch over the entire Eastern line."

"My God, that's astonishing I can't believe that it all worked, and you were able to get them to use it and pay us for it."

Ethan shrugged, digging his hands into his pockets. "It was a good idea."

"Doesn't mean people always like it though." Victor glanced in the direction of the shop. Thinking that it had been such a happy home for him and wondered if it would be happy one for Bartholomew that although had his freedom, still seemed to be in chains.

"And you're still able to keep the shop running?" Ethan asked, glancing a way down in the road towards the cabin.

"I'm still splitting my time between there and the factory, but so far so good," Victor said and looked down at the lights of his old house. "He's a good smith."

"I hear he's caught the eye of Widow Chomeau's house maid Judith, do you remember her?"

"Please! Widow Chomeau will have my head if Judith ever leaves."

"I guess there's no chance of that how old he is and young she is."

"I guess not."

Again, Ethan glanced up at the house, wondering if Celena had put the baby down and was undressed and waiting in bed for her husband.

"How's Abigail?"

"My mother? Why do you ask?" Ethan did not want to admit that his mother was becoming harder and harder to live with, and at times he feared she was losing her grip on reality.

"I don't know. No one ever sees her, and you never talk about her."

"What's there to say? She is fine. As disappointed and as irritated with me as ever."

"I know all about that. My pa never thought I did anything good or right. Always pissed off at me for something."

In the darkness Ethan looked at him. It was absurd to think of Victor not being good at anything, but since his father had so often told him, it had become part of his personality.

"I'll be different with my boys," Victor murmured.

"Oh by the way, Henry made the last payment on the farm."

"That's what Margaret told me, and he even did it without my help. Good ol' Henry."

"I gave him a clear deed, signed, legal, it's finally over."

"Thank you."

"Please...after everything my father did, after everything I let happen, please don't thank me."

"All right," Victor said with a grin.

Yvonne Riefler sat in the living room of her home on a summer night in 1853 and informed her adult children that she was pregnant again. Although surprised, they were pleased at the news. Yvonne was overwhelmed, having thought that her childbearing days were over.

That fall after two horribly long days of labor and the hushed fear of her family, she delivered her eighth child, a boy they named John after his father, but to avoid confusion immediately called Johnnie. Yvonne had not known how to answer the concerned questions of her grandsons, six-year-old Nathan and four-year-old Gabe, who wanted to know if Johnnie was *actually* their uncle when they were both older than he was!

It was the same year Eva surprised everyone and married Stephan Stoddard, *not* Danny Charbonnier, whom she had been courting for years, and Margaret suffered her third miscarriage and everyday thanked God for Hank, who so far was healthy and strong.

Chapter 28

"It seems to me like it was a bad law to begin with," Laurence said as he watched Victor work on a tie rod for him. "I mean I know the politicians were thinking they were helping the southern planters get their property back—but giving them federal officers at their disposal to hunt up the runaway slaves and do God knows whatever when they find them."

"I don't like it either, I want no part of all that. I don't like the way the southern delegates keep pushing the issue of getting increasingly new territories to be slave soil—they weren't supposed to do that with that compromise they all signed their names to years ago. Seems to me they get greedy every time a new territory applies for statehood," Victor added.

"I tell you this whole country is angry, and it gets a little angrier every year, like how the Whigs refused to nominate Fillmore again, their own incumbent after he signed that fugitive slave act into law—and the word I hear now is that the whole Whig party is pretty much disintegrating."

"Maybe it's just as well."

"It was not a friendly election...remember what the ailing Whigs said about Pierce—that he's fought many a *bottle*! And the Democrats' jeer, 'We *Polked* them in 1844 and we'll *Pierce* them in 1852,'" Laurence commented.

Victor grinned. "It's too bad politics is full of men that seem to forget their conscience."

Laurence replied, "That's the truth...Fillmore is nothing like old Rough and Ready that's for sure! what is it you said Pickering told you last time you were in Washington about him—something he said after a meeting with all the southern leaders when they threatened to secede—that he'd personally lead the army against them and hang them with no reluctance!" Although certainly not happy words, Victor found himself grinning at the memory of how Pickering had so colorfully related the story.

"It's hard to keep with all the different arguments they have in

Washington. I find myself confused by their bickering," Victor said tiredly.

Laurence laughed, and they both greeted Ethan as he walked into the shop. "You're just tired because you're not getting any sleep!"

Victor grinned and nodded, his eyes rimmed red. "I forgot how little they sleep in the beginning," he said, referring to his son Benjamin who had been born six weeks ago. "I don't know how Celena does it with Randy, the holy terror that he is running all around, and Ben not even able to hold his head up—and more often than not Carlene's daughter, Livi there too!"

"She can do it; my little sister is a tough one," Laurence said.

Victor smiled, but he did worry about her. He couldn't remember the last time he had seen her sit down for more than a minute or two.

Laurence grinned at Ethan. "Bet this baby talk is fascinating to a bachelor like you! When are you going to get married anyway, Ethan, how old are you now?"

"Twenty-eight."

"Well, that's still young enough, but let me tell you, you haven't *lived* 'til you've been woken up every night for three months with a colicky baby!"

Victor laughed in agreement.

"What? None of our Ste. Gen beauties has caught your eye yet?"

Ethan was glad Victor's back was to him. "No, not yet."

Laurence chuckled. "Well maybe it's just as well—you're probably getting more of that *stuff* then us old married men are. Seems to me every time I get near Lisette one of the kids cries, and when I am lucky enough to be in bed with her when she's actually awake—nine months later I'm right back where I started!"

Victor laughed, knowing from experience how many times he had been in the throes of passion with Celena only to have Randy cry and how abruptly she would shove him aside to tend the baby.

"I'm done here," Victor said and handed Laurence the repaired tie rod.

"Back to our earlier discussion—think President Pierce can keep order?" Laurence asked, trying to pay Victor, who shook his head at him.

"I don't know, but I hope he doesn't let all the southern delegates bully him into expanding slavery," Victor said.

It was then that Bartholomew walked back into the shop. He was still for a minute when they were all looking at him, and then ducking his head a bit, went quietly back to his work.

As much as Victor wanted to keep the arguments of sectionalism, expansion, and slavery far from his life, the bitter truth was right in front of him, and it got harder each year to brush it aside.

"I can't believe Eva married Stephan!" Carlene whispered to Celena after church. "I mean he's so—*stop it Livi!*" she screamed down to her daughter, who was whining to be picked up.

"Not now Carlene," Celena said, shifting a fussy Ben in her arms as Randy whimpered with his nose running, also wanting to be picked up.

"It's so obvious that Danny gave her the mitten and she went out and married the first man that asked her!"

"I don't want to talk about this now," Celena sighed, and then forced a smile at Ethan across the yard, but she was trying to get Victor's attention. Ben desperately needed changing and Randy was getting cranky, badly in need of a nap.

"Oh, here comes Mason! Tell him you need me at your house today," Carlene whispered, trying to hide behind Celena, ridiculous given that Carlene was four inches taller. "I don't want to go home with him."

Celena merely smiled at Mason but looked past him, still trying to get Victor's attention. He was talking with Jean Gustave, and she knew from experience that when those two got talking the sun could fall from the sky before they would notice it.

"Hello Celena," Mason said, seeing that she was having quite a time of it with Ben arching his back to get down, and Randy clamoring to be picked up. "I see you've got your hands full." Awkwardly he reached forward and took Ben out of her arms. He'd scarcely picked up his *own* child, much less someone else's. Livi was whining to be picked up too, and Mason leaned down and hoisted his daughter into his arms.

Carlene's mouth dropped open in disbelief.

"This is how Victor does it, isn't it Celena?" he asked with a smile.

Celena cringed seeing a damp spot on Mason's silk cravat from Ben's drool and reached out to take her son. "Oh, that's all right Mason—"

But he shook his head, obviously not intending to give him back yet.

Celena picked up Randy. "I'll be right back." She hurried over to Victor.

"What do you think you're doing?" Carlene hissed, straightening her back.

"I'm holding my child," Mason replied, but he knew what she meant and in truth, had no answer for her.

Celena came back a moment later having deposited Randy in Victor's arms, and took Ben from Mason. "Thank you, Mason, Randy's with Victor. I'll take Ben now, thank you for holding him."

"It was a pleasure, Celena," he said as his eyes drifted wistfully over to Carlene. "Maybe one of these days I'll have a son too..."

"You needn't slam the door I am already aware you are not pleased with how you stormed away after church," Mason said as they walked into their house.

"Not *pleased!*" Carlene shrieked, dragging a whimpering Livi into the house. "I'm furious with you, how dare you say something about us having a *son* in front of Celena!"

Sadly, he dropped his eyes and shuffled his feet. "I'm sorry. I suppose I shouldn't have."

Carlene knew all too well the argument that wouldn't follow. He would lower his head, close his mouth and the discussion would be over. It infuriated her the way he could be one minute saying something to enrage her and the next refuse to even speak! She wondered if his clients after seeing how weak he was wished they had hired a lawyer with backbone.

She was already in a bad mood. She'd had a terrible fight with Eva two days ago when Eva had called how she treated Mason 'cruel and immoral,' she had even gone so far as to call Carlene an adulteress because of Eddie. It had taken a tremendous amount of coaxing on Yvonne's part to get the two girls to agree to be in the same room together

"Is that all you're going to say? You're going to start a fight with me and clam up?"

"What good will arguing do Carlene? It hasn't done us any good in the three years we've been married." For a moment, the sadness in his voice took her off guard. She hadn't even realized he was unhappy.

"At least it would show you had opinions other than *yes*, no, or *maybe!*"

His eyes met hers. "I have opinions—"

"Oh no you don't, there's nothing to you Mason! You're so incredibly boring I don't know why I haven't died from it living with you!"

He opened his mouth to say something, but then thinking better of it shut it and again lowered his head.

"My point exactly!" Carlene snapped, placing her thin hands on her hips. "Nothing affects you Mason, you've got no reaction to anything, you have no feelings—"

In two strides he was across the room staring down at her. "I have feelings, Carlene, some of us just don't choose to show them at every public function they attend."

"Did I embarrass you, Mason?" she sneered, but she was embarrassed and ashamed about the scene she made.

"Frankly, yes but that's nothing compared to you and Eddie sneaking off behind my back."

She didn't think he knew, and for a moment it so shocked her that she was mute.

Livi, whining louder because of their arguing, gladly left her mother, and quieted when her father leaned down to pick her up.

"But...how did you know?"

"Come now Carlene, surely you didn't think I was stupid enough not to figure it out. Credit me with some intelligence please. I was furious at first when I realized you were still seeing him, insane with jealousy. But then I realized that the way things had happened so quickly between us, that you'd never had time to get over my charming little brother." He shook his head, recognizing his part in the foolish mess of his life. "I hoped that if I did nothing, you would get over him, and I had hoped that my own brother would have the decency to leave my wife alone." He shifted Livi in his arms.

"Why didn't you say anything sooner?"

The eyes that met hers were full of doubt and fear. "I was afraid you'd leave me. You must admit the hold I have on you is not exactly strong, and I am certainly not in the position to risk issuing ultimatums."

Although she tried to ignore it, she felt a sudden sense of pity for him.

"And besides that, you've told me more than once that if you left, you'd take Livi away from me." He turned then and kissed his daughter's cheek.

Normally such a display of affection annoyed Carlene. And even though he was not the type of father who roughhoused and threw their children up in the air, she knew he genuinely loved Livi.

"Why do you want me, why do you bother with me?" she snapped, thinking of all the times she'd yelled at him, laughed at him, been as disrespectful as she dare, and even more than she dare. How humiliated she had been when Father Tonnellier had shown up at her door scolding her for disregarding her marriage vows. "Why do you want me when you know I love Eddie?"

"You don't love Eddie, Carlene."

She could have clawed his face 'til it bled. But at the same time, she knew it was true. She *wanted* to be in love with Eddie. He was exciting and reckless, and their love was forbidden, and she'd committed a mortal sin with him.

Mason was not exciting. He was dependable, rational, and surprisingly enough still there. Even after three tumultuous years of marriage of enduring her temper tantrums and her leaving him. It occurred to her with an odd catch in her heart that he was still waiting for her. That despite everything she'd done, she still had a home to come back to.

"You might as well get over him once and for all."

"Why?"

"Eddie's getting married." The horrified look on her face confirmed that she had not heard this bit of news. "He's marrying Lorien Gustave, and I'm sure it won't come as a shock to you that she's pregnant. Besides, I had a little talk with him."

She was finding it difficult to breathe. "What did you say to him?"

"I told him that I was ending it between you two, that I'd had enough. I told him that if I ever caught him around you again that even though he's my blood, I'd seriously hurt him. My parents know all about it and they are furious with him. And you."

Carlene was having a hard time imagining Mason hurting anybody, but he said it like he meant it. It was also embarrassing to her to know her in-laws thought so ill of her, especially when she had always rather looked down on the Fisks. And the fact that Eddie had been with Lorien while still trifling with her was humiliating and degrading.

She dropped into the chair suddenly. She saw him gently place Livi down on the bench, heard him coaxing her to play with the doll Celena had made for her with the pretty blue buttons for eyes.

"What—what are we going to do now?" she asked quietly.

He looked up from Livi with surprise. "What do you mean?" he asked, sitting on the bench next to Livi, who was calmer but still looked like she might break into tears at any second.

"Surely you don't think I'm going to *stay* here now with you and live like this!"

"Why not? You might even find it agreeable, especially since Eddie will no longer be offering you amusement."

"I loved Eddie!" she shouted, indignant, even though what she was feeling for him now was the opposite. "And we would have gotten married if it hadn't been for you!"

Mason sighed tiredly. "Eddie was not going to marry you Carlene, we both know that. You knew full well that he saw other women while he pretended to be devoted to you. I wish now that I had waited longer so that you could have realized that. But I was so mad for you myself that I couldn't wait."

"You call how you act *mad* for someone! I'd hate to see how you treat someone you're *not* mad for!" Suddenly her eyes fell on her skinny, frightened little girl. Livi's pale hair would never stay in ribbons and her nose was always running. She always had a hurt look on her face that annoyed Carlene, in fact it was the same look on Mason's face right now.

"I can't stay here anymore!" she wailed, desperate for Mason to do something, to react. She stomped into the bedroom, making a mess as she pulled clothes from the armoire and stuffed them into a carpetbag.

"I'm leaving you Mason, I'm leaving you for good this time!" When she heard Livi crying, she turned to scream at her to shut up. But Mason had picked up the crying child and was gently rocking her back and forth. He had the gall to be whispering to Livi that everything would be all right.

Two days later Carlene showed back up at her own house early in the morning and as she started up the frosty steps Mason was coming out, ready to go to his law practice. He looked surprised but happy to see her.

There was an awkward moment.

Carlene wrung her hands nervously, and pangs of quiet guilt coursed through her. "Is Livi still at Celena's?"

He nodded.

"I'm going to put my things in the house and then I'm going to get her."

"There's no rush," Mason said, coming down the last of the steps, tentatively reaching to take the carpetbag. "I saw Celena last night and she said Livi's fine, you know how she loves Randy, Ben and Victor." He wondered if this would be a good time to tell her how happy he was that she was back. Wondered if this was the right time to apologize to her and admit his part of the mess that was their life. Wondered if he did all these things she might let him kiss her. It had been so long since he had, he had trouble at times remembering it.

"Carlene I'm so glad—"

"Well, I'm not *glad* about *anything!*" she interrupted and it annoyed her when he was immediately wounded. She wondered suddenly why he was so easily hurt by her, but then knowing the reason, hung her head in shame.

"I've just taken the coffee pot off the stove, and I bet it's still hot, shall we have a cup and sit and talk like two civilized adults?"

She had an impulse to smart back at him, but thinking better of it, said, "All right."

But once inside the house her irritation with him grew as he anxiously flitted around. The cups rattled when he put them in the saucers, he dropped one of the spoons. The noise of him dragging the chair close to hers grated on her nerves. When he finally got situated and poured the coffee, she found herself looking past him out the window. Wondering with a sigh if this was how dull her life was to be. She stared at him as he spooned sugar into his coffee.

Keying into her displeasure, his happiness at first seeing her faded.

Neither one of them spoke. She'd never been at a loss with words when she was with Eddie she thought with bittersweet longing, but then almost with a sense of betrayal remembered they were usually arguing, and as time wore on the arguments had gotten more heated. She wondered then which of the two extremes of her life was worse-quietness and boredom or excitement and heartache.

Then there was Livi, and Carlene fought back her tears when she saw one of her daughter's dirty little aprons laying on the floor. She knew Livi liked being at Celena's house more than she did at home. After all, Celena's house was a happy place. Even though she knew Livi loved her Livi cried a lot at home because of all the yelling she did and how tense their home was. Carlene knew she was taking out her frustrations on Livi *and* knew that it wasn't fair. Closing her eyes, promised herself she'd make it up to Livi.

Her thoughts again wandered to Eddie, and it surprised her that the thought of him getting married didn't bother as much as she thought it would. He was hard on her heart, hard on her soul. Maybe with Lorien he wouldn't be so bullheaded, so annoyingly opinionated, and loudmouthed. Never looking at things clearly, never stopping to think about his actions. It dawned on her that she had been comparing Eddie to Mason!

"Mason," she began softly, "you're not an altogether...bad person."

"Thank you. I think," he said with a smirk.

"But you're sort of..." Dhe paused, not wanting to hurt his feelings any more than she already had.

"Dull?"

She nodded. "Yes, dull. If I'm to stay here with you, do you think you could force yourself to show emotion sometimes? A little...feeling?"

He nodded, resting the spoon carefully on the table. "Yes. I suppose I could."

She sighed silently, discouraged again. "Could...*now* be one of those times?" she prodded, hoping to see a glimmer of life.

"Certainly," he said, and then cleared his throat and re-arranged his feet under the table. He accidentally kicked the table leg and sloshed coffee into the saucer. "I am glad you're home Carlene."

Silently she counted to ten. "Anything else?"

"I'm...I'm glad you're home."

"Yes. You said that already." When he nodded she felt her brittle hopes crumbling. It was how she felt when she left school. Expecting something to somehow happen, and to this day nothing really had! That was how it felt with Mason. And there was always enough work to do to keep life going, she surely knew that. But what was the point, if all that work had no bright spots. "Oh Mason!" she sobbed, shaking her head. "I can't live like this, and besides it's not fair to you either."

"Why not, what have I done?"

It hurt Carlene for one of the few times in her life to realize she had inflicted pain on another. "It's not what you've *done*, it's what you *haven't* done! I need more excitement than this."

"What do you need? Carlene I'll do *anything* please tell me!" He was suddenly more animated than she'd ever seen him. His chest was heaving, and his hands were fisted. "Carlene I love you!"

She felt terrible and a little embarrassed for both of them when she saw tears in his eyes. When he reached clumsily for her, she stood up to get away from him, but he followed her up.

"I'm sorry, believe it or not I don't *want* to hurt you. We're just too different." Her palms were flat on his chest to push him away.

"But we're *not* that different. I have feelings, I have passion. I feel all the same things you feel, I'm not good at showing them, but they're in my heart I swear they are! That's why I was so *enamored* of you, you have zest for life I lack, you say all the things I never can. Please, please give me the chance to prove it!" He wanted to die when she shook her head.

"I've given you time! And besides, I did just now. And what did you do? Nothing. You did nothing."

The unflattering statement hung ominously in the air. She could see him squinting a bit in deep thought, and it annoyed her that he was analyzing instead of merely feeling.

"But what is it that you want me to do?"

She looked up at the ceiling, frustrated. "If I have to tell you how to be romantic and exciting Mason, it rather ruins it all." She half expected to finish him with that blow and was surprised when he shot back.

"Don't be ridiculous, life is not actually like *that!* Did you have valentines and roses with Eddie when you were sneaking off behind haystacks in the dark? I think not."

Furious, she brought her hand up to slap him.

He caught her wrist. "I am your husband, and you will not strike me."

It was humiliating to have him still be in control when she was past the point of losing hers. She burst into tears.

"Here," he said, offering her his handkerchief.

She batted it away.

"Take the damn handkerchief, you need to wipe your nose. Sakes alive Carlene but you are such a *child* sometimes."

"I am not!"

He grabbed her chin and pinched her nose with the handkerchief. "Stand still!" he barked, wiping her nose. "It's no use fighting me, no matter what a patsy you think I am. I am much stronger than you."

She looked up at him wide-eyed—she'd forgotten how tall he was.

"Yes Carlene, I have been privy to the latest bit of libel you've been spreading in town about me."

She thought suddenly about biting him to get his hands off her.

"Now we are going to talk this through." It annoyed him how she squirmed to be free. "I want you back." It infuriated him that she interrupted what was to be the greatest oratory display of emotion in his life.

"No, you don't."

"Will you be quiet for once, listen and learn something?"

"It's too late Mason. Besides I'm ashamed of myself and looking into your eyes only makes it worse," she sobbed.

"I don't care," he began, and she jerked her face up to him in astonishment "I-I mean I *do* care, but it can be in the past if you'll let it." He tried to touch her cheek, but she moved back. "You're Livi's mother and my *wife*." He spoke with such pride that she winced in shame.

"Ive been a terrible mother to Livi."

"But she loves you and you have time to make amends."

She stared at him. "You're being brutally honest, aren't you?"

"Yes. I think it's time we both are if we expect any happiness out of our marriage."

"It feels like it's too late." Although she had not meant to hurt him, she saw it in his eyes.

"It doesn't have to be." He paused and swallowed hard. "We should take a trip, go down to New Orleans on vacation, I hear it's a wonderfully decadent city. We could leave Livi with Celena or if you prefer we could take her with us. Carlene I know you've never liked living here, I'll have a house built, one with more land so you can have the size garden I know you want." He stopped speaking suddenly and, taking hold of her hand, pressed it against his heart. "And since the reality of life is that we will have to come back here, we will have to make our own lives more interesting. You should read more Carlene—"

"If you think I'm so *ignorant* then why did you marry me?"

He briefly closed his eyes in frustration. "I don't think that, and I didn't *say* that. I was merely going to mention that there's a vast world waiting for you between the pages of a book, and we could discuss them together. It won't be perfect, there is no such thing, but I enjoy your company. And I am more than willing to forget the past and try again." She felt him pulling her closer to him.

"My brothers always said I was hard to get along with, and I've been so terrible to you."

"That's true. You are hard to get along with sometimes but that's because you feel strongly about things, and I admire the courage you have to voice your opinions." He reached up and touched a single tear that slid down her cheek. "You haven't been terrible to me," he whispered. "I mean, we had our moments, but it wasn't *all* unpleasant."

Despite everything she knew it was true. There had been good times, although she had worked hard to forget them.

"I want you to stay with me."

"But how can you forgive me? You're never going to be able to forgive me." She felt so inadequate suddenly, so unworthy of his and Livi's love.

"That's not true, there's a lot you don't know about me. I am capable of great love and forgiveness."

"*Great love,* Mason?" she said, a little harder than she meant to.

He nodded. "Yes. Even dull people such as myself." Awkwardly he reached for her hand and bringing it to his lips kissed it and looked into her eyes. "I am willing to forget the pain of the past, but I do ask that you promise me something."

"What?"

His eyes were full of love and longing. "That you'll never see Eddie again." Too choked up to speak, she nodded. "Or...anyone *else* for that matter."

She nodded again.

He moved towards her then and gently kissed her forehead, half expecting her to push him away. When she did not, he bent and kissed the tears off each cheek, then moved to kiss her mouth.

"Mason," she breathed, pulling back her heart pounding in her chest. "There's something I have to tell you."

"I know, Carlene."

"You can't know, what do you mean you *know*? You don't even know what I'm going to say!"

"I know about you and Eddie."

"But I mean—"

He put his hands on her cheeks. "I know. And I know that's why I was able to get you to marry me so fast." He stared at her unblinking. "I took advantage of you—"

She would not let him finish. "But how can you—how can you love me when I did something so horrible?"

"You made a mistake. I forgive you. It's my *brother* I will never forgive, for taking such hideous advantage of you." He stared at her, unblinking. "But I took advantage of you too in a way. You poor wretched young woman, both Fisk brothers after you from different angles. I hope you can forgive me. I wanted you for what I hope you believe are for the right reasons, and I *still* want you for the right reasons. Which is more than I can say for my little brother."

"You took advantage of me too." It finally seemed to make sense to her.

"I did. And I would do it again," he admitted with a shrug, "even if you hadn't married me, I would have done my best to see you didn't end up with Eddie. No woman deserves that."

Carlene was quiet a moment, considering. She knew he'd endured anger from his parents, the rumors in town, the fear that at any moment the woman he loved would abandon him.

When she said nothing, tentatively he moved closer, and slowly in case she wanted him to stop, bent to kiss her. For the first time in three years, she could kiss him without pretending he was Eddie.

She broke free a moment later and stood staring up at him. Not only was he taller than Eddie, but his hair was also lighter too. Reaching up to touch it was amazed at how soft it was. She remembered how Michelle

Christi always used to stare at him in church, which always surprised her because he wasn't as handsome as Eddie. But she realized there was something quietly appealing about him and felt foolish suddenly for being the last one in town to realize it.

"So," he began and had to clear his throat, "we have this all settled now. You've come back to me, you'll stay with me, and you won't leave me anymore, right?"

He sounded so much like a lawyer tying up loose ends that she smiled. "Yes."

When he pulled her to him again something strange happened. She felt as if something electric jumped from his body to hers at his touch. It was, foreign to her after all; Eddie's touch had never aroused such feelings.

"Were...were you serious about..." She stopped, embarrassed to outright ask. Especially with the pounding of her heart and the odd sensation that was building deep in the pit of her stomach.

"Was I serious about what?"

She bit her bottom lip, staring at his chin instead of his eyes. "About... wanting a son?"

"Oh God, yes!" His heart nearly burst out his chest. He'd show her how exciting, romantic, and even chivalrous he could be! Maybe with Eddie out of the way she would be open to liking, and in time even loving him.

Gallantly he swept her up into his arms, but he was having a devilishly hard time holding onto her with the stiff crinoline and the yards of fabric in the way. He took a step towards the bedroom and tripped on her skirt still dangling. They landed together in a painful heap on the floor.

"Are you all right?" he asked in horror, realizing he had landed on top of her. Mortified that she was going to laugh at him.

Carlene scrambled up from the floor, her elbows smarting. She turned and grinned at him, and made a mad dash for the bedroom. He was right behind her and when he flipped her on her back underneath him on the bed she was giggling up at him.

"I had no idea you had *this* in you Mason Fisk!"

"Oh, I've got it in me," he panted, "and trust me, it wants *out*! Have I proved to you that I do indeed have feelings, have I demonstrated enough *emotion*, for you today Carlene?" he teased. When he felt her hands reaching up and unbuttoning his shirt, he thought he'd died and gone to heaven.

"Perhaps, but let's see what *else* you can think of to do..."

Chapter 29

1856

"How do I look?" Celena asked, coming down the stairs while Victor, Ethan, and her boys waited in the hallway.

She was dressed in the deep purple gown she had worn in Washington four years ago to the opera that caused Victor's blood to boil, but she had added a lace tucker so that the cleavage was hidden. Since it was February and there were no flowers to decorate her hair, she had put a ribbon in it.

"You're *beautiful* Maman!" Randy cried, clasping his little hands together with delight, terribly excited to be going to a big Valentines party at Widow Chomeau's. Celena smiled down at all three of her little blond, blue-eyed sons. Randy and Ben stood proudly, dressed up in dark suits. Victor had done his best to keep clean but noticed a small damp spot of what looked to be applesauce on Ben's lapel. Both had their hair combed, but the little blond curls quickly sprung up. The newest baby Andrew was wrapped up tight in a blanket and gurgling happily in his father's arms.

"You're as pretty as a flower Maman!" Ben said and then began to hop like a rabbit, and they all laughed at his antics.

From the moment they walked into Josephine Chomeau's warm welcoming home, there was an air of excitement and happiness that embraced everyone that walked in. John and Yvonne came over to greet them. Kisses and hugs were given, and John shook Victor's hand heartily, putting a hand affectionately atop Victor's.

"Has that reaper given you any more trouble?" Victor asked.

John's grin was huge. "Not since you fixed it."

"Oh Celena," Yvonne exclaimed happily. Looking at Celena's radiant face she thought that she'd never seen anyone look happier than her daughter did, and it made tears of gratitude form in her eyes. Especially when Johnnie, clamoring to held by his big sister, reached his pudgy hands and laughingly Celena picked him up.

"Hello Eva!" Celena looked behind her. "Where's Stephan?"

"Right over there. He's with Laurence and Davey," Eva said with a proud smile at her husband. Stephan was not particularly handsome with his sandy hair and pale freckled complexion, but with how happy Eva was it did not seem at all important.

Suddenly Eva stole her arm around Celena's waist and hugged her tight. "This is all so fun; we should remember this night. All our friends here," she whispered, leaning near Celena as her eyes roved over all the friends in attendance. Smiling, she looked at Margaret and Hank who was annoyingly playing with the ribbons on her skirt. She smiled at the Stoddards, watched the Fisks talking with Jean Gustave, who was there with his wife and four of his five daughters. Eddie's refusing to show had caused a huge rift in his family with his wife Lorien wanting to be a part of such a special night, and Celena felt sorry for her.

The Charbonniers were there, including Caleb and his wife and children as well as the twins Davey and Danny. Danny was polite but cool to Eva whenever he saw her.

Of course, Ethan was there, handsome and charming as ever, and it occurred to Celena as she watched him sipping his wine, that he had no sweetheart, and to her knowledge never had. She had heard the whispered talk in town about he and Arvellen, but did not want to believe it.

Celena eyes rested lovingly on her own brood. Ben and Randy, both eating custards as fast as they could cram them into their mouths, laughing with Gabe and other children. Carlene had both Livi and Andrew on her lap, and she was now scolding Livi for feeding Andrew too fast. And shining in the golden light of at least twenty candles, she watched Victor talking with James and Alice as she showed off baby Charles.

She smiled when she saw Hank sneaking up behind Victor.

"Where's Hank?" Victor asked of his sister across the room, who was trying not to smile, knowing that at any minute her six-year-old son was going to jump onto his uncle's back like he was in the habit of doing.

Margaret shook her head, playing along. "Oh, I don't know, I haven't seen him for ages."

A moment later Hank jumped onto his uncle's back.

"There's the runt!" Victor said with a laugh.

Hank's small arms worked to get around his uncle's broad back. "I'm not a runt!"

"Of course you are! Are you as big as me?" Victor said, somehow able to tickle the little boy who was half sitting half laying on his back. "I never liked being this big—but I like it now because I get to toss all you little ones around!" He pulled Hank around to the front and flipped him down in front of him. "Good one Hank!"

Hank giggled with delight and immediately climbed back up on his uncle's back to repeat the trick they often did together. Seeing the fun, Randy, Ben, Gabe, and Nathan all lined up behind Hank. The little boys thought Victor a wonderful playmate. Especially since when he held them they could stretch and touch the ceiling even at Josephine's house which were at fourteen feet, the tallest in the village.

"I hear they've been fighting in the Kansas Nebraska territories," Laurence said as Ethan, Victor, James, Stephan, and Jean sat in the back parlor.

"Yes, that's what I heard too. Some fanatic by the name of John Brown's stirring up some serious trouble," Ethan said, shaking his head.

"But he's an abolitionist—thought you'd be all for him?" James jabbed. But no one since they all knew his opinions, answered right away.

"Do you know what he threatens to do?" Victor began, "In the name of Jesus he says he's going to drag slave owners out of their beds and hack them up into little pieces. The fool still believes in the Old Testament demanding an eye for an eye and a hand for a hand. Even if his message about wanting to stop slavery is *right*...his *methods* are all wrong—and I refuse to align myself with such a militant fanatic."

"They wouldn't be having all this trouble in that territory if President Pierce had any backbone and told the southern delegates no. Now everybody's all stirred up again about extending slavery into the new territories," Ethan said. Everyone but James murmured their agreement.

"I think it's got more to do with that damn Kansas and Nebraska act Douglas pushed through congress. He out and out repealed the ban in our Missouri compromise on slavery, which by the way is irritating to me that they can brush something like that aside that we've been abiding by for over thirty years. And it infuriates me that this act leaves it open for the territories to decide whether they want to be slave or free—says he's leaving it for popular sovereignty. And all it's done so far is stir everybody up!" Laurence said with disgust. "Now we got all the differences over slavery altering the political parties. In fact, the Whig party which had been so strong is losing out now as the national party, and the souths know nothing party—"

"I've always thought that an apt name!" Victor joked.

Laurence grinned but continued, "and now the democratic party is springing up in the south and now in the north we have this new republican party. And not only has that act got all the politics in an upheaval but they are stirring up some real trouble there."

"I heard that when the day comes for Kansas to elect members for their first territorial legislature, that the pro-slavery border ruffians plan to vote early, and *often!*" Victor said and the men grinned and nodded. "Which will no doubt only enrage those Kansas Jayhawkers."

"Oh, they will be fighting I unfortunately assure you," Laurence added grimly, having read reports from along the border in places like Independence and knew that if only a few men died they would be lucky.

"How did this all get so mixed up with the slavery issue anyway? I mean, weren't President Pierce and Senator Douglas trying to promote the railroad from up in Chicago to through the Nebraska territory and on to California?" Davey asked, confused, politics always bewildering to him.

"Yes, it was but I don't think Senator Douglas cares one way or the other about the slavery issue as long the railroads go forward—but what he seemed to forget was that an awful lot of us do."

"I like the idea of expanding the railroad," Victor began.

Jean laughed, interrupting. "Of course you do, wis your little coupler making you wealthier by za minute."

"That's true but the railroad by and large I think you would agree is a good thing—but where it seems Douglas gets into trouble with all that is that he tries to sweeten the deal for the new territories and allows them to decide for themselves the slavery nightmare."

"And then all the southern delegates get greedy, rushing into Kansas and Nebraska trying to make them slave soil," Stephan added quietly, and Victor was surprised he had spoken. Stephan was by and large a quiet person, and didn't usually join them in their discussions, even though they had encouraged him.

"It isn't fair if they don't! At least it should be balanced with half of country with slavery and half without," James said, trying to sound confident even though his voice shook a little.

"Seems to me the south is scared. Scared that if they don't keep adding slave states to the union, one of these days the majority of us will just up and tell them to drop the whole thing all together," Laurence said, careful not to meet the eyes of his brother.

"Then they'll up and go! You can't tell them to give up all their property!" James huffed, his eyes flashing.

"Oh God James, don't start in with succession and slavery bullshit!" Laurence burst out suddenly and then realized regrettably that he was chastising his little brother in front of the other men, which in turn he knew would only embarrass James and fuel his passion.

"It isn't only *that!*" James retaliated, still stinging. "Why do the abolitionists get to add all the new territory—while the south who only wants more states' rights and individuality gets nothing?"

"Don't cloak it under individuality. Don't cloak it under who wants more territory and states' rights. It's ownership of people. It's taking them, working them like animals, and legally having them do whatever you want."

James shut his mouth. First, it was difficult to argue with Laurence. He was smart to begin with and he read every single newspaper he could get a hold of from around the country that came in on the boats. Besides that, he had married Lisette whose grandmother had been black. In addition, Victor was looking at him, and although Victor didn't usually argue with him about slavery it was obvious the talk of it brought to memory his own Indian slave mother.

"James, I've told you this before, you've got to read! And not propaganda from the idiot abolitionists or the pro slavery, but *everything*. Then sift through it all and make your *own* mind up," Laurence urged.

James trudged forward. "I suppose you all believe every word that vile wench in petticoats Stowe, wrote in that hideous book! You think our benevolent host here Josephine is going to have one of her slaves beat to death in the morning?"

Sadly, Laurence shook his head. "I don't know James, probably not. And no, to answer your question I don't believe everything Stowe said. But you have to admit the book certainly paints a rather different picture than the *only* one you let yourself see of the happy-go-lucky slaves...singing their songs in the fields of Georgia...breaking their backs to make life in the 'plantation' house abundant...it puts a little different slant on the whole picture when they have to step over one of their own, beat to death on the ground, don't you think?"

It reminded Victor of that day he had heard the slaves singing as they brought in Josephine's harvest. He shuddered.

James stormed away then, leaving the group standing. Victor, like the remaining men around him, had the disheartening feeling, knowing that there were literally thousands of other men who saw things as James did.

"Sorry all"" Laurence said a moment later. "He's a little misguided, but he's my brother. And I can't help but worry about him."

A half hour later Celena watched Victor come up causally as she held Andrew. "For the second time in my life, I have purchased a slave."

Her eyes flew open. "Judith wants to marry Bartholomew?"

He nodded. "Yes, and a pretty penny Josephine wanted for her for too! I do hope you have the pantry well stocked!" he joked, but then he knew he had better tell her the other news. "There's a bit of catch though: Judith is bright and she knows Bartholomew didn't have enough cash to purchase her all himself, so she wants to work for you, to pay off the debt, now before you get all hot under the collar with me," he said, feeling an eruption coming from his wife—who he knew prided herself on being self-sufficient—"I wash my hands of all of it, I can't believe he talked me into *buying* her for him!"

"Well, I'll talk to her about it," she said, shifting Andrew. She realized he was wet. "I'm happy for Bartholomew, I hope he and Judith can be happy together."

It was confusing to him. She had never wanted any help that he had ever offered. He nodded, although he did wonder how much of a love match it could be. Bartholomew was at least twenty years older than Judith and they had only seen each other a handful of times. It must be he realized, the desperate desire to be free.

Celena turned her eyes on Victor. "It might be nice to have a little help, because I'm pregnant again."

He smiled down at her. "Kiss me."

"No, not in *here*," she admonished, embarrassed.

"Yes, in here," he said, pulling her chin up and kissing her. "All right then," he said, digesting the news. Seeing Randy and Ben wrestling each other to the floor he said, "Could you please make it a *girl* this time?"

When Celena came back from diapering Andrew, she noticed Victor had wandered over to the group of drinking men and smiled shaking her head at her husband as she walked by, blushing a bit because she could feel the weight of his eyes on her.

"*Damn* Victor, wait 'til you get her home!" Davey joked.

Grinning, Victor merely tossed back a shot of tafia.

Jean snickered, looking at Randy and Ben. "Victor, your children are so pretty and *blond!* Makes you wonder who sired them eh?" A thunderous laughter broke out.

"*Believe* me, I sired them all! And many pleasurable days and nights they were!"

All the men laughed.

"God Victor, you are a beast!" Stephan laughed.

Victor shrugged. "I've been called worse. Besides, look who's talking—I hear Eva's pregnant!"

Stephan's face went red, and he happily endured the teasing and back slapping by the men around him.

Jean stopped laughing enough to interject one last quip. "But Victor even *you* must admit, Celena is pretty, and ze idea of her wis you...it defies the laws of *nature* zat you two could even *mate!*" The laughter that followed the barb was so loud the other guests turned to look.

"Gentleman shall we have a toast?" Victor asked with a smirk, holding up his glass. "My wife just informed me that the laws of *nature* have been defied yet *again*, because there's already another one on the way!"

Ethan jerked his head up and looked across the room to Celena. He realized in a few months there would be another Gant child baptized by Father Tonnellier, and another celebration. And it occurred to him that his life was merely idling, while theirs went forward.

Chapter 30

Four weeks later Judith and Bartholomew were baptized and married by Father Tonnellier, Victor and Celena serving as their witnesses. As they walked back through town that Tuesday afternoon Bartholomew happily greeted everyone that walked by. Sweeping his hat off to the ladies-grinning madly at the other blacks and mixed people he saw in the streets-professing more than once, "Ah's a free man!" and proudly introducing Judith as his wife, bragging that she was 'free' too. It was heart wrenching to see how happy he was, and once he had even started to cry when they had gotten back to the shop. He offered Celena and Victor a drink to celebrate his marriage.

"Ah be beholden to yah," he said to Victor, big chin quivering, and then had to stop speaking, afraid he would break down.

Victor gripped his shoulder tightly and smiled. "No, you needn't be."

Judith too did not seem to know how to act with the sudden change in her life. She was quiet and subservient and yet at the same time, exuberant and happy. When Victor and Celena were leaving she surprised Celena by leaning towards her and hugging her

"Ah pays ya back—I don't have it now, but ah pays ya." Bartholomew struggled, knowing that Victor had spent a lot of money for Judith.

The old man's teary eyes were too much for Victor. "Please, don't worry about that now, we'll work it out someday." Victor stalled, but Celena knew he was never going to accept any money from Bartholomew. "Just keep up the good job you're doing in the shop. You have no idea how much I depend on you, and how it eases my mind knowing that you're here when I'm not." The praise had an immediate effect on Bartholomew, whose chest puffed out at the compliment.

As they waved goodbye to Judith and Bartholomew Victor wrapped an arm around Celena as they walked up toward their house in the chill of the March Day.

"Been an afternoon," he said with a smile, pressing a kiss against her temple.

"Yes, it has. Do you want me to go with you to Eva's to get the babies or stay home and get dinner on the table?"

"Start dinner I think, I'm pretty hungry. I'll go get our little brood." But then he stopped suddenly. Following his gaze, she saw Ethan stepping out of a carriage in front of their house, and he was not alone.

Exchanging curious glances, they hurried up their drive.

"Ethan!" Victor called, trotting up to greet them. "Where have you been? I went by the bank looking for you but was told you'd gone to Washington." As he reached the first step, Ethan's companion turned.

"*Penelope!*" he erupted with pleasure. He jumped up the last of the steps and enveloped her in a bear hug. "You look grand! What in the world are you doing here in Ste. Genevieve?"

"We're married." Ethan smiled.

Victor hooted with laughter and leaned to vigorously shake his hand, keeping one of his big arms clenched around Penelope's shoulders.

"Lena, did you hear? Our dyed in the wool bachelor here has finally gotten married!" Still not leaving Penelope's side, he reached for Celena, tugging her forward. "Penelope, I'd like you to meet Celena, my wife."

Penelope found herself looking at one of the loveliest faces she had ever seen. Celena's eyes reminded her of aquamarines she'd seen once for sale in a jeweler's window. Penelope felt suddenly betrayed by her husband. When she had asked him about Victor's wife, Ethan had barely spoken of her, saying only that she was shy. He could have at least mentioned she was pretty, and she knew her husband well enough to know he had noticed.

"Hello Penelope," Celena said, offering her hand.

Dully Penelope took it and couldn't think of anything to say, the wonderful feelings Victor had evoked only moments ago fading.

"Ethan why didn't you tell me where you were going, you took off and no one knew for sure where you'd gone. This calls for a celebration don't you think? Let's go out to eat, at Blays or Lawsons." Victor turned and grinned again at Penelope. "I can't believe you're here in Ste. Genevieve Penelope—welcome!" He bent and kissed her on the forehead. "Lena, do you think Eva would watch the children a bit longer while we go out?"

"I'm sure she would. She told us to take as long as we needed."

"Great! Hey, what are we doing still out here on the porch? What a terrible host I am, come on in!" Laughingly he began ushering his unexpected guests into the house. "How long have you been back?"

"Now, we haven't even been home yet," Ethan answered, his eyes dropping to the planked floor, wondering what his mother would think about his sudden, unannounced marriage.

Following them into the house Penelope was surprised by how nice it was, the exterior of the house with the bricks and roman columns had already impressed her. In fact, she had not expected to see so grand a house in the village, and never in a million years would imagine Victor to live in a house with such graceful lines.

"We'll have to let Eva know we'll be by later—but now we ought to have a toast," Victor said, grinning as they all stood at the sideboard. He happily filled the tiny cut glass cups with brandy.

Untying her bonnet, Penelope spied a cradle in the corner of the dining room and, trying to start up a conversation with the shy woman, said, "You have children?" She noticed with a faint wave of jealousy that at the mention of children, her eyes got even prettier.

"Yes. We have been blessed with three boys," Celena absentmindedly touched her stomach, "and we've another on the way."

"How wonderful for you," Penelope said, forcing a smile, relieved a moment later when Ethan was at her side handing her a glass of brandy.

"To us," Ethan began.

Victor made a face. "You made a terribly long toast at *our* wedding, and you think you're going to get away with that?" He grinned and nearing Celena, stole his big arm about her waist.

"I made a long toast?"

Both Celena and Victor laughed. "Yes, yes! You went on and on about how wonderful I was—which, by the way, was embarrassing *and* ridiculous! And then when it came to my blushing bride you got tongue tied and said bottoms up!" They laughed at the shared memory.

Penelope forced a smile , wondering why such an innocent story bothered her. Nervously she glanced up at her husband for support and blessed him when he smiled understandingly back.

Ethan was hoping his mother would have retired when they got home but told Penelope to freshen up anyway while he checked in on her.

Penelope quietly closed the door behind her, untied her bonnet and smoothed the hair back from her face. She smiled so happily at her reflection that she had opened her mouth, and then quickly clamped her hand over it to hide her slightly crooked teeth. She laughed then at her own silly behavior. Unable to help it, she smiled again when she saw the room reflected behind her. Ethan had not exaggerated when he told her about the beauty and grandeur of the house

She looked at what had been her husband's bedroom and now was theirs to share. There was a huge, canopied bed against one wall and on the windows, dark burgundy drapes, that although beautiful, regrettably blocked much of the sunlight. On the bed a gorgeous navy, and gold bed-spread covered the bed, and at the head, four fluffy goose-down pillows. Touching the luxuriant fabric of the bedspread, felt a flutter in her stomach knowing that they would sleep there tonight.

She saw evidence of her husband everywhere in the neat room. From the books lined up in the built-in bookcases, to the collection of stick pins and cuff links neatly stowed away in the small porcelain box on the long chest of drawers. Going to the armoire and opening one of the heavy doors saw her husbands' suits and shirts hanging. There was an array of tweeds, broadcloths and even silks, and as she lifted a sleeve of a gray broadcloth suit, gently rubbed it against her lips. It smelled faintly like Ethan, and she felt her pulse quicken. Wondered with a trace of amusement where in the big armoire already stuffed with her husband's clothes would her new trousseau fit.

She caught sight of her wedding ring and pressed the cool polished stone against her lips. It was an ornate ring with its two-carat emerald cut diamond surrounded by sapphires. She would have been happy with a simple gold band, but Ethan had insisted the jeweler show them the largest stone he had in the store. It was still too big on her finger-but Ethan had not wanted to stay in Washington even a day longer to get it sized.

She moved it back and forth on her finger, remembering when she had refused to go out with him even after the second night of pleading. It still made her heart pound how he had, just like in the romance novels pulled her fiercely into his arms and kissed her. It had been so hard to see him again after everything, especially since her father had lost the position in the university, and the rented flat they were living in was so rundown and she had been tutoring music to keep food on the table. There were so many bills and gambling debts piling up she didn't know how she'd ever pay them. Then like out of dream she opened the door one night to see Ethan standing there.

She tried not to fall in love with him again, but he said all the right things. He apologized for breaking her heart, tearfully telling her that he'd never stopped thinking of her.

When he saw the hopeful light burning in her eyes he set about in a whirlwind. He bought her an entire wardrobe (even though it was improper), took her out to expensive dinners, the theatre, the opera. And it was on the night after the opera at a midnight supper in a fashionable restaurant where he ordered a preposterously expensive bottle of champagne that he asked her. Looking across the table at her with those warm eyes of his, he told her how much he loved her, and begged her to make his life worth living by marrying him. Even when she agreed to marry him she worried about what her father would say. After all they had never gotten along, and she was not sure her father would consent. But Ethan told he would take care of things, and miraculously he had.

She thought back with a quiver in her stomach to the first evening in the Willard after they were married. She'd been nervous and apprehensive like any young bride, but he was so handsome and wonderful, and she was so in love with him.

What happened next, though, still confused her. It started out well enough with her handsome groom ordering yet another bottle of champagne in their suite. She had changed into the beautiful silk nightgown with the rows of delicate white Brussels lace, that with her cheeks flushing hotly Ethan had selected and purchased right in front of her!

Then he had begun to talk. And from what little she knew they had begun to consummate their marriage, because at one point she felt pain, but desperately not wanting to discourage him, masked her discomfort. But then she lay there in embarrassment as her groom fumbled clumsily below. His awkward apologizing and futile efforts were humiliating, she half wondered if there was something wrong with her.

They had had no opportunity since then. The sleeping berths on the trains were too small for one person let alone two, and for Penelope the thought of having only flimsy pull drapes separating them from the dozens of other passengers was not appealing.

There was a knock on the door, and two male slaves walked in carrying wood for the cold fireplace and water. They were silent as they went about their work of lighting the fire and putting water in the basin, and unable to help herself she crept to the door when she recognized Ethan's voice down the stairs. She wavered a moment wondering if she should wait like he had asked her, but feeling happy and excited, went down the staircase.

She wasn't sure where to go at first, but then heard the murmuring of voices and saw light from the half-opened parlor door.

"...I am certainly old enough to be married, mother," Penelope heard Ethan say as she walked towards the door. A wonderful shudder went through her. *Yes, and to me!*

"I guess it shouldn't surprise me—what's she like, this girl?"

Suddenly the expression on his mother's face changed and Ethan swung around to see Penelope. With all eyes suddenly on her she forced a nervous smile.

"Good evening Mrs. Stanfield." She was then going to say how wonderful it was to meet her; how happy she was to be in Ste. Genevieve—but something in the old woman's stare stopped her.

Abigail was dressed in full mourning regalia—the black bombazine, the black crepe over the dress, even black knitted half gloves. Her husband, Penelope knew, had been dead over three years, and her donning of full-blown mourning attire was unusual that long after death. But what shocked her was the unmistakably cold stare she received.

Penelope turned to Ethan, her frightened brown eyes pleading for help. For a brief terrible moment, he did nothing.

"Mother...this is Penelope."

Summoning all her courage, Penelope approached the old lady seated on a blue velvet couch. "I'm so happy to meet you, Mrs. Stanfield."

The old lady did not bother to mask displeasure as her eyes flicked over her. Although Ethan had seen to it that Penelope was dressed stylishly in a dark green traveling dress, smart with its deep maroon trim, her figure Abigail noticed was straight up and down with no curves and small breasts. *She'll never be able to keep him!* Abigail knew her son's taste when it came to women. She also noticed the tameness in the brown eyes, the slightly crooked teeth, the ears peeping out from her chignon. *Inferior stock.*

"I hear you are originally from Boston, my husband and I lived there many years on Wimple Street."

Thankfully, Ethan pulled a chair closer for her, and with her knees trembling, Penelope sat down. She did not answer, not knowing what Abigail expected her to say. Boston was after all a large city, was she supposed to know this street?

"Have you family?"

"Yes, well no—I mean it's always been my father and me. I-I was an only child and my mother died when I was four."

There was no smile, no small nod of sympathy.

The grandfather clock ticked noisily, and outside the window a bird called.

"What is it your father does?"

"He was a history professor." Realizing she had referred to it in past tense, she looked up nervously to recant.

"Yes, he *was* a professor, so Ethan has told me. What does he do now that he's no longer a professor of history and has my son to support him?"

"He's not well, Mother," Ethan explained.

Penelope looked down and gave a small nervous cough into her hand.

There was another awkward silence in the room, and Penelope suddenly heard the fury of the wind outside. Funny she hadn't noticed it earlier. The floor to ceiling drapes on the parlor windows hadn't been fully drawn and she could see and almost feel the cold March wind whipping the leafless limbs against the windows.

"Has there been any correspondence that I need to see since I've been gone?" Ethan asked quietly.

His mother waved a bony hand at him. "I've no idea. You should have thought about that before you took off recklessly for Washington, that's to be your responsibility. Enough of all this. I'm tired, I'm going to bed." Even though she was thin, she had trouble getting to her feet. "Where's my Arvellen?" she cried, and Arvellen, who had been hovering outside the door, sauntered in.

"*Arvellen?*" Ethan cried in shock.

Ethan had told Penelope that there was a great deal of intermarrying within the village—and he had related it in a positive light that Ste. Genevieve was open minded towards people of color. It was obvious when Penelope laid eyes on Arvellen, that through her veins ran not only African but Indian blood as well. She was a gorgeous brown color, and her skin was flawless as it stretched tight over the structure of her face. Her lips were full and deeply red. Her brown hair was pulled back in a bun, with long curling tendrils winding their way down her slender back. But it was the exotic and beautiful combination of clear green eyes in the dark face that caught Penelope's attention. They were hungry catlike eyes, and Penelope felt the hairs go up on the back of her neck when she suddenly felt them on her. Arvellen was also shapely and obviously not in the habit of bothering with the top three buttons on her dresses.

"Mother, what is she doing here?"

"*Oui*, Madam I am here," Although she did not look at Penelope, Penelope had the feeling that every slave in the Stanfield's house would know by morning that the young master had married—and that his mother didn't approve of her son's choice.

"I dismissed you before I left," Ethan said, taking a step toward her. Even though he was a great deal bigger, and presumably in charge, it was clear she was not at all intimidated by him.

"I wanted her back! Besides what right do you have of dismissing one of the few good servants that help me? I'm going to bed Ethan," Abigail said firmly gripping one of Arvellen's shoulders for support.

"Mother, things have changed—"

"Not for me they haven't!"

Shaking his head and looking dejectedly at the floor, Ethan mumbled, "Good night Mother."

"Good night," Penelope called, but Abigail ignored her.

It was cold in the room suddenly and Penelope shivered. She watched Ethan cross to an enormous carved sideboard. Heard the little *ting* of the crystal stopper being taken out of the carafe and watched him pour a healthy brandy and then in surprise watched his head snap back as he downed it. He cleared his throat and without turning to her said, "I'm afraid I have rather a lot of catching up to do. I-I need to do some work." He poured yet another drink, facing her. "You must be tired from the long trip, aren't those sleeping berths awful?"

At first Penelope smiled back, but her smile faded when she noticed the sad tinge in his eyes.

"Do you think you can find your way back to our room in this dark God forsaken house?" The question broke the tension.

"I think so." She stood awkwardly, not knowing exactly what to do. He had warned her that his mother would not be thrilled at their marriage, and although the meeting with her mother-in-law was not as warm as she had hoped, it was not surprising. But she had dealt with difficult situations before. She shuddered remembering how her father had often hinted to her that to help, she marry one of the old, rich men that he knew. Thank God Ethan had saved her! Besides the entire homecoming had not been unpleasant, and a sudden warmth of gratitude washed over her remembering how Victor had hugged her. He had been so genuinely happy to see her, and her presence she realized, had that effect on so few people in her life.

The wind whipped against the windows again, rousing her from her thoughts. "Good night then."

He looked up abruptly, already seated at the desk, unaware she was still in the room. "Oh...yes, good night." He smiled briefly at her and went back to his papers.

When Penelope awoke she was met with the sight of the enormous canopy above her and marveled at how beautiful the fabric was draped above her. She sat up looking around the room for any sign of Ethan. Spying the armoire open and his discarded suit and shirt on the tufted chair, realized he had changed, but had not come to bed. Pushing the covers back she jumped out of the bed to hurriedly dress.

She walked slowly down the staircase, her hand lightly trailing down the polished banister, wanting more than anything to feel the security of those warm brown eyes on her. She nervously walked into the dining room with as much dignity as she could muster.

"Good morning." She was startled to see her mother in-law seated alone at the table, again clad dreadfully in black.

The beady eyes swept over her, and Penelope laid her hand at the back of the chair, trying to appear ladylike—in reality she wanted it for support. Despite her sour temperament Penelope could tell Ethan had inherited his good looks from his mother, for there was a faded beauty about her.

"Has Ethan breakfasted?" she asked, hoping at any moment to see her husband's handsome face turn the corner.

"Yes. He's long gone." Abigail poured thick cream into her coffee.

Penelope's stomach muscles tightened. "Oh...I see." She sat suddenly, her skirts fluttering louder than they should have.

Abigail frowned. "Patsy," she called and a black maid appeared a moment later to pour coffee for Penelope. Looking around the lavishly set table. she noticed there was another place set. Since Abigail was at hers, and Ethan's had been cleared away, she wondered who it was set for.

"You've a lovely home Mrs. Stanfield," Penelope began, taking a tentative sip of her coffee. "I must say I was surprised to see such a grand home here in Ste. Genevieve, Ethan has told me so much about the village with the river and people that your gracious home here is rather a surprise—a gem."

Abigail snorted. "Yes, I suppose he would say that."

Penelope nodded encouragingly, but Abigail looked away from her. It was clear she was not going to reward Penelope's attempt at polite conversation. Thankfully, a minute later Patsy appeared with her breakfast, and after two more failed attempts at small talk, resignedly Penelope ate her breakfast in silence.

"I've letters to write," Abigail explained, hoisting her herself up. "That's a very becoming frock you have on."

Penelope quickly swallowed her eggs, smiling. It was a pretty dress with a forest green velvet skirt and petal pink sash. Looking down appreciatively at it, remembered Ethan said the pink in the sash matched her cheeks, and she looked like a *nymph from the forest* when she wore it.

"My son always did have good taste in clothes," the old lady remarked snidely. It was not proper after all for men to purchase clothing for their wives—*before* they were married as Ethan had done—and Penelope found herself blushing. "It's a pity though, a waste of money...this is a house of mourning and you'll not be able to wear things such as that. Have you mourning clothes?"

"No...I-I haven't," Penelope stammered, knowing that Abigail's full-blown mourning so many years later was not in line with the practices of the day. Most widows wore black for the first year, then gray or lavender the next, and ending their formal mourning by the second year.

"Then tell my fool son to buy you some." She shook her head unpleasantly at her daughter-in-law, but before walking out turned around. "Are you a foolish girl, Penelope?"

"Excuse me?"

"Are you in love with my son?"

Penelope was embarrassed and shocked to be asked such a question.

"He'll only end up hurting you, you know that don't you?"

"Who?"

Penelope shivered when the old lady smiled. "My son of course. He'll abuse you and hurt you take advantage of you like my poor Arvellen." She sighed then, bored with Penelope. "No matter. I've got letters to write."

Penelope spent the rest of the day alone. She instructed one the of huge slaves whose name was Ephram to take her trunks to the bedroom, and disregarding what her mother-in-law said, carefully unpacked all the lovely, lovely dresses Ethan had bought her. It was hard to find space in the armoire because Ethan being the well-dressed man that he was-had it nearly filled. But she managed by shifting things of his from the armoire carefully to the chest of drawers.

She unpacked the few cherished possessions she had such as her mother of pearl brush and mirror, which she carefully laid next to Ethan's silver brush on the chest of drawers, as well as the diminutive china tea set that Rebecca her old maid had given her years ago. Two of the four cups were chipped now, but still she lovingly arranged the gray and pink set on the corner of the chest of drawers, cautiously out of harm's way. It was one of the few things she had that reminded her of a time in her life that had been happy. Even now there were times when she could calm herself simply by looking at that little tea set and remembering the woman who had loved her.

She placed her beloved violin carefully in the corner by the bed and had a sudden wonderful vision of playing on some sun filled morning for her husband. Envisioned him sitting up in the bed shirtless, his thick brown hair tousled, smiling broadly at her while she frolicked with her nightgown fluttering behind her as she played Bach or Mozart.

She then spent in inordinate amount of time working on her hair, trying to get it right. Ethan had said so many wonderful things about it being softer than silk and lustrous with all the dark brown and auburn highlights. *He certainly has a way with words*! She thought dreamily and wondered anxiously when he would be home.

She fell asleep in the big, overstuffed chair she'd pulled over closer to the window to get more light, the heavy curtains she found blocking far too much sunlight for reading. The book of poems she'd crept down to the library and made off with, must have fallen out of her hand when she dozed off, and when she awoke it was laying on the floor. As she bent to retrieve it, noticed guiltily that two of the pages had been creased when it landed and quickly smoothing out the wrinkles, shut it.

It was late afternoon, and she shivered in the cold room, noticing despite a big, beautiful marble fireplace was against the wall, it was of little use with no fire in the grate. She realized that either the servants had forgotten to light it for her—or worse, had never been instructed to. She also realized that she had forgotten to eat lunch, and that no one had thought to tell her when lunchtime was. Feeling a bit forgotten she got up, rubbing her hands against her shoulders for warmth and made her way down the stairs. She felt a wonderful burst of relief when she caught a glimpse of Ethan through the partially opened door of the back parlor.

"There you are!" he said, and the smile that lit up his face made him even handsomer. "I just got home, and I was about to go up and get you," he said, crossing the room, placing his warm hands on her shoulders.

"You must be freezing." He bent to kiss her and led her to one of the blue wing chairs.

She noticed though that he'd been home long enough to have a drink of brandy; she could taste it on his lips. His suit coat was off, and his shirt and hands were warm, as if he had been sitting for a time by the fire.

"And how," he said, pausing to place a kiss on each one of her hands, "did you spend your day?"

She blushed at the sweet way he was looking at her. "Nothing much, I put away clothes and did some reading. I was so surprised when I awoke, and you were already gone this morning."

He got up and poured himself another brandy. She politely declined his offer of one for herself. "Like I told you, I've been gone for almost a month, there are a lot of things that I needed to address." He sat back down. She noticed the whites of his eyes were covered with tiny red blood vessels, and the shadow of a beard was on his chin, and that he'd undone the top button to his shirt. She'd never seen him that way, but his less than perfect appearance didn't make her think any less of him. If anything, it made the tenderness she felt for him increase, realizing how hard he was working.

"You look so tired," she said suddenly and stood, taking a step toward him, but then worried what Abigail would think.

"It's all right," he said softly, sensing her hesitation, "my mother uses the morning room. This room has been mine alone for a long time. We'll not be disturbed."

She came near him then, nestling gently by his feet as he sat in the wing chair by the fire. She reached up lovingly and wanting so desperately to be alone with him laid her cheek innocently against his thigh. "Where did you sleep last night?"

He wished she would not kneel before him like that, not rest her cheek against his lap! It reminded him ferociously of what Arvellen used to do for him when he sat in that chair. He could almost feel Arvellen's slender hands on his thighs now, rubbing slowly up and down, could feel her hands unbuttoning his trousers, could almost feel the warmth of her mouth around him.

He shook himself violently. "I-I didn't. Like I said I had much work to do." Finished with his brandy and urgently in need of another, he tried to get around her. It was annoying to him how long it took her to clumsily get out of the way.

She watched him pour another frightfully large brandy and gulp it down. It was odd; she didn't remember him drinking so much in Washington.

"It's a pity it's so dark," he said, looking out the windows at the blustery evening descending, still trying to shake off the sexual arousal. "I would have liked to show you the gardens and the orchard." He forced himself to face her. "Maybe this weekend I could show you off and around town."

"I'd love that."

He dropped his head and looked so sad suddenly she wondered what could have possibly gone through his head to make his expression change so dramatically. "I'm sorry," he began and then looked up. "I'm sorry about my mother's ill treatment of you. I should have better prepared you. She's not at all fond of *me,* it's no surprise that she'd be less than overjoyed to meet you." He gave a short laugh and she did too.

She was delighted a moment later when he reached for her.

His mouth was warm and wet with brandy against hers. He'd only kissed her like this once before on their wedding night—and it had been new to her then this open-mouthed tongue kissing. And she wasn't sure how she felt about it, it seemed unsanitary after all.

He had one hand on the back of her head forcing her mouth against his. The gentle arms that had reached for her only moments ago were now crushing her against him and confused by the animal like change in him she squirmed to be free.

He jerked away. "Why don't you kiss me back?"

"I-I am."

"You kiss like a *child!* I'm a *man,* dammit, your husband, Penelope! Now *kiss* me like it!" He let go of her, dropping his arms from her and turned without a word. He stood staring into the fire, his hands on his hips, breathing heavily, trying to collect himself. He faced her finally and swallowed hard. "I'm...I'm sure it's time for dinner. Shall we go?"

Humiliated, she had to choke back tears, unable to speak.

"You're not going to *speak* to me now?" The anger in his voice rendered her mute. "Fine!"

She heard his boots thud over the hardwood floors, and then she dissolved into tears as his footsteps faded.

He came into the bedroom much later that night, carrying a lantern turned low, and when he closed the door she sat up in the bed.

"I'm sorry, I didn't mean to wake you," he said, setting the lantern opposite her side of the bed.

"I wasn't asleep."

"You missed dinner, I brought you something to eat."

She was famished, especially since she had missed her lunch. She took the proffered plate and greedily wolfed it down. For good measure she took an extra biscuit and slathered it with butter, and downing the milk so fast she had to wipe her mouth with the back of her hand.

"Penelope," he whispered in the darkness after changing and joining her in bed. "Please come here." He softly turned her towards him. Gently he traced her cheek with his fingertips. "I'm...sorry about earlier." His thumb brushed across her lips. "Can we try and start again?"

"Oh yes. Please. I want that more than anything, I love you!" Realizing how desperate it sounded she stopped and bit her lip.

"It's all right," he murmured, kissing her forehead.

He was so good at this, so good at making her feel better instantly.

"It was my fault, and I apologize. I was rushing you." He kissed her softly on the mouth, and when she did not object, kissed her again. "Let me love you," he said against her neck.

She found herself wondering how he knew to do all the wonderful things, then realized with a sharp pain across her heart that she was not the first woman he'd ever been with, and that he'd had literally years of practice with scores of different women. And for a moment it so depressed her that she wished her body would not respond to the warmth of his touch—his touch that had been on so many others.

"Tell me that you love me," he pleaded a few minutes later.

"I love you."

"Tell me that you want me—that you've *always* wanted me."

"I-I want you."

His entire body was trembling above her. He was suddenly unlike the ultra-assured lover he had been only moments ago. "You *love* me!" he whispered, collapsing against her, his chest heaving.

She was bewildered by the tortured sounds of his words. It was almost as if he asked her these things as if he had never *heard* them before.

"Are you all right?" she asked, touching his cheek, but he moved abruptly away from her. But not before she felt his tears, warm and wet on her hand.

"I'm fine," he said, and then spent a ridiculous amount of time rearranging the covers over them.

She sat in anticipation of a good night kiss, wanting more than anything to sleep nestled against that warm chest, to feel those wonderful arms around her. But he merely sunk against the pillows with his back to her.

Penelope closed her eyes and tried to calm down her pounding heart. There was a dull throbbing ache between her legs, but it was all right; she was happy. He had made love to her. He was hers forever now.

"Where in God's name are my *shirts*?" Ethan shrieked, rifling angrily through the armoire. Turning, he stared accusingly at Penelope still in bed.

Standing there half-dressed looking so handsome, her heart fluttered and she felt a sudden wave of modesty, remembering the things they had done the night before.

"I-I had to move them to put away all the gowns you bought me. I folded them and put them in the dresser."

She watched him stomp to the chest of drawers like a spoiled child. "Well, you should have asked before you started moving all of my clothes, or—better yet have told me there wasn't room for all your things and I would have gotten you another armoire!" Shaking his head in disgust, he stared down at the shirt and tossed it carelessly to the chair. He sat heavily on the bed. "I like my shirts to be hung. There wasn't room, I understand that, and I'll get you an armoire." He nodded, figuring he had fixed things, but looking at her saw that her face was white and her eyes were brimming with tears.

"Come here," he sighed.

She did not look up at him, but fell into his arms, burying her face in the warmth of his neck.

"You'll have to excuse me; I've never shared a room with anyone or shared much of anything for that matter. I was an only child and I guess I never learned how to behave as well as I should with others."

Her arms were so tight around his neck they nearly choked him.

It was horrifying to her after what happened between them last night, to have the morning dawn this way! She felt so terribly vulnerable, so far from everything she knew. Even though Victor had done everything to make her feel welcome, she was embarrassed to admit she was jealous of Celena. Jealous and caught off guard by her beauty, jealous that she knew Ethan so well. And although she tried not to let Abigail's chilly reception bother her, it did.

"Please don't be angry with me! I don't want to quarrel with you." She pulled back, searching his face, marveling anew at how handsome he was. "I love you so much! Do you have any idea how *desperate* love can make you feel?"

For a brief, mad moment, he almost answered her.

She leaned toward him, expecting him to murmur how much he loved her too and to kiss her.

"I've no wish to quarrel with you either, I'm sorry." He stood. "I seem to be apologizing a lot to you, don't I?" he mused reproachfully. "Fine husband I am." He forced a grim smile and then, clearing his throat, picked up the shirt and finished dressing. "I'll let you dress, and I'll meet you downstairs."

Chapter 31

Yvonne smiled when she turned and saw Victor walk out of the church. Watched in amusement the way his big hands fumbled with the blanket over baby Andrew.

"Morning, Yvonne—guess you knew the Gant crew was here today!" he said with laugh, smiling as Celena came out of the church firmly holding Ben by one hand and Randy by the other.

"Morning Maman," Celena said with a smile and then shook her head looking down at her little boys. "I guess you heard my boys." She looked at her husband. "Do you have to be so loud?"

He grinned self-consciously as the rest of Celena's family and assorted friends gathered, hearing her admonish him, a ripple of laughter went through the group.

"They were saying the Lord's prayer like I do," he defended.

She sighed. "What am I going to do with you?" and laughed at the humorous way he was looking at her. She took the baby from his arms. "I'm going to change Andrew."

"Victor!" Laurence called, walking toward him holding little Estella by the hand. "Heard Ethan married!"

Victor nodded.

"Who is she?" Lisette asked, standing next to Laurence.

"He'd known her since his school days, her name's Penelope." He scanned the crowd and, seeing them, called out, "Ethan!"

Ethan led Penelope toward the group. "Morning Victor, Laurence, Lisette, I'd like you all to meet my wife—Penelope."

The gaggle of women greeted her and immediately began to ask, Penelope thought, too many questions, while happily introducing her to their extended families-pointing out their rambunctious children that were running around now that the solemnity of mass was broken.

She shook hands with the men, most of which squeezed her hand too tightly and, though they looked proper enough in coats and starched shirts, she sensed a wildness in them. They laughed too loud, touched too much.

"Hello Penelope, I'm Laurence, Celena's oldest brother. This is my wife Lisette." Meekly Penelope said hello. She noticed a little blond boy dashing toward Victor, and was surprised when Victor lifted the tot and noisily kissed his cheek, wondering idly where in the world the child's parents were! Penelope wanted children to like her, but she had been around precious few in her life and was not sure how to behave.

"This is Ben, Penelope—he's our second. Ben, say hello to your new Aunt Penelope."

"Hello." It warmed her heart the way he smiled shyly, snuggling his face into his father's neck.

"Hello Ben, you look just like your Mama!" Penelope exclaimed and laughed when the tot nodded as if he heard it all the time.

"It's a good thing, don't you think!" Victor said with a chuckle. "She's a lot prettier than I am."

"Good morning Penelope." She felt a friendly hand on her shoulder. It was nice to be recognized amid meeting so many new people, and yet at the same time Penelope was not sure she appreciated the instant familiarity. "It's nice to see you. I see you've met Ben. This is Andrew." Celena smiled at the child whimpering in her arms. "Randy's around here somewhere," she said, glancing amidst the children playing tag.

"Look for the one getting into it," Victor said with a grin. He reached a hand out to shake Will's as he gingerly approached them.

"Morning Victor, Celena. Billiards today?" Will asked, smiling. He said hello to Penelope and, after mangling her with a handshake, introduced himself simply as 'one of Celena's brothers.'

"No, not today Will."

"Come on! You've turned into such a bore!" Will turned to Ethan. "How about you?"

When Ethan also turned him down, Will said goodbye to Penelope and stalked off in pursuit of more willing prey.

"Ethan, is this your wife?" Carlene asked.

Penelope, reeling with surprise at meeting so many new people, forced a smile.

"Penelope, this is Carlene Fisk and her husband Mason, and their daughter Olivia," Ethan said.

Letting go of her daughter's hand, Carlene shook Penelopes.

"Pleased to meet you Penelope." She turned to her sister. "What are we doing today, Celena—can we quilt and make candles? Penelope, on Sundays the men usually do something they shouldn't, like play cards or billiards," Carlene said with a laugh, "while we women congregate at Celena's and do things that *need* to be done. We have a good time laughing and eating, my sister is a wonderful cook—sometimes I'm disappointed when Mason comes to get me, I've had such a good time."

"Your sentiment is quite touching dear!" Mason said with seriousness, but the glint in his eye gave him away.

Celena reached out and again touched Penelope on the arm. "We'd love you to join us, do you quilt or sew?"

"No...not well."

"We can teach you," Eva said, wandering over to the group. "I'm Eva, the sister in between Carlene and Celena."

Penelope noticed she was pregnant, that she took no pains to hide it, and found herself wondering what sort of wild river town was she to live in? She realized that the three sisters were pretty and it made Penelope's already weak confidence dwindle.

"I don't want to pressure you...I mean if you have plans, life in our little village is probably a lot different than you're used to in Washington," Celena said.

Penelope thought back to her life in Washington. No bright sparks appeared.

"Of course, if you've already made plans for your day..."

Penelope thought of spending another day in that house, not knowing when Abigail would turn the corner and be annoyed at seeing her or when Abigail would start talking some disgusting nonsense about Ethan and Arvellen.

"I'd love to come over."

"Like this?" Penelope asked, her head bent over the huge rack they had set up in the dining room with an unfinished quilt stretched tight over it. There was a silence, and although Eva did not want to be unkind, felt she had to tell the truth.

"No." All the women in the room laughed good-naturedly, and despite herself Penelope did as well. "You have to link them up," Eva explained, taking the needle and thimble from Penelope's unskilled hands. "Make them tight and even," Eva made a few more stitches as Penelope watched. "Would you want me to do the rest of the square?"

"Do you mind?"

Eva shook her head. "Not at all."

Penelope watched Eva neatly stitch, and then aimlessly looked around the comfortable, welcoming room. She picked up her tea, even though it was cold by now, and took a long satisfying drink.

"So..." Carlene began deftly pulling the thread through the square, "you've known Ethan a long time?"

Even though she assumed Carlene meant it kindly, Penelope was shy to speak of Ethan with all these women she did not know. Besides, Penelope and Carlene had been talking about candle making earlier and Penelope had been embarrassed because she did not know that in order to get the wicks to adhere, they had to be dipped in wax *first*, then water, then wax. And that every other women in the room new this simple fact made her feel inadequate.

"Yes. He was a student of my father's."

"Is your father still teaching? I think Victor told me he's a history Professor?" Celena asked.

Penelope dropped her eyes. "Yes, and he's doing well."

"It must have been fun to have a father who knew so many things," Celena said, her smile bright. "It's one of the reasons I like Ethan so much. I can ask him all sorts of things from history to literature to politics, and he'll know the answer to most of them!"

Again, Penelope felt at a disadvantage with how close Celena was to him. She spent the next few minutes politely answering their questions and was glad when at last their curiosity was satisfied and was content to listen to their conversation.

They did their best to include her, although it was tiring with having to explain who everyone was, along with a thumbnail sketch of their histories. But she did not mind not being intimately part of the conversation. And she was secretly surprised how much she did enjoy quilting when Eva again gave her the needle and thimble. It was such a mundane task, and yet at the same time there was something satisfying about pulling the neat tight stitches through the cloth, that was soothing to her troubled mind. She'd never done any needlework, her father thinking it "mindless women's" work, thereby discouraging it in the house, telling her she was not "well suited to it." Penelope thought impatiently *When did you ever know anything about me!*

Ethan, Jean, Stephan, and Victor had gone to try their luck "squirrel barking" and she had felt silly when she asked why they called it that, how Victor had merely chuckled and explained, "We call it squirrel barking because you aim for the bark on the tree to knock the squirrel down, because if you hit the squirrel with the shot, even *Celena* wouldn't be able to make it taste good!"

It was surprising to Penelope, having never imagined Ethan hunting or interested in those sorts of things. She was glad he had not gone to play billiards, not wanting to have anything to do with gambling in her new life. But it was all bit disheartening to Penelope how well everyone knew Ethan, even Lisette and Alice in passing said things about him that she was not privy to. Even though they were little things like he didn't particularly like cherry pie—but loved apple tarts—to the fact that they all seemed to know and understood his odd family life, or rather lack thereof and had simply adopted him into their own. She had felt especially foolish when she had remarked to Celena how lovely the house was, and how everyone had giggled at her saying: *It's no wonder you like it, your husband designed it!*

Like Carlene said, Penelope found she was disappointed when she heard the men at the back door and wanted to clamp her hands over her ears when all the "papas" came home, and the noisy bunch of children clamored towards them. But it was fun to be part of such a warm family of neighbors and friends.

"Ooh! Something smells good, what did you make?" Victor asked, rubbing his hands together and hoisting up a grinning Ben, who was always delighted to see his father.

"We made your favorite Victor," Eva teased, looking up at him. "*F-o-o-d!*" Everyone laughed.

A little prick of jealously went through Penelope. No one had ever teased her in her entire life and she found herself wishing for family and friends who knew her well enough to do so.

Close to half of the group, along with the recently arrived Margaret, Henry, and little Hank, stayed for the enormous meal Celena had managed to cook. When Margaret greeted her Penelope tried not to stare at the ghastly scars on Margaret's arm.

The meal Celena cooked in the afternoon while quilting and caring for her eight-month-old son as well as the assorted children that seemed to be drawn to her house like magnets was superb. Penelope had never had such perfectly sautéed venison, never eaten such wonderfully seasoned soup loaded with succulent peas, cabbage and onions, and the bread was crusty on the outside, but warm and moist on the inside. And the tarts; she couldn't imagine when during the afternoon Celena had managed *that*. She never would have guessed the scruffy inhabitants of the village would possess such discriminating palates.

Penelope and Ethan rode the short way home in silence, and even though the house was a great deal warmer than the outside, Penelope shivered when they walked in, and was relieved when she felt Ethan's hand fumbling clumsily for hers as they went up the stairs.

"Tomorrow, if you're still interested, I'll show you the house, one needs the benefit of sunlight before daring to venture all the way through it!" he said with a laugh. "And the gardens—if you'd like a spot of your own I can arrange it. And I'll take you to the bank so you can see where I spend much of my time."

"I'd like that."

Although it took Ethan a month to find the time, he finally showed her the house, and he was smiling and charming as he related the humorous stories. How as a young boy, he had been afraid of the house, the gloomy third floor in particular. Penelope had to admit the house was a bit foreboding even with the sunlight streaming in the tall windows. Wondering why they had chosen such maroons and dark blues with which to adorn it. It made it morose, it made it unfriendly.

And as she listened to his stories she realized that he had been alone most of his life, and at a young age was left to his own devices. She thought he had turned into a remarkably pleasant and sociable man given his parents' horrible example. She could also tell with pity, that he loved them anyway, even when they repeatedly proved to him how little he meant to them. It occurred to her that he masked his loneliness with his jokes and stories and was glad again that she had married him. And not only because she was in love with him, but because she thought with a little tremor in her heart, that now as his wife, she had the power to make him happy.

He took her to the bank, and she was impressed its orderliness and how competent and secure he was with his occupation. He had taken her to lunch at Lawsons and as they walked home, he began to talk about Victor.

"How long have you known him?" she asked, holding his hand.

"Fifteen years give or take."

"And you've never quarreled? Not even with that business with his father and yours and the farm?"

The night of the barn raising loomed unpleasantly in his mind. "No. Never."

"I can't believe your father let him pay on that farm for two years thinking he was paying down the principle when he was only paying interest; that's deceitful! And that your father did that on purpose to your friend. How old was Victor when that happened?"

"Thirteen when it started."

"And Victor and Margaret started living with the German blacksmith?"

Ethan nodded.

"And that's when Victor started working an extra job at Celena's parents' farm to make money?"

"Yes, they ended up there, after Victor's father died." Ethan remembered the horrid story. Robert had been dead over a week when Victor made the grisly discovery and buried him. It was over a year before Victor slept without a nightmare.

"Jonah got something in his hands, a stiffness that didn't allow him to control them. Victor was doing all the smithing by then."

Penelope nodded as they walked. "And the old blacksmith's land, your father tried to take it from him, right?"

"It's an old custom of using pecan trees as markers, and there was a dispute of some sort. It was bogus of course but my father was relentless." He wished he had not told her so many details, unsure why he had bared so much of his pain to her.

"I guess you couldn't stop your father because you'd already left for college."

Ethan hadn't left yet, but hadn't the courage to stand up to his father.

"Is that how Jonah got burned so badly and died, going back into the shop? You said he couldn't work anymore because of his hands, and Victor was gone trying to earn more money to stop the foreclosure?"

Ethan had to look away, so deep was his guilt.

"*Oh my God!*" Penelope said and stopped walking. She put a hand on Ethan's arm and turned to him in horror. "Is that why Margaret's arms are burned, because she tried to save him?"

"I-I don't know. I was not here. I don't want to talk about it anymore."

They walked in silence for two blocks.

"I hope you'll be able to help my mother run the house. She's—she's getting on in years and the Stanfield house certainly could use a mistress who was capable and cared."

Penelope nodded.

"I'll talk to the staff and let them know your requests are to be honored...it may be a bit difficult at first with my mother. And Arvellen if she gives you any trouble—"

"I can manage it."

Although he smiled as they walked, he wondered if she had any idea what she was getting herself into.

Ethan was hardly through the door when he heard Penelope frantically shout his name and come running down the stairs.

"Ethan! I thought you'd *never* get home!" She bound into his arms and buried her face against his chest, crying.

He looked around quickly, half expecting to see Arvellen lurking in the corner. "What's the matter?" he asked, trying to get her to look up. He felt a tightening in his chest to see her face so swollen and blotchy from crying.

"She burned...everything!"

"Who?"

"Your mother, she burned all the clothes, everything you bought me!"

"*What?*" his hands gripping her arms hurt.

"She said it was a house of mourning and I wasn't to wear anything but black. She had them go into our room when I'd gone to post a letter to my father and she took everything I own...and *burned* it!" She leaned against him, crying , wishing he would wrap his arms around her. Thinking that the letter that she had mailed to her father about how wonderful everything was, was suddenly so far from the truth. She tearfully looked up at him. "What are we going to do?"

He sighed once and dragged a hand through his hair. "I'm sorry Penelope, but it is...only fabric—I'll buy you more clothes."

She let go of him, incredulous. "But it's not *just* the clothes, it's—it's that she dislikes me so much! Ethan, she waited 'til I left the house and then snuck up and took everything I owned and burned it! If she does that...what else is she capable of? She frightens me!"

"Don't be ridiculous," he said, and tried to move from her, but she gripped his shoulders.

"Ethan, do you know she still writes your father everyday? And the letters are in the present tense—as if he's on a trip or something."

"She's dealing with her grief."

"She's not *dealing* with it! One minute she says it's a house of mourning and burning everything I own and the next she's writing him letters and still has a place set for him at the table!"

He gently pushed her hands off him, moving a step back.

"Don't leave me, I'm afraid here!"

He swung around angrily. "I'm *not* leaving you. I am simply going to speak to my mother and try to figure out what to do."

"Let me come!"

"No, you're behaving like a child. You let me talk to her. Sit and wait for me."

She burst into tears again and, hurrying into the parlor, shut the door behind her. It was over an hour before she heard him at the door, and she smoothed back her hair and tried to compose herself. He said nothing as they walked up the stairs together to their room, and once inside he merely closed the door and leaned against it.

"Did you speak with her?" she asked, her heart jerking uncomfortably in her chest.

"Yes, I did." Sighing, he moved from the door and began tugging off his coat.

"Well?" she asked, on his heels as he draped his coat over the chair.

He turned to her tiredly and gently put his hands on her shoulders. "I am sorry she upset you. She can be difficult to live with." When she stared at him dumbstruck, he bristled back. "What? What else do you want me to say?"

"Did you ask her about my clothes?"

"Yes, I did. She says she asked you not to wear the bright colored dresses and that she has no idea about any clothes being burned or what you accuse her of."

For a moment Penelope was speechless. "You...don't...*believe* her, do you?" Her heart went cold when he turned to unbutton his waistcoat, obviously not wanting to discuss it further. "Ethan, I'm your *wife!*"

He swung around. "And she's my *mother*! I don't know what or who to believe! You come flying at me crying and saying one thing...she cries to me swearing to another." He sat on the bed. Normally, when he hung his head, she wanted to comfort him. But tonight, his plea for sympathy angered her.

"Did you ask her about the letters?"

""No. Why should I?"

"Ethan...she's writing to your father daily—"

"She's old, Penelope, and she's sick in body as well as her mind. Leave her be. She's my mother for God's sake! I gave her a thorough tongue lashing now what else do you want me to do? Throw her out?" He sighed, trying to be reasonable. "I understand how all of this would be upsetting to you. Tomorrow if it will make you feel any better I will order a new lock made for the door, that way no one will be in the room that you don't want." He paused, trying to gather himself. "And I will call a dressmaker and you can order some clothes—"

She jerked her chin up defiantly.

"Fine. If you don't want a dressmaker, Celena is an excellent seamstress."

Her eyes shot up to him in horror. She'd rather *die* than have Celena know her mother-in-law hated her so much that she'd burned her clothes! "No! Don't you *dare* tell her!"

"*Damn it!*" he shouted, jumping up from the bed. "You dislike Celena too now, is that it? With you and my mother at me every day—I'll be *mad* by the end of it all!"

"But Ethan, your mother also spread the vilest rumors about you *abusing* Arvellen," she began.

He shook his head, interrupting her. "My mother...do you know what she told me? She told me that every day, *every day* when I leave for the bank that you have Ephram come up and rearrange the furniture for you."

She did not like the way he was staring at her. "Just—just that once so I could be closer to the window and read my music."

"My mother said that you asked him to stay up here. Stay up here so you could play for him—and that he comes up every morning now. And that while I'm gone you play for him and that there's laughing coming from behind the door. And do you know what I did when she told me this over a *month* ago? *Nothing!* Did I confront you with it, do I check up on you Penelope, do I *accuse* you of anything?"

"But...but it's not the same thing!" she stammered, horrified. "I have *proof* of my accusations! I'll show you!" She ran to the armoire and flung the door open. Seeing her clothes hanging in the armoire, she let out a strangled gasp. She stood there in shock, mouth gaping as the heavy door of the armoire bounced against the wall and hit her on the shoulder. "But they were *gone!* Ethan I *swear* it! She told me she'd burned them, and when I checked it earlier...there was nothing there!" She jerked her head back to the armoire and realized someone had moved the clothes. Looking closer, she saw that two dresses were indeed missing. But when she turned to inform him, she knew it was too late.

"I suppose now you'll be telling me that Ephram *does* stay upstairs with you?" he asked, shaking his head as he walked out the door. "I pity him."

Chapter 32

That night when Ethan came home, Penelope showed up in the parlor, and it was annoying to her that he seemed surprised to see her. He was already in the habit of stopping there first for a drink before he came to her, and it hurt her that a brandy and the dark paneled walls of the parlor were able to comfort him more than she could.

"Oh hello," he said and forced a short smile. Turning his back, he poured himself another brandy. "Victor get the lock in?"

"Yes." Not knowing exactly what to do, she crossed the room and sat down nervously in one of the wingback chairs. "Dinner should be ready at half past the hour." Silently she folded her hands in her lap. It was more daunting than she ever dreamed to try and run such a big house. There were always so many of them coming up to her asking her when and how to do things, and she had the sense that they asked her these things, knowing she would not have the answer, and that they laughed at her when she was out of sight.

"*Should,* Penelope? You're the mistress of the house, merely tell them when you want it done, and they'll do it! Do you want me to talk to them again?"

"No, I can take care of it," she murmured, knowing exactly how he would oversee things. He would bark at all of them, and to *him* they listened! But knew they would only think of new ways to torment her when he was gone, like the ridiculous dress-burning incident.

He sighed and turned away from her. It hurt his heart to look at her. She certainly did not look happy these days with her head always bent, and her pale face. He knew she was having trouble running the house, but he knew it was almost beyond Penelope to be assertive. As a result, the slaves quickly learned that the new mistress had, as he had overheard them say, "no teeth" and he knew it was Arvellen who was running the house.

"I'll talk to Arvellen," he said softly and again she nodded, but it only added to her feelings of frustration and inadequacy. "I'm not upset Penelope, I didn't marry you so you could run the house, it doesn't matter to me." He feared his consolation did little good, and found himself hoping that maybe when Penelope got pregnant things would be happier for them. "Would you like to play chess until dinner?"

"Yes, that would be lovely."

They played until dinner, and dinner was surprisingly pleasant, especially since Abigail was not feeling well and did not dine with them. Happily, Penelope had taken a second helping of everything.

She laughed when Ethan told her a story about Victor's son Randy; he had pinned his younger brother Ben by his overalls on the clothesline. Instead of scolding him when he came home, Victor pinned him up as well to teach him a lesson. But the only one that had been taught much of a lesson was Victor, who had had to fix the entire clothesline when it collapsed under Randy's weight.

"Those boys, I never knew such rambunctious children!" Penelope laughed as they climbed the stairs.

"Victor and I did our share of foolishness."

"Really? I can't imagine you doing anything like that."

"There's a lot you don't know about me!" He grinned and closed the door behind them.

"D-do you think our children will be so energetic, so lively?"

"I certainly hope so! It's normal and healthy. Especially boys. Men live to antagonize one another."

"What if it's a little girl?"

His face lit up. "Well then I'll let her wonderful mother tend to her—and I shall be the overprotective father." He paused. "Do you have something to tell me—are you expecting, Penelope?" He asked hopefully—he'd noticed she had put on weight.

"Oh! No, not yet." She watched him shamelessly undress. Tugging off the boots, carelessly unbuttoning the shirt and waistcoat and tossing them both to the floor, knowing someone would clean up after him like they always had. When she found herself the sudden target of those warm brown eyes, she wished she had hurried to undress hidden by the open door of the armoire like she normally did

"Get in here, you must be cold," he said after she had changed and edged shyly near the bed. He flipped back the covers and gingerly she slid in. He pulled her against his bare chest, and she suddenly found her nose in the hollow of his throat. He kissed her sweetly on the top of her head as his arms went around her shivering form.

It had been such a wonderful evening! Reaching up she touched his cheek lovingly, and was about to tell him how happy she was, how much she'd enjoyed the chess game, how much she had enjoyed their conversation, when he pushed her flat on the bed and rolled on top of her. She felt the unmistakable hardness between his legs. "W-what are you doing?"

"What do you mean?"

"I-I didn't mean to get this started. I mean...can't I ever touch you without you—you getting all..."

"Horned up?"

"Don't be so crude, Ethan!"

"It's what you meant isn't it?"

Although she hated the term it had been what she was thinking.

"Well, pretty much...*no*! I can't simply kiss you," he explained, swallowing hard, "especially not when you're in bed with me undressed." It was humiliating the way she was gawking at him. "Do you think I'm unique in this sense Penelope, because I assure you, I'm *not!*"

"But it seems like that's all you're interested in. I mean once a week!"

"Christ Penelope, you're my *wife*! Am I *wrong* to want to have sex with you? And while we're at it, here's a little insight on men. We do get married because we want sex, and we want it *regularly.*"

She pushed him off. "Why do you insist on being so disgusting and crude?"

"I'm not! I'm merely stating the truth. What do you want me to call it?"

She turned from him and wrapped her arms defensively around her.

"Besides..." he said gently, touching her arm, still hoping all was not lost, "you mentioned children earlier...and I naturally thought—" When she went rigid under his caress a slice of annoyance went through him. "How do you think children get here Penelope, the stork? You'll need to have sex with me for us to have children!"

"I-I know that!" she wailed, her cheeks going positively scarlet. She couldn't bring herself to admit what was truly bothering her. Something happened to him when he reached for her in the dark. "Can't you ever come to bed with me without grunting and pouncing on me and trying to pull my nightgown off?"

He stared down, hoping to God she wouldn't make any more unflattering observations of his behavior. "Yes," he said quietly, and moved away from her in the bed to blow out the lantern. "I suppose I can."

Chapter 33

"Evening Penelope," Victor said, smiling.

Nervously, Penelope stepped into the house and heard the loud squawking of Randy and Ben as they sat on the floor rolling a ball between them, cheering loudly whenever they caught it. She wondered why Victor's children seemed to be louder than other children. But it also occurred to her that they were about the *only* children she had ever had the chance to spend any time with.

"Hello Ethan, Penelope," Celena greeted.

She looks beautiful, Penelope thought with a pang of envy. More beautiful than a pregnant woman had the right to look at the end of a long day.

Penelope tried to be helpful as Celena got dinner to the table, but Celena was so adept at putting the meal on Penelope finally stood to the side, tired of being in the way. After dinner it annoyed Penelope the amount of time Ethan and Victor spent talking about the factory, and how they made no pretense of including she and Celena in the conversation. It did not seem to bother Celena who had been content to clear the table, do the dishes and then sit with Andrew on one side of her lap and Ben on the other.

"So, have you decided what to plant?" Celena asked as she simultaneously rocked Andrew, corrected Ben on his letters, and encouraged Randy's printing.

"Oh, no not yet," Penelope said, forcing a smile and then glancing back towards the men trying to find a space in their conversation where she could interject her own opinions.

"If you need any seeds I save them from year to year," Celena continued, and Penelope gave a short silencing smile and again turned her attention back to the men. "My sister Carlene is the devout gardener of our group and if you need any seeds or thoughts I'd be glad to ask her for you."

Penelope didn't answer.

"I put in a huge garden again this year and most of it did well, the string beans were good, but I must have done something wrong with the squash because they only got about half the size they were supposed to, about like this." She realized that Penelope was not listening to her. "Anyway, I figure it not only feeds us but it's one of the few things I have control over these days. Not that God and nature don't have a fair amount of influence on it too!" she said, thinking that nursing and diapering ruled her life. Thank God Judith had so generously offered to take over the laundry; it was wonderful to have help. "Besides, it already takes me twice as long to get down on the ground to weed it and three times as long to get back up!" She smirked, looking down at her protruding stomach. "I had no idea how difficult it was to raise children." She kissed Andrew's upturned face. "In the beginning they are so tiny that you worry every moment. You've got to be wary of feeding them, and if they aren't choking on it, they're spitting it up back on you, and when they're sick and you can't think of anything else to do for them but rock them. Then when they learn to walk it opens up a whole new world of dangers with trying to keep from the fire and the well. Then you have to teach them right from wrong, how to share, be kind and not hit! Then their alphabet and numbers, and to love God...and then it starts all over with the next one. It's a daunting prospect at times."

"That it is," Victor said, coming over to them. He smiled at Penelope, and she flushed with embarrassment realizing he knew she had not been paying attention to Celena, but he seemed to forgive her.

"Which one do you want me to take?" he asked. "They never want me when their mother is around, but I know Celena's got more than her hands full with the three boys, the house, and another on the way—besides, she has *me* to work around!"

Penelope noticed with a pang of envy the way Celena smiled up at her husband. It was almost as if something spiritual passed between them.

"All right you two, up to bed," Victor said to Randy and Ben.

"But Pa! Uncle Ethan and I were going to start playing chess!"

"You'll see your uncle again," Victor said, motioning for Randy to get up. Although Penelope had seen Randy and Ben literally climb all over Victor, it was obvious they knew when he was serious.

"Will you read to me Papa?" Randy asked hopefully, his arms eagerly reaching up for his father and Victor leaned down to hug him back.

"A short one," Victor answered and then, smiling down at Ben, followed Celena who had Andrew in her arms up the stairs

"Goodnight Uncle Ethan," Randy said and hugged him hard, and then stopped in front of Penelope, not sure what he should do. "Good night Aunt Pen." It surprised her when he hugged her too.

"We'll be back in a few minutes, continue making yourself at home." Victor grinned at Ethan, who had his feet propped up against one of the benches near the table.

"Shouldn't we be leaving now?" Penelope whispered when they had gone.

"But we've only recently arrived, why do you always ask that?" Ethan cried, thinking that the last thing he wanted to do was to go back to their silent house. "After the children are in bed sometimes we play cards or chess, or we read the great works of literature and Victor murders them with his hideous pronunciation."

She stared at him.

"You don't understand, this is my life. How I choose to spend my time—they would be offended if we left now, and besides I don't want to go..." Although he did not say it, the meaning was clear that a wife and her tastes were not going to affect it.

"Let me see what we were reading the last time," Ethan said, rummaging through the bookcase. "He does not have a large collection—in fact, he borrows them from me mostly."

Penelope resigned herself to sit back down and wait, and folded her hands tightly in her lap. "Does Victor actually read them?"

"Sometimes I think he does, but mostly I think it's Celena."

"Now that surprises me."

He turned and looked at her. "Why does that surprise you?"

"Well, I didn't think she would. I didn't think she was the type, oh I don't *know*—we can't talk about this now!" Penelope said, thinking it the height of rudeness to talk about one's hosts while still under their roof.

"What are you trying to say?"

"Nothing! I-I just didn't think she cared at all for literature or poems." She didn't like the way he had been so quick to defend an attack on behalf of Celena.

"Well, she doesn't have the time, she is not afforded as much leisure time as you and I are, but I assure you her heart feels as yours does—"

Penelope jerked her chin up at him, then jealously watched the way his face lit up when he saw Celena coming back down the stairs.

"Victor will be down in a minute. After he reads, he has to arm wrestle them."

Ethan laughed. "What shall it be tonight, Celena—epic poems of

Coleridge? A rousing reciting of *The Rime of the Ancient Mariner*, or Shakespeare. I think I saw *Macbeth* in here—"

"Oh no! Murder and bloody spots on her hand that aren't there, not tonight thank you. Besides even though the words sound lovely together, you know half the time I have to ask you what he's saying." Celena rolled her eyes.

"Surely not the infamous trio again?"

This time it was Celena who laughed.

"What trio?" Penelope asked with annoyance. When she was with them she always had the feeling if she came into the room late, that she was missing something.

"Byron, Shelley, or Keats?"

"Keats."

"*Again*, you want him every night?"

"I can't help it. I love him."

Ethan laughed. Penelope felt another stab of jealousy—he'd laughed more this evening than he had in a month alone with her.

"Surely the passionate handsome, Lord Byron would be a more natural pick for a woman to admire? No great speeches from *Don Juan* this evening?"

"I don't think so, it's too ambitious a poem—what is it, something like seventy-four stanzas?"

Another tinge of jealousy went through Penelope at the sound of Celena's laughter. It was unnerving the way Celena reminded her of a debutante flirting with a suitor when she was a married woman, nearly eight months pregnant and whose shoulder had baby spit on it.

"Yes, and halfway through I'll be nodding off to sleep." She turned to Penelope to include her. "Has that ever happened to you?"

"Shelley then! Surely sensitive, impractical Shelley is more worthy of your admiration?"

Penelope looked at her smart, handsome husband, wondering why the two of them had no such 'poetry' night.

"He was wonderful, and I love him too, but he was so caught up in the politics and the revolutions of the day. Let's just say, he looked farther outside his door than I do," Celena answered.

"He does not affect your heart the way Keats does?"

"I don't know why. Maybe it's because unlike Byron he wasn't wealthy and handsome, unlike Shelley he wasn't publishing radical treason, perhaps it's because Keats was rumored to be plain and that his love for that girl was never was fulfilled, and he died so terribly young, so before he should have."

Their eyes met and Penelope forced herself to think of something to break the connection. She was relieved when Victor came down the stairs.

"They are down," he said with a smile, placing his big hands on his hips. "Lena, is there coffee left?"

Murmuring that there was, she went to the kitchen.

"What are we doing tonight?" Victor asked with a smile and sat, Penelope thought, too close. He was so unmistakably *male*.

"We were discussing what works to read tonight, I was working on Coleridge but—"

"She wants those damn poets again doesn't she?"

They both laughed when Celena came into the living room bearing the coffee pot and the necessary cups on a tray. "What?"

"I was saying to Ethan you want those poets again. Those three poets who talk in riddles and can't ever come out with it! Those three that you think the sun rises and sets on!"

Laughing, Celena handed Penelope a cup of coffee. "You have nothing to be jealous of Victor, they're dead. Besides, the sun rises on Byron and Shelley—but for me it never sets on Keats!"

"Oh, good God!" Victor chuckled, rolling his eyes up to the ceiling. "You weren't like this when I married you."

"Under my tutelage she has become a student of poetry, but I agree Victor, she does seem stuck on those three!" Ethan chuckled.

"Let's play that game," Celena said brightly.

"Oh, Lena please no! I hate that game."

Penelope tried to push away the uncomfortable feeling of not belonging, after all the three of them had no trouble carrying on witty conversations with or without her input.

"That's merely because you're no good at it, and if you'd read more you would be!" Celena teased.

Victor's eyebrows went up humorously. "Oh, is that so? I'm no good at it, well then we'll just see!" He straightened. "Penelope, do you know this game? You have to spout a line of sappy poetry, or some other words written by some rich, idle fool who spends his time loafing when the rest of us are working—and they have to guess the author and the work if they can." He leaned in, lowering his voice. "I always lose. I only know parts of about three poems, and they slaughter me every time. Do you think you can help me?"

"I-I suppose—"

"Of course she can," Ethan said, smiling at her. "She is well read and quite a student of literature." Although it was a compliment from her husband, it seemed odd to her how they had been paired up.

"All right then," Ethan said, "Victor, you start."

"*Christ!*" Victor mumbled and blew out a long breath, struggling for more than a minute. "Something's...something's rotten in the state of... Dunsmore—"

"*Hamlet*, Shakespeare, and it was Denmark, by the way, Victor," Ethan said quickly.

Victor shrugged, glad that his turn was done.

"Celena, my dear," Ethan said sweetly. The endearment annoyed Penelope, who took two shortbread cookies from a tray and began to eat.

"Let me think, forgive me I may get a word or two wrong—"

"Like I'd be able to tell!" Victor quipped.

"*They say that hope is happiness but genuine Love must prize the past; And memory wakes the thoughts that bless, they rose the first and set the last...*"

"Keats, *Ode to*...something or other?" Victor chirped up.

Celena shook her head.

"But you *always* pick Keats!" he cried as if betrayed.

"I know, that's why I didn't this time."

"Lord Byron," Ethan said, and Celena smiled to confirm it. "But I don't remember the work!" He shrugged and they laughed.

It's 'They say hope is Happiness,' Penelope thought, but since no one seemed interested, she didn't speak.

"Well done Celena." Ethan grinned, then turned to Penelope. "Have you got one Pen?"

She was caught off guard, not knowing she would be next. Besides, she thought it was sweet that the children used the nickname but was not sure she liked it when he did.

Because they were all looking at her, she blurted out the first line that came to her. "*Then window, let day in, and let life out—*"

"That Juliet person!" Victor burst out.

Surprised, Penelope turned to him. 'Yes, how did you know?"

Victor shook his head, afraid by the admiring look she was giving him too much credit. "Sounds like something she'd say to him. It was daytime, time for lover boy to go home so her father doesn't run a sword through his heart, seeing as how her father didn't like him—I had a little experience with that sort of thing once!" Victor said, winking at Celena. "I don't know the title or who wrote it though."

"For God's sake, Victor, you have half the title. It's *Romeo and Juliet!* Shakespeare of course, I don't understand if you can remember the passage why you can't ever remember the author?" Ethan scowled.

"Because they all sound alike to me," Victor defended. "Anyway, I guessed right. It's your turn, *poet boy.*"

Ethan turned to Celena and burst forth as if the words came originally from his own heart. "*She walks in beauty like the night, of cloudless climes and starry skies, And all that's best of dark and bright, meet in her aspect and her eyes, thus mellow'd to that tender light, which heaven to gaudy day denies...*" He was staring so adoringly at Celena that it caused the hairs on the back of Penelope's neck to stand on end.

Penelope turned to Victor for help and was surprised to see a look of bored impatience on his face.

"Keats, ode to pretty girls...in the dead of night?" Victor offered, breaking the spell.

"Why do you guess him *every single time?*" Ethan barked.

"Well...one of these times it's going to be right."

Since her husband had apparently forgotten Penelope was in the room, she piped up. "Lord Byron, *She walks in Beauty,*" she said, and when Ethan turned and smiled at her, the smile faded from his face when he saw how she was staring at him. "Do you know the last stanza as well Ethan?" she asked. "*...but tell of days in goodness spent, a mind at peace with all below, a heart whose love is innocent.*"

"I have one, you all," Victor began, flexing his big arms and cracking his knuckles. "*Under the spreading chestnut tree, the village smithy stands—*"

Both Ethan and Celena groaned.

"*The smith a mighty man is he, with large and sinewy hands, and the muscles of his brawny arms are strong as iron bands!*"

Celena giggled. "Yes Victor, *The Village Blacksmith,* Longfellow! You recite it so well sweetheart, and so *often!*"

"All right, your turn." He tapped Celena playfully on the nose, but he kept his arm around her as he moved his chair to sit by her.

Celena concentrated. "*My heart aches and a drowsy numbness pains, as if of hemlock I had drunk.*"

"Keats. You have your 'ode,' Victor, *Ode to a Nightingale,* surely one of his loveliest."

"*Loveliest*, isn't hemlock poison? And we're all happy sitting around here knowing this poor wretch wants to *kill* himself?" Victor scoffed.

"That's one possible interpretation, but the one I am more inclined to believe is that he wishes he too was a nightingale—"

"He wants to be *bird?*" Victor choked, looking at both as if they had suddenly lost their minds. He turned pleadingly to Penelope. "Have you ever wanted to be a *bird*, Penelope?"

She merely smiled at him, but thought that right now would be a wonderful time to turn into a bird and simply fly away.

Chapter 34

"Did you hear what happened on the floor of the senate between that senator from Massachusetts Sumner and Brooks from South Carolina?" Ethan asked. The meal was over on a warm June night, and they were seated outside on the front porch listening to the night sounds of crickets and cicadas.

"Yes, I heard—horrible isn't it? Makes you not want to have a difference of *opinion* doesn't it?" Victor agreed.

"What happened?" Celena asked, realizing that it must be unpleasant if Victor neglected to tell her.

Victor sighed. "Sumner delivers a scathing abolitionist, anti-slavery speech. In which he goes undoubtedly too far toward provoking anyone with a trace of southern sensibilities. I heard that he compared pro-slavery men to drunken spew, that they were vomit of an uneasy civilization—" Celena recoiled at the words. "It gets worse," he warned grimly. "He delivers this blistering anti-slavery speech about among other things, the crime of bleeding Kansas—which in my mind wasn't doing anything toward *helping* the antislavery cause with a vigilante like John Brown, but anyway—Sumner's words infuriate this southern senator Brooks-who wants to challenge him to a duel."

"A...duel?" Celena asked, thinking that the south was taking their chivalry too far.

"But he *can't,* you see, because the code of honor in the south forces people to only fight with *social equals,* and not with a Yankee who he figures would reject the challenge anyway. Instead, he decides to chastise the senator. Brooks comes at Sumner as he's sitting at his Senate desk and starts to beat him with his wooden cane—he beats him there, openly in front of everybody on the Senate floor, and only stops because his cane finally breaks! till Sumner is bloody and unconscious on the floor. And all these senators just stood there and watched."

Celena's mouth dropped open.

"Laurence showed me in the Petersburg Intelligencer, you know it's the paper from Virginia, that it more or less said that Brooks should have picked a different spot to call out the villain, but it also goes on to say that if he had broken every bone in Sumner's carcass it would have been just retribution on this slanderer of the South and her citizens—"

"That's so...vicious," Celena said softly

"What bothers me the most about it is that you can't have a discussion with any southerners about slavery intelligently. I don't mean to criticize their intellect, what I mean is they get quicksilver furious and then can't seem to listen to any point of view other than their own," Victor said.

"I agree. And all the compromising and concessions in the world will I'm afraid never give them what they want," Ethan said.

"What *do* they want?" Celena asked, still trying to get the gruesome visions out of her head.

Victor thought, rubbing his chin. "From the best that I can piece together, I think what they want is their lives not to change. Their whole economy after all is based on slave labor, its entrenched in their entire makeup. All the way from the wealthy plantation owners with three hundred slaves down to the poor white farmer, who proudly scrapes together enough money to buy himself a slave. It's easy to sit around and say what the south *should* do, it's easy to sit around and talk about how morally wrong slavery is—especially when your livelihood is not dependent on it."

"Well, it is morally wrong," Celena interjected quietly, thinking about the whipping scars she had seen on Bartholomew's massive back, the fright that was still at times in his eyes. The elation that had been on his face when Victor had purchased Judith for him and he had been able to marry her, and that they were both free.

"Well, yes I think so—still, I don't know how happy I'd be if for instance the government all the sudden came in and took my anvil—it would be impossible for me to make my living. And besides, *telling* a man you think he's *morally* wrong will no doubt enrage him."

"Don't compare Bartholomew to an anvil, Victor," Celena said, her eyes wide.

"I'm sorry, that's a bad analogy, but you get my point."

"Do you know what I heard? I heard that the pro-slavery groups were trying to prove that the Negro's *brain* was smaller. They say then that's its morally correct then to enslave them because they suffer from certain affliction that renders them incapable of voluntarily working, they said they have some sort of disease, oh I can't remember what they called it, but it's supposed to be the reason they run away," Celena said, appalled at what she had heard.

"Drapetomania," Victor said and Celena turned her huge eyes on him "That's the name they give the affliction. Of course, the ills of *slavery* could be *one* reason they were running away!" Victor said with a grin, but he bristled at the way she was staring at him. "Lena, settle! Do you honestly think I believe Bartholomew's brain is peculiarly small? Because I assure you if that was the case, he would *not* be in my employ."

"No, but you aren't being kind."

"*Kind?* Life is cruel. I think the Negroes are getting a raw deal, but they will have to prove themselves capable and fight their way out. Besides most slaves, I see, don't do much to dispel the myth—though they might if any-one ever took the time to *teach* them anything," he added ruefully.

"I can't believe you're saying this!"

"What? What am I saying? I'm simply being honest. All right, I'll say it about myself, about Indians: we're all drunks and can't handle our fire-water. It's partly true, and they should pull themselves up—and I hate to sound trite, but by their own moccasin straps! I did."

"You had lots of help, with Jonah."

"I know that and I'm grateful, but I've also worked hard to take care of myself and not fall prey to things like alcohol. Why do you think I don't drink much? it's in me you know that weakness, I have it from both sides. My father was a drunk and it's in my mother's blood, but I refuse to bend to it. I refuse to let my life slip away with drink." He sighed when he saw the tight look on her face. "I don't mean to sound cruel; I am merely try-ing to be realistic. If tomorrow slavery were suddenly done away with, thousands of slaves would find themselves with no way to make a living and feed themselves. They'd have to learn all new skills, and I'm sure that they could do—but it would take time. I am merely trying to point out the fact that it won't be an easy road. Doing away with slavery will not wipe out the prejudice we have been made to believe about the Negro. There's no easy pat answer to this problem—no quick solution. And I tell you it scares me the way the abolitionists keep backing the southerners into a corner. They are only going to make things worse."

"What do you mean?" she asked worriedly.

"You know how I feel about owning people! But I think they should do away with it *slowly* over a few years. Telling the south to give up their slave's tomorrow would not only ruin their whole economy but infuriate the hell out of them as well! This is a powder keg waiting for a spark, and we all need to settle down—the abolitionists included. I don't know, maybe we could pass a law where the slaves could work off their debt or whatever. Then little by little they could adopt a different system in the southern states—maybe using more reapers and machines as opposed to slave manpower. Because I tell you it worries me. If we keep pushing the southerners into a corner, poking at them with a stick I guarantee they will come out blind, and furious!"

"I know what you're saying about their lives depending on it," Ethan mused. "I have my slaves, but my livelihood does not depend on them thank God—and I've thought from time to time about freeing them, but to tell you the truth I'm not sure some of them would be able to feed themselves if I let them go."

"That's still no reason to keep them," Celena said quickly.

Ethan shrugged. "You're right, but then I'd have to get bond servants or free Irish girls or something. Frankly, I'm too lazy to do anything about it, when the time comes, and I think the time is coming, they will all be freed. Then I'll deal with it."

"What do you mean the time is coming?" She had heard the whispers, the words secession and states' rights; they chilled her because she feared what they ultimately would lead to if cooler heads would not prevail.

"I don't know for sure," Victor mused, shaking his head again, "but in the worst-case scenario it could mean...war."

"But we'd be fighting...ourselves," she said softly and couldn't help but think of her brother James and his impassioned defense of slavery, states' rights and virtually everything the southern states touted.

"With the things I read, I sometimes think there are two separate nations—two countries. Neither half of the country feels like the other. How is something like that ever going to be resolved? Half of the country is always going to be feeling like they got a raw deal?" Ethan asked rhetorically.

"It's not two nations, it's one. It's a shame that our president is so weak," Victor countered, and Ethan merely shrugged his shoulders.

"President Pierce is weak? Why do you say that?" Celena asked, her alarm growing. Not wanting to think about the bad argument James and Laurence had gotten into only last week concerning states' rights and the expansion of slavery into new territories.

"There's lots of reasons," Victor sighed. "He's surrounded by strong men, strong pro-democratic and southern men. I don't think he stands a chance." Victor glanced at Ethan who nodded in agreement.

"Don't worry Celena," Ethan said, patting her hand. "Nothing's going to happen right away. You know southerners, they talk a good game, and we've been fighting about this for over fifty years now, I doubt whether tomorrow they'll suddenly wake up and make a move."

Momentarily Celena was pacified, but wondered what would happen when the country fought, not a foreign power, but itself. "How's Penelope?" she asked, smiling down at Andrew sitting happily at her feet, playing with a wooden bowl and spoon. "We don't see much of her these days." She wondered if she'd somehow offended Penelope.

"She's fine," Ethan lied, forcing a smile, "busy with that violin."

"Arvellen still there?" Victor asked.

Ethan looked up at him suddenly. "Yes. Why do you ask?"

Victor picked up Randy and nestled him awkwardly on his lap. He had his mother's coloring but inherited his size from his father. Because he was only seven and already too big to fit on anyone's lap, even Victor's.

"Just wondered."

Ethan was tired and irritable by the time he arrived home. It was puzzling because normally he was content after an evening with Victor, Celena, and the boys, but there had been a tension in the air with their political talk and questions about Penelope and Arvellen. A tension that even two brandies quickly downed, couldn't quite dispel.

He was glad that the lanterns were lit and waiting for him in the parlor—he liked to have them lit before he got home; wanted something to welcome him.

Penelope was struggling running the house and any given night she had a list of complaints and woes to tell him. There had been kinks in the beginning with his mother screaming at him, and the servants not wanting to serve a new mistress—especially when the former mistress often gave them orders that contradicted the latter, but it was working out now. Especially, since he had told Arvellen to simply take care of things.

Things were good with the factory, and although he had yet to entice any other railroad to use the coupler, he and Victor were quietly making a fortune buried down in Ste. Genevieve. He had invested wisely, and together they were the wealthiest men in town—although neither of them advertised it. He could still remember the day he had told Victor what he was 'worth' in net terms, and the expression of his face had been priceless! Instead of resting on his laurels, Victor kept thinking of ways to as he liked to call it 'spread the wealth' by either increasing wages or quietly funding things for the town like he had done by paying for a new levee on the river.

"We did well," Ethan said, toasting the flickering lanterns with his third brandy.

The bank too continued to flourish. There were some bumps along the way, what with each president that came along trying to overhaul the banking system and creating and then destroying their own rules, but he was lasting during all the turmoil and that in and of itself, was an accomplishment. It was a daunting task to run a bank when there was so much foreign currency in circulation. There were Russian kopecks, Dutch rix-dollars, and various French coins. He heard rumors that the government was going to outlaw foreign coins and make the silver dollars, halves, and quarters the standard. As far as he was concerned it couldn't happen fast enough. He smiled at the memory of Ben's surprised face when he did that simple magic trick with the coin and thought how wonderful it would be to have a child. Smirked at the way Victor often mixed up the boys' names, and how the boys insisted he match the correct child to the name before they did what he asked.

His thoughts turned to Penelope upstairs, and he knew what she would be doing. She would either be reading or playing the violin, and she would scold him when finally, he went upstairs. Scold him that he was drinking too much, working too hard, and annoyingly at times she even tried to put him to bed like he was a child. He knew she meant well, but it was certainly not what he wanted from her and yet, she did not seem capable of giving him what he needed.

Finishing his brandy, he got up and placed it on the cool polished mantle, but as he turned to leave Arvellen walked in. Silently she slid the pocket door closed behind her. He smiled grimly, thinking she had housekeeping details to talk over with him.

She crossed the floor and wound her hands up his chest and, leaning up, kissed him. He knew he should pull away, knew it was not right. But her mouth was so warm and kissing her was so very satisfying and familiar to him. She never pulled back after he kissed her and wiped her mouth.

"Arvellen, *don't*."

Paying no attention, she laid her mouth against his again as her hand slid down his chest and lower. He felt a sudden lurch of heat and arousal as her hand fondled his groin.

"Let me take care of you," she said into his mouth, "ah know you need me."

"I said *no*." And the hands gripping her wrists hurt.

"*Porquoi?*"

"She's one floor above us Arvellen, I...I can't do this to her." Letting go of her hands, he walked to the desk, trying to calm his heart, and put out the flame of desire she could so easily ignite in him. He moved papers around needlessly, unable to meet the gaze of those inviting green eyes.

"I only meant to comfort you like I alwayz have—and I know zat you need me."

He turned and smiled resolvedly at her. He knew no one else would ever understand that for Arvellen, sex had only to do with friendship and pleasure, and nothing at all to do with what she considered to be the silly confines of love or marriage.

"I know...in your own way, you meant well." He let out a breath he had been holding and hung his head.

"Are you ah right?" The compassion in her voice was too much for him. He remembered once when he had been young and naive, telling her that he was falling in love with her, and still remembered how laughingly she had then explained to him the difference between love and *lust*.

"I'm fine," he lied.

There was a short silence.

"I'm trying wis Penelope, but Ethan I don't think ze understands or wants to learn how to run ze house."

"It's all right. I appreciate you trying to help her, and I'm grateful that you are here to take care of things." He had to turn away then.

"*Mon gentilhomme*, you're not happy." Her hands were on him again, but tenderly this time, with no motive. "It breaks my heart to zee you so unhappy. Es a shame that your marriage has to change everyzing."

He moved out of her embrace and began needlessly moving papers. She had waited for him to come to her, knew things were strained in his marriage and had been surprised there had been no knock on her door.

"I don know why it should bozer her zat you take pleasure wis me."

"I'm supposed to be married Arvellen. It's generally frowned upon to be unfaithful."

"*Porquoi?* I've seen you with her in za evenings, you're attentive to er. You're za same kind, considerate man you has always been. And I don't sink she realizes all za effort you put forth, especially when ze gives you so little in return."

"Well, apparently I'm not putting forth enough effort."

"Oh, *mon amor!* She is not for you; she couldn't handle all you if she ever even got it! And I zink what zes's doing to you by pushing you away all zee time is spiteful and mean." There was a small silence. "Seems to me marriages would work out a better if when ze partners aren't pleasing to each other—find ones zat are."

He gave a pathetic laugh.

"She only wants your *mind* and she has zat! Truly, why should she care what your body does!"

"Only *you* Arvellen, could make adultery and sin sound so reasonable."

"I'm sorry for you Esan."

With a flush of embarrassment, he jerked his head up. "Why is that?"

"Because," and it seemed to pain her to have to tell him, "I've watched za two of you, she doesn't like it when you kiss her, and I can tell by the way she pulls up from you before you want her to."

With a flush of humiliation found he could not contradict her words. "Well. It's my problem, and you can't help me," he said, wishing the feel of her warm sweet mouth was not still on his lips. "Let me...wallow in my own frustration will you? I assure you; I'll survive."

"I've seen you look at her, and I can tell you're searching her eyes for et but you can't find it. You sot zat marrying her would take your mind off how happy za are, but it hasn't worked." For moment he felt so exposed he was speechless. "I don't think za two of you have any chance...at least not here. Not in Ste. Genevieve." Thankfully the wind rattled the windowpanes; otherwise the silence would have been unbearable. "Ze ones you want to love you never has, have zey? Not your *maman,* not your *pere,* not *elle—*"

He looked down, still unable to speak.

Nearing him, she laid her hands on his chest. "Especially *elle*...and I know you've tried, but you jus can get over her can you? No matter what you do or who you marry." She smiled sadly, wishing she could help.

"No," he whispered, and it was a relief to admit it. Admit it to someone who he knew could merely know the sorry facts, and yet not judge him.

Her eyes caressed his handsome face that still looked so innocent she thought, despite all she had taught him. Leaning up then she kissed him sweetly. "It will be a long time, but *je promets,* you'll have her one day."

He frowned. "You've missed your calling then, Arvellen, if fortune telling is your forte." It was said with such bitterness that she couldn't help but laugh.

"If zats true then for you *ma douce,* I zee a wonderful future!"

"I *said* you were out awfully late last night!" Penelope huffed, annoyed that she had to repeat herself, and peered curiously at Ethan across the breakfast table.

"Yes, I was...I'm...sorry about that," he said, rubbing his face vigorously with his hand. Not only was the little scene with Arvellen in the parlor weighing heavily on his conscience, but he'd dreamt fitfully of Celena again and woken later in the parlor, cold and cramped in the chair.

He looked at the breakfast set before him on the dainty pink and blue china plate. The eggs were sunny side up and steam still rolled off the top, the bacon looked crispy and perfectly cooked, and the toast had been made just the way he liked it, with chunks of butter in even little clumps. For the life of him, he could not pick up the fork to eat it.

"When I questioned Arvellen she said you'd come home earlier, but you didn't come up." She sighed, feeling neglected, and stuffed a mouthful of waffle dripping with syrup into her mouth.

"You—you talked to Arvellen this morning?" Without realizing it he gripped one of the silver knives.

"I don't usually, I mean I try not to."

Ethan pushed back from the table standing up suddenly. "I need to go. I'll be home early tonight, I promise." He paused, wondering if he tried harder if he could perhaps feel more. He went to her and leaned down to kiss her. "Penelope...please kiss me."

She jerked her head up, wiping her mouth with her napkin, pushing him away with the other hand. "For goodness sakes, I had a mouthful of waffle, can't you wait?"

He nodded, but noticed even after she'd finished her mouthful she still did not accept the kiss. "Goodbye." He walked out of the room without looking back.

He went to the bank but got little done and in the middle of the afternoon, simply left. Surprising the staff, after all he'd only left early once before in all the years they'd worked for him, when there had been an emergency of sorts at the factory.

He bought some ridiculously expensive and he feared stale chocolates from the Woolrich's, and talked Mrs. Blay into parting with purple cone flowers, and yellow black-eyed Susans and they laughed at the rather pathetic bouquet it made with the muddy roots dangling. As he walked back to his house with his store-bought chocolates and awkward bouquet, hated that he was behaving like a guilty husband.

"Good afternoon!" he said, breezing into the room.

She looked up at him shocked and pulled the violin from the crook of her neck. He shut the door behind with his foot and then sweeping his arms out from him behind his back and awkwardly said, "Candy and flowers for you my dear!"

"Have you done something you need to make amends for?"

A bit of red crept into his neck. "No...I simply realized that I've been gone a lot lately, and well...I missed you." He noticed with a tinge of guilt how she blushed.

"Shall we have one?" she asked, smiling and holding the little box of chocolates.

He pulled a chair closer to her. "By all means." He watched her unwrap the white box and politely offered him the first one, and then ate one herself. They were both pleasantly surprised at how good they were.

"Can I put them in here?" Ethan asked of the flowers, moving toward the chest where a basin sat.

She nodded.

"Shall we take a walk and enjoy the sunshine?" he asked cheerfully. Thinking that if he was to breathe new life into his marriage he would do the things he'd always heard women wanted. Her happy, startled expression encouraged him.

"Ethan! My goodness what's gotten into you?"

He tried not to stammer. "Nothing. I thought you might enjoy it."

Thankfully, she stood. "I'd like nothing better."

They spent the rest of the afternoon walking through the garden, and even into to town and looked at the flatboats, keelboats, and barges on the muddy waters of the Mississippi. He bought bread from the bakery and a bottle of burgundy that at first Penelope thought scandalous to drink, not only during the day but out of the bottle! But relented when a rather large piece of the thick crusty bread lodged in her throat. They sat and ate their small picnic by the river watching the water and the boats.

The sun set as they made their way home. Penelope shivered as the air cooled and clumsily Ethan put his arm around her, still relating to her the humorous story of James' barn raising as they walked to the house.

"I can't believe Victor didn't get hurt catching that falling broadside!"

"He told me the joints in his arms hurt for days after that."

"And then you had the dance?"

"I'm sure we'll have another one before too long and you'll get to see what I mean. I think 'dance' too elegant a word for what we do out here, but it's fun. Everyone brings a picnic and we stay out all day and long into the night." He thought of Celena in his arms that fated night. Remembered the moment he had leaned down and almost kissed her.

"But isn't if awfully dark to dance outside? Doesn't it get cold, and don't you trip dancing in the grass? Where do you put your wraps? I can't imagine you all do that when there's perfectly agreeable dancing inside."

He did not have the strength to answer. As they walked into the house, he grabbed her hand and began leading her up the stairway.

"Ethan I need to see about dinner—if I don't keep on them nothing gets done."

"Can't—can't it wait?" He desperately hoped she would not pull away from him again. After all he'd nearly drank the bottle of wine himself, and it was making him affectionate. He bent to kiss her.

"It'll only take a minute."

He climbed the stairs alone.

Inside the room he took off his coat, tossed it to one of the chairs and then stretched. Sleeping sitting up in the chair was torturous on his back and he sat down on the bed, mindlessly rubbing his lower back as he looked out the window watching the afternoon shadows gently glide across the green garden. Watched the sunlight dance against the shadows as the wind blew the foliage, listened to dozens of different birds that called goodnight to one another from the trees. The familiar sound of cicada's drone made him smile, and he knew the crickets would not be far behind them. He chuckled when he saw the familiar wink of a firefly in the twilight and wondered if Victor's boys would be out trying to catch them.

Even though he had wanted her to come up with him, he was disappointed when he heard her noisily enter the room, complaining. She had, he realized an uncanny knack for ruining moments.

"Dinner will be ready in a half hour. Oh, by the way the household budget I've been meaning to ask you about—" She stopped when she saw him coming towards her, obviously meaning to kiss her.

She leaned away, preventing it.

"Do you need more money to run the house?" he asked.

"Well...er...yes."

"That's fine." Gently he drew her near.

"I can explain where I need it."

"Maybe later." He bent to kiss her.

"Ethan it's—it's still light outside, and we haven't had our dinner."

"What difference does light make? I'm not hungry." This time she was unable to get away from him and he kissed her, but she pulled back sooner than he wanted, like always.

"I think you've had too much wine." Her palms were flat against his chest, keeping him away. She hated the hurt look that was suddenly all over his handsome face.

"Why don't you want me Penelope, why don't you ever...want me?"

Her eyes dropped guiltily from his. "I-I do want you."

"You do? Your hands are pushing me away, and you avoid me whenever I try to kiss you." He let go of her, dejected, and turned away. "Have I...*done* something?"

A bright red crept into her pale cheeks. "No."

"Are you...not *attracted* to me anymore? After what, five months of marriage?"

She looked away knowing the exact opposite was true. She was so in love with him it frightened her. And she thought with a tremendous longing that maybe it would be different when he made love to her this time.

"I-I love you very much."

He turned and looked at her. Thought about asking her if she loved him so much, why could he count the times she'd let him make love to her on one hand? He felt guilty for resenting their unsatisfying and infrequent lovemaking. It was a source of quiet but constant irritation to him-especially when he had tried so hard.

"Do you...*love* me...Ethan?" Her eyes glistened with unshed tears.

He swallowed hard, unable at first to answer. He'd said the words boldly the night he swept her off her feet with lies about how much he had missed her and couldn't live without her, he said it to her that night in the Willard, but there was no way he could say it to her now.

"Of course. Let me show you."

Penelope let him kiss her. She even gave in and let him do some of the things he had asked for that she had not been comfortable with—like his desire to slowly undress her. She found that when his hands slowly unfastened her clothing she was trembling. She forgot about how the corset when she took it off, left red and white marks all over her stomach with how tight it had to be laced for her to get into her dresses even though she added an expander in back, forgot about everything else shaking with anticipation under his warm hands. Her body responding to everything he did. After all he was so good at it.

Yet at the same time it was too much for her. His kisses were too passionate, too consuming. Something inexplicably changed between them when he reached for her in the dark. And no matter how much she gave him; it was never enough.

When it was over and she was laying weak and vulnerable in his arms, her heart still pounding with the excruciatingly wonderful release, she was sure that this time the pain wouldn't come. Surely this time after she'd given everything to the man she loved, the hollow emptiness would not take root in her heart. When it did, she couldn't help herself and began to weep.

"Pen! What's the matter, have I...hurt you?" Ethan asked worriedly, knowing the sexual frustration he was living with had made his performance quite athletic.

"No...leave me alone."

He innocently reached for her.

"Don't touch me!" she screamed, flinging his hands off. "*Get out!*" and then began to sob.

Chapter 35

"Penelope...Penelope!" Ethan called, running up the stairs two at a time, wanting to relate the happy news that Celena had that afternoon delivered her fourth baby, a boy they named Samuel. Yvonne had been there all night, and by the time Ethan arrived, John was celebrating drinking glasses of tafia to welcome the latest grandchild.

Carlene, who had had a baby girl they named Marie two weeks earlier, and Mason and Livi were already there, as were Eva, Stephan, and their son, David. Both Carlene and Eva had been cooking, and there was a huge meal being prepared for everyone. Laurence was on his way over with his family as well as James and Alice with baby Charles, and Will was bringing over his little brother, Johnnie, who desperately wanted to see his cousins.

Ethan wondered as he ran up the stairs if maybe he had been wrong to keep Penelope from the things he loved, maybe if he tried harder things would be different between them. There was an infectious happiness in his heart after having been with Victor toasting the latest boy and he flung open the door startling Penelope as she sat looking at music.

"Penelope my dear! Victor and Celena have had another boy, everyone's going over to their house to see them, there's to be a celebration!" His handsome face was flushed with excitement.

"Do you think we should? It's going to be all family," she stalled, not wanting to be in a house with so many happy people when her own heart was so heavy.

"Of course, we're family!" he exclaimed. "Come along—they're waiting for us."

It was indeed a celebration, the talking and laughing animated and loud. The children kept running up and down the stairs to see the new baby, and the men talked and drank, while the women fussed around them.

Even though everyone was kind, Penelope couldn't help but glance up often at the china clock, wondering when they could go home. But more than anything, she did not want to go upstairs when it was their turn to see Celena and the baby and felt helpless when Ethan's hand dug into her elbow ushering her upstairs.

The minute the door was opened, she wished she'd made an excuse not to see them. Victor was sitting in a chair by the bed, and the tender expression on his face as he looked down at his wife and latest child, made something violent and jealous jump in Penelope's heart. She could have murdered Ethan for shutting the door loudly behind them, interrupting the intimacy.

"Penelope...hello," Victor said, getting up from the chair, and bending down to kiss her cheek. She noticed his eyes were bloodshot and rimmed in red. She did not often see his hair unbound, and simply tucked behind his ears. He looked indeed like he had been up all night—which of course he had, helping his wife give birth to their fourth child. It was a curiosity to Penelope that he took such an active role in the birth of his children. Usually, it was a midwife with the relatives or friends of the wife helping—never the father himself. It annoyed her the way Ethan made fun of *Victor's part-time job as midwife* because she admired the way he helped.

"We're glad to see you." Victor did not let go of her hands as he led her to the bed. "Here's the latest boy."

"He's beautiful Celena," Penelope heard her husband say, and saw that he sat on the bed opposite Victor's chair, stroking the baby's tiny cheek.

"Thank you, I'm quite fond of him myself," Celena said with a smile, her eyes not leaving the infant nursing at her breast.

Penelope noticed that a bit of Celena's oversized breast was exposed, and a shudder of embarrassment mingled with jealousy came over her realizing how close her husband was to Celena's nakedness.

"I'm sorry Penelope, this is the first time he's eaten, hopefully in a few minutes he'll stop, and you can hold him."

Penelope nodded, hoping to God Samuel Gant would want to eat for a good, long time.

"How long did this one take?" Ethan asked as Victor sat down opposite him, leaving Penelope stranded by the foot of the bed.

"Well let's see," Victor said, rubbing his face tiredly, "about eighteen hours." He looked to Celena for confirmation, then nodded. "Yeah that's right—faster than Randy came, but slower than Ben and Andrew!" Both men laughed.

"Is Laurence still downstairs?" Victor asked and Ethan nodded, smiling at the way Sam was nuzzling his face against Celena's breast.

"I need to tell him something—I was supposed to fix that damn adze for him, and I didn't get to it." He stood. "I'll be back in a minute." Leaning down, he tenderly kissed Celena's forehead. "Here, Penelope, sit."

Although she would have rather died, not wanting to attract any more attention, she reluctantly did so. She sat and looked anywhere but at Celena, who Penelope couldn't help but notice looked remarkably well for having only hours ago given birth. Even with her hair tangled around her shoulders and dark circles under her eyes, Celena was still pretty.

"I guess that's that," Celena said, wincing in pain as she pulled up from Sam, who apparently thought sleeping more enticing than eating.

"Here, let me take him," Ethan said, jumping up.

It surprised Penelope how good he was at holding him but then realized that since this was Victor's fourth child, Ethan had already had practice.

"Thank you...I'm a bit sore." Her frankness caused a small flush in Penelope's cheeks, and she noticed too that it took Celena a few moments to pull the sheet up and cover her swollen breast! Penelope's eyes grew wide with embarrassment the way her husband took it all in. It was not exactly sexual, but it was not how she expected her husband to look on another man's wife. It was too familiar.

"Did you bring your violin?"

Penelope dragged her eyes from her husband suddenly and looked at Celena. "Victor keeps telling me that the next time you come over you're going to play for us?"

Penelope forced a tight smile. "No, I didn't. I'm sorry, we were in such a rush to get here that I forgot."

"Oh well, next time." She smiled at Ethan holding her child. "I keep telling Ethan to bring you with him when he comes Wednesday nights, but I guess you've been too busy." Ethan was thankful that Sam was in his arms, thankful that he could look down at the infant and not have to meet Penelope's eyes.

"Yes...next time..." Penelope choked out, feeling foolish for believing all these months that was the night he did the accounting for the bank. She imagined him laughing and talking with Victor and Celena and their children. Eating and drinking around the table enjoying Celena's cooking and Victor's hospitality. Happy without her.

"Maman I'm hurt," Andrew said, toddling in with a pretend hurt, not sure if one of the adults were going to shoo him out like they'd done count-less times today. He beamed when his mother patted the side of the bed.

"Let Maman see."

Climbing up on the bed he nestled close to his mother.

"Ooh that's terrible—Uncle Ethan look at that!" Celena said, holding up the fat little hand which did not have a mark on it.

Right on cue Ethan gave a gasp. "Andrew! You've been wounded dreadfully! What was it, a bear?"

Penelope saw that the little boy was enjoying her husband's role play-ing, and realized he was good at it. Andrew nodded his little blond head, the bright blue eyes getting bigger each second.

"A large bear, but you were brave weren't you?" The boy gave a wide-eyed stare and nodded. "Is he still in the yard, should I chase him away?"

This time Andrew shook his head.

"You did it? You chased away that ferocious bear—how brave you are!"

"And he was scared, he ran away scared when I chased him!" Andrew said, taking his thumb momentarily out of his mouth to relate his valiant deed. Both Celena and Ethan laughed sweetly at him, and feeling warm and loved in his mother's bed, he settled. After all he'd had quite a day with his Grandmaman and aunts here all night shuttling him back and forth, not letting him see his mother. And he hadn't liked the awful noises she made from behind the bedroom door, and no amount of reassuring from his father had allayed his fears, and was glad that it was all over. Cozy next to his mother, he happily stuck his thumb back in his mouth.

Penelope looked out of the window at the darkening September sky, and never felt more alone than she did right then in Ste. Genevieve in that house so full of happy people.

Chapter 36

"Penelope are you ready?" Ethan asked, tapping lightly on the bedroom door, hesitating before he walked into her room. He no longer slept there with her, hadn't since the ill-fated afternoon she'd ended up sobbing in his arms and screamed at him to leave. And it was sad he thought how things were turning out, but he squared his shoulders and plastering a smile on his face opened the door when she bid him enter.

She was delighted with the way his eyes jumped all over her, glad she had spent so much time and money. "Do you like it?" she asked, smiling, turning a bit to make the hoops sway underneath the yards of dark green velvet trimmed in black. It had a sweetheart neckline and was scandalous to show so much cleavage, especially since she had more to show these days with the weight she kept gaining. She hoped Ethan would think she looked pretty though she was past the point of merely plump now. She had fixed her hair in the latest low chignon and thankfully her ears because of the tight hairstyle were lying flat against her head. It was wonderful to have her husband look at her, it had been such a long time since he had.

"Yes. I like." He smiled, offering her his arm, thinking she looked ridiculous, over-done and round.

She was jittery as they made their way up the snow-covered steps to Victor's house on Christmas eve, and she could already hear the happy voices of many children and of Celena's brothers, sisters, and parents. She had to smooth the front of her dress, trying to calm the pounding of her heart.

The minute the door was open the happiness and warmth of the home hit her. Victor grinned broadly when he saw them, and was as dressed up as Penelope had ever seen him in a dark suit coat over a white shirt buttoned to his throat, and unlike her husband, flatly refused to wear cravats. That coupled with the fact that his hair was long and either he had neglected to tie it back or wanted it loose, it hung now, black around his shoulders, making him look like some sort of bandit. He had Andrew in his arms who was adorable with pearly little teeth.

"*Joyeux Noel!*" Victor said with a grin. "Evening Penelope, evening Ethan."

Randy was clamoring at them to take their wraps, explaining to them that was his duty that night. He was proud he had been entrusted with this task because he jumped around excitedly waiting for them to hand them to him.

"Watch out for the mistletoe, Aunt Pen!" Randy said and Penelope looked up to see mistletoe hanging right by the door. She nervously moved away from it.

Halfway through the evening Penelope watched Ethan as he talked animatedly with two of Jean Gustave's daughters, Loralie and Loriel. He was clever, and easily made the young girls laugh. He was acting so carefree and happy; it caused a lump to form in her throat knowing that no one there would ever suspect how quiet and melancholy they were at home. It occurred to her that if he could still be this way in public, that it was not gone—that there would be some spark to bring their marriage back to life

By the evening's end the families were headed off to church, which to Penelope's surprise was open all night on Christmas eve, and she waited impatiently for Ethan to say goodnight as they stood on the threshold.

"Hey Ethan, don't look now but you're under the mistletoe! Aren't you going to lay one on your old lady?" Will joked, to a round of laughter.

"Will, you have such an eloquent way of phrasing things!" Ethan smirked.

"No matter how he phrases it—are you going to kiss her or not?" James taunted, folding his arms in front of him.

With everyone staring at her Penelope felt ridiculous and embarrassingly chubby.

"Of course." She was shocked to hear her husband say it, and before she knew what he was doing, he kissed her.

The loud cheers immediately went up and flushing with embarrassment she quickly moved from the mistletoe, only to have Stephan drag a laughing, smiling Eva over and kiss her, then the humorous shouts got louder when it was *Carlene* who dragged Mason over and kissed him. Jean and Margot had been next, and Laurence and Lisette had tried to kiss but with all three of their children clamoring at their feet they had started to laugh and eventually gave up!

But what got the crowd laughing was Celena trying to escape from Victor. "Don't even bother running from me, you know I can catch you!" And he did quickly. He then refused to put her back on her feet until she gave him four kisses, one for each of their children. Even though it was a bit earthy for Penelope's tastes, she had to admit it had been fun, and laughed along with everyone else.

Ethan and Penelope were still laughing as they climbed the stairs later that night.

"Oh Lord, Victor's singing! He's abominable, I don't know how Celena puts up with him!"

Penelope smiled. "I don't think she minds. Besides, I don't think I've laughed so hard in years! And poor Carlene, she thinks she has Mason under her thumb. Do you realize half the time Mason is chuckling at her behind her back, turning things around on her without her even knowing?"

"You know, you're right! I've always thought the *same* thing!"

From downstairs Penelope heard the clock start and grabbed his hand in the darkness.

"What's the matter?"

"Listen." She froze on the stairway, waiting for all twelve of the chimes. Overcome then with nostalgia, she turned to him in the darkness. "It's Christmas, Ethan," she breathed, bittersweet tears filling her eyes. "Merry Christmas."

"Merry Christmas, Pen." He felt her fumbling with his hand and was surprised when she laid it against her heart. A second later she led him the rest of the way up the stairs, her heart beating faster with each step.

It will be different this time. It will be all right.

She threw herself into their lovemaking, reached out and touched him like she never had before. It was intoxicating to kiss him and be in his arms once again. *"I love you Etha,"* she whispered in the darkness, thinking that it was sinful what he was able to make her feel. It was so wonderful, and she loved him so much.

Later, when she was laying exhausted in his arms, gloriously reveling in the after throws of passion she was certain this time the feeling of loneliness wouldn't come. Surely not after all this time the dull ache, the terrible emptiness, would not pierce her heart. But when she felt the icy chill start up her back, abruptly pulled away from him with a cry.

"What's the matter?"

She turned her face from him, avoiding his concerned gaze.

"Pen, what have I *done?*" he pleaded.

Part of her truly felt sorry for him. After all she realized, his heart too was broken, and she knew first-hand how that felt.

"Penelope *please!* What is it?" he begged, rearranging his arms so that she had to look up at him.

"Oh *Ethan!*"

He watched her face crease in pain, saw the tears slip past the tightly shut eyes. "What's *wrong?*" His helplessness and alarm grew by the second. "What *is it?*"

She couldn't stop the words from tumbling across her trembling lips. "*Who* is she Ethan, who are you making love to when you hold me? Who's in your *heart,* Ethan, when I'm lying in your *arms?*"

He sat in the chair with his blue silk dressing gown tied tightly around his trim waist, and she was relieved he was across the room. The farther he was from her, the better she liked it. She too had put on a dressing gown and had it closed protectively to the throat.

"I-I don't know what to say to you," he began weakly. "Does...telling you I'm sorry help at all?"

"Well, yes. Being sorry for your mistakes does generally help things... but I don't think in this case it's going to be enough." She let out a sob, and then fought to control her breathing. "I feel...so stupid!" she choked, still trying to catch her breath. She blew her nose noisily into one of Ethan's monogramed handkerchiefs. "As much as I wanted to believe you...loved m-me," she sputtered, and Ethan's eyes guiltily left her face and stared at the rag rug on the floor, "I knew...something, *something* had to have happened. You were too handsome and too wonderful not to have had a sweetheart! And you married me...so quickly, that I knew something had to have happened to you. I liked to tell myself—" Her hand went to her lips to stop the sob breaking forth. "That someone had broken your heart, and that you'd come back to me so I could mend it for you. But then when you made love to me, I realized that she was still in your heart. And it was hard for me to want you so much and love you so much knowing that this woman still held your heart. You have no idea the horrible emptiness I felt every time after we were together." She took a deep breath. "I kept thinking that if I gave you enough time, you would forget her and love me. I thought that, in time it would be...*me* you were making love to."

There was a long silence.

"God Penelope, I'm so sorry. I thought you were pulling away from me, well...for different reasons—"

She laughed grimly. "No, it's not that you weren't setting my heart on fire, but rather because you *were*."

He got up suddenly and even though she tried to push him away he put his arms around her. "I'm so sorry I hurt you! *You* of all people, you've never been anything but good to me."

She couldn't help herself and shut her eyes, clinging to him. Hoping that if they discussed it, this woman's mysterious charms would somehow dissipate. "Did you love her...very much?"

"Yes."

"Did you know her from your time in school, in Boston?"

Feeling more wretched by the second, he did not know what to say. "No."

"Europe then?" Into her mind sprang the images of him kissing a beautiful hazel-eyed Parisian girl.

"No."

She realized that left only Ste. Genevieve. "What happened, did she leave you?" She wondered what woman would be insane enough to let him go. But he paused so long that she repeated herself. "I *said*, did she leave you?"

He was unable to meet her eyes and she watched in horror as he shook his head. "Maybe we shouldn't talk about this—"

"Why not, what harm could simply talking about it do? I mean she's in the past—" He flinched at the word 'past' and she dropped her hands from him as if he were diseased. "She is in the *past* isn't she? *Who is it?*" Penelope screamed, her heart pounding.

He moved from the bed and turned away from her.

"Oh my God Ethan! Is she...*still* in Ste. Genevieve, do I *know* her? *Have I met her?*" She racked her brain to think of anyone he'd ever spoken of. Wildly, she thought of everyone leaving church on Sundays, thought of any woman she'd ever seen in the bank or in town. Then like the slamming of a door when a gust of wind catches it, it came to her.

"Oh, *Ethan*," she whispered, the anger sliding into despair. She dropped her face into her trembling hands. Into her mind tumbled all sorts of torturous bits. He had designed the house for Celena, he knew when all her children's birthdays were, he taught her to appreciate poetry and the things he loved.

She got out of bed and neared him, but she was shaking so badly she needed to grip the chest of drawers for support. "How...how could you *do* this to me? How could you bring me here to Ste. Genevieve where she is? How *could* you take me to her house...expect me to *befriend* her?" She swallowed to keep the bile that was building in the back of her throat from choking her. "It never was me you made love to, was it? When you begged me to tell you that I loved you, it was because you dreamed it was *Celena* saying the words..."

He looked up, desperately not wanting to hurt her, his eyes full of remorse and guilt. "Penelope—"

"Do you *deny* it?" she shrieked, and Ethan could not have been more shocked if she had struck him. "*Don't lie to me!*" She slammed both fists on the dresser and the little teapot fell to the floor and shattered.

Silently she stared at splintered pieces and felt the flame in her soul gutter. The flame she had nurtured since she was a child. The flame that had in it what little sparks of happiness she had ever known as well as all her hopes and dreams for the future. She had tended it so carefully, and for so long, and in one, horrendous, agonizing second felt it simply go out.

The second day when he knocked at the door, he was relieved when she opened it, and merely stood to the side and let him enter.

She looked terrible and he wondered if he should summon Dr. Casey. Her complexion which had never been rosy, took on an ashen tinge. And her dark hair which was not arranged looked almost greasy as it hung loose around her face, and her thin lips looked dried and colorless. But the worst was the haunted, defeated look in her eyes. He hated himself knowing he was the cause of her torment.

"Are you all right?"

Nonchalantly she nodded. "I'm fine." Crossing the room, she sat.

He studied the floor, not having the slightest idea what he should do, and was relieved when she began to speak.

"I've been thinking that the best thing to do..." Even calm and collected, her eyes filled with tears when she thought about what she was going to say. "Is for me to go." It wounded her that he did not immediately beg her to stay. "I'll go...and you can do as you please, with *whomever* you please."

He shifted his weight as he stood leaning against the wall. "But—but where would you go?"

"Back home, back to my father."

He shook his head and let out an impatient sigh. "I don't want you to go. Please stay and let us try and work this out."

"There's nothing to *work out* Ethan. You are in love with someone else, I will go, and that will be the end of it."

Ethan rubbed his face viciously. "I've done wrong—terribly wrong, but please don't leave."

"I want—" Annoying tears filled her eyes and she was angry with herself for breaking down. "To go home."

"Penelope, don't. Please stay with me."

When she felt his warm hand on hers she jerked back like he had leprosy. "*I'm going home!*" she cried, tears stinging her eyes. She had to wipe the mucous already running from her nose with the back of her hand.

He grabbed her by the arms and shook her once. "You can't!"

Her breaths were coming short and fast, but still not allowing enough air into her lungs.

"You...*can't*," he whispered again.

"What—what do you mean?"

"He doesn't want you." Reluctantly Ethan dropped his hands from her. He crossed to the chest of drawers and handed her a handkerchief.

She took it as if sleep walking. "But he's...my father."

It looked as though it pained Ethan to speak. "I know."

The reality of the statement made her knees weak, and she grabbed on to the chair and sat down, pulling at the starched handkerchief in her hand. She didn't want Ethan suddenly at her feet, looking up at her with sadness and pity, didn't want to feel his warm hands gently stroking her.

"He told me you were mine now to take care of, and he meant Penelope, from now on."

"I want to go home."

"My sweet, you don't even know where he is!"

"But—but I do! I have his address and I've—I've written him letters!"

"And how many letters have you received?"

"But he wouldn't...*abandon* me."

"He didn't abandon you Penelope...he *gave* you...to me."

She sat for a few seconds, handkerchief against her mouth, feeling the painful jerk of her heart in her chest. "How—how much...did I cost you?"

"Please, it isn't like that—"

"How much?"

He paused, both afraid to tell her and afraid not to. "Six thousand."

She swallowed bile. "My God, that's nearly three times what a normal slave would have cost you. I was an...awfully *expensive* purchase wasn't I?" She put her hand against her stomach and could feel her insides trembling. Looking up, she met his eyes. "Tell me...do you feel like you've gotten your money's worth?"

"Penelope please—" He reached for her, but she batted his hands away.

"Don't touch me. Don't *ever* touch me...again." She dropped her face into her shaking hands. Her top lip and temples were sweating, and yet she was cold. "But why—why would you *do* this to me? There was no need to *pay* for me. I would have married you...willingly. I thought I *did* marry you willingly!" The irony of it all tumbled painfully in her brain.

She tried to push him away. She hated the soft way he was apologizing and saying her name. "I don't feel good right now, would you please *leave* me?" Feeling the cold sweat trickling down her sides and the bile she had been forcing back made her nauseated. She had to think of a way out— there must be a way out of all the pain!

"No, Penelope you're my wife, and I won't leave you. I am so deeply sorry. Please let me explain."

Feeling suddenly like an animal trapped in cage, she wanted to hurt him. Wanted his heart to be ripped out of his chest with veins and arteries still attached as hers was. "It's too late for sorry, *it's too late for everything!* Besides, your mother told me all about you and Arvellen—"

He jumped up from where he had been kneeling before her, hauling her up so high she had to stand on tip toe. "*Don't believe her, she's lying! Don't believe a word of what she tells you.*" His eyes were wild, his hands bruising her upper arm. "It's been over between Arvellen and me for ages! I *swear* it! Even these last months when you refused me in your bed *still* I didn't go to her! *I've not been with her* in *years!*" He stopped talking when he saw the shock and horror register in her eyes.

"Oh my God..." she whispered, wishing more than anything else in the world that she was dead. Gone.

He saw her breaths becoming shallow, and realized she was going to faint.

"*Penelope!*"

Chapter 37

Penelope sat by the window during those next few weeks in January peering out at the gray depressing overcast skies. Staring at the lifeless, black skeletal trees that shook perilously when the cold wind blew. At first all she could do was sit and cry, but as they days wore on she tried to organize her thoughts. Night after night as she sat by the same desolate window, wild thoughts flitted through her brain as she searched for a solution. But she quickly realized solutions had problems too, like trying to return to her father. The father who, she reminded herself, cared so little for her, that he'd sold her to a man *he* despised. He did not want her, and besides, she would rather *die* than to show back up in front of him now. Could almost hear him laughing at her, *you couldn't even succeed as a wife Penelope*! She had no other relatives and no money. But still perhaps, she could somehow strike out boldly on her own. But devising this plan required a strength and a faith in herself she no longer had. Besides there was no solution from what really tormented her, there was no release from loving him.

A few weeks later she awoke, like she did all the time, and sat up in bed. Defeated, depressed and melancholy she gazed out at the dark starless, sky. Each day was more desolate and painful than the last, and the only respite from the pain was the dreamless nights. If she stayed with Ethan it was painful, if she somehow left it was painful too, and she realized simply that she didn't want to do either anymore. She didn't want to 'be' anymore.

She smiled slowly at how easy it suddenly seemed. Laying back down she sighed with a relief she hadn't felt since that horrible night when her little world shattered in front of her eyes, and knew soon all the pain and heartache would be gone.

Penelope held on tightly to the banister as she came down the stairs, noticing that her breaths were annoyingly loud, and felt a clammy sweat underneath her arms. She stumbled down a step, then held her breath in the darkness, hoping she would not wake anyone. She wondered dully where Ethan slept these days and was assaulted with visions of him making love to Arvellen. As much as she hated to admit it, it still made her heart hurt.

She crossed the dark hallway, and, placing her hands on the heavy doorknob, pulled it open. It groaned in the darkness, but she didn't care suddenly if it did wake anyone because she felt a wonderful freedom escaping from that dark, stifling house.

I should have brought a heavier cloak, I'll catch cold, she thought when the cold air pierced her skin, and then laughed at the absurdness of it. Looking down with dismay she realized the afternoon's little snowfall had gently blanketed the ground and that her kid slippers were a poor choice to go walking in.

It was crystal clear night, and as she walked the stars above her were so bright in the inky sky that the world looked beautiful and full of promise that she doubted her decision.

He certainly wasn't worth dying for. She shivered, wrapping the wool cloak tighter around her. But she'd already given him everything she had to give. She'd given him her heart and instead of taking care of it, he'd shredded it.

There was no one out and she was glad, having no idea how she would explain why she was out alone on a dark, snowy night with only a sliver of a moon. When a raccoon scurried across the road in front of her it startled her. It took nearly ten minutes to make it to the river's edge, and when she finally made it let out a little gasp, and felt herself trembling not only with cold, but with a sadness that suddenly surprised her.

"I'll make him so sorry!" she cried, but wondered if it would trouble Ethan much at all, and then amending her thinking. "At least....I'll embarrass him." She tried to imagine his face when someone brought him the news that her body had been found. And it annoyed her suddenly that she knew nothing of drownings and hoped her body didn't merely sink— and thereby cause him no trouble. She shivered again when she heard the water lapping at the shore. Knowing that it was the dead of winter and that the dark water looked unfathomably cold. Especially now with the edges of the river iced over and covered with an inch of new snowfall.

Shaking herself against the cold she struggled again with her decision. He'd paid for her. Humiliated her and made a mockery out of the tender love she felt for him. It embarrassed and degraded her that he had cared so little for her intellect to go behind her back and buy her like one would a horse. It was inconceivable to her that the man she was so in love with would do such a thing.

Then there was Arvellen. *I've not been with her in years!* But he *had* made love to her in the past, hundreds of times Penelope realized knowing as she did the sexual appetite of her husband. She understood without having to be told that Arvellen was able to please him in ways that she could not; that Arvelllen would allow him to do all sorts of things that she was too shy to do. Although she tried not to, she knew that he had to have compared her to Arvellen, and with a fresh flush of humiliation knew that she did not measure up.

Lastly, he was hopelessly in love with Celena. Despite her anger and humiliation felt a sort of pity for her husband who loved someone who she knew had never given him a second thought.

Shivering uncontrollably she wondered where her father was; wondered if Ethan would get word to him that she was dead. Then realized her father didn't care. After all he'd sold her, he had the money and wouldn't care that she'd drowned.

She took another step toward the river, and realized with dismay that she could not merely walk into the river toward the path of the moonlight like she had romantically envisioned, because there was as drop of at least four feet, and suddenly wondered how she was going to get down there, angry with herself for not planning better.

Climbing down the snowy, frosty embankment turned out to be easier than she thought, and when she landed in a heap at the bottom of it, she laughed triumphantly as she struggled to her feet, brushing the snow off her skirts. She could almost smell the crispness in the air, and half expected to be able to smell the damp, muddy, earthy scents, like she had that day she and Ethan had picnicked near the river. But it was winter, and no such wonderful smells emanated from the huge dark river.

With a little catch in her heart, she realized that she'd left no note, but then thought bitterly there had been no one to leave a note for. No one cared about her. Not her father who'd thought so little of her that he'd callously sold her to a man he himself detested, certainly not her husband, who was in love with someone else. Her absence, she realized, would inconvenience no one. In fact she knew Abigail would be overjoyed she was gone, and Arvellen could have her lover back. There would be hushed talk in town for a few days about her death, and then like a dried leaf blowing away, she would be forgotten. The pain in her heart at the depressing revelation was so strong that she gripped her chest with anguish.

She suddenly thought back to that night at Victor's, the night they had played the poetry game and that Keats poem about the end of life and tried desperately to remember the words.

"*When I have fears that I may cease to be—*" She bit her lip then frantically trying to remember the poignant lines, stamping her wet feet now which were numbing from the cold. "*...When I behold, on the nights starred face, and think that I may never live to trace their shadows with the magic hand of chance...that I shall never look on thee more...then on the shore of the wide world I stand alone, and think, till love and fame to nothingness do sink...*" She hoped she had done Keats' work justice, and then looked at the dark water in front of her.

"It's all right," she whispered, wiping the tears from her face, trying to talk herself into it. "I know. No one will miss me, no one will care. But it's still all right to go." It seemed odd that there wasn't any more to it suddenly, and she found herself with nothing left to do but walk into the water. A bitter wind whipped about her shoulders, and the hair she had hastily braided was coming undone and blew across her face.

"I couldn't have picked July to do this, no, had to be damn February!" She scoffed, swearing on purpose. It was something she had never done and it seemed fitting to at least swear once in one's life.

As she took a step toward the river, the thin ice along the edge cracked loudly and she jumped back with alarm when her foot slipped into the piercingly cold water. Victor's face flashed into her mind. She imagined his big strong arms fishing her lifeless body out of the icy water. Imagined the horribly sad look on his face. She would miss Victor, and she would miss his children, always hoping that one day when she married she would have children to love. More than anything she felt guilty leaving Victor. *Victor* of all people! He was fond of her, and been kind. And because there had been so few that had in her life, she remembered them all.

She thought of the night in Washington when Ethan had yet again swept her off her feet talking about Ulysses voyage and the love of the devoted Penelope. "Out with Penelope and in with Ophelia!" she joked and forced herself to take another step towards the frigid water, but the foot that had slipped through the ice was so shockingly cold it was throbbing, and besides being terribly cold, she was afraid of water.

In the darkness the river was frightening. It was huge, and she noticed that the current was strong. She'd been amazed that day she and Ethan had picnicked to see whole tree trunks being born down by the river's force, and realized with a distasteful shudder how easily it would bear her lifeless form away.

"Oh, I'm *cold!*" she gasped, shivering hysterically with the wind whip-ping around her head stinging her ears, and she was trying to re-arrange the cloak tighter around her. The numbingly cold water swirled around one wet foot, and she scrambled, terrified, back a few steps, and stood trembling maniacally. Frustrated with herself for not being able to simply do it and yet terrified that she would.

She took another step, but for one last moment, she was afraid. Afraid to go, afraid to die, and as much as she did not want to admit it, afraid to leave Ethan. "It's all right," she whispered, and then smirked thinking that she had indeed lost her mind since she was now having conversations with herself. "Go into the path...of the moonlight," she urged, staring at the surface of the water watching the faint glimmer of the silver light of the moon rippling and waving in front of her. One foot again broke though the thin ice on the edge, and the water was so excru-ciatingly cold, it woke her from the trance.

She realized with a hitch in her heart that she was afraid of what lay beyond. She had never been religious, but the fear of what might be wait-ing for her—or worse of what might *not* be waiting for her—made her cry and she knew suddenly she could not go through with it. She stepped back toward the shore, shaking her numb foot, crying with cold and fear.

Voices!

Frantic voices in the dark. Turning, she saw the yellow light of a lan-tern, and then horrifyingly recognized one of the voices as Ethan's!

She cursed silently, knowing he would think her a fool to go to such drastic measures, and even more humiliated and embarrassed than be-fore turned, frantically to flee.

"I don see her!" Arvellen called.

Penelope gritted her chattering teeth thinking that she she'd rather die any day than have Arvellen rescue her! With tears stinging her eyes she took a hasty step but slipped on the ice and fell. Scrambling back up she slipped again, and screamed when she broke through the brittle ice and fell halfway into the excruciatingly cold, black water.

"*Penelope!*" Ethan called, following the tracks she left in the snow. When he heard her scream, he jumped down the embankment. "Penelope! Where are you?"

Frantically Penelope tried to scramble back up on the ice, but she was panic-stricken when she realized she could no longer breathe with the shockingly icy water ripping at her skin. Her heavy soaked skirts were like weights around her legs. The black ice water felt like it was strangling her as she flailed in the water. But as the piercingly cold water went over her head she realized with her heart feeling like it was going to explode out of her chest that it was over. It was so horrible and so cold and she was so frightened she wanted it simply to end.

She felt something tug at her and at first fought it off, but then realizing they were hands trying to rescue her and clung to them.

"You're all right! You're all right Pen, I have you!" Ethan was saying as he pulled her drenched body to the shore. He was panting and they both fell onto the frozen riverbank, shivering, coughing, and choking as they gasped for air.

Looking up through the plastered hair across her face, Penelope saw Arvellen running towards them. A second later she was at her side wrapping a blanket around her, vigorously rubbing her numb arms up and down. She looked down at Ethan still panting in the snow, threw another blanket at him and began to yell at him in French.

"You'll be aw right—it will be aw right," Arvellen said, switching back to English, rubbing Penelope's frozen back. She said something else to Ethan in French. Then, like a dream, Ethan was picking her up and trudging up the steep embankment. He fell once, but the force of masculine adrenaline propelled him up the hill.

She trembled as he hurried her over to the wagon, all the while murmuring all sorts of endearing things—he was worried about her—why had she done this—he would take care of her. She nodded weakly, simply to get him to shut up. More than ever she wished she was dead, but hid it knowing the sooner she acted rational, the sooner they would all relax and she could try again. And she promised herself that next time she'd have a better plan.

"It's turned into pneumonia now, and Dr. Casey is doing everything he can think of to ensure Penelope's recovery."

Victor nodded as he pumped more draft into the fire. "With Dr. Casey doctoring her, you might as well leave her in that river like she wanted."

Ethan jerked his head up, horrified.

"No one *falls* into the river in the middle of the night!" Victor scoffed not believing for a minute the story that circulated around town. "She must be pretty unhappy about something."

Ethan could not bring himself to look at him.

"Any idea what's wrong?"

For a moment Ethan considered telling him. Victor of all people might somehow understand, might even pity him instead of hating him. But it would take courage to stand in front of Victor and tell him, a courage Ethan was not sure he would ever possess enough of.

"No."

He watched Victor shake his head, and had the unsettling feeling that Victor didn't believe him.

Penelope vaguely remembered people hovering over her, but fevers being what they are, she slept most of the time. Since her motivation to get better was nil, she lingered feverishly for nearly three months. Most days she was too weak to sit up. And it occurred to her happily in one of her lucid states that if she continued weakly at this pace—she would simply die. Although not as dramatic as her taking her own life, the result was the same. She would be dead; she wouldn't hurt anymore.

She had been dreaming about her old nurse Rebecca. She could see Rebecca's round face smiling at her and remembered how much fun they used to have playing a rhyming game while Rebecca did the wash. She could feel the steam from the hot water in the tub, smell the lye soap, hear the rhythmic sound of Rebecca rubbing the garment against the washboard.

"Have you got one Miss Penelope?"

"I do. Rub a dub dub three men in a tub—"

Rebecca laughed and brushed the hair out of her sweaty face with the back of her soapy hand. "That's not a new one Miss! And I sure do wish I had three men here to help me!"

"I'll help you," Penelope offered; she hated the way Rebecca's hands would crack and bleed after she did the week's laundry. It hurt Penelope to see the woman she loved work so hard.

Rebecca shook her head and leaned back, resuming her work. "Not you my pretty little Miss. You're meant for better things than washing."

But then the happy images of her nurse faded, and Penelope realized where she was. An emptiness filled her mind, then her heart, then her soul.

Penelope was perversely happy with the thoughts of her soon-to-be demise that she was smiling when Ethan walked in the next morning with her tray of food. She even let him prop her up gently on the pillows, and spoon bits of broth into her mouth.

"You look much better today."

Alarmed, she jerked to face him. "I do? Why?"

"Because your eyes, they have that wonderful warmth in them again that I always liked." Annoyingly she felt his hand on her wrist. She had to resist the impulse to fling it off.

He moved the tray to the table, taking an inordinate amount of time to leave. Then he turned back to her, and to her horror he took one of her hands and pressed it to his warm lips. His head was bent, and she couldn't see his eyes, but noticed that his hair was neatly trimmed. That was certainly her husband after all, no matter that his wife he had made so unhappy she tried to drown herself, he still found time to be groomed.

He lifted his head. "We need to have a talk."

She pulled her hand away.

"I want to tell you first that I am sorry about everything. That it was all my fault, and that you did nothing wrong. I take all the blame myself."

Of course you're to blame! she wanted to shout, but then an odd pain started in her heart when she realized how many times she pushed him away. "All right," she answered weakly, and was angry with herself for not biting him hard like he deserved.

"If you will let me, I would like to explain about my relationship with Arvellen—"

"Don't! Please...*don't!*" She shut her eyes against the vision of that beautiful green-eyed whore.

"I know I have no right to ask for your forgiveness, but still...I'd like to explain."

She was irritated that he'd even asked for forgiveness. She would never forgive him. *Never.*

"I dismissed her before I left to go to Washington," he said, making sure to relate the one decent thing he had done to prevent what he should have known would happen. "That's why I was so surprised when we got home and Arvellen was still here. I knew she should not be in your house, but my mother is so attached to her that I was afraid that if I forced

Arvellen to leave again—"

"Are you a *child*? Are you still afraid of your *mother?*"

He took her blows to his manhood and character quite evenly, and it rattled her that he was maintaining his composure as she felt hers slipping away. "No, but I realize how attached my mother is to Arvellen, and her leaving would distress my mother greatly. She's ill. I worry about her."

"Arvellen...do you love her?"

"Of course not."

"But you—"

"One doesn't have to be in *love* to do *that.*"

She looked away suddenly, thinking the exact opposite. "Does she love you?"

"No."

"But how do you know?" she wailed, wondering if he had any idea the depth of love she felt for him, and how his little conscience cleansing was hurting her.

"I know," he sighed. Knowing there was no way he could explain to her the number of men Arvellen took to her bed, barn floor or whatever surface suited her at the moment. How the look in the flashing green eyes was immediately understood by every man who'd ever been lucky enough to be the recipient. "Like I told you, I've had nothing to do with her in a long time. I wanted you to know that." He then told her a brief history of his relationship with Arvellen, and at first she did not grasp his euphemistic words, relating that Arvellen had been the maid for the upstairs, and that one of her winter duties had been to put warming bricks into the beds at night. But that for his bed, she had always gotten in his bed to warm it— and it took her a few moments to realize that he meant *with him!* When he finished a short time later she found it difficult to look at him for many reasons, one of which was that she had already been bothered by the fact that he'd been with other women, but before they had been faceless entities—and now Arvellen's cat green eyes loomed in her mind.

"Do you have bastard children somewhere hidden about the place?"

He was offended, and this pleased her. "No. I most certainly do not."

She stared at him skeptically.

"I've never actually...had *sex* with Arvellen. She did not allow that. If she'd gotten pregnant, she would have lost her position."

"But you said—"

"We did...*other* things."

Horrified, Penelope remembered the time he had asked *her* to do those things! And not only because she thought the acts themselves lewd, but that as an educated, affluent man he agreed to the disgusting, wanton relationship with Arvellen on *her* terms.

"Well, she's leaving isn't she?" Penelope asked, then wondered why she cared. She would be dead before too long—what difference did it make to her who he was sleeping with?

"Yes, she's leaving as soon as I can find a place for her."

"Why do you have to find a place for her? Throw her out!"

"I can't."

"Can't or *won't!*" she shrieked, and her heart started to pound, her body reminding her mind how weak she still was. "If you don't love her why do you care so much about what happens to her?"

"Not everything is so cut and dried Penelope, everything is neither black nor white. There are shades to things, even Arvellen. She was brought to her first masters' bed when she was only eleven, and she's been abused by different men ever since—"

"So, your name's added to the list of those that abused her?"

He took a full step back from her, shocked that his sweet even-tempered Penelope was spewing such hate. "Well, frankly no. Since I was only twelve at the time and she was twenty, I'd say it was *she* who abused *me*."

"Am I supposed to feel sorry for you then?" The sarcasm in her words caused Ethan's stomach muscles to tighten.

"No. I was only telling you this so you'd understand something about her. And me too."

"I don't want to understand about her. I don't want to understand how you could touch someone like that when you don't love them."

"Then you still know nothing of men, Penelope."

The calmness of his words surprised her, and when she met his eyes she knew what he meant. She couldn't help but wonder if her pulling away and always stopping him was also wrong.

"Obviously, it was the wrong decision to tell you any of this," he said, looking down at the floor.

A bitter humiliation welled up inside her. "Obviously, it was the wrong decision to put your hands on someone other than your wife!"

"It was a...long time ago, before I knew you. I'm not trying to defend what I've done, I only meant that it happened, and I am sorry for it. I tried to have her gone before you came, and I hoped that if I—came out with it, perhaps you could find it in your heart to forgive me. And if not that, at least understand how sometimes...things happen."

He sat back down on the bed and taking one of her hands gently rested his weary head against it, and when he felt her pull it away, stood up.

"All right, I suppose I deserve that."

It was an awful dream. She was laying fitfully on the bed as her weak body tried to live out her mind's torment. She was in the icy river trying to drown herself, only this time no one showed up to save her. She could feel the horrifyingly cold water closing in over her, paddled and flailed frantically—yet no matter how much she struggled, she only went deeper into the icy darkness 'til the circle of light above her disappeared.

Gasping for breath, she woke, her chest heaving. In the darkness she gripped the sheets of the bed, trying to convince herself they were real—and that she wasn't in that dark, freezing water getting ready to end her life. Unsettled and groggy she sat up, and then froze when she heard breathing. Peering over the bed in the darkness realized it was Ethan, asleep on the floor next to the bed.

He was on his back, wearing his night shirt, and even though he had doubled up the rag rug, still it could not be comfortable. She saw that the quilt had fallen away from his legs and that his feet and ankles were exposed to the cool night air. She watched him, looking with a tenderness she could not suppress. He looked innocent and gentle with his lashes against his cheeks. She imagined him at the tender age of twelve, saw him shy and naive, and it made her heart hurt for the boy who was so bereft of affection and found it in the form of a lewd, sexual relationship with a woman eight years his senior.

"Well, I guess I know now where you've been sleeping..." she whispered, realizing he would be gone in the morning before she woke. She leaned down and gently covered him back up. With the terrors of the dream gone, she laid back down and fell asleep.

"I've come to take you outside," Ethan said with a smile.

"I don't want to go outside. It's cold," Penelope barked, wrapping her arms defensively around her, wishing she hadn't gotten dressed and sat in the chair. But she had been in that bed for so many months—she was restless, sore, and bored to death from laying in it.

"It's warm."

"It's cold."

"It's warm. It is an abnormally warm March afternoon, and we had better take advantage of it before winter again rears its ugly head!"

"But I'm—I'm too weak to walk," she lied.

"Then I'll carry you. Come on—put your arms around my neck."

He scooped her up. She thought about fighting to get down but feeling the density of the arms that held her decided she'd rather endure it than have him laugh at her. She noticed he smelled faintly of soap, and his smiling face was irritatingly handsome. Before she knew it he was whisking her down the stairway

It was wonderful suddenly to be out of the cursed room! A moment later he was fumbling with the doorknob from their parlor that led to the garden, and then in one glorious motion, it opened.

She filled her lungs with the fresh, clean air, gazed in delight at the gorgeous garden full of ornamental trees and flowering bushes-all budded green and ready for spring. She turned her face up to the cobalt sky which looked like it stretched onto forever.

"Isn't this much better now?" he asked. Even though they were near the little round table and two white painted Adirondack chairs, he made no move to put her on her feet.

"No."

She realized she wanted him to keep trying, so she could keep hurting him. He walked her over to the budding forsythia bushes that had tiny yellow flowers dotted haphazardly along the willowy stems. "There's a spot here that I've always thought needed work. I was hoping when you're feeling better you might tend it—if you wanted, that is."

At his hopeful words about the future, she dropped the hands from around his neck. He sat down then in one of the chairs, but carefully kept his arms around her, as if he knew she meant to escape.

"You act as though...I'm staying."

"You are." He felt the tensing of her muscles against him. "I mean, I want you to. When you were delirious with fever, I wrote your father two frantic letters. Neither of them was answered...then I wrote to the woman I'd hired to take care of him. He's gone. Truly, I don't know where he is."

There was a long silence.

"I need to tell you something, and I am hoping it might change things for us—"

"Are you suddenly over your pathetic love for Celena?"

It took him a few moments to collect himself enough to answer. "No, that's not what I was going to say."

"Then nothing else matters. I don't care, whatever it is, it won't change how I feel, and how much I-I hate what you've done to me. It's unforgivable!" Having said it, she wished she hadn't. It was too strong, too final. What she felt was not hate, but betrayal and as much as she did not want to admit it, underneath the hurt and anger she knew the last thing she wanted was to be apart from him. She wanted him punished, not banished.

"Don't you even want to know what it is?"

"No. No matter what it is, it won't make any difference how I feel about you, it won't stop me from leaving—not after what you've done."

"This is insane Penelope! With all the *evils* a man can do, all the vile things, you're lumping *me* in that category? What I did was wrong—but *unforgivable*? I cared for you and married you. Rescued you from a life of misery with a father who cared *nothing* for you, and I *had* a relationship with a woman *before* I met you! And for all this...I should be banished to *hell*?"

He was confusing her with his logic, and she felt hot tears in her eyes. "Don't you think I know what you're doing? Bit by bit explaining to me all the foul things you've done, explaining them away so that everything will go back to the way it was. You've explained your way out of your sordid relationship with Arvellen, and now you're explaining your way out of the ugliness with my father. And now that he's gone, and since I have nowhere to go, somehow makes your *buying* of me less heinous. I suppose your love for Celena is next! Tell me, is there any way you can explain your way out of *that* one?"

He was not as upset as she wanted him to be, and it was confusing to her because she realized she *wanted* to fight with him.

"I didn't think about it, but yes...I suppose I was doing that; I was trying to do that." When he said no more she struggled to get off his lap, and he let go of her.

"Well, don't just sit there! Aren't you going to come after me? Aren't you afraid I'm going to try and kill myself again?"

Sighing tiredly, he looked away. "No. I don't think you will try to kill yourself, at least I hope you don't."

"Why not?"

He seemed defeated, broken. "You don't want to die Penelope."

"What makes you think that? I tried it once."

"You have to be...*empty* to want to die." The way he looked at her told her that he knew intimately what he spoke of. "And you're *not* empty Penelope. You're full of hate, full of hate for *me*."

It shocked her this sudden serious change in him. He had been so pleasant when he swept her up in his arms only minutes ago. With a pang she realized she had been able to single-handedly dispel his fragile momentary happiness. But she bolstered her anger back up, wanting since he had accused her of it, to prove to him how full of hate she was.

"Now, I suppose, is where you start telling me all about your love for the beautiful Celena." She intended her tone to be mocking and thought triumphantly she was succeeding even better than she thought possible when he lowered his head.

"I don't think we need to talk about this—"

She snickered. "Oh, I think we do...Celena, who is the object of your fantasy riddled nightmares. But your love for her is to be forever chaste and unrequited! Where you tell me how you have loved her for years, and that it's not *your fault*, you didn't *mean* to fall in love with her, and you've never told her and you live in desperate anguish loving her from afar. You try to be noble and a friend to her husband, even though it cuts at your heart a little deeper each day, that she chose him and not you, that she loves him not you. And even if he were dead she would *never* love you like she loves him. Yet still you trudge bravely on, your devotion unfailing. And each day a little part of you dies. Every time she kisses him your heart is breaking because it's not you, every time you look at her sons your heart breaks because they aren't yours. Day after day you harbor the secret...and you live in quiet agony...loving someone who will *never* love you."

Finished, she looked over at him still sitting at the table with his head bent. After a few moments he looked up, and she was stunned to see that his face had gone white.

Penelope felt a horrible, painful catch in her heart. Never in her life had she *willingly* inflicted such pain on another human being. She suddenly wished she could take it back—*take it all back*! She had only been guessing! Merely rambling on to be cruel and hurt him. She had no idea she was treading so vilely on his heart, so unerringly close to his soul.

"Well," he began, swallowing hard. "I see you have...quite an understanding of the situation here." He smiled grimly. "You even managed to grasp the subtleties and nuances of my...sorry life." He wished suddenly that he'd never come back to Ste. Genevieve, wished he'd never seen Celena on that ill-fated harvest night, wished he hadn't married Penelope and hurt her so. "I suppose that takes care of all the explaining." He stood and when his eyes met hers, she knew she had gravely wounded him.

"I won't...stand in your way anymore if you want to leave. I hoped I could salvage something from the mess I made. But I see—I see now that I have done *irreparable* damage. I have plenty of money, and I'll see to it that you have everything you need, anything you want. You can go, wherever you wish. You can divorce me if you want or not. I'll not fight it." He sighed, knowing it made no difference to him; he had no plans to ever remarry. "I have been foolish. But I see clearly now that you can't stay with me."

He turned and walked away, but stopped abruptly and faced her. "I know I have no right...to ask you for any favor," he swallowed hard, "but...I do ask that you give the child my name, and that you let me see him or her, from time to time."

"*What?*"

"My child...our child. You're pregnant, Penelope."

"But what do you *mean?* How could *you* know, before I did?"

"Dr. Casey told me. Apparently one of the times he examined you, he discovered it."

She knew she had not had her 'monthly' since her convalescence but attributed it to her illness. "Oh *Ethan!*"

"Please, in six more months, it will all be over, and you won't be carrying my child, and be reminded of all my wrongdoings. You have my word; I won't bother you these next months...but I *desperately* want that child!"

He left her speechless and trembling in the garden.

Chapter 38

Watching from the upstairs window two days later, Penelope saw Arvellen start up the drive. She was dressed in a dark plaid traveling dress complete with the navy woolen cloak Ethan insisted she take, and a carpetbag.

Penelope didn't know how Ethan managed it, but Arvellen was leaving. Penelope could still hear Abigail screaming at Ethan—pleading with him not to send Arvellen away. But because Ethan didn't raise his voice, Penelope never heard the whole conversation. She felt guilty knowing he was absorbing all his mother's fits and tears, and that she was the cause of so much turmoil in the house.

When Arvellen was halfway up the drive, Ethan suddenly came out the front door and jogged to catch up to her. He didn't have a suit coat on and wrapped his arms around himself to ward off the cold.

Penelope wondered what he could be saying to her. Arvellen had been his friend for over seventeen years—even if Penelope still flushed thinking about Arvellen's twisted concept of friendship—still he was saying goodbye to someone he had cared about, and who had cared about him.

She saw Arvellen drop her bag and hug him tight. She held his handsome face gently between her hands, and she must have been saying something dear because her lovely eyes filled with tears. She kissed him innocently. Grabbing her carpet bag, she walked to the end of the drive, waved once, and was gone.

Penelope stared at him still standing in the drive. She had been so angry about his relationship with Arvellen—so insanely jealous. But now that Arvellen was gone, there was no righteousness in Penelope's heart, no feeling of virtue, but instead a sense of guilt. The sort one feels when they find out too late they've been mad at the wrong person, unwittingly punished the innocent. And even apologizing never quite makes it right again.

Ethan looked up and realized Penelope had been watching from the window, and a flush of shame coursed through her. Nervously she forced a smile at her husband, a smile he was unable to return.

Celena and Victor were the only ones that went with Penelope and Ethan back to the house after Abigail's funeral. Ethan was pleasant as always, but Penelope knew that behind the polite smiles and accepting of condolences that he was more depressed and desolate than he let on.

Penelope would never be sure exactly what happened, only that three days after Arvellen left, her mother-in-law was dead. All Ethan would tell her was that when he had gone into her room in the morning, he had found her dead. What he chose not to tell her was that Abigail had ended her own life by taking a triple dose of laudanum left for her by Dr. Casey for her arthritic legs. It was horrifying to Ethan realizing what she had done, and close on the heels of anguish was guilt. He couldn't help but think she was the second person in no less than three months who tried to kill themselves to be free of him.

The staff was dressed in black, and it was a depressing sight—the house had always been somber and this only made it worse. Penelope was glad the minute the four of them stepped into their parlor, that a fire had been lit, and that immediately Celena sensing the need for sunlight stepped to the window and opened the heavy brocade drapes.

"I need a drink," Ethan said, the facade cracking a bit now that he was in his house with his dearest friends. Celena went to the sideboard, poured four drinks, placed them neatly on the tray, and brought them over.

Not knowing what to say, Victor merely looked at him. "To your mother Ethan, God rest her."

Ethan nodded, thinking it a remarkably civil toast given from a man who had only heard hateful things directed at him from the deceased. He upended the snifter. "You don't have to go yet do you?" he asked, a trace of worry in his voice. He poured himself another brandy while the other three were still politely sipping theirs.

"No, we can stay," Victor replied.

"Good. I don't want to be alone."

Victor and Celena glanced at each other in surprise but said nothing.

"Well...I guess that's the end of that." Ethan sighed, staring despondently into the fire. He had never been able to be close to either one of his parents, and he found himself wondering then why it still hurt him when they died and left him. He sat down in one of wing chairs near the fire and for a minute rubbed his tired eyes. Feeling then a bit like they were all looking at him began a conversation.

"Have you thought anymore about the repairing of the steamships? I've written to Pickering about our idea, and he's interested. I was thinking I'd go to Washington before too long and talk to him about it—"

"No Ethan, I'll go for you. I'll talk to him since I'll be doing the repairs."

"No, you've got more than your hands full here," he said, smiling, referring to Celena and the children. "I'll go. I have nothing here that prevents me from going, there's no reason I can't go and get the work done."

Again, Celena and Victor exchanged curious glances.

"All right. If you're sure."

Ethan got up to get himself another brandy. "I'm sure." He stood at the sideboard, but he wasn't pouring a brandy. He was staring down at it, his hands resting on the smoothed polished surface. He stayed that way silently for better than a minute, and it was torturous for the three of them to watch him, simply standing there silent, in his private grief.

He felt awful about what he'd done to Penelope—knew he had made her terribly unhappy. And even though there was no one who would ever understand, he missed Arvellen. Missed her because she knew him—all of him, even the dark corners that people hide and never show anyone. And he couldn't help but feel that he caused his mother's death. He knew what Arvellen's leaving would do to her, and even though his relationship with his mother had been strained at best, still it weighed horribly on his conscience that she was dead now, because of what he'd done.

Then there was the child. The child that he was sure Penelope didn't want. It pained him every time he thought about the horrified look that had crossed her face when he'd told her. The child he was sure she would take from him after it was born—the child that he'd never get to know, never get to love and be loved by in return.

Suddenly it was all too much for him. He'd been alone for the first thirty years of his life, and here he was poised to be alone again for the next thirty.

A terrible lump formed in Penelope's throat when she saw Ethan's shoulders trembling, watched as he tried to force down his tears.

Celena neared Ethan, put a hand on his shoulder. Bent at the waist, he turned to her like a hurt child. She said something to him Penelope couldn't hear, and his arms went around her in a death grip. He let out one tortured sob. But Celena held on to him, kissing the top of his head.

As they sat watching the odd, tender display before them, Penelope turned to Victor. He seemed neither embarrassed nor repulsed by his friend's tears. There was only compassion in the gray eyes and the understanding that Ethan needed Celena, that only she could console him. Penelope realized Victor was loaning to Ethan the person most cherished in his life. *He knows,* Penelope thought, her heart beating painfully in her chest. *And yet he still loves him. He has forgiven him.*

Watching them, Penelope felt little pains in her heart. She wished it had been her arms he had turned to, wished she was the one whispering soothing words like Celena was now. But she'd had the chance to go to him before Celena did, and yet couldn't. Penelope was surprised that at the sight of them embracing, no raw jealously burned in her soul, but rather a dull ache from misunderstandings and missed opportunities.

"I'm sorry," Ethan croaked.

"It's all right," Celena murmured.

Embarrassed, he moved to get his handkerchief to wipe the tears.

Victor handed Ethan his own handkerchief. "Blow your nose. That sniffling is annoying, you remind me of Andrew!" It broke the tension and the three of them laughed.

"Well," Ethan began, forcing a weak smile, his eyes and nose still red. "What I always say is, if you're going to make a fool out of yourself, do it early in the day and get it over with!"

Victor smirked. "And what I always say is, eat early in the day and you can eat again! Are we having any food at all today?"

Ethan smiled at him—not only because of the joke to lighten the mood, but because he knew Victor still loved him. Dark corners and all.

"Ethan, I want to talk to you," Penelope said, walking into their parlor a few nights later.

He looked up from his desk, papers spread out and two ledgers open. She could tell he was annoyed at being interrupted but did not refuse her.

He pulled one of the small straight-backed chairs over. She folded her hands in her lap and tucked her feet underneath her. "There's been so much—" she searched for a neutral way to describe it, "turmoil in the last few months, I wanted to see if we could have a civil conversation without either of us raising our voices."

"I'm willing to try."

"I've decided to stay here at least until the baby is born." Her voice quivered on the word *baby*. He did not look at her but nodded his approval. "I can't imagine leaving right now, not...like this," she said placing her hands gently against her midsection.

"And after? After the baby's born, do you still plan on leaving?"

She had to look away from him, not sure what to tell him. Not wanting to think that far into the future. Found herself ridiculously wishing she could stay pregnant for a few years, giving her time to think and her wounded heart a chance to heal. "I-I don't know."

This time it was Ethan who looked away. "I understand," he said tiredly. It was the sound of someone who was wearing down, the sound of someone who knew defeat was coming and no longer had the will to fight. He looked back down at his papers and picked up his pen. He furiously wrote five lines and looked back up. "What is it now Penelope? Is there something else?"

"Why—why are you angry with me?"

He tossed the pen to the desk and stood at the window with his back to her, hands clenched behind his back, then turned and faced her. "I'm not...angry. I'm disappointed Penelope, I don't want you to leave me. I know that I've done things wrong. But I have also apologized repeatedly to you and tried—to the best of my ability to make up for them. The situation with your father. I wanted to marry you, and he was going to make it painful for me, you know that don't you? He'd always hated me. I thought paying him off was the best solution. And besides, I knew I could offer you a better future than he could."

As much as she did not want to admit it, she knew it was true.

"And Arvellen—"

"I don't want to talk about this," she interrupted and suddenly felt nauseated, not knowing if it was because of her pregnancy or the mention of Arvellen's name.

"You *still* don't believe me do you? Don't you understand how frustrating that is for me? Especially after I've gotten rid of her and now the guilt of my mother's *death* hangs over my head?"

She wiped a tear away, hoping he would not bring up Celena.

He sat on the desk in front of her. "Like I've told you before, there are many kinds of marriages, and they aren't great love matches but they can still be good marriages that last a lifetime. Companionship of having someone to tell your troubles to at the end of the day, someone to share the happiness. We can't all have these passionate loves we read about—it's not realistic. As we sit here pining away for what we don't have, time is racing by us, it's a delicate thing. And take a hard look at our life, Penelope," he said, glancing around the room, thinking about the real and serious problems that were threatening the solvency of the nation, thought about all the poor he had seen in his travels through Europe. "I'm the wealthiest man in Ste. Genevieve, I have more land and more money than I hardly know what to do with! And I can give you anything, *anything* you want! We are going to have a child now Penelope, don't we owe it to that child to put aside our differences and give that child a loving, stable home?"

He was so persuasive she had to stop herself from nodding, because a small part of her would still not give up. The part of her that was still young and naïve and still dreamed of knights in shining armor, and of love being most important. "I can give you the world," he whispered, thinking of the hefty amount of money he had already made that month and the wonderful education and experiences his money would give their child.

"But I don't want the world if you're not in it!"

He shook his head in frustration, and it was humiliating to her knowing he thought her childish.

"Ethan, you're asking me to stay with you. Stay in a marriage when I know you don't love me? Where we don't love each other—how can you expect me to live like that?"

"I'm not asking you to do anything that I'm not prepared to do as well." It took a moment for the meaning of his words to sink in, and when they did all the wounds she tried to close broke open again and bled.

He'd had four brandies at Victor's by the time he left, two more than he normally did, and he could only attribute the need for additional drinks because it dulled his senses when he returned to his unhappy home.

He was whistling off key when opening the door, he saw Penelope standing on the bottom step. He stopped, whistling when he saw her, and smiled. When she dropped her eyes distastefully from him, resumed his bad whistling and went into the parlor to promptly pour another drink.

"Oh!" he exclaimed, not realizing she had followed him in. "Didn't see you there. Want one?"

She shook her head. "Where have you been? You've been gone since morning."

He let out a breath. Even though they were better than a yard apart she could smell the brandy on it. "Well...let's see." He rubbed his face tiredly. "On the hill eating after church. Watching Victor do an...amazingly horrible job of minding his children, then blacksmithing, then eating again, then chess with Victor, then here." He turned from her and looked out of the doors that led to the garden, wondering if she was going to scold him. When she said nothing, he turned back around. "And how was your day?" he asked too cheerfully

Looking at her he noticed she was showing; he could see the roundness on her, even though the loose cotton dress was designed to conceal it and was pudgy all over. She might have looked healthy if it weren't for the way her cheeks were pale and drawn. Downing the last of his brandy he realized he'd never seen a woman in his life who looked more unhappy to be carrying a child.

"Lonely," she answered and then looked up at him and took two tentative steps nearer, and then nervously took one back.

"Penelope, what is it?" he asked gently.

"I want to try..." she began. "I want to try to have a...friendship again with you."

He was so surprised by her change of heart that he merely stared at her, dumbstruck.

"I'm so terribly...lonely without you," she admitted, and her eyes dropped wistfully from his. "And even though I know how you feel—still you've cared more about me than anyone else ever has." He noticed her hands gently resting on her stomach. "And if you want to know a secret I'm afraid of having the baby. I mean I want it—it's just that I'm...afraid. And Ethan you are so good with babies."

He smiled at the compliment.

"Would you mind if we...tried? Is there anything kind left in your heart for me after I've told you I hated you and damned you to hell?" Embarrassed suddenly, she laughed and was relieved when he did too.

"Yes," he answered, "there's something left." Silently he thanked her for not asking for more than he could give.

It was an incredibly hot evening in mid-June and annoyingly Ethan kept batting the June bugs away when they banged into the lantern on the table where he and Penelope sat at the table in the garden playing cards.

"They have to be some of God's stupider creatures," he remarked, watching the same June bug battering itself to death against the glass of the lantern, "and when you get in there you'll only incinerate yourself you stupid spider."

"It's an insect Ethan."

"Spider, insect, whatever."

Triumphantly she slapped her cards down. "Gin!"

"You evil *wench!* That is you *wonderful, intelligent, savvy* card playing wench!"

Smiling, she got up from the table.

"And just may I ask, do you think you are going? I demand a rematch!"

She could only giggle, "I'll be right back."

He sat back in the chair with a thud. "You have to—*again?*"

Embarrassed, she nodded.

"Good God! I don't know why all pregnant women don't expire from dehydration with all the trips to the privy!"

By the time she got back he had shuffled and dealt the cards and she smiled as she watched him still swatting at the large June bugs that she had to admit could be awfully annoying sometimes. She watched him reach for his glass of sassafras and take a long drink, realizing since she had asked him not to drink so much, he hadn't had a single drop. She was not against all drinking and thought nothing wrong with an occasionally brandy, but he didn't even do that anymore, and it touched something in her heart how hard he was trying.

When she returned to the garden, she noticed that his hair needed a trim because the soft brown strands were resting on his collar. Reaching out she placed her hand on his back. He froze under her touch, and she bent and lightly kissed him on the back. Closing her eyes laid her rounded pregnant body against him, sliding her arms around the front of him.

It had been so long since they had touched each other that he was paralyzed at first, not sure what to do. He pulled the hands up from around him and sweetly kissed the backs and then the palms. He stood up and pulled her into his arms, innocently embracing her.

"I've got it all dealt out," he said into her hair. "We may have to resort to playing chess to cover up my humiliation at the pitiful way I am losing to you!" He laughed.

"I-I don't think I want to play anymore."

"Why?" He had been enjoying himself, and thought she had been too.

She reminded herself that he did not love her, and that no matter what she did she would never have all of his heart. Reaching up she placed her hands on his face and kissed him. It had taken a long time, but she finally figured out how to show him the passion and love she felt for him.

He pulled back from her warily. "What-what...are we doing?" he asked, trying to free the hands she had clasped about his neck. "Penelope please. Don't get me started, all right, I am....only *human*." It had been many months since he'd had the benefit of female companionship.

"Why not?"

"Because." A trace of shame crept into his voice. "The minute I get going, you're just going to ask me to stop—"

"No I won't!" Blushing, she had to look down. "Don't you want to...?"

"I assure you, I'd like nothing better. But I can't do that to you. I've hurt you enough already. And I remember the last time—"

She put a finger to his lips to silence him. "I know, I know you don't love me. But you *like* me and you've been kind to me. And I've realized, I don't care anymore. I know I can't have...everything but you were right." She lightly caressed his cheek, realizing that she couldn't stay angry at him. Not when she loved him so much, not when she had forgiven him. "Life is both fragile, and fleeting, and some happiness, some love, is better than none at all..."

They had been arguing for weeks what to call the baby. Penelope was set on Ethan Jr. if it was a boy, much to Ethan's displeasure, never thinking it a particularly inspiring name, but it was if the child were a *girl* where the arguments got heated.

"Absolutely not! Arabella sounds like a name for a cow!" Penelope scoffed.

"It is not! Luanne and Bessie are names for cows," Ethan defended, "and it's a far better choice than Prudence. What do we call her for short—*Prue?*"

Penelope bristled, not liking the sound of the nickname or any nicknames for that matter. "We don't shorten it at all, we will call her by her formal name, Prudence."

"We most certainly will not."

"*Ethan!*"

"She's half my child, and I'll not saddle her with a horrible name like

Prudence."

"Oh, all right. I don't know why you have to be so difficult!" In reality she loved how attentive he was being, how pleased and excited he was about the baby they would soon have. "Rebecca then—"

"That was the name of your *nurse!* You want to name our child after a servant? We've a few more weeks...we'll decide later."

Things were surprisingly good between them, she had to admit, a remarkably good imitation of being in love with her. He was witty, always able to make laugh, and he spent increasingly more time with her, especially since she had let him back into her bed. And he listened to her play the violin and was learning to appreciate the works of the masters. He was acquainted with Mozart, Vivaldi, and Bach, but had no knowledge of Paganini who was her favorite because he was technical master at the violin.

They talked about the financial panic that crushed many banking institutions from the in pouring of gold from the California territory. She had been relieved that her husband's bank was still solvent and in no immediate danger, and she could only attribute this to the fact that he was cool and dispassionate when it came to business matters and unlike others had not overestimated the need for grain in the Crimean war, and although he had speculated in railroads he had done it prudently. And finally, in 1857 the government banned all foreign coins, but then *Wildcat* banks started popping up in the frontier, and it only fueled Ethan's aggravation with dishonest bankers with their worthless paper money.

They talked about the issue of the slave Dred Scott who had tried to sue for his freedom in St. Lous and was thus told by Judge Taney that he was *not* a citizen and therefore had no rights to sue-and how the judge's ruling had delighted and surprised the southern delegates; although it drove a lethal wedge through the northern and southern wings of the once-united Democratic party and infuriated the northern free soilers and Republicans. The ruling also broke open a rather nasty scar about the extension of slavery into new territories-rendering the almost fifty-year-old Missouri Compromise null and void. And it seemed to both Ethan and Penelope, as they talked of these things, that the sectional differences between the two parts of the country became worse each year. It was wonderful, she thought, how he listened to her views about the happenings and did not immediately discount her opinions simply because she was a woman.

He ordered things to be made for the baby, like the cradle, highchair, and bookcases. She had laughed the first afternoon when he had begun loading up the newly finished bookshelves, reminding him that it would be a long time before the infant could read the likes of Sophocles! He had merely chuckled, and then showed her the nursery rhyme books and special leather-bound copy of Aesop's fables.

Although he had not asked again if she had forgiven him, she knew he still longed to hear it. Longed to hear that she had exonerated him from his wrongdoings. But she could not quite bring herself to tell him, even though she knew it would free her to simply let go of the pain of the past.

She decided when the baby was born, and he held the physical proof of her love and devotion in his hands, she would tell him that she had forgiven him. Tell him what she knew he desperately needed to calm his troubled soul.

Ethan frowned at the document in front of him. Mason had drawn it up and it seemed that he used more words than necessary, and seemingly tried to make the blasted document as difficult to decipher as possible! He gave a short laugh realizing how seriously Mason adhered to and upheld all the rights and privileges afforded by his law degree.

"Maybe Carlene's right...you need to undo the top button a bit Mason..." he mumbled under his breath.

The bank door banged open loudly, forcing him to look up.

"Mr. Stanfield—ya need ta come now," Patsy said, her chest heaving, worry creasing her forehead.

He knew immediately what was happening. "Have you told Dr. Casey? Is he on his way?"

She nodded, and it alarmed him to see tears in her onyx eyes.

"She's hurtin' bad, been hurtin' bad since this mornin'—"

"Why did you wait so long to come get me?" Ethan asked, glancing up at the clock realizing it was almost dinner time.

"She didna know what happinin' fo shur," Patsy said, shaking her head ominously, "she knowin' it now..."

"Penelope *please,* let me get someone, Celena—Victor even!" he whispered as the clock in the hallway chimed one, not wanting Dr. Casey to hear.

Ethan was worried about the way things were progressing. Victor had tainted Ethan's views about Dr. Casey's skills as a healer. The doctor, Ethan had to admit, had a rather dismal success rate with his patients surviving postpartum.

"No...no I'll be all right," she said, not wanting Celena to help her with anything, and the thought of having Victor helping her give birth would be more embarrassment than she could handle. It was bad enough the way Dr. Casey kept 'feeling' around on her, and swearing at her when things were not happening.

"You're not helping the situation here, you're upsetting her by all your talk of breathing and relaxing," Dr. Casey complained.

"But it's past one o'clock in the morning, she's been in labor for hours! Shouldn't something appreciative be happening by now, can't we do something to help her?"

"No, women give birth, Mr. Stanfield, *not* men! I would appreciate it if you would wait outside."

"Outside—why?"

"It's totally unheard of to have the fathers hovering about upsetting the women—"

"But I want to help her."

"If you don't mind I believe that is the reason your frantic slave came running for *me* is it not! And if you don't let me attend to your wife as I see fit, then I'll have to leave."

"You'd *leave*? What sort of Hippocratic oath did *you* swear to?"

"Ethan—I'll be all right!" Penelope gasped, not wanting them fighting. Besides, while they stood arguing no one was paying any attention to her! And she was frightened, more frightened than she had ever been.

"Are you sure?" he asked worriedly

"It..it probably won't...be much longer now..." she said desperately.

"I takes caya of huh..." Patsy said, ducking her head to Ethan, and Rosa too nodded. Ethan had the unsettling feeling that neither of them had any more faith in Dr. Casey than he did. As he reluctantly left, he had the sinking feeling that Victor would have never left Celena in such unskilled and careless hands.

Penelope awoke sometime later. The hot throbbing pain between her legs robbed her of sleep, and she wondered feverishly if someone had put a hot rod there. Disturbing images filled her mind of Ethan and Dr. Casey shouting obscenities at each other, of Ethan throwing him out of the room. Then she heard weeping—whose she wasn't sure.

"H-how do you feel?" Ethan said softly, suddenly at her side.

"Tired." Her eyes closed. "What was it...?"

"A-a girl," he choked out, bending his head so she couldn't see his eyes.

"Is she all right?"

He wondered now what he should do—wondered if he should tell her that the child was dead, but feared what the news would do to her in her already weakened condition. Wondered if she would forgive him later when she learned the truth. "Yes she's fine. Patsy is taking care of her. You rest now."

Rosa and Patsy assured him that Penelope's bleeding—called 'flooding'—was normal, but when they had to change the linen cloths for the fourth time that night, they all knew something was dangerously wrong.

The two slaves did everything they could think of to help Penelope. They gently wiped her with clean water and cloths, and as Rosa had with her old, gnarled hands *'closed up the loin,'* Ethan had been amazed at how calmly the old slave had delicately extracted the placenta from Penelope's body, all the while keeping her other hand on Penelope. Patsy handed her the dry cloths to lay between her legs to soak up the bleeding.

"I gotta keeps my hands here to keeps air from gettin there."

"What will air do?"

"Sometimes the air, it cause too many afterpains—"

"You mean she's going to have more pain than she's already had?"

Rosa shrugged, solemnly wrapping a binder around Penelope's knees, as if tying them together. "I don know...that be a bad one," Rosa said, hoping the bleeding would slow. The color of the bright red blood was a bad sign—old blood was darker and even brown. The vibrant color of her mistress's 'new' bleeding concerned her.

Yet for all the tender care given to her postpartum, Penelope got steadily weaker and her bleeding remained alarmingly heavy. Sick with worry, Ethan refused to leave her side.

"I've been thinking," Ethan began in the twilight of a humid September night as he wiped the sweat off Penelope's clammy face. He had to swallow a lump in his throat, realizing that she was getting weaker with each hour and that her breathing was labored. It had been a grisly, horrifying birth and Penelope was not recovering like he hoped she would. It was bad enough the child had been mangled and ripped from her womb and before even taking a breath, died in his arms. "That we should go away." He forced a smile as he sat close to the bed and was assaulted with guilt when her brown eyes trustingly looked up to him. He saw that she was trembling even while she perspired in the muggy air. He got up to rearrange the quilts around her, not knowing how else to comfort her.

"I'm so cold Ethan...can you hold me?"

He dragged a tufted chair over to the bed, the legs groaning in protest against the floor. Reaching down he gently gathered her into his arms, hating himself when she winced in pain. It was frightening to him how limp and lifeless she already felt, how feverish and damp. "Better?" he asked, draping the quilt around them both.

"Yes," she managed. Too weak to hold her head up, it rested against his chest, and the sound of his heartbeat was soothing.

"I've been thinking that we could start again, Penelope. Start over with our lives and our marriage—"

"The three of us?"

He wondered what he should do—if he should tell her that the child was dead—but feared what the news would do to her in her already weakened condition. Wondered if she would forgive him later when she learned the truth. He had to swallow hard. "I should never have brought you to Ste. Genevieve. It wasn't fair to you, and for that I am truly sorry." It made his heart ache the way she weakly hugged him then, as if to console him. "I was thinking we could go to Italy...buy a villa that looks out over the blue waters of the Mediterranean. It's beautiful, have you ever been there?"

"No," she whispered, enjoying the feel of his arms tight and warm around her. She tried to hug him again, but her arms would no longer respond.

"Then you must let me take you there. Do you know that flowers in pink, blue, and yellow, every color imaginable bloom year-round there? We could learn to sail or take up painting." When she looked up he gently kissed her parted lips.

Feebly she shook her head.

"If not Italy, how about France? Paris is a city like no other! The first royal palace has a chapel inside, called the Sainte Chappelle built in the thirteenth century and the story of the Bible is told in more than 1,000 panes of stained glass. We could see the hill where the French people were attacked by the Huns—where our own Sainte Genevieve fasted and prayed them to victory. We could buy a chateau in the hills by the Alps. Out one window we could perpetually see winter on the snow topped mountains, and out the other, the greening hillsides and the cattle grazing, and know that way beyond it, the grape arbors were somewhere blossoming below."

"What about...the bank?"

"I'll leave it. We've plenty of money to go abroad for years, or if you want, forever."

"What about...Victor?" As much as she longed to go, she felt guilty knowing she would be forever separating them.

"We'll still be partners, but I suppose he'll have to make do without my guidance." Although it was said in jest, she knew how hard it would be for him to leave Victor.

She sighed in the growing darkness, thinking about all he was offering to give up. Giving up the bank he so cherished, the town he grew up in, the man who was like a brother to him—and although neither of them would mention it, the woman he loved. All this he painted for her like some wonderful, impossible dream.

"You'd...you'd do all that, for the baby and me?" she asked, her voice nothing more than a whisper.

He nodded, knowing that he had no choice if they were ever to find true happiness—Arvellen had been right. And selfishly too he thought that if he made the sacrifice it might be a way to be absolved of his sins, and that someday she would forgive him. Even though it was the right thing to do, he knew that he would regret for the rest of his life leaving. Leaving Celena.

"You love our daughter...very much...don't you?"

He was thankful her head was cradled underneath his chin and could not see his eyes. "Yes," he choked out, "and I love you too."

She found the strength to squeeze one of his arms. It was comforting to simply listen to the romantic plans. Wonderful to pretend they could have this magical dream.

"Or Greece. The warm countryside basking under the sun near the Aegean—it's only fitting don't you think that I should take *my* Penelope to the places where Odysseus wandered so many years trying to get back to his?"

She smiled faintly at the memory of that night in Washington when she had again fallen so hopelessly in love with him.

"Hmm? Which one do you prefer my sweet, where should I take you?" He placed a delicate kiss on her damp forehead. "Italy, France, Greece?"

"Greece," she whispered breathlessly, wanting simply to please him. She knew she would never see the cobalt waters of the Mediterranean, never see the vibrant bougainvilleas blooming along ancient stone walls, never sail the sea of Odysseus. She struggled to look up at him, and gently stroked his cheek in the darkness. "You should have told me," she began, but speaking was almost beyond her now. "You should have told me that you loved...someone else."

"I'm sorry Penelope, but I wanted you to marry me—"

"I still would have," she gasped, interrupting him. "I would have...anyway." She sighed wistfully and closed her eyes with exhaustion, imagining Ethan and their daughter together in one of those lovely sun-drenched Greek villas. At least he would have their daughter to cherish and love. And besides, it would cause him, if only occasionally, to think of her.

She sighed, her cheek heavy and damp against his chest. She imagined him walking hand and hand with their daughter through one of the cosmopolitan markets in Greece. She thought wistfully of all that she would never see, all that she would never do, all that she would miss. "At least I had...a nice...summer."

Even before Ethan awoke fully he shivered, strangely cold and wet. Confused as to what was on top of him rendering the lower half of his body immovable. His legs were utterly numb and couldn't figure out what had cut off the circulation. He also noticed the faint smell of urine.

"Penelope," he said, trying to rouse her, simply to get the blood circulation going in his legs again. He noticed that even though she had been laying against him all night she was cold. "*Penelope...Pen!*" He gasped when he had to wrench one of her hands from around his arm, realizing to his horror that they were already stiff.

He knew then that sometime during the night, as she lay in his arms, she had died. While he had peacefully slept, she had silently left him.

He stared at her white face. Her bloodless lips were cold and her brow, last seen creased in pain, was smooth. The sickness and torment gone.

For a moment, his numb mind was unable to process. Glancing up to the window he looked out to the lush green trees in the garden. He waited for the tortured anguish to rip across his heart, waited for pain to assault him. But then it dully occurred to him, it was far too late for all that.

She was, after all, free now. Free of the immediate pain of her illness, free from the knowledge of her daughter's death, free from all the heartache and pain being married to him had caused her. She could be happy.

Tears pricked his eyes and he leaned down to gently kissed her cold mouth, tracing his thumbs across the smooth cheeks. "I am so...sorry," he whispered, his warm tears wetting her cool cheeks. "Forgive me my sweet, please forgive me."

Victor got out of the wagon and hurried around the other side to take Sam out of Celena's arms and help her down.

"When do you want me to come back?" he asked, ignoring Sam's wail at being taken from his mother.

"I don't know. It's going to take me a couple hours."

"Can I go with you Mere?" Ben asked hopefully, not liking the way the mood had changed in their house since Uncle Ethan's slave Tillman had come over to the house with the sad news that Aunt Pen and her baby had died. Although he felt bad for his uncle and aunt, what upset him was the melancholy way his parents were behaving. It unnerved him to see his mother crying and his father so gloomy.

"No, not today Ben," Victor said and handed Sam to Randy, who sometimes balked at having to hold his little brother. But realizing his father was in no mood for antics, he put his arms protectively around his little brother and shut his mouth.

"Are you sure you don't want someone else to help you—Margaret or Eva? I don't like the thought of you there alone with him."

"I can do it, and I want to do it." Seeing the impatience cross his face, Celena gently touched his shoulder. "I feel so bad for him Victor...it's a tragedy to lose them both."

He nodded, unable to contradict her words. "All right. I'll be back at supper time to get you." He didn't get back in the wagon right away. Ethan's tragedy only reminded him again how fragile and short life was—and he loved his own family so much it made him crazy to think of anything happening to them. Besides, part of him was angry with Ethan for not coming to get help when things started to go wrong. He couldn't help but wonder if he, Yvonne, or Celena had been with Penelope, she would be happily showing off her baby girl rather than being dressed for burial.

"Boys, kiss your Mother."

Squaring her shoulders, she headed toward the dark house. As she passed under the shade of the old hawthorn tree, a little shiver went through her. The feeling of gloom only deepened when she heard Victor and the boys driving away.

"Ethan," Celena said in the doorway of the parlor.

He turned. Opened his mouth to say something and then shut it, and simply looked down. A moment later her arms went around him, and he felt her lay her head against his back

"I'm so sorry—I'm so sorry all of this has happened to you."

He nodded, unable to speak, and then freeing the hands she had clasped around him took a full step away from her.

"Are you hungry, have you eaten anything?" she asked, taking in his ragged appearance. She didn't expect him to be the model of fashion a day after his wife and child died, but had never seen him so disheveled. His hair was tousled, he hadn't shaved, his eyes were rimmed in red, but there was something else. It was the look of desolation in his eyes; of bone deep sadness. The loss of a sort of innocence that one has a seemingly unlimited supply of when they were younger. The hope always for better days, better tomorrows. The optimism and blind faith had simply gone out of his eyes.

"No—but I don't want anything."

"I'd like to get started then." She made a move toward the door, but he put a hand out to stop her.

"I don't want you to do this."

"But I want to, I want to help you."

"It's...unpleasant. I don't want you to have to see it," Tears formed in his eyes when she put both of her hands around his to reassure him.

"I think you forget sometimes; I was raised on a farm. I can do it."

He led her upstairs to the room where Penelope's body lay after being washed by Rosa and Patsy so it could be dressed. He watched Celena as she entered the room, seemingly unaffected by the ghastly sight he thought Penelope made in her shift, lifeless on the bed. It was unnerving the way her eyes were only half closed, and it made him shiver, feeling like she was watching him.

Celena merely untied the bonnet from under her chin and began to roll up the sleeves of her calico blouse. She moved to the window then and opened the curtain letting in the sunlight. She then picked up a brush and began brushing Penelope's hair.

Unable to stand it, he turned away.

"Have you decided what you want me to put on her?" she asked after a time and Ethan, sitting grim-faced, head bowed in the chair, answered that he didn't.

Celena went to the armoire and gently went through Penelope's clothes. She caught the scent of soap Penelope washed with and felt a lump form in her throat. Celena recognized the pretty maroon traveling dress she'd seen her in that first day on the front porch, remembered how her eyes had sparkled when Ethan had introduced her as his wife.

Celena carefully pulled out a dress. She could not resist tracing her fingers against the forest green velvet of the skirt, lightly touched the four-inch petal pink sash around the waist. "Would this be all right?"

He looked up. When he'd bought the dress he remembered he'd said the pink of the sash perfectly matched the pink in her cheeks, and that she looked like a nymph form the forest when she wore it. Glancing over at her now-white face, he shuddered. "Yes, that would be fine."

It touched something deep in Ethan how strong Celena was being for him by dressing his wife for burial, the wife that had never been particularly nice to her. He wondered if Celena ever guessed why, but as he watched her dutifully putting the last touches on Penelope's clothing, he did not think so.

It was not until Celena saw the little bruised child that any outward sign of emotion crossed her face. He knew she must be thinking that the poor little creature had been mangled to death being born, torn out of its mother's womb, and how it had suffered—but he couldn't think about it. The baby hadn't cried, and therefore there was no audible sound of her pain, unlike her mother, whose sobs he feared would haunt him forever.

"My Grandfather used to say when a tiny one like this dies, they go straight to heaven," she mused, prying the little arms through the tiny burial shroud.

It occurred as he watched Celena work that even though she was small she was strong. It had not been pleasant the work on Penelope and it took a fair amount of physical strength to dress the dead. Yet Celena did it while preserving the dignity of the bodies she wrestled with.

"He says they are still connected to God. She's all right you know... your little girl is with my little girl. After all, when they leave earth this quickly they haven't had the time to do any wrong, therefore they bypass purgatory and go straight to God," she explained, tying the garment around the infant's neck and then turning the lifeless baby gently on its back, adjusted the collar neatly.

He found himself wondering what path Penelope's soul had taken to heaven, wondered if her troubled heart had found redemption immediately upon leaving her body. He tried to imagine them together, his daughter and wife flying on white angels' wings towards a bright heaven.

"Penelope's there too then...there would be no need for any stops if you will," he said, adhering to Celena's Catholic faith. He had fallen away from his own Protestant upbringing that any faith, he figured at a time like this, was better than no faith at all. "She's done her penance on earth. She was married to *me*, after all." He had not meant to make Celena feel sorry for him, and when the big blue eyes filled with compassionate tears he waved her off. "I'm neither asking for nor desiring your pity, I was merely stating a fact."

"Oh Ethan, how can you say that? She loved you, truly she did!"

"I know she did, and for that, I feel the most guilt."

"But why—why do you feel this way?" She was right in front of him, looking at him with those kind caring eyes. He could not keep the tender feelings he had for her out of his consciousness, and suddenly hated himself for it. Could not help but think of how much he loved her, even now as he stood in a room with his wife's body cold and stiff and infant daughter dressed in a burial shroud. Celena's eyes, voice, everything about her still affected him in a way that Penelope never did.

"I'm merely relieved that she doesn't hurt anymore. I had no idea childbirth was so painful for women."

She smiled a small, understanding smile.

"At least she's happy now, she can finally be happy," Ethan finished.

"Ethan she was happy with you!" Celena burst out, remembering all the times she had seen Penelope's eyes adoringly caress the face of her husband.

"No...she wasn't." He wondered suddenly how much he should tell her. It was true those that have committed crimes can't help confessing; can't help unburdening their consciences no matter how grisly the details. "I made her terribly unhappy for most of our short marriage. There was a brief period at the beginning where I think she was happy, and then, well...she said she'd had a nice summer."

There was an exceptionally long pause.

"Well, whatever you think you did, she loved you. And when you love someone, you can't help but forgive them."

He looked up at her, startled that she had keyed directly into his torment. He sighed. "It's too late now to make amends, they are both gone. And wretchedly, I am still here. Why God would take an innocent child, one who'd never even gotten to live a single day; why take Penelope, a woman whose biggest sin had merely been to love me?" He shook his head despondently. "I wish she had forgiven me. I don't know, maybe I don't deserve it, perhaps I'm unworthy of forgiveness like she said. But I wanted it from her, I *needed* to hear it. Now I'll never know." He had to look away from the caring face of the woman he was in love with. "I suppose that's to be my *torment*. My own little private hell. After all, God took *them* didn't he, he took the innocent and the good, and what he left behind...was *me*."

Ethan ordered marble tombstones for the graves of his wife and infant daughter who had, two days after their respective deaths, been buried side by side in the small Protestant cemetery of Ste. Genevieve overlooking the muddy far-off waters of the Mississippi. The marble stones would not be placed for months over the graves to allow for settling, and in the meantime he asked Victor to carve two wooden crosses to mark their graves.

On the first Victor carved *Beloved wife, Penelope Harrison Stanfield,* 1830-1858. And on the other was carved *Beloved daughter*—and below that the name of the only child Ethan would ever have, *Rebecca Prudence Stanfield.*

Chapter 39

"I don't like it," John said, resting his thin hand against his even thinner knee, watching Victor repair the wheelbarrow he brought in.

Victor nodded in agreement.

"It's one of the scariest things I've ever heard of—how many men did he end up killing?" John asked.

"I don't know but seventeen men are dead because of it." It scared Victor—the lengths that John Brown had gone to in his abolitionist zeal by seizing the federal arsenal in Virginia and trying to get the slaves to rise up at Harpers Ferry.

"Doesn't the fool realize that his going after things this way only gives the southerners more to scream about? Now you can't be an abolitionist without the southerners thinking you're a *murderer* too!" Don said, the heavy jowls of his face flushed with emotion. "Heard that they're calling all abolitionists 'Brown loving' Republicans!"

"You know what irks me the most? Is how they cloak everything with states' rights and sectionalism, when all they mean is they want no sanctions or no limits on slavery," John said and Victor nodded but he wished the discussion of states' rights, which always turned into a debate about the ills or glories of slavery had not been started again. Besides, he found it unpleasant to have these conversations with Bartholomew present.

John said, "Do you know what James told me after he purchased his first slave? Told me he didn't care what the US government said about slavery…said that states' rights were more important, and that he didn't want those wealthy politicians in the north or wherever telling him what to do with his property-mule or slave." John was quiet for a minute, listening to the noise Victor made with the hammer on the anvil.

"I tell you one thing, Buchanan has no idea what's going on. He keeps thinking the compromises will take care of it." Don stood and took the repaired adz from Bartholomew, who pretended he was not listening.

"How much?"

"Fifty," Bartholomew answered.

Paying him, Don got ready to leave. "Yes siree—I tell you if we ever get a strong president in there, there could be real trouble."

John quietly watched Victor and Bartholomew work after Don left. Remarkable how well the two of them got along. It irritated him the rumors he heard from a few in town about Victor being a *'nigger lover'* because he worked with Bartholomew, and yet others referred to him as a *vile slave holder* saying that he was talking out of both sides of his mouth by saying he was *against* slavery with two slaves in his old house.

"What am I going to do with James, Victor? What am I going to do with him?" Victor looked up from his work to see John's head bowed, his shoulders slumped. He felt badly for his father-in-law who he knew loved his son despite disagreeing with his politics.

"Don't think there is anything you can do."

John nodded in bitter agreement. "Even when they're all grown, and you shouldn't care or worry so much, still..."

Victor plunged part of the hub of the wheel for the wheelbarrow back into the fire. He couldn't help but think about Randy, Ben, Andrew and Sam and the daughter he hoped Celena was now carrying. He scolded them constantly for Randy and Ben were always getting into it—and Andrew too to his extreme disappointment was mixing it up with his brothers almost as much. It was a constant struggle to keep them safe, fed, clean and from beating on each other. He wondered sometimes why Celena hadn't lost her mind years ago! And yet it was the thought of them and what he wanted for them that kept him late at night down at the forge, made him stop by at the factory, made him stop by their rooms at night before he finally went to bed.

"You hear everything down here Victor, you hear all the news from the up north, and I know Laurence gets all the papers he can from the south...what do you think's going to happen? Because I tell you the truth even though I don't let on to Yvonne, I think there's going to be only pain and suffering come out of all this. I don't truly see how it could end up any other way."

Victor couldn't help but notice how much older John was looking lately. The lines around his eyes and mouth had deepened. Victor knew it wasn't because his life was getting any harder; if anything, it had gotten better with Laurence, James, and Will farming with him. And Yvonne still doted on him like she always had, and yet there was air of sadness around him.

"I agree. I think it will only be resolved-violently. Do you know what else worries me, we're sort of the 'buffer' between the northern and southern opinions—we're the border so to speak and divided within our own state. Rather a precarious position to be don't you think?"

John nodded again. "Well maybe it won't be happen, maybe we'll all come to some sort of agreement."

Victor said nothing knowing that neither of them believed it would work out that way.

"How's my little girl and my grandbabies?" John asked, trying to be more cheerful, changing the subject.

"Your grandbabies are fine," Victor said, grunting a bit as he worked to re-fit the rivet through the hole, "Randy lost two teeth yesterday while eating an apple and threw a fit when he when he realized he swallowed one of them, Ben fell out of the redbud tree by the back of the house and got a whopping goose egg on his head, Andrew is too scared at night to go down and use the privy and keeps missing the chamber pot—"

"Good God Victor!" John said laughing, remembering fondly when his own house had been so full of children.

"Sam is...Sam is—" This time Victor laughed, "Sam is into *everything*! Celena had me make a gate off the front porch so he wouldn't tumble headfirst down the steps."

"And my little girl?"

"Your little girl is fine, a bit cranky. I don't know if she's told anyone yet, but she's expecting again."

John nodded quietly. "Tell her I want a granddaughter this time—we have four scruffy boys now, that's enough."

Victor laughed and, finishing with the wheelbarrow, rolled it over near the door.

"She was always so pretty. The prettiest one I had," John mused, shaking his head.

Although Victor said nothing, the way John spoke about Celena embarrassed him. It was like she was dead. And she wasn't dead, she was exhausted, pale, and worn out.

"And sweet, there wasn't a sweeter child than that girl!" He looked up and forced a smile. "You tell Celena, hello from her Papa—"

"She's up at the house, I know she'd be glad to see you.

But John waved him off. "Don't want to trouble her. She's got her hands full."

Victor opened his mouth to say more, then shut it. He had the feeling

John did not want to see his little girl; she had changed so much.

In May of 1860, Celena delivered her sixth child (six because she always counted baby Anna), another boy, and was embarrassed to find out that Victor had taken bets that the latest child was to be a girl—and when Myles Gant entered the world, his father had to pay back his lost bet to half the town! Everyone laughed at the blank look on Victor's face when he related how he had begged his wife to present him with a girl.

"I don't know what I'm doing wrong!" Victor laughed while he endured the jokes of Jean, Danny, Stephan, and all Celena's brothers. They offered all sorts of advice while drinking in the living room after the birth.

Stephan was grinning at he watched his own wife Eva helping Carlene with the chores in the house.

"You're too...*male,* Victor, to have girls. I don't know how Celena puts up with you!" Carlene scoffed, getting in between the men and clearing away glasses and fussing at them to make sure and spit their chewing tobacco *into* the jar. "Don't be offended! I'm fond of you, but be happy with your boys because that's all you're going to get!" She leaned up and pecked him on the cheek.

"He is handsome isn't he?" Carlene exclaimed, inspecting the picture in the newspaper of Elmer Ellsworth the dashing colonel who had for the summer in 1860 been touring with his volunteer militia. He had awed countless crowds with the men he trained. He transformed a lackadaisical group of Chicagoans into the national-champion drill team. He modeled his unit after the exotic French Zouaves of Crimean war fame, dressing the men in baggy-trouser uniforms. He also developed his own variations of the Zouave drill, featuring hundreds of swift acrobatic maneuvers with musket and bayonet. He became a celebrity almost overnight-embodying patriotism to millions of Northerners and was the Union's most promising military talent.

"Yes, I suppose he is," Eva said, nodding.

"That's a Byronic pose if I ever saw one," Celena said with a smile, not failing to note the wave of his long hair, the hand thrust into his trouser pocket, the cape resting daringly on his shoulders. "He's not very tall though—I heard they call him '*the greatest little man!*'"

"Oh, everyone seems short to you, you're used to Victor. They say nobody can outdo his men," Carlene remarked about the famous unit.

"Let's hope so, seeing as how he wants to be the first, I've heard, to invade the south," Eva said and her smile faded a bit as she looked at the picture of the young man.

"If anyone can do it, he can," Carlene said confidently.

"How old he is?" Celena asked suddenly.

Eva scanned the article. "Twenty-four."

"He's three years younger than I am," Celena mused, shaking her head, trying to imagine how it would feel to be embarking on such a difficult quest.

Victor surprised Celena three months later by showing up at the house with a short, curvy Irish girl who was an immigrant bond servant he had employed to help her with the household chores. Embarrassed and furious, Celena could barely contain her emotions long enough to force a smile at the bewildered young girl and march back into the house, Victor hot on her heels.

"Why would you *do* such a thing?" she cried, holding baby Myles in her arms while a two-and-a-half-year-old Sam whimpered at her feet. "I can do it! I can take of the house and the boys."

"I know you can, but I feel terrible with the way you look."

She shrank back from him, a hand across her lips to muffle the little cry of humiliation.

He took a step toward her. "You know I don't *mean* it like that," he said. "What I mean is, if we have the money, which we *do*, it's foolish for me not to get some help for you." He leaned down to pick up Sam who was bewildered at his parents arguing and starting to cry.

"But I-I already have help—I have Judith doing the wash."

"I know that, but you obviously need more." He had not meant to hurt her and felt terrible when he saw a sharp look of pain slice through her tear-filled eyes.

"But *I'm* supposed to do those things, that's *my job!* I'm your *wife!* And I can do it, I *can!*" she wailed again, feeling like a failure. She had been sick again with a fever last week and had to call both Carlene and Eva to help her.

"Lena, you're tired, anyone who looked at you could see that! and it's nothing to be ashamed of. You're trying to take care of a big house and six people, five of whom are under the age of eight. I see no reason to run you ragged and into an early grave when we have more than enough money to pay for help!" He had seen it before with women in town. They could do it all right, have child after child after child every year. A lot of them simply wore themselves down to nothing, and he noticed died much sooner than their husbands, and he was *not* about to become a widower.

"I don't want any help," she said tearfully, turning her head and protectively kissed Myles' little cheek. They had so few arguments that she found herself in tears every time they did.

It had been a bad week. Andrew had been waking up two or three times a night with what Celena called 'night terrors' and the only thing that calmed him was Celena rocking him. Sam had been sick and vomited off and on for three days, and Myles still woke every two hours to nurse. Although Ben and Randy were older, they still relied on her for so many things.

"You're just plain worn out."

Irritation built up in her. "It's *your* fault then. It's your fault I'm worn out."

He stood straighter, annoyed. "It is *not*. I am the one who is trying to help you, I am the one trying to get you some much needed help—"

"It's *your* fault!"

"It is *not*! It is not my fault that you're wearing yourself down to nothing because you won't let me help you! My God Lena, you're pale as a ghost and getting thinner every year!"

"It is too!"

He threw his hands up in exasperation. "This is ridiculous! It is *not my fault*—"

"It is *too* your fault, I'm *pregnant* again!" Realizing the Irish girl had to have heard her, embarrassed, she brushed past him and ran up the stairs, a wailing Myles in her arms.

She heard muffled talking downstairs sometime later and then heard Victor's big feet coming up the stairs, he knocked once and opened the door.

She was not crying anymore, but her face was still blotchy and her eyes red as she gently rocked Myles asleep in the cradle. He closed the door quietly behind him and sat on the bed next to her. Hearing her sniff he rummaged around in his pocket and handed her a handkerchief.

"Thank you," she said, her voice muffled as she blew her nose. "Where are the babies?" They must have left—it was far too quiet downstairs.

"I took them down to Judith's. Told her I'd be back in a bit for them."

She nodded silently.

"Come here," he said and tried to hug her.

She pushed back from him. "Where's that *girl?*"

"Brigid? Well, you scared her half to death with your yelling. She's sitting on the front porch now, waiting."

"You shouldn't have done this without asking me first."

"All right, I'll give you that." He was successful then in his attempt to pull her against him. He settled her on his lap, kissing her tear-stained face. "Another one eh?" he said, his hand gentle on her middle. "Even with the nursing, huh?"

Blushing, she looked down. "Yes...I should have had my monthly by now, and I'm so tired." She leaned into him, burying her face in his neck.

"It's not that I don't think you can do everything, it's not that I don't think you're capable—"

She looked at him. "But that's what I'm supposed to do Victor. I consider it my job to take care of all of you."

He took one of her hands and kissed it. "And you do a wonderful job of it."

"So *wonderful* that you have to go get me help?"

He frowned.

"How would *you* like it if someone told you *you* needed help with your job?"

"I *do* need help with my job! Smiths don't work alone, believe it or not. I *need* Claude and Thomas. And I couldn't even *begin* to do what you do, Lena. The cooking, baking, canning, diapering, and the sewing...I'd be *bats* if I had to put up with what you put up with every day." She smiled, and he took the opportunity to kiss her forehead. "Besides...I'm selfish I suppose. I want you in the evenings. I want you to be able and sit with me and talk sometimes, and I know you can't do that when you're working your head off with the cooking and taking care of everyone. I know that you will still have plenty to do taking care of the soon to be six children. She'll only be here if you need her, give her a few nights off a week, whatever you want to do. And if you still don't like it if it doesn't work out—I'll let her go."

"But what about her, who is she, where is she from?"

"She's from Ireland." He found that it pleased him to be in a way helping someone like Jonah, who had started as a bond servant when he'd first come to America. "I expect she has family back there, but came here to make a new start."

"I can't imagine leaving my home, my family."

"I'm sure she didn't want to either, goes to show you how bleak her future looked there to leave everything and come here."

"All alone? How frightening for her! What if she came to someone who would hurt her?"

"Well then I guess she's lucky that she came to this household, because she'll have you as a mistress, and you'll not mistreat her."

"Oh, don't say that, mistress, makes me feel old and mean."

He laughed. "Anyway, she's here to help you."

"What will she do?"

He shrugged. "Whatever you want her to do. Watch the children, help you with canning, cleaning." Seeing the look of look of horror creeping back into her eyes, he quickly added, "I did tell her that you more than likely would still do the cooking." Sensing that she was still unconvinced, he went on, "When you said you'd marry me, I promised you I'd take care of you. Please let me do that. Let me take care of you."

"Only for a few years and then she'll go?"

"Like I said, if it doesn't work out, I'll let her go—tomorrow."

"But with her freedom? With something to at least get started with or at least money for the passage back home?" she asked, still caught up with admiration and the courage Brigid had to leave her entire world, gambling on the promise of America, and blind hope.

"Of course." He wondered if he should tell her that he had already told Brigid that if things worked out he would be happy to book passage for her cousin, who she had tearfully told him wanted more than anything to come to America.

"Where will she sleep?"

"I thought I'd build her a room off the kitchen, she'll be warmer there in the winter."

"Make it a nice room Victor, not too small and cramped—and a real door, she'd want some privacy—and a window. I know they are monstrously expensive, but she has to at least have a window."

In November Celena miscarried what would have been their sixth child. Although Victor knew she was saddened, privately he was relieved, not sure she would have so soon after Myles lived through another birth.

Neither of them had the luxury of time to dwell on their misfortune for a storm of controversy was raging around the country at the coming Presidential election. Everyone had heard the wild rumors, the grumbling of the south that if the 'rail splitter' won they would secede.

It wasn't until a particularly cold December afternoon when looking up Celena saw Victor walking up the drive. His head was bent, and his coat was buttoned all the way up against the cold, but there was something in his step that made a sense of gloom descend upon her.

"South Carolina has left," he said, taking off his coat and bending down to pick up Myles, who had been sitting on a pile of cozy blankets.

"Left?"

"The union, our United States, or *dis-United States*." He smiled at Sam when he felt his son's chubby little hands on his thighs.

"What does this mean?"

"Well, it certainly doesn't mean anything good."

"Can't he stop them—can't Mr. Lincoln stop it? He's the president after all?"

"His hands are tied; he can't do anything about it. Besides, he doesn't even take office for four more months, we've got ol' Buchanan to deal with till then. And you know what that means don't you? It means nothing will happen—nothing except maybe *more* states following South Carolina's lead that is."

In April of 1861 Celena listened in shock to Victor and Ethan talking about how President Lincoln had asked for 75,000 troops to dispel the "uprising" and had to stop herself more than once from breaking into their conversation and begging them both to promise her that no matter what, neither of them would join up. It still felt far away to her being in Ste. Genevieve. Although Missouri was a slave state, it had not followed her wayward sisters and departed the union as had eight others. Only last month the vote in the capital, Jefferson City, was a surprise to everyone and a supreme disappointment to southerners when not a single advocate of secession was elected, although the state remained divided on slavery. The people had spoken not so much against secession, but rather for a delay and compromise for the preservation of the Union. She hoped whatever was going to happen, it would be over quickly like Laurence and those with pro-union sentiments told her. But she was not so sure, after all these were the same men that had emphatically told her the southern states would never *actually* secede. And her faith in their optimism was dwindling.

"But why? Why would they fire on Fort Sumter, their own fort?"

Victor looked up when she interrupted. "They mean to break off from us—they consider us the enemy. They are forming a new government, the Confederate States of America."

"But wasn't President Lincoln sending provisions to the fort?"

"It doesn't make any difference what our intentions were provisions or reinforcements the south unfortunately sees it as an act of aggression. Like it or not Lena, there will be fighting."

"But that's *ridiculous*, we'd be fighting against each other!" She racked her brain to think of another solution. She adjusted Myles on her shoulder and kissed a hurt on Sam's finger.

"I heard Lincoln is declaring martial law in Maryland. He's sent troops in because the state threatened to cut off Washington from the north-he's supposed to be sending troops here too," Ethan said.

"Here, to Missouri?" Celena cut in.

Victor stared at her and sat back hard in the chair. "Why does this surprise you so much?"

She was at a loss for words suddenly, especially with the way he was staring at her. "We don't have slaves—"

"It's *beyond* that now. They've broken off, and we can't let them do it."

"But why not? If we have such terrible differences, if we simply can't agree? If they want to go, do we have the *right* to force them to stay?"

"All right Lena, suppose for a minute we did that," he began calmly, and she felt the terrible welling up of fear because she knew how strongly he felt about not breaking up the nation. "How would we separate, tell me, what would the boundaries be? The Appalachian Mountains? No, they run the wrong way. How about the Mississippi? No, it too runs the wrong way. We can't separate; we can't allow them to go. It's physically, geographically impossible. Besides that, separating would only start a whole new host of problems like the money the government owes! Do you think the confederate states of America are going to want to help the vile United States with that one? How about all the federal territories waiting to be states, who gets them, how do we decide? And the Under-ground Railroad trying to free all those supposedly *contented* southern slaves—you can bet those efforts would double up! We have to settle this problem once and for all."

"Another thing that bothers me," Ethan began, noticing how white Celena's face had gotten, "is that the European nations would be delighted if the United States were to break into two parts, it's much easier to deal with an enemy if it's half the size."

"But we're not anyone's enemy!" Celena exclaimed, thinking of the wonderful calmness and prosperity that they had enjoyed ever since she could remember, except of course with the Mexican war and a few other unpleasant things she'd rather not think about right now.

"Not at the moment but don't you think England would love to sit back and smugly watch us Yankees get our asses kicked pardon me Lena. Besides, for them it's a game of divide and conquer."

Ethan nodded. "I think that Europe identifies more readily with the south than the north anyway. The aristocracy in England has long cherished something of a fellow feeling for the aristocratic society of the south. Besides, we must face the fact that the world does not like our American democracy—probably because the system built on self-governing, is working, by the way. I think Britain and France would like nothing better than to see the breakup of the union and they want the south's long coveted independent cotton supply." He shrugged. "And perhaps they figure they can make a fortune or two selling the confederacy weapons and warships."

"They are against us too?" Celena asked, feeling vulnerable suddenly with the southern states blasting cannons at them, and Britain and France eagerly waiting for the United States to fail and opening their purse strings to reap the benefits.

"War is business," Victor said flatly, but she could see the tension building in him. She could tell he was trying not to fall too deeply into the impassioned rantings of the abolitionists, because she knew first-hand how he felt about the slaves. Felt that even when they were rightly freed, it would only be the first step down a long and problematic road. But she noticed his patience was ebbing away, and the slurs thrown at the north by the southerners no longer rolled so easily off his back. It was becoming more personal to him this secession, than she ever dreamed possible.

"You know what's especially unnerving is that right here in our own Ste. Genevieve, we have friends, neighbors who are on both sides of this problem. I can't imagine anything worse than that, can you?" Victor asked. Celena had to look down, thinking painfully of James.

"The whole thing raises some intractable, perennial questions of when, and for what cause, reasoning men should resort to force when they can no longer persuade their compatriots. Do we resort to force and thereby mark a supreme defeat in my mind, for democracy? Or simply let them be?" Ethan philosophized.

"I think we have to resort to force if we want the country to move forward, and slavery is nothing to move forward with, in fact if anything slavery is a blatant step backward. I had hoped slavery would fall off—I mean they abolished it in Washington what nearly ten years ago, and in England and other places by—"

"1830 or so I believe," Ethan offered.

Victor looked down and Celena could not see his eyes. "It's certainly not a forward way of thinking, this forced labor. I hoped they would follow a more industrial lead like what's happened here with our factory and farther north with industrialization. It's ironic that while the southern farmer tries to get more land and buys more slaves to make his life better, somebody like me is employing workers and buying equipment."

"And with the southern man's fear that someday slavery may be abolished, their rational seems to go out the window!" Ethan exclaimed. "I unfortunately entered into a conversation with southern merchant en route back to Georgia. He immediately attacked me in his defense of slavery—before I could even tell him that I indeed *owned* slaves and began emphatically to defend himself! It was pathetic almost as if he was standing in front of a judge—and as he did so, barred all intelligent opinion! what surprises me is that the southerner's refusal to recognize *anything* of merit in the case against slavery. By their insistence that slavery should be encouraged to expand into the western territories—they extol the virtues of their agrarian society. When he found out I had a factory he made sure to point out to me that the slaves have escaped the horrors of the factory system, and that the slaves were treated far better than factory workers—like your *regular* abusing of the Christi brothers!"

"I *would* abuse them, if they showed up for work more often!" Victor said with a grin, but he too had heard about the terrible conditions of the factories of the north and had heard the horrors of the textile mills in England. "Working a man to death is wrong—wherever it is. But at least the Christi brothers can leave. That's where I have the biggest problem with all of this. If we keep expanding and adding new states and we will with how land hungry we all are with all the newcomers and immigrants—the south will demand slavery in the new states."

"But it's their *right* to secede" Ethan jabbed, playing the devil's advocate. "The government has no rights to force them to stay. In fact, they liken it to our own war for independence from Britain, the American colonies led by the rebel George Washington when they seceded from the British Empire by throwing off the yoke of 'ole King George. The 'rebel' Jefferson Davis is throwing off the yoke of 'king' Abraham Lincoln and the union. Without the unions burden, the south is, I'm sure, convinced it can work out its own destiny more prosperously."

"But it's *not* like our war for independence, it's one nation. And besides our supposed enemy is after all, not across an ocean."

They were quiet for a moment.

"Did you hear what our governor Jackson did when Lincoln issued that proclamation requiring that an army of 75,000 men be raised, and that each state contribute its share?"

Victor shook his head, wondering how with all he had been reading lately he had missed it.

"He told Lincoln his requisition was illegal, unconstitutional, and revolutionary. He even was so bold as to say not a man will the state of Missouri furnish to conduct such an *unholy* crusade"

"We'll be lucky if Jefferson City doesn't fall to the confederacy when it's all said and done," Victor said, having no idea how right he was.

"*Jesus,*" Victor said, shaking his head as he read the article in the *Democrat* Laurence had brought him to read in the shop. "What a mess! I can't believe Davis was able to move all those muskets and ammunition to Camp Jackson without anybody knowing." It was ingenious he had to admit how Jefferson Davis had secretly moved heavy artillery on a steamship up to St. Louis in boxes cleverly labeled 'marble.'

"Where's Camp Jackson Papa?" Randy asked, sitting on a stool, not liking the worried look on his father's face.

"St. Louis," Victor answered without looking at his son. "It's a training camp for the militia on the outskirts of town."

"You know what Davis and Governor Jackson were after though don't you? Not merely Camp Jackson but the armory," Laurence said.

"How much was in it?"

"What's an armory, Papa?" Randy interrupted worriedly.

"Where they store muskets and ammunition," Victor answered.

"I heard there were 60,000 Springfield and Enfield rifles, something like 500,000 cartridges and at least 90,000 pounds of powder. The prize if they had pulled it off."

"Jesus," Victor said again, still thinking it was a wonder Missouri hadn't seceded since the men with power had southern allegiances.

"I read in the paper the common expression around the campfire was 'that if the United States Regulars attack the camp, no one would lift a finger of resistance, but if the Illinois, Iowa, or *German* troops made the attack, they'd be more than ready to fight."

Shocked, Randy turned his face to his father. He loved his grandfather and couldn't understand why someone would be willing to fight simply because he was German.

"Sounds like it got out of hand. It's stupid, guess we'll never know whose fault it was; Frosts or Lyons," Victor said, refolding the newspaper and handing it back to Laurence.

"What got out of hand Papa?"

Victor sighed. "General Lyon commanded General Frost to...leave the camp, surrender. And they do, but then they're all standing around waiting because nobody knew where to take them, when the crowd of people who had come up to gawk start—" He was embarrassed suddenly to admit something so childish to his son. "Start throwing clumps of dirt at the Union soldiers. They shouted, 'hurrah for Jeff Davis.'" He left out the other epithet 'Damn the Dutch' knowing it would confuse and hurt Randy to know how the Germans were disliked. "Somebody fired and then... more people fired."

"Did anyone die?" Randy asked, his eyes wide.

Victor nodded. "Twenty-eight, and a lot more hurt."

"But I don't understand. Why is anyone asking anyone to go, why did General Frost have to surrender?"

"Because General Frost was sympathetic to the southern cause," Laurence answered, putting a comforting hand on his nephew's shoulder. "He even told General Lyon that he considered the orders he was given illegal. He said he couldn't understand how Lyon could justify attacking citizens of the United States who were only lawfully performing duties involving the militia of the State."

"Is that what they were doing Papa? Or were they doing something wrong?"

"Not in their minds," Victor answered.

"The paper says St. Louis was panicked that night. Tons of people left town, and those that stayed locked their doors and shuttered their windows fearing a riot was going to break out."

"Did one?" Randy asked.

Laurence tried to smile at his nephew. "No, thank God. It's a shame," he said, shaking his head, "taking over Camp Jackson I'm sure was meant to crush out all those secessionists in the state."

"You mean all *ten* of them?" Victor joked, remembering that in February a vote of secession had been submitted to the people of Missouri and that it had been declared *against* by a majority of 80,000 votes. Apart from Governor Jackson and a handful of followers, Missourians wanted to stay in the Union, wanting no part in this 'civil war' already underway in other states.

"But it seems to have had...rather the opposite effect," Laurence said, knowing that men who had remained loyal to the union before the Camp Jackson fiasco found themselves now driven toward secession. Still others like himself, were inclined to protect the Union and as trite as it sounded, fight slavery at all costs.

News of the capture of Camp Jackson was telegraphed to Jefferson City while the legislature was in session and caused a panic. *"Captains Blair and Lyon and the Dutch have seized camp Jackson!"* A military bill conscripting all able-bodied men into the state militia that couldn't get a vote earlier was passed within minutes.

"But don't they just want..." Randy paused a minute, trying to remember the real reason these men were always arguing. "States' rights? Uncle James says states' rights should come first, and that if a state doesn't want to stay in the Union, it shouldn't be forced to by a President they didn't vote for."

"States' rights. That's what he says this is all about doesn't he?"

"Aren't states' rights good? Uncle James says they are?" Randy asked gently, knowing that his father and his uncle didn't always agree.

Victor nodded. "States' rights *are* good. But that's not what everyone is really arguing about. They prefer to call it that because no one wants to admit they are *for* slavery. You call it whatever you want, but it doesn't change what it is..."

In the last half of May 1861, Virginia officially seceded from the union and the newspapers were full of how Federal troops had been ordered to cross the Potomac and seize critical points on the Virginia side. The dashing Colonel Ellsworth had wrangled a choice objective for his Fire Zouaves at the port of Alexandria. He was dressed for the assault in a resplendent new uniform and pinned to his chest a gold medal that was inscribed in Latin, *Not for ourselves alone, but for country.*

Ellsworth and his men encountered no resistance when their steamer came ashore in Alexandria, and he dispatched one group of men to take the railroad station while he and a small detachment set off to capture the telegraph office. As they made their way up the road the diminutive Colonel noticed a Confederate flag waving from the Marshall House Inn, and wanted it taken down immediately. Stationing guards below, he dashed upstairs with four men and after cutting down the flag started back down the stairs, where the innkeeper James Jackson stood waiting with a double-barreled shotgun. Brownell one of Ellsworth's men instinctively batted the shotgun with the barrel of his musket, but the innkeeper fired, and Ellsworth was hit. Ellsworth's men turned to see their heroic leader laying in a heap on the floor his blood staining the Confederate flag. His gold medal driven into his chest by the shotgun blast.

Ellsworth's death plunged the north into mourning, bells tolled, and flags flew at half-mast. It was said that President Lincoln was grief-stricken when he saw the body of his young friend and ordered an honor guard to bring the body to the White House where there was a funeral attended by Cabinet members and high military officers. The casket then moved to City Hall in New York where thousands filed by to pay their last respects. And his death caused various emotions in the north-sermons, editorials, songs, and poems lamented his loss, and from the union's grief sprang new enthusiasm '*Remember Ellsworth!*' became a popular slogan. Enlistments in the army soared.

Celena and Victor had been surprised by the mixed emotions in the town; most people they knew felt it was a tragedy, but some like Alvin Woolrich said, "*Served the scoundrels right!*" and James had, much to his parents and family's displeasure, more than once, loudly proclaimed that Jackson was shamelessly "Killed in the defense of his home and private rights—it's *he* that's the hero!" James said to anyone who would listen to him, and not above arguing hotly with those who did not agree with him.

Jackson became a hero to the south as Ellsworth did to the north and as one northern newspaper thundered: *We needed just such a sacrifice— let the war go on!*

And it did.

Chapter 40

Will was beating on the door so fiercely, Celena barely had time to pick up Myles and run to it, fearing he would break it down with his bare hands.

"It's Pa," he said, swallowing hard. "Maman needs you to come to the house right now...can Brigid watch the babies?" She was shocked to see him choking back tears and shushed Sam, who, keying in on the tension, was tugging on her skirts wanting to know what was wrong.

"What's happened?" she asked, her heart in the throat as she handed a wailing Myles to Brigid as Will pulled her out of the house.

"James is gone, he left this morning."

"*Gone,* where did he go?" She had trouble finding the buggy's step in her haste and fell off, painfully scraping her calf.

"Gone to join up with a confederate regiment in Arkansas. Pa was so shocked when he read James' note, that he started shaking something terrible after he read it. Then he got real red in the face, and it looked like he couldn't breathe, almost like he was choking. He fell to the ground before I could get him, he was making *awful* noises, I never heard anyone make sounds like that—" Will looked down as they started off in the wagon, "Pa's dead, Celena."

A horribly cold wind passed over her, and she knew with an agonizing pain inside that Victor was right. The war was not going to be a skirmish-fought deep in the south or some other remote place, far removed from her and those she loved. It was to be right next to her, right beneath her. And that her father had become a casualty of this civil war.

Yvonne closed the door after having said goodbye to the friends that had come over for her John's funeral, and although she was doing her best to keep up a front, the sudden departure of her son and death of her husband had severely rocked her, and her depression was deepening every day. She was functioning normally, still doing the chores and had attended the funeral with dignity and composure, but the brightness had gone out of her blue eyes. A part of her soul had been buried when John Riefler had been laid to rest, and Celena was afraid that nothing would ever make up for it. She kept hearing the words her mother had whispered to her when she looked at her husband's grave, the grave of the man she had been married to for almost thirty-five years.

"I had a lifetime with him Celena, and it still it wasn't enough."

It was unusually quiet in the house considering so many of her children and grandchildren were still there. The dismal meal they were all vainly trying to enjoy had been interrupted by the wild-eyed Alice. She was tormented by James' leaving and had already started three arguments with a distraught Laurence before she got the desired rise out of him.

"Alice please! I've said no such thing!"

"You did too, James told me! He said you said you were saying our governor was a traitor!"

"No, you've misunderstood me. I was quoting from the paper which I regularly do. It *enlightens* the mind to read." But the subtlety was lost on her. "It does not necessarily mean that I *agree* with what I've read."

"We *are* a slave state after all, and I don't know why all of you don't accept it. It won't stay a border state like Maryland and—and—" She sputtered angrily, hating herself for not having listened more closely to all the things James had told her.

"Delaware and Kentucky," Laurence added, but it only further enraged her because she feared he knew more about it than she did and was better prepared to argue.

"And what did that nasty splitter say, something about *God* only being on their side?"

Again, Laurence fought for control. "No, Alice, what President Lincoln reportedly said is that he *hoped* to have God on his side during this conflict, but that he *must* have *Kentucky!*"

Confused and embarrassed now about how many states had seceded and when, and why this was significant, she trudged on. "Why, why must he have Kentucky?"

"Because I am sure you will be happy to know the Union is now, being precariously held together by a thread. If Missouri or Kentucky or one of the other teetering states fall it will be enough to tip the scales and mark a defeat for the north and no doubt the confederacy will succeed in destroying the union. As it is Claiborne Jackson our *own* governor, nonetheless, has made off into the night with the state's records and seal. God only knows what will happen to this state now since we have some sort of ridiculous government in exile, linked no doubt to the confederacy!"

"You think James is wrong, don't you?" she burst out.

Celena immediately felt sorry for her. It was obvious she felt as though she was in the house of her darkest enemies, instead of in a room with her husband's family all of whom she had known her entire life.

"You hate that he's gone off to fight."

"Yes, I do," he answered evenly, amazingly in control Celena thought despite the way Alice was snipping at him. "I hope he comes back to his senses—and comes home safely."

"Comes to his *senses*, isn't that an arrogant attitude! I suppose you think he's wrong, I suppose you think all those—those southern states are wrong!" When Laurence said nothing, she attacked again. "What makes *you* so right? What makes you think you have the truth, what makes you think *you* know more than anyone else?"

"I may not be *right* Alice, but it's called an opinion. Taking ideas, sifting through the facts and fables, and coming to, if possible a well thought out decision. Not merely following a rebel yell toward a war which will no doubt be bloody and painful for all those involved."

"You're just a *coward*, you're afraid to fight! It's true what James says all the Yankees and free soilers are afraid, when push to comes to shove none of you will have the guts to do anything to defend your *precious* Union! None of you will have the guts to do what James' has done!"

The hair went up on the back of Celena's neck, and even though Laurence did not change outwardly, she did notice a flicker of something like anger mingled with pride in the depths of his eyes.

"Alice please, I know you're upset about everything, but truly we're all family and we're as worried about James as you are," Celena began, but Alice angrily cut her off.

"Oh, don't you start now too Celena! I suppose you're going to start about the vile southerner who only wants states' rights! What would you know anyway, you've no sense for what is right in the world, you who married a man who isn't even *white*! You who married a *dirty Indian!*"

"*Alice!*" Celena exclaimed, thinking she must be hearing things. After all, Victor, who the town still joked was responsible for not letting Alice and James' entire barn fall down that day!

Celena turned to Victor for support, but he had gotten up quietly and simply walked out.

"Victor," Celena said later, finding him in the barn with his suit coat off and shirt sleeves rolled up. He had the top of the reaper up and was oiling it. She smiled thinking that Bartholomew was right, he never could leave well enough alone.

When he turned and looked at her the tears she had been pushing back all day could no longer be repressed. Lying against him she began to cry. "I'm so sorry. I don't know why Alice would say such a terrible thing."

He kissed the top of her head. "She's upset that's for sure."

She turned her face to him. "What do you think is going to happen? what's going to happen to James? Why would he do this?" she wailed and buried her face against the warmth of his chest. It was bad enough to be struggling with the grief at losing her father only to have the pain compounded with worry about James and now an ugly family argument.

"He's doing what he thinks is right. Hopefully, he'll make it back."

"Laurence thinks it's going to be a long-bitter thing, but then Will thinks we'll have it all tied up in month—what do you think?"

He hated to see the fear and worry in her eyes but respected her too much to lie. "How long have Laurence and James been having this exact same argument now?"

She had to swallow hard. "Almost as long as I can remember..."

"And in all that time, no matter who's right or who's wrong have you ever seen either one of them give in or give up without a fight?"

"No," she sniffed.

"You have your answer then."

Summer of 1861, Laurence was among the first to join the fight for the Union, and it shocked everyone. Laurence who was always calm and even tempered, who had held on longer than anyone else to the beliefs that it would be resolved peacefully, who always said that fighting was the most barbaric way to solve anything.

Half the town turned out to watch the would-be soldiers getting on the steamship to take them up to St. Louis to join their regiment, and the giddy hysteria that was in the air Celena privately thought was, heart wrenching. The newspapers talked of the embarrassing Union defeats-of the confederacy with its skilled officers trouncing on the young untrained troops who had last week been farm boys and factory workers. The word *casualty* chilled her. It was such a nice, antiseptic word, a word by its sound, seemed to deny its meaning. But it was clear to her, clearer she thought than it was to half the wild-eyed women who were waving the stars and stripes crazily over their heads. Because it meant somewhere, for some mother, father, or wife, that someone was not coming home. And it made no difference to her on what side she heard these casualties, because they evoked in her the same heart constricting feelings, the same breathless sadness to know that somewhere a man had fallen and for those left waiting for him, he was never coming home.

Celena was glad she had deviated so from her personality and openly, hotly, violently argued with Victor the week before, begging him not to join up. It had started out calm enough, but because she was frantic to extract a promise, it had escalated into a bitter argument. In fact, all other arguments that they had during their twelve years of marriage paled compared to this one. She had shamelessly been reduced to using every deceitful tactic she could think of—from shouting at him that he did not love Margaret enough to stay—after all with Henry's illness she needed Victor more and more, that he did not love *her* enough to stay, which she had felt ridiculous even at the time saying—she had even gone so far as to accuse him of not loving his *children* enough.

She had been afraid at that last when his gray eyes had blazed down at her. Had never been more acutely aware in her entire life how strong he was-especially when his big hands had slammed the small chair so forcefully against the floor, he had splintered one of the legs. For the first time in her life, he would not touch her when she reached for him-would not allow her to put her arms around him when apologizing; she had begged him to take her into his arms.

She knew he had been angry with her, and part of her did feel guilty for behaving so crazy. But the thought of James and Laurence becoming one of those "casualties" was almost too painful to contemplate—but if *Victor* were to become one, she was not sure she would survive.

By late July 1861, the disastrous stories of the Union defeat at Bull Run began wilding circulating around Ste. Genevieve, and scores of men began joining up. The numbers themselves were shocking-at last count nearly five hundred were dead, over a thousand wounded, and nearly the equivalent of two regiments were missing and presumed captured or killed, raising the total to more than 3,000.

"And that was only...one day," Celena said, her voice resonating with shock when Ethan showed her the newspaper. "It's not going to be over quickly, is it?"

He shook his head, looking down at her. "No. Did you hear the confederates are referring to their General Jackson as 'Stonewall' because he repelled the Federal assault so valiantly? They say his men adore him and vow to *'meet death for his sake and bless him when dying.'*"

Celena shook her head, thinking it was dangerous to have such a hold on people, to have their leaders raised up to godlike status.

"Do you hear anything from your brother James?" Ethan asked folding the newspaper, trying to blot out the disturbing report.

She glanced out over the river, noting that with the cloud cover the water looked very dark. She swallowed hard. "He doesn't write to us, but yes, Alice has received a few letters from him." She paused, shifting a sleeping, sweating Myles in her arms. "He's a corporal now—and she's so proud of him." Ethan saw a glint of tears in her eyes.

"And Laurence, have you heard from him?"

"Yes. He has written to all of us. Mostly about the boredom and monotony of army life with the constant drilling and marching, about the terrible food." She did not feel at liberty to reveal the desperate anticipation she gleaned from his letter, the sense that if was almost as if he was holding his breath—waiting. "He's with the army of the Tennessee. Lord, I wish he was home," she said and surprised him by laying her cheek for a moment against his chest.

He felt a painful little burst of joy at being able to touch her, even if Victor's sleeping child was in between them.

"I'm sorry I'm behaving this way. I'm just tired."

To Ethan's regret, she straightened and moved away from him.

After Bull Run Celena was reluctant to read the papers—they were always full of bad news, more defeats, more casualties. And every day it seemed she heard a story of someone else leaving.

The four Christi brothers had walked into the factory one morning, informed Victor they were going to fight for the Union and had simply walked out! Claude and Thomas had shocked their mother and amidst bitter arguments said they were *'joinin' the confederacy to fight the Yanks!'* Victor had in the span of one week lost all his employees, leaving only he and Bartholomew left to run the blacksmith shop, the sawmill and factory.

Unlike Celena, Victor could not stay away from the papers, devouring all the news, and shared it with her. All the battles concerned her but the ones closer to home, like Wilson's Creek were especially alarming to her because even though it was west of Ste. Genevieve and two-hundred miles away it still happened in Missouri.

It had been a victory for the Confederacy. The Union was exhausted, low on ammunition their general dead, and they retreated to Springfield and then to Rolla. When the battle of Wilson's Creek, the first battle west of the Mississippi was over, nearly 2,500 men would be dead. And the ground the Federals had charged up and the confederacy had held, would be ominously dubbed "Bloody Hill." General Lyons of the Camp Jackson incident would have the distinction of being the first US General to die during combat, but unfortunately not the last.

"In a six-hour battle," Victor began, doing the numbers grimly in his head, "that comes to approximately seven men dying per minute..."

Chapter 41

1862

In the turbulent year that followed, Celena had another baby, a boy they named Luke, and with all the Union defeats she was terrified that one of these months Victor would tell her he had enlisted. He was a bit past the median age of conscription at thirty-four, and she desperately hoped it would all end before she could no longer keep him from leaving.

"Lena," Victor said as she nursed Luke by the fire on a surprisingly chilly April night. "Did you see the paper? There's been another battle fought."

"Was it like Bull Run?"

"Well...in a way yes, except we won this one, if you can call it *winning* when you have almost 13,000 casualties."

She was silent as tears pricked her eyes at the thought of so many men dead or wounded before their time.

"And those numbers are for our side. The final toll is something like 22,000 dead and something like 20,000 injured. Lena," he began, wanting to break it to her gently, "it was a battle down in Tennessee near a town called Pittsburgh landing, but they are also calling it Shiloh because it was fought by a little church by that name—"

"Was the army of the Tennessee in it?" The tears that had been welled up in her eyes spilled out when he nodded. He came to her and held her, and she wondered desperately what happened to Laurence on that Sunday morning in April near a church that ironically in Hebrew meant *place of peace.*

By September 1862, the rest of the country read in shock the reports of latest horror, Antietam. The quiet creek near Sharpsburg Maryland became the battleground where General Lee commanding the Army of Northern Virginia, met US General McClellan. In a series of charges and counter charges both armies poured men into what at first appeared to be a futile battle, with neither side being able to win a decisive victory. For hours and hours thousands of men crossed through the East woods and West woods—a thirty-acre cornfield in between, firing and shelling.

On the night of September 18 when General Lee led his army back at night across the Potomac and into Virginia, he left behind him a battlefield which would become unique in American history. For on no other field, in no other one-day battle would so many men be killed. Some 12,000 Federals and 10,000 Confederates fell dead or wounded. And a well-used farm lane, so worn down over the years by travel and erosion known as Sunken Road-was ominously dubbed 'blood lane' after Antietam.

Antietam would prove to be a turning point in the war, because even though McClellan had been too cautious to pursue Lee, still it served to forever thwart Lee's attempts to invade the north—and his hopes of finally winning a decisive battle on northern soil in 1862.

The Union armies' ability to survive the battle was enough for President Lincoln on January 1, 1863, to issue his legendary Emancipation Proclamation. What before Antietam had been a war waged only for the Union-now became a war against slavery as well. And this proclamation against slavery, forever doomed the South's feeble hope for foreign intervention, and forever melded the ideas of the union and freedom.

1863

"I don't have any choice," Victor said, his arms crossed in front of him as he and Celena sat quietly in their living room on a bitterly, cold February night. The boys keying in on the tension surrounding their parents were silent. Randy and Ben, eleven and ten, played chess, but they did not annoy each other like they normally did. Instead, their eyes were glued to the board as they listened unhappily to their parents' conversation. Eight-year-old Andrew was working with his letters on a small chalkboard and intermittently helped six-year-old Sam on his own chalkboard. Even Myles who was only three and a half seemed to know that the hushed tones with which his parents spoke meant something was wrong and was content to lay in Brigid's arms his thumb stuck firmly in his pink mouth. Little Luke was asleep covered up by a blanket in a cradle by Celena's feet.

"Not anymore. I have to go," he said quietly and glanced into the fire. But staring at the fire he could only see Laurence, and how he looked these days when he saw him after church. Although Laurence seemed happy to be back home and was doing his best to act like nothing had happened as he awkwardly got out of the carriage. Tried not to notice how both his boys didn't seem to look anywhere but at the ground. How his twelve-year-old daughter Estella simply would not let go of her father's hand, and because he needed his hands to walk with his crutches since his right leg was amputated at the knee, instead hung on to the sleeve of his coat, following him every step he clumsily took.

And he'd read in the paper about Stones River fighting in Murfreesboro, Tennessee. The casualties were high, 23,000 men and it only served to solidify Victor's commitment to end the war. Besides a confederate soldier was quoted in the paper as saying the *"Yankees can't whip us, and we can never whip them, and I see no prospect of peace unless the Yankees themselves rebel and throw down their arms and refuse to fight any longer."*

"How soon before you leave?" Celena asked so softly that at first he was not sure he heard her. Then he felt a jolt of love for her when he watched her calmly darning one of the boy's socks, and he knew that as much as she did not want him to leave, she understood that he had to.

"The twenty-seventh."

She stopped darning briefly and caught her breath—she would have two weeks with him.

"Ethan and I are leaving together."

"You're going to war, Papa?" Ben asked, looking up from his chess game. "But why?" He dropped his head, his big eyes beginning to tear.

"He has to Ben; he has to go fight in the war. To try and keep the states together right Papa?" Randy said, looking the father he idolized.

"But I heard it's to free the slaves, but we don't have any slaves cept Bartholomew and he only works for you right Papa? And Brigid you're not a slave and you're only staying here 'til you save enough money and can bring your cousin from Ireland," Ben argued. Begrudgingly Brigid smiled, but she was too upset at the prospect of the man she admired leaving and merely looked back down, tightening her arms around Myles.

"That's all true—but I still have to go."

"What if you get hurt like Uncle Laurence, I don't want you to get hurt Papa!" Ben said and tears gently rolled down his plump cheeks—which would have normally given Randy a wonderful opportunity to tease him. Although Randy was still dry eyed, he too was looking pleadingly at his father.

"I'll try not to get hurt," was all Victor could think to say, not wanting to start making promises to his boys that he couldn't keep.

"Don't go Papa," Sam piped up and left his chalkboard and began to tug at his father's sleeve. Victor hoisted him into his arms.

"I don't want you to go anywhere. I want you to stay here with Maman and all of us," Sam said simply, and possessively laid his head against his father's big shoulder trying to wrap his small arms which would not meet around Victor's back.

"I don't want to go either; I don't want to leave you," he said emphatically, looking at each of his children and at Celena, "any of you."

Ben had his arms around Victor's waist now, and Randy joined his brothers against their father, nearly knocking Andrew out of the way to get a coveted place to lay his head against him.

"Papa!" Myles said suddenly pulling his thumb out of his mouth with a little noise. Even though he did not understand why all his brothers were leaning against his father, only knew that he wanted to be there too. Brigid let go of him and he ran over to Victor, pushing Ben out of the way and Victor lifted him up too while still holding Sam, and couldn't help but laugh while holding the two youngest, as the older three all clamored around him, jockeying for the best position.

"Would you have ever thought there wouldn't be enough of *me* to go around?" Victor said with a laugh to Celena as he calmed down a squabble which erupted between Randy and Ben both wanting to lay their head against him in the same place.

Celena smiled, thinking they made a sweet picture together, and found herself trying to sear the vision into her memory. Then shook herself violently, trying to banish the horrifying thought that she would need to.

Ethan looked up and saw Celena standing in front of him. When she reached out and touched him gently on the sleeve, he dropped the pen he had been writing with and came up from behind his desk at the bank.

"Can I speak with you for a moment in private?"

"Of course." He led her to the small office in the back.

"I know you and Victor will be leaving next week—and I have a favor to ask of you." She paused for a moment, looking at her hands and twisted the iron wedding ring. He knew Victor had bought her a gold one ages ago, and how Victor teased that it was a waste of good money because she had never once worn it.

"I don't know what to do. I'm packing more socks for Victor. Laurence said when his wore out he never got more." She closed her eyes, painfully thinking that Laurence would only need one sock from now on. "I know you don't have anyone looking after you. I feel so foolish Ethan, I feel like I should be doing something to help you and Victor, but I don't know what to do."

"You're doing enough, you care that we're going."

A desperate sob escaped her lips, and he came closer to her and to his delight she laid herself against him. "Have you got everything worked out?" she asked weakly.

He nodded. "I think so. Tillman and the rest ran off I think the day South Carolina seceded, but Patsy, Rosa and Ephram have decided to stay and take care of the house for me but I'm paying them now. Rosa was quick to inform me she is no longer a slave. They are going to live in the house. And I've seen Mason and he's written a will in case anything happens to me, which if it does by the way, will make *you* a very *rich* woman."

"If anything happens to either of you—" She broke off with a sob and he pulled her against him again.

"It will be all right," he whispered, closing his eyes and holding her so close he could feel the swell of her breasts against him.

"I'm so afraid! If anything...happens to him—"

"It won't, he's a strong and he's big," he soothed.

"But I'm afraid being *big* will only make him a larger target."

He laughed grimly. "Well, I'll tell him to keep his fool head down."

She pulled back from him. "You will? You'll...look after him a bit? I feel silly asking anyone to look after him, he's so capable and smart. But he's been everything to me for so long that I don't know what I'd *do* without him. Everything I have is tied up in him, and the boys. I don't know what the boys would do without him. And he' such a good father, and they so look up to him. Without him I don't know if I could go on. Ethan, please make sure he comes back to me...*promise* me!"

"I promise," Ethan whispered and closed his eyes tight as she hugged him, weeping quietly. He would gladly watch over Victor and sacrifice his own life if need be. After all, there weren't six children waiting at home for him, there was no woman trembling and in tears at the thought of him leaving. Although he did not consciously hope for his own death, it would be, he thought, a fitting way to die. A glorious way out of a rather disappointing life. Besides maybe it was what he deserved, to die on the battlefield after having hurt Penelope so much. He found himself trying to imagine Penelope tearfully saying to goodbye to him, but it was difficult to envision her weeping for him or feeling anything except, disappointment.

Victor left a bewildered Bartholomew in charge of everything. The sawmill Victor had re-staffed with four boys Celena thought that barely looked older than Randy. The factory after the Christi brothers had walked out he had to simply close and lock up. Besides the railroads were busy fighting the war these days and changing over their link and pin system was the last thing on their minds. As far as the blacksmith shop went Bartholomew knew what to do but still, he nervously followed Victor around the shop the morning after a hellacious storm knocked down the old sign.

"Wat do ah do wif da sign?" Bartholomew asked, bent as he watched Victor retrieve the splintered sign from the frozen mud. "Ah cain fix it," he said, noticing the fondness that was on Victor's face as he looked at it. But as he reached out to take it from him, Victor straightened and shook his head.

"No, it's past repair," Victor said. "I'll keep it. I was hoping I could ask you a favor while I'm gone."

"Wat you won me ta do?"

"Help Celena if she needs it, check in on her from time to time. Sometimes she's stubborn and won't ask for help. Keep an eye on my boys for me. They can be a handful and I don't want them getting into trouble while I'm gone. I've done my best to put the fear of God in them while I'm gone, but they are *my* sons after all and...well, they might need reminding." They grinned at each other, and Victor unfolded a piece of paper and awkwardly handed it to him.

"Ah cain't read—"

"I know, but Judith can. It's the deed to the shop."

There was a long pause.

"I've been trying to give it to you for years." Bartholomew did not reach out his hand to take it. "And you'll find a rather tidy sum in Ethan's bank under your name," he said, almost afraid to tell him the 'wages' he had taken from his own time down at the shop he had instead saved in the bank for Bartholomew since Bartholomew had refused to take any more money from him. "It's only under your first name because I didn't know your last name—"

"Doan hab one."

"That's why it's only under Bartholomew." He grinned.

There was an uncomfortable silence.

"It be too much," Bartholomew said.

"It's not. In fact, it's the least I can do, after what you've...been through. Like I told you before my mother—" Even twenty-five years after her death there was still a roughness in his voice when he mentioned her. "My mother had very few chances shall we say—few opportunities for her life to go differently—and God knows where I would have ended up if it hadn't been for the kindness of Jonah Schaeffer." He couldn't help it and glanced down at the sign again, and then back up at the empty brackets. "He helped me at a time when I desperately needed it. Wouldn't the country and the world for that matter be a lot better if we all simply did that, simply helped each other out a bit when we needed it?"

There was another silence.

"But wat do ah owe ya fer it?"

Victor shook his head. "Nothing."

"You cain be givin me aw dat!"

"Why not?" Victor saw the turmoil rising in the big chest. "I don't need the money," he offered, trying to appease Bartholomew's pride. "I have been...*unbelievably* fortunate in my life," he said, thinking not only of the wonderful successes with the carriage factory and coupler, but of his boys and Celena.

"But wair yur boys goina work wen de grow up ifn ya gimme da shop?" Bartholomew argued. Although he would love nothing better than to have the shop be his own, it was an awfully large gift, and he thought Victor was letting his excitement and about leaving go to his head. The anvil and tools alone would, Bartholomew knew, take years to save for, to say nothing of the shop, and house.

Victor shrugged but couldn't keep the prideful smile from crossing his face when he thought of someday Randy, Ben or one of the others taking over the factory. "I have the sawmill—and the factory and two businesses in Washington, there will be plenty of places for them to work. Or who knows, maybe they'll go to college."

Bartholomew looked up straightening his big shoulders, but then looked back down at the frozen ground when he felt his emotions rising.

"Folks still be needin a sign ta fine da place—wats yah want me ta make it say?" he asked, thinking he would have to ask his smart wife how to spell Gant and blacksmith *before* he started carving.

Victor shrugged. "I suppose *Bartholomew's* would work well."

It was a cold, gray February morning that the latest batch of enlistees were to leave Ste. Genevieve. No clouds broke up the horizon, instead a bleak monotonous gray hung above them as the men stood waiting with their families at the banks of the frosty Mississippi to board the steamer that would take them up to St. Louis.

Sam had woken up with a bad cold and Celena had already wiped his nose ten times since they had left the house. "Better?" she asked, holding a sleeping Luke, forcing a weak smile down to her son. He tried to smile back but couldn't. In fact, none of the boys—apart from Myles who was too little to know better—were smiling.

Randy ambled over to his mother, head bent and hands thrust deep into his pockets, staring despondently at the snow beneath his feet that the traffic at the shore had turned a dirty gray. Nearing her, Ben slid under one of her arms as they watched Victor talking with Mason and Stephan who had, to both Carlene and Eva's displeasure, opted to leave with Victor and Ethan and the others.

She went over in her mind everything she had packed for Victor in the tiny case—three sandwiches, a coat, three pairs of socks, another shirt, a knife—she'd even smuggled a bottle of whiskey, having heard it was good for wounds. Shuddering, she pushed the thoughts from her mind.

She smiled seeing the glint of silver threading through his hair, and how he laughed when she teased him about it. He had said that living in a house with *six wild little boys,* was turning his hair prematurely gray! She told him then that it was not *premature* since he was already thirty-four. He had merely laughed and told her that her hair would be gray too one day when they were both sitting in rockers on the front porch. A hitch caught in her heart, and she had to rid herself of the image of her, *alone* on that porch.

"He's bigger than everyone else Maman, do you think I'll get that tall?" Randy asked hopefully as he looked at his father who because of the new boots stood at 6'7" and was more than a foot taller than the rest of the men. She looked back at her son who was already four inches taller than she was and smiled.

"Yes. I think you'll be like him." She gently touched her son's chest and noticed with a surge of motherly warmth that he blushed at the compliment. He adored his father and hung on every word Victor said. Even at eleven, Randy still ran to the door when his father came home.

"Morning Celena."

Turning, Celena saw Margaret forcing a smile. Letting go of Randy and Ben, she gathered her into her arms, careful not to wake Luke.

"I can't believe he's going," Margaret whispered and Celena heard the anguish in her voice though she was doing her best to hide it. Pulling from Celena, she hurriedly wiped the tears out of her eyes. "He'll be mad at me if he knows I've been crying."

Celena nodded, understanding. "You packed him food too?" she asked, noticing that Margaret had a basket slung over her arm, and despite everything the two of them laughed.

"I figured you would—but I brought something anyway. Think Ethan could use it?" Margaret asked.

"Yes, I'm sure he could." It was sweet that even with as long as she had been taking care of Victor, Margaret still retained some small possession of him. She watched Margaret approach Victor, how she touched his sleeve. Watched Victor's face soften, and then laughingly he opened the basket and happily took out a bit of bread and stuffed it into his mouth.

Margaret's black hair was starting to silver too, and she was much too thin and the lines around her tired eyes unfortunately made her look older than she was. She had been pretty, but it was rapidly fading, and Celena couldn't help but worry about her. Worried what she and Henry would do now that Victor was leaving.

"How's your Pa?" Celena asked, smiling at Hank.

His head was hanging, his shoulders slumped, he held his hat nervously in his hands. He was gawky, so tall and thin, and it was shame Celena thought, that although he had inherited his stature from his mother's side, he had inherited little else of her good looks. He had a sad look about him, like all the Wilburns did with their bland eyes and dull brown hair. Celena found herself wondering if it wasn't because by and large their lives *were* sad that they always looked that way.

Hank shrugged, wondering if he should merely smile and say 'fine' like his mother always told him to when people asked the dreaded question-but this was family, his *Uncle Victor's wife.* And he was as upset about

Victor leaving as much as he would have been had it been his own father.

"He couldn't get up today," Hank said and then looked at the ground. "Nor yesterday...I don't understand. Some days he can work and he's almost like he used to be and then the next day he's using the cane to walk, and then the next he can't even get out of bed...Ma had me carry him to the privy this morning—he can't even do *that* alone anymore!"

"I'm so sorry Hank."

He nodded, a bit embarrassed he had divulged so much, but felt better having said it, especially when he saw only understanding and warmth in his aunt's eyes. He glanced up at his mother and uncle and wondered how he was going to keep everything going on the farm with his father so often laid up, especially since he would not have Victor to help and advise him. Even though he loved his father, because he was sick and often in an ill temper, Hank transferred a lot of his love and affection onto Victor. He liked his uncle. They laughed at the same things and Victor had more patience with him than his father did.

"Wish I could go with him," Hank said, eyes on the man he so admired.

Celena's eyes flew open wide with horror, thinking that at thirteen he was far too young to even contemplate such a thing. "I feel bad no Wilburns are going to help," Hank said and lowered his head to absentmindedly kick a stone with the toe of his worn boots.

"Oh Hank," Celena sighed and then swallowed hard. "That's not true—your uncles Claude, Thomas, and Isaac have gone—"

"Yeah, but they're on the *wrong* side—things haven't been the same since they left."

Celena shook her head knowing that it was true. Things hadn't been the same in her family either since James left to fight for the Confederacy. Alice was still vehemently defending him, even though no one was accusing her of anything, and alienating nearly everyone who wanted to help her and little Charles. It was obvious to everyone that Alice felt like the enemy surrounded her, and Celena wondered if James ever stopped to think what his running off would do to the wife and child he left behind.

"Hank, please, you are far too young for this!" she exclaimed at the risk of injuring his pride. "Do you know what would happen to your mother if..." She stopped, not liking to think of all the terrible things she knew could happen, especially when she was getting ready to send Victor off to fight.

"I feel like I'm letting everyone down." His eyes again rested on his uncle, who having seen him grinned broadly and began making his way over.

"You're not, please Hank don't think of it that way," she implored and wondered if it was a burning desire in all men to rush off to war. Because even with the risks and the terrible stories of death and suffering, even with the grisly visual of Laurence back without his leg, here they were all clamoring to get on the steamer—to join the fight.

"Hank!" Victor said and loudly slapped his hand into his nephew's and shook it vigorously. "You take care of your mother while I'm gone, we talked about it. You know what to do." Begrudgingly Hank nodded, and a current of silent understanding seemed to go through them.

"Papa!" Sam said, lifting his arms. Effortlessly Victor leaned down to pick him up.

"Do you know where you're going?" Hank asked wistfully, and Celena felt a painful tug in her heart when she saw Hank embarrassingly wipe his eyes when Victor wasn't looking.

"Not yet. I think we go to camp Jackson in St. Louis, then we get orders, but other than that I don't know, but you'll hear from me," he said and smiled at Celena, who was trying to pick up Myles while still holding Luke. He picked up Myles for her.

Before long there was a flurry of activity when the steward of the ship started the loading, and holding Luke firmly pressed against her they watched, almost holding their breath, the image of Stephan walk up the plank and turning waved goodbye to shouts and cheers of his parents and friends.

It was curious to Celena how happy the Stoddards looked when they had no idea where Seth was since he had left six months ago and no one had heard from him. Yet here they were, smiling and waving goodbye to another son.

"Wave to Papa!" Eva said, holding little Stephan in her arms. Although she was smiling, there were tears in her eyes.

It was loud all the sudden, with all the kissing goodbye to wives and family and the squawking and crying of children, some of whom seemed giddy to see their fathers and brothers off to war, and yet others were crying and reaching arms out to prevent their leaving.

"Goodbye Hank," Victor said, putting Myles back on his feet and grabbing his nephew to hug him hard. "Take care of your mother. Make me proud while I'm gone, all right?" He turned to Margaret and hugged her too, but gently. He then kissed her twice on the cheek. As he drew away she pulled him back.

"Please," she begged with worried eyes, "please be careful Victor."

He nodded. "Randy," he said, straightening to his full height, and Celena watched her oldest son swallow hard, looking up at his father. "Take care of your brothers—you and Bartholomew are in charge, but you're *not* leaving school."

Immediately Randy shot his mother a look of fury. "But Pa I'm going to need to work—"

When Victor shook his head, Randy shut his mouth. "You can do both. Bartholomew oversees things—you do what he and your mother tell you." Randy, who was hoping he could stop going to school, lowered his head. He then felt his father's chest press into his downturned face. Victor kissed him on the top of the head and then moved down the line.

"Bye Ben," he said, and hugged the boy who made no attempt to hide his emotions and cried openly at his father's leaving. "Counting on you to help your mother."

"I will Papa. Goodbye."

"Andrew, Sam...be good, you hear?" Simultaneously they nodded their blond heads and Victor chuckled when four blue eyes looked up at him trustingly. He kissed them both.

"Myles my man," he smiled at the tot at his feet and planted a noisy kiss on his pudgy cheek. "Be good for your Mama."

Celena suddenly laid against him, Luke between them.

"I'm going to miss you so much," she whispered and he managed around Luke to plant a kiss on her head. Celena, like Ben, made no pretense at trying to hide her emotions as two glistening tears slid down her cheeks.

Brigid intervened then and took Luke from them, and Celena turned a bit shyly to Ethan.

"Goodbye Ethan...good luck." She hugged him and surprised him by kissing him on the cheek. "Please take care of yourself," her eyes darted back to Victor, "and each other."

"I will." Ethan paused and, realizing he would never get the opportunity again, bent down and kissed her lightly on the mouth, tasing the tears on her lips. It was his right, he reasoned for the first and last time in his life, to touch the lips of the woman he was in love with. "Goodbye Celena," Without looking back, he boarded the ship.

She was instantly in Victor's arms again, trying to blot out the sounds of the ship's whistle, the men boarding, and families saying goodbye.

"Kiss me goodbye, Lena."

With her heart hammering in her chest, she looked up as he stooped to kiss her, much to the delight of the already loaded men who began to hoot and holler at the tender display of affection. But they were not the only ones kissing goodbye because Mason was having quite a difficult time disengaging himself not only from his daughters Livi and Marie's overzealous embrace but of Carlene's as well!

"I love you," Celena whispered, holding him as tightly as she could. When their eyes met a terrifying feeling of doom passed between them. "Promise me you'll be careful, promise you'll come back to me."

"I will," he said and gently kissed the spot under her eye. "Goodbye." Horrified, she felt him pull away.

She watched him board the ship, waving goodbye to friends and neighbors who were calling out well wishes. Eva came to stand next to her, biting her bottom lip to keep it from trembling as she held little Stephan so he could wave goodbye to his father.

Trying not to transfer all her heartache and worry to her children, Celena forced a smile. Besides, she didn't want the last thing Victor to see was the image of all of them sobbing on the riverbank.

"Wave to Papa!" she said, smiling through her tears, and Myles, Sam and Andrew waved, but Randy's chin was on his chest, and Ben was in silent tears.

A sudden horrible pain gripped her. A cold fear went through her heart that she was looking for the last time on the face of her husband. She knew suddenly with an agonizing ache in her heart, that she was never going to see him again.

But when she looked at the faces of her sisters and the countless other women next to her, realized they were all having the same horrifying premonitions. That all of them were terrified they were looking for the last time on the faces of the men they loved.

Chapter 42

"*Gant!*" the Sergeant bellowed.

Nimbly Victor stepped forward. The astonished look on the sergeant's face caused the new recruits to laugh, but quickly shut their mouths when they saw irritation cross the burly sergeant's face.

"Well *damn*, you are one *big* son-of-a-bitch!"

Victor sighed, having heard the same phrase from no less than three men already that day, and it was embarrassing to be stared at so much. He hadn't realized how happily buried he had been in Ste. Genevieve.

"We ain't gonna have nothing to fit ya. We got four sizes of regulation clothing, but none of them are going to work," the Sergeant said, shaking his head. "What ya got there in your hair?" Rudely he reached forward and pulled the leather band out. "I'll be *damned!* I think we got us a *mutt* here!" Several of the men in line bent forward, craning their necks to stare at Victor. "What kind of mix are you, boy?"

"An American mix."

"There is something *in* you boy, you ain't all *white* that's for damn sure!"

Victor sighed, thinking it was no wonder the Union army was floundering when its officers were wasting time discovering the bloodlines of their soldiers rather than training them.

"Sergeant Bellamy!" his commanding officer barked and immediately the scruffy sergeant straightened, as did everyone else at the tone of his voice.

"Yes Captain?" Bellamy asked, standing as tall as his five feet could muster.

"Is there a problem here?"

"No Captain, taking down their names and information is all," the Sergeant replied, his round eyes respectfully glazed as he stood at attention.

Captain Smyth stopped in front of Victor and eyed him up and down, and then back at the mangy little sergeant who he could smell had an aversion to bathing.

"Name, private?"

"Victor Gant."

The captain nodded approvingly. He was dressed beautifully in a new blue uniform. He was fair and blue eyed and had a soft, rather gentle look about him. Victor wondered if he had seen any of the horrors they had all been hearing about but noticing the pristine condition of uniform complete with shinning buttons, didn't think so.

"And Private, you hail from?"

"Ste. Genevieve," Victor finished and when he felt Ethan nudge him, added, "sir."

"That's a little town south from here on the Mississippi isn't it?"

"Yes sir."

"Mostly French is it not?"

"Yes sir, and German."

"But you're not French, or German?"

Victor shook his head.

"But that's where you were born?"

"Yes sir," Victor answered, wondering what in the world where he was from had anything to do with enlisting in the army! Laurence was right, he decided, with how caught up in trivialities the army could be.

"I've been in those parts before. Ah, I see *metis* aren't you?"

It annoyed Victor that discovering his parental origins were being investigated so thoroughly.

"Kaskaskia, or Sauk perhaps?"

Victor stared down at the captain, realizing he did know the area well. "No. Osage."

Proud of himself then, Captain Smythe began walking down the line to inspect the rest of the troops. But this bit of information seemed to undo the sergeant.

"You mean he's an *Indian?*" the sergeant asked, horrified. "But captain sir...do we *want* an Indian in the army?"

Captain Smyth turned around abruptly then, his pink and white hands pressed firmly behind his back. "Sergeant Bellamy at this point, we want *everyone!*" He grinned and, turning back to his new recruits, said grandly: "Welcome, gentlemen, to the army!"

Sergeant Bellamy had been right, there was nothing to fit Victor in way of the uniforms, but he put the dark blue flannel coat on anyway, even though he could not get the last two buttons to meet across his chest and more than four inches of bony wrist showed. The blue kersey trousers were as bad, hitting him about mid-calf and would have looked entirely ridiculous had he not been able to get his big feet into any of the army issue 'gunboats' and kept his own new boots on instead. In fact, the only part of the uniform that did fit was the blue forage cap, and when he pulled it down, the black leather visor made him appear quite sinister.

When he was fully loaded with the accouterments of soldiering: cartridge box, blanket, canteen, a haversack holding all personal needs such as essential eating utensils, a cup, a sewing kit humorously dubbed 'the housewife,' as well as small picture of Celena, a hinged match safe, and spiked iron candle holder, it was heavy. All held in place by leather straps crisscrossing his torso and on his waist a large buckle with US insignia on it. And adding to the already fifty pounds. the average infantryman was carrying he had to, of course, carry his rifle with bayonet. Thus, garbed Victor turned to Ethan and quipped: "I can appreciate the feeling of an animal in harness now!"

The first few days of 'mustering in' were completely confusing to both Ethan and Victor but they quickly learned to get up the minute the bugle sounded reveille at 5 A.M. and stand outside their tents. And even Victor had to admit they made a sorry sight as he looked across from him. Some of the men only had one shoe on, some were shivering clothed only in their linens, and they stood ludicrously like apprentices and clerks trying to act like soldiers.

"What are we doing?" Ethan whispered, standing next to Victor in his army-issued kersey trousers, the white shirt buttoned up but the suspenders hanging down.

"Roll," Victor said and then shut up. It had not taken him long to realize the first sergeant of their company, Bellamy did not take kindly to talking. It made no difference to Sergeant Bellamy that scarcely two days ago all of them had been civilians, they were *in the army now!* as he had bellowed to them so many times in the last two days and he expected them to act like it.

Monotonously Sergeant Bellamy began the roll, which they soon found out would be only the first of three roll calls taken each day. When the first roll was done, they put the camp in order and eaten breakfast being coffee and something almost inedible called hardtack. A cracker so hard that one young blonde-haired recruit from Illinois broke his tooth trying to bite one.

About every two hours the company guard was changed—which seemed ridiculous to Victor since they were still in St. Louis and no enemy in sight—but it was what the army wanted them to do, and he would do it no matter how ridiculous it seemed.

After the fifth session of drill, each of which had been two hours Ethan nearing exhausting had turned to Victor who was next to him in line and said, "Do you realize we've been at this for nearly ten hours?"

"Well, since none of us know what we're doing," Victor said in a low voice when he was sure Sergeant Bellamy couldn't hear him, "we'd better get it right *here*, rather than out *there* where mistakes may dearly cost us."

As the last golden rays of the sun's light sunk behind the hillside dozens of candles lit up the tents, and the recruits gathered around the campfire to either to write letters home or talk.

"Where are you from?" a red-haired man asked, seated across the fire from Ethan.

"Ste. Genevieve," Ethan responded, not wanting to talk. His hands were raw from digging new latrines, and four large blisters had broken up during the afternoon, and right now they were throbbing.

"What were ya on the outside before yah come in here?"

Ethan wished he had merely gone back to the tent, but not wanting to seem rude especially when so many of his company were looking at him answered as politely as possible. "A banker." He noticed the heartier recruits were nudging each other and laughing.

"Told ya!" The red-haired man grinned, and a short dark-haired man dug deep into his pockets to pull out a filthy coin and hand it to him. "Had a wee bit of a wager on ya! They thought you must have been a schoolmaster or somethin' on account of how pale and proper you looked, I figured yah to be a money man though!" He laughed. "Name's George Dugan. I come from Ireland to your great country—and when I get her—yah have the *gall* to be havin a war going on!" He offered his hand to Ethan. "Everybody calls me Rusty though."

"Pleased to meet you I'm sure!" Ethan said and again they laughed.

"Hey, what's your name?" asked another young man, whose face he tried not to notice was covered with blemishes.

"Ethan Stanfield."

The young man smiled, which not surprisingly helped his appearance. "I'm Amos Norton," he said and then his voice dropped lower, and he looked around him as if at any minute a beast was going to pounce. "That big guy—your friend, is he really...an Indian?"

Ethan nodded. "Half. And half English too."

"Oh, so he's an enemy on both counts!" a dark-haired man quipped, and when he smiled devilishly by the firelight it was apparent that his front two teeth were missing.

"How do you figure?" Ethan asked absentmindedly, looking at the raw marks on his hands, wondering if he had digging detail again tomorrow how he was going to do it.

"All the Indians are the white man's enemy and the English, well, they're from England—we didn't fight that war with Washington for nothin'!" There was a good deal of agreeing and stupid laughter around him. Sighing, Ethan found himself wondering how he would endure the company of these men for a *year!*

"What's your name?" Ethan asked. Looking up he was met with a cool stare.

"What's it to ya?" the man replied and then laughed openly at Ethan to the delight of his hangers-on. Uninterested, Ethan looked back into the fire only to shriek a moment later when a four-inch knife thrown at him stuck in the ground an inch from his foot. The resounding laughter at his fright, embarrassed him.

"Lord boy, you can move quick when you have to!" the dark-haired man grinned.

"You aren't supposed to have that Gideon, that's against army regulations!" Amos squeaked as he bent down to retrieve the knife.

"Give it here."

Amos shook his head. "You're not supposed to have that—that's contra-contraband!" the young boy managed to get out much to the humor of the older wiser friends of Gideon Plummer.

"Give it here Amos!" an older man said and, laboriously getting to his feet, easily wrestled the knife from the boy and then knocked his cap off his head.

"It's against the rules," Amos huffed again, picking up his hat, inspecting it for dust.

"Hey, you, banker boy," Gideon began.

"I'm not a boy," Ethan interrupted.

"Where you from?"

"Down the river a ways—and you?"

Gideon put his hand to his chest, mocking Ethan. "Kentucky."

"Where abouts?"

"Up on Black Mountain near the Appalachians. Greenest, wildest, prettiest place you ever did see—"

Ethan snorted. "That explains it."

"That explains what?"

"Your...deficiencies."

"My *what*?"

"Probably caused by inbreeding."

"*Inbreeding*?"

This time it was Ethan's turn to laugh. "You know, your sister with your brother, your brother with your aunt. In fact, it all but ruined the greatest societies of the world. Take ancient Egypt for example—Cleopatra after being forced to marry her brother, later poisoned him. The inbreeding has been known to render the offspring either mentally retarded, insane, or both."

Enraged, Gideon jumped up. "You're a God damn wise ass is what you are!"

"I thought I was a boy?" Ethan asked and found himself being yanked up by his shirt collar.

"Whoa, gentleman," Victor said, laying hand on Gideon's holding Ethan's shirt up choking him, "what did I miss?"

"Gideon here threw knife at your friend 'cause he's sort of pale, well, meaning no disrespect, sort of a pretty boy, then your friend told him he was the product of inbreeding because he's from the hills of Kentucky— oh, by the way, my name's Amos Norton."

"All that happened in the time it took me to write a letter?" Victor queried, looking at Ethan.

Letting go of Ethan's shirt, Gideon stalked off angrily and sat back down.

"Making friends quick I see." Victor smirked as Ethan tucked his shirt back in. They both sat down by the fire.

"I'm Rusty."

Victor, grinning, reached out his hand, as did the others around the fire.

"Trigg Dikeman," the man sitting next to Gideon offered warmly.

When Victor offered Gideon his hand, Gideon refused to take it.

"I'm from Cahokia," Trigg said.

Victor's grin was huge. "Then you don't live far from us, we're from

Ste. Genevieve!"

A smile bloomed across Trigg's face. "I'll be damned, we are practically family then! What did you do back there? I had me a job on good sized farm for a while."

"What happened?" Amos asked, his innocence and naivete so blatant it reminded Victor painfully of Hank.

"The farmer, he got conscripted on and he sent me instead—since I couldn't find no work anywhere else anyway." He shrugged. "I joined up instead of him, so I figure let the army pay me and an feed me for a while, 'til I figure out what to do."

"You mean you joined the army because they was paying you?" Amos asked, incredulous. Victor had the desire to shut the young boy up, before one of the crustier enlistees did it for him.

"Aren't they payin' you lad?" Rusty said with a quirk of his bushy auburn eyebrows. "They're payin' me thirteen dollars a month by God!"

"Well yes, but that's not why I joined up—"

Victor shook his head at him quietly. "Amos, let it go."

But the boy foolishly would not be put off. "Aren't any of you here because of the plight of the Negro? My father's a preacher and it's against God;s laws to enslave anyone! slavery must die, and if the south insists on being buried in the same grave, I shall see in it nothing but the retributive hand of God," he said boldly.

"Is that so?" Gideon said with a malicious grin and Victor found himself wondering which of the ragged enlistees would pummel young Amos first.

"I got a $200 bonus for enlisting," Gideon said, the firelight flickering unbecomingly on what teeth he still had. "And besides that, I get to kill them asshole Reb's, within the limits of the law that is. Those arrogant bastards who think they can do whatever they want."

"What did you do—I mean what were you before you became a soldier?" Victor asked and curiously looked over the fire at Gideon, who didn't like being put suddenly on the spot. But he had noticed how big Victor was and decided he had better answer.

"I was a carpenter, you?"

"Blacksmith."

"Did you join for the money?" Amos asked with no small horror, and to his relief Victor shook his head at him.

"You?" Amos asked, straining his neck to see around Victor to Ethan.

"No."

"For glory and honor?" Amos asked hopefully.

"Something like that," Ethan mumbled.

"Well, I'll be *damned!*" Trigg whispered, marching next to Victor as they joined the trained veterans of countless other regiments in the camp.

Even Victor had to admit there were several good-looking groups as they passed, smartly snapping off salutes, and he found himself wondering if he could learn to adjust to the constraints of army life—of life in a strange city of tents. He shook off the cold feeling of fear like he had already done several times since leaving Ste. Genevieve months ago, wondering if he would have the courage when the time came.

The camp was situated on a beautiful stretch of land. It was a lush valley with towering pines and deep woods, but the army was already having rather negative effect on the woodsy landscape. It had denuded part of the forest, and each day the army encroached a bit more on the habitat. Chopping down trees for firewood and for building the officers cabins. The camp had been laid out in the common army fashion of a grid pattern with officers' quarters at the front of each street and enlisted men's quarters aligned to the rear. There were regulations Victor discovered which spelled out the width of the streets, the location of the kitchens and sinks, where the baggage trains should be parked, how far in front of the camp the pickets should be posted-nothing was left to chance.

They were a full-strength infantry regiment that spring of 1863, composed of ten companies of hundred men each. And enough animosity and bullheadedness among the lot of them to cause a fight to break out nearly every day. Victor had written to Celena telling her that he'd never heard so much swearing, and disgusting language before in his life and that he had regrettably picked up the habit, and she was hereby given permission by him to pinch him when he returned home every time he swore!

He quickly learned the discipline necessary to survive in the army. He honed his skill at drill, watched in rapt amazement and wonder at the army's mysterious organization and chain of command. He was expected to be proficient in the handling of arms and the care of his equipment, a detail lost on such men as Amos who Victor had tried repeatedly to explain the rudiments of *Hardee's* 9 tactics to correctly load his gun. When Amos had at last mastered the complicated set of instructions Trigg had laughed and said, "*With the time it takes him to load up, the war will be over!*"

Victor took his turn with all the other recruits standing guard in the night in the snow and sleet and as the weather turned warmer in the rain as well. He learned how to quickly pitch not only the large spoked twelve-man Sibley tent, but the smaller wall tent with flaps. Some of the men were even in wedge tents which were nothing more than a six-foot length of canvas draped over a horizontal ridge pole and staked to the ground at the sides. Flaps closed off the sides giving the four to six men who slept in them privacy, but with only about seven square feet of space per man, sleeping was a cramped exercise. And even smaller than that were what Victor jokingly wrote home to Celena was a *dog tent* because as he wrote to her it *would only accommodate a dog, and a small one at that!*

Four months into their tour an incredible tedium set in. And as the boredom that set in while they waited for something to happen-the men filled their time with leisure activities of their choice which ran the gamut from the checkers, card playing and drinking to snowball fights, boxing matches and gambling. He was glad Celena would never know how a whole host of prostitutes hovered around the camp—especially once a month when the men were paid and how men partook heartily in *horizontal refreshments!*

But even with all their bawdiness, gambling, and carousing, their thoughts and conversations around the campfire inevitably revolved around two central themes—the fear and excitement of battle, coupled with the desire to simply have it all end, and go back home.

Victor and the rest of regiment watched the floundering of Captain Smythe. The recruits soon discovered the man meant to lead them knew little more about the army and maneuvers than them. It was painful to watch him give an order and then change his mind and give another, or tell them one day a drill was to be one way, only to change it the next.

"How old you think he is?" Ethan whispered, standing next to Victor during the second drill on a chilly April afternoon.

Victor snorted. "Hank's age."

"He has no idea what he's doing!" Ethan said, exasperated. "The problem is none of us do either. How well do you think that will hold for us if when we ever do meet the Confederate Army?"

"Not too well," Victor agreed and, seeing Sergeant Bellamy nearing, straightened. "I tell you what bothers me is the fact that Captain Smythe's pretending that he knows what he's doing doesn't do much for morale," he said, noticing the sideways looks some of the men cast at their officer as he repeated the same blunder as yesterday. "And when the time comes and this regiment falls apart, that only means *more* of us will get killed."

Victor stopped to wipe a line of sweat from his forehead, and then out of habit inspected the ax making sure the seasoned wooden handle driven through the loop was wedged in tight. He leaned down to haul limbs out of the overgrowth for 'wood detail' when he heard something.

Realizing it was a man's voice, walked a few steps brushing back the tangle of vines and crept closer to the sound. It was Captain Smythe and Victor wondered suddenly if he'd taken part of the regiment out into the woods to perform some mysterious maneuver. Through the underbrush Victor could see him underneath the shade of gigantic oak tree.

A grin spread across Victor's face when he realized the young Captain was practicing. He felt sorry for him suddenly, realizing the Captain must know his troops were losing respect for him. Otherwise, why would he have walked from the earshot of camp to orchestrate army maneuvers? He shouted with more authority to the trees than he ever did to his men. Not wanting to embarrass the Captain, Victor turned to skulk away, but snapped a small twig and the captain spun around. A faint blush rose steadily from the collar of his pristine suit to his freshly barbered hair.

"You make a remarkably *bad* Indian given your bloodlines. I doubt you could sneak up on a dead man."

"I didn't mean to be tracking you, sir."

"What were you doing?" the Captain asked nervously, wondering if by nightfall all his troops would be laughing at him due to the embarrassing story that would no doubt be circulating around the camp.

"Wood detail, sir."

The Captain nodded and looked behind Victor, wondering if the smart fellow that was normally in his company was with him. "You alone?"

"Yes, sir." He watched as the captain visibly relaxed.

"Well..." Captain Smythe began, but before he could tell Victor to 'carry on' he interrupted him.

"Captain—sir." Victor tried not to smile as the handsome young man came closer to him, having—since he was only 5'5"—to look up to Victor. "Could I...make a suggestion?"

Again, faint pink colored the young Captain's face and Victor wondered if his poor mother was getting any sleep at night with worry for him. "And what suggestion would that be, private?"

"Sir, Captain. We men, that is," he paused, hoping his next words would not garner him extra work detail or some other punishment. The army he had already found out did not take kindly to suggestions.

"Yes, private?" Captain Smythe prompted, standing directly in front of Victor. The young captain so reminded him of Hank that he found himself wanting to wrestle him into a headlock.

"I think you'd stand a much better chance if you just came clean with your men."

"Came clean with them about what?"

"We all know you don't know what you're doing. And it's not your fault, the Union's running out of trained officers, and you're trying your best. Besides you're...if you don't mind me asking, Captain, how old?"

"I'm twenty," Captain Smythe answered.

"I think your men would respect you more if you admitted you don't know something. We can probably all learn what we need to do together, sir."

"Well," Captain Smythe began, wanting to put this outspoken and surly recruit in his place, wanted to come back with a tongue lashing that would make the private wish he had never so much as opened his mouth. "That's your recommendation for me—to admit my faults and weaknesses openly to the men?"

"One of these fine days, Captain, all these drills and maneuvers we practice are going to be put to the test—I sure would like to think you had as much faith in us following as we'd like to have in your leading..."

For the next few days Victor noticed Captain Smythe did not look at him, but he also noticed that a subtle change came over the captain. He was still barking orders, but he made more eye contact with the men, used the pronoun "we," and the drills, although still sloppy affairs, improved.

But it was not until Major Marks marched over to a flustered Captain Smythe and in front of the entire regiment asked him a long, complicated question, using, it seemed to the men, as many extra words as possible. In fact, it was such a ridiculous way to ask a question that Victor had to decipher it for Trigg. What it came down to was how Captain Smythe intended to deploy his troops when meeting the enemy.

For a long minute the entire Missouri regiment agonized silently while their young Captain floundered, and then his blond head shot up suddenly and he glanced at his troops, straightening his thin shoulders.

"Well Major, I cannot answer that according to the books," he began and then swallowed hard. Again his eyes drifted over his regiment. "But I can tell you, Major Marks...that I would risk myself with the men of Missouri any time day or night—and I would go in on our main strength, and I trust my men!" There was an annoying silence, but Victor could see the men around him grinning with pride.

Although, Major Marks was not awed, when he saluted in leaving and Captain Smythe turned back to his troops they erupted into shouts of approval and hoots of laughter and only the bellowing of Sergeant Bellamy could get them to settle down and stay in rank

As Captain Smythe dismissed his men he glanced up at Victor, tightness around his mouth and wariness in his eyes. But when Victor smiled and nodded, the captain gave a small smile of thanks.

Chapter 43

It was quiet in Ste. Genevieve in the months after the boats of able-bodied males left, and Celena sighed as she walked back home after visiting with Father Tonnellier through the silent streets. She passed Dolph Adders shop and the closed sign in the window only caused the tightening her chest to worsen. He had left before Victor and his wife had still had not heard from him. She hadn't heard from Victor either, and her depression was only lessened when she realized how many other wives and mothers in town were feeling like she did.

At first Carlene snickered at Celena talking with Father Tonnellier weekly. Celena would talk to him about her fear and worries concerning her husband and friends. Sometimes they would pray the rosary together, other times she would merely sit quietly alone in the church. Afterwards she would stop by the cemetery and pull weeds out from along Anna's small tombstone, as well as of her father's, Jonah, and others. She found herself gently touching the decorative wrought iron fencing Victor had put up years ago to encircle Anna's small grave. She had been pregnant with Andrew and had both Randy and Ben by the hand when he had led her into the cemetery to show her. He had simply explained his installing it by saying: *'I didn't want her to think we'd forgotten about her.'*

"There, Anna," Celena whispered, having tidied up the grave and then sat for a minute silently amongst the dead, listening to the sound of the wind rustling the leaves, the far-off sound of the river lapping at the shore, the occasional twittering of the birds. As she walked quietly out of the cemetery she gently traced her hand over Jonah's stone, whispering' "Watch over your son."

Celena's hands were shaking with excitement as she closed the bedroom door. The children were finally asleep and even though she had already read Victor's letter to them, wanted to read it again, alone. Her eyes immediately filled with tears when she recognized his handwriting, and she stopped for a minute before reading it to trace her hand along the rumpled letter, wanting simply to touch what he had touched.

"*My dearest Lena,*" she read aloud in the privacy of their bedroom and blushed even though she was alone at the intimacy of his salutation.

"*I am well.*" Celena shook her head, smiling. "*Hope this letter finds you and the boys healthy. Ethan and I have been assigned to a regiment.*" She sighed, trying to calm the happy pounding of her heart.

She laughed later reading his humorous anecdotes about the monotony of drilling of which he said: '*In the morning we drill, then drill, then drill again, and then drill a little more and lastly drill!*' He wrote about the endless digging of latrines and trenches, caring for the horses, mules and repairing equipment. How the army clothes were too small and did not fit him and jokingly the men in his regiment called him little *boy blue* because he looked like he had put on children's clothes. How the army food made him yearn for one of her cream soups, or roast pig seasoned like she did with baby onions—how he was making friends almost as fast as Ethan was alienating them! How he felt sorry for his commanding officer, Captain Smythe, who he thought was too young to be in command and had been a student at West Point when the war started.

He gushed about the feeling of pride the troops had, the feelings of camaraderie and fellowship which had been forged in such a short time. Told her the fear he had of going into battle, the fear of turning 'coward' in the time of need. Although she knew it bothered him to admit his fear, almost worse was the fear that his cowardice might get other men killed.

He went on for more than a paragraph about the unpleasantness of life in camp. The cramped quarters, the mud, the boredom, the vices. Jokingly promising her he was not engaging at all in multitude of leisure activities afforded the common solider—most of which were lewd.

But he did tell her he had, because he was the biggest out of the hundred men, been selected to box a particularly bellicose Irish recruit by the name of Chester O'Connell. Who was, he was to find out *after* the first fight, a professional fighter in Dublin. And the first time they boxed, Victor had been beat and badly! However, the second time a bit wiser and better boxer he quickly became and since his reach alone was longer than the shorter man's, it had been a decent fight. And because the stakes were as high as every man in camp could afford; the unresolved draw of the winnerless second fight had made every single man in his regiment who'd bet on him money. Even Captain Smythe and Sergeant Bellamy had been screaming with the rest of the men during the fight.

He did not tell her that measles was running rampant in the camp, and that even before meeting a single confederate soldier thirteen men had died. He also purposefully did not tell her that he'd never in his life seen so many rats and mice that had, almost the minute they moved into camp, settled in with them. It had to do with the amount garbage located scarcely fifty feet from the camp. He also left out the fact that although he did not have lice yet—it was in camp and begrudgingly knew by the shoddy washing and hygiene habits of his companions before long he too would be as they joked *'inhabited.'*

He ended the letter asking questions about her and the children, and about Margaret, Henry, Laurence, and others. She could tell that he was torn by his probing need to know what was happening at home and his wanting to do his part. The last line of the letter he asked if Ethan too, could write to her, and it touched a sentimental chord in her heart when she read her husband's plea: '*...he has no one that cares and worries about him as I do, and I have been so unbelievably blessed in my life, to have the children and you...'* He ended the letter on a rather somber note, his optimism dwindling by the end of the letter, simply signed "V" because he had run out of room on the paper

It amazed her how quickly her loving husband had, in fact, become a soldier.

November 1863
Battle of Missionary Ridge

"What do you think we're going to do?" Ethan asked, turning to Victor, rubbing his arms against the chill in the air.

"I don't know. But one thing is for sure—we're not leaving." Victor thought of the disorganization of the army, the intense lack of morale following the Union defeat and bloodshed at Chickamauga. "Besides, we're getting reinforcements every day," he said, looking up at the new regiments swelling the size of the fragmented army.

"Besides, you know what I heard? Heard President Lincoln said General Rosecrans was acting 'confused and stunned like a duck hit on the head' with all the depressed telegrams he's been sending him." Victor shook his head, looking at the mud underneath his feet. "Must be why General Grant's in command now."

Ethan nodded in agreement. "That's so like Lincoln to say something like that. I heard that when Lincoln was considering Grant for command of the Union army, he was warned that Grant was a heavy drinker."

"And?"

"Lincoln asked if anybody knew where Grant got his whiskey because he wanted to give a barrel of it to *every* general in the field."

Victor laughed.

"Maybe his victories in Vicksburg will rub off on all of us. It would be nice this next time to win."

"We're still alive, that's victory enough," Victor said, looking up in the darkness toward Lookout Mountain, knowing that the Confederate army was poised on the top. Between them was Orchard Knob, a foothill three quarters of a mile to the front, and beyond that a rugged escarpment known as Missionary Ridge. Looking at it in the darkness, he realized that to win or at least drive the Confederates back, they'd have to take that ridge.

At daybreak they heard cannon fire, and got orders from Major Marks to be the third regiment to be sent in. And while they were waiting muskets poised and nervously resting in their hands the crack of musket fire and shells and bullets began taking off the limbs of the trees around them.

"Oh, that's great! I'll be killed by a damn tree limb falling on me today before I ever get a shot at one of them rebels today," Gideon hissed as they moved, backs hunched, toward the smoke and noise.

"Remember," Captain Smythe said behind them in a cool, even voice, "keep your lines and hold your fire 'til I give the orders."

Victor could see Ethan beside him out of the corner of his eye, and he could hear Amos on his other side praying annoyingly loud.

The closer they got the smokier it became and at times it was difficult to see and a panic hit Victor and he hoped he could remember again what he was supposed to do when the time came. He'd already been in combat, but it didn't matter. The fear welled up just like it had the first time.

They could hear the confederate soldiers yelling.

"What the damn devil are they always yellin' for?" Rusty scoffed as they halted at Captain Smythe's command. Curiously they listened, and heard the decidedly high-pitched yelling of the Confederate soldiers as they charged into battle. They had, of course, heard the infamous 'Rebel yell' before.

"It is a bit...effeminate isn't it?" Ethan said.

"Why they sound like a bunch of women!" Trigg joked nervously, even though he was terrified.

"Like old women trying to shoo the crows out of the garden!" Amos grinned.

"Well," Victor said, gripping sweaty hands against his rifle for reassurance, "they aren't *women*, and you better get ready with your *own* yell."

"Fire!" Captain Smythe bellowed

Like in Chickamauga, the jokes of what a poor shot he was resounded in Victor's head. He took aim and, with his second shot, hit a Confederate soldier down, and laid back down and began to reload.

"Amos get your ass down!" he yelled and yanked Amos to the ground next to him. It was the scariest moment of a soldier's life sitting on the ground reloading a rifle—it took time to reload; time that seemed like an eternity as bullets whizzed by and screams of men erupted all around.

"Reload!" Victor shouted at Amos, whose eyes were huge with shock.

"I-I can't do it!" Amos wailed over the din of gunfire

"The *hell* you can't! Fire the damn thing!" Victor barked, tearing open the cartridge paper with his teeth. Seeing the dazed, frightened expression on Amos's face, he crawled near him. Inspecting Amos's rifle he realized that it was still loaded and that he hadn't fired a shot.

"Amos, it's already loaded—you haven't fired yet!" Victor yelled to the confused boy, who he knew would have done more damage to himself than to the enemy with his frantic reloading of the unfired rifle.

Victor heard Captain Smythe yelling at them to get up and move, and scrambling to his feet took off into the smoke and gunfire with the rest of the regiment. He looked briefly next to him to see Ethan or Trigg or Rusty, but only saw Gideon stopping to take aim. When he'd hit his target he let out a blood-chilling yell.

"Get *down!*" Victor shouted. Amos was the last of their regiment behind a large rock on the foot of the steep hill. His face was beet red as he looked at Victor, his eyes wild with fright, his chest heaving.

"I-I killed one!" he said in shock, and Gideon merely wiped the sweat off his forehead and spit, unconcerned with the look of terror and shock in Amos's eyes.

"Good boy, now help me and kill some more, will ya!" Gideon yelled.

At first the bullets whistling by his head had shocked and frightened Victor but he stopped dodging them after a while, especially when Rusty, his face blackened by powder, asked, "Why ya flinchin'—them's has missed ya? You'll know when they don't!"

"Company—fire!"

Victor had never seen such pandemonium in his life, with the screaming, cannonballs exploding yards away plowing up the ground, and everywhere smoke and gunshots. He tried to listen to Captain Smythe, but some of the men behind him were so caught up in the battle hysteria that they couldn't keep their lines and ran ahead. Much to his dismay he would sometimes pass them a few minutes later, lying dead on the field, guns still clasped in their sweaty hands.

"Damnit Amos, you're gonna get your fool head blown off—stay where you're supposed to!" Victor yelled, having noticed a decided change come over the young man, who had been at first afraid to fire, but now was showing a remarkable amount of courage—and foolhardiness. "Your Mama's going to want you back in one piece!" Victor barked, reloading and glancing next to him to see Ethan covered with dirt, surprising him with his newly acquired skill at crawling on his stomach.

"Are we winnin' do ya think?" Rusty asked, jamming the rod down the barrel.

"I don't give a shit—it'll be a victory if we live through this day..." Gideon hissed and at Bellamy's command began to run toward the enemy

"I'm going!" Amos announced bravely, and charged into the smoke.

"*Amos!*" Ethan shouted and he and Victor watched him take the first bullet in his leg, then his chest, and crumple to the ground amidst the noise and smoke.

As Union Generals John Breckenridge and Ulysses Grant watched the battle in the late afternoon, they realized that two regiments kept advancing. At first they were pleased as the gallant federal forces seized the line of Confederate rifle pits along the base of Missionary Ridge—but what alarmed them was when the soldiers continued to charge up the hill *without* orders.

Grant mumbled to the other generals near him that someone would dearly "pay for" for blunder if the assault failed. But the Confederate position at the center of the line was badly located, and in a moment of panic at the federals' relentless charge, the Confederate center broke and the soldiers fled.

It was dark by the time the opposing armies stopped firing at each other, and it started to rain lightly sometime during the night, loud cracks of ominous thunder shaking the earth as the heavens cried down on them. Victor jumped each time a blast of white lightening illuminated the battlefield. It was a scene from a nightmare—the field littered with dead soldiers in the mud as the rain poured down on their bodies.

He tried to eat but couldn't. Still wondering what had compelled him to keep running up that hill. He shivered with rain running down his neck even with the rubber blanket around his shoulders. His ears were ringing, and he couldn't keep the disturbing images of Amos being shot out of his mind.

He wanted to see where everyone was. He hadn't seen Ethan since the morning, nor Trigg, Rusty, or Gideon. He was too exhausted to look for them, and too afraid if he did what he would find. Looking down at the water in his little cup, he thought about trying to drink. But hearing someone in front of him he glanced up.

"Well, God damn. I thought you were dead."

Ethan slumped down next to him, wincing in pain. "Came close." He drew back his coat to show a ghastly red stain on his right hip. "Thankfully, it went *along* me rather than *through* me."

They fell silent listening to the rain splatter against the muddy ground and the occasional rumble of thunder.

"Did you hear our regiment alone lost thirty men? God knows how many we lost in other regiments." Ethan hung his head, jumping when another crack of thunder rattled the ground under their feet.

"That's low compared to what we lost at Chickamauga," Victor remarked, looking back toward the littered field. When the lightening again illuminated the dead he thought for a minute he saw the soldiers walking on the field. They looked like ghosts when the lightening flashed, and he found himself staring at the hundreds of bodies, willing them to get up.

"Have you seen Amos?" Ethan asked.

"Not since he was hit."

They fell despondently silent again. "Killed for the righteous emancipation for the Negro..." Ethan mumbled, wishing he had stayed closer to Amos; he was so young after all.

"It's ironic, isn't it, heard the Major say this was a victory..."

Everyone in the regiment was happy and relieved when six weeks later Amos rejoined them, still slightly injured but ready for duty. He let the men examine the wound on his leg and the bruise on his chest where a bullet had pierced his coat, but had been stopped from doing more damage by the thick Bible he always carried.

"You see—the good Lord saved me!" he said proudly, showing off not only the dark bruise but the battered Bible as well.

"Yeah, *this* time," Gideon mumbled under his breath.

"Gant! You have two letters," Sergeant Bellamy said.

Taking them, Victor went off to find a somewhat secluded spot to read. Finding a tree, he sat and leaned against it. He glanced at Celena's letter and could feel the warmth of her small hand within him so strongly he shuddered. Wanting to save her letter for last, he opened Margaret's.

Ethan couldn't help following him, even though he knew how private Victor was.

"*Oh shit!*" Victor exclaimed, stopping Ethan dead in his tracks. "It's my nephew Hank," he explained, looking back down at Margaret's letter, shaking his head with disgust, "fool's gone off and joined the army!"

"But he's only what, sixteen?" Ethan asked, dropping down next to him.

"Fourteen, but as big as he is and as desperate as the army is—they'll think he's of age." Victor shook his head, sighing. "Stupid young cuss...I'll break his scrawny neck next time I see him!"

Ethan raised his eyebrows in agreement.

"Margaret says he wanted to help out since his Pa is too sick...what a crock of shit is that? Do you know what this will do to Margaret if something happens to Hank? She asks me to watch out for him—how the hell am I going to watch out for the little ass when I don't know where in the hell he is?" Disgusted and worried, he refolded Margaret's letter and stuffed it into his shirt pocket. Even though Ethan was sitting next to him he opened Celena's letter and began to read. Ethan watched curiously as shock once again crossed his face.

"Well...I'll be God damned," Victor mumbled, dropping his head into his hand and tiredly rubbing his forehead.

"What's the matter now, more bad news?"

"No, not bad news...she had another baby."

"*What?*"

Victor nodded. "I must have gotten her pregnant before I left. Here I am a father again, and I didn't even know she was pregnant!" He wondered what day he had been endlessly drilling or marching that his beloved Celena had, without him there to help her, given birth to their seventh child. He read further. "Eva had a boy, David and Carlene had another girl, Emiline—they all had babies within two weeks of each other." He turned to Ethan. "It's a girl! I finally have a *daughter!*"

"A *girl?* Well, it's about time, Victor! Tell me, what are we calling this miraculous Gant *girl-child?*"

"Catherine."

"That's a fine name."

"It was my sister's name."

"Your *sister?* I wasn't aware you had another sister."

"She was stillborn, it was the child my mother died birthing." It touched something deep in him that Celena had named her that. And despite being hundreds of miles away and unsure of his future, he smiled. Overjoyed that he had a precious daughter to finally call his own.

"Have you ever been this damn cold do you think?" Victor laughed, noticing that even though there was a fire in the tent he could still see his breath. Grinning, he moved a bit in the frigid tent to let Trigg sit.

"Colder than a witch's titty out there!" Gideon added and rubbed his hands near the smoky fire.

"I never thought soldiering would be this boring," Ethan said.

"I agree! It's not about battles, it's about *boredom!*" Victor grinned and they all laughed in agreement.

"I never thought a youngin' could fart so much!" Rusty chuckled at an embarrassed Amos.

"It's getting deep in here," Victor said with a laugh and, leaning over, brushed away the flap of the tent to look out at the snow that had been steadily falling since early morning, blanketing the ground. It was beautiful to have the snow cover all the mud they turned the grounds into where they camped. He wondered if Ste. Genevieve too was being gently covered by snow. He sighed.

"Ah...ya homesick Blue?" Gideon jabbed.

"Well to tell you the truth, as fond as I am of all of you—I'd rather be many places than a cold stinking tent with five grown men who haven't had a bath probably since they enlisted!"

Everyone laughed.

"Ya must be married, 'cause even outside of the army I didn't take so kindly to bathin'! You have a wife at home?" Rusty asked, fiddling like he always did with his pocketknife and whatever bit of wood he could find. It was strange—for the most part these men had been together for over a year now, but none of them had talked much about their private lives. They had talked about their work and taunted each other, but the things that were most dear to them had not been much discussed.

"Yes," Victor answered, careful to avert his gaze, knowing how his heart thumped whenever he thought of her, afraid it would show in his eyes.

"Youngins?" Gideon asked.

"Yes, seven."

"Ooh! Been busy, ain't ya! Boys, girls?"

"Six boys and one girl."

"Your wife, is she pretty?" Amos asked.

Victor nodded. "I've always thought so."

"What's she look like, your lass? I was married once—she wasn't particularly bonnie, but she had sort of way of grabbin' on to your arse during fornicatin', it was a beautiful thing!"

They all laughed.

"What happened to her, your wife?" Amos asked.

"She left me for a damn peddler. He came to the house sellin' his wares—and samplin' the wares of my wife too I think!" There was a trace of sadness that went across him even though he was smiling.

"Do you have children?" Amos asked.

Rusty shook his head. "We had two babies, but they both died before they could walk."

Amos turned to Gideon. "Gideon, are you married?"

"What are you, a damn matchmaker?"

"No, I was only curious."

"Well shut your damn mouth runt!"

"Cursing is the work of the devil," Amos began as both Rusty and Trigg began to laugh.

"Oh, shut up Amos before I haul your ass out into the snow and bury ya in it headfirst!" Gideon threatened.

Amos ignored the put down and looked to Ethan. "Surely an educated man such are yourself is married?"

"I was...once."

"Children?"

Ethan shook his head.

"So, Victor's the only one of us who's married?"

The six of them looked to one another blankly.

"I'm married," Gideon said, though he did not seem happy to admit it. "I got eight youngins too, maybe even nine by now." Victor grinned at him and begrudgingly Gideon grinned back.

"She pretty?" Trigg asked, thinking about the girl with the green eyes he had known a long time ago and wondering if she ever thought of him.

Gideon thought. "No, not really." A round of laughter ensued.

"Why'd ya marry her then?" Trigg asked.

Gideon shrugged. "Had to. She was my brother's wife and he up and died on her." He paused, blowing out a breath. "She had three youngins by that time and no way to feed any of 'em, so she come up to me while I was in my shop one day. Closed the door behind her, dropped to her knees in front of me and—" He made a sweeping gesture across his groin.

"Oh, you're *lyin!*" Trigg said, his eyes wide with envy. "She didn't come up to you and do *that!*"

"Do what?" Amos asked, his eyes huge.

Victor shook his head at him. "Don't worry about it Amos—you'll understand when the time comes."

"It's something vulgar isn't it?" Amos asked suspiciously.

"Depends!" Gideon said with a laugh and a nudge to Rusty. "My brother's wife...or *my* wife now...she's missing some teeth...makes it good for doin' certain things!"

"Oh Jesus!" Victor said, dropping his head against his arms propped up on his knees, and laughed.

"Hey, little boy blue! Your wife—" Gideon laughed, "tell me...is she as pretty as *mine?*" and he laughed even harder when he watched a puzzled Amos still trying to figure it out.

"Well, I don't know, she has all her *teeth* if that's what you mean!"

"You are all despicable talking about your wives this way!" Amos huffed, and Gideon took the opportunity to reach outside the tent and squeeze a handful of snow to throw at him.

"Oh, shut up Amos! You ain't been laid or even touched a tit yet!" Gideon barked.

"Have you been married long?" Amos asked Victor, looking ridiculous as he flung bits of snowball into the smoky fire.

"Me? Uh...yes, a long time," he answered, not wanting to talk to them about Celena—she was too precious to him.

"Is she an Indian like you?"

Ethan snorted. "No, she most definitely is not!"

"Oh, that's right, you two are from the same hometown," Trigg said, nodding, pleased with himself for not getting lost during the conversation, which happened to him more than he liked to admit.

"Is she pretty?" Amos queried.

Wishing all of them were not looking at him, Victor merely nodded, not wanting—even as friendly as they were—to share her with them. "Yes, she's pretty."

"That's how you describe her, *pretty?*" Turning with another snort, Ethan glanced into the fire. "She's *beautiful*. Absolutely, perfectly beautiful. Everything about her. Her gentle voice, her long sun brightened hair, her angel's face—and my God those eyes! They are the most astonishing pale blue eyes I have ever seen. And they pierce your heart, your very *soul!* In fact, they have always rather reminded me of early spring violets, and not the ones in full bloom, but the tiny ones that blossom in spring, deep in the woods near streams. But there's more to her than physical beauty; there's goodness, honor, and virtue in her heart. And she sets such a good example that it makes me want to strive to be good too—she brings out all that is decent in my heart, and when I gaze into those eyes of hers, I see all that is wonderful in the world, all that is shining and bright."

"*Well God damn!*" Gideon howled. "Banker boy, you've got it seriously *bad* for this little blue-eyed gal don't ya, *whose wife is she again?*"

Although it took Victor a moment to answer, he finally did. "Mine. It's my wife he's talking about."

It wasn't until two days later that Ethan had a chance to talk to Victor without the eyes and ears of all the others. He gingerly approached Victor as he sat by the fire outside the tent. He noticed with a sickening lurch in his stomach that Victor somehow managed a tight smile up at him.

"I don't know what to say to you," Ethan began, sitting down. He silently watched Victor poke the fire with a long stick. The embers glowed, and the breeze sent the sparks up in a slender orange swirl into the black night. "I guess...you know now?" Ethan asked warily.

There was no anger flashing in the cruel gray eyes, no murderous rage. "I think I've always known."

For a moment, Ethan was embarrassed, shocked into silence, and felt a sudden terrible nakedness at having been exposed for so long. "Oh, that transparent, was I?" he trilled in a horribly failed attempt at humor.

When Victor turned and looked at him, Ethan hated himself for trying to make light of something that he knew was not trivial.

"Yes," Victor said at last, then looked away again. Done rearranging the glowing logs, he rested his long arms against his knees. They heard an owl hoot, and Victor wondered what rodent the owl was after.

"Why didn't you ever..." Ethan had to swallow to bolster his courage, "say anything to me?"

Victor shrugged, still not looking at him. "What was I going to say?"

"How long...how long have you known?"

"I had my suspicions, but the day I married her, your toasting and drunken boasting pretty much confirmed it."

"Suspicions? You had suspicions *before* that?" Ethan balked, wondering how Victor had managed all these years to deal with the unsavory knowledge. He found himself wondering, if the tables had been turned, if he could have been so civil to the man in love with his wife.

"Remember the night, it was a long time ago, that huge harvest? The night you'd first come back from school," Victor began, fiddling with the stick in the fire, sending more amber sparks up into the sky. "I always thought...that you saw Celena and me that night, and that you knew how I much I wanted her, and you would have known I was..." He shook his head, not finishing.

"I did," Ethan admitted painfully, and then shut his eyes tight when he saw a quiet flash of disappointment cross Victor's face, "I did see the two of you that night."

Victor turned, looked at him, and sighed wearily. "Oh...well. Then that means the night of James's barn raising when you followed her and wouldn't leave her alone, you already *knew* how I felt about her, and yet... you did it anyway."

The silence was painful for Ethan but apologizing so many years later seemed inadequate and he was finished with lying.

"But it was a long time ago...I guess it doesn't matter anymore." Victor sighed.

"I wish I hadn't! I didn't mean to—fall for her...and I knew I shouldn't pursue her...but I couldn't *stop* myself!"

Victor made no reply to the confession, and they both simply watched the lights of the fire.

"Did you...hate me for it? *Do* you hate me for it?"

Victor glanced at him, his gray eyes devoid of warmth. "Why should I hate you?"

Ethan shrugged. "Most men would."

"Then most men are fools." They fell silent again as the wind sent the flames leaping haphazardly into the inky sky. Another owl screech pierced the night. "I must admit I feel a sort of...pity for you," Victor mused quietly, "in a way, I even understand how sometimes things just happen. I got lucky after all because she wanted me, she could have easily wanted you. I don't know what would have happened to me if she had not loved me." It was the first time in the entire conversation that a truly distraught look crossed Victor's face. "I can't even begin to imagine the pain of it, because when I do I can't *breathe*. Without her my life would have been...*empty*." He looked over at Ethan. "And I imagine that's how your life has been without her. You've been living with this pain, this emptiness...for years."

Ethan stared into the intense blue light at the fire's base. Remembering all the crazy things he thought were going to happen when he talked to Victor. Ethan imagined things ranging from the violent like Victor assaulting him to the ridiculous like Victor spitting on him. Ethan felt a sudden strange sense of detachment, able to look at the situation almost outside of himself. Part of him was relieved she had fallen in love with Victor and not him, knowing with a painful lump in his throat that Victor proved himself to be the better man time after time.

"I never...did or *would* have touched her," Ethan said softly, swallowing hard. "You know that don't you? I mean once I realized I...knew there was no hope."

"I know. Besides, you'd never have gotten anywhere with her if you'd even tried. And if you had," he shook his head grimly and Ethan knew it would have simply ended the friendship. "Penelope knew, didn't she?"

Ethan looked down guiltily, trying to push from his mind the unsavory thoughts that assaulted him whenever her face came into his head.

The innocent look in her brown eyes had been replaced by the humiliation and anger that had been in them when she'd learned the truth, and then been replaced by sadness and disappointment when she died.

"Yes."

"I hoped when you married her, things might change. I hoped you might forget."

"I did too. And I did try, I did. But I simply *couldn't*." Ethan stared up at the stars in frustration. "Celena didn't mean to but she...put a *spell* on me."

Victor nodded. "I know. She put one on me too."

"Does this...ruin everything? God willing if I live through this wretched war, am I banned from your home, am I barred from seeing her?"

"What good would that do, except hurt you and confuse Celena?"

Ethan had to look down and again thought how lucky he was to know Victor and made a vow to himself that he would return him to Celena no matter what had to be sacrificed. After all Victor's life was worth far more than his own.

"Besides, I haven't forgotten, Ethan. I haven't forgotten that after Anna died and Celena and I were at odds, it was *you* that suggested the trip to Washington. You were responsible for making me realize how much I had to lose. You brought us back together, despite the way you felt."

Overcome with emotion, Ethan had to look away. It was strange, when he looked back on his life, he could only see all the wrong he had done.

"I've spent my life wanting what you had, jealous of your happiness, hating myself for it," Ethan admitted painfully. "I apologize—"

Impatiently, Victor waved him off and for a moment their eyes met. The accumulation of their years of friendship passed between them. Their shared happinesses, disappointments, pains. Through all of it, they had always been able to depend on the other. And silently the need of forgiveness sought by one, was granted by the other.

"You felt this *pain* for me all these years and yet you wouldn't give her up and let me have her?" Ethan joked weakly, but it had the desired effect of breaking the tension.

Victor smirked. "Would you?"

"Let's blame God then shall we? For the sorry state of my pathetic life! After all I suppose it's his fault for sending down to earth such an exquisite creature to capture my heart. We couldn't both have her—she couldn't love us both!"

"You're right. God should have made two of her."

Henry Wilburn had the unenviable task of telling his mother that two of his brothers Claude, Thomas had been killed. It was hard for Celena to imagine Claude and Thomas dead already. She thought of them working with Victor in the shop all those years and it didn't seem possible that they were both already gone.

The Charbonniers too received bad news—Caleb had been killed and one of the twins had been too, but the army had never been able to keep them straight. In the upper half of the letter, it said it was Davey and in the last it had said it was as Danny! Esther was beside herself not knowing which son to grieve for. *'They were two different boys even if they looked alike! It makes a difference to me which one's gone!'*

Alice heard James had been killed, but it only hardened her more. She would take no one's condolences. In fact, she refused to allow his family to grieve for him which upset Yvonne so badly that her daughters feared for her health when she would not eat and continued to slip each day toward despair with the loss of her husband, and now James. Celena thought that God had sent Johnnie to force their mother to continue living, to anchor her. And Celena shuddered wondering if she too didn't have seven *'anchors'* to keep her from drowning in that ocean of grief.

The war continued delivering bad news. Stephan's regiment had been captured and sent to Vicksburg to a prison camp. They were relieved in one sense and terrified in another having heard nothing but horror stories about starvation, disease, and the filth in those camps.

Carlene had not had a letter in months from Mason, and although she tried to act like it didn't bother her, she was more cross than normal and given to screaming fits whenever the mood seemed to strike her. Which was often these days and only made things worse for poor Livi, Marie, and baby Emiline who longed for their quiet, competent father to balance their emotional mother. There was no consoling Carlene, who amidst her fear that something happened to Mason still said horrible things about him.

"I bet he deserted, you know what a sissy he was! I bet he deserted, and they shot him, or he shot himself with as clumsy as he was."

"Carlene, don't," Celena warned, her patience with her sister's lack of feeling for the countless neighbors and friends who had confirmation of their loved ones' demise infuriated her.

"Why not? He was my husband and I know what a sap he was!"

"Will you *shut up!*" Celena snapped. "You don't even know how *lucky* you were he married you. You could have ended up with that bastard Eddie and been left abandoned like Lorien! I bet Eddie didn't join the army, I bet he up and left Lorien with those babies! Mason has been kind and wonderful to you, and you *don't deserve him!* You've *never* appreciated him! For God's sake Carlene how can you talk about him like that in front of your girls? He's their father, and they *love* him! If you're going to talk about Mason like this I don't want you coming over any more! Go ahead Carlene, make all the sarcastic comments about the men we love dying every day, but don't you *dare* do it in *my house!*"

Carlene left in a huff with her whining daughters, but she came back the next day, her eyes still red from crying. "I'm sorry," she sobbed, then looked down at the ground, not sure her sister would welcome her back. Truthfully, Carlene didn't know what she'd do if Celena didn't let her return. Carlene had, since Mason left, been looking to Celena for direction. It was Celena who helped her organize the garden, Celena's house she went to everyday to cook or sew. Celena's house she ate dinner at almost every night—where Livi did her school lessons under the patient tutoring of her cousin Ben.

"All right," Celena said at last, "but consider yourself warned."

Celena did not panic when the letters from Victor stopped. The war made mail dangerous and unpredictable at best. He was wounded and any day a letter was coming, or he had been sent like Stephan to a prisoner camp. Victor would be all right. He was strong, always so strong. She tried not to think about the hideous stories they heard of men going into the camps weighing a normal 170 pounds and being exchanged weighing only 100. How packed into the camps they came down with every communicable disease and died while waiting to be exchanged or for the war to end. The thoughts themselves were too terrifying—too paralyzing for her to think of, so instead she refused to contemplate—to wonder, to imagine.

To keep the frightening thoughts from taking over she immersed herself in taking care of everyone. Which with her own children and the added pressures of both her sisters and their children suddenly dependent on her for support, was a daunting task. Although Randy and Ben and even Andrew were old enough to be useful and helped immensely there were still lots of things they couldn't do. She was trying to keep their lives as normal as possible, and did not hide her fear from her children, nor did she enlarge it. When they asked her like they did so often, "When's Papa coming home?" she did not blindly reassure them and would merely say, "When the war's over—God willing."

The boys begrudgingly went to school and did their never-ending chores. Did their homework at night in the living room in the company of their cousins and aunts. They went to church and to their grandmother's house. But it was obvious to everyone that they were all doing the same thing. They were silently waiting for the men they loved to walk through the doors, for the war to end or for dreaded official letters bearing bad news. Breathlessly they waited.

Celena tossed and turned at night, often waking in a cold sweat with an ache so painful in her heart she would rear up in bed with a start, with bitter feelings of guilt and selfishness. After all her mother had lost her father-and even though her mother had indeed changed, she was still living-still going on. Celena had an infant daughter and six boys who looked to her for answers to everything from; *why Luanne wouldn't stand still while you milked her—why had their uncles fought on opposite sides of the war?* Their daily demands were all-consuming, and it was good because it kept her mind off the horrible; the unthinkable. They depended on her—she would have to go on.

As she silently walked the floor night after night as winter turned to spring and sleep eluded her, she would look up at the dark sky and find herself staring at the stars and the moon. Wondering if in a far-off army camp Victor too was looking up at the moon thinking of her, his children, and the home he'd left behind. Wondered if his heart ached with loneliness as hers did. But the melancholy thoughts never stayed for long because they would be replaced by torturous thoughts—that maybe he was dying under the same peaceful sky she gazed at.

May 1864
The Battle of Wilderness

"This is a God awful country," Trigg complained, marching next to Victor, who merely shrugged, too tired from marching to look at the scenery. "Ground may be all right," Trigg mused. He liked to think about farming—it took his mind off the relentless marching and moving the army did all the time, and off his fear. "But this is the worst kind of forest—"

"I didn't know there was a *bad kind* of forest!" Victor joked, turning briefly to look at Trigg, too tired to do more than that.

"Of course, there are. Looks to me like somebody once upon a time tried to tame this place—they cut down the good trees and left the straggly ones, the bad ones." Trigg shook his head in disgust seeing the small pines, scrub oak, and cedar trees and other vines and underbrush. "And now there's a scrubby thicket of bad trees, second growth trees—why, you can scarcely see ten paces ahead of ya!"

"Don't want to be doing any fighting in there," Amos agreed.

Victor too could think of no worse place to meet the Confederates and wondered as the long blue line of soldiers marched towards it—what strategies the Generals were planning and what awaited them there. He'd heard the rumors. Their commanding officers General Mead and General Grant's object was plain. Engage the Army of Northern Virginia in battle, and as always, if possible defeat it. But under no circumstances allow it enough freedom to upset the vital Union plans elsewhere. It was a 'squeeze play' of sorts Victor realized, knowing as he marched north other Union forces were marching aggressively against Atlanta, Petersburg, and the fertile Shenandoah valley. But unfortunately for the Union the Wilderness presented probably the worst possible condition with which to maneuver a large army. But for the Confederacy the dismal forest would help offset their opponents' numerical advantage. But he also knew enough to know that more than likely General Lee was not going to along easily with General's Mead and Grants plans.

A shell exploded by Ethan's feet. Startled, he dropped his gun and scrambled to the ground to retrieve it. He heard mini balls whiz above him and knew he would have been dead had he not dropped his gun.

Victor was not far behind him, but the vines and infuriating brush obscured his view. Through the dense brush Ethan saw Victor furiously shoving the rod down his rifle. Ethan heard Captain Smythe yelling at them to fire, and Victor slid down next to him, re-loading.

"You've gotten rather good at this soldiering thing!" Ethan grinned, thinking it was odd to be joking at time like this, but it was a release of the fear that otherwise would paralyze him.

"Well, it's either do it right, or die," Victor grunted.

"Move out!" Bellamy shouted, and they moved into the smoky, dense woods. Victor heard a shot nearby and realized it was another regiment.

"Forward...double quick!" Bellamy yelled.

Again, they scrambled to their feet running toward the smoke, dodging the bodies of the fallen men in front of them, and the tangle of brush undergrowth that made it nearly impossible to move or even see what they were firing at. Ethan stumbled and fell, smacking his head hard against the ground. Dizzy, he felt a hand under his elbow hauling him up and looking up saw it was Victor.

"I am *not dying* today in this godforsaken place!" Gideon barked as he viciously loaded his gun. Turning over, he closed one eye and shot.

"Well, we'll see about that," Rusty said and spat out part of the paper from the cartridge, noting the horrible taste of the gunpowder. "Seems to me the Good Lord is the one who decides that!"

"The *Good Lord* ain't here today, you're gonna have to look after *yourself!*" Gideon barked.

"Come on!" Victor urged when suddenly Trigg stopped in front of him—but when he looked up through the smoke he froze with the frustration of their fight. They had made advances, but the confusing tangles of the Wilderness knew no allegiance, and time and time again they were ordered to retreat and forced to find a different route back, the way they had come in flames. "Company back!" Sergeant Bellamy yelled.

Victor saw a gravely wounded Confederate soldier giving his last by bayoneting a young Union soldier who had fallen. But something about the young Union soldier's cry was horrifyingly familiar.

Ethan saw Victor sprinting toward the two soldiers, dodging the brush fires as he went. Before the Confederate soldier could drive a second wound, Victor wrenched the gun from him and stabbed him until he fell back dead.

"*Hank!*" Victor yelled, staring down at his frightened, bloodied nephew.

Tears made clean marks on Hank's dirty face. He was bleeding from the chest and trembling with fear and stunned, dumbfounded relief as he stared up at his uncle.

A shell exploded near them, and Victor yelled, "*Go back!*" He grabbed his bleeding nephew when a shot hit him in the shoulder blade, spinning him to the left.

Turning at the sound, Hank screamed. He screamed again when

another shot caught his uncle in the chest, and amidst the smoke and noise he watched Victor stagger and fall.

"Damnit Hank! *Get back—go on!*" Ethan shouted at Hank, who was trembling and crying so hard he couldn't even crawl. "I said *go!*" He gave Hank a vicious shove.

"*No God...no...please no!*" Ethan prayed as he crawled through the tangled undergrowth to where Victor lay. He grabbed Victor under the shoulders and dragged him away from the field, grunting under the strain. He propped Victor's bleeding body against one of the small cedar trees that mercifully hadn't been splintered by the shelling.

Frantically Ethan struggled out of his coat, using it to sop up the blood from his friend's wounds. The first shot in the shoulder looked to have gone through, and a steady band of bright red was already down the front of him, but it was the second shot, near his heart, that Ethan knew was serious.

"Did Hank...get back?" Victor gasped, looking up.

Ethan nodded, kneeling over him, still trying to stop the hemorrhaging.

"Good," Victor whispered, grimacing in pain. He closed his eyes.

"*Damnit, Victor!*" Ethan grabbed him by the shoulders, shook him once hard. "Open your eyes, don't you God damn die on me! *Don't leave me!*" Ethan cried, seeing that Victor was struggling to breathe.

Victor saw the tattering of his flesh, the blood leaking from one wound and pulsing from the other, and knew.

"*God damn you!* Don't *leave* me!" Ethan wailed, still trying desperately to mop up the blood. But looking down, realized that his own coat was already soaked, and knew how useless it was. He dropped his head against Victor's chest, and feeling the warmth of Victor's blood against his face, began to sob. Uselessly, he gripped Victor's hand tighter, as if he could by his own will keep Victor with him.

A moment later Ethan felt a gentle hand on the back of his neck and looked up.

"E-Ethan," Victor choked, blood leaking into his lungs, drowning him. He coughed and spit up, blood bubbling on his lips. "Tell... Celena...that I'm sorry."

As the light began to fade around Victor into his mind darted the wonderful images of home. The soaring sycamore trees with their peeling tan bark that exposed white wood, the thick green moss growing on the side of a long ago fallen elm tree, the way the morning sun could make that muddy river look like gold. Of Jonah robust and young before he was sick, of Margaret scolding him, of his boys and how they liked to hang from his arms like they were branches of a tree, of the daughter he'd never seen. And of Celena. *Lena.*

"Victor...*Victor!*"

Ethan's sobbing nor the sounds of battle dimmed. Victor could barely feel Ethan's strong warm hand in his, and he managed for the last time to smile at the man who had been his lifelong best friend. Looking over Ethan's bowed head, amidst the tangled forest of Wilderness littered with bodies of men dead and dying, Victor saw the serene image of his mother. She smiled at her son, unbound black hair blowing wildly in the breeze. She reached a hand toward him, and this time, he went with her.

Hank Wilburn was delirious from his chest wound. They had patched up as best they could, then sent him to an army hospital. Even though the hospital was used to dealing with frantic, hysterical men, the majority of which had never witnessed the horrors of battle, his tortured wails of "*I killed him—oh my God I him killed!*" tore at even their hardened hearts.

"Poor young pup, bet he thinks twice about enlisting to see the *glories* of war," scoffed one of the hospital attendants, shaking his head at the distraught boy, doubting seriously as he glanced at his wound that he would live through the night.

In the end at Wilderness, although there was no victor, the Union army met its objective. For the first time, General Lee faced General Grant, an adversary who had the determination to press on despite the costs. There was a decisive moment for the war in that tangled underbrush at Wilderness that marked the beginning of the end for the Army of Northern Virginia, and the end for the Confederacy itself. The casualties had been staggering for both the Confederacy, nearly 13,000 and for the Union-17,000 had been killed or wounded between May 5-12 in 1864. A total greater than all Union armies combined in any previous week of the war. Within Victor's regiment, Captain Smythe had been wounded and Sergeant Bellamy had been killed, and accounting for the large number of dead and wounded soldiers at the end of the days was a wearisome task for the burial detail.

Privates Trigg Dikeman, Rusty Dugan, and Gideon Plummer all had taken bullets through their brains, but they were identified. Amos Norton, though, was not because he had been blown to bits by a shell. Private Ethan Stanfield's body was not found, and when he did not answer at roll was presumed to have been captured.

Although it took the burial detail two days to identify the partially charred body of a Union solider they found propped up against a singed cedar tree, they finally accounted for and listed Private Victor Gant as killed in action.

Chapter 44

It was to be called Camp Sumter in southwest Georgia, named after the confederates' victory at the fort on the auspicious beginning of the war. But like many things in life, it didn't turn out that way, and the place Ethan was transported after he was captured was known simply as Andersonville.

It was already hot on that May afternoon in 1864 when Ethan and 200 other captured men walked through the crude seventeen-foot stockade fences of Andersonville prison, which had been squared on all sides to keep the prisoners from seeing out. Immediately, the stench of the fouled stream—ironically named *Sweet Water*—defiled Ethan's senses, but it was the sight of the prisoners gawking at the new men that horrified him.

"They—they look like living *skeletons!*" a young man exclaimed, standing next to Ethan.

Their clothes were tattered rags. They were so filthy it was difficult to recognize their features, and they all seemed to be alternately scratching at the lice and fleas that had infested them and the mosquitoes that Ethan heard humming even in his own ears. Appalled, Ethan looked across the grounds, and the desolation of thousands of men living in the open in such a cramped space made him want to cry out.

"Awl right yawl lisen' up!" one of the guards called in an almost incomprehensible southern drawl. Ethan realized he had to be at least seventy because his hair was snow-white and his face was lined and wrinkled after working his whole life under the hot Georgia sun. Next to the old man was a young boy whose childish face was riddled with acne; he couldn't have been more than fourteen. These were all the Confederacy had left to guard them, and he shook his head with sadness knowing how many men in their prime had already been killed.

"I gotta few things ta tell ya newins'," the old man started, but his eyes Ethan noticed seemed apprehensive as the men kept pouring through the gates. "Once a day ya get your rations—and we don't want no fightin' about it neither...ya do your own cookin'." Ethan found himself suddenly looking at the red dust of the Georgia clay beneath his feet, and not seeing a tree in sight wondered suddenly what they were to use for fuel. "And those of you that wants it can make yourself a little shebang or place to live—" Ethan glanced to the crude hovels the prisoners had fastened. They used skinny limbs, small brush, and sometimes blankets or old clothes draped over them to provide protection from the merciless Georgia sun or rain. But he noticed that the men inhabiting the 'shebangs' had their shirts, and a shiver went through him realizing where they had to have come from.

"This here is the deadline." The old man pointed to a long flimsy looking fence that would have done nothing to keep a small child in much less a grown man bent on escape. It ran the interior of the rectangular shape of the prison—almost like a smaller box inside the stockade. "See them sentries?" He pointed to the men placed ominously every forty feet or so, each of which held a member of the Georgia reserves rifle. "If'n ya cross that line," his eyes for a moment glittered as if with sadness when he looked directly at Ethan, noting the incredible youth of the boy standing next to him "...we shoot ya...that's why it's the deadline, you cross it, you're dead." He turned from them, pointing to the latrines which it seemed to Ethan were placed dangerously close to the creek, and as he looked closer he saw with disgust that the fecal waste indeed ran into the stream from which they were to get their drinking water.

"Thems there are the latrines...that's all." His short, grim tour of Andersonville prison was over, and he walked off.

Ethan knew then that was it. He would either wait out the rest of the war, or die there. As he looked at the other emaciated prisoners around him, noting that many of them simply laid in their shebangs to get out of the hot sun while flies and mosquitoes flitted over their filthy bodies, realized that most of them were too weak and malnourished to even think of escape. The agonizing thought occurred to him that Andersonville was merely a camp where the confederacy was 'housing' union soldiers until they died.

He glanced up at the guards placed evenly around the huge stockade fences, with their long muskets poised, noticed the two huge gates one on the south, one of the north, and the enormity of suffering and torment that he knew was to come almost broke him.

He heard a lumber wagon bumping along and looking over saw it was piled high with bodies. They were buried naked, the other prisoners desperately needing their clothes and transported in full sight of the stockade, piled like pork with stiff limbs sticking out in all directions from the wagon. The Union's brave soldiers.

He must have made some small, horrible sound because a prisoner, who had been there awhile by the looks of his arms and legs misshapen due to scurvy, turned to him. "Twenty is a full load," he commented, watching the grisly sight of bodies pass by.

"How long have you been here?" Ethan asked, noticing gnats were swarming in the wounds festering on his feet.

"What month is it?"

"May."

He thought for a moment. "Five months then."

In only five months Ethan realized he would look like the man before him.

"If ya see somebody dead—don't say nothin'," the man said, edging near. He was so covered with lice and filth that Ethan had to resist the impulse to immediately move back, especially when the man merely licked off the lice crawling on his lips.

"Why?"

The man looked around for a moment, grinning like a mischievous child. "We hide it from the guards," he said, nodding his head. His hair was matted and scaly, encrusted with months' worth of dandruff, his bright eyes oddly gleeful. "Hide it as long as we can thata way we get their rations, and mind ya tie 'em to ya after they die, so nobody steals 'em from ya—that way while you're doin' your burial detail, ya can get ya a piece of wood to do your cookin'..." The man seemed inordinately pleased that he had imparted this knowledge to him, and Ethan felt an uncomfortably large lump forming in his throat.

"What's your name?"

"Edward Fitzsimmons," he said brightly and reached out to shake Ethan's hand like they were old friends meeting pleasantly on a street somewhere. "Yours?"

"Ethan Stanfield."

"That little feller come in with you?" he asked, referring to the young private who stood next to Ethan when they had been given their introduction to the camp.

"Yes," Ethan managed and had to look down when he realized the young man was huddled by the stinking latrine, arms wrapped tight around his legs, his hunched shoulders shaking with the force of his sobs.

"That ain't gonna do no good," Edward said, viciously scratching the flea bites around his ribs and under his armpits. "Somebody's poor boy." He shook his head despondently "I suppose it's a good thing his Mama can't see him now..."

It was as if a heavy wooden door had been slammed behind him, and Ethan's already aching heart shriveled up inside his chest. He glanced up in despair at the foreboding walls of the prison comforted only by the thought that he'd be dead soon enough. It was just as well. He'd never be able to live with the pain, could not live with the guilt. Would never have to look into Celena's eyes and tell her that he'd broken his promise.

There was no hope, there was no tomorrow. A sense of gloom and utter defeat took over his soul. Ethan was terrified suddenly, more terrified than he ever had been before in his life. Not because he knew he was going to waste away and die slowly in Andersonville, but because he was alone. Victor was no longer with him.

Shaking his head, he swallowed hard, and lifting his face stared up at the unmerciful blue of the Georgia sky and hated God. Hated that God had done it again. He had taken the good and the innocent, and left him, behind.

"No," Celena managed to get out as she stared at Hank sitting at the table, white as a ghost, newly home from an army hospital that August, still sporting his badly mending chest wound. "No...please, please don't tell me this—" A numbness took over body, her mind rejecting the words she so dreaded hearing.

Hank dropped his head into his hands and began to weep bitterly, and Margaret and Henry who were both seated at the table with him were silent. Margaret was so distraught, that she could not find the strength to comfort even her own son.

"I'm sorry! I am so *sorry* aunt Celena! He'd have been all right if he hadn't been coming back to save me—" He broke off in a tortured sob and dropped his head against the table and wept.

"Maybe...you're mistaken," Celena said, but even to her own ears her voice sounded feeble, "maybe he's somewhere...with Ethan."

"No. Ethan's probably dead too, I think they're both dead now! Uncle Victor...he yelled down at me to go back, and he was yelling at me when they shot him, *twice!*"

He dissolved again into uncontrollable tears and wished like he had so many times in these last months that he had listened to his uncle and never enlisted. Now not only would he have to live without him, but he would carry forever the weight of his uncle's death. "It's all my fault, it's *all my fault!*"

The fear Celena had been fighting to keep at bay gnashed viciously at the hope in her heart as if it were a mad, snarling beast. She stood from the table and backed away from them as if they were diseased. "No. He...*couldn't* be dead! I would have known it. I would have known in *my* heart if *his* had stopped beating!" Even though all along she knew there was a chance he could be killed, she realized dully it didn't help; now that the unthinkable had happened, the horror she felt in her heart was even worse than she had imagined. And amongst the excruciating pain engulfing her was guilt. The *guilt* of knowing that somewhere Victor had painfully drawn his last breath—and she hadn't even *felt* it.

"But I saw him Aunt Celena," Hank sobbed softly, "I saw him fall..."

She stood motionless, refusing the words. The room darkened suddenly and afraid she was going to faint; she gripped the doorjamb for support. She took a shaky step out the door and leaned against the house. Looking up at the sky she wondered suddenly why everything looked gray, wondered why the leaves of the mulberry and elm trees no longer looked green, wondered why the sky was no longer blue.

It was over. In a horrifyingly brief moment, it was all over. All the worrying, and all the waiting and all the wondering, and all the hoping, it was all over. Knuckles white and hands fisted, she leaned over the railing and vomited.

For two days she could hardly speak. She forced herself to tell her sons, and her heart would have ached when she saw them go white and how grief stricken they were if her heart wasn't already so full of anguish she couldn't take on any more pain. They sobbed against her, and she stroked their faces and hugged them when they clamored against her. She told them not to be angry, it was no one's fault. She told them to pray to God for his soul and for the wonderful time that they had him, and that somehow they would get along without him. Told them that in time the pain would go away, that it wouldn't always hurt so bad. And they trusted her and believed her. But she did not believe it herself. Not any of it.

She tried to eat, but everything she put in her mouth tasted like dirt, and often came back up. She lost an alarming amount of weight, and her complexion took on such a sallow tone that she shocked those that had not seen her in a while with her gaunt, sickly appearance made worse by the bleak mourning attire. She was silent, private, and tormented in her grief.

During the windy cool nights of fall that followed she found herself thinking wild, mad thoughts. She'd not seen his body—maybe the army had misidentified him. Maybe he was merely wounded and too delirious to write home—he had been captured and was any day going to be exchanged and would return home. And during the desperate night hours she would imagine all sorts of explanations for his absence, explanations that made her mad, wild brain pound. But in the chill of early dawn, she would lose her optimism, her hope and know with an agonizing pain in her shattered heart that he was dead. Cold and lost to her forever, buried in a hastily dug mass grave near some lonely battlefield in far off Virginia. Buried somewhere she could never visit, never mourn him. Never lay wildflowers on his grave.

Six weeks later she received two official letters from Captain Smythe. Although he could not write letters home to all the men he had lost at Wilderness, could not bear the thought of Victor's family never knowing what happened to him. The first letter was about Private Stanfield; since he had no other relatives, she had been listed as his next of kin. In it, the captain regretted to inform her that, even though he had been gallant on the battlefield, unfortunately, he had been captured by Confederate forces. In the next letter, he also regretted to inform her that her husband, who the captain assured her, had also been gallant on the battlefield, had been killed in action. Because Captain Smythe had been so fond of Victor, went on for another short paragraph telling her how he had paid the ultimate price in service to his country and that he hoped her heart was eased some knowing how bravely he had performed during the battle, and that he had died a hero.

She sat simply staring at the letter, refusing the words before her, as her heart seemed to slow down in her chest, then ceased even to beat.

It all broke then, the last remnant of resistance, the last shred of denial, the last bit of hope. She felt her heart break.

Victor was dead.

Chapter 45

Ethan woke with a start, shivering in a damp sweat underneath his she-bang. For a moment he could not fathom where he was. He had been dreaming he was playing chess with Victor, and since Victor had beat him he was demanding a rematch. Celena was telling them their dinner was ready and Victor and he and the boys were all noisily coming to the table. He could smell the roasted chicken fresh out of the oven.

He sat up in the darkness, huddled with his knees under his chin.

Food.

It was almost the only thing he ever dreamed about, that or when he was going to die. He swallowed the bitter taste left in his mouth by the tiny piece of slimy beef he'd eaten for dinner, trying to settle the rumbling of his still-empty stomach.

He dropped his head on his knees in the darkness, hearing the young private Allan—who had pretty much attached himself to Ethan since they'd arrived—crying. Ethan turned and looked at him huddled underneath the filthy shebang. Allan's shirt was no more than a rag, his body a mere frame, his hair fallen out and his ankles and wrists riddled with scurvy and grotesquely swollen.

It made the muscles in Ethan's throat constrict to hear him sob so.

"You poor boy..." Ethan whispered. "You're somebody's boy and here you are dead and yet still breathing." He hung his head and cried. Ethan had done his best to stay alive so he could protect Allan, but it was difficult to do either.

The rations were appallingly small, enough to keep them alive long enough to allow them to starve to death slowly. Most days they got a quarter loaf of bread. The problem with the bread was that it was made of such inferior wheat that it increased the dysentery and other bowel complaints which were already at an alarming level. Then there was the six ounces of pork or beef so rotten they could be smelled at a great distance. At first Ethan couldn't bring himself to eat it, the smell had so nauseated him, but he ate it now even though it was often full of wiggling white maggots.

The stream, was so fouled that it was a veritable cesspool of filth, occupied much of Ethan's thoughts. In fact, when he was not trying to scramble for food or spending his every moment scratching the incessant bites of fleas and lice, he pondered the architectural and planning mistakes so obvious to him in the camp.

"The cookhouse and bakery: putting them upstream only pollutes the water before we even get it. Did Captain Wirz not understand the flow of the river before he put it there?" Ethan had remarked to Edward Fitzsimmons, who unlike most of the men was interested in these sorts of things. "That's probably more detrimental to us anything else. And the sinks," Ethan said, referring to the latrines, "it should have worked." He was able to see by the beginnings of two dams across the creek that the intention had been to open one of the dams once a day and flush down the river the bottom of the stream. But like so many things in Andersonville it had been hastily erected and ill conceived, and with other projects requiring attention it had been mostly abandoned. Leaving the stream to become a quagmire for disease.

"The maggots in the water," Edward said. "I strain them out of the water with my teeth." He forced a grin, but it did not lift Ethan's spirit as he thought it would.

"You know what I heard? I heard one of the guards say 120 men died yesterday. Andersonville is claiming on average 100 men a day."

"Starvation, disease, murder, despair...take your pick," Ethan said, looking up at the deadline.

Only yesterday four men had been shot and killed going over the deadline. At first Ethan felt sorry for them, compassion when he witnessed their malnourished, filthy bodies fall to the ground. But he wondered now if they weren't merely freeing themselves from a hellish existence.

At the same time there was a gang of prisoners who preyed on the weaker ones, stealing their blankets, their food—sometimes even murdering them for it. They had terrorized the camp for months. Finally, Captain Wirz caught them and all six had been hanged. Ethan had watched the hangings, surprised that their deaths affected him so little.

"If a man were to tunnel under that stockade, say twenty yards, do you think it would be far enough not to be seen?" Edward asked.

Ethan merely nodded, having had this exact same conversation with Edward, who he learned owned a large mercantile in Dayton. He had two brothers who were also in the army and he alternated between the two subjects—his brothers and their welfare, and his desire to escape from Andersonville. Other than those two subjects his only other conversation was the oft-repeated rumor that any day the war was going to end, and they were going to be liberated.

"I don't know," Ethan mumbled, uninterested in digging. Although in the beginning he had thought of escape, the months of imprisonment, filth, and starvation had left him apathetic and silent. In fact, he barely spoke to anyone anymore since he had been humiliated two nights prior when Edward, who had been sleeping next to him, shook him asking, *"Who's this Celena you keep crying about?"*

"I say we slip out quietly on work detail," Ethan suggested.

"Then what happens in the morning when our benevolent Captain Wirz here finds out we're gone?"

Ethan shrugged. "With the influx of prisoners crowding into this place day after day, they'd never miss us."

"What about the dogs? You know that scum Turner has bloodhounds and he'll hunt us down like foxes."

"Well then..." Ethan let out a desperate breath, raking a hand through his matted hair. "Suppose we pretend run off during burying detail."

"No! It will never work," Edward said, his eyes abnormally bright against the filth of his skin. "We'll think of something. We can't give up hope."

Ethan merely nodded, waiting for Edward to leave him to his thoughts, knowing that he had abandoned all hope the day Victor had died at Wilderness.

"Father! I was hoping to have a word with you," Celena said, catching him after mass. She was quick on her feet, Father Tonnellier thought, given how gaunt and unhealthy she looked.

"Yes Celena, what can I do for you?" He couldn't help himself and reached out a touched her arm, trying to remember how old she was. He'd baptized her, as he had every child of John and Yvonne, and realized she had to be at least thirty. But she looked younger, and it made him want to protect her. It saddened him to see how much she had changed.

She had always been petite, but she was past the point of thin, and it made her appear like a little girl masquerading in her mother's clothes. Rather than the effect being charming, it bordered on the macabre.

"I wanted to ask you if it would be all right if I put up a—a memorial for Victor." She blinked back the tears that were always just under the surface. "I know because I don't have his body that I can't...bury him, and since I know that I'll never get his body back, I wondered if it would be all right?" She stopped suddenly and, sighing, looked away, doing her best to fight back tears. She knew she'd already grieved too much in front of the boys. "May I put one up, Father? I must have; I mean I'd like to have...somewhere. A place to go...a place to think about him. It tears at m-my heart that I don't know where he is." She closed her eyes trying to blot out the gruesome images of his bloated, unburied body decaying on the battlefield. "I don't want him to think I've forgotten him." She glanced past the priest to the place where little Anna was buried and smiled sadly remembering Victor had said the same words about their daughter.

Father Tonnellier couldn't help but think no one in their right mind would ever think that she had forgotten him, because there was a forlorn, haunted look about her eyes. They had always been such pretty blue eyes, but now they mainly looked cold. He wanted to comfort her, but had tried so many times already, and always had the feeling that his words no matter how well-meaning did little good.

"He was a good man. He was a good husband and father. He is at peace Celena; you know that don't you?"

She nodded even though she felt no peace for Victor, nor herself. "May I, Father, may I please put up something for him-near our Anna?"

He nodded and immediately she leaned against him and surprised him by holding on tight. He could feel the bones beneath her skin.

"Thank you," she whispered a moment later, sniffing and wiping her face free of tears. "I'm sorry. It's been nearly a year now and I still cry... every day..." She wished she hadn't admitted it when she saw the shadow of disappointment cross his face. "Father," she began tenuously when he turned to walk away.

"What is it Celena?"

She was unsure suddenly if she should ask him, not sure even a Jesuit priest could understand the restlessness and agony that filled her every moment. "Where is he, is he truly gone?" Her eyes dropped to the ground. "I mean, I know he's dead." Right on cue two glistening tears fell from her eyes, wetting her cheeks. "But why didn't I know?" She sniffed,

fumbling with a handkerchief. "We were close, I don't know about anyone else's marriage—but believe me when I tell you Victor and I were
incredibly happy together...we were *connected*. And not just because we
were married those years and had all the children, it was more than that.
I should have *felt* it when he died, I should have *known* when his heart
stopped—" She pressed hard against her stomach and for a moment he
was afraid she was going to faint. "I don't understand." She blotted viciously at her eyes. "Why didn't I know when he left me?"

"Because he didn't leave you, and it isn't over. You'll meet him again
in our father's kingdom. Let your faith be your rock—"

"Victor was my rock," she interrupted, and having said it could not
meet the priest's eyes. "Was God being cruel, to give someone so wonderful to me only to break my heart by taking him away?"

"Celena my child, you know better than that."

"Father, I don't think I'm strong enough for—for this."

"But you are." He put his reassuring hands on her shoulders. "It is
normal to grieve for a *while* Celena, but you must go on. It's what he
would have wanted for you."

"I'm not interested in...*anything* anymore. With Victor gone, I don't care
if I wake in the morning. The enchantment has gone out of life for me."

"What about your children?"

Guiltily Celena looked away.

"They are Victor's children, and they need you. They are God's children too and they need their mother back."

She nodded dutifully. Although she tried to make herself believe these
things, she couldn't. "Everything reminds me of him. There isn't a corner
in Ste. Genevieve that I don't look and see something he either worked
on or paid for. I miss him Father. I miss him so *much*. He said what he
felt for me would last long after he was gone. And he promised me he'd
come back. And I believed him...I trusted him." She shook her head again
with disillusionment, then flustered and annoyed at breaking down
again, forced a weak smile. "Thank you again about the memorial." She
left him standing in the cemetery, fearing he had failed her again.

It was never quiet at night in Andersonville. The air was always alive with
misery. The hospital if one could call it that, was full of men with any
number of contagious diseases and the sounds of their coughing and

moaning made even the night no respite from the horrors.

Another month, maybe two at the most? And I'll be dead, Ethan thought. *It will be over. It would be a relief.* What he was living was not life; it was torture—a slow, agonizing death. There were no battlefields around the prison, but the thousands of men that were laid side by side in the mass graves had still fallen in war, killed at Andersonville.

Ethan sighed and rubbed a raw spot on his hip. It was oozing pus and hurting more each day, and his boot had a hole and it had rubbed his heel raw now. It was strange, it had started as a little thing, but as it was with everything there, became infected. He'd seen men with little cuts that became gangrene that ended up killing them.

What a way to die, in a stinking hell hole, slowly by disease and starvation.

Only two days ago, he had tried to rouse Allan in the morning only to find that the young boy had died during the night, his tiny frame huddled underneath the shebang while flies and mosquitos lit on his body. Ethan had almost cried, but found his tears, like his hope, all used up.

Ethan pushed himself wearily to his feet in the darkness, deciding not to wait for death to claim him. His life was already over, and yet he was still breathing, and it was time for it to end. He took a step. When his aching heart started to tremble at what he was about to do, he calmed himself by whispering, "It will be easy...and it will finally be over."

He took another labored step and stumbled over something in the darkness, landing shaky and weak on the ground, fighting back tears. Summoning his courage he staggered weakly to his feet and again started towards the deadline in the darkness.

No one would ever know. The identifying of the dead was sketchy at best and the cause of death was usually not even documented. No one would ever know what he had done. Besides, who was there to care? He had no family, Victor was dead, and he knew he could never in life, face Celena again. There was nothing left for him. What difference would it make if he hastened it? He was going to die anyway.

As he took another step found himself thinking that since his mother had killed herself, that it was a good thing his daughter Rebecca had died. Not wanting the weak gene or whatever caused the Stanfields to commit suicide, to be passed down to the next unsuspecting generation to deal with. But without warning the sudden thought of Rebecca made pains go across his heart.

Would it be true? he wondered—when he killed himself would he go to hell as Celena had told him was taught by her faith? If he were banished to hell for eternity, surely he would never see his daughter, Penelope, or Victor again—and for a moment these horrifying thoughts paralyzed him in the eerie darkness.

He shook his head, wishing like he had so many times, that he had been killed and not Victor. He turned his anger and frustration up to God.

"It should have been me! Have I been so awful that you'll never release me from this torment, why do you leave me here?" he whispered, looking up at the stars, tears filling his eyes, thinking that despite shining down on him in Andersonville, they still looked beautiful with their pale blue light.

He was dangerously close to the deadline now and in the darkness heard one of the young guards in the pigeon roosts—who he knew had been too afraid to shoot anyone—yell out to him.

"You're going the wrong way!"

And Ethan detected a warning in his voice too. And for a moment Ethan felt badly that the young boy would finally have to shoot someone. He went towards the line, his heart thumping inside his sunken chest.

It will be over...at least it will be over.

He took another step.

"Ethan no!"

Startled to the depths of his soul at the sound of the voice, Ethan jerked his head up to the deadline. Gasping, he slammed his eyes shut, then reopened them when the vision had disappeared.

He staggered back from the deadline then and finding his own tattered shebang collapsed underneath it in a shaking, sweating heap and began to sob. He sobbed for Victor, sobbed for Penelope, sobbed for Rebecca, and Celena but more than anything he sobbed desperately to God to release him from his torment.

The next day Ethan Stanfield and Edward Fitzsimmons were found dead lying next to each other underneath their shebangs and taken outside of the stifling walls of Andersonville prison to be buried.

"I feel so...strange," Celena confided as she sat with Eva one spring night. The lantern light was turned low, casting eerie shadows against the walls. The low light illuminated the gauntness of Celena's face and made her eyes look like black holes, giving her an almost demonic appearance. The children were asleep and most evenings they had mending or darning to do, but tonight Eva noticed Celena was quieter than usual.

"I know Victor is dead, and yet I keep thinking...it *can't be*." Celena dropped her head into her hands for a moment, trying to force her tears away. "I walk into a room sometimes...and I swear to you I think he's going to be there. I always get the feeling that he's just left, and that I barely missed him. At night sometimes when I'm sleeping, I feel him, right next to me. It's like his breath against my forehead and I open my eyes thinking he'll be right there. And it makes me wonder...if he's gone— or if he's somewhere else, and that if I try hard enough, maybe I can find him. Am I...crazy, do you think?" Her troubled black eyes met her sister's, and for a minute Eva was so paralyzed with worry that she could hardly bring herself to speak.

"No, I don't think you're crazy. I think you loved him, and you miss him. Besides, he *is* somewhere Celena, he's in heaven with Papa and James—"

But she was overly kind, and Celena suspected Eva thought she was, indeed, on the brink of losing her mind. It had been ten months since she'd learned of Victor's death and her grief, instead of lessening, seemed to be getting worse.

"No, he's not in heaven, although he should be," she said, ignoring Eva's kind, patronizing look. "He's not here, but he's not *there* yet either. And where should I go, what should I do? I feel breathless and rigid waiting—but I don't know what I'm waiting for!" She stopped talking, thinking that she didn't want to wait any more. That she didn't want to live at all if she had to live the rest of her life without Victor. It would be too long, and it would be too painful. She would not be able to bear it.

Celena didn't sleep well anymore, and often when she did, she had bad dreams. They didn't always start out being about Victor, but somewhere during the dream she would either hear his voice or see him, and she would always wake then. Not crying, but rather breathless, tense, and so incredibly sad.

It was no different this spring night when suddenly her eyes opened, and she found herself staring at the shadows the leaves were making against the curtains. It must be a full moon she realized to make such shadows and watched them glide effortlessly across the floor when the wind swayed the trees.

She heard the faint breathing of Catherine in the little trundle bed and getting out of bed peered down at her and smiled when she saw Catherine sleeping. She'd had chicken pox last week and had been so irritable and uncomfortable that Celena had cried with her, for a want to soothe her. Now she was sleeping peacefully, and Celena leaned forward and brushed her damp dark hair from her face.

I gave you a daughter, Victor.

She sat silently, listening to the quiet. It had to indeed be late because all the night sounds of insects had slowed, and yet the moon was still high in the sky.

The floor felt cold her under her feet, and she shivered. Finding her stockings, she put them on and grabbing the quilt, slung it about her shoulders as she went silently into the hallway. She passed the boys' room and heard the steady regular sound of their breathing, and it too comforted her. Six healthy boys, and when the all too familiar prick of tears hit her eyes, she pushed away the torturous thoughts of them growing to adulthood without the influence of their wonderful father.

The house was dark and cold as she went down the stairs, and once there, merely stood in the silence looking around. Tracing her hand along one of the iron sconces on the wall, felt the unevenness where Victor had hammered it at the forge. Touched the oak mantle he had carved and smiled remembering how proud he had been when it had turned out so well. Looked down at the table in the darkness, remembering the countless meals they had eaten there with their family and friends. She went to the bookcase and took out the book Victor had been reading before the death had taken him from her. It was about steamships, and when she opened it the blue jay's feather Victor liked to use a bookmark fell to the floor. Stooping to retrieve it she brushed the feather gently against her cheek and then sighing, put it carefully back between the same pages.

Restless, she opened the door and walked out to the front porch in the darkness and sat down on the step. Shivering a bit in the coolness, wrapped the quilt tighter around her.

The moon cast silver shadows across the front of the house, and it had a trance like effect on her. Leaning her head against the big column she closed her eyes, trying to let the peace and stillness seep into her troubled, aching heart.

She knew she had to find a way to get over him. She didn't care about herself, but for the boys and Catherine. After all they'd lost their father and needed a mother. And she felt intensely guilty about the pain she saw in their faces every time she went to pieces. She knew they too missed Victor, and realized she was only hurting them more each day as they watched her fade farther into that abyss of grief. When Victor was alive, there never seemed to be enough hours in the day to get everything done, and the years had raced by when they were married. But now without him, her life and future seemed to stretch on into forever. A forever of empty, aching loneliness.

"Victor," she whispered softly, simply for the pleasure of saying his name. Having said it so many, many times in her life, she knew there would not be little reason to say it anymore.

"*I'm here.*"

Startled at the sound of his voice, her eyes flew open.

There he was, walking toward her in the moonlight.

Certain her eyes and tortured mind were playing tricks on her, she blinked hard. "*Victor!*" she shrieked, tears springing into her eyes as she leapt off the step into his arms. "*Victor, Victor!*" She pressed her face into his chest and began to weep when she felt the familiar warmth of his arms around her. "*Oh God how I've missed you! I've missed you so—oh let me look at you!*" she gasped, pulling from him, swiping at the tears that blurred her vision.

"What happened, what are you doing here?" she questioned. It was unbelievable that he was here and her heart began to pound. "Hank said that...you'd been..." she choked on her sobs, broke into a tortured cry, and leaned against his chest again, sobbing.

"I know. It's all right though, please don't cry," he soothed and she wiped her face against his shirt to rid it of her tears. "Here." He handed her a handkerchief and she dried her face and blew her nose. Wanting to cheer her up, he clumsily handed her a little bouquet of wildflowers.

Despite everything she laughed. "Picked these along the way did you?"

He nodded and she quickly laid them on the step behind her, and then leaning up kissed him. "I'm so glad you're home! I missed you *so much!* You have no idea how it's been this last year thinking you were dead—I've been so terribly depressed and unhappy!" Her heart shivered with relief and joy, and thought fiercely that now that she had him in her sight again, she would never, *ever* let him go!

"I know," he said, "I know you have been."

Even in her giddy joy his words struck her as odd. "What's happened? Have you been furloughed—are you wounded?" She began inspecting him, scrutinizing his shirt for the wound Hank had so gruesomely described, but saw only that he was thinner and that his uniform was worn. She wondered anew with fright if he'd deserted, having heard the horror stories of deserters being executed.

"No." He took her hands from his shirt front and brought them gently to his mouth, tenderly kissing each one. He then simply looked down at her face as if trying to memorize it.

A stab of wild pain went through her heart. "Hank said you were shot, and that Ethan tried to help you, but that he couldn't—" She was even more alarmed when she noticed his eyes were wet.

"I know." His voice was kind and full of understanding as he leaned down to kiss her sweetly—though she spoke before he could.

"He said that...you were...dead."

"I am."

She darted back in shock. "But how can that be? You're *here!*" She touched him again, feeling flesh and bone underneath her fingertips.

"I know, but I am dead. Hank was right."

She dropped her face into her hands and began to weep bitterly and let him lead her blindly to sit on the porch. Cursing herself, thinking that Eva and Father Tonnellier and everyone else was right—she *had* lost her mind! She hated herself; hated that she was so weak and tormented; hated the way her desperate mind sought to torture her in her dreams.

"Let's sit for a while," he said, pulling her next to him on the porch and looking down at her small hand between both of his, bent and laid a tender kiss on the back of it. "I-I don't know where to begin—"

"I guess you could start by apologizing to me for getting yourself killed. You promised me you'd be careful," she jabbed, wondering what her tormented imagination would conjure up for him to reply.

A hint of a smile showed on his face. "I'm sorry, I-I didn't mean to be killed. You know I meant to come back."

She looked up at him, sniffing.

"I saw Hank..." He shrugged. "And I couldn't stop myself. I wasn't thinking. I'm sorry. I truly meant to come back to you. I apologize for dying so young." He grinned self-consciously. "At least *relatively* young."

They fell awkwardly silent.

"Did it...hurt badly when you were shot?"

"Yes, at first, but it didn't hurt long."

She nodded and looked down, thinking she'd had her share of odd dreams before, though never one *this* odd. "I miss you! And I've been so worried about you!" she cried and felt the hot sting of tears, and the lump forming in her throat.

"I thought you might be," he began, and, sighing, took her hands and placed them snugly inside his again. "That's one of the reasons I came back." He looked at her intently. "Please don't worry so much about me, don't miss me so much. I am all right." He broke off suddenly and looked away impatiently, although it was clear he did not want to hurt her. "You're getting along all right without me, you and the children?"

She had to swallow hard. "Well, yes mostly. Bartholomew's doing all right in the shop now—but someone burned the shop a while back, said no blacks could own anything. Thankfully, Judith and Bartholomew got out without being hurt. He rebuilt it though and wouldn't even take any money from me, said he had some in the bank. It was a good thing he had the deed otherwise he couldn't have proved it was his, but I have good news too. Judith had a baby—they finally have a child, Teddy."

He nodded with approval. "And the boys? Tell me about them." Although he was listening, his eyes seemed far away.

"They complain about school and I've had a ghastly time with Randy not wanting to do what he's told regarding school—but it still amazes me how I can threaten that child, and merely the thought of you angry with him makes him straighten up immediately! Ben took it worse than anyone when he heard...he always followed what the papers said about the battles, he was always scanning for your regiment with that worried expression of his. Andrew, Sam, and Myles are all right, they all had the chicken pox but the only scars they have are on their backs. They were pretty broken up when I told them and Luke...oh—" She gasped, breaking up again. "We're getting along but we miss you dreadfully Victor!" She leaned up and kissed him. He hadn't been prepared to be kissed or wanted it because never had he ended the kiss before she wanted to.

"It all seems like such a waste now. So many of us killed. I suppose none of us realize how little time we have, and how precious life is. I thought I'd have more time."

Celena reached over and wanting to chase away the melancholy, took his hand and squeezed it.

"But you'll be all right," he urged. "I never was good at words was I? Here I've been given this wonderful chance to say goodbye to you again, and tell you things and...I can't." He hung his head, discouraged. "Remember when I asked you to marry me that day in the shop, I even managed to mess that up, didn't I? I asked you to marry me before I even found out it you were fond of me!" He laughed lightly, and despite the impossibly cruel dream, she laughed too.

"Yes, you did, but it didn't matter because I understood!" She smiled, searching his eyes a moment later and saw a strange sort of longing, and a trace of bittersweet sadness.

"Do you remember that harvest night?"

"It's not something I'd ever forget." She smiled, remembering well that wonderful night her soul had been forever linked to his.

"I was truly, *truly* mad for you by then. I could hardly wait for you to grow up so you could love me too. By the time that night rolled around I was so pent up I could scarcely look at you without wanting to throw you down underneath me. I nearly scared the daylights out of you that night when I kissed you! It's a wonder you agreed to go to the shop with me the next day after that display of lust!"

"I didn't stay scared long, besides the attraction was certainly not one sided—" There was mischievous sparkle in her eye that hadn't been there since he had left. "I was simply mad for you too!"

"And then you actually *married* me," he said, ginning, hardly able to believe even after all these years that the miraculous thing had happened. "The night of our wedding after I made love to you—do you know what I said to God?"

She laughed. "I didn't know you ever talked to God."

"Well, I did *that* night! I told him that I didn't deserve you, that I was just a plain, ordinary man, but that since he'd been kind enough to give you to me that I'd take care of you and love you the best that I possibly could—"

"You did. You have," she whispered.

He looked deeply, lovingly into her eyes. "I never told you, never in all those years we were married."

She desperately wanted to erase the sadness in the gray eyes. "But it's all right, because I know you loved me, and I loved you too!" She pressed herself against him.

"That's what you always did for me, I'd falter trying to say it and you would say it for me. Was it irritating all those years never hearing it?"

"No. Because even though you couldn't *say* it, you certainly showed me how you felt."

"Still, though...I'd like to tell you—at least once." He looked down as if summoning courage and then back up at her, tenderly. "I love you, Lena," he said softly, shaking his head with the finality of it as one of his hands caressed her cheek. "And I always loved you. Loved you since that day you comforted me and cried for me when my mother died. Loved you that Fourth of July celebration when you were a little girl and fell asleep in my arms after we counted stars. And all those years I worked on your parents' farm, it was true I needed the money...but I got to see you, and I think I would have done anything to see you. You have been in my thoughts, and in my heart...constantly, for all my life."

They were silent for a minute with the memories.

"It was *good* wasn't it? Our life, our marriage. We didn't fight much you and I, no one's ever believed me when I've told them that. I mean had I not lived it myself, I never would have believed I could have been so happy." He smiled at her gratefully. "Thank you for being my wife."

She buried her face against his chest, tears rolling down her face. "Oh, Victor...don't go back! I miss you so much! Can't you stay?"

"No, of course not. I'm dead." He couldn't help but laugh then when he saw the horror in her eyes. "I never could say the right thing, and not only did I spend my *life* saying the wrong things, but I'm doing it in *death* too!" Standing, he pulled her up with him. "I want to see the children before I go."

Silently they went into the house and Celena watched with bittersweet sadness how tenderly he touched Randy as he slept, how he touched Ben, Andrew, and Sam—the way he tenderly bent and kissed Myles and Luke. When they made their way into their bedroom his eyes which were already filled with tears, spilled down his cheeks when he beheld his daughter asleep in the little bed. Without giving a thought that he might awaken her, reached down, and picked up the sleeping child.

"A *daughter*!" he whispered in awe. "When I opened that letter, you have no idea how happy I was! She—she looks a little like *me!*"

Tears of pride formed in Celena's eyes. "She does."

Victor kissed his black-haired daughter and laughed in delight when her sleepy gray eyes opened and she stared at him.

"The boys dote on her and love her to pieces. Sometimes they even fight about who gets to play with her!"

"What an *angel* girl!" he cooed and sat down on the edge of the bed. His daughter in his arms, his wife holding on to him for dear life. "Cathy my sweet! Cathy my angel!" he said, kissing her. "What gifts I'd been given," he mused softly, and bending kissed his daughter's forehead.

"Yes, we were extremely blessed," Celena said, smiling as a drowsy Catherine yawned widely in her father's face, making him laugh.

"You still are Lena. You have the boys and Cathy, and you're healthy and you're young."

"I don't feel young anymore."

"But you are," he consoled. "And you still have you whole life ahead of you. And I expect you to live it."

"But I can't without you! I don't want to live it without you—"

"Of course, you can. It will merely be different. But you *must* get over me, I want you to. And not only for the children's sake, but for yourself as well."

"I know they need me," she said thinking guiltily about the poor job she had done lately as their mother. "...I feel like I'm failing them Victor, but I am so lost without you that I don't want to go on."

"You're not failing them," he sympathized. "Things will be better from now on, I promise they will."

"I wish you could be here with me. I'm afraid to raise them on my own."

"I wish I could too—but I can't anymore. You're still anchored to the earth, and I am freed from it. But you'll be fine. I know it because you're strong."

"But I feel so lost without you—"

"You're not, you're more capable than you think. It was always easier for me to do things for you, and besides," he said, dropping his head a bit guiltily, "I liked doing things for you. You're an incredibly capable woman in your own right, and I suppose now you'll realize it." He sighed quietly, trying to find the right words. "I really...liked my life. And not everyone can say that. I liked my work. I liked being your husband, I liked having people joke to me about our rambunctious boys. I liked all of it," he said with a quiet air of finality, and then gently kissed Catherine's plump cheek. "I was a lucky man; I had a good life. I have no regrets."

"Nor do I."

"Would you...promise me something?"

"Anything."

"Promise me to go on with your life without me, I want you to. Please don't wait. Don't wait to be happy—do it now while you still can. I want you to live, I mean *live*. Laugh again—love again—"

She jerked up with surprise.

"You're young, Lena, and you're beautiful, do you think I expect you to be *alone* the rest of your life?"

"But I couldn't! I could never be with and love someone again—I still *love* you, I'm your wife!"

"I still love you too, I'll never stop loving you. But you must stay here awhile longer." He paused, trying to decide best how to explain. "Someday you'll feel differently. And when the time comes, I want you to know that it's all right."

"I could never betray you."

"It's not like that. I can't be here anymore. And if it will comfort you, if you need it, know that you have my blessing to go on with your life." He kissed her once more lightly, almost like a gentle breeze against her lips. "Promise me?"

She nodded, unable to speak, and he sighed contentedly, like someone who finished what they'd set out to do. "Come here, let me hold you both. Hold you 'til I have to go." He moved toward the bed.

She slipped under his arm and laid her head against his chest, Catherine nuzzling cozily between their bodies as they laid down on the bed.

"Don't leave us," she begged. Her eyes pressed tightly shut, but tears slipped past them anyway. "I don't want you to go, please don't leave me."

"I wish I didn't have to."

She gazed up at him. "Is it...wonderful where you are?"

His face suddenly lit up with such a radiance that it lightened even her heavy heart. "Yes, very much so."

"What's it like?"

"It's beyond...words. I can't even *begin* describe it."

"Try." She felt guilty for asking him when she saw him struggling, knowing how hard it was for him to express himself with words.

"Just know that everything you've ever dreamed or imagined is possible, and there is no such thing as discontent."

"Are you an angel now?"

He laughed. "Hardly."

"Then why did you get to come back to me?"

He shrugged. "I promised you I would."

"But I meant *alive*," she wailed and felt his chest shaking underneath her with his laughter.

"Sorry about that. I did my best." The laughter was replaced with tenderness. "I came because I wanted to tell you that I loved you, but even more importantly because I was worried about you and I wanted if I could, to bring you some peace."

"Will you...come back again?"

Even before he spoke she knew what his answer would be.

"No."

"Will you watch over us then?"

"I always have, I always will."

"You know Victor, this is the strangest dream I've ever had! I mean I usually don't *know* that it's a dream until *after* I wake up, not during, not while it's happening."

"Is that what you think this is—a dream?" In his eyes there was a trace of regret but also a gentle sort of understanding.

"Of course. What else could it be?"

Begrudgingly he smiled, brushing her cheeks with the tips of his fingers. He rearranged his arms comfortably around her and leaning down whispered: "Then wake up my sweet. Wake up knowing that your future is to be happy and that your heart will heal."

He kissed her then for the last time, gently, on the small place under her eye.

Celena felt a feather-light kiss under her eye, and opening her eyes turned her head, expecting to see him there. She sat up slowly and looked around the room bathed in the early morning light, staring at the familiar surroundings like she'd never seen them before.

Getting out of bed, she looked down at Catherine and sighed with relief when she saw her daughter sleeping soundly. Celena walked a few steps into the room, her palms up, feeling the air as if trying to decide if any of it had been real or not.

"Victor?" she whispered, almost afraid to say it aloud. Afraid quick movements and loud noises would disturb the remnants of such a vivid and strangely wonderful dream. She stood silently in the middle of the room not knowing what to do, not sure if it was over or if it had even happened. Sighing she swallowed the lump in her throat and felt the painful prick of tears behind her eyes. But the tears that formed in her eyes that morning were not the product of tortured thoughts of him dead, not borne of agony like they had been nearly every day since she'd learned of his death.

She was different, better, stronger. Realized that for the first time in over a year—she'd slept well. It was as if she had finally crested the slope to an impossibly high mountain, and although there were still mountains ahead of her, felt strong enough to climb them. Victor was not in pain.

He was all right. He was happy. And he was gone. She would learn to live with it, accept it finally in her heart and in her soul.

It was the most intensely cathartic, and cleansing dream she had ever had, and felt a bittersweet tear slide down her cheek. She felt suddenly more intensely loved and more blessed to have been lucky enough to be his wife, and found herself for the first time, thanking God for the years she had with him, instead of raging bitterly against the injustice that their time together had ended.

"You were right, we were so lucky," she said softly. "You are so good to me." A smile of gratitude burst forth. "Even in my dreams, you come back to take care of me." She closed her eyes and said a thankful *Our Father*.

Glancing up at the window she was suddenly drawn like a magnet towards it. Looking up at the sky, happy tears slipped from her eyes. It was blue again.

"Good morning boys!" Celena said happily, Catherine planted on her hip, and Luke's hand in hers. Her voice was more cheerful than it had been in months and her sons looked up at her in surprise. She pushed away the guilt knowing she had come down so many mornings, gloomy and depressed—she'd barely smiled in the year since Victor's death. When she thought again how close she had come to wanting her life to be over-and leave them, her heart skipped a beat.

"Mama!" Myles cried, interrupting her thoughts.

Looking down, she was overjoyed to see Victor's child—her child. "Morning, Myles," she said, placing Catherine in the highchair and Luke at the table. She crossed the room and kissed his upturned face three times, deciding that night she would have a long talk with her boys about their father. They had lost him too, after all, and she had done nothing at all to ease their pain.

Even though he was dead, she would keep his memory alive, and they would love and remember him from the stories she would tell. But in perspective and respectfully in the past where it needed to be. Because if she didn't, they feared they would grow to hate to him—grow to hate the memory of the man whose death had tormented and possessed her.

"Here, Mama, for you," Myles said, pulling from behind his back a bunch of withering wildflowers. They were decidedly worse for the wear being out of water all night. The spring beauties were beginning to wilt, as were the wild geraniums and blue violets.

"W-where did you get them?"

"I found them outside on the front steps. They're for you!"

"Are you all right Mama? You look like you've seen a ghost?" Randy asked, concerned.

She shook her head, then dropped to her knees and hugged Myles so hard that for a moment he couldn't breathe.

"I love you, *I love you all so much!*" she cried, then stood up shakily and wiped her eyes, looking adoringly upon her family.

"We love you too Mama!" Myles exclaimed, confused suddenly, having thought the flowers would make her happy. "But please don't cry!"

"All right Myles," she said, straightening her shoulders. "I promise all of you, I won't cry...anymore."

Two weeks later the war ended and Ste. Genevieve like every other little town and big city in the country heard the news that General Lee had surrendered. Celena could still remember Bartholomew, running up to the house, and banging on the door telling her in excited, jubilant tones what he'd heard.

"It been a long time a comin', ah sure am glad it's over."

"I am too," she had answered and smiled up at him. There was a tenseness between them, there always had been, and since Victor was dead Bartholomew found it even harder to look at her.

She could still remember the look of sadness that had crossed the big man's face when she had told him Victor had been killed. She could still see him standing there, his big chin thrust out in defiance. He'd offered to make a wrought iron base for the marble angel that had arrived for Victor's memorial, and without even asking her what she wanted he'd etched Victor's name and dates in the base and put it together with the tall lone angel to stand sentinel in the cemetery not far from Anna's grave. Although it was all much larger than she had envisioned, it was so beautiful and finely done that she had wept when she'd seen it.

"Just think Bartholomew, your boy Teddy is free, and he'll always be free."

Bartholomew shook his head. "But ma boy was already free cuz he was born to a free man, ahn I was free cuz of him...ah reckon I don know what a happen ta me if hadna been for him..."

Yet the jubilation at the war finally being over was tarnished when only five days after Lee's surrender, President Lincoln was assassinated. Celena agreed with Laurence that not only was it a tragedy because a kind and reasonable president had been killed, but it only made the over-zealous victors of the north more aggressive towards the ailing south.

The south had at first rejoiced in his death, and hundreds of bedraggled ex-Confederate soldiers had cheered at the news. But as time wore on they would come to realize that Lincoln's death was nothing short of a calamity for them, and only served to increase the bitterness felt towards them from their northern brothers partly because of the fantastic rumor that Jefferson Davis had plotted it. Belatedly they came to realize that Lincoln's kindliness and moderation would have been effective shields between them and the vindictive victors. Lincoln's eloquent words in his moving second inaugural address delivered forty-one days before his death. *"With malice toward none, with charity for all...to bind up the nations wounds, to care for him who shall have borne the battle and for his widow and orphan, to do all which may achieve and cherish a just and lasting peace."* Celena feared the words would not be heeded, and she always had the feeling that if Lincoln had lived, a certain amount of suffering and heartache that was to come from reconstruction would somehow have been eased.

Chapter 46

"Hello, is your mother at home?"

Myles looked at the man standing before him. "She's at my Aunt Eva's bringing back some canning jars and lids, but she'll be back soon."

"Oh, all right." The man looked so distraught that Myles felt bad for disappointing him.

"You want to wait on the porch?" he offered. "It's awful hot in the sun."

"All right, thank you."

Myles watched the man limp to the front porch. He seemed to be in pain when he lowered his body. He turned then and smiled, and wanting to comfort the man, Myles smiled innocently back.

"Are you Sam?"

A wide grin showed a missing tooth. "No, I'm Myles," he said, straightening himself, proud that he had been mistaken for his older brother. "Do you know my brothers? I have lots of 'em."

The man was shaky, and Myles was glad he was sitting down, afraid he might suddenly slither to the ground if he stood. It was confusing—he didn't look that old, but the tremors in his hands reminded him of how the old peoples' hands shook in church holding the hymnals.

"You'll have to excuse me, the last time I saw you, you were much littler," the man explained.

Myles nodded politely but couldn't help but think the man a little strange. He was awful skinny for one thing, and although he was washed and shaved, the clothes he had on looked like they belonged to someone else. And he looked sick, what with the dark circles under his eyes and the unhealthy color of his skin. But his brown eyes were still kind, even in the haggard face.

"That's okay!" Myles soothed. "Everyone's always getting us mixed up—even my Mama calls me the wrong name sometimes. I wait 'til she gets it right though before I do what she tells me."

The man nodded.

"You want a drink of water or something?" Myles asked, still worried about the man's health.

"No, thank you. I'm fine. I knew your father; I was a friend of his."

Myles watched as the man struggled to keep his tears at bay. "My Papa's dead. He died in the war."

"Yes, I know he did. I was in the war too."

Myles looked at him quizzically. "My Mama says he was brave and that I ought to be proud of him."

The man nodded distantly.

"She says he's in heaven and watches over us, and that I shouldn't do bad stuff because he can still see me. I miss him though. He used to arm-wrestle me after he read to me at night."

The man smiled faintly, as if he'd reminded him of something from long ago. They fell awkwardly silent, but Myles' curiosity was getting the better of him.

"Are you, by any chance...my Uncle Ethan?"

It caused a large lump to form in Ethan's throat when Victor's son recognized him, the endearment especially touching since he had no other family and felt like he belonged nowhere. "Yes," he said hoarsely, "as a matter of fact, I am."

Myles lunged over and wrapped his small arms around Ethan, hugging him hard and patting the skinny back. "We were all afraid you *died* Uncle Ethan! Mama will be so glad you're alive and be so *glad* to see you!"

Ethan's shriveled heart actually moved in his chest.

"Randy—Ben—Johnnie come on out here!" Myles called suddenly, wiping his nose with the back of his hand. "It's Uncle Ethan! He's back!"

They came charging out of the house, and suddenly Ethan found himself staring into the eyes of Victor's sons. He recognized Randy first, who he realized must have grown a foot, and then turning saw Ben, who was already taller than he was. Johnnie too looked so old he realized if the war had lasted much longer more than likely he would have been in it!

"Uncle Ethan!" Ben exclaimed. "We thought—I mean Mama knew you'd been captured, and then we never heard anything from you again. How long have you been back?" He reached out and shook Ethan's hand.

"You've all grown so much—I hardly recognize you!"

"That's what Mama says—says we grow like weeds!" Ben grinned. It was easy to tell they were Victor's sons; they had inherited his muscular build and height, but they looked like Celena. Every one of them had the pale eyes and summer lightened hair, it was like looking at male versions of her.

"You've been missing too many meals Uncle Ethan—it's a good thing you're home!" Randy quipped. "How are you?"

For the first time in months Ethan smiled. "I'm better." He then saw yet another blond child ambling shyly from behind the bushes wanting to see who his brothers were talking to. "Now that has to be Andrew."

The boy laughed. "No, I'm Sam!" he said proudly, and then a moment later Andrew popped out from the bushes, along with Luke.

"I'm obviously confused!" Ethan chuckled, and gratefully took the glass of water Myles had gotten for him.

"How are you all?" Ethan asked as he sat on the steps surrounded by Victor and Celena's children.

"We're fine," Randy said, his voice reminding him so much of Victor. "Pa's factory is not running yet, but Uncle Mason and Uncle Laurence are trying to get in touch with the men at the railroad and get it started up again. Sawmills doing well though—whole lot of folks needing lumber these days and Ben and I have been running it for Mama, and so far so good." It occurred to Ethan that Randy was taking over where Victor had left off, and that Randy was going to be as capable as his father.

"How are your uncles?" Ethan asked, hungry for news of his old life.

"Uncle Laurence is fine. His stump bothers him a lot when it's cold or rainy, but he and Nathan and Gabe are still farming." The look of surprise on Ethan's face prompted Randy to continue. "He walks pretty well with the leg my Papa made him, and he doesn't want anybody feeling sorry for him."

Ethan nodded, wondering when in the world Victor had figured out a way to make a leg!

"Uncle Mason got home a few weeks ago. Walked up to the house without a word and scared the daylights out of Aunt Carlene!" Randy's grin was infectious. "She sure was happy to see him though, we all were. And he's up to eyeballs in work already and Aunt Carlene says he's going to run for Judge."

"Did he come home all right?"

"Oh yeah, he's not missing any parts if that's what you mean. He's skinny as rail like you though! Bet you didn't hear about Uncle Will, he was decorated for bravery at Petersburg for leading a charge. He was shot though in the thigh, and he's home now but he's still pretty weak."

Ethan nodded, relieved that nothing worse had happened to anyone. "Aunt Brigid had her baby, a girl."

"*Aunt Brigid?*"

"Yes siree, she married Uncle Will right before he enlisted. And he is furious with her right now! While he was gone she named the baby Wilamina *after him!*" They all laughed. "But I guess you couldn't have heard about Uncle James. He was killed, and Aunt Alice won't talk to any of us anymore though. She won't even let Mama see Charles..." He shook his head, and Ethan did too, thinking it was a shame. "Uncle Laurence and Mama sent her a big check with a letter asking if they could see Charles, but she cashed the check, and no one has seen her since. Mama tried to find them, but sort of lost the trail once they left St. Louis."

Ethan nodded, taking it in. "And Stephan?" he asked.

"He was captured like you were and sent to a prison camp in Vicksburg, and he was on his way home on a ship, the Sultana. But one of the boilers burst and the ship blew up when they were heading up on the Mississippi towards Cairo. We don't know if he drowned or if the explosion killed him. Aunt Eva tells her boys that a nice farmer fished him out of the water. Looking through his pockets he learned his name. She tells her boys the farmer buried him on a bluff overlooking the Mississippi, and that he carved a cross with the name Stoddard on it. She says one of these days they'll go to Illinois and try and find it." It was clear to Ethan that Randy did not believe this tale, and that it was made up to console something that would never quite be all right.

Ethan looked down and shook his head at the irony of the tragedy. Living through the war was hard enough, and living through a prison camp was absolute hell, but then to die when he had only been a two days journey home seemed saddest of all. And it might have been comical were it not melancholy to have seen every blond head bowed when Randy had spoken of the death of their uncle.

"And...Hank?"

"He's fine now that he's home. Still farming." He paused a moment. "It's a good thing he came home because his Pa is so sick these days he can't work anymore. I don't know what Aunt Margaret would have done without him. She wouldn't come live here when Mama asked her." Randy grinned again. "Guess it's that proud Osage blood."

Ethan smiled in agreement. "And your grandmother, how is she?"

Randy jumped up like something had bitten him. "Grandma! There's someone out here!"

A cold panic hit Ethan suddenly, wishing Randy hadn't said anything, not sure how she would react.

"Oh my God—*Ethan!*" Yvonne cried upon seeing him, and smiled warmly, scampering out of the house and into his arms. She smelled delightfully like the peaches she had been slicing and she still had a dishtowel in her hands when she hugged him. "Es so good to see you!" She kissed him on the cheek. "We sot somezing had happened to you!" He felt intensely guilty when tears sparkled in her eyes. "No one heard from you."

"I'm sorry," he said feebly.

Ethan spent over an hour sitting at Celena and Victor's table alternately talking with Yvonne and the boys. They caught him up on everything. He learned more sad news about the Wilburn brothers, about the Charbonnier boys, and Jean Gustave being killed. But then Randy trying to talk of more pleasant things informed him that in his spare time he was leaning blacksmithing from Bartholomew.

Ben, he found out quickly had no such aspirations and read incessantly, none of his brothers understanding his love for books and he confided in Ethan that he had hopes of being a doctor. During one of Andrew's rather lengthy stories about a certain coyote that he met up with every time he went into the woods (how he was so sure it was the same coyote-Ethan had no clue) when they heard little feet scampering up the steps, followed by the sound of feminine voices.

A little dark-haired girl bounded in the room and started happily to dash for her grandmother but stopped in her tracks when her gray eyes warily beheld Ethan. Deciding she did not like what she saw, ran out of the house to loudly voice her complaints to her mother.

"Oh, Cathy hush!" Celena said, walking up the porch as Cathy danced on the step complaining. "For heaven's sake Cathy," she scolded, walking into the house, "Oh!" she exclaimed when her eyes fell on Ethan sitting at the table. Eva walked in a second later and let out the same strangled noise.

It was awkward and involuntarily Ethan felt his head going down.

It should be Victor who has come home—not me.

"Oh *Ethan!*"

When he looked back up she was right in front of him, tenderly leaning toward him. He felt her arms go wonderfully around him. He had to force back his tears of relief and joy, fearing Randy would never understand tears from a man who had been a friend of his father's.

Ethan stayed for dinner, and the children did their best to entertain him—in fact, he learned many things about them from their schoolwork to their chores, and it warmed his heart how innocently they welcomed him. They still remembered that he owned the bank, and that he lived in that 'monstrously big brick house' as Andrew had referred to it. Celena had obviously kept his memory alive because he had been gone nearly three years, and although that in and of itself not a long time, for the young children-most of which had changed so much he hadn't even *recognized* them, it was an eternity. He found himself wondering what if anything Celena had told them about him being there when their father was killed. And if she had, he realized she had painted him a good light because they showed no faint anger, no blame whatsoever.

Although he was happy to be there, it was strange being in Victor's house-without him there, and a flash of pain crossed over him as he looked around the room, sat in the house Victor had built. He'd been dead well over a year now, but the anguish that was flooding over Ethan's heart suddenly made it seem as if it had recently happened. In Andersonville, he had been so sure he was going to die, the need to mourn Victor had not consumed him like it was now.

Later that night as Celena headed off to put the children to bed, he was restless and felt out of place. Not sure what to do, went on the front porch and sat in one of the rockers, watching the darkness quietly descend. Part of him desperately wanted to stay and talk with her about Victor, and yet another part wanted to slip away silently, longing to keep the torturous knowledge far out of his mind like he had done in Andersonville.

"Ethan?" Even though her voice was gentle it startled him. He glanced at her, but looked away nervously as she sat in a chair next to him.

She hadn't changed much, still sensibly dressed in a simple skirt and blouse; her long hair braided. And although at thirty-three she was past the fresh bloom of youth; it made no difference to him. Childbirth eight times over had thickened her middle some, but as far as he was concerned, she was as beautiful as she had always been. And her eyes, those marvelous blue eyes that had been haunting his dreams for over seventeen years—there were faint lines around them now.

"How long have you been home?"

"Two days. I'm sorry. I should have come to see you sooner, but I think I slept for a solid day and a half."

As she looked at him, emaciated, pale and bedraggled thought it was a wonder he was able to even come today. "That's all right, I understand."

"Things look good here—I mean the house, and the children, and keeping the sawmill going. You must have had your hands full with the children and all the rest."

"Thank you, I did my best. Laurence helped me and Randy has been wonderful. He grew up a lot while Victor was away." She rocked quietly for a moment. "I was wondering Ethan later when you're up to it if you would help me write the railroads. I'd like to start the factory up again and I want to try and force all of them to change over. I still think it should be a law—that way no one else will be needlessly killed. Lord knows we've had enough of that. Did you hear? All four of the Christi boys made it back, I think they are the only family in town that didn't lose someone."

A silence fell.

"Your boys are something else."

Celena laughed, and it was refreshing sound, especially for someone who had for so long been immersed in pain and suffering.

"Randy, Randy." She shook her head, smiling. "He analyzes every-thing! If I say the sky is blue—there's a discussion about what *shade!* Oh, he drives me crazy, he is so meticulous; he's so like his father! But he's a good boy and I love him, and he's worked hard since Victor left. They all have. I love them all."

"Your little Cathy is irresistibly sweet, and not shy at all!" he said, thinking about the pains she had gone to tell him how well she could print and how she knew all her colors and half of the alphabet and why it was all right to gloat about it, even when her mother said it *wasn't!*

"Thank you. She's a handful though, and she knows I love her to pieces as do her brothers and she tries to take advantage of it! I don't know where she gets that because she's much more talkative than either Victor or I," Celena said, shaking her head. "Must have been something else...some wild Indian on Victor's side!"

This time it was Ethan who laughed. "And she looks so much like him, I could hardly believe it when I saw her. She is without a doubt, *Victor's child*." Although he was smiling, his voice faltered. "You should have seen him Celena. He was beside himself with happiness when he received that letter and found out it was a girl…" Ethan looked down despondently at the step beneath his feet, painfully reliving the memory. "I can't believe he never got to see her."

For a moment Celena considered telling him that Victor *had* seen Cathy. That before he had come no one had called her anything but Catherine, but since his visit—miraculously she had been *Cathy* from then on. But she didn't think he'd believe her, and besides, it was private and special, something she was not sure she would ever share with anyone.

"I wasn't sure if you'd…want to see me."

She gently laid a comforting hand on his. "Why wouldn't I want to see you?"

He shrugged his skinny shoulders. "Oh, I…don't know." He grimaced. "Maybe because I failed you, and Victor died. That I promised you I'd watch over him."

"You didn't fail me," she began gently. "And please, I don't want you feeling guilty. I don't blame you any more than I blame poor Hank. It was no one's fault, it just happened." She reached out to touch his face, forcing him to meet her concerned eyes. "Lord knows this war has caused enough pain and misery without everyone laying blame." She looked in the direction of the blacksmith shop and sighed like she did every time she saw it. "Please don't think I blame you or I'm angry." She was kinder and more understanding than he had imagined she could be.

"I still can't believe sometimes he's dead. I'm sorry Celena, I know I shouldn't say that to you, but it doesn't seem possible to me that he's gone. I thought he'd always be there."

"I know, I thought so too." Another silence fell between them. Part of her wanted to keep talking about Victor, but she also knew if she did more than likely she would be crying again. Something she had promised the children she would not do anymore.

"Did you have a…bad time where you were?" she asked, changing the subject though she did not want to; always wanting to talk about Victor.

"Andersonville? Yes, I suppose so."

"I'm so sorry you had to be there." As she looked at him, it was like looking at the shadow of the man she had once known. His hair had thinned and he was deathly gaunt, even though he had obviously taken pains to dress and look decent. His face was a sickly shade, the whites of his eyes yellowed, and she noticed the few times that he laughed two of his molars were missing. Although she never would hurt his feelings by saying anything, his eyes—which had always been so warm—had lost their luster. It saddened her to see the once handsome man so changed.

"The newspapers are saying terrible things about Andersonville, some are even calling for Captain Wirz to be tried for the horrible conditions he allowed and all the misery there, they call him the 'Andersonville Savage' and say it was the worst of all the camps—"

"There's no such thing as a *good* prison camp," he interrupted, and then shook his head tiredly. Even though he had grown to hate Captain Wirz, Ethan knew all the horrors that happened in Andersonville hadn't been Wirz's fault but realized with all the negative publicity Andersonville was being given, more than likely Wirz would be hanged anyway. "Besides the war made all of us do things we never would have dreamed doing normally..." He shook his head again, thinking despondently about the men he'd killed, and to the depths he had sunk while waiting to die in Andersonville.

"Are you all right?" she asked, and tenderly placed a small hand on one of his that still shook, and she had noticed that he limped when he got up from the table.

"I will be, in time I think. It's been a rough few years what with the war, measles, dysentery, scurvy, malaria, malnutrition, flea, and lice bites, I think I've had them all!"

The smile she bestowed on him was so warm that he had to look away when he felt his heart start to pound inside his sunken chest. Wondering if she had any idea he'd endured them all because of her.

"How did you get out—were you exchanged?"

"No, the exchange system had long since broken down."

"Did you...escape?"

He gave a pathetic laugh. "Well, I suppose if you classify pretending to be dead and letting them pile you in a wagon full of other dead bodies, taken outside, and lain among the dead, that you miraculously rise up like some gruesome Lazarus in the night—then yes...I escaped. And I was incredibly lucky I did it when I did, because it was later realized to be a ruse, and they started stabbing the bodies to make sure they were indeed dead." He was disheartened by the horror in her eyes and wished he hadn't told her. It certainly was not an honorable way to escape. No brave tunnel dig—no daring escape route, just praying to God they would believe his performance. He wondered if she was more horrified by the fact that he had so cowardly masqueraded, or that he had been willing to lie among those other foul dead bodies.

"What happened then?"

"I ran."

"Did they come after you?"

"Yes. Guards and dogs."

"For how long?"

"Not long. The guards were nearly as malnourished as we were." It was still astounding to him that it had worked; that somehow he had found the will to escape after all those months, and the strength to run when he had to. Miraculously he had made it. Edward had not.

"But you got away,' she breathed, reaching over. She took one of his hands and held it warmly between hers, and the tears in her eyes were tears of relief.

The old ache in his heart began to throb again. "Yes, I got away."

"How did you get home?" she asked, having unfortunately spent nights looking at maps, finding places like Shiloh, St. Petersburg, Chickamauga, and the Wilderness, and knew they were far away.

He shrugged. "I walked most of the way, hitched a few rides, ate what I could. Ironically the war ended while I was making my way home."

"That must have been awful for you."

"I've enjoyed other things in my life more." Her first reaction was to feel sorry for him, but she stopped herself and suddenly realizing how he answered, let out a nervous laugh.

"Well, I'm glad you're safe, and I'm so glad you're home." Celena couldn't help but think of the many nights she had spent like this, sitting on the porch in the twilight. Letting go of his hand, she closed her eyes pretending for a minute that Victor had gone into the house for something and that at any moment he was coming back.

"God Celena...I miss him."

"I miss him too."

"He...said something to me at Wilderness Celena...right before he died, he asked me to tell you—"

"I know," she said quietly. Even in the coming twilight he could see her eyes brightened by tears, "and I forgive him, I know he's sorry." She was silent for a moment lost in her memories. "He was so big and healthy. It never seemed like nothing would ever hurt him." He watched a tear cling to one of her lashes. "I thought I'd get old with him Ethan, and now I'll get old alone..." A tear slid down her cheek and impatiently she brushed it away. "I'm sorry, I shouldn't be doing this, and I've been so much better. It's just that seeing you again and talking about him, and yet I *want* to talk about him, I don't ever want to forget him, but we don't have to be sad when we do."

Ethan wanted to reach out and console her, but her words had caused his throat to nearly close.

"I'm sorry." She stood up, straightening her shoulders, and he saw a tenderness flood her luminous pale eyes. He stood then too, stiffly. "Thank you for coming tonight, Ethan, and I'm so grateful that you're safe. Please come as often as you like." She leaned in to awkwardly hug him, then turned and went into the house.

As Ethan made his way silently back home, everything in town seemed different. He knew it wasn't only that it had changed in the years he had been gone, but that he had. That a part of his soul had died with Victor at Wilderness.

"Hold on Mr. Woolrich I think I have it," Eva said, reaching deep into her purse while holding her son in her arms, paying for her groceries. Suddenly, she had the oddest sensation that someone was staring at her. Turning, her eyes flew wide with astonishment.

"*Danny!* Oh, my heavens!" she exclaimed and felt her heart skip a beat at the sight of her old beau. "Oh, I'm so glad you're all right—your Maman and Papa have been worried sick about you!"

"Eva," he began, a flush of embarrassment creeping up from his shirt as he nervously glanced around, trying to quiet her.

"How *are* you, how long have you been home? Oh, let me look at you!"

He took her by the arm and drew her out of the shop and into the sunshine. "Eva—"

"Were you hurt Danny, were you ever wounded? Were—"

"I'm not Danny, Eva...I'm Davey," he interrupted as gently as he could. "I know the army got my parents all in a tither with both our names on that letter, but it *was* Danny that was killed." He had to drop his eyes when he saw the shock and disappointment cross her face.

"Oh I'm—I'm so sorry Davey! I of all people should have known!"

He glanced back up at her, feeling badly. Everyone had always confused the twins when they were younger, and Eva of course had always been able to tell them apart—she had nearly married Danny after all.

"It's all right." He shrugged.

"I'm sorry...it's just that you—you...look different," she said, and then wished she hadn't when a shadow crossed his face. He was thinner than looked good on him, and so tired looking. And his eyes—so like Danny's—were sad now.

"I know. I guess it's because I am different."

She forced a smile.

"Done and seen a lot of things in the last three years—I never thought I would." He looked down and, attempting to lift the gloom, smiled at the child beside her. "Is this your youngest boy?"

"Yes." Her smile came easily when she looked at her son.

"What's his name?"

She swallowed hard—it was awkward suddenly. "David."

A glimmer of quiet pleasure showed in his eyes. "He's fine looking."

Eva smiled again.

"I heard what happened to Stephan on that boat, I'm sorry."

"Thank you."

They fell uncomfortably silent.

"You and your boys are living with Celena now?"

"Yes."

"Heard about Victor, too..." He shook his head. "Damn shame."

"We miss him."

"Is that where you're headed?"

She nodded.

"Mind if I walk with you? I haven't seen her since I've been back, and I want to pay my respects—do you think that would be all right?"

He was so like Danny, with his dark hair and quiet ways. It was strange. Almost like being with another version of Danny, and yet again, not like him at all.

"I don't think she'd mind a bit," Eva said, adjusting her packages.

He wrestled to take them from her. "Give them here, I'll carry them."

Celena's happiness at seeing Davey overwhelmed him and even when he declined the dinner invitation found himself happily seated at their noisy table with all the boys and Cathy. He had been surprised when later Ethan walked in, apparently perfectly at home and a regular visitor. Davey had enjoyed himself so much he was reluctant to leave when the time came.

He thanked Celena, and when it was he and Eva alone on the step, he turned to her. "That was nice of you to have me over. I haven't felt this normal...in a long time," he said, thinking about what the years of living in tents, eating horrible food, and war had done to him. "Thank you."

"How are your mother and father?" she asked, knowing they had been distraught when Caleb had been killed—and the dilemma of not knowing which twin was dead, had almost been too much for them.

"They are still pretty tore up about Caleb, and they miss Danny." He shrugged. "And I'm not him."

Eva felt a flash of sympathy for him.

He took a step down the drive, and she simply stood watching him on the porch, hugging her arms against the chill. Suddenly he turned back around. "I...I always thought Danny..." He shook his head, looking at the ground, not sure he should continue.

"You always thought Danny what?"

Looking up, his sad eyes met hers. "I always thought Danny was a fool for letting you go." He looked back down at the dirt. "Goodnight Eva."

Chapter 47

1867

"Celena," Eva said and paused for a moment, watching her sister tug at the weeds around Victor's memorial. "Davey has asked me to marry him. Do you think I should? I asked Maman, but, well you know. She didn't answer." She fidgeted nervously, wondering what Celena would think.

It had started out innocently, but before Eva knew it Davey was stopping by the house weekly—and then on Sundays too, in fact he was there almost as much as Ethan was! He began doing little things like helping Celena's boys with the chores when he came by. And he often brought meat for them to cook, or cloth he had found at a bargain and thought they could use. He'd even after two months, began reading to little David. One night as he was leaving he had simply pulled Eva to him and kissed her goodbye. Almost year and half from to the day they had run into each other at the store, he asked her if she would marry him. It made her heart miss a beat how he had apologized for not being more like Danny—apologized because they were so different, having no idea that she too had noticed the differences but that she liked *him* better.

"Are you fond of him?" Celena asked, rousing Eva from her thoughts.

"I wasn't sure at first...but this last year it's been so nice to have someone." She paused a minute, thinking hard. "Yes, I am."

Celena went back to her weeding. "Well then I think you should. I think you should marry him."

"It's not too soon?" Eva had to wipe the beginnings of tears out of her eyes. "But Stephan's gone, and he's not coming back, and I have to think of what's going to best for my boys. And I can't live with you forever."

Celena stared at her. It was on the tip of her tongue to contradict her, to tell her that she enjoyed having her, Stephan, and little David—but at the same time she did not want to make Eva feel guilty for leaving her.

"No, he would want you to go on and live your life. We should talk to Father Tonnellier as soon as possible," Celena said, realizing she was echoing Victor's sentiments exactly.

Eva dropped to her knees and hugged her. "Thank you so much. You've been so good to us; I don't know what we would have done without you!" Celena hugged her back and then sniffing, Eva got to her feet. Looking up, she was surprised to see Ethan standing there.

"Congratulations are in order?" he asked with a grin.

A faint blush of pink started in Eva's cheeks. "Yes!" she laughed and rushed back to a waiting Davey, whose heart started to pound when he saw the beaming smile on her face, and realized it was his soon-to-be-wife running toward him.

"You know that is a... *gaudy* memorial Celena."

Celena looked up at the giant memorial. The marble angel was bigger than she had wanted, but it had come all the way from St. Louis and there would have been no returning it. She always thought the base Bartholomew made was too large, but he had put his heart and soul into it, and she would never hurt his feelings by saying it was anything but perfect.

"Yes, I know." She smiled and continued to tug at the dandelions that were growing haphazardly around the giant stone, tidying it up like she did for all the graves of those she loved. "But I suppose it fits who it was made for don't you think?"

Ethan laughed. "I suppose Victor *had* been larger than life!" He knelt beside her and began to tug at weeds.

"I always think that angel looks a little lonely up there all by itself. And Victor was never lonely—or *alone* for that matter with me and all the children!" She smiled over at her new weeding partner. He was dressed nicely in a gray suit. Although he had gained weight back in the time he'd been home, he was still too thin, and she had the feeling he always would be. Whatever had happened to him during his almost ten months in Andersonville, had permanently weakened his health. The limp that he had come home with had not left. And although he tried hard not to walk with the cane, at the end of the day when he came for dinner, she would hear the familiar sound of it on the wooden steps. But his eyes had their old life again, and his wit had come back, and he made her laugh more often than she thought possible.

"They will make a good pair, don't you think?" Ethan asked, but wondered ruefully if there would be any greenery left around Victor's stone with the ferocious way she was weeding it.

"I think so. Davey is crazy about her. And all I want is Eva to be happy. Who would have ever thought—" She shook her head, not finishing.

"What do you mean?"

"Oh, I don't know, she was married once; she might not have wanted to marry again."

Even through her gloves he caught a glimpse of the iron ring still around her finger and stood up. Glancing toward the church, Ethan wondered if Victor's memory would ever fade enough for her to love him. He could still feel Victor in the air, like a gentle ghost that, although it meant no harm, never left.

"But she wants to, and she seems like she'll be happy," he said, and then looking back, watched with annoyance her kneeling on an old quilt on the ground, weeding her dead husband's memorial, and suddenly found himself wishing she would stop taking such tender care of those who were dead and worry a bit more about those that were living.

"I hope so. Davey has been good for Eva. He's chased away the shadows, showed her that there was still sunlight," she smiled, "like you've done for me."

His heart nearly leapt out of his chest. "It was good advice you gave her. To go on. Perhaps you'd consider taking that advice yourself?"

It was a minute before he spoke again. "Would you consider it? Taking your own advice that is?"

Her head raised slowly. "I have taken my own advice; I have gone on."

He thought about telling her that although she had made great strides in dealing with Victor's death, still had a long way to go. Considered telling her that it was useless to go on loving a man who was no longer of this world. But not wanting to risk and argument with her, left her where he found her. Weeding the graves of those she'd loved and lost.

Chapter 48

1869

The next years were hard ones for Celena. Shockingly Yvonne died, leaving her fifteen-year-old son, Johnnie, orphaned and out of place with his older siblings. He moved in with Celena, and although she tried to remind herself that he was her brother and not her son, the lines were blurred. In a short time, it turned out not to matter much, he simply fit in.

Ethan had been good to her. Acting like a surrogate father to the boys and Cathy. When they were younger helping them with their schoolwork, and as they got older listening to their different points of view about the reconstruction that was still happening in the south. Randy, Ben, and Andrew were enthralled at how Ethan, with his savvy banking knowledge, had explained to them that the war had not only been costly in the terms of life, but in dollars too. How the government was not in debt sixty-five million, like it had been in 1860, but now three billion dollars!

She found herself wondering sometimes what Ethan gained from this strange relationship. After all he had plenty of money and his bank. There was no need for him to come every night to their home and bear the trials and tribulations associated with raising six adolescent boys-and six-year-old Cathy, who repeatedly asked her uncle why he wasn't married and didn't have children.

Celena was content that this was to be her life and did not want to analyze what his motives might be. Ethan, however, was not so resigned, and one cool September night, he sat her down.

"Celena..." He glanced down at the table, feeling foolishly like he had waited so long, was not sure he could even say the words anymore. "Are you...happy?"

"Yes, I'm happy."

He snorted and looked away from her for a minute, and when he glanced back wore an expression she had never seen before. "Well... I'm not."

"Oh!" she said and couldn't think of anything else to say—it was a bit embarrassing.

"But I will tell you what would make me happy. I am in love with you, Celena." Trying to ward off the response he knew was poised on her lips, he added quickly, "I love you. Would you please marry me?"

"Oh, Ethan," she began, and he abhorred the pitying sound of her voice. "I—I couldn't."

He reached across the table and gently took her hand, and his warm brown eyes darted across her face like a lovers would. "Why not?"

"Because..."

"Because...why?"

She cringed. "Because...I don't love you."

He shrugged as if it was of little importance. "You *like* me don't you?"

"Well of—of course I like you. You've been good to me."

"Then marry me and make me happy."

It was a moment before she could collect herself enough to answer. "I can't," she whispered, and pulled her hand from his.

"Yes, you can."

"Oh Ethan—"

He silenced her with a look. "Don't apologize to me. Don't feel sorry for me. Marry me."

She was suddenly speechless, wanting not to hurt him, but there didn't seem to be any way out of the messy little situation she found herself in. "But I can't marry you. I still *feel* married."

"You're not married anymore. He's gone, Celena. He's been gone nearly five years. And even as strict as the Catholic faith is the marriage vows are only 'til death do you part. And I want you, I want you very much."

"I know he's gone, but I haven't stopped loving him. I still love him Ethan—and I don't think I'll ever stop."

"I know you do, and I'm not asking you to stop."

"I don't know what to say—"

"Say yes."

"I can't."

"Why?" The question, she realized as he sat back stubbornly in the chair, was a dare. It was obvious he was not going to give up so easily.

"It wouldn't be fair to you."

"Why don't you let me worry about what's fair for me all right?" he countered rudely.

Looking down she swallowed hard and could feel the weight of his eyes on her and couldn't help but think it was all so impossible.

"Don't act so *damn surpris*ed Celena!"

She jerked her head up. "I *am* surprised!"

"Oh, for God's sake! Don't tell me that all these years you had no idea how I felt about you! I mean you must have had some inkling, some *suspicions?*"

"I didn't! And I'm *sorry* if that disappoints you! I was happily married. He was the only man I ever even thought about. I *loved* him! I never saw anything past Victor. He was everything!"

"But you had to have *known*, everyone else did!" Embarrassed that *he* could still remember that Sunday afternoon when she had nearly slapped him, even if *she* couldn't!

"What do you mean everyone *knew*? How long have you felt this way?" A flush of humiliation went through her wondering who was talking about them—when there was nothing at all to be talking about.

"Since that night of the harvest when I'd first come back—"

Her eyes flew open with astonishment. "My God Ethan, but that was *years* ago!" she shrieked, incredulous, reeling at the thought. But it vaguely came back to her—that unpleasant moment on the front porch. She thought he'd gotten over that silly little crush *years* ago.

"I tried to get over you," he began, trying to keep the desperation out of his voice. "I knew you loved Victor and I knew it was hopeless. I even married to try and forget you, and honestly I did try to make my marriage work. But I couldn't. She realized I loved someone else."

"Did she know...who?"

He nodded.

"Oh Ethan, how terrible for her!" She was embarrassed and humiliated that she had been made an unwilling and unknowing party to Penelope's unhappiness. Celena had always been suspicious that things were not as good between them as they should have been, but never dreamed *she* was the cause. "But I loved Victor and you *knew* it! I never did anything to encourage you. She should have had no reason to be...*jealous* of me!"

"I know you didn't, and I am sorry about making you part of it. But I couldn't help it."

"Did Victor know?"

Again, he nodded, and she turned away from him and couldn't help but wonder what her husband had felt with this unpleasant fact.

"When? I mean how long did he know?"

Uneasily Ethan looked down. His professing his love and asking for her hand not going at all like he hoped. "He was suspicious, but he told me he knew for sure the day you two married—although if it comforts you at all, we never spoke of it until the war."

She stared at him, aghast, and could not even begin to imagine what *that* conversation would have been like. "He knew all that time. Everyone knew but *me*, I feel like such a fool!"

"Please don't feel that way."

"What did he do, what did he say when you told him?"

"He...forgave me."

She felt weak suddenly, and closed her eyes, missing him. Missing that wonderful, wonderful man she had been lucky enough to have fall in love with her.

Ethan swallowed hard and looked down, thinking that if there was ever a time for honesty and truth in his life, this was it. "I never told you this, or anyone for that matter...but the night before I escaped from Andersonville, I was...out of my mind. I was dying...slowly, starving to death. Victor was dead, and I couldn't help thinking, that it was all my fault, and that you'd never ever be able to forgive me or look at me—"

When she looked away suddenly, he had to take a deep breath before he could go on. "And I decided I couldn't take it anymore. What was there left for me anyway? Victor was dead, I'd let you down, Penelope and my child were dead...there didn't seem any reason to prolong it. I was going to walk up to the deadline and...have them shoot me...get it over with. Get death over with."

She waited for him to continue, and when he didn't asked, "Why didn't you, what stopped you?"

"Victor."

Suddenly her eyes were on him unblinking, and he hoped she would not think he'd lost his mind. "I saw him that night. I don't know...what he was...ghost, spirit...*angel!* But I know I saw him across from the deadline, and he told me no. And I didn't do it. I knew then he didn't want me to die, and that I had to try and escape or that I was going to die there. And I didn't want to die there, Celena. Even though he *knew* I loved you, he still saved me. He still sent me back. And I think maybe...he was sending me back to you."

Standing up, she turned away from him.

He stood up too. "Please believe me!"

"I do," she whispered quietly, and dropped her head. Although she realized now would be a perfect time to tell him of her own angel's visit from Victor, did not. And knew suddenly, she would never share it with anyone.

"So, if that's what's stopping you, because you think he wouldn't want you to remarry—"

"No. That's not what I think." A single glistening tear slid down her cheek. "Ethan, I want to be honest with you. Victor and I had a *wonderful* marriage. I don't think I could feel that way with anyone else ever again, and I would hate to disappoint you."

"It's a risk I'm willing to take," he said quietly and took a step toward her. "I know it won't be like it was between you two, but I promise you I'll do my absolute *best* to make you happy. Please. I've been waiting all my life; won't you give me the chance?"

"But will it be enough for you, this kind of marriage?"

"It wasn't for Penelope, but it will be for me, I know it. Of course, in all fairness to my dear departed wife, she did not have the benefit of knowing I did not love her going into the marriage as I do." He swallowed hard. "I promise you I won't ask for more than you can give...I won't even ask you to love me. It will be enough for me just to have you in my life." He reached out to hold her, but she placed her hands on his chest to keep his away.

"I was married to a healthy man..." She swallowed hard, looking down, but then surprised him by looking up again determinedly, "and I know what men expect from marriage, and I can do that Ethan—"

He felt himself flush at the rapturous thoughts.

"But if it's children that you want—"

"I don't care!" he exclaimed. "Children are not the reason I want to marry you. God knows if I could even *sire* a child anymore after everything...besides, you and Victor have seven children that I love, and I want to take care of." He paused. "I just want you."

She had to look away. "I don't know. It feels like...maybe it's too soon. I need more time."

"For God's sake Celena, I've given you time. It's been five years. I'm here nearly every night, and Cathy is so used to having me around that she scolds me when I miss a day and asks me where I was!"

Despite everything Celena smiled, knowing it was true.

"The only difference will be that I won't have to go *home* every night!" He let out his breath impatiently. "I'm not—shall we say—*young* anymore! I'm already forty-three and in bad health I might add, are you waiting for me to get too old to marry? Or simply hoping I'll die before you ever get around to it?"

Suddenly they both laughed.

"Will you...let me think about it?"

"All right." Reluctantly he dropped his hands from her. "Will it make your decision any easier knowing that it would complete my sorry life and that I would be happier than I've ever been before, if you would please marry me?"

"No! that makes it harder."

"Good. I want it to be difficult for you to tell me no."

Later that night she sat quietly and thought about what the next years would bring. Randy was eighteen already and was taking care of the factory and the sawmill as well, and Ben planned to go to medical school. Ethan had already helped Ben write the letters. She realized that one by one, they would live their own lives and leave her. And she sat quietly and thought about it. She could be alone, she knew she could, and knew marrying Ethan would change little in her heart. Yet at the same time the thought of making him happy, pleased her-almost as if she was giving back so much of the good Victor had done during his life.

Besides, it was what Victor had told her to do and he'd been right s about so many things, maybe he was right about this too.

She smiled thinking of Hank. He had married the youngest Stoddard daughter, Arlette, last spring, and they had a son. It touched something wonderful and deep in Celena the timid way Hank had asked if her it would be all right if they named their son Victor. When they hugged each other, he still reminded her of that frightened, young boy Victor died saving.

In the morning she felt surprisingly clear-headed considering she had been up so much of the night thinking. But she felt calm, not at all how she imagined she would feel. She decided to treat Myles by milking Luann for him, but when she opened the back door, was startled by the sight of Ethan asleep on the back porch.

He was curled up in the corner on the wooden floor and was shivering in the cool dampness of the morning. He had taken off his suit coat and used it as a makeshift pillow. She could see the outline of his ribs through the thin shirt and the wet spot on his hip from the wound that broke open periodically and never completely healed.

A gentleness stirred in her heart.

"Ethan." Rousing him, she helped him groggily to his feet. "What in the world are you doing out here, have you been here all night?"

He nodded as she led him back into the house and helped him stiffly ease on to the chair. "Your hands are ice cold. That had to have been terrible all night on the porch with no blankets." Quickly she fetched one of the quilts from the living room and draped it around his thin shoulders. "What on earth possessed you to spend the night on the porch! Why didn't you go home?"

The eyes that looked up at her were full of worry. "I couldn't wait any longer...have you thought it over, have you made your decision?"

She was kneeling by the stove, lighting it. "I'll have coffee going in a minute, and I'll fix you something to eat. It's bad enough your still thin as a rail but sleeping outside all night, you'll catch your death of cold—"

"Celena please, don't." Something in his tone made her stop. There was a long pause during which he shook his head as he stared despondently at the table. "I don't want coffee. I don't want anything to eat. I simply need to know...will you marry me, or not?"

A bittersweet pain went across her heart when she looked at him-saw the tiredness and doubt in his eyes, and understood how precariously in her hands was his future happiness.

"Yes, Ethan, I will."

He stared at her mute. He got up finally and crossed the room, leaving the quilt in the chair behind him. Softly he put his hands on the sides of her face and when she tried to nervously look down, gently forced her face back up to his.

"Thank you."

"You're welcome."

Her automatic response made him smile, and for a moment it transformed him into the Ethan of the old days. "May I..." He paused, unsure. "May I...kiss you?"

"I suppose you could."

Bending, he gently touched his lips to hers. A moment later he turned his head and wrapping his arms around her, hugged her hard against him. Overcome with gratitude and relief that the thing he had wanted his entire life, would finally be his.

She too was relieved.

No shiver had gone through her, no desperate feeling of disloyalty or betrayal. It would be all right.

Two days later, they were married and would have married sooner but had to wait a day for Father Tonnellier to baptize Ethan into the Catholic faith.

For the rest of his life Ethan would remember how it felt to go up the stairs with Celena that first night, go into that room with her and close the door behind them. How he had watched her take the combs out of her hair and undress, how it felt to slip into that bed beside her. When he reached for her in the dark, he had been overwhelmed by her tender welcome of him.

It was a feeling he hadn't felt in such a long time he'd nearly forgotten it. That feeling of security and of belonging and of being...home.

Epilogue

1898

Cathy knelt and laid the white spring beauties down neatly on her mother's grave. She smiled seeing the wilted bunch of violets near them, knowing that Randy's wife Naetha must have come while she had been in Washington, and put them there.

"You finally did it Mama. It took a long time, but it's done now. Papa's coupler is a law, it's a requirement on the railroad." Cathy sighed. Her mother had made three trips to Washington in the last few years and written countless letters to Congress, fighting to have the coupler enacted as a safety requirement on the railroad, but had died before it had been made a law. Since her death, Cathy had taken it upon herself to continue her mother's fight.

"Are you all right?" her husband Paul asked gently, his hand touching her shoulder.

She nodded and stood next to him, looking at her father's enormous stone, gently tracing her fingers over his name, which had been etched there so long ago.

"I wish I'd known him," Paul said, having heard so much about his wife's father through the years that it did not seem possible that one man could have influenced so many people, had been dead for so many years.

Amazing to him the story Cathy told how he had been the son of an Osage slave, and how the little factory he had started was now one of the largest and most profitable in the state and had even begun to search out markets internationally. Remarkable to him his invention of the one-piece rim which had forever revolutionized the way wheels were made, and that he had been granted a US patent for his invention for the railroad. And that all his wife's brothers, except for Ben who had become a doctor, had inherited their father's passion for machinery and become engineers.

"You would have liked him. He was wonderful," Cathy said, smiling through her tears. "My mother loved him so." She looked down at her mother's grave, over to her stepfather Ethan's, her father's memorial looming between them.

They had not meant to bury them that way, but Ethan had died first, and it seemed only natural to bury him next to his friend, and then five years later when their mother died, felt they had to bury her next to their father. But it was fitting, Cathy thought, that they were all buried so close together. She knew the three of them had been connected all their lives.

"It's so strange Paul. I was born after my father left for the war, I know in my head he never came home. Yet I swear in my *heart,* I can remember him."

"Maybe it's just all the stories you hear. I mean both Ethan and your mother talked about him all the time. Perhaps it's the stories they told that made it seem like actual memories for you."

"But they are so *real,*" she whispered, shaking her head. "I saw him once. I *know* I did, although I never told my mother. He came home one night. I can still remember him picking me up out of my bed. He held me and kissed me...called me his angel girl. He laughed then, and I can still hear that wonderful sound even to this day." She bit back her tears, feeling a twinge of guilt. Ethan had been a kind, considerate husband to her mother during their marriage, and wonderful stepfather to all of them as well, and she had loved him too. But still he was not her father, he was not the man in that faded picture her mother kept in a drawer beside her bed. The giant of a man with the long hair and cruel eyes. The man that had been dead for nearly three decades now.

"My mother loved my father so much. I hope somehow, somewhere they're together and happy now."

"I'm sure they are," Paul consoled, taking her into his arms.

Looking up, Cathy let out a strangled gasp, never in her life expecting to see such proof.

"What's wrong?" he asked, alarmed at the way she suddenly trembled under his hands.

"Did Randy or Andrew...*do* something to Papa's stone while I was gone?"

Squinting, he looked up at it critically, seeing nothing amiss. "No, not that I was aware of. Why, what's wrong?"

"Nothing...it's nothing," she stammered, knowing that her sensible banker husband would never believe her. She let the tears of joy fall down her face as he led her out of the cemetery and away from the stone memorial bearing the name of her father, which she did not fail to notice was now adorned with *two* angels entwined for eternity in a loving embrace.

Two angels together, where all things are possible and there is no such thing as discontent.

About Atmosphere Press

Atmosphere Press is an independent, full-service publisher for excellent books in all genres and for all audiences. Learn more about what we do at atmospherepress.com.

We encourage you to check out some of Atmosphere's latest releases, which are available at Amazon.com and via order from your local bookstore:

Dancing with David, a novel by Siegfried Johnson

The Friendship Quilts, a novel by June Calender

My Significant Nobody, a novel by Stevie D. Parker

Nine Days, a novel by Judy Lannon

Shadows of Robyst, a novel by K. E. Maroudas

Home Within a Landscape, a novel by Alexey L. Kovalev

Motherhood, a novel by Siamak Vakili

Death, The Pharmacist, a novel by D. Ike Horst

Mystery of the Lost Years, a novel by Bobby J. Bixler

Bone Deep Bonds, a novel by B. G. Arnold

Terriers in the Jungle, a novel by Georja Umano

Into the Emerald Dream, a novel by Autumn Allen

His Name Was Ellis, a novel by Joseph Libonati

The Cup, a novel by D. P. Hardwick

The Empathy Academy, a novel by Dustin Grinnell

Tholocco's Wake, a novel by W. W. VanOverbeke

Dying to Live, a novel by Barbara Macpherson Reyelts

Looking for Lawson, a novel by Mark Kirby